PURCHASED FROM
MULTNOMAH COUNTY LIBRARY
TITLE WAVE BOOKSTORE

REDSHIFT BLUESHIFT

THE PENDULUM OF TIME

Leslie Peterson

Order this book online at www.trafford.com
or email orders@trafford.com

Most Trafford titles are also available at major online book retailers.

© Copyright 2011 Leslie Peterson.

All rights reserved. No part of this publication may be reproduced, stored in a retrieval system, or transmitted, in any form or by any means, electronic, mechanical, photocopying, recording, or otherwise, without the written prior permission of the author except for brief quotations embodied in critical articles or reviews.

This is a work of fiction. All of the characters, names, incidents, organizations, and dialogue in this novel are either the products of the author's imagination or are used fictitiously.

Printed in United States of America.

ISBN: 978-1-4251-7057-8 (sc)
ISBN: 978-1-4251-7058-5 (e)

Trafford rev. 04/14/2011

 www.trafford.com

North America & international
toll-free: 1 888 232 4444 (USA & Canada)
phone: 250 383 6864 ♦ fax: 812 355 4082

*To my best friend and brother, Win,
who kept me interested in the universe
since we were kids*

CONTENTS

Part I	**DORT**	1
Part II	**ORIGIN**	139
Part III	**ORIGIN'S CHILDREN**	233
Part IV	**THE ISLAND**	383
Part V	**CRYSTAL LIBRARIES OF TIME**	487

APPENDICES

Appendix A	Characters	554
Appendix B	Isomorphs	561
Appendix C	The "Others"	562
Appendix D	Miscellaneous	565

Part I
DORT

ONE

Laura Shane was in her favorite lotus position taking tea beside her pool. She was perched there on the grass beside Ned Keller, her occasional lover; but at the moment was paying little attention to him. For the previous two weeks she and Ned, along with several thousand others, were being smeared across light years of space on *the Great Cone of Transformation*. It was Ned's latest transformation vehicle; but it was Laura's fresh interpretation of *Transformation Theory* that made those Cone creations possible. She was therefore responsible for all that was happening to them, but could hardly grasp it emotionally. *What a trip! she thought. This thing is no toy!*

She took another sip of tea. It was hot and sweet with an eye-opening tang.

To think I volunteered for this. . . . It's real—I guess. But everything's different; so how come nothing's changed? The garden is in bloom. Its scents are still floating across the pool and wafting around me. The grass is moist. My house hasn't changed. Everything's as mundane as ever—even our names! Ned. What kind of a name is that? Names are tough for me; numbers easy. Hmm. He looks cute today in those crappy shorts. What a great dancer he was—still is! He's an all-around hoofer! I'm not. Darn! I need to change. How many times have I thought that, I wonder? And so, on and on she thought and thought. As a genius, thinking was, after all, her job.

Laura's best friend, Judy Olafson, a chemist, appreciated her trusting nature, her scientific brilliance, and her—more often than not—eager, naïve optimism. She was kind and caring to people and tolerant, even admiring, of the alien Dorts—huge, awkward, translucent, hulking and amoebalike though they were.

But Laura was less than attentive to matters important to many others: the momentous social issues of the time; opportunism and incompetence in government; and careless, even aggressive, environmental degradation (no small amount of it caused by the very Cones of Transformation that her work made possible).

Instead, Laura occupied herself with things *she* considered important— time with friends, her fascination with the aliens, the beauties and mysteries of science, sex, and other universals. As a scientist, her grasp of visual and mathematical abstractions was without equal; but the realities that emerged from those were often beyond her emotional grasp—arousing a struggle between her exceptional mind and her ordinary feelings. This was one of those times. Mostly, however, her intellect was busy with the great and all-embracing concepts—the infinitely large and the incredibly small—and, of course, she also had to consider her nails.

To the public Laura was a lovely, impossibly young, twenty-six year old genius—a virtual child in a world where the average lifespan for a woman was a hundred and eighty—twenty years longer than for men—and where beautiful, healthy babies were commonly born to still-young women in their late sixties.

Laura was thought to be a sober-minded physicist—not a fuzzy-minded dreamer. But today, after hours of concentration that led nowhere, her thoughts became reminiscent and scattered, even as she tried to relax beside her pool.

What a trip! she kept thinking. *My body—smeared across light-years of ordinary space!*

Fortunately, she was not *in* ordinary space. Happily for Laura, Ned and everyone else on the junket, cruising Transformations never took place in ordinary space. If that were so, they would all be dead. As a passenger on the Great Cone of Transformation, the particles that composed her body and soul were, in theory and fact, just so many transformed quanta and forces, sailing along in a sea of energy within another reality—another dimension in an alternate membrane of all that is.

Ned Keller, Laura's senior by a decade and a half, kept reminding her that the description for this was almost the same that one could use for ordinary space, matter, and life on Earth. "The Transformation," he said, "is just a dancing step-step-slide away from ordinary spacetime. This arrangement of mass and energy is highly stable. A Cone of Transformation," he emphasized, pointing a finger into the air, "maintains its internal integrity down to the last quark and beyond. So nothing much has changed and you of all people know that better than anyone!"

To this Laura replied simply, "Yes dear, nothing's changed—except everything."

Several hundred years earlier the first version of Transformation Theory was brought to Earth by the Dorts. No other aliens had, to anyone's knowledge, passed this way before. The turf-conscious, busy-with-our-own-projects-thank-you physics establishment studied the Theory reluctantly. Over time, however, a few physicists looked deeper and had to admit it was brilliant. Then others, not to be left behind, climbed aboard. In time they all came around, magnanimously pronouncing it the most revolutionary advance in physics since the ancient Dyon-Twist Theory of Matter and Energy. The Dorts had gifted Transformation Theory to humanity—on a silver platter.

Over those centuries the theory went through many minor changes, but it was Laura Shane's insights that gave it the "finishing touch." It revolutionized the Dort Theory. Laura said it was "*just* a finishing touch," as if that were a small thing. But the physics community realized those changes had significantly advanced the theoretical and practical ideas latent in the Theory—and made possible the incredible journey that she, Ned, and several thousand others were experiencing.

Dorts began to arrive on Earth from their "Settlement Planets," humankind was told.

On first arrival, they were insubstantial. They did not arrive at full mass, but waited patiently for their particles to catch up to the rest of their substance. When a Dort arrived by that process, one could pass a hand through its body, as through a mist. They were of little help at first, but within days a new arrival accumulated enough solidity to generate sounds, to "hear" and learn languages. Soon after that—strangely soon—a Dort might be at a college lectern teaching a one-credit minicourse entitled, for example, Transformation Physics 101, or would simply start giving physics lectures on street corners. In all their years on Earth, that was their only assertive activity in the public domain—aside from several notable acts, including lifting collapsed bridges off vehicles and assisting in other difficult situations.

As human scientists made their own advances in Transformation Theory and its related technologies, the process for Dort arrivals coincidentally improved—rather dramatically—raising many suspicions and questions. The Dorts claimed that *before* their earliest arrival on Earth, they were already far ahead of the recent human advances in Transformation Theory and resultant practices. Some wondered why, if they were so technically advanced to begin with, the first arrivals were so slow to materialize. Later on, concerns about Dort candor was comfortably sidetracked to the satisfaction of many—including Laura Shane. She was not noted for her skepticism; but suspicions coming from the outside, "nonscientific groups," never diminished.

Certain fringe groups were antagonistic and fearful—despite the Dorts' nonviolent, even shy, behavior. The scientific community called those groups paranoid, but did note that Dorts brought with them something to be paranoid about—or at least to be jealous of. That was, of course, the most fruitful silver-platter gift—the apple of Theory from the tree of Transformation, bestowed without strings or expectations—none, at least, that any but the radical groups could imagine. They had other reasons, valid they believed, for their revulsion against the aliens: Dorts simply did not look, act, or speak like people. To produce utterances and expressions of any kind, they set up vibrations on their external layer creating sounds aversive to human ears. In fact, scientists and other professionals who regularly worked with Dorts on corporate or governmental teams had to admit that, unlike pets, it was impossible to care about them or to identify with them—as individuals or as a group.

Ned Keller admitted this. He knew the Dorts in his role as founder and Director of 3T Corporation and had worked with them for years. He would not publicly admit to anything like suspicion or foreboding about the Dorts. Elites in the broader scientific community and even his closest peers would have met such a politically incorrect attitude with derision and scorn. That community's jealousy of Dorts was still there, beneath the surface, but over the centuries it had become suppressed and deemed unworthy, for the sake of their nobility, to even remember such shallow feelings, much less mention them. The openly hostile groups were not considered among those noble elite; but in truth, a wide, if only unconscious, overlap did exist between them.

Not all of that overlap was unconscious. There were a few areas of open agreement. The scientists admitted, for example, that *descriptions* of the aliens—by even the most paranoid fringe groups—were accurate. Dorts *were* disgusting-looking things by any human standard. They were couch-sized and translucent, like gigantic amoebas. They frequently demonstrated an awesome intelligence—or, more accurately, extraordinary intelligencelike capabilities. Like amoebas, they could send out false arms, or pseudopodia, from their main body; but those appendages had greater versatility than any amoeba's. At will, depending on a job's requirements, they could extend one or more false arms, or even thousands of small, cilia or tentaclelike excrescencies. They used the small tentacles for intricate scientific or mechanical work. Larger pseudopods were seldom extended, but powerful when they were.

During their centuries on Earth, no Dort had been known to reproduce, and none had ever died or been killed, even under the most extreme accidental—or deliberate—circumstances. If one had wanted to, no one, not even the scientists, knew how to kill them. Little wonder the Dorts aroused loathing and terror in so many for so long. To most observers—academic or fringe—their full potential and purpose had not yet been seen. As before, the academics expected more helpful potential to emerge slowly. The fringe groups feared that potential contained an already ominous purpose.

In the century before Laura's theory advances, the pace of practical applications had already moved ahead, allowing Ned's 3T Corporation to thrive.

The earlier 3T applications were exciting, not only for scientists, but for the general public—especially its *individual Transport Through Transformation*—the "i3T." Laura called the i3T a "mere toy;" but that invention made it possible to transit inanimate and animate objects between linked platforms. The platforms could be stationed at home or office and linked to other platforms on or off the planet. In practice, such transport took only minutes or seconds, depending on distance or the model and upgrade. For animate objects, like people, the user-friendly i3Ts created subjectively invisible spacetime corridors between platforms. Distant platforms could be dialed as easily as a radio station or a cell phone number.

The i3T was 3T's primary cash cow before expiration of its main patents. Competition did cut into business, but not badly at first (thanks to the competition's excessive interplatform losses). Most of 3T Corporation's profits went into R and D and the implementation of increasingly ambitious projects. Ned described those projects to politicians and the public as "undreamed of."

The most exciting *undreamed of* applications were 3T's "Cones of Transformation"—gigantic creations described by the world's media as the "ultimate spaceships." The latest, most immense of those, was 3T's *Great Cone of Transformation*—the one on which Laura, Ned and a community of technicians, scientists and others were traversing the Galaxy.

The Great Cone itself was a conical chunk of planet Earth, many kilometers across on the circular surface, the Cone's "base," with it descending sixty-four kilometers to its vertex. In the first instant of a Transformation, the Cone's great mass was expelled at ultraCeleric speed (faster than C, the speed of light) from Mother Earth—including everything on it, over it, and in it—minerals, people, atmosphere, trees, everything.

The advent of this achievement was a source of professional gratification and celebration, but on a popular level it was marred by mass protests, negative editorials, and marches by all manner of groups, conservationists and, in Laura's opinion, "Paranoids with no appreciation for progress." She said to her friend, Judy Olafson, "Even David Michaels, the Chief Geologist on this very Transformation, has been protesting these Cones for years! I don't know how Ned got him—with David's way of thinking and his ridiculous *non*sense-of-humor—to join us. Ned must have been at his best, or just caught David at one of his 'funny' moments."

The Great Cone was launched two weeks earlier—after its irreversible ten-hour start-up time, erroneously and informally called a "countdown." (Stopping one would be possible, but a bad idea.) In that moment of launch, it *transformed* from one set of familiar dimensions into another—and was gone—leaving behind a cavity of indescribable immensity. That and other Cones created voids in planet Earth that would at once suck in the atmosphere from kilometers around those cubic kilometers of emptiness. As the atmosphere rushed in to sate the monstrous vacuums inside those round, gaping mouths in the planet, they created tortured, high-pitched wails heard halfway around the world. The sound was the broken-hearted shriek of an anguished Mother for her dying child. It was Earth—Gaia—screaming.

The project's significance and moral legitimacy, however—according to Ned and his "boss," Jack Lewis, Chairman of 3T's Board of Directors, and a scattered few favorable editorials, was the Great Cone's purpose—the advancement of science. Such pompous pronouncements mollified most of their supercilious social investors. With such rationalizations and generous financials firmly in hand, many busy and dedicated scientists were able to eschew the concerns of paranoid groups, protesters, and other "uninformed" outsiders, and join the enterprise.

In their movement through spacetime at multiples beyond the speed of light, cruising Transformation Cones were, as Ned kept reminding Laura, "incredibly stable." In theory, the only possible *instability* was during its ten-hour countdown. If that were stopped before its completion, the entire Cone would instantly dissolve into a radioactive lake of goo. Only wild-eyed experimenters, extremist do-gooders and terrorists would give serious consideration to such an interruption.

There was, however, one *inaccurate*, but widespread destabilization theory. It was a false rumor. It stated that being on a Cone's *surface* at the first moment of Transformation was dangerous. The rumor apparently arose to explain why there were kilometers of subterranean corridors deep below the surface in every Transformation Cone. That naive concern failed to take into account the monumental spaces needed for the mass-energy conversion generators in every Cone and the space required for related living and work areas.

One unknown physicist did come up with a destabilization theory that could affect an entire Cone, not just its surface. It was humorously called a "Twister" by the scattered few scientists aware of it. The article was published in a minor physics journal without editorial comment or a single peer review. Laura thought the "Twister" mathematics worked out well, based on another hardly-known theory by the same author and published in the same journal a quarter earlier. Like the ancient M-theory, there was no further proof in experiment or practice for the truth of either theory. After that, the article was all but ignored, with few references in other journals, leaving its author, still unknown. Even Laura forgot his name.

Laura glanced over her cup at Ned. He was in his lounge chair reading. His trim and muscular build made him look younger than his age. *He's like a well-kept thirty-year-old*, Laura thought, with a wry smile. *Too bad he's here right now or I could put this lotion all over.* (She was well on her way to an almost complete tan anyway.) Lover or not, she was not going to be brazen—not today. After all, it had been quite a while. *Oh well, there's no rush.* She knew Ned's feelings were stronger for her than hers for him. She thought it possible he loved her. She thought he looked distinguished most of the time; but she also enjoyed the lusty way he looked at her when she wasn't supposed to notice—and especially when she was.

Laura was accustomed to that from men, and knew she deserved it—despite the prominent occipital bulge at the back of her head. She kept it luxuriously covered with her long, silky black hair.

Finished with the lotion, she reversed the position of her legs and took another sip of tea. Ned leaned toward Laura from his lounge chair with a twinkle in his eye. "Nice legs," he said.

"Shut up. I'm thinking. Yours aren't bad either—for a guy. What are you reading?"

"About Dorts—their history on Earth, their supposed ethics, and a lot we think we know about them. I hadn't read this one before. It's good. By the time we reach Settlement Planet Three I don't expect, or want, any major surprises, but we'll be able to dig a little deeper. You know my suspicious mind. Jack Lewis says I'm wasting my time—that I'm paranoid about Dorts, as if I'm from one of those nut groups. What do you think?"

"Obsessed, I imagine. Or maybe you are just a bit—around the edges."

"I knew it! You're all against me!"

They both laughed and took more tea; but Laura still seemed somewhere else.

Ned eyed her, as she floated back into her private thoughts.

"What are you thinking, Laura?" Ned asked quietly. "You've been day dreaming for an hour—a couple days, in fact."

"Have I?" she said, almost startled. "I guess I have. It's just . . . what's happening to us."

"I think it's love," Ned said, shamelessly admiring her long and lovely legs.

"Oh, cut it out. You know what I mean. I never know when you're serious."

"I'm sorry. What about what's happening to us?"

"Well," she began, tapping the back extension of her head with a forefinger, "I understand it here . . . but I can't relate to it with the rest of me—not when it's me out here getting shoved across a transparent universe like so much slush in front of a squeegee. It's my first Transformation so maybe I'll get used to it. If we were in a real spaceship, the old kind with roaring engines, strapped into crash couches, feeling the g-force of acceleration, even weightlessness!—then I could believe this. But we're sipping tea in my back yard for Pete's sake! The only difference is the artificial sunlight coming in all directions from the Luminaerie on our 'horizon.' It doesn't . . ."

"—Compute?"

"That's it. It's too much!"

"You're right," Ned said. "It is a bit much."

"So is this Transformation. Way too much—too much for a human to grasp."

"Yeah, it could be even bigger than anything the Dorts have done. We know what they tell us about *their* Transformation Cones—or whatever they're using. We haven't seen one of them yet. Maybe they brag."

"Oh, come on Ned! You know they don't brag, and they don't lie. At least we haven't caught them at it, not in three hundred years!"

"Not actual lies, maybe—but okay, so even this Transformation may not be big stuff by Dort standards. But I can question that. Opinions are still allowed."

"It's still a weird feeling—this trip. That's my opinion."

"You keep saying that! Oh well, why shouldn't you? At your tender age it makes sense for you to feel weird."

"How's that supposed to follow? You're not all that old, and you're the Director of 3T. Sure, physics may not be your field. I think of you more as a classy dancer. But even you know enough about Transformation physics and what this Cone is doing to feel weird yourself. Hmm—and what does age have to do with it?"

Blinking provocatively, Ned said, "Yeah, but a competitive dancer I am no more. I'm just a layman devotee of your physics. That's your arena my dearest. I'm just an administrator."

"*Just* an administrator?" Laura exclaimed, taking the bait. "Who else could have organized the scientists and technicians, to say nothing of the Dorts and the politicians, to leverage Transformation Theory into this creation—the *Great Cone* and all its predecessors?"

"I thought the Dorts were supposed to be ahead of us on that."

"Yes, I'm sure they are, but you know them as well as anybody and got them to help. You organized the Dorts, the scientists, the engineers and everybody into an integrated array of design and production teams. That was fantastic, Ned."

Laura said all that before realizing she'd bitten on Ned's provocative little hook; but she caught herself—". . . And as for Dorts, you probably *are* a total paranoid on the subject—the top one! Besides, you could have done much better. I know you don't like it when I tell you this, but you could have been a famous dancer. Never forget *that* my dear!"

"You never let me!"

"You'd have won that stupid contest—that tango thing and all those other dances—if that scatter-brained partner of yours had bothered to show herself—to just disclose who she was. I couldn't believe it—she even wore a mask! But no—she had to be incognito! What a silly rule for an international contest. Why did they have to know who she was? Both of you had to forfeit all that recognition, not to mention the award—just because of her. Maybe she was wanted for murder somewhere. Except for her, you'd have been famous!"

"I am anyway." Ned smiled.

"As I said, it could have been better. Why *did* you quit those competitions?"

"You're right," Ned said, becoming very serious. "I shouldn't have quit. But you know what happened after the contest. I got more and more involved in all this 3T stuff. After that, I never looked back. It took everything I had."

"*Of course it did*," Laura said, dripping bathos. "Anyway, the Directors . . ."

Laura noticed her porch light and stopped speaking. There was a long silence. Ned looked on expectantly as Laura's mouth became a distinct pout. "*What?*" Ned said.

"Why is it right for *me*," Laura asked, "at my '*tender age*,' to feel weird about this trip?"

"That again? Jesus you're sensitive. I just meant that you, one of the top three human experts on Transformation Theory in the universe, maybe the top one, author of the famous—"

"Enough! You know how I love all that bullshit, but you're avoiding my question. . . . Anyway, the Directors must be here early. Somebody wants onto the property. They turned on the porch light, it's blinking—that's my signal." Laura got up to return to her house.

"You didn't let me finish," Ned said. "I was going to say, when I look at you I'm like that light. I too must blink at you, in purest admiration—not to mention, you also turn me on!"

Wincing in disgust—and blushing—Laura said, still walking away, "That's sick. Worse—its pathetic! It's more of your BS, Ned Keller. You're so goddamn impossible—you know that—and so goddamn cute! You and that geologist should get together. Your humor is as bad as his."

Hurrying to catch up with Laura, he complained, "What an insult. And, hey!—I wasn't being funny. Really!"

"Thanks for the explanation," Laura replied, picking up the pace as she crossed the lawn to her porch, "How else could I have known?"

TWO

They passed under the blinking porch light into Laura's living room where a signal light was flashing in unison with it on her computer console. Blinking lights were Laura's compromise to avoid certain modern "conveniences"— astroprojected telemetry alarms, bellers, and the recent craze for cranial implant notifiers. She touched a key on the console panel and a hazy, half-meter-high figure appeared on a small metallic plate beside the console.

It was Jack Lewis, Head of *3T* 's Board of Directors. Jack was a biologist. At the time he joined *3T*, he was involved in several other ventures. He was first-rate in his field, but his main strengths, for *3T*'s purposes, were in business and political lobbying.

"Hi Laura, Ned. What kept you? I've been standing here for half an hour."

"Hi Jack," they replied together. Laura went on, "No excuse, we just didn't notice. I'll hook in the sound from now on." That was a lie. "We were expecting the division Directors at the gate, not you on this thing. I'm off schedule. They should be along soon. Nothing special. Just a routine staff meeting."

"How about fattening me up a bit. I'm at a disadvantage down here."

Laura made a few more keystrokes and Jack's hazy image was transferred to a much larger disk-shaped platform in the center of the room. The platform, four meters in diameter, was decoratively tiled for the dual use of *i3T* connections and for disco dancing at her parties—but mostly for the dancing. Laura moved another dial and the ghostly manifestation grew to twice Jack's normal height.

"Don't be funny," Jack said.

Laughing, she again fiddled with her console instruments and Jack settled down to his normal height. He still appeared indistinct and colorless, like one of the early Dort arrival.

Jack said, "I'm glad to see you're both looking well, except for a certain pale transparency, of course."

"Look who's talking!" Laura replied. "But just wait till I get my tan."

"I noticed the outfit," Jack laughed; but then became serious. "I know you didn't expect me; I'm sorry to butt in, but I came for a couple reasons. We've been getting your reports regularly Laura, and, as usual, they're excellent. I wanted to tell you personally how important and helpful your information and your analysis has been. It's really appreciated!"

Then there was silence as they looked uncomfortably at one another. At last Laura said, "Okay Jack, what was the other reason for coming?"

Jack slowly sat down cross-legged on the raised platform, bringing him to eye level with Laura and Ned who were still standing. He was gradually becoming more opaque as his mass increased.

Laura persisted, "What is it, Jack? Has something happened? You didn't make this dangerous individual Transformation just to give me a pat on the back. You could have sent a memo instead of your whole body."

"Hey! We never tested the $i3T$ under these conditions before. In a few more days an individual leap like this *would* have been dangerous. You'd be too far out. Even your reports wouldn't make it back to Earth."

"Right," Laura said, "but you have to get back, or you could be stuck here, not only for safety reasons, but we need you right there on Earth to keep things running smooth. Really glad to see you, of course, but why are you here now?"

"Well—hmmm—what can I say? It's not out yet and I'm trying to keep the cap on it as long as I can, but I had to see you about it, and get your advice. Both of you. I'm afraid it . . . may affect you. You and the others on this Transformation. If it isn't handled right we can expect problems back home—even riots from the fringe, the paranoids."

"For God's sake, Jack, what is it? Spit it out!" Laura exploded.

Ned knew Jack very well—for years before Laura met him. Ned turned to Laura and put his hand on her forearm to settle her down and said, "Take it easy, honey; Jack has to say it his way."

"But . . . ?" she said helplessly.

"Trust me!" Ned said with finality.

Jack continued, "As you know, the previous Transformation expeditions to the Dort Settlements returned with tons of data. We thought it would take years to study and integrate, so we farmed out some of the work to other companies.

The expeditions also brought back more about the Dorts themselves, but that material doesn't add up to much. It's to your credit, Ned, that you never published your fears and concerns about the Dorts. Your publications always stuck to the facts. But after your Dort studies you started to have some rather frightening ideas."

Ned looked uncomfortable. He remembered that on several occasions he told Jack what he really thought—that everything the Dorts told the world for the past three hundred years was a fabric of lies and misdirection, and that those on planet Earth, and who knows how many other inhabited worlds, were being led down some prearranged path.

On that politically incorrect point, past discussions between Ned and Jack had been vehement. But their arguments helped Ned crystallize what had been vague areas of suspicion—and whet his determination to plan this most ambitious Transformation yet—to get at his unanswered questions.

"Ned, are you all right?" Laura asked, looking at him with concern.

"It's nothing. Just remembering things. Go ahead Jack."

"Four weeks ago I was talking with our jovial old friend, Reinholdt Dietzman, about your . . . paranoia." Jack gave an embarrassed laugh and continued. "He listened more intently than I'm used to from him, and he asked a lot of questions. His Corporation for Biological Studies has been helping us analyze the Dort materials and the usual physical debriefings on our returned Transfonauts."

"Hasn't Dr. Dietzman been studying Dort physiology and chemistry right along?" Laura asked.

"They've tried, and did the best they could, short of autopsy, if they could get one. But none of the Dorts has ever died. And besides, didn't you write something, Ned, about their value system not allowing anything like that?"

"Yes, but for Pete's sake, Jack, lay it out will you!" Ned barked.

Laura touched Ned's arm and looked at him slyly saying, "Let him say it his way, honey. Trust me!"

Ned rolled his eyes and soundlessly mouthed, "Okay."

"Dietz asked a lot of questions, like I said. We discussed things that worried *you*. Then Dietz, of all people, confessed that he, like you, had come to similar apprehensions. He has studied the Dorts as thoroughly from the perspective of his field as you have from yours. I decided right then that I'd better take a closer look. So, for the next two weeks, with Dietz's help, I studied everything relating to the Dorts that his group had found."

"And? And!" Ned prodded impatiently.

Laura shot Ned a scolding frown that changed to a smile that changed into a frown again.

"Everything fit a hunch Dietz had. It gave me the creeps. The biological data on the Dorts themselves was virtually useless. Even though they are almost transparent to their innards—they may as well be in a black box for all the insights that provides. The Dorts themselves claim they can't, or won't, explain the functioning of their parts—that *values* thing again. Very convenient. We know nothing of their eating habits, if any. Imagine, after all this time no one has seen them take nourishment, nor are there any known excretions. An old joke suggests they should be really mad by now. All the hypotheses we've tested about their ingesting and expelling through the air have proved negative. Hell! They don't even breathe! And they do just as well under water—even acid. They appear to be chemically inert and impervious. I wouldn't want the job of figuring out how to kill one."

"Jack!" Laura said with shock.

"I was just being ironic."

"Go on, Jack. What else?" Ned prompted.

Jack shot a peevish glance in Laura's direction, but continued, "We did learn a couple new things about the Dorts from their participation in several underwater tests—nothing fundamental, mind you, but provocative. For instance, not only can they talk to us by vibrating the atmosphere with their body surfaces, they can do it under water."

"You mean like sonar? Or whales?" Ned asked.

"Yes. They can communicate under water in exactly that way. But that isn't the half of it. With sonar, you need underwater detectors to pick up the sounds. Or, if you're under water swimming or scuba diving, you can hear sounds directly, but since sounds travel four times faster under water than in the air, that screws up our directional hearing. Anyway, Dorts have gone further. You can hear them speaking with the naked ear when they're under water and you're above it."

"You don't mean, do you, that they can send speech sounds through the *air* when they're under the surface?" Laura asked.

"Yes I do. More than that, they could adjust their volume from barely audible, to an ear splitting roar of sound, like listening to a powerful loudspeaker at close range."

Laura snorted, "That's not only incredible, it's impossible!"

Jack shrugged, "I know. But it happened. In a lake, or even in an ocean, they could kill a lot of marine life with the sound volume alone. They never have, that we know of, but there it is! Some recent whale beachings have been suspicious—because the pattern is different—but nothing we could pin on the Dorts. Those beaching episodes have gone on for all of historical time. Our sonic experts are trying to figure it out, but don't hold your breath. Granted they can do that, there is something just as surprising. From under water, when their volume is down to a normal speaking level, they can impersonate human voices!"

Laura cried out in astonishment, "Human!" Her surprise then turned to delight. It fit her Dort fantasies. "But that's wonderful! I knew they weren't just protoplasm robots. They must have spirits—souls!" As she said these last few words, she turned her radiant face to Ned. He was not smiling.

"That's a bit of a stretch," he said blandly.

Speaking again to Jack, Ned asked in a curious tone, "Was there one voice, or more than one. Was the voice, or any of the voices, recognizable?"

"Yes. They could reproduce the voice of anyone they had ever heard."

"Could they improvise—music, voice sounds, whatever?"

"They could reproduce a symphony—one they'd heard. But, no, they can't improvise music. On their own, the sound was worse than an orchestra tuning up. They can improvise *words*, but not voice sounds. It's always a voice they heard before."

Laura slumped as though she'd lost a personal battle. She mumbled something about parrots being able to do that—even her "Keeta," a beloved parakeet she had as a child.

"Did you notice any other behavior in the water?" Ned asked.

"Yes. They change their form more often, and more dramatically—spreading themselves flat, or sending out enormous pseudopodia, like a starfish, taking on the shape of a ray or an eel and swimming smooth and fast, unlike their lumpish movements on land."

"Anything else? What about other studies. Were X-rays tried?"

X-rays gave us nothing at all. No bones. Nothing solid. Some shadows, nothing more. We do know something of their external, more observable and measurable behaviors. We do know about their general size and density—that, as you know, they vary at will. And that's a mystery—especially since they have no known material exchange with the environment. There must be some such exchange—from somewhere. We just haven't found it. Their intelligence is high, although different from humans. We know how they ambulate, how they 'vocalize' from their surfaces, and of their extraordinary pseudopod development and manipulative skills, and some of those things. But we know nothing of a verifiable nature about what goes on inside their skin. And I wouldn't call it skin. And that's another thing . . . but it's a long story and I won't bother you with that. We don't even know how they reproduce, if they do."

"*If* they do?" Laura repeated.

"That's right. All the Dorts came from outside. None was born here. Even on the other Transformation expeditions to the Settlements there were no observations or proof of pregnancy, cell division, egg laying, or any other form of reproduction."

"Their value system won't allow such observations!" Laura said. "Even *we* don't have babies in the middle of the street!"

"What's this leading to, Jack?" Ned asked. "A little earlier you said something might affect us—all of us on this Transformation, and possible riots back home. What is it?"

Ignoring Ned's question, Jack returned to his own. "What do we know of the Dort personality, Ned? I mean first hand."

"I don't know why you're asking this again, Jack. We've discussed it before—many times. How is one more time going to help your perspective?"

Jack looked at Ned in obvious distress, jerked his head slightly and allowed his eyes to dart momentarily to Laura, as if trying to point to her with his eyes. Laura was looking at Ned so she didn't notice. Ned suddenly realized that much of this review was for Laura's benefit, for *her* perspective, and to set the stage and prepare both of them for whatever was coming—for whatever Jack had really come to tell them.

Ned returned a microscopic nod of understanding to Jack and began by saying, "Never mind, I'm sure you have your reasons for asking. Let's see, the Dort personality. Okay, they're flat; compulsive on details; total lack of imagination; they all give more or less identical answers to the same questions. Their intelligence seems to be identical—extremely bright, of course; can memorize hundreds of digits at a glance—God only knows how they see; and the same with books—perfect memories. Their conversations are boring; they answer questions without elaboration, except when teaching things about Transformation—then they go on and on; they never ask questions of us in conversation. Without questions, they just sit there. They listen. They learn fast—not social things, but everything else. They never get angry or sad—or show anything like an emotion. Their 'voices' are—except under water as we've just learned—a mechanical, vibrating drone, with an almost metallic quality. No one who's ever met one or spent much time with them can say they like them. They don't appear to have either likes or dislikes—except, as I said, they must like teaching certain things. We infer that because it's something they do spontaneously. They never dodge a question in any area, except if they believe it violates their value system, or if they simply don't know the answer they say so. They all, sooner or later, come to possess the same knowledge. No more, no less. They're interchangeable for most purposes."

"Like computers?" Jack asked.

"Not exactly. Computers are more likable. Take teaching machines. Some verbal goodies, like 'well done,' or 'very good' can come back from them."

Jack pushed the point further with, "Who programs teaching machines?"

"I see what you mean," Ned replied.

"Well I sure don't!" Laura proclaimed. "What I think is, you're *both* nuts—folie a`deux! I think they're real beings and not computers or anything of the sort. Ned, you say they have no imagination. I suppose you think it took no creativity or scientific imagination to develop Transformation Theory and all the gadgets that go with it! That took no motivation of spirit and intellect?"

"I wouldn't argue with the 'intellect' part," Ned replied, "but think about it a minute. Let's suppose what Jack's driving at is true. What inventions have we seen the Dorts develop since they've been with us? What have they created that proves they have imagination?"

"I just told you. Transformation Theory and the gadgets. Furthermore, they can build gadgets and fix them—and you know the level of complexity I'm talking about. What more proof do you need?"

"Yes, but hold on. They *arrived* on Earth with Transformation Theory and gadgets."

"So what?"

"And they are endlessly building the gadgets."

"See!"

"But they're always building the same, identical gadgets."

"Aha! I've got you! They've also built new gadgets; many of them—even in the time I've known them. Besides that, the new equipment and technology is almost always based on advances in the Theory itself, and those new gadgets help to advance it even further, and so on." She took a deep breath, and then added victoriously, "You're now on my turf, gentlemen!"

Ned groaned inside, but did what had to be done. "Yes, your turf," Ned said in a barely audible voice, then more distinctly, "And, aside from your own, who made the latest Theory advance?"

"Dr. Loren McNally, founder of the McNally Institute. What about it?" she snapped, getting the feeling her turf had just slipped a little.

"Is he a Dort?"

Silence.

"And that theory advance of his was made possible by a special piece of new equipment, was it not?"

"Yes," she said uncomfortably, with less bite.

"What equipment was that?"

"The tele-micro lens. We have one with us."

"Which does what?"

"Allows microscopic observations across long distances. You could observe anything down to the size of a microbe as far away as the moon from Earth; or larger objects for that matter."

"That got Dr. McNally's foot on the next rung of the theory ladder, did it?"

"Yes. But you don't expect the Dorts to outshine us on everything. Obviously, humankind has a contribution to make too. I think we've even proved their equal in theory building!"

"I don't doubt that for a minute. Now, who invented the tele-micro lens?"

"This is ridiculous. It isn't a lens anyway—it's an extension of Transformation Theory. It sends out nested parallel sets of 'blanks' from a Transformation field and then returns them 'loaded,' so light coming from the distant object is unnecessary. The transmitted 'blank field' literally finds the object, 'loads up' on it, and brings back the three dimensional image almost instantly by returning through the incoming negatives, or blanks—very similar to the way Jack got here today, and similar to this whole Transformation, except that Transformation Cones use only the 'loaded' Fields. In theory, we could bring an object back to our lab without the need of a 'loaded' Transformation Field at the source. In fact—"

"Skip the rest, Laura. I didn't understand a word of it anyway. But tell me, who invented the tele-micro-whatever-it is?"

"We did. All of us—Dorts included, at $3T$. It was a team effort. McNally leveraged off of that."

"What role did the Dorts play in that team effort?"

"They answered questions put to them."

"And the contribution of those answers to the development of the *whatsit*?"

Laura was losing some of her color, but her integrity was more important than her turf. She responded, "Mostly calculation and memory stuff, I'm afraid—things we could look up, but we knew the Dort would have the answer without our having to bother. That and complex calculus and a million other kinds of math or logic questions we could have done on a computer in a matter of minutes or hours—sometimes it would have taken weeks. The Dort gave the answer instantly. They're very handy."

"How were the blueprints for the tele-micro lens developed?"

"Once we had the main elements in hand, we did the preliminary experiments, made the necessary modifications, and then drew a rough plan for the first prototype—practically on scratch paper. But I tell you, the Dort took those scratchings and made a beautiful set of blueprints in nothing flat. All the exacting curves just right; and absolutely straight lines—'free hand,' with all the right notations. Everything."

"Could a human draftsman have done the same?"

"Yes, but it would have taken him longer," she said peevishly. "Besides, the Dort went ahead and built the prototype. Yes, yes—I know—a human could have done that too. Anyway, the first full-scale model needed a few more changes, and we went through the same process until the thing worked perfectly, just as we did with the Gravity Tug in historical times—a thousand years before anyone ever saw or heard of Dorts. Yes, mankind can be clever too."

Laura became thoughtful, and then with simmering eyes she snapped, "Humph! Ned, you knew the answers before you asked! So why ask?"

Jack hesitantly moved back into the fray. "You're right, Laura, he did know. That's the thrust of what Ned was telling me when I called him *paranoid*, back when. But there's more. In area after area the Dorts have the same MO. Ned should know. He's headed up more of these teams than anyone at $3T$. The Dorts always come across as very bright, but never where a new insight or a deep flash of understanding is needed. Those things have always come from people—people like you, Laura. Ned has traced this ladder of theory-invention-theory back a long way. Tell her, Ned, what you told me."

Ned turned to Laura, and in a matter of fact tone said, "Not a single independent step in theory, and not one independent invention has come out of the Dorts since they arrived on Earth three hundred years ago."

Laura felt more stunned than defeated as she murmured, "My God—what are they?"

THREE

They remained silent, knowing there was more to come. Jack was becoming more solid and felt the gravity enough to move off the platform. He stood up, stretched his legs one at a time and took the few steps down from the metallic, tile-covered disk. "I was getting a little stiff. Mind if I move around?"

He walked to the expanse of bay windows behind Laura and Ned and looked across to the familiar scene. It was a lovely little chunk of modern suburbia. Laura's house was on the hillcrest of the highest point on the Cone's surface, well above the verdant lowlands and lesser hills. Curved dirt roads connected the aboveground homes. Laura's and the other Directors' nicely painted houses and landscaped yards, and the homes of several dozen other crew members could only be seen from Laura's hilltop as random flecks of color and highlights where the trees and other greenery happened to part. At night, their lights flickered through the same spaces between the trees.

Only a fraction of the Transformation personnel were lucky enough, or rich enough, to live on the surface. Their work usually kept them below—deep in the Great Cone's core. Living arrangements in those depths were comfortable, but not plush.

Laura's house was in the center of many square kilometers of circular terrain—the surface land uprooted from planet Earth along with a sixty-five kilometer deep conical core of underlying rock and mineral upon which that landscape was formed. On the surface's perimeter, towering steel balusters supported the Luminaerie, a ring of light surrounding the entire terrain. It was their man-made "sun"—a high-powered hoop of luminosity, synchronized to vary its brightness with the day-night pattern on Earth.

Rising vertically from the surface of that picturesque terrain was a cylinder of air that thinned as it extending upward more than five hundred kilometers. It was maintained there by the same field of Transformation forces that kept the rest of the Cone together.

Jack leaned forward in concentration, his head tilting to one side, and then the other. His eyes moved rapidly, as in a dream—carrying on an internal visual and auditory dialogue, blurring the scene before him to see and experience the rest of the miracle that existed below.

Living and working together deep within the Great Cone was a throbbing community of workers, scientists and professionals—engineers, technicians, support staff, shop keepers, carpenters, bar tenders, counselors, and dozens more.

Before returning to Earth, this would be a long journey. The planners tried to anticipate every imaginable and unimaginable contingency, including the need for a wide range of talents, social services and institutions, and the physical materials needed to compliment and sustain the project. They took vast stores of supplies, building materials, modular habitat components, entertainment facilities, hydroponics gardens, well equipped medical and dental clinics, and all the other trappings required for a smooth running space-age bedroom-working community. The earlier Transformations demonstrated the need for such a full range of human and material resources, especially for sustained, rigorous and complex voyages of several months. The thousands of trained and skilled men and women who came to inhabit the Great Cone on its maiden journey brought with them a rich assortment of acknowledged and visible assets—their specialties—along with an even greater diversity of overt and covert motives.

Within this subterranean edifice, far below the tube of atmosphere and picturesque landscape were numerous subcenters and specialized complexes, each with its own chambers, corridors, observatories, labs, and networks of computers and consoles—all supported by a range of transportation systems that went beyond the cone's intranet and other electronic needs and capabilities. Those included a small fleet of commodious, but secondhand space shuttles—useful only when a Cone was in "hover position" above a planet—and a modest caravan of large and small conveyances that would hurry and slow, like insects feeling their way through the Cone's labyrinthine burrows, channels and ducts, moving past individual cubicles and groups of apartments and across a dozen miniparks and recreation areas.

Jack stood at the window visualizing all of that and more; but he especially marveled at the Transformation's energy systems. First was the glowing energy center in the heart of the complex—the Tesla Tank containing a suspended, undulating ten-meter ball of lightning. It was just a secondary backup energy source, but Jack appreciated its superior manageability over the matter-antimatter and fusion "primaries." Even those, however, were only secondary to the big one. Jack's greatest admiration was reserved for the true engine within this and all other Transformation Cones: the toroidal mass-energy converter—the machine that took them beyond the confines of relativity, being the true embodiment of a dynamic conversion of Transformation Theory into the realm of practical invention.

For this living and working community, only a small fraction of the Cone's many cubic kilometers of available "space" was required, using only the upper layers of rock and mineral strata. In decades to come, Jack knew additional capacity would be needed, but to add that new capacity would merely require more digging. Even currently, the population within the Great Cone could be doubled with room to spare. To Jack and others on the Transformation, this interstellar transport was more than a marvel—it was the archetype for all future space travel and for intimate, firsthand research into the nature of the universe.

They stood beside Jack, sharing with him this silent moment in feeling and understanding. For years they had talked, dreamed and worked together for this. Ned and Laura could almost read Jack's mind and emotions, but they were unprepared for Jack's next statement.

He turned toward his two friends and said, "I don't believe the Dorts ever had anything close to advanced Transformation technology." Ned and Laura shook their heads in total surprise. Jack continued: "I've slowly come to believe all they had was the most elementary Transformation Theory, the same level of theory they revealed to humankind when they first arrived—along with a few good experiments, of course, to prove that much of it. Who knows where they got it from originally."

Ned shrugged and said, "I know I haven't given them credit for much creativity and accused them of resting on their laurels for many years, pretending and playing the you-learn-from-us game; but after all, they did reach Earth from across interstellar space and kept on doing that for over three hundred years. They couldn't do that and still be doing it without a practical Transformation vehicle like this Cone or something similar. They must have gone beyond the Theory, that's obvious."

"It's obvious if your premise is right," Jack responded.

"You think the premise is wrong?"

"Yes. Think of it in a different way. Consider some other way the Dorts could have gotten to Earth without highly developed Transformation Technology."

Laura joined in. "Sure, we could consider our heads off, but right now I'm wondering why you're bringing this up now. The reason you're here—it has something to do with the Dorts, doesn't it? We've been talking so much about them lately, and naturally so. One of their planets, and their society on it, will be an object of study for this Transformation. At least that's our physical destination—the Third Settlement. But we're not out here to just be checking on Dorts. Our main focus will be the most important physics and cosmology verification projects to date. Most of the resources for this Transformation are centered on that side of science—not the aliens."

"We all know that," Jack said.

"But we don't know why you're here. You've been skirting around that. You're trying to ease into it, probably more for my feelings than anything. You underestimate me. I'm not good at these games. I think we're both ready to hear. I know I am. For once, Jack, say it."

Jack shrugged and did just that. "The Dorts are gone." Then he went silent and expressionless.

Laura screwed up her face. "That's it?"

"That's it. You wanted me to belt it out. So there it is. That's it! Well, I've got to be running along now." Jack turned and headed back toward the platform.

Jack smiled despite himself. He couldn't help it. He knew it would happen, and it did: Laura's otherwise sweet voice scraped the atmosphere like a diamond-bitted hacksaw—"*Just one moment!*"

Jack turned around, hands palms up in a helpless gesture, an open-mouthed look of innocence on his face.

Laura folded her arms tight across her chest, her mouth held a hard line; her eyes glistened through slits.

Despite all the dire consequences inherent in Jack's curt announcement, Ned could not help himself either. Behind Laura, he doubled over in agony, trying to maintain inaudible laughter. The implications of Jack's announcement could be gravely serious, but Jack's uncharacteristic by-play, under such a circumstance, was so absurd Ned dropped to his knees and, holding his sides, roared aloud—completely out of control. Any serious implications would have to be sorted out later. It took another minute, but by then Laura and Jack had also lost any semblance of their own composure.

When the laughter abated they still could not look at each other directly lest the laughter begin again. After a series of such episodes, however, Laura was able to remind them the Directors would be along soon. "We were going to have a short meeting, mainly for progress reports," she said between subsiding giggles, "and then just socialize for a while." Becoming quite serious, she added, "Jack, you said this information about the Dorts should not get out. When the Directors arrive, do you want your presence here to call attention to the fact that something's up? If that's the case, we've got to talk fast. Personally, I don't see how we can reasonably keep anything important from the Directors—especially Doug. Besides, you know how curious he'll be. He'll be social, and go slow at first, but he'll get it out of you one way or another!"

"Of course," Jack said. "The Directors have to know everything."

"Then you should stay for the meeting. In fact, why don't you stay for a couple days? In three days we'll be too far for you to get back safely, but a couple days should be okay."

Jack shook his head saying, "I wish I could, but I can't stay that long—but for today's meeting that would be fine. I have to get back to Earth. Problems there may already be starting."

Laura said, "Sorry about the problems you're left with, but I'm glad you can stay to share this with the Directors; but I'm still not sure what the problem is you'll be sharing. What does that statement, 'The Dorts are gone' really mean, and how do you know it's true?"

"No one has seen nor heard from any of the Dorts for almost two weeks. They've simply vanished," Jack said. "Their nests have been checked, they haven't attended staff meetings, they haven't reported to the labs—they haven't even been teaching their classes. I've tried to cover up by making the excuse they were needed on a special emergency project, but some people are starting to talk. It's not entirely out of hand, but we can't keep the lid on indefinitely." Jack finished with an exasperated shrug.

"Any speculation about what happened?" Ned asked.

"That's part of the problem," Jack continued. "There's been too damn much speculation. Oh, the speculations are still confined mostly to insiders, but some of their guesses would stand your hair on end. If the paranoids got wind of what's being talked about, they'd believe their worst fears were realized. They'd be on the media in a minute, stirring up the public and trying to bring the house down on us—and trying to get rid of the Dorts permanently. It could set us back a hundred years."

"What are the speculations?" Laura asked.

"Well, some in Dietzman's group think the Dorts may have taken to the ocean to reproduce. If that's true, or if people only think it's true and the idea gets out we could have panic."

Laura frowned. "Isn't that a bit dramatic? Even if it were true, why should that cause panic? The ocean's a big place, and we could stand to have a few more Dorts around—after their little fling. I fail to see their disappearance as cause for alarm. So, go ahead—alarm me."

"It's the unknown, Laura," Jack intoned with a trace of condescension. "And they are aliens. Even after all these years we do not know their life cycle, their biology, their psychology, or much of anything else about them. Now this. It's as if humanity has been waiting all these centuries for the other shoe to drop—for their true nature to be revealed. Now they're gone, and God only knows what that means." Jack was speaking faster and his face was turning red. "Why have they gone?" he continued. "Where have they gone? Will they reemerge, and if so when, and if they do will they be the same? If they're reproducing in the oceans, will they return in small numbers or by the millions? Or the billions? What's their plan? What's their game? It's getting to the point—"

"—You're getting distraught," Laura interrupted calmly. "And you thought Ned was paranoid. What's come over you, Jack? Are you afraid of Dorts? Or are you afraid of people's reaction to ideas about them? Do you really think the Dorts are plotting something dire for the human race? Good Lord, Jack, even frogs and turtles are alien to our species, but we get along in the same world. Dorts are different too, but we've gotten along with them for hundreds of years, so don't panic and get paranoid. They've been so consistent and predictable the slightest deviation has everybody in a dither. They've raised our expectations too high. Maybe we've become dependent on their regularity of disposition. If they had any sense, they'd have done this a long time ago—frequently and on a random schedule. Then where would your suspicions be?"

Laura took a deep breath and Jack moved in again, saying, "You're preaching, Laura, but you're right. This break from their predictable pattern is what has us worried. It isn't like them. Every day the Dorts are gone will bring more questions. Reporters have already approached me, and another reporter contacted one of our technicians in a bar. He asked if she'd heard any rumors about disappearing Dorts. She said no. She *hadn't* heard any such rumors—not till then. If another reporter asks her the same question, she'll have to say yes. That's how reporters generate their own news. Dietzman is aware of similar approaches to his people. There is bound to be a major lapse eventually. It wouldn't be so bad if 3T were the only organization with access to Dorts. But they're all over, including Silverman Electronics, USK, and International Minerals, Ltd. I heard from their CEOs directly. They're all madder'n hell at us. They think we spirited their Dorts away for that supposed 'emergency project' I mentioned earlier."

"Not a good cover story," Laura commented.

"I know. But that's the fiction I started with—so now we're stuck with it. There was no time to dream something up. About the same time we realized what happened, I got that first call from a reporter and made up the story on the spur. Even then I didn't know the Dorts had vanished from *everywhere*. I thought it was just us."

"I'd like to get back to what Reinholdt Dietzman's outfit is saying," Ned persisted.

"He doesn't believe the Settlements are their place of origin. He thinks the Dort Settlement Planets could just as well be the resting place or part of an expansion. He also believes that the Dorts never did have advanced Transformation capability when they first came to Earth."

Ned asked, "Then how could they have gotten to Earth?"

Jack said, "That was my question earlier. Now it's yours. So, I'll repeat our question back to *you*. If the Dorts didn't come by advanced Transformation, and all they had was its barest beginnings, then how could they now be on Earth?"

"I can't imagine, but I'll play along. All right, let's see . . ." A look of surprise came to Ned's face. "Hey! They would have to have been on Earth all along. They would have to have *evolved* on Earth, somehow undetected, as they have been undetected for the past couple weeks, and then emerge to reveal themselves as they did three hundred years ago. How's that for a guess?"

"That's one theory Dietz and his staff considered, but we're all just guessing," Jack said.

Laura took another deep breath. "Jack," she said, "I believe there is one more way the Dorts could have gotten to Earth—a way that might account for their form."

"What would that be?"

Then, shaking her head, she said, "Never mind. On second thought it's impossible."

Jack looked at her with a mixed expression, saying, "I hate it when people say '*never mind.*' That's right up there with '*skip it.*' But I'm ready to consider any other possibility. Let's hear it."

"Sorry. It's too silly to say. I'd sound like a nut case. Besides, the idea keeps getting more complicated the more I think about it."

As a stall for time, and to think more about her idea, she said, "Let's take a break. I'm starved. I'll fix a snack and pour a few drinks. Any takers before the Directors start arriving?" Ned and Jack wanted to keep going, but did agree.

They wandered into the kitchen where the two men sat at the table and Laura donned the most trifling suggestion of an apron. They watched as Laura moved about her galley performing the age-old routines that, from the beginning of time, warmed the hearts of lazing men. The scanty swimwear beneath her dainty apron did not detract from that effect—not in the least!

FOUR

After changing into conservative apparel, Laura sat with Jack in her living room to finish their cocktails. They were waiting for Ned. He had a few changes of clothes in her spare room and was bellowing operatic discords from its shower when the first gyro-car leaned into her front drive. Douglas Groth stepped quickly from the two-wheeled g-car and bustled his short, round body up the front walk. "He's always first," said Laura, laughing on her way to the door.

"Hi, Laura," Doug said in a high, cheerful voice as he fairly twinkled through the door. His round, ruddy, elfin face, sparkling tiny eyes, large ears, and flowing sea of red hair were no less startling on first sight than his ungodly green plaid pants and yellow sport jacket.

"Hi scamp," she said bending down to kiss the small island of baldness in the center of his Red Sea. "And to think," she said, now shaking her head with feigned concern and looking across the room at Jack, "that our lives and the safety of this Transformation depends on . . . *this*!"

Doug chuckled and turned to see who Laura was talking to, and gave a little hop of surprise and pleasure when he saw Jack smiling and strolling across the room to meet him.

"Well, for the love o' Mike! Nice to see you Jack. This is a surprise. Seems like we just left ya, though."

"Nice to see you again, and so soon too, Doug," said Jack as they shook hands.

The friendly interaction continued for some minutes—a not altogether unwelcome situation. Talking business would become repetitious if each new arrival for the Directors' meeting immediately demanded to know what brought Jack to this improbable meeting place. Doug was curious—even suspicious—but tried not to show it; and Jack did not want to cause Doug any undue apprehension—not without a lot of people around.

Douglas Groth was not one to add anxiety to any situation without good cause; but as Physical Systems Director for this and the previous Transformations, his responsibilities were staggering. For good cause, his pleasantness could give way to apprehension and frightening conniptions. Such outbursts were rare and short-lived—a fact that was always a relief to the two groups of Operations Managers reporting to him. One set of Managers handled the technical side of the Transformation. The second group saw to the basic creature comforts. The first group included particle engineers and other professionals overseeing the gravitation, electromagnetic, strong, and weak force field equipment; plasma engineers; magnetohydrodynamicists; the toroidal mass-energy control monitors; spectroscopy specialists; biocomputer technicians; astro-pilot navigators; and a dozen others. He shared the management of Navigation with the Astrophysics Department.

Doug's second group managed the janitorial, kitchen and cafeteria, laundry, recreational, and other such services. In a nutshell, his job was to direct and coordinate the operation of those areas so that the Transformation not only held together physically, but also got to and from its destination in a timely, safe, and comfortable manner. That, at least, is how his job description read.

Sometimes Doug's Managers were called upon to control his turbulent behavior, to the point of almost sitting on him from time to time—and on two occasions, *actually* doing so. Doug fortunately possessed the insight and good nature to later realize he needed that kind of damper on his sprawling sense of direction and attempts to multitask beyond even his abilities. When he was settled down, and that was most of the time, his Managers listened to their leprechaun leader with respect, loyalty, admiration, and love. His deep and comprehensive grasp of the entire Transformation as a system was second to none—and his people knew it.

On the earliest Transformation expedition to Settlement Planet One, Doug had walked beside a row of consoles when he noticed a minor deviation in an indicator measuring toroidal integrity fluctuations, and noticed this in conjunction with insignificant deviations from displays on two other related consoles—insignificant, that is, if each display was gauged in isolation. He realized the *combination* was anomalous and would cause a cascade of interactions to negate the forces maintaining the Transformation's integrity. He ordered the three technicians to step aside and moved to where they had been. Standing by each console in turn, he keyed in a series of commands. The technicians looked on in amazement as he worked the touch screens and keyboards, even as a rain of perspiration fell from his face onto his stubby fingers. Finally he struck the last enter signal, stepped back and shook from head to toe. One by one, together and in rapid succession, chains of adjustments took place throughout the Transformation in its most critical systems. It happened quickly, and just in time. The toroid system had begun cycling nearly out of control when its support systems and energy stabilizers were triggered. In another second there would have been destabilization, and the molecules and particles of the Transformation—including those of every person aboard—would have gone sailing on disconnected courses throughout the universe.

The nano-biocomputer networks on that and all subsequent Transformations were "tweaked"—a euphemism for their receiving major overhauls—to avoid such problems in the future. The $3T$ computer and systems experts were never able to decipher how Doug, or anyone, could have taken those few cues to come up with the exact diagnosis, prognosis, and cure for that crisis as Doug had—and he did it with a glance! Even Doug could not explain it. His only comment was that looking at the displays gave him a "hunch," and after that everything was a blur until he hit the final Enter key. Even before that, his technical skill was well known; but from then on his "hunches" were never questioned.

The approach of several more gyro-cars relieved the growing awkwardness of their chitchat. Another breather came when a dripping, hairy-legged being appeared from the back hallway. "Where's your hair dryer, anyway?" it asked with irritation, while adjusting the sash on a bright blue terry cloth bathrobe. Ned added more cheerfully, "Oh, hi Doug! Nice to see you. I'll be along in a minute."

"It's on the shelf under the sink—where it always is," Laura replied with a pained sigh of resignation. "Klutz," she added under her breath as it vanished down the hall. Doug and Jack exchanged amused glances.

Doug went to the front room window and waved. "Looks like they're carpooling again," he announced over his shoulder, "Everybody's here." Laura and Jack joined Doug at the window to smile and wave to the approaching group. The smiles of anticipation quickly faded from their face. "There's something wrong," Laura said in a tone of distress. "They're all serious, worried looking, frowning. This isn't like them."

First through the door was bearded, graying and allergy-ridden Stanley Lundeen, Director of the Astrophysics and Astronomy Department for the Transformation. He had a small group of professionals reporting to him and several graduate students on internships. Entering behind Dr. Lundeen was tall and stately Debra Anderson—a buxom Scandinavian from a land area on Earth still designated as Louisiana. She was in charge of Information and Communications, personally disparaged laptops as lacking the touch of personal immediacy, and instead carried notepads and several multicolored pens with her at all times. Among her many tasks was production of the Great Cone's "Daily" newsletter—printed in hardcopy (at her insistence) and on the intranet. Debra and Stan went on in to where Doug and Jack were waiting. Although pleasantries had been exchanged all around, there was an undercurrent of discomfort.

Next in the door was forty year old Clinton Bracket, Director of Security—a stocky, square jawed, ruggedly handsome, thick necked and notably bowlegged man of average height who projected a gruff, no nonsense military demeanor.

Close on Clinton's heels, as usual, came the petite thirty-seven year old Ellen Stone, a physician with an additional Ph.D. in physiology. She, in turn, was followed by two of her Operations Managers, Dr. Roger Flanders and Dr. Henri Lufti.

Despite her relative youth and quiet manner, Ellen was highly competent in her role as Medical Director. Introverted or not, she struggled to keep a relationship going with Officer Bracket who, at least in public, hardly seemed to notice her. She was fascinated not only by his brawny good looks, but even more by his sheer, robust size. Although he was an adequately schooled and fairly bright man, Ellen and Clint had no common interests and were rather apart intellectually, but those matters seem never to have crossed her heart.

Dr. Roger Flanders, who also headed the Transformation's Biology and Genetics Program, was on loan from Dietzman's corporation; and Henri Lufti was the doctor responsible for the small clinic and hospital. Both physicians would like to have been protective of their boss, Ellen, but she was at no risk except for her own relationship choices. As they entered, Laura was met by more restrained cordiality, causing her distress to escalate.

As the remaining Directors filed in—except for Judy Olafson who came last—Laura merely held open the door, making no more attempt at pleasantries. George Sachs, Personnel Manager, gave Laura a worried headshake as he entered. Tall, skinny and bushy-browed Ernst Berman of Mathematics and Statistics frowned on entry. David Michaels, a geologist and Director of Geophysics and Mineralogy offered some inappropriate humor and was the only one to laugh. David's crew was already below preparing to delve into the geologic mysteries of Settlement Planet Three. Anthropologist Cameron Greenberg, Director of Social Dynamics, headed a group that included a variety of scholars in history and the social sciences, and several counselors. He, Ned Keller and Stanley Lundeen were close friends and colleagues. Cameron appeared less distracted than the others. He managed an ambivalent smile that came across much better to Laura than David Michaels's "humor."

The last to come was timid, asthmatic, Judy Olafson, who joined on as the Transformation's Chief Chemist, and was Laura's best friend. A cautious and fearful person, she was prone to anxiety attacks; but, when it counted, she could eschew her fraidy-cat status and be surprisingly brave. She also had a strong aversion to any kind of profanity. Laura had to talk long and hard to get her to join the Transformation. She told Judy to think of the job as a *vacation cruise.* That helped, but the clincher was her mention that David Michaels would also be going.

Judy was last because she returned to the g-car to get something. Laura walked halfway to the car to meet her. As Judy came back up the walk she saw that Laura was biting her lip, almost in tears. Judy wasn't looking very confident herself as they came together. Without a word they embraced each other for a moment of comfort and reassurance. Turning to go in, Laura said in a hushed voice, "Tell me quickly, what's going on—everyone is so . . . so strange."

Judy's eyes went wide. "We were talking about it in the car," she said. "I hadn't heard anything earlier. Stan and Debra found out before we left. Somehow, don't ask me how, the Transformation seems to be . . . *off course.* Stan and Debra got it from one of the astronavigators just minutes before we left to come here. Stan started everybody working on it. In an hour or so there should be a preliminary report. It could be a human navigation error, a nano-biocomputer glitch, or some other mistake. Anyway, being off course, if we are, is causing all the long faces."

"That can't happen!" Laura gasped as she stopped in her tracks. "Transformations are virtually *unsteerable.* Speeds can be adjusted to some extent, but once a Transformation is under way the direction can't be changed, except slowly, and even then only with a tremendous energy drain. Our guidance technology and capabilities for Transformations are prehistoric. Once we're committed, that's it! If this were a conventional spaceship built for sub-light velocities, we could make all sorts of adjustments. All we can do in a committed Transformation is go, stop, make some minor speed adjustments, and, with *great* energy consumption, make one or two extremely minor midcourse directional corrections! On all the previous Transformations, midcourse corrections were never needed. Not once!"

"Take it easy, Laura!" Judy said, and added, without conviction, "Maybe it'll turn out to be nothing at all."

Without hearing a word that Judy just said, and becoming more agitated, Laura continued: "Don't you realize that even the slightest hair of deviation from our original course could send us *light years* off target—into nowhere! We could be lost . . . forever. HyperCeleric Astronavigation is primitive. Cruising Transformations only have *internal* integrity; so, to the galactic stars we're as invisible to them as they are to us. To the outside universe we're just so many scattered, invisible particles moving randomly through a trillion 'double slits.' Our navigation cannot be optically anchored. Even gyroscopes are totally unreliable on Transformations. We don't know why, but think it has something to do with Transformation gravity. To get anything approaching a navigational fix, we have to rely on a special combination of instruments tied to mass-particle detectors. *Transformation Navigation* is one of the primary investigations for this expedition. As things now stand, if we are off course, there's not a chance in a million we'll ever get back. We simply do not have the energy for a midcourse correction—even if we had navigational accuracy. The navigation research from earlier Transformations moved us in the right direction, but at this stage I wouldn't give you two cents for any of it. The only reason for having an in-flight Navigation Program at all right now—aside from research to improve it—is for morale; not because we thought we'd ever need it!"

"I know," Judy said, shaking, as she led the way into the house. She was in the midst of an anxiety attack. Laura, unthinking, said all of that to the wrong person.

They entered the living room and saw that Ned was dressed and talking to Jack, Doug and the others. Their expressions showed they too had heard.

When everyone was seated, all eyes turned to Laura. She touched a key on her console and the room began to plunge—into the Transformation's core.

FIVE

Half a kilometer below the surface, the Directors exited Laura's room-lift to enter a nearby chamber where they reassembled around a brilliantly illuminated conference table. Ned Keller glanced around the room to survey the periphery of glowing, flickering screens. At last he called the meeting to order and asked Stanley Lundeen and Debra Anderson to summarize the recent news of a possible course problem.

After their fragmented presentation Ned said, "We need more facts from the Navigation and Astrophysics groups to know if this will be a problem or not. Their reports should be along soon. In the meantime there's an unrelated matter you should know about." He turned his head, nodded to the man beside him, and said, "Jack."

Jack leaned forward and looked from one familiar face to the next. He said, "I hope that Ned is right to say that this is 'unrelated.'"

Ned and Laura darted surprised looks at one another, but said nothing.

Jack spoke rapidly. He announced the disappearance of the Dorts, summarized the earlier discussion between himself, Laura and Ned, and reviewed the reasons for not including Dorts on this and previous Transformations. Although there were public relations reasons for precluding them, the main reason was a widespread attitude of prejudice and fear among crewmembers against the Dorts. The Dorts had urgently requested inclusion, but the 3T Board overruled their petition.

Dr. Flanders waved his hand as Jack concluded his remarks. "Thank you, Mr. Chairman," Roger began with unusual formality after a nod from Ned. "Jack, your remarks were thought provoking. I was interested in your conversation with Ned and Laura about the nature and origin of the Dorts. You said that Laura had another idea that might explain their arrival or emergence on Earth and a possible reason for their present form. I've long had a special interest in that, if you could elaborate."

Jack shrugged and said, "I don't know. She didn't get around to that. Perhaps," he said turning to Laura, "you could tell us now."

Laura looked uncomfortable. She shared the unspoken, growing tension that was becoming more apparent around the table. Expressions were taut. Some appeared angry, others fearful. Doug and Clint were mumbling to each other as they both stared at one of the screens in the far end of the room. George Sachs had his eyes closed. Ellen Stone was watching Clint. Henri Lufti was watching Ellen. Cameron Greenberg was watching everybody.

"I don't think this is the time to go into that," Laura said. "We're all on edge about our course and navigation problems. I know I am."

There were mutterings of agreement, but Doug, who hadn't appeared to be listening, turned his head toward Laura and said, "It may seem irrelevant to you, but I think Roger's interest in this is on the mark. Jack's remarks implied a connection between the Dorts and our present crisis. If that's correct and the connection is there, any linkage should be explored. If you've given thought to this then your ideas could help."

Doug's remark changed the volatile atmosphere again and everybody became intent to hear from Laura.

She began methodically, "The Dorts came to Earth with the basics of Transformation Theory. That's not news. That began their relationship with human society. Until today, I never seriously questioned their possessing advanced theory and technology similar to what we now have. Most of us believed they had it all along. We thought they were simply bringing us along, rather paternalistically, little by little to make our own connections and to assimilate each new advance. That's been drummed into our heads for as long any of us can remember. Through the years that caused a lot of anger and frustration; but we adjusted—most of us anyway. Now it appears that *they* learned the new technological advances and theories from *us*. If true, then we've been subjected to a long-term deception. The motivation for such a fraud eludes me, but Ned and Jack convinced me. It's been a three-hundred year deception. We've just gotten used to it."

"Then how did they get here?" Judy asked.

It was a good question coming from the one person in the room who knew less about Transformation than anyone there. Despite her tendency toward anxiety attacks over small matters, she could handle the big problems better the more she understood them.

"If they didn't have our current Transformation technology," Laura replied, "then they couldn't have come to Earth that way. Ned's idea that they may have evolved on Earth and somehow remained hidden until three hundred years ago is a possibility. The fact that they have been on the Settlement Planets could still be explained by their use of more recent Transformation vehicles to get here. If that happened, then a sizeable recent Dort migration from Earth to the Settlements could have happened. Either that or a small number migrated and then multiplied like crazy on the Settlements. We have no direct evidence that they can reproduce at all, much less rapidly—although their very existence tells us that they must once in a while, or did so with a vengeance at least once. As I've considered these scenarios, they seem impossible to believe. On the other hand, if they came—"

"Excuse me, Laura," Judy interrupted. "I've seen a few Dorts just after they arrived on Earth. That was years ago, when I was a little girl. They were, well, misty. They weren't solid yet, and didn't become solid for quite a while—for days. That's consistent with an *extended* Transformation, isn't it?"

"Yes. It is consistent if by 'extended' you mean Transformation across a distance of many light years at superceleric speeds. Most of us are now familiar with that technology and the fact that Transformations, large or small, must be controlled in terms of 'speed,' but that's a long story, Judy."

Controlling her breathing for the moment, Judy pressed on: "If the Dorts arrived 'solid' to start with, then they didn't get here by any form of Transformation technology. Is that right?"

"Again, yes. If a chicken crosses the road without a mishap, then it will arrive on the other side as solid as when it started. Chickens don't exceed the speed of light and don't use Transformation to cross the road."

"But *Dorts* do—now anyway, and back when I was a little girl; but with all the most recent Transformation deliveries we've seen—deliveries of things and people and Dorts—they became 'solid,' not over days, but in minutes, or a few hours at most. Why is that?"

"Improvements, Judy. The revised and advancing Theory is more powerful. The new Transformation vehicles have been upgraded in step with those advances. . . . Is that enough tutorial, Judy?"

Judy remained on edge. "Well," she said, "as long as we're waiting for the navigation report, there is still one area where I need a booster review."

As she spoke, Laura was surprised to see some of the Directors taking notes, even on such elementary material.

"Sure Judy, ask away."

"You told me before that if we are off course we'll need a lot of power to get on track again, but that we don't have that kind of power. You just mentioned that speed, even here in space or whatever this is we're in, has to do with power and control. It's important then, but I don't really understand it."

"Speed, power, control, distance, and time. I'll explain that—the easy version."

"Thanks! That's the version I need for my nerves. If we're going to die out here, I don't want the confusion of not knowing why!"

"Okay. None of us would consider slow individual transport for any distance. That would be silly and inconvenient. Even at this distance from

Earth, in Jack's short time here, after his i3T transport, he is almost solid already. That's a tribute to the modern technology—even for those little i3T toys. Our i3Ts are *always* set for rapid Transformation. They are set in the factory with a rheostatlike control for slow or fast delivery. At the slowest, it could take months or even years just to transport across a room. . . . Or a road. Most *local* individual transport equipment is set to transport at speeds *slower* than light. Transformation Cones are many times *faster* than celeric speed, but not a fraction of the speed possible. The main dynamic in ordinary space is the speed of light. Anything moving faster than light is no longer in that space, but another dimension. As far as we can tell, things outside the speed of light are beyond the reach of relativity, but they are there. We, in this Cone, are there right now—unnoticed and unaffected by the forces of our familiar universe. The two, even if they might look and feel alike in many ways, are not the same. On launch, a Transformation Cone makes a quantum leap from 'ordinary space' to 'ultraCeleric space' without so much as slowing down. It vaults past the light-speed barrier. We just jump over it without passing through it. In order to return from there back into ordinary space the Transformation *de-Transforms*. That is how it makes the jump back. The Cone's smeared and spread out molecules, *consolidate*—analogous to the way a light wave 'becomes' a photon."

"Why don't we travel at exactly, or close to, the speed of light?"

"We don't mess with anything close to the speed of light—for two reasons. First, it would destroy the Transformation and the universe, and second, it's impossible anyway. Only weightless particles, like photons, or virtually weightless particles like neutrinos are allowed to mess with the C-barrier. In fact, they're apparently supposed to. They spend their 'lives' running around at that speed—so they never 'experience' speed or time. At that speed there is no time and everything is an eternal now."

"If a Transformation Cone is traveling at only a fraction of its possible speed, then why don't they go faster and get where they're going . . . more or less instantly?"

"That's theoretically possible if experiments based on Bell's ancient theorem could somehow be combined with Transformation, but I never could figure out how to do that. Getting somewhere, in almost nothing flat, isn't the problem anyway. It's 'stopping'—de-Transforming—on a dime. And that has to do with energy. It takes a transfer of energy, or power, to stop, to consolidate the Transformation. Much of the borrowed energy of a Transformation is given back when that happens. It goes back into the universe it came from or a nearby planet or star. In either case, the Transformation Cone becomes low on power. That's why having a planet nearby is essential." Laura dabbed her brow with a tissue, looking hopefully at her best friend, the one she roped into coming on this now dangerous "vacation cruise."

"I still don't understand why Transformations don't go faster—forget about infinitely fast," Judy said.

Laura blinked hard, but continued. "In a cruising Transformation, much of our energy of mass is expended to *prevent* greater acceleration and speed. This is tied to the fact that it takes greater and greater force to approach the light-speed barrier from *either* side of it, but if we go too many times over the C-barrier our mass goes down along with the available energy needed to make the quantum jump back to our universe. We derive some energy directly from our original mass as a solid Cone—as one might visualize it before its Earth launch—but most of its energy comes from harvesting energy from the planet's own mass and concentrating it in our gigantic, deeply buried mass-energy toroids. That energy is collected prior to the ten-hour countdown. Once in Transformation-mode, the toroids keep 'recharging'—enough to keep things going, but it's always a tight balance. The more we slow down and get closer to the speed of light, the greater our energy of mass becomes. That's because our mass becomes greater. But we don't get so close that we become an infinite mass or anything close to it. But, as I said, that would be impossible."

Judy frowned. "If it turns out we *are* off course, remind me why we don't simply de-Transform into ordinary space then and there, here and now."

"We dare not consolidate and come to 'rest' in normal space outside the close proximity of a large planet, such as Earth or one of the Settlement Planets. From any nearby planet we can 'borrow' some of its mass-energy in order to hover above it or to put the Cone back into full Transformation-mode."

"Kind of like a gyro-car battery, it won't start without it?"

"Right! The planet's mass gives the Transformation its starting energy."

"What if there's no planet around when we de-Transform back to plane ol' vanilla space?"

"Well, once we are in Transformation, we could do that at any time. It is feasible to come to 'rest,'—that is, to 'stop' or, as I said, to consolidate in real space. But only a fool would want to do that. In a normal-space consolidation we would just float there, forever circling the center of the Galaxy. Even as large as this Transformation is, its rest mass could not efficiently provide the energy necessary to get us going again. At minimum we need a planet-size object nearby. Even a nearby star would be excellent—if it weren't so dangerous.

"At the other extreme," Laura continued, "if we exceed the speed of light too many fold, then we would again become helpless because we'd lose too much of our mass-energy and could no longer de-Transform. We'd be out of control and unable to slow down. We would speed up endlessly, like our universe. Even within the safe limits of our current Cone of Transformation, our energy will be used up in 'stopping.' Jack's little transporter was set for particle speeds faster than this Transformation, but was still in the safe range. He insisted on his own control of the speed 'rheostat' when he obtained his i3T from our 3T factory several years ago—in case he ever wanted to join us on one of our Cones of Transformation and still be able to get back to his office unscathed. So here he is. He made it this far."

"Thanks," Judy said. "That helps. But what I'm wondering too is this: Um, is it impossible for the Dorts to have had advanced Transformation technology when they first came, or appeared on Earth. I can see that they could be using *current* methods to fool us into thinking they arrived from a Settlement planet."

"Right," Laura said. "They *could* be trying to fool us that way. I couldn't prove it either way. As for their arrival three hundred years ago by Transformation, you've heard me say that today I've come to doubt it. I don't believe they had a practical Transformation vehicle then; just the early form of Transformation Theory."

"Perhaps I can add something to this," Ned interjected. "Transformation Theory from its earliest beginnings predicted the insubstantial, hazy appearance that such a traveler would have for a period of time. But so far in my studies of the very earliest Dort contacts, right on up to recent years, I have not found a single unimpeachable source indicating first hand observation of that phenomenon, not until recent times. Historically, there were many rumors and secondhand accounts of it. They could have been planted. Only since *we* improved the Theory and the technology has it been confirmed that newly arriving Dorts have come in the hazed form, and therefore by some form of Transformation technology."

The Directors went on to discuss and reject many other "possible" ways the Dorts could have arrived on planet Earth. Debra Anderson asked, "So what does that leave us with?"

"I believe it leaves us with just one reasonable possibility," Laura said. "There had to be a single place of origin. Ruling out Earth as that place, and ruling out their having advanced Transformation technology in the beginning, they must have traveled to Earth at sublight speeds."

"Like the chicken crossing the street," Debra said, laughing nervously.

"In other words," Laura continued, "even if they came from the relatively nearby Settlement *Planets*—and they are far more distant than nearby *stars*, like Proxima Centauri, they would have to traveled through conventional space, not ultraCeleric space. Such a trip would take thousands of years."

The group sat in dumbfounded silence. Finally, Cameron Greenberg said, "Could that be any more likely than all the other possibilities we've talked about today? We know the Dorts must live a long time, but don't you think that's a bit much? Besides that, there is no known fuel system that could push an ordinary space ship *anywhere near* the speed of light—hmm—so I guess that's why such a trip would have taken thousands of years. Anyway, fast or slow, most of their voyage would have to have been in zero gravity, or at best with some acceleration to provide a little artificial gravity."

There were murmurs of agreement around the table before Laura responded. "I agree," she said. "It's unlikely that any individual, even a Dort, could have lived *that* long, short of a mothball approach such as hibernation, taking on a spore formation, cryonic preservation, or stasis. If that happened, they wouldn't have changed much and I don't think we'd see them in their present form. But suppose they did reproduced in those early days and continued to do so for untold generations—in zero gravity. Whatever their original form, whether they once had bones, an exoskeleton or whatever, their long development in zero gravity could have given them their undefined, bloblike shape. Even humans after many generations, assuming they could keep reproducing in zero gravity, would start to look something like that."

"That could explain a lot of things," Roger Flanders said. "Before I left Dietzman's group for this Transformation there were some ideas like that floating around. The ideas didn't get far, though, because we thought the Dorts always had the Transformation methods we have now. It seems likely to me now, that they didn't. Since they must have come from a single ancestry pool, they could just as well have reached Earth and the Settlements from some other source, without the Earth Dorts having to come from the Settlements, or vice versa."

Stanley Lundeen stroked his beard. "If that were the case," he said, "then they could, as you say, be on other planets, in addition to Earth and the Settlement planets. If they started those voyages more than mere thousands of years ago, but eons ago, then they could be widespread—by now the most prevalent intelligent life form in the Galaxy. Where they came from, their original form, and why they undertook such an exodus is incomprehensible to me. What do you think Ernst?"

Stanley habitually sponsored Ernst Berman. Ernst seldom volunteered, but when asked he often contributed freshness and clarity to a discussion. In readiness for one of his usually welcome pontifications, the Directors became especially alert. Ernst folded his bony-slim hands on the table, leaned his tall, thin frame back into the cushioned chair and, through bushy eyebrows, gave deep consideration to the ceiling.

"Their motivation," he began sonorously, "exceeds the rational." Lowering his gaunt head to look directly at the group, he said, "Their nonrationality is in the service of an internal drive—probably instinctive. Their urge to possess and extend Transformation capability may not be an end, but a means. The diaspora of their kind across this Galaxy that began so long ago—voyages of sacrificial proportions—were not for *exodus*, but for exploration. It was a search for the creativity they do not possess, in order to have an advanced tool—Transformation as it *now* exists.

"Whoever or whatever set them on this course, or even created them with that built-in motivation, had its own motivation—one that even the Dorts may not be aware of. They needed us, or some other creative intelligence to hone the Theory they brought to Earth. They now have it within their reach, but may not be there yet. They may require more from us. I believe they have no interest in the Settlement planets as such. It seems their internal mandate is to return the advanced Theory and its technology to their place of origin—to whoever or whatever sent them to find it.

"Let's remember this: They never before requested anything that we know of—except to be included on our Transformations and for places to give their physics lectures—lectures that have improved, by the way, along with the Theory changes created by humans. But now they have again pressed us to be on this Transformation. Those requests were denied. Now we find that, for the first time, a Transformation may be off course, heading light years from the Settlements. Combining that with the disappearance of the Earth Dorts, I think their location and the reason for our navigational and course problems are obvious. None of you will be surprised at my conclusion. The Dorts are here, with us now on this Transformation. They are here as a hidden multitude. It is not us, but they who control of this Transformation. My friends, we have been hijacked."

SIX

Beneath a stunned silence, brief though it was, Ernst Berman's pronouncement brought out their defenses. At some level, even before Berman had said a word, they all knew, but did not want to. He'd stopped talking, but his words continued their work, surgically removing protective layers of denial as they tried frantically to repair them. Half the group came to its feet. Some were yelling angrily or babbling to one another. There were shouts of "That's just your opinion!" condescending "Tut-tuts," and "Let's consider this with at least a little rationality." Some ran around aimlessly trying to make sense of flickering screens. Debra was becoming distraught and asthmatic Judy was gasping for air. Some sat down again, immobilized. Their efforts were useless. The mechanisms and supports for continued inaction were destroyed from within, for Ernst had spoken directly to their fear.

The din and turmoil seemed endless, but had, in fact, lasted only a few minutes when silenced by a voice of power and authority. It took a moment for the group to realize that it was Ned. In that vacuum of silence he delivered a cascade of instructions, first to one Director, then to the next. As Ned continued his rapid-fire orders the expressions of fear and confusion were replaced by understanding nods and looks of determination. Together, the assigned tasks made a pattern for focused action.

Laura watched and listened to this in astonishment. Her gentle, studious, kind, tentative, and often klutzy Ned had just turned, before her very eyes, into a dynamo. She gasped with the chill of excitement as his final words rumbled across the room—"That's it for *Step One*. Do it! Get it done and meet back here for conference in one hour—sharp! Now *HAUL ASS!*"

Except for Jack and Laura, the exodus was immediate. Ned watched the others leave, and then sank into his chair.

"That was a hell of a performance, Ned," Jack said with admiration. "Is there anything I can do?"

"Yes," Ned replied in a calm voice. "You could climb back on that transporter plate right now and get back to Earth while you still can."

Jack looked insulted for a moment, but he soon recovered. "There are still a couple days to go before that'll be necessary. Technically anyway."

"Maybe," was Ned's wooden response.

Jack chattered on. "I wish we could line everybody up and send them all back on the transporter. This Transformation cost billions, but it isn't worth the loss of a single life."

Laura said, "That's a noble thought, Jack, but not a possibility. That little transporter toy of yours can only handle one at a time, and this many parsecs from Earth it could only handle one person every couple of weeks. Returning from a cruising Transformation takes a lot more than getting to it."

Jack wasn't ready to give up. "What if we stopped the Transformation? Then there wouldn't be that growing distance problem, except for drift."

Laura was starting to become edgy. She was thinking about the assignment Ned had given her, and time was moving on. Jack was supposed to understand these things!

Laura tried again: "Two problems with that idea, Jack. First, given the numbers of our crew, it would take forty years to get everyone off, even without drift. And second, if we weren't near a star or other body of considerable mass when we came to rest, or *drift*, as you called it, then our energy of mass would be too weak for even you to get back. You'll have to go while we're on the move."

Ignoring Laura's obvious discomfort, Jack said, "How close would the Transformation Cone have to drift toward such a mass to make the transporter, the $i3T$, effective?"

Laura sighed, but went on. "Depends on the other's mass," she said. "If we were close enough for geosynchronous orbit of Earth, or a planet of similar mass, for example, or even, say, half the distance from Earth to the Moon, that would be close enough for our mass-energy transformers to regain some power. After that, we could descend slowly to any level, or even—in theory at least—*land* on the planet. We would gain more energy the closer we came to the planet's center of mass. It's a process that allows enormous energy borrowing, even from orbit."

Jack frowned and said, "How close would we have to come to a star, say the size of our Sun?"

"Somewhere between the distance of Mercury and Venus from the Sun," she said with a hint of protest in her voice. She raised her hands, palms out as if to stop the next question, she said, "Excuse me. I have a lot to do and no time. You understand."

After an apologetic look to Jack, she turned and walked over to Ned. She kissed him and squeezed him hard around the neck in a quick embrace. "I love you," she whispered. Then she turned and left the room. Ned watched her go. He felt a surging lightness in his chest that took him by surprise. She'd never said that to him before.

"I'm no Transformation physicist," Jack went on, "but from what Laura just said it would seem feasible to me for us to—"

"Forget it Jack," Ned cut in. "The Dorts, I believe, have altered our course and are still at it. We'll know definitely very soon. Do you realize the power that's taking? Our own toroidal mass-energy converter is almost thirty kilometers around. The Tesla Tank provides for our minor internal energy needs *and* triggers the converter, when it is ready. But the Dorts must have a Tank of their own *and* an independent converter. Either that or they're somehow supplementing whatever they've got by hooking into our equipment. Most likely they already have enough of their own power that we couldn't de-Transform now even if we wanted to. We'd have to coordinate."

"I see what you mean. Okay. What can I do to help? I'm staying at least a while longer. Maybe for the duration."

"Not for the duration, Jack. If we . . . never . . . get back, someone has to tell the story. Every year more Dorts will come to Earth from their eons-long flights—all with the same goal: To grab any Theory or equipment upgrades and then, like salmon, try to get back to their place of origin—with more human hostages under their pseudopodal fins. So you can't stay, Jack. You're the only one who can guarantee the word gets back. Humanity will have to know. Defenses will have to be worked out."

"You're right," Jack said, "but let's hope the navigation report will prove our worries wrong."

"Yeah, well I worry about your getting stuck here. In a while it'll be too late. If the Dorts are taking our energy right now, getting out could already be a problem. If they're brewing up something else to surprise us with, you may not get out at all. I think you should leave immediately."

Jack shook his head. "You told the Directors to be back here in an hour. If they've had any luck at all on the jobs you've given them, then we should have strong clues, or actual proof, of what we're now assuming—that they're *here* on this Transformation and up to dirty tricks. If I go back without witnessing that proof, then I'll be branded as a garden variety Dort-paranoid. In that case my *warning* won't be worth a damn. I have to stay until I've heard or seen that proof. It's just an hour more. It won't make that much difference."

Ned knew he was right. Just then a signal light on screen seven began to blink. Ned said, "Okay boss. You win. You're a biologist so go help Ellen, Judy, and Flanders figure out how to kill the bastards! Prelims are coming in already. I have to get busy now. See you back here for conference in forty-five minutes."

SEVEN

Jack left and Ned moved to screen seven. He touched the flashing signal key and Doug's face appeared. As they made eye contact, Doug raised his right forefinger and began.

"First," he said, "Navigation confirmed course alteration by the time I got here. Since then, some of the other details have been analyzed. We're heading in excess of a full degree more toward Galactic center than before, and heading north of the Galactic plane by three-quarters of a degree. Before, when we were on course for the Settlement planet, we were heading south by close to half a degree. So, saying we're *off course* is putting it mildly!"

Doug's second digit now appeared.

"Second, I immediately gave the approximate coordinates—as close as Navigation could figure them—to Laura and Ernst to determine the power needed to do that. It must be a hell of a lot to have diverted us that much! The Dorts must have additional power sources we don't know about." Doug gave Ned a moment to absorb that; then continued. "In order to get those directional updates, the navigation probes required a broad range of spot checks using normal-space techniques. That really sucked the juice! Getting a few photons from outside the Transformation is like turning it inside out. But you already knew that."

Now three fingers were up.

"Third, the location of any Dort power source within this Transformation has not yet been detected. Stan and David have pooled staff and equipment resources with half a dozen of my units as per your orders. Looks as if it'll take a bit longer. The Dorts must be blocking our probes—continuously, it seems. They can't possibly keep up that kind of energy drain for long. Again, a power problem—theirs this time. The deeper they are in this Cone, the more energy it'll take to detect their location—but that's *nothing* compared to that outside navigation scan we just did. One good thing though, if they're blocking our internal scan nonstop, it's taking more of their energy to block us out than it is for us to detect. They have to be wasting a lot of energy just to remain hidden, to make things look normal. Our instrument checks show they aren't tapping into or diverting our energy. They obviously predicted we'd use the probes if we suspected they were here, but at the same time that gives us an incremental advantage. When their blocking system is in operation there is no way they can detect our scan. So they may not know, at least from that, that we're on to them."

Four fingers.

"Finally, some of David's people have joined Debra's and my forces to work out communications possibilities. We can tune in and focus all modalities simultaneously—all channels, wavelengths and circuits, all the traditional ones and one nontraditional. If the Dorts refuse to talk back to us, assuming we want that, we still have a good chance of threatening them. Using *traditional* approaches, we presume the Dorts would have had the foresight to bug our equipment, but I believe our communication consoles are safe from that. They were the last things we installed. They couldn't have gotten near them. We've already checked everything we're using. These systems have the usual radio, microwave and other remote two-way sensing devices. We've shut all that down for now. No remote spying possible till we turn it on again.

"Even without that shut down, there's a strong likelihood that none of the usual systems could reach them anyway. We've never seen a Dort anywhere near the complex, and this Cone was a hive of human activity a full year before Transformation. In that case, they and we are incommunicado. Anyway, as you suggested, David Michaels's people and mine are working on that. Debra Anderson's traditional methods are energy efficient, but probably won't work even after we reopen the remote systems. Dave's last-ditch approach is a nontraditional one if we have to use it. It's a kind of code sender using small earthquakes that will center wherever we find the Dorts—if and when that happens. That'll make the scoundrels sit up and take notice!

"That's it so far, Ned. Any comments?"

"Just one. If the Dorts are hiding their power source by blocking our internal mass-scanner probes, then the readout graphs could still give us a clue to their location."

Doug looked quizzical. "How do you figure that?"

"Blocking takes what? Fifty to a hundred times more energy than a search probe, right?"

"Right! A lot of energy," Doug responded. "A tremendous amount, in fact. To prevent discovery, they have to smooth out the bounce signals we get back from the ones we send. So what?"

Ned smiled. "So . . . if you had to save energy, and we know they have to, or else we could gain a significant advantage—not just an incremental one—would you, as a fairly bright Dort, leave the blocker on full time, or, as you said, *continuously*?"

Doug gasped. "Great Gibbering Lemurs! Of course not! They'd use a detector to pick up our probe. That, in turn, could almost instantly activate their blocking system—a great energy saver! All this time we've been looking for the *high* readings. In that fraction of a second—that *almost* instant activation—all we'd get is an *insignificant* spike at the location of the energy source. The faster their blocking system kicks in, the smaller the spike. *But it would be there!*"

Doug looked off-screen and said, "Did you catch that, Stan?" Then, looking back at Ned, "He heard. Stan's already digging through that pile of graphs and readouts. If you're right, we should be able to pinpoint their location."

"Good. Anything else?" Ned asked.

"No."

"Then I'll see you in thirty-five minutes."

Ned tapped another Accept. It had been flashing for several minutes.

"Cameron Greenberg here," the face said unnecessarily. "As ordered, George Sachs and I have figured out an ingenious strategy for informing, and interpreting, this whole mess to the crew. And we can do it in a way that will cause little upset and preserve the crew's morale."

"What's that?" Ned asked, "Honesty?"

"Why yes. How did you happen to think of that? It was even simpler. You see, once you got all the Managers going on this activity, including most of our Operations personnel, it didn't take long before everyone knew something was up. In fact, I guess they already knew. My staff has been busy making inquiries. They've been doing that for a while now, and calling in. Seems that news of a possible course change seeped out of Navigation even before Stan and Debra got hold of it. Why is it that us top guys, hehehe, are always the last to know? It's humiliating! Anyway, combining that knowledge with the assignments we've been handing out, it was only minutes before everybody down to the last sanitary engineer had a pretty good idea that the Dorts are probably here in numbers, that they screwed up our course, and that we're looking for them now. Everybody is madder'n hell and loaded for bear. The morale, in a word, is *marvelous*!" He added that Debra would be composing regular information bulletins for rumor control and "preservation of esprit de corps."

Ned allowed himself a chuckle; then asked, "How about those other matters?"

Cameron replied in a glum voice, "Oh yeah. That'll take a little longer. Priorities you know. If such a catastrophe were to happen, such as a de-Transformation into normal space, or a mythical *Twister* hit, then—if we were still alive—we'd be at least halfway ready with contingency plans. But that's another six or eight hours anyway. We're having some of our people from Social Dynamics and Personnel meeting with Dr. Lufti as you suggested. It would take some flexible redeployment of personnel and semimajor physical plant reconstruction and expansion of the hospital facility itself, but I think we can at least be ready with *plans* by then.

"But, frankly," he continued, "I think it's overkill to consider such unlikely events. But if you insist! The biggest unknown is the *number* of psychological casualties we would need room for. Who knows how many additional beds we'd need! Another question is the number of deaths. We can only guess at those kinds of unknowns. But we will! We'll guess till the cows come home. But

Twisters are just a theory, and unintended de-Transformations can't happen, except, maybe, through sabotage. Hmm—I see what you mean."

"Somehow, Cameron, I knew you'd figure it out. Now get motivated and accelerate those casualty plans. I hope your optimism is right, but don't rule out that sabotage idea. See you in conference in twenty-five minutes."

Ned cut over to the next call. It was the Security Director. "Hi Clint. How's it going?"

Clint Bracket looked formal and austere at the best of times. Now he looked grim. "Not so good. We've been going over our arsenal. If ordinary weapons can kill Dorts, then we may be all right in a one-on-one situation. But if we are attacked in large numbers, we don't have enough weapons. This Transformation was set up as a scientific expedition to the supposedly friendly Settlements. I've long said I needed more weapons and more trained men. We'll just have to recruit from other areas and do some training. But that's beside the point now. We're not ready for a war. Another possibility is to catch them in their lair and use biological or chemical means to kill them. I talked with Ellen Stone. Her group has been pooling its ideas on that with Jack Lewis, Judy Olafson, Doc Flanders and a few others. There are many possibilities, but their present opinion is that Dorts are invulnerable to the usual poisons and microorganisms. My preference is to search and destroy using incineration and lasers."

Ned sighed, "So much for extremes. Are there any less drastic options?"

"Just a couple ideas on that. Containment is one; but we'd have to isolate them from their equipment. Intimidation's another. We could just threaten to incinerate them, or blow up their part of the complex, wherever they are. Tactics would depend on a lot of things in either case, such as our estimate of their capabilities to defend, and so on. Until we know more about those things we'll just have to keep exploring the whole range of possibilities."

"Speaking of exploring, how's the search going?" Ned asked.

"The Directors have been helpful there. Especially Doug. They've been able to free up half the personnel for the search. They're checking every corridor, passage and closet, the walls, ceilings, floors, ventilation shafts, pipe alleys, the works. So far they haven't found anything unusual. No passages we weren't aware of, no unusual equipment, nothing. A special group of technicians is double-checking the energy gear to see if the Dorts could be tapping into our power. The first sweep on that was negative. I'm sure our instruments would pick up an energy drain, but to make sure we're also searching through the instruments themselves for tampering."

"Thanks Clint. Keep your people working on those options. That's a crucial search operation all right, but I'm having second thoughts about the destroy part. I'll be asking you more about our defensive situation later. Have to sign off now. See you in conference in ten or fifteen minutes."

Ned switched back to Doug's signal. It started blinking halfway through the report from Clint. The screen was blank except for a view of his empty office. *Doug must have gotten tired of waiting*, Ned thought as he turned off the screen and walked back to stand before the empty conference table. Bright, low hanging lights illuminated the dark polished table and the glistening, cushioned leather chairs. Ned's head and shoulders were in deep shadow above the hooded brilliance. His profile flickered in silhouette against phantom-pale screens on a distant wall. He felt alone and uneasy. *Is this a nightmare or reality?* he wondered.

But there was no time for fear or whimsy. Within minutes the shiny leather seats would receive impressions, and anxious eyes would be turned his way in search of comforting reality—not for the security of certainty, but for the solace of further action. Could he deliver more than paralysis, and preserve the Transformation?

Ned sat, took his pen in hand, arranged the pad, and began to write. He wrote with savage speed in phrases and key words. To anyone else, the outline would appear as the illegible and meaningless scrawl of a madman—except for the printed words on top of the first page: STEP ONE.

EIGHT

The conference was about to begin.

The Nine, led by one called Doyan, filed past the multitude to enter a giant geode of dim-glowing and changing colors. The Integrator's ultrasonic signal to begin the meeting originated from there and was itself occasioned by a series of probes from high above in the Great Cone. Those electronic probes were met by activation of a signal-blocking system, canceling the probes and making them useless.

The Nine spaced themselves at regular intervals to circle the lone central figure—the Integrator that emitted the signal. Ringed by fifty glowing, color-changing disks, the Integrator extended its sensitive, translucent arms above the disks and touched them delicately as conditions, signaled by the colors, required.

High above, nitid minerals encrusted in the immense natural geode returned the flickering disks' light through a million faceted, prismatic reflections. From that cavernous, glittering, vaulted dome shone the likeness of the firmament.

Beneath that shimmering skyscape, the meeting began.

An arm-width protuberance merged from each individual in the Circle of Nine. The feeler-protrusions slowly extended upward for seven meters to touch and intercoil above the Integrator's central hump. Like a gigantic blister, the hump bulged to a full meter, as high as it was wide, before folding in upon itself to create a circular, vaselike lip that continued its quavering, upward movement toward the entwined and now descending tentacles. The lip then closed to seal in the entwined extensions. The Nine, now Ten, became One—and the conference began.

The meeting was of great importance and lasted much longer than usual. During that time, they exchanged thousands of quintillions of information bits, discussed matters at length and argued endlessly. Many items were unresolved and tabled, others were agreed upon and assignments accepted. The protracted meeting lasted, by human measure, less than a nanosecond.

Following the conference, the procession of Nine left the geode and retraced the entry routes. Only one item of agreement was now clear and paramount: There would be no communication with the humans until *after* the Twister.

NINE

"Where's Doug?" Ned asked after everyone else was seated.

Dave Michaels answered, "Navigation called him back twenty minutes ago. Something urgent and confusing. He tried to call you but couldn't wait. Said he'd report as soon as he could."

The status reports were quickly summarized. Stanley Lundeen had located a number of previously unknown energy sources some fifteen and thirty kilometers below and believed that was where the Dorts had to be. The most powerful sources were at the deepest levels.

Ernst Berman had been working with Doug. "We estimated," Ernst said, "that the Dorts' energy potential is no less than thirty percent of the Transformation power 3T had installed. That's a minimum estimate based on our most reliable figures. To gauge their maximum potential would require a little experiment. They are using their power to divert our course, but it's ours that keeps us moving. So it's a cheap piggyback ride they're taking at our expense."

"From that, what do you recommend?" Ned asked.

"We recommend that our energy resources take a rest by gradually being reduced. That would force the Dorts to increase their energy output to keep the Great Cone on whatever new course they selected. Then we can make a better estimate of their maximum energy resources. After our power installations rest a bit and develop a little extra capacity, we can then abruptly reengage to full capacity. That would divert the course, as minute as that might be, thus foiling the Dorts. Then they'd be just as screwed up and lost as we are."

The other reports were equally brief. George Sachs and Cameron Greenberg, along with Debra Anderson's help, believed their staff would soon be ready to broadcast and publish detailed announcements about the crisis. They repeated the idea that this was essential for morale, rumor control and general readiness. Clinton Bracket agreed, but was pessimistic about their defensive posture. He thought it would be necessary to go on the offensive. Ellen Stone reported no real progress from her group. Dr. Lufti feared that under certain negative scenarios the planned hospital expansion would be inadequate. Debra Anderson announced that traditional communications were ready and that Dave Michaels had arranged, with staff and engineering help from Doug's group, for a simple toroidal power diverter that could, using code, focus small earthquakes near the main Dort energy source. That, she explained, would initiate a frank and symbolic interchange with the Dorts. Clinton was irritated about any attempt to communicate with the Dorts, "symbolically," in "code," or any other way.

Laura explained how a long shaft, four meters in diameter, could be "excavated" to reach the Dorts. Such cavities had been made before in some of the smaller Cones of Transformation, but for other reasons. This one could be made by de-Transforming a focused part of the Cone, starting from their present depth, and "boring" right through the bottom of the Cone. It would be like coring an apple. The core would be left to float in ordinary space, leaving behind a kind of bottomless silo or elevator shaft within the Transformation Cone. In Doug's absence, she announced that a crew of his engineers was already at work modifying one of their torpedo-shaped cargo conveyors so it could act as a "crawling" elevator within the shaft. Additional tread belts and related sections were being forged to operate with it.

Ned asked, "How long will it take to expel that core into normal space to create the shaft?"

Laura replied, "Once the portable de-Transformation equipment is set up, the excavation can be done instantly, like de-Transforming a Cone into real space. That setup will be ready in another half-hour, and the 'torpedo elevator' would take an additional hour. Doug assigned the most capable of his lead engineers, Zachary Parker, to be in charge of turning one of the cargo conveyors into a kind of creeping elevator."

Clint again grumbled about so much effort going into the "communications option." He said, "The shaft should be blasted right through their energy source." But he backed off that idea when Laura explained it would "turn the Great Transformation Cone into the Great Mushroom Cloud."

The meeting continued without pause until everyone seemed to have said his or her piece. During the pause that followed, the Directors noticed Ned's now famous and furious note taking. He'd finished logging the gist of the reports and began to modify another sheet in his usual illegible hand. The Directors soon began to talk among themselves and were becoming louder and more animated as Ned gave those last scribbled pages a neat and legible title. He thought of something else and continued to write even as the din grew louder. In the midst of this, a tense and distraught Doug Groth entered the room unnoticed. He remained, for a moment, catching his breath, and finally croaked, "I have news," but he was ignored.

Finally, Ned stopped writing and looked up. Everybody became quiet. "I believe we're now ready to roll," he said, holding up the scribbled plan. "This is

Step Two, if you hadn't already guessed. We will be following through with the goal we set before—to contact and negotiate with the Dorts."

Doug tried again, in his high voice, to speak, but Clinton Bracket, beet red, jumped to his feet and bellowed his outrage at the idea of talking to the enemy without so much as a show of force. "This is a military operation and our task is to crush them—not to dicker with them!" He glared at Ned.

Ned looked coldly at the seething hulk and said, "I have no intention of arguing with you or trying to pacify you," and then added, looking around the group, "or anyone else for that matter."

Doug cringed.

"The time we have available to act is unknown, but I'm going on the assumption that we're talking hours or days at most. Not weeks. We don't have time to wrangle about approach, philosophy, strategy or tactics. And I'm not going to fight about who's in charge. If there were all the time in the world, we could develop sixty options and then vote on the best one. The work and input from all of you is essential, but we can't have divided leadership. You of all people, Officer Bracket, should know that."

"I really must interrupt," came Doug Groth's high, intense voice, again from a shadowed corner of the room. Everyone turned toward Doug as he approached. "I hate to tell you this, but we're not going to have those days, or even the hours that Ned just spoke of. I'm afraid we're talking only minutes—minutes at most. We're headed straight for a gravitational wave center the mass of a hundred million suns. It exceeds our worst, most improbable fears, and it's as immense as anything yet discovered in all of space. We'll not be able to avoid it. It's a twis...s...s...."

As Doug tried to speak the last word, it happened. His head and body bloated and gnarled into shapeless and undulating waves, ruptured and split apart—along with the table, walls, all the people—and the entire Transformation.

Not only stars, dust and gas were orbiting that most monstrous of all black holes, but other black holes were themselves trapped in its swirling gravitational pull. The killer Twister was beyond anything even theory had envisioned.

TEN

Ned's first impression was the storm of pain in his head and joints; and worse, the feeling of nausea. He realized he was lying face down on a floor in some dark place, but could not remember how he'd gotten there or what had happened. He knew he'd been unconscious, but had no idea how long. Sounds began to penetrate his consciousness. Far-off vibrations and droning machines reminded him of the Transformation, but the connections in his mind were loose and disordered as he struggled for control. He felt as if moving in sickening, slow motion through layers of mist. He slipped into unconsciousness once more before arousing to a nameless horror. It crept through him before the realization of its source. The distant sounds seemed to come closer—the groans, the retching, the sobs.

A wall screen began to shimmer in the background, and the swirling cloud of confusion in his head began to lift. With dawning visual orientation he struggled to get up, but fell back. He tried again and managed to prop his shaking body on two elbows, but his head still hung limp between his shoulders. He tried to lift his throbbing head but it would not budge, and again he was roiled by nausea and weakness. But this time he remained conscious. He turned his eyes and then his hanging head as far as he could in the direction of the sounds. The topsy-turvy view was further distorted by the pulsating, shadowy gloom cast by the solitary flickering screen.

From his capsized position he saw bodies scattered on the floor—some as writhing mounds of shadow; others, still and silent. Through the horror of the passing moments Ned came to realize that a Twister had come and gone and that the agonized sounds and movements, as dreadful as they were, were also those of life.

Almost without thinking Ned dragged himself toward an unmoving shape—a familiar one. The vertigo and nausea had lifted somewhat and he was strong enough to raise his head. In a minute he reached her.

"Laura?" he called, but there was no answer. He felt the pulse in her neck and saw she was breathing. He suddenly found himself sobbing deeply and holding her in his arms.

Ned had been holding her for an hour when she began weakly to thrash around, whimpering and snorting. Finally, she seemed to relax and in a few moments opened her eyes. "Oh darling," she said faintly, reaching an arm around his neck, but it relaxed and fell limp to her side. She was asleep again, but this time a restful one.

As he held Laura, and the minutes continued to pass, he became dimly aware of other activity in the room. Doc Lufti was moving from person to person with his stethoscope. Earlier on, he noticed that little Ellen Stone was, by turns pushing forcefully and rhythmically on Clinton's chest and breathing into his mouth. She looked frantic.

Doug Groth was hunched over the keyboard of the only working console, punching things in and checking feedback on the screen.

Lufti checked Ned and Laura. He told Ned he thought they'd both be all right. In a low tone he said that Clint's best friend, George Sachs, was dead, but the others would probably make it—except he wasn't sure about Clint. He moved on to help Ellen.

One by one, after several hours, most of the screens and equipment began to function and the lights returned.

The next four days were hellish; but the first two were the worst. The death toll had mounted to several hundred. The Transformation's population had been decimated. The small, unprepared hospital overflowed into the halls with critical cases. Less critical patients and those well into rapid recovery, were treated and returned to their own quarters—Clint Bracket among them. Dozens were derailed mentally and a special section was set up for them.

Doug recruited the Transformation's soul Bible-banger, Elmer Slattery, the Recreation Coordinator, and former Chaplain, to handle the looming mass funeral service, and a few smaller ones in the days that followed. There were no embalmings. Just a simple, dignified service with prayers, songs, commemorative speeches, the playing of taps, a few twenty-one gun salutes and the somber sequential clang of eight bells. The burials took place by the de-Transformation ejection of the bodies into normal space—where they lingered briefly before exploding.

Slattery had been a Chaplain in the army and an undertaker years before that. He quit both professions to get away from bloodshed and cadavers. He hated to be called Reverend because he associated the title with death, but regained the title without being asked.

Except for several of Stanley Lundeen's Astrophysics sections, the hospital, and some support services, everything else was either shut down or operating with skeleton crews. Barely sixty percent of those still living were physically and mentally able to function, even marginally well, and most of those were recruited for hospital and quasi-nursing tasks or for food service and the hydroponic gardens.

By day four following the Twister, the death toll had leveled off and most of the remaining hospital patients had responded well to treatment. They were discharged to their own quarters with scheduled monitoring through office or home nursing visits. Many returned to their regular duties. Gradually, all the departments began to functioning closer to normal.

In the meantime Stanley Lundeen, Laura Shane, Doug Groth and all their combined teams worked together to better assess what had happened. Their conclusions were extraordinary. On the fifth day, Laura presented those findings to all the Directors. She explained that deep within the Theory of Transformation was the unlikely, virtually unbelievable possibility of a cruising Transformation being seriously effected by a Twister. Except for one scientific paper, the physics and mathematics of that kind of event had never been explored. The paper was erroneously ignored. To produce a Transformation Twister, the paper stated it would have to pass close to a black hole. To meet the criteria for a Twister, however, the Transformation could not enter the black hole's event horizon. If that happened, the Transformation would be destroyed. On the other hand, the physical result of a Transformation's particles passing close to an event horizon would cause a major, but temporary, disruption of its unique particle-wave structure. Rapid reassembly of that structure would take place as the particles moved beyond the super gravity of the black hole. The final outcome of a "minor" Twister—major Twisters had never been explored, even in theory—would be a minute rearrangement of the original particles in ultraCeleric space and a slight alteration in the Transformation's spatial direction in ordinary space.

On that much, the "experts" were now agreed. Their opinions, however, of what would happen to electronic equipment, and to living creatures in a Twister, differed widely. Arguments ranged from total breakdown, including death without exception, to minor changes of little significance. Of the few "experts" to eventually comment on the original article that postulated the possibility of a Twister, they fell into two camps. On the benign side of the argument, the likelihood of humans experiencing inner ear and dramatic visual distortions for a brief period of time were described; but the likelihood of death, insanity or even temporary unconsciousness was thought to be remote. Theoreticians holding this view were the Transformation "optimists," and Laura included herself in that group.

The optimists had high confidence in the power and stability of Transformation forces, even near the event horizon of a black hole. This was because of the inherent independence of a Transformation from ordinary spacetime dimensions.

The theory pessimists expected more harmful results. They were less confident of the stability of forces operating within a Transformation. They noted that energy borrowing by a Transformation is, by definition, temporary. Their argument stressed the temporary part of the borrowing, rather than the independence from relativity that the optimists pinned their arguments on. The pessimists believed that payback of the borrowed energy would become urgent at the interface between an event horizon and a Transformation.

Laura explained further that no theorist, optimist or pessimist, had ever imagined what actually happened in this Twister. They had experienced a continuous series of Twisters, amounting to one long one.

The Transformation had been passing through the "empty" space between Galactic spiral arms. The black holes should have been made visible, but from a cruising Transformation they could not use x-rays or other techniques to detect it until almost the last minute. What they came upon, and what the Dorts had evidently known in advance, was a circle, or wheel, of black holes, numbering in the hundreds, that were orbiting just outside the event horizon of a common gravitational center—the mammoth black hole. The "smaller," satellite black holes were so close together that many of their own event horizons actually touched or overlapped. Like a Ferris wheel, the "wheel" of black holes they encountered was at right angles to the Galactic equator and edge on as the Transformation approached its southern rim.

Had the Transformation passed within this wheel of black holes or any of their event horizons, rather than barely skirting its edges, its particles would have diverged in a spray of chaos, and that would have been the end of the

Transformation. As it was, it neared the wheel's southern edge, was turned, or twisted—originating the term Twister—slightly north, then neared and passed the next event horizon, then the next, and so on; but each time it edged farther away from the next event horizon than the previous one, until it broke away and continued on its journey.

The consequences were twofold. The physical effects on people and machines were more serious and longer lasting than the optimists predicted, but less serious than the pessimists expected. Secondly, the change of course for the Transformation was greater than the theory predicted—at least for a close encounter with a single black hole.

Laura concluded, "From this experience, we can now be sure that if this had been a single Twister instead of a series of them, the devastation would have been minimal. The fact that we survived, to the extent we have, powerfully proves the real stability of Transformations."

"That's all very interesting," Clint Bracket snarled, "but where in hell are we? The Dorts have been shoving us around, but where to now?"

Laura sighed and said, "I think I'd rather have Doug or Stan answer that one."

With a look and a nod, Stan deferred to a fatigued and tousled Douglas Groth, whose shock of red hair straggled across his eyes and cheekbones.

"We were off course," Doug said, stroking back the locks from his bloodshot eyes, "even before the Twister—as you already knew. We were on the mean plane of the Milky Way heading in the direction of the star Kolob, in the center of the Galaxy. That's supposed to be as close as you can get to where God lives. Now we're heading away from there in a new direction. The Twister turned us sharply northward. How far north we were unable to determine until late this morning. Gentlemen, and ladies, we are now heading directly to Galactic North—at a right angle to our previous course! To be a little more precise, we're at right ascension thirteen hours, and declination twenty-eight degrees. And furthermore, I'd say—"

"—What!" several interrupted at once. Judy Olafson, who rarely swore and hated profanity from others, finished their thoughts by saying, "I don't know shit about ascensions and declinations, but I know something about what's straight up from the galactic disk. There's nothing, not a damn thing out there!"

Astrophysicist Stan Lundeen raised his eyebrows and said, "Oh yes, there are some things out there—way out there. A couple hundred globular star clusters used to halo our Galaxy. It's a lot less now. If we're lucky, the Dorts have us headed for one of those that are left."

"What do you mean, '*if* we're lucky'?" Judy asked.

"I mean, if we don't encounter a globular cluster, then we really have a long trip ahead."

Everyone looked at Stan in disbelief. This time he deferred to Ernst Berman who, although a mathematician, also knew his elementary astronomy. He accommodated as usual by saying out loud what everybody was afraid to admit, but already knew.

"The next stop, if ever, after missing a star cluster, would be somewhere in the super cluster of galaxies called Coma. Things that far from our Galaxy are not getting any closer. Everything out there is moving away very fast. Centuries ago, the Coma galaxies were over three hundred and fifteen million light years away! They're twice that far now. Like everything else giving off light from that far away, their wavelengths are getting longer. Their spectrums are redshifting more every day. Everything that far out is getting farther away from our Galaxy every second—in Coma's case, over fourteen thousand kilometers farther away every second. Centuries ago it was moving away at only half that speed."

"What's speeding it up?" someone asked who already knew the answer.

"We can thank negative gravity, or dark energy, for the explosive acceleration of the redshift and the expansion of our universe. Dark gravity is even more powerful than the gravitational influence of dark matter. So, if we miss a star cluster, our journey will be long indeed."

"Star clusters are close to us, nearby, right now . . . right?" Judy asked in a quavering voice.

"Even reaching a 'nearby' globular star cluster will take a decade in this Galaxy, even at our current hyperCeleric speed. Either way, this Cone is going to be our home for a long time!"

"If that's the way it is," Judy exclaimed, "I'm getting off right here—right now!" And then she laughed.

And then she cried.

ELEVEN

Slap!

"Christ! A mosquito!" Laura groaned, brushing its corpse off her thigh. "How did they get here? You'd think the Twister would have killed the pests."

Ned laughed at that as he wrapped the shredded sash of his blue terry cloth robe around his waste and sat down beside her on the grass. They were dripping wet from the night swim in Laura's pool. The distant man-made Luminaerie formed a soft, parhelic ring of light around the Cone's horizon. It was at full moon intensity, it's highest "night" radiance. There were no sharp shadows across the landscape, only diffuse contrasts from gray to black, except near the Luminaerie itself where fuzzy, Milky Way-like clouds of scintillation seemed to float unmoving and mysterious in the atmosphere above it. Closer in where brighter "stars" and "constellations" formed by lights from houses in the valleys surrounding Laura's own hilltop aerie.

It was the first time in over a week that Ned had laughed. Those days had depleted everyone emotionally and physically. No one had been laughing, or even smiling. There was little to smile about, much less laugh. Ned was surprised he still could.

In addition to his usual administrative duties, Ned, the other Directors, the Operations Managers and supervisors, the counselors, and Elmer Slattery—the new and now very busy Chaplain—spent every spare moment composing letters of condolence to relatives of the deceased. Most of the letters were eventually dispatched in a bundle via i3T to Jack's wife for distribution back on Earth. At best, it would now take some weeks before the packet could arrive there, if at all, given their now unfamiliar and only vaguely understood location. With that package, Jack also enclosed a long personal letter to her, and information about what had happened. He also enclosed a related dispatch for her to give to the media. And there were other communications for delivery to a variety of organizations and agencies, including a lengthy private note to his friend, Reinholdt Dietzman.

Before a letup in their immediate duties, the stress of recent days was telling on Ned and Laura. Like everyone, they were exhausted. With that first opportunity for rest, Ned slept most of the day and all the previous night, as did Laura. The rest and swim gave welcome relief and was long overdue for them both.

The scheduled plan to confront the Dorts was delayed by the crisis, but tomorrow everything would be ready. Or so Ned hoped.

Ned complimented the Directors and their staffs. They had done well under difficult circumstances. Many staff had been killed or temporarily incapacitated—some permanently. Had the Twister resulted in resentment and rebellion against the Directors, no one would have blamed them or been surprised. Miraculously that did not happen. If anything, it was the opposite. Detailed and timely information was communicated to every person aboard, including Ned's "Step Two" plan to penetrate the enclave of those kidnappers and murderers. Motives of hatred and revenge infused the crew's work with special inspiration. Although major portions of Ned's plan had been postponed, they were more relevant now than ever. Ned shook his head and scowled. *We'll have to be careful,* he thought. *Hatred and revenge could be a two-edged sword.*

Ned had, indeed, become contemplative, but, sensing something, turned his head to look at Laura. He found her looking at him intently, as if into his soul. For a second he thought to lighten the moment by saying something humorous, but her look, the line of her cheek and the curve of her body put that out of his mind. A surge of warmth passed through him and he felt her closeness as never before. Hesitantly, she moved her arms apart. It had been so long. Eternity had come and gone since they last touched. They moved closer, their bodies barely touched, then came together with mutually welcoming arms.

They held each other, and kissed for a long time, their bodies pressing and moving together, their hands now wandering without inhibition amidst loving words and sounds. Their pent-up longing was for release, to reexplore the mysterious and familiar tributaries of their rapture, their passion, their ecstasy—whether harsh and demanding or gentle and loving. They would have it all.

Their long day and night of rest gave them the strength for that liberation. As though their lives depended on it, they came together in a dance of extravagance and control, like acrobats on a high wire, maintaining the thrill as long as possible before tumbling to the net below.

An hour later they made love again, but more serenely. Tired and mellow, they returned to Laura's house where they went to bed and slept in each other's arms another night of deep sleep and rest, only to wake the next morning with renewed vigor and desire.

This time, for Ned's part, the sense of tenderness outweighed his ardor. Laura had the same feelings, but in reverse. Unconvincingly, he fended off Laura's genteel, but determined approach, explaining that his morning arousal meant nothing. Laura believed him, but was insistent. She turned him gently on his back, and assumed an engulfing ascendancy over him. Like the night before, she managed an uninterrupted succession of high wire performances—of finely sustained climaxes.

She lingered there, just outside of return. Ned watched for the subtle signs. Her face become gaunt and her eyes defocus upward with each fierce and exquisite contraction. From the past, he knew that Laura's remarkable occipital-dominant brain was somehow carrying her far beyond visualization into stunning realms and dimensions of feeling unknown to any man and probably, he thought, to any other woman. Less subtly, she was sweating profusely.

For his part, Ned had a perfectly adequate, although undynamic culmination. But that was nothing beside the awe he felt as he responded to Laura's luxurious and decisive movements and her amazing countenance. Her mounting pleasures continued to soar beyond his meager comprehension. She was the creator of an experience he could only admire and worship. To Ned it was the creation of beauty—and the beauty of creation.

He would have let it continue for hours, except he could not last, and it was over. From the great height of an intensely apprehended reverie, she descended gracefully, giving Ned only the slightest glance of reproach on her return. They snuggled down for a final half-hour of rest.

* * *

Breakfast was bacon, scrambled eggs, hot toasted English muffins smothered with butter, and lots of coffee. They were very happy.

Ned chewed thoughtfully on a large mouthful of egg, followed by a sip of coffee. "Is there something wrong?" he asked with pseudo concern. "You hardly said a word to me last night!"

Laura chuckled. "It wasn't necessary. Like all the king's horses and all the king's men, I was busy. Perhaps you noticed. I was . . . sort of . . . being put back together again. I prefer younger men, but you weren't bad for an old guy." She then added matter-of-factly, "It was really kind of urgent—it was clinical necessity."

"Clinical? Yeah! It probably was. But, as I've often said, I prefer more experienced women." Ned laughed, with a tilted smile. "You mean clinical, like taking a tranquilizer?"

Leaning her chin delicately on the back of one hand she looking directly into his eyes and responded, "Something like that, I guess." With her own wry smile, she added, "Actually it was glue—for my Humpty Dumpty soul." She reached out, touched Ned's hand, and said, "A big part of that is . . . I feel close to you again."

Ned lowered his head and squeezed her hand, then looked up into her dark, expressive eyes and said softly, "Me too."

After breakfast Laura loaded the dishwasher. They each took their turn in the bathroom and were dressed and ready to go when the gyro-cars arrived right on schedule at 10:00 a.m.

"Well," Laura said sourly, "its back to reality. I don't look forward to this day."

"What 'reality'?" Ned asked.

"You're right," Laura said. "The real reality was here, last night, this morning. Down there is that . . . that horrible dream. Will we ever wake up? Will the nightmare end?"

Laura watched them coming up the walk. Tall Debra Anderson was looking more proud and stately than ever, holding her shoulders back—effectively lifting her ample bosoms more aloft than usual. But there was something different. She was on the arm of equally tall, but skinny, Ernst Berman. He was looking so pleased! That was different. And her friend Judy Olafson was being especially solicitous of David Michaels. Why, she even tried to tickle him just then! Laura noticed.

Soon they all seated themselves in Laura's living room. Ellen and Clint were together on the couch, very close, and surreptitiously holding hands while maintaining expressions of saintly innocence. Laura touched a key and the room began to move. As it lowered into the depths of the Great Cone, Laura smiled to herself and murmured under her breath, "It's not just the peasants cohabiting these days. The king's horses and all the king's men must have been very busy last night." And then she thought, *Maybe we should have had a Twister a long time ago!*

TWELVE

The downward slide began slowly, accelerated to a free-fall plunge, and finally slowed to an unnoticeable stop in the subterranean corridor next to the Director's conference room. Without a word they rose from Laura's couches and chairs and hurried down several different passageways to their respective department centers. By one o'clock they had met with their Operations Managers and had returned to the conference room.

Astrophysics and Navigation reports remained essentially unchanged. Stan Lundeen, Doug Groth, and Laura Shane explained the situation. Stan then summarized: "We're headed for the Coma Supercluster of galaxies, but we're still well within our home Galaxy. We've made every possible effort to change course toward some star or open cluster within range. All our efforts have been countered by the Dort energy system. No individual stars in the disk of the Milky Way are now within reach on this trajectory. Failing that, we're heading out of the Galactic disk. The only remaining survival possibility is somewhere in this Galaxy's halo of globular star clusters. We'd have to de-Transform near a star or planet in one of those clusters."

The Directors muttered nervously.

"That, gentlemen and ladies," Stan continued, "is the gloomy picture. On the bright side, the Dorts have made no attempt to accelerate the Transformation to light speeds beyond the standard considered safe. If their intent is to go to the outer limits, then what are they waiting for? The theoretical answer is simple. It is possible to accelerate without limit, and they could reach the Coma cluster in days or for that matter in seconds or nanoseconds. It would make no difference then because the Transformation would never be able to stop. At such speeds the energy potential of the entire universe would barely be sufficient for us to de-Transform back to normal space. I suppose we could call that an instance of Dort Rationality."

The Transformation's ultra-proud Information and Communications Director, Debra Anderson, delivered her ex cathedra remarks. She began with several courtly wriggles that elegantly redistribute her fundament. "For the past five days," she announced, "except for a single two-hour gap, continuous attempts to contact the Dorts have been made using conventional means. They did not respond. Either they did not receive the communication or they're still pretending they're not in the Cone. In any case, less conventional means of getting their attention have been made ready."

David Michaels, Director of Geophysics and Mineralogy, had also been working feverishly for days with a number of other departments. "Tremors of any magnitude," he reported, "can now be centered at the Dorts' location. The extent of the tremors can be controlled, along with their frequency and duration. The small 'earthquakes' could be sent in a kind of dot-dash Morse code. There is, however, a danger. A violent quake could break up the Transformation, so that will have to be controlled. We know they'll notice even the smallest tremor and, being exceptionally bright, they'll receive and decode any message so delivered. If they still pretend they can't 'hear,' then we can turn up the 'sound.' Unfortunately, as the tremors increase arithmetically in strength the chances of a Transformation breakup rise geometrically. Still, we could give them a hell of a fright before any high probability of danger."

"How certain are you of the point where a Cone breakup could occur?" Ned asked.

"Well," David said, chewing on a thumbnail, "we've never done anything like this before, so it's just an educated, wild-ass guess. Somewhere out on the end of the normal curve even a small tremor could blow us apart—a version of the ol' uncertainty principle, I guess. Externally from us (back in our normal-space dimension that is, aside from running into more black holes) passing through a solid body (like a thousand light-year thick cube of lead) would not destabilize this cruising Transformation in the least, but internally we can wreck ourselves without much trouble. Anyway, if we can settle on the odds we're willing to accept, then we can crank up the 'communication quake' to that level. Say, for example, one in a thousand—that would be the safest—or one in a hundred, or five in a hundred. Whatever is decided, we can do it. But I must emphasize again—there are no safety guarantees!"

After discussion, the Directors came to a firm consensus. They decided that, as a maximum, one in one-thousand would have to do. To start with, the tremors would be much lower than that. If there was no response, then they could work up to that maximum. Initially, a short message would go forth in the form of vibrations barely strong enough to be felt and understood—not strong enough to be called a quake. If that brought no response, they'd gradually move up that shaky ladder to the approved maximum. Another option would have to be considered if that approach failed. Unfortunately, they had no other options. The Directors would then have to increase the level of danger, maybe to one in five hundred. None of the "decisive" Directors wanted to think about that.

Then Doug Groth gave the status report on "Operation Core Bore," as the engineers had come to call it. It and the makeshift torpedo-shaped tractor-elevator were ready to go. "The core," he explained, "will be four meters in diameter and the torpedo's treads will fit tightly, but flexibly against the sides. The cylinder of the vehicle itself is three meters in diameter and nine meters in length—longer if one counts the laser drill in its nose. For the last two days the engineers have been teaching Clint to run the torpedo-tractor and its equipment."

Jack Lewis had been silent and morose for a number of days after the

Twister destroyed his chance of returning to Earth on the i3T so now he spoke: "When that tractor goes down the core, I want to be on it."

Asserting his role as Director of Security, Clint Bracket said, "The thing will only carry four—myself and three other soldiers. In times of war, and I don't know what else to call this, you have to use fighting men to do the fighting. We don't know what we'll find down there. I'm sorry sir, but I'm afraid you'd be in the way."

Jack tensed momentarily; then thought what he would say. The room became very quiet. "What do you plan to do down there, Clint, with your four-man army? The Dorts aren't totally unsophisticated in weaponry, and there may be a hundred or a thousand of them; and we now know they aren't above killing to get their way—whatever they want."

Clint responded, "It would be foolish for a President to be on the front lines in a war, you and everybody else at this table, excluding me, are needed here. You can suggest the nature of our military action, but the direct action itself must be in the hands of those trained for it. We will carry hand lasers, one laser pack, grenades, and some high explosives. We will find their energy centers and destroy them. Dorts will have to be killed. If we lose our lives in the attempt, then so be it. There is no other chance and no other alternative."

Debra Anderson made a "tsk" sound with her tongue as she drew an audible breath that caused her breasts to thrust forward accusingly. "My dear Officer Bracket," she intoned imperiously, "just where have you been this past week? Do you think we've been trying to communicate with the Dorts merely for the sake of conversation as a preamble to wiping them out?"

"I'm aware that you'd wish to dicker with them," Clint snapped back. "I thought it was foolish from the start. This past week has seen the murder of hundreds of our fine people and my best friend, George Sachs. As for your communications, we all know where that's gotten us. Nowhere. And the reason is simple. They have the position of strength. Everything has gone their way so far. If you want to dicker with them, it'll have to be done when we have the upper hand. And when we get in that position there'll be no need for talk. We'll have this Transformation back in our hands and the enemy will have been neutralized and punished."

"And if you four men are killed . . . ?" Jack asked.

Clint's reply was vigorous. "We go in shooting with the surprise element on our side. We won't be killed. Our hand lasers will last for hours. And we'll bring along the big one, the laser pack—like the one on the nose of the torpedo vehicle. It's usually used for drilling tunnels. I doubt that any army of a thousand could be better equipped. In fact, in the cramped conditions we anticipate, a larger contingent would get in each other's way."

Ned, Doug, Laura and Stan spoke quietly and intently to each other as Clint continued his argument. At last Ned broke into Clint's polemic and said, "We have another problem, Clint—one that may change your view of the needed tactics."

"What! Change the tactics—for what?" Clint snapped.

"Consider the tactics required to keep us all from dying of old age, right here."

Clint opened his mouth to speak, but Ned's hand went up for his silence, as he continued. "I respect your comments, Clint, and your arguments are not taken lightly . . ." (Clint looked from side to side with a glimmer of pride), "however there are facts that have a direct bearing on the tactics we use if we are to optimize our chances." (Clint glowered and set his hulking jaw, but again held his tongue.) "We have to sort out what we know, what we don't know, what our goals are, and in what order, and the level of risk we are willing to accept for each, and . . ."

Clint's chair went flying as he jumped to his feet and barked, "What a bunch of academic bullshit! We'd grow old just doing all that cataloging. Our course is clear and we're wasting time counting angels on the head of a pin. Either we regain control of this Transformation or we die. It's as simple as that. You say that we have another problem, that we need to consider the facts, and then you give us bullshit—no new problem, no new facts."

"Give him a chance, Clint," Ellen said, replacing his chair.

"The fact is," Ned went on calmly, "that we can no longer divert our course to any star cluster within this Galaxy on our own power. Destroy the Dorts' power center and we'll die out here. There'd only be the dust of our bones in flight a million years from now—probing the Coma Supercluster. We'll need our power *and* theirs to survive."

Clint contracted like a worm feeling the first touch of a hook. His eyes became piercing highlights beneath sphincter-tight lids; his fists became massive, white-knuckled lumps of armor. His whole musculature billowed visibly beneath his uniform. But it was neither fight nor flight. It was undulating, congested paralysis—awesome to behold!

Haltingly, Clint's words came, but they did reveal the early beginning of some understanding. "Then . . . we must . . . COOPERATE . . . with them?" It was too much. Clint's paralysis lifted. He sank limply into his chair, in utter dejection and denial.

After what seemed a long silence, Ned continued. "Anything we call it—cooperation, coercion, or whatever—one thing is certain, we'll need both their energy system and ours to reach a star cluster. Even then it may not be possible. Their system will have to be very powerful. Let's hope it is. It is not to be destroyed.

"We know that when they develop technical equipment on their own it is incomprehensible to humans. That's one reason we've had to include them on human technical teams and not turn them loose on their own. They don't build things creatively, but they've been known to obfuscate even the makings of a simple toaster. We know about their energy system, but if they automated everything and really aren't here, there is little chance we could fathom their version of system controls. That leaves us with just one choice. We have to negotiate with them."

Clint looked beaten. "Negotiate," he said limply. But, with a little more animation, and seeming to get the idea, "What'll you use as leverage?"

"Whatever leverage we have will depend in part upon what they want. As you made quite clear, we could threaten to kill them. Not that we know how to do that. We could try to push their energy system to the limit by pitting our system against theirs in a navigation and piloting duel. Over a period of years by that means we could send them, and us, in some arbitrary direction that would make their own destination impossible to reach. We could threaten that.

"We may have other leverage as well," Ned continued. "For one thing, they need us. It's improbable they hijacked this Transformation out of any inability to build their own. They may not have had that ability decades ago, but they do now. They're as up on our technology as we are. If they could build the power and control systems we know they must have on this Transformation, then they didn't need this one. They must have wanted us too. Why, I can't imagine, but if these ideas are correct, then they will be looking for our cooperation. They may find that our cooperation comes high—that is, if they need us. If kidnapping us was optional to their plans, or if they have no use for us at all, then that won't help much."

"If they're looking for our cooperation, they've got a hell of a way of asking for it," Cameron grumbled.

Ned nodded. "They have no understanding of human beings. If anything, they understand our nature and psychology less than we understand theirs. And that's not much."

Ellen Stone spoke up, a bit flustered. "I can't believe they miscalculated us to that extent. They know we are capable of anger and aggression; and they must know that we don't take kindly to murder and hijacking or the threat of spending our lives on a Transformation to nowhere."

"We have a little leverage," Ned continued, "and maybe a lot. We'll just have to see. I take it that our first priority is to stay alive, and close behind that is to return to Earth—as young as possible. Any discussion about that?"

"What do you mean by putting 'return to Earth' as a second priority?" Judy Olafson squeaked.

"It would do no good to return to Earth dead," Ellen said reasonably. "We don't even know if it's possible. To remain on the Transformation for the rest or our lives might be preferable to a short life. Others might prefer to die. I'm not one of those. I think Ned's statement of priorities is right."

There were murmurs of agreement, and a frightened nod of understanding from Judy. Clint remained impassive and mute.

"Then it is time for us to begin," Ned concluded. "Dave and Debra, I want you to arrange the tremor signals after we're through here so that it's ready to go when I give the okay. I want the message to read, 'Agree to negotiate now or Transformation will be destroyed. You have ten, blank, to respond.' In the 'blank' garble the transmission."

"Shouldn't something definite go in the 'blank'?" Doug asked. "Ten what? Seconds, hours, years? It's too vague."

Everyone at the table began talking at once, asking Ned what he thought he was doing. They were upset. Except Cameron Greenberg, Director of Social Dynamics. He just observed the reaction, and noticed that Ned was watching him. At last, Ned raised his hand for silence. "I haven't discussed this ahead of time with Cameron, but judging from his expression I think it would be safe to ask him to explain."

"Okay, I'll give it a try," Cameron said. "It's really beautiful. For instance, look at your own reactions to this message—every negative emotion in the book. All based on anxiety—the natural reaction to an ambiguous situation—especially a dangerous ambiguous situation. That's what this message creates. Were we the receivers of such a message rather than the senders, just imagine how we'd react then!"

The explanation brought nods and frowns.

Judy spoke up for the frowns. She directed her comments to Ned. "Dort psychology is an enigma. What makes you think they're capable of anxiety? What if they work like computers, or even let computers make their decisions, such as decisions regarding that vague message?"

Debra Anderson answered for Ned. "No problem. . . ." Using technical terms, she made a clear conclusion. "A Dort computer would be flashing the equivalent of red lights, and setting off Dort versions of alarms and sirens. They'd all go off at once if the program was even the least bit sophisticated."

More discussion. Ned waited for silence, and then continued. "After we send the message and receive a reply, I want that four meter core de-Transformed and the descent vehicle swung over the shaft for immediate departure"

"If you want things to move that fast, then wouldn't it be better to have the shaft de-Transformed and the vehicle ready above it before the message goes out?" Judy asked.

Doug Groth said, "Early in the planning for this, I made the suggestion that it be done in the order Ned just called for. No particular reason. Call it a hunch. I think it would be better in that order." (No one ever argued with Doug's hunches.)

Clint had another concern. "What if they don't respond at all, Ned?"

"I'll be very surprised if they don't. Two days ago we discontinued all conventional communications for a couple hours—just to get their attention if they were tuned in. After the two-hour period elapsed, we sent the same message that I gave to you a few minutes ago. If they got the message, they could not avoid responding to it. I concluded that the Dorts have no communications equipment intercepting our transmissions."

Clint sneered, "If your right and they didn't get the message, then what makes you think they will send back a message? I repeat my first question, what if they don't answer."

"I believe they will. The quakes should get their attention."

Then, looking nervously at Clint, Ned added, "Somehow.... Call it a guess. But if they don't answer, then you, Clint, and your three best men, can have at it!" Even Clint was startled.

"However," Ned went on, "if they do respond, in any way, then the group to go down will consist of Jack, you, me and, if she will, Laura." Laura nodded. "Do you agree to that, Clint?"

Clint nodded his agreement, but with an oddly changing expression of triumph and doubt. He then asked, "How long is that wait supposed to be before we can assume they won't reply?"

Ned's answer to that was also a shocker. "Ten minutes and no more."

Preparations for de-Transformation of the shaft were ready. To create it would take less than an instant. One moment there would be solid rock, and in the next a sixty-five kilometer hole straight down and exiting somewhere near the apex of the Great Cone. The "Core Borer" would be wheeled aside and the torpedo-elevator winched up and swung into place with its passengers already aboard.

The two contingent teams were waiting beside the descent conveyance. The torpedo shaped vehicle had tractor treads up the length of four sides. Each team had taken time to become familiar with its cramped interior. They were suited up and ready for any surprising atmospheric risk that might hit them when they stepped into the world of the Dorts.

All they were waiting for was the message to be sent, and in ten minutes they would know which group would be leaving—the negotiators or the warriors.

It was exactly 1500 hours when Ned spoke quietly into the communicator, saying, "Okay Debra. Send it."

THIRTEEN

Debra Anderson's voice rang out from every loudspeaker. Letter by letter and word by word she announced the message as it was sent. When the "blank" was reached, interference and static sounds made the letters and word impossible to interpret. The tremors themselves could not be felt or heard, but they were being felt some thirty kilometers below. Everyone knew that, and some smiled. When the last word was completed many people looked at their watches, including Ned and Clint.

The loudspeakers went silent; but all receivers of every description were wide open on every channel and wavelength awaiting a response. Any response.

Minutes came and went. Nothing. Seven minutes had gone by and Clint was giving last minute instructions to his men—who already knew their duties. Clint was just letting off steam. Eight minutes—and Ned was shaking his head.

At nine and one-half minutes the ground shook violently, knocking several crewmembers completely off their feet. The tremor was brief, followed by two more. The quakes subsided briefly, only to be followed again by tremors even longer and sharper than before, knocking Ned on his back. There were shouts and screams of panic up and down the passages. Thirty meters down one passage Ned saw a cave-in just miss a running girl. Ned shouted into his communicator, "What the hell is this, Michaels? We weren't supposed to feel the shocks. Now they're coming back magnified!"

"No Sir!" came the metallic reply. "Those vibes aren't ours!"

Then another one hit, then another and another.

When it was over, Clint directed his men into the "Torpedo"—the name someone painted down its length the previous night.

The loudspeakers crackled and Debra Anderson was on the air. Three of Clint's commandos were already inside the vertical airlock tower and his own foot was also inside through the open access door. He registered confusion as he heard her report:

"We have still received no message from the Dorts through conventional communications media. However, there is reason to believe that the strong tremors we just experienced may have been an attempt by the Dorts to send us a message. If we assume the communication was in Morse Code, as was the message we sent to them, then it is significant that we received nine tremors, the middle three lasting longer than the first and last three. The message would then be simply, 'SOS.'"

Ned was happily surprised when Clint made no attempt to argue with him about the content of the message received or the method of its delivery. He merely looked disgusted, shrugged and had his men leave the vehicle.

Ned did experience a moment of near panic, however, when Debra Anderson wondered if she should communicate a request for "clarification" of their message. If Ned's communicator could have been affected by vocabulary, it would have melted in his hand as he expressed his opinion of that suggestion, and made a few of his own.

The clattering, jerking, eight kilometer per hour descent of the makeshift "elevator" was under way for two hours before Clint stopped manipulating dials, checking calibrations, adjusting contraptions and generally hovering over the vehicle's controls. He used the rest break to have some iced tea from a thermos, and a sandwich. He looked casually from Ned to Jack to Laura while chomping noisily on the sandwich. They looked back with blank expressions, like dignitaries on an ancient passenger train observing the eating habits of a provincial.

"This is it," Clint said breaking into a smile. "In another three hours, if this tin can holds together, we'll either be talking to the Dorts or fighting them."

"You may be fighting them," Laura said, "but we intend to talk. If they won't talk then I don't even want to think about it."

Jack gave Clint a questioning frown and said, "Three hours? I thought we were halfway there. You mean two hours, don't you?"

Clint glanced at Jack, shrugged indifferently and stuffed in the last of his sandwich.

Still doubtful, Jack shrugged too and looked at the others.

"It's like this Jack," Ned explained, "twenty or thirty minutes will be needed for the laser drill in the nose of this Torpedo vehicle to create a tunnel into the Dort passageway. During all that drilling, a lot of rock and gaseous debris will spew back into this shaft. After another twenty or thirty minutes, the tunnel will cool enough to walk through. Even then we'll need our insulated boots, air conditioned suits and helmets."

"The nose laser is a lot like this one," Clint remarked, taking an interest in the conversation. He patted a metal box that looked like an ancient home movie projector. "I'll be taking it with us, just in case—and this," he said touching his side arm.

Ned continued. "The nose laser will make a tunnel two meters in diameter, but we don't know yet exactly how long. We expect it won't be more than three or four meters. We de-Transformed this shaft as close as possible to one of their passages. At first our instruments only gave us a crude idea where their passages were. Their efforts to block our probe scans were successful for a long time. But over the past several days, by focusing our scan, we were able to locate a definite passage segment. The layout and full extent of their passage system is still unknown. It could be limited, or it could be vast and wind around for many kilometers. So far we don't know what the layout looks like. The only other things we know for sure are that their Tesla Tank is much deeper and a kilometer closer to the central axis of the Great Cone than the shaft we're in now. After we bore our tunnel we'll still be a good three kilometers above their Tank. We can also infer from their use of energy that their torus mass-energy converter is at least nineteen kilometers in diameter. That's smaller than ours, but they could have one or more in reserve."

"What confuses me," Laura said, "is how they could have built all that so fast, so far down, and without being detected."

Jack looked at Laura a bit surprised. "Haven't you figured that out? Hmm, of course not. It would have to be a puzzle if you didn't know the history of the selection process for the site of this Transformation. We began zeroing in on this location long before the Director's and others' homes, including yours, were built. The Dorts were in on those decisions from the beginning. They even presented compelling arguments for making this Transformation exactly what it is, its proportions, its location, everything. They may well have had most of their construction done and their massive machines and toroids installed for years before we began this project."

Laura looked askance at Jack and Ned and said, "For creatures who supposedly understand human psychology so poorly, they knew how to manipulate you—not just a little, but in detail!"

Much to their relief a voice cut in from the speaker and asked, "How's it going down there?"

"Hi Doug," Laura said, "We're fine so far. How's everything up there?"

"Not bad. The quakes caused one major cave-in and eight or ten small ones. No injuries though. It's getting cleaned up. The big cave-in may take a while. Anyway, since their SOS, the Dorts have lightened up on blocking our probe scan—at least in one place.

"What do you mean, 'in one place'?" Ned asked.

"It's some kind of a chamber. Very large. Like an auditorium. Only a lot bigger. It's a kilometer west of where you'll be getting off, and its base is a thousand meters below that. I think they're deliberately letting us know it's there."

"Maybe that's where they want us to go," Laura said.

"Yes, and maybe it's a trap," Clint growled.

Ignoring Clint's reasonable remark, Ned said, "If they're telling us the meeting place, I wonder why they're continuing to block the rest of our scans."

"If it's a complicated maze down there then how would you know which location to go to unless they made it simple?"

"Good point, Doug," Ned said. "I guess we'll just have to use dead reckoning to find it; although they could make it easier by sending us a tour guide."

"Maybe they will if they know where you are. They must know we de-Transformed a core and that somebody is on the way down. That's elementary. If they're using a second-generation probe scan like ours, they know where you are right now—in that case they could have lasered out to the core shaft, then aimed the laser straight up and picked you off. Since they haven't tried that, we can assume they intend to talk."

Clint fidgeted. These ideas and dangers had been discussed before they had embarked, but being reminded brought beads of sweat to his forehead. A defense for that contingency had been programmed into the Torpedo's nose laser. At best, if that defense had to be used, it would ruin the shaft for further descent. The thought reminded him of something.

"Say, Doug?"

"Yes Clint?"

"How did you figure out that the Dorts were going to use tremors to send their message back to us?"

"I didn't know. It was just a hunch."

"Well it was a good one. If this shaft had been here before the tremors came, that would have been the end of this shaft. It would have broken up quite badly."

"I don't think so, but keep your fingers crossed that they don't send another one before you get back up here!"

"You had to say that, didn't you." Again, fresh beads of sweat adorned Clint's forehead.

Debra Anderson's muffled voice could be heard reproaching Doug for his bad taste in bringing that up. She urged him to change the subject and stop making callous remarks.

"Ahem!" Doug said.

"Yes Doug," Ned responded.

"Um, let's see. Oh yeah. Be sure to keep your collar communicators and tracers on open when you get in there and make contact. But leave the tracers off until there is some kind of contact. We'll want to know what's happening and where you are."

"Sure thing Doug," Ned replied. "Unfortunately you won't be able to hear us once we get far inside. A little too much terra firma between senders and receivers."

"Oh yeah. I forgot. Anyway, we'll be able to locate your tracers with the scan equipment. But just in case, you'd better keep the tracers off until you're sure they already know your location. If they're using first generation scanning equipment, it's not likely they have you located. Ours is second generation. So keep them off for now. Once they're on, they'd spot you in a minute."

"Thanks for the reminder," Laura said politely, even though they covered these points before. Doug's repetition was becoming tiresome. She thought he was trying to keep them company, or more likely it was the other way around.

The conversation went on for several more minutes before Doug signed off. Talk inside the vehicle also stopped, leaving the passengers to their private thoughts and to the clattering and groans of the capsule.

Clint brought the Torpedo to a halt, adjusted the nose laser and began the drill. Twenty minutes later he announced the breakthrough and closed down the laser. The inside temperature of the well-insulated capsule had risen ten degrees, but began to cool from there. Half an hour later Clint started the capsule into motion again and descended another five and a half meters to align the airlock exit with the freshly bored tunnel. Insulated boots and pressure suits, helmet seals, collar communicators, tracers and life support backpacks were given final checks.

Standing with his back to the sealed door, Clint faced the others. "All ready?" he asked over the collar set.

"I'm nervous about this breathing equipment," Laura said. "Are you sure it won't spring a leak or something?"

"Don't worry about it," Clint said reassuringly. "This isn't a space walk, you know."

"Is that so? Never mind. Just one last review, please, before we leave this contraption."

"Okay then! This gauge," Clint said pointing to one of a dozen on the bulkhead next to him, "shows the atmospheric pressure outside is safe, and it hasn't changed since the breakthrough, but the air is moving fast. A lot of wind whistling around out there, but pressurewise it's good. The big question is what the air quality inside will be. We have no reason to believe it's any different from ours. If it's no different, we won't need our helmets, unless it's bad to start with or changes for the worse. The transceivers are in the collars of your suits—not the helmets. And the outside sound receivers are on the front of your suits. We all know how to adjust those. As for the atmosphere in there, I have this gas analyzer." He reached into one of his kangaroo pouches and removed a tube-laden instrument that looked like the cross between a hand calculator and a small squid or octopus. "The tunnel we just lasered out is the shape of a large drainage pipe—a little over four meters long. It'll be blazing hot, but nothing like it was half an hour ago, so your insulated boots and suits will be needed for sure. Don't walk slow. Get through as fast as you can. And be careful on the gangplank—it's only two-thirds of a meter wide. One false step and down you go . . . for quite a few kilometers! There may be toxic fumes, so keep your helmets on till I check it out with the squid thing. Keep low in there—real low! Head clearance is only one and two-thirds meters. When we reach the end of the breakthrough into the Dort tunnel, we'll need light. For now, Jack will carry the beacon. After we get across the breakthrough, we'll be there! Once there, turn right, keep going, and start looking. Any questions?"

"No questions here. I'm ready now. . . . I guess," Laura said.

Clint turned toward the airlock door and the others moved close behind him. The hatchway slid easily aside, the gangplank extended, and four earthborn beings entered another world—a realm of Dorts.

FOURTEEN

The airlock door opened to a slow-cooling, but still seething breakthrough. A strong airstream from the far end the burrow met an equally sharp downdraft from the core itself. The earsplitting resonance from the confluence of currents came at them like an unending human shriek—or more accurately, an inhuman one. The cry from that freshly bored throat gave a prosthetic voice to an unspeakable horror somewhere within. (Had they not sent an urgent distress call, that SOS?)

Fork-tongued ripples of flamelike vapor lapped at the walls of the burrow—wafting through the blistered tube like an endless, fiery vortex.

Bending low, they moved quickly through the disorienting tunnel of noise and illusions. At the far end of the breakthrough they entered the Dort passageway, turned right, and kept going. The plan was to move toward the center of the Cone, and downward to find the immense chamber that Doug had described. Even with that information, it would be difficult to find. In a brief mood of amusement, they hoped to come across a cooperative Dort to be their guide, but if they ran into hostility, Clint would "handle that." He was itching to do so.

After they'd been trudging along for a short distance, Clint suggested they stop for a quick check on the atmosphere and their surroundings. Jack flashed the beacon around. It's power was on a low, but still brighter than the high-beam of a g-car. They'd been moving along the right-hand wall, but knew that any side passage to take them inward would have to be on the left. Jack turned the beacon to that wall. They were surprised to see the opposite wall was at least as far from them as they had already come—about fifty meters. He shined the light to the ceiling. It was twice as high as the corridor's width. He commented that it looked "parabolic." He then turned the light in the direction they were moving and saw . . . nothing!

"My God!" Laura said, "What's this cavern for? Turn up the beacon, Jack, to full power. Let's see if we can make out the end of this."

Jack turned the beacon to full power. The light shone for many kilometers—far enough to detect that the cavern curved gradually to the left. He then turned the light in the opposite direction. It was the same, and curved as gradually to the right.

"This excavation could be in a complete circle," Jack observed. "Another thing is strange. It's empty—just blank walls and a rock-strewn floor. And no Dorts." He turned down the beacon's power and again illuminated the arched ceiling, following up to it from one side and down to its base on the other. "Looks primitive enough," he continued. "Just a standard lasered tunnel, except it's bigger than anything of its kind that I've ever seen or heard of. Our own passages would collapse without reinforcements. With or without parabolic arches, this granite grotto is impossible!"

"I think you're right, Jack," Laura said. "I can't imagine what's holding it up, but it seems to be built for the ages. I'm beginning to have an inkling of what it's for. If this cavern does go all the way around it could, some day, hold an immense mass-energy converter—a torus laden with hundreds of converters. My guess is that they have other excavations, some containing converters, others empty like this one, awaiting installation. We know they have at least one already."

"Yes," Ned agreed, "but at some point the internal diameter of the torus is less important than its length."

Clint interrupted. "The atmosphere is safe for breathing," he said. The squidthing wriggled in his gloved hand. "You can flip your helmets back now. It'll save your air. We may need it later. It's not fresh air and it'll smell a bit, but it's safe."

Laura lifted her helmet. "Smell a bit, you say. Good yuck! It's awful!" Laura said.

The others followed suit by turning back their own helmets. Their remarks were similar. The smell was not strong, but had a sweet, sickening quality.

"We'd better move along," Clint said. "We won't find any side-passages standing here."

They walked another half-kilometer when Laura stopped and said, "Wait. I hear something."

"What you're starting to hear," Ned said, "is silence. We're getting away from all that weird wind."

"That's probably why I didn't hear it before. There's water running somewhere. Can't you hear it?"

Ned tilted his head. "You're right. It seems far away though. Either that or a small trickle nearby."

"Or a large one behind all this rock," Clint said.

They walked on. The wind they left behind became almost inaudible, and the delicate trickle of flowing water became clearer. Clint stopped and placed his ear to the stone wall. Jack trained the beacon on him. The moist stone glistened around the motionless figure.

"Nothing here," Clint announced. "I'll try the other side." He trudged the fifty meters to the right-hand wall and again placed his ear to the stone. He looked back into the beam with a shrug. "Nothing here either," he shouted. He then placed his ear to the floor of the cavern, listened for a while, got up shaking his head in wonder, walked to the center of the cavern and again listened, ear to the floor. Then, returning to the group, he lifted his palms in a helpless, frustrated gesture, kicking pebbles as he walked.

Laura got down on her hands and knees and, holding her long dark hair to one side, placed her ear to the ground. She shook her head and said, "The flow seems to be coming from everywhere at once. Let's keep going. It must be up ahead." Then, in mild disgust, she threw one of the numerous pebbles with an awkward right arm and marched ahead to lead the group.

After walking another half-kilometer, they moved to the center of the cavern with Jack shining the light to the left and right walls as they went. There was still no sign of a side-passage. They continued to stride on through the ever-present sound of flowing water.

A crackling sound suddenly came from their collar transceivers followed by, "Hello down there! Can anyone hear me?"

"This is Clint. Yes, we're receiving you. Is that you Doug? We're getting a lot of static."

The crackling continued, but Doug's voice was understood. "Yes, this is Doug. I didn't want to interrupt anything. The static is bad on this end too, but it hasn't interfered enough to keep us from listening in on your conversation. We'd have lost contact a long time ago if you'd found some side passage to follow in all that rock. Until that happens we should be able to remain in contact."

"Can you hear the water, Doug?" Laura asked.

"No. Not over all this static, but we can hear you talking about it. Does the floor of the cavern slant up or down, or is it higher in the middle or on one side?"

Laura responded, "So far as we can tell it's perfectly flat and level, except for a few stones. Why do you ask?"

"Nothing specific. It's just that we've continued our probes and the Dorts are still blocking them—effectively, except in the few places we've already located. The thing that's confusing is the scan at your level—where you entered the cavern. We keep getting a fluctuating signal. The graph is impossible to explain. When you were talking about a mammoth cavern instead of an ordinary passageway, we started varying the depth of the probe to see if we could measure its dimensions. That should have been easy. But what we're getting is a continuous reversal."

"Would you describe the graph for me and whatever dimensions you're getting," Laura said.

"Sure. The distance across the cavern is no problem. It's 47.82 meters—a little over 52 yards. And the surface appears flat, all right. We pick up a lot of pebbles and stones, but it's flat, as you've described it. When we scan for the shape and dimensions of the parabolic vault you talk about, that's where the graph goes crazy. In theory, the graph should be a miniature cross section of the cavern—a parabola or something close to it. Halfway across, at the top of the cavern, the graph should show a maximum. What we get is the opposite—a minimum."

"That's more impossible stuff," Laura said. "There's nothing in Transformation Theory to allow for anything like that. A functioning Transformation is coherent, a unified field, not a bunch of incongruous internal polarities."

"Hold it. I have an idea," Ned interrupted. He picked up a hefty rock and heaved it down the lengthwise direction of the cavern at a steep upward angle. Jack's light caught it as it bounced and clattered a short distance away.

"That wasn't much of a throw, whatever you're trying to do," Clint said.

"Yeah? Well let's see if you can do any better," Ned said.

Clint chose another stone and threw it a long distance. He looked self-satisfied, but said nothing.

Ned shook his head. "You're missing the point of this, Clint. The distance you throw the stone doesn't matter. What I'm after is height."

"Why didn't you say so?" Clint said. He then doffed his pressure suit, picked up a stone that just fit in his palm and, standing in his loose security habit, wound up as if to make a pitch. He let the stone fly with all his might, sending it high into the air. Again they heard stone striking against stone as it bounced somewhere in the distance. Jack held the beacon steady on the distant floor of the cavern, but the stone was not seen. Only its "clack... clack... clack... clack," could be heard as it kept bouncing against the granite, and then—Kerplunk! The stone splashed into water; but no bouncing stone or splashing water could be seen. It was as if the stone had vanished from the visual dimension without a reduction in sound.

Clint stood with his mouth open in awe, staring in the direction of the light beam. "There must be water down that way. I heard the rock splashing into it; but I didn't see it. I don't understand this at all!"

The collar speakers crackled again and Doug's voice came through excitedly. "What's happening? What are you trying to prove by throwing stones? How come you couldn't see it hit the water?"

"Keep your shirt on, Doug," Ned replied. "The answer to this may give us an even tougher puzzle. Clint, throw another stone just the way you did before. And Jack, this time keep the beacon focused on the stone itself, not where you expect it to land."

Clint selected a stone the same size as before and hurtled it high. The beacon followed. The stone slowed toward the top of its trajectory, but suddenly gathered speed and continued forward and upward where it hit the side of the cavern dome with a loud "clack!" The clacking continued several more times and ended with a loud plunk at the peak of the arch. A splatter of water jumped downward from the apex, and then upward again.

Jack turned the beacon to full power—and there it was! The rivulet was flowing along the length of the summit as if through an inverted flume—defying the laws of nature!

They continued their march down the mammoth corridor and were becoming tired. As they walked, they finished talking with Doug and the other Directors about the strange phenomena and, again, about their overall situation. They thought that perhaps the newly discovered gravitational polarity demonstrated a basic error in Transformation Theory. To explain this would, no doubt, keep the Transformation Physicists busy for a long time.

In the meantime, it was after 2300 hours and there were practical facts of human fatigue, hunger, and the disappointment of finding no easy access to the Dorts. They were prepared for a stay of several days, but had hoped that contact would come sooner. Every passing hour plunged them farther into space, reducing their chances of diverting their course to some kind of safety.

There would be no chance to keep going that night. They had to rest. They ate and drank their day's rations, after which urgent modesty requirements were attended to at a distance in the relative darkness of indirect beacon light. The sleeping pads were inflated and, according to plan, they had to sleep in their protective suits in case of any sudden atmospheric changes, although the helmets were not required so long as they were kept nearby each sleeper. Clint's gas analyzer, or "squid thing," as he called it, would give plenty of noisy warning. Laura and Ned arranged their pads close to one another. They reached out and touched hands, but the events and anxieties of the day, and pure exhaustion, swept them into restless slumber, and then into deep sleep—and the quiet, trickling stream still flowed—from the conscious into the unconscious.

A new sound integrated with slumber and escalated slowly—just below the threshold of notice. Clint was the first to stir. It took him several seconds to realize the difference. He shook Jack awake, who turned the beacon to full power. Its beam reflected off the glistening, vaulted walls of the cavern. Clint then went to Ned and Laura, shook them and shouted, "Wake up!" Jack had gotten to his feet, alert and tense.

Ned squirmed around drowsily and glanced through half-opened eyes at his watch. They had been asleep almost six hours.

"What is it, Clint?" Laura shouted. (Shouted!) Together she and Ned jumped to their feet in wild-eyed awareness of the change—of the thunderous sound that enveloped them during their sleep.

Clint moved quickly, waving his arms to get everyone's attention. He secured his helmet to its collar and gestured for the others to do the same, and for them to turn off the chest receivers of outside sounds. The collar transceivers were checked and operating. As their helmets were secured, the outside din became a quiet undertone—a distant murmur. Standing, they turned and looked all around. Nothing they could see had changed. They could hear each other's breathing and the muted din outside their helmets, but nothing else was disturbed.

Jack picked up the beacon and turned it's high beam in the direction they had been traveling the night before, and then in the opposite direction. In each direction the great, looming cavern narrowed and curved into the distance, its features unchanged from before. As he was about to turn the light again, at the extremity of the beacon's powerful reach, there came a flicker.

"What's that?" Jack said, pointing into the distance. They all saw it. The specs of reflected light took shape and were moving toward them at great speed. Within their helmets the distant murmur became louder and louder. There was no response to Jack's question. Nor was there any need of a response—the answer was terrifyingly obvious. Laura instinctively moved into Ned's arms as they watched and listened and waited.

The deluge approached pell-mell, its tumultuous, frothing ramifications pouncing and lunging as it crashed from one side of the cavern to the other. Even within their helmets the sound, amplified by the parabolic structure above them, soon became deafening—again. As it reached its crescendo, the roiling ferment surfed over the huddled figures—and the noise abated.

The group reflexively jumped and sprawled on the floor of the cavern as if under attack by a low-flying airplane. The beacon went out, completing their plunge into darkness. Minutes passed before anyone moved. The sound of rushing water could still be heard, but its moving front became more distant. Within the darkness, their realization of still being on a dry surface came slowly. Tentatively, one by one, they began to move.
"Is everybody all right?" It was Ned's voice.
"I'm not sure. I think so," Laura replied.
"In one piece, I guess," Clint said.
Jack responded with irritation, "I can't find the goddamn beacon."
"Here it is," Clint said, "I've got it."
"Well, turn it on!" Jack snapped.
"I'm trying to!" Click and the floodlight came on.
The imposing river swirled and coursed above them, nearly filling the top half of the cavern. Standing agape below the fearsome torrent in the "sky," they hoped the river-god would not notice its mistake and set it right!

FIFTEEN

There was little discussion about it. They decided not to turn back. The idea of returning to temporary safety was outweighed by the dangers of failure to make contact with the Dorts—and soon. With beacon in hand, Clint set the pace. They moved out promptly, leaving their pressure-helmet visors unclamped and open. The overhead river was becoming tolerably quiet as it receded, and even without protective headgear the cavern's ill-smelling sweetness was still endurable.

They walked two kilometers before they spotted, far ahead, what Jack described as a "wall-opening." The small opening seemed to lead inward from the left wall. That's what they were looking for. Their viewing angle was such that they could not be sure. Still, their hopes were raised and they walked faster; but, like a desert mirage, the opening appeared to move farther away as they drew nearer. The pace increased again and they moved in cadenced steps behind the reflections from Clinton's beacon—a light that also bounced along in perfect time with his hurried steps. It seemed he was trying to catch up with the fugitive wall opening. His bobbing light enlivened the moist walls and the flowing river's wavelets with the pulse of flickering gleams and shadows. Whatever they were chasing—crazy wall-openings, crazy rivers, or Dorts—it all seemed strange or unreal.

But the wall opening was not a mirage. In another half-hour—it was 0700 hours already—they reached the elusive side passage. Clint's odometer showed they were only six and a half kilometers from where they entered the cavern late the previous day.

The passageway with the "small opening" was huge. It was big enough for a truck to enter. It led off at a right angle from the much larger, noisy cavern, but its shape was similar, with a parabolic dome and a flat base. The glistening walls were similarly textured with a wavy, sometimes scorched surface of fused rock, looking more like colored glass or polished, speckled terrazzo than ordinary granite. The sweet, musty smell also hung in the air, but was noticeably worse. There was no trickling stream at its dome, and where the moisture on the walls was sufficient to cause running, it was in a direction they were glad to identify as "down."

They moved along the newly found passageway and welcomed its quiet. The silence settled in as they moved farther from the cavern and its crazy river.

And that's what they named it—"Crazy River."

Ned was again on his transceiver talking to Doug, but the transmission was breaking up. Doug wished them luck as the connection severed. Ned felt a twinge of anxiety and loss with the termination of this last communication from the "outside world."

"Finally, we're going in the right direction!" Clint said. "Sooner or later we'll need to find some way down to a lower level—stairs, a sloping tunnel, something like that." He was smiling and patting the hand laser at his side.

"I don't think you'll find stairs in Dort country," Laura said. "They wouldn't build them unless they were trying to make things convenient for humans, and I haven't seen any signs of that."

"Yeah. I know what you mean." He was still smiling.

They tramped forward in silence for a considerable distance. They saw no sign of other passageways, no equipment or artifacts, and no signs of life. The corridor curved left, then right, then left again. It became difficult to estimate their location. They traveled two kilometers along the side tunnel before their light picked up a fork in the passage. They hoped that one of the forks would slope downward, but the one on the left was level and the other slanted upward. They chose the left fork.

Some distance into the fork Jack said, "Have you noticed that the farther in we go, the narrower it's getting to be? The dome is lower too."

"Yes," Ned said. "And the floor seems to be lower in the middle—not flat like before. The dome looks different too. The curve seems wider—not as sharply parabolic at the crest. Not that it matters, I suppose, so long as it's in solid rock."

As they walked, they continued to talk, occasionally noting that the tunnel was still becoming rounder and smaller, and the twists and turns in the passage had no discernible pattern or frequency.

At five kilometers from the fork they'd still found no other side passages, and the tunnel itself had become a circular tube, barely two and a half meters in diameter.

They began to consider turning back to take the other fork. The air was becoming stifling and extremely humid. Twice they stopped to rest and to secure their helmets. That provided temporary relief from the humid stench and gave them a breath of "fresh air." Still, the squid atmosphere analyzer showed the air was safe. At Clint's insistence they agreed to continue farther, but grumbled about throwing good time and energy after bad, and his insistence on keeping their visors open to save the air tanks for when they might "*really*" be needed.

Two kilometers farther on, the tunnel had become a narrow oval requiring them to move in single file, and the temperature had continued to increase. The walls became moist to the point of runny. Where the base was low and uneven they slogged through puddles.

The topic of turning back took up the next rest period. They could have overruled Clint's insistence on continuing, but came to a compromise instead—one they all agreed to. If no promising downward passageways were found in the next three kilometers, they would retrace their steps to the other fork—the upward sloping right fork. Three more kilometers would put them exactly ten kilometers from the fork. Clint admitted that would be a fair exploration—and a nice round number.

They traveled in silence for another kilometer. The air continued to get worse, but the squid made no fuss. Jack, who was now in the lead, suddenly stopped.

"What's the problem?" Clint asked impatiently.

"It's different again. It happened so slowly I didn't notice till now."

"What's different?"

"Everything. Look at the ceiling. It's flat."

"Oh for Christ's sake. So what! Let's go. We can't keep stopping to admire the scenery."

"You're missing the point, Clint," Jack said. "Take a look at what we're walking in, and the walls, and then that ceiling. Remind you of anything?"

"Now it's puzzle time," Clint said with irritation.

Laura gasped, "We're walking in the apex of a parabola."

"You're right!" Ned said. "Either this tunnel has turned upside down or we have." He reached up toward the flat ceiling, but could feel no gravitational difference. Superstitiously, he tossed a pebble the short additional distance that he couldn't reach. It bounced off the ceiling and fell back down—whatever *down* meant at this point.

Clint took the beacon and handed the portable laser to Jack. Clint, as usual, kept the hand laser—his trusty sidearm—in its holster. Jack moved to the end of the line. Clint said, "Let's go!" and led the way. There was nothing more to discuss. They followed.

In another five hundred meters the tunnel they were in made a distinctly downward turn. The four spelunkers looked incongruous and ungainly in their "*space* suits" as they crowded together at the top of the slope. Clint focused the beacon down the incline for what appeared to be a great distance. The slope was free of angles or curves until leveling off far below. It was not too steep for walking, but steep enough to require care on its wet surface. The side walls were close enough to reach with both hands to brace against for support. Clint strapped the beacon to his chest to free his arms. Laura helped Jack attach the heavy laser to his backpack.

They moved forward slowly at three-meter intervals. Walking single file was already bad enough, especially with all the light in front. Those behind the lead person had been in deep shadow—a condition more confusing than total darkness. Now, on the narrow, slippery slope there was added uncertainty to every step.

One-third of the way down Ned slipped and skidded into Clint who fell backwards onto him. They slid sprawling together for a dozen meters before managing to stop. Clint delivered a loud, random selection of oaths. Ned groaned. Neither was seriously hurt, although Ned's right shoulder, right fundament and upright pride were bruised in roughly equal proportions.

The descent continued for another half-kilometer before leveling off. From that point the passage went straight for a short distance, followed by a series of familiar twists and turns. With each turn the smell became more unpleasant, verging on intolerable. Clint's kangaroo pouch suddenly chirped like a canary and erupted into vigorous activity. They all gathered close to Clint as he removed the wriggling squid. It registered danger. He reset the distressed atmosphere analyzer and that seemed to tranquilize the thing. There were sighs of physical relief as they donned their helmets, but anxiety was mounting and tempers were close to the edge.

"We have to turn back," Ned said with irritation. "The hours are slipping away. We may not have another day. Maybe two. No more than three. After that, it'll be too late to get this Transformation back on track—even with Dort cooperation. We have to find them. We won't find them here. *This* fork of the passage is just a stinking sewer."

"I agree," said Jack. "Even getting back up that incline will be a bitch—and then that endless trek back to the other fork. We should have turned back long ago. We can't afford to squander another minute. Let's get out of here! Everyone agrees to that, right?" Ned and Laura nodded.

"Gentlemen, Laura, I can appreciate how you feel," Clint began with uncustomary tact and composure. "But earlier we made an agreement to complete ten kilometers. That was the plan. It seemed reasonable then. I don't see that anything has changed to make it unreasonable now. Sure, it stinks down here and the air's gotten to be unsafe. We're all getting tired and on edge. So am I. But you don't change a battle plan every time the troops get tired and irritated. You stick with the plan. If conditions change in some fundamental way, then I can see taking another look at it. But throwing in the towel to ease frustration is something you scientists call 'irrational by definition.' If we start to cave-in to excuses and rationalizations every time we get uncomfortable with agreed-upon plan, then we'll have lost our discipline. We must continue on."

"But... but," Laura's voice quavered, "what about the dangerous atmosphere reading? Isn't that a fundamental change?"

"Not at all, Laura," Clint said in a modulated, compassionate tone. "First, because we never were sure the atmosphere would he safe anywhere down here. We were lucky. It stinks. But it was safe until now.

"And second, the air became dangerous gradually. It didn't fundamentally change. Our crawly little chirping analyzer threw a fit because the safety criterion was exceeded. It *snuck* into the yellow zone—no sudden change."

"All right," Ned said. "A deal is a deal. Let's finish the damn ten kilometers and get it over with. We're already tired. In the next fork any plan, agreement or deal will be different. For one thing we'll decide how far in we go before we enter the thing—not after hiking seven kilometers." Clint agreed. Laura and Jack made helpless gestures of protest, but also finally agreed. They felt constrained to do so, but thought Clint's use of reasonable arguments was hitting below the belt. "Just one more kilometer, Laura," Jack said, "and back we go." He put his arm around her and gave her a gentle squeeze of reassurance.

Just one more kilometer, they thought, as if that would end their troubles, as if turning around and retracing their steps was an end in itself. Frustrated by failure, their intrepid, hopeful quest had become a bad dream. As they trudged onward to complete the arbitrary, pointless, ten-kilometer march, it soon became a nightmare.

SIXTEEN

Clint took the lead. Ned glanced at his watch. It was 1051 hours. No wonder they were tired, he thought. After being on the move for over five hours, they had nothing to show for it. "Nothing!" Ned grumbled aloud.

"What did you say?" Clint asked without slowing.

"Nothing."

"Oh."

After a while Ned said, "I've been thinking. When we start back to the right fork, we should increase our pace and skip a couple rest periods. That way we could reach the other fork around 1430 hours and start making some real progress."

Clint said, "Fast or slow, we'll have to spend the night in there anyway. And then what?"

Laura said, "*And then what* is right! Another day will be wasted. *Something's not right. It feels wrong.*"

Nobody responded. They slogged on behind the beacon with resignation and stoic silence. The bends and twists in the passage were coming closer together than before. Into the sixth turn past the slippery half-kilometer descent, Clint's suit again came to life. The atmosphere analyzer practically crawled out of his kangaroo pouch. Without slowing his pace, Clint pulled it out and checked the readings. He pushed some buttons on its surface and the writhing stopped. He crammed it back into the pouch and did increase the pace. After rounding another turn Ned asked, "What was the reading?"

Clint hunched and continued another dozen paces before responding, "Don't ask!"

Ned thought about it and decided Clint's answer was eloquent if not numerically precise. He didn't ask, nor did anyone else.

During the next few passage twists, the air became more bluish and Clint was again observed resetting the analyzer. Still farther on, Clint's pouch became a frenzy of thrashing tremors. He impatiently pulled it out by one of its many-ducted prehensile tubes and raised the trembling thing to eye level. Its other tentacles stroked and clung pleadingly to his forearm.

"Oh shit," Clint said quietly as he came to a halt.

"Are you going to tell us now?" Ned asked.

Clint nodded inside his helmet. "Guess I'd better," he said. "Danger levels have been increasing. We've reached a point where one breath of this stuff . . ."—he gestured toward the thin haze—"would kill a man. An elephant for that matter!" In a more reassuring tone he said, "Of course we're perfectly safe so long as we keep our hoods clamped on and the air holds out. No problem, really. Just thought I'd better tell you. So leave the helmets in place—even if you get sick!"

Jack asked, "How much worse will it have to get before we're in any real danger—in our suits and helmets, I mean?"

"These readings could go to the moon and we'd still be safe. The danger would come if we ran into another kind of condition—like corrosive substances in the atmosphere harsh enough to eat through our softer suit materials."

"But, right now, you believe we're in no danger?" Laura asked.

"Right now we're safe. The analyzer shows insignificant corrosive levels."

"Then why are we standing here?" she said. "Let's finish the damn ten kilometers."

The next turn in the passage was a sharp right angle. That was new. Clint shone the beacon along the passageway but did not enter it. The stragglers saw him in a slight crouch, shoulders and helmet forward, hyperalert.

"What is it, Clint?" Ned asked in a quiet but urgent tone.

Clint began to relax and straightened up. "You'll see."

As the others caught up and looked at what held Clint's attention, they gaped in wonder. There was another meter and a half of the usual tunnel, but beyond that its shape flared out to become a broad rectangular-shaped funnel.

It extended upward and to the sides and farther inward for a full six meters where it abruptly ended against a five meter square of interwoven metal rods. The tempered-steel grid of bars was set in the surrounding rock at twenty-centimeter intervals. Lazy curtains of bluish mist drifted back and forth through the latticework.

They approached the rigid portcullis for a better look between its bars; but the bright light of the beacon rebounded off the haze to dazzle their eyes and obscure any visibility. Clint lowered the beacon's intensity and turned its beam in several directions to find a glare-reducing angle. Even after the angle-correction, the languid vapors still streamed and curled in uneven veils, shrouding some vistas, but spreading elsewhere to uncover others. Fragmented revelation by random glimpse, the semblance of their surroundings beyond the grid began to appear. Slowly, vista by vista, most of the features within were revealed, except for anything that lay below a thick, gently roiling cloud at their feet—an impenetrable mist that crept and swirled around their ankles. At ground level it not only covered their feet and the surrounding platform, it extended outward beyond the grid and across the entire room. It was a large room and a round one—about seventeen meters across with a vaulted ceiling directly above that floor and the circle of eight more rectangular grids about the height of a man.

Laura described it this way: "It's like we're standing in an alcove or gallery—or a less than fancy skybox—in a minitheater or arena with a lattice of small windows for watching the movements in the smoky room. With that floor somewhere below us, it could be for anything. Yes, that makes sense to me. Let's call where we're standing, a porch or a gallery, and down there—that's a sunken theater."

They made guesses about the mist-covered floor. They thought it could be flat and only a meter's step down from where they were standing; or perhaps it was a bottomless pit; or a floor with bottomless potholes and wells.

They were not sure of their first estimates since the shallow sunken base, or abyss, was so cloud blanketed. Jack tossed in a rock through the bars. It clattered close. The sunken area was no abyss.

To their right, and separated from their grid by an arm's length of supporting granite, was another latticed opening identical to theirs, and to the right of that was another, and then another and another, all the way around the room.

Counting the grid they were standing behind, there were nine such openings. Except for one of the alcoves, each was partitioned from the main expanse of floor in the same way. The second opening to their left was the exception. It had no metal grid and was truly open.

The fourth grid to their right—the one opposite theirs—was almost completely obscured by a particularly oppressive-looking, bubbling cloud—the main source of the haze. The other alcoves were also frequently obscured, but never to that extent.

The third opening to their right was also of special interest. The room's most ephemeral veils were drifting through its grid as though drawn in by sluggish exhaust fans.

Soon they began to notice large boulders scattered haphazardly around the floor and realized once again that the floor could not be very far below the granite sills that secured the steel grids. They only caught glimpses of the boulder tops through the heavy, slow-moving brume. The boulders were in greater profusion near the "vent" rectangle on their right and below the unbarred opening on their left.

Laura said, with quiet revulsion, "The sickness of this place hangs in the air . . . and it's not just the poison vapors."

"Yes," Ned said in an equally hushed voice. "This place is like a medieval dungeon—and eerie."

"I wonder where all those galleries lead," Jack said.

Clint said, "We'll never know if we just stand around talking. I think we've seen all we can from here. We'd better laser through and take a closer look."

Everybody readily agreed—out of pure curiosity. Ned took charge of the beacon and Jack handed back to Clint the heavy metal case with the powerful laser. They backtracked into the narrow tunnel they'd come through when they found the barred gallery. Around that tunnel's sharp corner they were protected by solid rock between them and Clint's target. He placed the heavy laser outside the narrow passage and aimed it toward the metal bars. He knelt over the apparatus and looked into the viewer. After making an adjustment, he pressed the control key, readjusted the viewer and again pressed the key. He did this over and over. In ten minutes the laser was programmed to cut through the metal rods in fifty-six places to create a large enough opening for them to duck through.

Clint turned his head toward the others and said, "Get back a little farther. She's ready to go." After they were well back, he set a timer and joined them. Within seconds the red glow began, followed by a fireworks of sparks. It ended by a loud crash of the one and a half meter latticework falling outward onto the floor of the sunken theater.

Ned held the beacon and guided them through the opening. The exposed tips of grid-bars were still aglow and sizzling as they stepped across to gather on the narrow sill. They moved off the ledge onto the mist-submerged floor and walked cautiously to the next gallery. With each advancing steps they were accompanied by a waist-high wake of dense haze.

"This looks like the cage we just left," Clint said.

"Maybe so," Ned said as he climbed onto the sill and shined the beacon down the passage. Unlike the curved and twisted passages they'd come to expect, this one extended far back in a straight, unobstructed vista before it seemed to dissolve into thin layers of haze.

And there was another difference he could see from his perch. He did not explain, but had the others come up to see for themselves. The gallery and narrow passage behind it contained hundreds more large boulders—each emitting thin, smoky-blue vapors.

They started for the next gallery. Ned still had the beacon, so Laura stepped back to clear the way for him to lead, but she screamed with fright and surprise as she fell backwards over something. Ned quickly turned the light toward her, but she was gone.

In a moment they saw her gloved hand appear above the layer of mist. "What was it?" she asked in a shaking voice as they helped her to her feet.

"You fell," Clint said in an expressionless tone.

"I know I fell, damn it! What was it I tripped over? Something was right here!"

They milled around, kicking into the mist, but found nothing.

"Are you sure you didn't fall over your own feet?" Clint said unsympathetically.

"No!" Laura shouted. "I tripped over something. It was here, and it was large and soft. Now it's gone."

Ned shone the beacon around the room. The boulders were there, but nothing else and nothing was moving—unless it was under the blanket of fumes. He walked all around the room, but still found nothing. "Except for all these boulders, I can't find a thing," he said just before sitting on one of them.

"AHAAG!" he bellowed as the "boulder" caved in under him, spurting out voluminous clouds of thick brume. He attempted to get up, but slipped and fell again.

"Quick, help him!" Laura said, moving in Ned's direction.

"No! Stay back. I'm all right."

Ned slid himself a short distance before making it to a dry spot, and from there to his feet. He took a few steps and looked back. "That stuff is god-awful slippery," he said shaking his head behind his helmet. He turned to the group and added, "So much for the theory that those are rocks!"

Moving with greater caution, they approached another of the dark shapes. The surface of the floor around it was sticky, but not slippery, as though whatever had oozed out of it had been there for a long time. Jack tested the surface of the object with his gloved hand. It yielded to the pressure of his hand. Like a bad case of dropsy, the indentation remained when he took his hand away. The object's surface was shriveled like an immense raisin.

Ned set up the beacon in the center of the room and aimed it at the ceiling to provide a spread of indirect light. This turned out to furnish the least blinding glare, and the best overall visibility within the compass of the circular room. Several other dark objects were examined and all were similar to the first.

While the others were doing that, Laura walked over to the third gallery—the one that seemed to be acting as a vent. Aside from more "rocks," she saw nothing special beyond that grid.

She gave it a half-shrug, and moved to the fourth opening—the one that was least visible from their first views of the room. Standing back several meters from the large rectangle that loomed above her, she could only stare and say in a barely controlled, but urgent tone, *"Come here!"*

They assembled on either side of Laura and looked up at the massive screen. Piled almost to the top of the screen were hundreds of the black objects, many of them partially protruding through the small square openings. Several were halfway or more inside.

The heavy blue fog was drifting from the objects and dark ooze ran slowly down the surface of the pileup, like sap from an injured tree. The flowing material collected in a high, glistening drift in front of the sill. "Dear God," Laura said. "What happened in this place?"

They quickly checked the remaining grids. Those were less congested and fouled, but each contained many more of the objects farther back in the passages. At last they headed toward the open gallery—the one without a barrier.

"Why are you shaking your head, Clint?" Jack asked as they walked.

"Nothing much. I've just been wondering."

"What?"

"What are those things?"

Jack stopped in his tracks. "You don't know?" he said. "Well," he continued, as he started walking again, "I couldn't prove it right now, but I imagine 'those things' are dead Dorts."

"Yeah. I thought they might be. They're still plenty big, but they're a lot smaller than live Dorts, and I never heard of one dying."

"Are you sure they're dead Dorts and not just some kind of mushroom that grows in caves?"

"As I said, I couldn't prove it, but I believe those withered objects were once living Dorts."

Then another voice said, "you are correct doctor lewis dorts they were but now they decay"

It began as a metallic sounding vibration, refined into understandable words, and ended again as meaningless resonance.

"What the hell was that?" Clint bellowed.

"It was I," came the reply as they watched a live Dort humping itself with great effort from the pit onto the ledge of the open gallery. It was unlike any live Dort they had ever seen, and unlike the dead ones. It had lost its translucence and had darkened to an awful gray. It was dying.

SEVENTEEN

The gray Dort had already lost whatever semblance of grace it might once have had. Like a played-out walrus, it plopped forward, bulged and craned, hunched and plopped again, all the way to the center of the gallery where it stopped to gather its strength—and to wait.

"The poor thing," Laura said.

"zvzvfeel sorry not for me. I have zvzvlived thousands of your years zvzvand not known before zvzvwhat you call pain. this will not last zvzvlonger"

Laura climbed onto the ledge, walked over to the Dort and knelt beside it.

Clint whipped out his blaster and aimed it at the Dort. "Stand back from that Dort!" He snapped, "The thing is dangerous!"

"Oh, shut up, Clint," she said matter-of-factly, "and put that thing away." Then, placing her hand gently on the Dort, asked, "Does this hurt?"

"nn zz no ... yes ... no"

She quickly removed her hand.

"vzvz it all right ... touch ... is good.... wantzv"

Again she placed her hand on the Dort and said, "Touch you? I'd hug you if I could. I never knew a Dort who cared one way or the other if he was touched—or that ever had a want." Her voice was low and delicate. "Why are you different?"

"vvzv because I quit mad ... Twister unaffected some ... dead is our multitude ... first mad ... now dead ... The Ten ... nine now dead ... untouched ... one only... possibly others...

"last chance vz vv zz ... was unpredictable, but.... possible vzvvv so vvzzvv many of us came ... some would survive ... and ... be yet ... sane"

"But you, you're not 'mad.' To me, except for your form, you seem close to ... well, maybe not human, exactly, but ... I've always thought that you—the Dorts—had much more than reason and intellect. Now I know you can feel pain, have wants—needs." There was sadness in her tone.

"Jesus!" Clint snapped, "you're such a damn bleeding heart. Let me blast it!" Laura just ignored him.

"vvzz can not i rationally longer think ... the twister ... pain gave ... not before in all memory ... the memory ... our memory ... it opened chain ... and all was felt ... not just pain ... all that ... you accuse me of ... vzvv feelingszzv"

With surprise, Laura said, "You never had feelings before?"

"only one ... not a vvzzv feeling ... like feeling ... but greater ... always had ... our very being ... the being ... pervasive ... eternal ... all ... not before noticed"

"What feeling could ever be that strong? Love? Hate? Fear? And yet not be a feeling?"

"not hate .... vvzzvv not fear ... closer is love ... much more than ... much"

"What feeling is greater than love?"

"Drivel!" Clint smarted under his breath, but for all to hear.

" zzvzzbeing ... total ... pervades all .... that which is .... the changing is ... must preserve"

"Must preserve? You must preserve 'that which is' that is changing? That sounds like . . . like duty or responsibility. What is the responsibility you have? What are you talking about?"

"to keep all that is ... the chaging is ... without void."

"I . . . I don't understand. What are you talking about?"

"eternal ... so great ...infinity of infinities ... without void—"

Clint turned to Jack and Ned, agitated. "The Dort's delirious—out of its mind. Makes no sense! The thing is insane. Totally mad. Laura's in danger. Allow me to remove her now!"

They hushed him impatiently and continued to listen.

"—without end ... but is not ... is not perpetual ... all can end ... entropy ... then void ... must not end ... being is responsible ... all is responsible"

"Oh hell!" Clint blared. He was almost beside himself. "Is that thing trying to excuse this hijacking by saying they're on some kind of great mission! Gimme a break!"

Laura glanced at Clint, then back at the Dort. "Is that what you are saying? That you believe you have some—some great mission?"

"all being ... not dorts only ... all that is ... is responsible ... is in you ... in me ... in this "—a pseudopod came out and slapped the stone floor—"in all that is"

Ned had come up on the platform and was sitting cross-legged nearby. He now addressed the Dort. "You said that you are 'mad' and that death will follow that. When you are dead you will not be able to pursue your 'duty,' whatever that is. You implied that feelings, such as those of human's, are madness. Do you say that all humanity is mad?"

"the questions ... so many"

"And another thing," Ned went on, ignoring the Dort's words, "You and your kind have been so durable these many hundreds, perhaps thousands of years—why did the Twister kill most of you, and fewer of us? We may be more durable than Dorts, after all?"

"durability ... no virtue either way ... just is ... conditions ..."

"The Twister all but wiped you out. Why you, the Dorts, and not us?"

"man already knew pain .... other feelings ... your nature ... not nature of dort ... to dort is madness ... to man ... is natural .... to dort not shameful ... merely lethal"

"But feelings," Laura returned softly, "must be in your nature too, even if they kill you. Otherwise why would so many of you have been affected? You were vulnerable because you were open to feelings. The pain opened the door, but the feelings were always potentially there. It is your nature too."

"potentially there ... of course ... natural not ... things were not ... at origin ... so arranged ... even stone"—a pseudopod again slapped the surface of the gallery—"... can feel ... if things are so arranged"

"I can't believe that," Laura said, shaking her head.

"the rules ... would have to change ... but potentially there ... is there ... and ready"

With confusion in her voice, Laura asked, "You think a stone could be responsible?"

"yes"

Ned was shaking his head. "In your so-called 'madness' have you lost your ability to be responsible?"

"entirely not ... arrangement changed ... all-pervasive focus lost ... less responsible now ... when dead ... will be even less ... entirely lost will never be ... unless all being .... all existence ... loses ... then all is lost ... if high entropy ... should win ..."

"Most of you are dead now, or dying. Looks as if you're going to lose." Ned said, without expression.

"perhaps ... I know not all ... the ONE knows more ... this much i know ... we ... the dort ... are crucial ... was never intended we do all ... alone"

"What do you mean, you're 'crucial'?" Clint snarled again from the sidelines.

"dort is so arranged for this ... you call it specialized... is not enough ... need all else ... organized energy ... matter ... for change ... to evolve ... change ... evolve ... then ..."

"And then what?" Laura encouraged after a long silence.

"... it begins again ... never a certainty ... always a responsibility ... on us ... onus ... but always chance ... the rules ... never the same ... chance is rulemaker ... holds the dice ... entropy ... chaos ... it's goal"

"What 'begins again'?" Laura asked, her voice betraying bewilderment.

"no time left ... must follow me now ... the Ten ... remains one only ... the ONE ... knows more than i ... than all ... other dorts ... vv zz vz ... without the ONE ... then entropy the master ... hurry ... zzzvvzv"

The Dort turned and began humping and plopping toward the open passage. As it was about to make the first turn it stopped. "hurry." It then disappeared around the turn.

They caught up with the Dort seconds later. It was not moving; its gray surface was becoming darker. They gathered around and listened to its vibrations—more distorted and indistinct than ever:

"vvzz vzthe pain ... opens wider ... the window ... more clearly see i now ... of what i spoke ... our task ... as madless dort was duty ... without joy ... in my madness now i see ... as ... act of ... pain ... and more as act of vvv ... vvz but vvzmore than ... love"

And then the Dort expired.

EIGHTEEN

The Dort's last word," Laura said with restrained feeling, "was 'love.' He said their mission was an act of love."

"Act of love, hell!" Clint snarled irreverently. "What sentimentality! Have you forgotten what they did to us? What got us here? That Dort give not one iota of useful information. It led us by the nose—right into this passage. It's a trap. We have to be careful . . . . Can't trust 'm. They don't give up even when they're dying. That junk about 'eternity of eternities,' and the rest—I almost puked. It sounded like a Dort lecture—just as crazy and meaningless. They're all mad. Even the healthy ones."

Shaking with remorse and anger Laura cried out, "For Christ's sake, Clint! Who needs you?"

"Take it easy, Laura," Jack said softly. "Clint looks at these things differently than you."

"I'll say!" she snapped.

"We need your perspective, Laura; and we need Clint's too. You keep us sensitive to what's happening, and Clint keeps us wary and alert to what might happen. Clint's just giving us a different slant."

"Bias, you mean!" she snarled.

Ned put a gentle arm around Laura and said, "We can't afford to quarrel. Not now. We have to keep going. It's almost 1230 hours. The day is only half gone and we're already tired and short-tempered. Let's move on. The Dort said to hurry. There must have been a reason."

Clint mumbled, "Now we're taking marching orders from a dead Dort."

"Clint!" Jack said with exasperation. Clint crouched visibly, but only for a moment.

Ned persisted, "How about it, Laura. A little peace in the family?"

"All right!" she said stoutly, throwing her head back. And then, with a final pout, "But his remarks were uncalled for!"

Clint bristled, but said nothing as they again took up the trek.

They threaded their way through the narrow passageway that led from the open gallery. The straight channel led them past a dozen small openings on either side. The chambers were barely two meters square, barred with the familiar trelliswork, and crammed with dying and putrefying Dorts. Perception was down to arm's length. Viewed through their helmets, the enwrapping shroud was oppressive. They could as well have navigated the passage in the dark.

A quarter-kilometer farther, the passage became several meters wider. A few steps more and Clint came to a sudden stop. Displayed before his beam, glinting blue through the surrounding cloud, was a massive bulwark of polished steel. Frustrated by the obstruction, the group gathered before it to observe and touch it. Clint removed a small, hammerlike tool from one of his pouches. He listened as he tapped it on the metal.

After examining its surface with care he announced, "I'm sorry to say we've reached the end of the line. A dead end. This is the wrong side of an airlock door . . . or something of the sort. It won't do us any good. There are no controls on this side. We won't be able to get through."

"How do you know it's an airlock door?" Ned asked.

"I don't. If it is, it's not like any I've seen before. It could be, though. Notice this hairline crack." He put his finger on an imperfection and traced it all the way around—a perfect circle just over a meter in diameter. "That could be an airlock hatch; or it could just be a thin groove—a manufacturing flaw. Either way, it's useless."

"We could laser through, couldn't we?" Jack said.

Clint replied, "It would be too dangerous in a space like this. No place to hide. The laser returns would be deadly." Clint looked around. There were no questions, just helmets glistening through the haze. "The only thing we can do now is turn around and go back."

They continued to stand in silence realizing that Clint was right. Jack and Ned were stunned at the thought that their chances of returning home safely were slipping away. Laura was less optimistic than that and thought their chances were gone. She sat down and hugging her knees, placed her helmeted head on them, and quietly began to sob.

Squatting beside her, Ned placed a comforting arm across her back. "It's all right, Laura," he said, without much confidence in his voice. "We still have time. Not much, I know, but with a little luck . . . ." His voice trailed off.

After a minute Laura sat up straight and looked directly at Ned through her helmet's reflective shield. She'd stopped crying and said in an almost cheerful voice, "What's the matter with us? We're going to make it. We don't have to turn back!"

Through his helmet she could not see his face either, but behind it he was looking at her as though she had lost her mind. "What are you talking about?" he asked in a voice half an octave higher than usual.

"The Dort!" she answered with excitement. "He said 'Hurry.' He was taking us into this passage before he died. That thing"—she pointed to the barricade—"is a door that opens from the other side. If it opened from this side then there wouldn't have been any hurry. It would have known we could get through in our own good time. Obviously we're not operating this . . . this airlock on our time. We can't leave now. We have to wait. I'm sure it won't be long. We got here much sooner than if the crippled Dort had been able to bring us. It moved slow. We're ahead of schedule!"

There was a long silence as Laura looked from one to the other. Their helmets reflected unreadable highlights through the drifting, alien ghosts between them.

"Don't you see?" she said with renewed agitation, "the Dort said . . ."

"The Dort," Clint interrupted, holding his tone in check with difficulty, "was, by its own admission, 'quite mad.' It was either lying about that—in which case it could have deliberately sent us on a wild goose chase—or it wasn't responsible or competent to know what it was saying. Either way, this is still a dead end—or a trap. We must leave now. Time is running out!"

"Those aren't the only possibilities, Mr. Either-or." Her voice dripped sarcasm.

Clint spun around, turning his back on Laura, and stood slowly clenching and unclenching his fists. Struggling for control he said, "Whatever you say now, Laura, has lost all credibility as far as I'm concerned. There is no more time to pacify your tender feelings. We have to turn back and we have to do it now!"

"You'll have to carry me!" she shouted.

"That can be arranged. No more time can be wasted on misplaced trust in a dead Dort."

"Wasted time!" she said cynically. "You're the one who insisted we cover a full ten kilometers in these Godforsaken passages!" She was almost screaming now. "We wanted to go back but you drove us on. Good for you. You got your way. This is almost exactly ten kilometers. Your way, Clint. But does everything have to go your way?"

"Yes, Laura," he said in a stone cold voice. "This time I was wrong. I admit it. Now we can spend no more time on either of our errors. Let's get out of here!"

"I see what you're up to," she said with breathy amazement. "This is a power struggle! A dumb, stupid power struggle! I don't even know if the struggle is with me or . . . or a dead Dort, or whoever! And all I'm asking is that we stay here a little while longer. Just minutes. We could spend hours and hours on your ten-kilometer error. I don't think it was an error. Now you can't wait a minute to get out of here. You accomplished your goal. You got us to walk ten kilometers against our better judgment. A power struggle. Okay, I can play that game. I outrank you and I say we stay!"

"You'll have to take that up with Ned and Jack," Clint snarled without changing his posture, "They outrank both of us."

After moments of silence she spoke, and her voice was calm. "All right," she said. "I accept. Ned. Jack. What do you say?"

Ned stood up. "This isn't easy," he said. "Unfortunately this has gotten into personalities. I say we talk this over a little more."

Clint commented, "The sands of time keep falling—even as we talk."

"How poetic," Laura sneered. "And you, Jack? Whose side are you on?"

Jack looked at Laura, shaking his head. "Now who's into a power struggle, Laura?"

"I thought that was clear," she said in a tone of total reasonableness. "Clint and I are. A pure power struggle. Only now the game has shifted to you two, and so it's become a popularity contest—to win the hearts and minds of the highest ranking. But I notice that neither of you want to decide. Ned wants to discuss it more, and you want to shame me with a rhetorical question. Can't either of you decide?"

"Laura," Ned pleaded, "why are you being so bitter?"

"Now Ned is into rhetorical questions," Laura said absently. "I still hear no decision."

"For once," said Clint, turning around to face the group, "I have to agree with Laura. We need a decision."

She stretched out her arm and pointed accusingly toward Clint from her sitting position: "I thought you said I'd lost all credibility. Now you're agreeing with me. You're taking my side. What is this, Clint? What are you up to?"

Clint suddenly looked grotesquely awkward as he hunched forward, almost imperceptibly, within his outsized suit and helmet. He spoke in a helpless, human tone, "I just want us to be saved, that's all."

His humility was too much for Laura. She began to shake as she got up and ran to him, putting her arms around his great bulk as far as they could reach. "I'm sorry, Clint," she said with breaking voice. "I didn't mean all those rotten things I said." She turned to the others without leaving Clint. "I didn't mean anything rotten to either of you either. I just thought we should stay. I thought something might happen. I don't know what. Something. *I was just stalling.*"

Laura went on. "Jack said that my point of view and Clint's both had value. Maybe I was testing to see if my opinion, reasoning, or intuition was right or worth taking seriously. I don't know and it's too damn hard to find out.

"I thought I was really communicating with the Dort—that he would lead us out of here to—what did he call it? . . . 'The One.' I must have been wrong about the Dort. I felt so sure."

She noticed Clint was holding her in a caring, gentle manner. She looked up at his inanimate helmet reflections, but knew from subtle movements that he was trembling. She wondered if he was shivering from a chill or . . . . She placed her hands on his arms and slowly extricated herself, and said, "There'll be no more stalling. We can go now. I was wrong."

"No," Clint said in a husky voice, "We'll stay a bit longer—until you think it's time."

No sooner had Jack and Ned nodded their agreement than a bright circle of light opened beside them. A strong and healthy vibration came from within: "PLEASE ENTER THE AIRLOCK. THE HATCH CLOSES AUTOMATICALLY IN THIRTY SECONDS!"

NINETEEN

The airlock chamber was spheroid in form, except for a flat, circular floor just under two and a half meters across. Laura was the first to step through the small hatch onto the inner deck, followed by Ned and Jack. They moved without haste, as though they'd merely been waiting for an elevator in a department store. Clint, however, held off nervously until the last possible second. Then he jumped in, brandishing his side arm. As the hatch snapped shut behind him he whirled around at the sound and threw himself against the bulwark. Groaning, he slid to the floor holding his right shoulder. The others helped him to a sitting position against the curved wall.

"Just what was that all about?" Ned said reproachfully.

Clint panted, "I have a . . . a responsibility to . . . to keep you all safe, damn it!"

"How do you expect to do that if you ruin yourself?"

"Oh, shut up!" Clint snapped, more like his old self, and clambered to his feet still caressing his shoulder.

Then, as though he'd suddenly remembered something, he crouched with his weapon poised. "Where's the Dort?"

"Clint, you're really making me nervous!" Laura said. "There is no Dort. The voice we heard must have been a recording."

The resonant voice came again: "IT IS IMPERATIVE THAT HELMETS REMAIN IN PLACE UNTIL ATMOSPHERE IS CLEARED OF TOXIC IMPURITIES. WHEN IT IS SAFE YOU WILL BE NOTIFIED."

"That's no recording. We're being monitored!" Jack said.

"How do you know?" Laura asked.

"Dorts don't use helmets. They do just fine in any kind of atmosphere—with or without 'impurities.' That message had to be for us."

The hissing sound of an air exchanger began and the blue wisps of dead Dorts that had entered with them began to curl and rise toward the ceiling and out a small aperture. Laura watched the whorls with fascination and noticed that some were still reluctant to go.

Then her interest shifted to the wall directly opposite the round hatch they'd entered. It held another circle, but this one was recessed; its concave reflective surface deformed their images. She moved closer to it and her reflected form spread weirdly across its entire surface. With irritation she said, "Dort, if you hear me, what is the purpose of this curved mirror?" And then with accusation in her voice, she asked, "Are you watching us from the other side?"

"NO INDEED, DOCTOR LAURA SHANE. OBSERVE—"

The interior lighting dimmed, and then went dark. At the same time, the circular reflective disk became transparent and an exterior beacon of growing brightness began to illuminate the expanse beyond.

Just outside the oriel, not more than four meters below, they could see a familiar looking curved groove of rock. The ravine extended for many kilometers to their left and right, and down its center a slender stream trickled past. The curved bay protruded from the stone wall of the gorge, providing a panoramic view.

Far above the base of the chasm they could see a great, flat roof of stone. "My God!" Laura said in hushed, but driven tone, "What's holding all that up? The slightest earthquake and that granite roof would be all over us!"

"I really don't know," Ned said. "It defies the imagination how they could have—"

"Wait! Look up there!" Jack interrupted. "It's a half-kilometer to the right—where the rock ceiling meets the top of the gorge. Do you see it?"

"No! What *should* I see? It all looks the same to me." Laura was chagrin she'd missed what Jack saw clearly.

"Well, I'll be damned!" Ned said in disbelief, "It's our breakout point. This has to be our Crazy River Canyon!"

Laura squinted and pressing her helmet against the transparent bay. "Yes, I see it now. How do you know it's *our* tunnel? And how did it get up *there*? We walked on a level all through that ten kilometers of tunnel, except once, and that was *down* a slope—not up!"

Ned said, "From the point of view of a guy standing at the breakout, the slope we took that you call 'down,' would have been 'up' for him. That means we did some kind of—what can I call it?—gravitational walkover. The flat surface of the passage we were in became curved, and the curved ceiling became flat, and was circular in-between."

"I see what you mean." Laura said.

"Look," she said, turning and pointing to the airlock's ceiling, "they're leaving." The last of the blue specters was being exhausted.

A sudden scratching and grating of static was heard through their transceivers. Then came a familiar voice saying, "How's it going down there? We've been listening, but haven't heard the usual bickering one expects from our top Directors."

"Doug!" Laura yelped with elation. "You're a voice from heaven—static and all! As for bickering, you should have heard us earlier."

"Thanks. It's good to hear your voices too. We've been catching your conversation ever since you entered the airlock. Apparently it's right on the side of Crazy Canyon. And what's that about 'toxic impurities' we heard some Dort mention?"

Before anyone could answer, Doug began talking fast, almost agitated, throwing out questions and comments: "Where have you been? What's happened? Have you made any useful contacts with the Dorts yet? It sounds as if you haven't. If you're in an airlock chamber, have you figured out how you're going to get out? Ellen sends her love to Clint and 'Hi' to the rest of you. It's been a fright up here worrying about you. Do you realize how many hours it's been? We didn't know if you were alive or dead. Everything depends on you and there isn't much time. We've been recalculating our position and the location of any star clusters we might be able to reach before we're flung out of this Galaxy for good. A few hours ago there were ten good possibilities using our own power—if the Dort energy system wasn't fighting us all the way. Now we're down to two. Figure five if we had the Dort system working with us right now. In another *hour* we'll be down to zero possibilities on our own, and only one with Dort cooperation. As you can see, our earlier estimates were too optimistic. That's why it's been a fright up here."

"We'll do the best we can," Ned said. "From what you're saying, the timing on this is too close for comfort—far worse than anything we feared—by several days! Just an hour left, at best! God help us!"

Ned's tone became conspiratorial. "Hold off as long as you can on my next order to you. Give us another forty-five minutes. If we don't have total cooperation from the Dorts by then, you have my order to sink as many shafts, like the one we came down in, as necessary to completely destroy their Tesla Tank and their mass-energy converters."

There was a long silence. Everyone knew that if that order were followed, it would be suicide. The destruction would not only eliminate the Dort power systems, it would reduce the entire organized Transformation into so much disorganized energy and scattered subatomic particles—a tiny nebula expanding into the void. And the Dorts knew it too.

In seconds Jack, Laura and Clint were signaling with gestures and nods to Ned that they approved and understood his "order." It was a bluff! They knew that such an action was beyond the pale of acceptance. Life was life—even on an interminable journey to nowhere. And the Dorts, without great understanding of most humans would *not* know that.

"We have your orders, Sir," Doug's voice came tense and shaking. "We understand them completely, and they will be carried out to the letter." The other Directors had gotten the message too. "In the meantime, since the Dorts know where you are, either as guests or captives, we suggest you turn on your tracers so we may know where you are at all times.... Aha! Very good. We now have your location."

"THE TOXIC FUMES HAVE BEEN EXPELLED. YOU MAY REMOVE

YOUR HELMETS. ALSO, KINDLY ASSEMBLE IN THE CENTER OF THE AIRLOCK."

Clint turned and barked a question at the walls, "Why should we?"

"TIMING IS CRUCIAL TO PREVENT THE FLOODING CHANNEL FROM ENTERING YOURS."

"Flooding channel," Clint mimicked sarcastically. "What channel? What flood? What the hell's that supposed to—"

Before completing his statement, he rushed to the bay and looked down at the little stream. It had not changed. He followed the gorge as far in one direction as he could see. Nothing. Then the other way... and there it was—the rampaging torrent of Crazy River—less than four kilometers off and coming at great speed, careening from wall to wall on its forward surge. Clint and the others stared, paralyzed.

"IF YOU PLEASE... INTO THE CENTER OF THE CABIN."

Without thinking, they responded as requested. The reason immediately became clear. Four safety couches rose out of the floor around them.

"WILL EACH OF YOU KINDLY SELECT A COUCH AND STRAP YOURSELVES IN. REMOVE YOUR HELMETS IF YOU HAVE NOT ALREADY DONE SO, AND PLACE THEM ON THE MAGNETIC PLATFORM BESIDE YOUR ARM RESTS."

They complied instantly, and with rising hope. In seconds the airlock sphere began to swivel and turn. "I think we're going somewhere, Doug!" Ned said. "We'll be in touch."

"Make it soon," Doug replied. "And good luck!"

As the sphere pivoted, the couches moved within it until the seated occupants were visually oriented toward the circular bay. The bay darkened as the chamber rotated turretlike past a wall of rock. A narrow, floodlit channel came slowly into view; its brightness crept across the bay's disk like a waxing moon. The spherical conveyance rearranged itself, moving down, sideways and up in unpredictable, jerking movements, until its occupants found themselves looking down the barrel of a jagged conduit of granite. The sphere began slowly on its downward movement into the gullet of rock, but in seconds it accelerated in an explosion of velocity.

The passengers were pressed deep into safety couches that wrapped womblike around them. In sudden turns they were pressed left and right, forward and back. They watched the serrated channel whip past them as they barely missed the most perilous of its outcroppings. Then the cushions fell away. All that kept them from slamming into the ceiling and walls were their safety belts.

The Orb made another downward plunge, but this time it led to an oddly inverted weightlessness. For those with their eyes open—and theirs were bulging—it was no benign floating experience. The sphere fell faster and faster past the blurring jaggedness. Laura screamed in terror as the floor of the shaft rushed to meet their craft. With a final shriek before the deadly impact she covered her eyes; but the "impact" became normal gravity. It crept in and replaced their weightlessness. The bay's disk darkened, the sphere came to rest, and its interior became a blaze of brilliant light.

Ned tried several times to get Doug back on the transceiver, but the relays failed—or were blocked.

"YOU MAY DISEMBARK. YOU HAVE ARRIVED AT THE CENTRAL GEODE AND OPERATIONS CONTROL POD. DOYAN, THE ONE, AWAITS."

TWENTY

The round hatch opened to fresh-smelling air and darkness. The frightened passengers exited the bright interior and the circle of light closed behind them. They walked a short distance from the sphere with the surface crunching like crisp cereal beneath their feet. Laura removed a glove and felt the noisy material. As she expected, the crystals they were trampling were small and fragile.

They soon noticed a many-colored penumbral glow some ninety meters to the left of the exit hatch. The light's source and character was unclear, but the faint light was coming from an area behind an intervening landscape of man-sized crystals and even larger rocks. As their eyes adapted to the darkness, the colorful half-light seemed to increase. They picked their way toward it, avoiding the boulders and the large, slanting crystals that jutted upward like tilted, razor-edged obelisks. Jack was not so careful. He shoved and kicked at a number of the larger rocks. Some, already on the edge of imbalance, tumbled short distances. "They're real rocks this time," he mumbled.

Halfway to the light source, Laura grabbed Ned's arm, stopping him. Clint and Jack stopped too and looked above them where Laura was pointing.

"The stars!" she said, in a tone of wonder. In truth, the stars did appear all around them—and below them too, as though they were suspended in space. Even the boulders and shadows that lay between them and the mysterious light looked like interstellar clouds obscuring nearby suns.

The mammoth crystalline cavern they were in was larger by far than any planetarium or stadium any of them had ever seen. As their night vision continued to improved, they could pick out hundreds more of the large stones and mammoth, jutting crystals, not only nearby, but directly overhead. The chamber was a colossal geode.

Moving forward, the fragile reflective crystals still glittered, but behind them the trail of their steps left footprint-shaped patches of blackness—as though the procession of mere mortals could grind out the stars. Laura preferred the breathtaking illusion overhead.

Still captivated, she continued to watch the "stars" while Ned led her as though she were blind. When they had again halved the distance from the sphere to the light she stopped. "My God!" she said, "What's that?" High overhead, they saw something floating and rippling in the center of the sphere like a great, translucent manta ray, its fluidic undulation distorting the dots of light. It slowly spiraled downward, then gained speed and soared in a high arc to transit the meridian, and finally returned to its original position where it seemed to stop in mid air, billowing in place, waving its diaphanous foils. It had soared with grace and beauty, and now hovered at zenith in elegant, lacy ripples—a flowing, responsive, membrane in space.

They passed the barrier of crystals and rock and came upon a low, flat field that contained the wellhead of lights. The clearing itself was nearly thirty meters across, and in its center was a great necklace of fifty raised disks—all in glowing, flickering hues and arranged in a three meter diameter circle. The disks were fifteen centimeters across with two-centimeter intervals between them. They wondered at the precision and purpose for this circle of color-changing lights.

The cosmic spelunkers were duly impressed. They took their places on the random rocks and crystals that surrounded the circle of iridescent fires, and waited. The celestial troglodyte was again circling downward like a condor from its invisible roost on Olympus. Its descent was graceful, but the landing heavy. The Dort's weightless maneuvers in the center of the geode had been exquisite, just as they were known to be in water, but in the stronger gravity on the periphery of the geode it lurched awkwardly and fell the last meter with an inglorious plop—a graceless performance redeemed in part by the precision of the fall, landing flawlessly in the center of the circle of lights, with fifty thin spatulate pseudopods extended to cover each of the disks.

This is where the bargaining would have to begin—within this starry, imitation universe, unearthed from the belly of the real one. This shadowy, coruscating cellar universe should have become their courthouse of mediation; but the long awaited negotiations were not to be. To negotiate there must be options and choices. There were no options to consider. It was a fait accompli, and the Dort did most of the talking.

The Dort began its vibrating sounds with reasonable politeness. Its buzzing tone was matter-of-fact. "I am pleased," it said, "that you arrived in time. I know who you are, but allow me to introduce myself. I am called Doyan. I am the last of The Ten still alive, and therefore called The One. The Twister killed them and The Integrator, so I now serve all their functions. In your administrative structure you would have called them Directors. As Directors, you no doubt have many questions and concerns to discuss, but first there is an urgent matter that must receive our undivided attention. To begin—"

"Just a moment!" Jack interrupted. "There are urgent matters, all right, but ours will be presented first! Our goals and grievances include—"

"I UNDERSTAND," the Dort boomed at a decibel level that made their ears ring and the spacious geode resound. Then, more gently: "You see, there is *no time left* for us to discuss anything. It is now 1320 hours. Twenty-eight minutes remain before you intend to destroy this Transformation if no accommodation and agreement can be reached. Unfortunately your scientists' estimate, as reported to you minutes ago by Doctor Groth, is far too optimistic. *Less than four minutes remain* before our *combined* energy sources can be utilized to bring us safely to the last possible livable planet of the last possible star of the last possible star cluster in this Galaxy. To reach it is now your immediate goal—and ours. To reach it you must now, this minute—*this instant*—place your mass-energy converter on passive mode so that I, Doyan, can integrate its energy with our own systems and set a course for that planet."

"But we have no communications. We lost it minutes ago when—"

Ned was interrupted by Doyan stating, "I have just patched you through."

Then came the crackling sounds of static. "Doug! This is Ned. Are you there?" There was no response.

"You can't do it, Ned!" Clint roared. "You can't seriously be going along with that . . . that Dort-thing. He'll grab the power and lead us to oblivion. We do have time. Doug told us. The Dort is lying! And what makes it think there's a planet out there that we could reach that we could survive on for even a minute, and—"

Loud static stopped Clint's railing. "This is Doug." His voice was hysterical. "I heard you, Clint. I don't know how we got connected. I don't know what's happening down there, but whatever you said about the amount of time I predicted, it was wrong. New update on that is in. There's no time left. Three minutes at the outside. Furthermore—"

"Quiet Doug! This is Ned. Do as I tell you right now, and do it on faith. This is an order. Place the mass-energy converter on passive mode—immediately!"

"What! I don't—"

"Don't think, just DO it!"

"It's done. . . . But I'm afraid that mode won't be able to kick in for another two minutes."

There was a brief silence before Doyan commented, "Vzzvzthat should just do it."

"Doug? Still there?"

"Yes, Ned. What?"

"If the Dort pulled a fast one on us and we don't change course for that last star cluster in exactly two minutes, blow us up—Transformation, Dorts and all."

"I understand," Doug replied.

The Dort seemed to hunch momentarily; and Ned, out the corner of his eye, saw another subtle movement. It was Clint—nodding his approval.

TWENTY-ONE

The four watched Doyan, The One, and time crept by. After two minutes, that felt like hours to the humans, fifty glowing disks began to brighten and the translucent mound began to move, pressing the colored disk controls with precise sequences and timing. The moves looked random, but were dictated by the lights and the Dort's purpose. In seconds the activity stopped and the pseudopods withdrew.

Static crackled again, and Doug was on the air. "We're starting a slow course correction," he said. "It's extremely minute, of course, but four or five hundred times greater than we were getting from our system when it was bucking the Dort interference. If this correction continues for another two hundred and sixty hours there's a chance we'll be on course for the outer fringes of that last star cluster in the Galaxy. It's the only one reachable. After the course correction, however, there's some news. Good news and some not so good news. I think we're on our way. That's the good news. The bad news, which is still better than the alternatives, is that it will take at least a decade to get there. That's a biocomputer estimate. The accuracy of the estimate will improve as time goes on. A lot of things could change, but so far so good. At least we've still got a fighting chance for survival. As for our ever getting back to Earth, I don't know."

"I hope that ends the bad news," Ned said.

"Well, not quite. We're trimming it close. The Dorts could double-cross us the last minute—even ten years from now—and we'd still miss the cluster. There's no fail-safe on this. Seems as if we still need to work something out with . . . er . . . what's-his-name—Doyan?"

Ned replied, "So, we're still not out of the woods."

"I guess not," Doug's voice crackled. "If there were just some way to be sure. We need to stiffen our plan and do more thinking. . . . Hmm. I have an idea. Give me a few minutes to talk this over with the other Directors. I'll be right back."

"Okay. We'll stand by."

When Doug's voice came on again it was theatrically confident saying, "We have a comment and a suggestion." From his melodramatic style it was clear to the four that Doug was well aware that every word he said could be heard by the Dort.

"Go ahead," Ned replied.

"Much as we value our lives and would hate to destroy the Transformation, we're in full agreement with you about what to do if there is a deviation that would take us out of this Galaxy. In that case, we're as good as lost anyway, not only for those ten or more years, but forever. None of us would still be alive by the time we were near the Coma Cluster of galaxies but, judging by their known longevity, the remaining Dorts would still be alive. So, if our course correction to some safe planet in some star cluster in this galaxy fails for any reason, then our first point is to reaffirm our determination to destroying the Transformation."

Ned looked at the others. They nodded their understanding. They knew Doug's comment was a continuation and reinforcement of Ned's earlier bluff.

"Good," Ned said. "Then we're all in agreement—and not just from some order I might give." He watched the Dort as it again humped and arched in its subtle way—uncomfortably, he hoped. "Now what's your suggestion?"

"That we send down several teams. Security people and teams of technicians to monitor the mass-energy system and its controls, set up a communications center, and regain control of this Transformation. To do that we'll have to learn what the Dorts have, how their controls are different from ours, and a lot of things we can't even think of yet. We may have to build a completely new control system if we can't operate theirs. The only other alternative we can think of right now is to trust Doyan—and we don't!"

Clint Bracket cleared his throat for attention. "That's right. Send in the Security. There's no reason to trust the Dorts, and we have to get back the control. I think we'd be well advised to take hostages—especially this one," and then with great sarcasm, "It calls itself 'Doyan,' or 'The One,' or the 'Integrator,' and God knows what else. Right now it isn't even touching the controls, so everything must be on automatic. The Dort is no longer needed here. I'll take it into custody and—"

Doyan interrupted. "I can appreciate your reasons for distrust. Nevertheless I will cooperate in every way to assure a safe arrival within this Galaxy. We now share that common goal. Without your timely arrival and immediate cooperation this would not have been possible. From our throng, the Multitude, there are only six others and myself remaining. The rest are dead or mad—that is, dying. They were needed for many tasks, including the building and maintenance of our mass-energy converters. The Twister was far more devastating than our worst projections. No loss of life was expected. The seven of us are deployed on tasks of systems maintenance, but we are too few for the jobs that must continue in order to keep on track. The technical teams you intend to send down to establish something approximating a 'fail-safe' system will be no luxury. From our viewpoint they are a necessity. Without the assistance of your technicians it is unlikely we will ever arrive at this Galaxy's last star cluster before an uncontrollable trajectory sends this Cone into the distant Coma Cluster of galaxies.

"As for the idea of taking me or the other remaining Dorts into custody, as hostages, you can forget that right now." (Clint bristled.) "Without myself and those few other Dorts, your technical teams would never have the time or knowledge to determine how to run our unique equipment, much less how to keep it operating and maintained. As Integrator, I must coordinate everything from here, first by sensing the data disks, and then responding. From this location, I handle dozens of routine problems at once. However, many require on-the-spot correction. Most problems, as I stated, can be located and corrected from here; but much repair must be on location. That last type of problem is already getting out of hand—which would have been expected even without the Twister. Your help is needed for the on-site corrections and repairs. After that, go ahead and build in as much 'fail-safe' as you wish, but those essentials must be handled immediately."

"What about computers?" Clint growled, turning to his friends. "Couldn't we just replace this Dort with a computer? We can't be dependent on this, this Doyan-thing, and gain control at the same time. It has to be replaced."

Not unlike the human response to many of Clint's pronouncements, the Dort continued as though there had been no interruption. "Everything here is operated from these lights—this circle of data controls. Many computers are involved—hundreds for each lighted disk. But there is no central computer. The complexity of this system would not allow it. No known combination of biocomputers could handle it. Nor was such a computer necessary. The operation of this complex requires more than a powerful memory. It requires the ability to make detailed, instant judgments based on the totality of dynamic data changes across the entire system. As Integrator, I serve that function. I know of no way to transfer my memory and comprehensive systems judgment to one of your super biocomputers."

Doyan then extended his pseudopods to cover the fifty disks and again began working.

"Are you saying that our biocomputers could never be adapted to these systems?" Laura asked.

"Such an adaptation would be radical. There wouldn't be sufficient time in this universe. It would take virtually forever for the programming. Even in theory I do not know how it could be done."

On a more practical note, Laura continued questioning. "How much of your time is needed to keep us on the right course?"

"Very little at first. Under these power conditions, I need to check our coordinates at least hourly and then make the necessary corrections. The closer we get to the final correction, the more frequent the adjustments will have to be—until the last twenty or thirty hours when the monitoring must be continuous."

Doug's voice scratched its way through again. "Maybe Doyan is right to say we can't modify their systems. At least not on time for us to gain control before heading into that last globular cluster. Then again, maybe he's wrong. I'm betting their technology and science is no more advanced than ours. He could be bragging. It may be differently engineered for their convenience—for the physical, mental, and psychological differences between men and Dorts, but a toroidal mass-energy converter, for instance, is still the same. It has to be."

"Not to quibble with you, Doug," Jack cut in, "but their equipment may have uses for some unusual phenomena we hadn't known before. For instance, we can't explain those screwball gravitational events in Crazy Canyon. Another thing is that sphere that brought us here through all those kilometers of rocky, jagged sidewalls without so much as touching them, even in the narrow spots. I wouldn't underestimate them, Doug. They still have a few things they can teach us."

"Oh, details!" Doug said with a frustrated sigh. "Right now we have to get those teams down there. 'The One' has said the Dorts will cooperate, so let's take him at his word. At least for now. They did send that SOS. Anyway, we have no choice right now. If it wants to start proving its good will, it can begin by lifting that block to our scanner. That should increase the energy available for course changes."

Doyan's pseudopods quickened their drumming on the flickering disks.

Then commotion crackled from the speakers. "Blessed mother of frosted horn toads!" Doug whooped. Other voices clamored in the background, but with none of Doug's delicate expression and excitement. "What's the matter, Doug?" asked Laura, her voice shaking. "Is something wrong?"

"It's a long story, Laura. You'd have to see this to believe it. The Dort came through on this one. The scan block is lifted. If we'd seen this a few days ago, I don't know what we'd have done. We'd probably have sent down an army."

"What is the scan showing?" Laura insisted.

"The computers are translating the scans to visual on four of our screens—layer by layer and in perspective views, and from different angles. In a few minutes we'll have it on hologram. So far all I can say is, it's immense. They have four conventional operating toroids, each much smaller than ours, and a Tesla Tank. Nothing unexpected there. But there are two other structures I can't figure out. One, the smaller of the two, is operating at high energy, and the other, a really immense one, is dormant."

"What do they look like?" Laura asked.

"Like stretched-out spiral springs that double back at the top and bottom to form a continuous connection. The smaller one is four kilometers across, and the spiral runs up and down the center of the Transformation Cone for over fifty kilometers. The dormant one is at least three times larger in all dimensions. Those are just the larger structures. There are hundreds of other machines, devices, and complex equipment spread throughout the Cone below our level that I couldn't even begin to describe. Some are either generating or using energy, and others are just there, dormant or incomplete. And there are passageways upon passageways—and caverns! The lower two-thirds of this Transformation is honeycombed with them. Some are filled to the roof with equipment, and others—like Crazy Canyon—are still empty. . . . God! It makes you wonder what the Dorts have been preparing for!"

"Let's ask him," Laura suggested. Turning to the Dort she said, "Doyan, would you enlighten us?"

The Dort hunched and tucked—this time less subtly. "The closed spirals are not unlike extended toroids," Doyan explained, "but they require relatively less space to increase their length and power. Achieving a simple Transformation would be its nominal mission. The main purpose involved in their obvious difference from ordinary Cone-torus rings, however, is to promote and generate a field to stabilize and energize a Cone of Transformation, and send it through multiple *Reo-Spheres* by hurtling each of their hyperCeleric barriers. This complex function has never been tested. A byproduct of its internal field at present is the gravitational anomaly you are already familiar with."

Laura placed her fingertips to her temples and shook her head in bemusement at what she'd just heard. The implications of this revelation, if they were possible, were too staggering for even her immediate comprehension. If true, the Dorts, something or someone, had made a theoretical, and practical, quantum leap—beyond anything dreamed of in Transformation Physics. It would reduce the principles of Transformation Theory to a special case of a broader, more fundamental explanation.

It was a year since Laura had, for the first and only time, heard the term "Reo-Sphere." It was in one of those pipe-dream postgraduate seminars on cosmology. The guest lecturer that day was a physicist of middling credentials and the CEO of an inconsequential rival company. Its "CEO" was the company's only human employee. Like 3T, it worked with Dorts. The "CEO" lecturer had spoken of "spheres of reality" or "Reo-Spheres" for short. He shortened that to "R-Ss." She couldn't remember the speaker's name, but recalled it sounded silly, like chicken wings or some other protein. The theory postulated that the universe, "The one we live in," he said, "is only one R-S of a possible infinite number of R-Ss—not to be confused with parallel universes. They are not in parallel, but in hierarchy, as in a chain or necklace of slightly overlapping Venn diagrams."

He also told the conference that within each R-S the maximum local speed was, as usual, the speed of light. The only point of "contact" between R-Ss was in relation to that limit. The R-Ss were said to exist "unaware" of each other because the "slowest" velocity of one R-S was the maximum—the speed of light—of the one just "below" it. Thus, he claimed, the speed of light limit is never violated when traversing Reo-Spheres. The sum total of all R-Ss he called the Macrosphere. The seminar speaker defined the ultimate cosmology as the study of the relationship between R-Ss, the evolution and promulgation of additional R-Ss, the dynamics of their demise, the n-dimensional nature of the Macrosphere, its genesis, future and limits. He'd also noted that Transformation was a limited, special case of a single, not multiple, R-S progression, whatever that meant.

As if those ideas were not enough to completely destroy the lecturer's credibility, the real clincher was his assertion that it was theoretically possible to momentarily transfer particles, or "entities," from one R-S to another and back again—and in the process to have fleetingly traveled, with respect to the first R-S, at any chosen multiple above or below the speed of light, while in actuality never exceeding the speed of light in any one of the alternate Reo-Spheres. Thus, the actual "traveling" would take place in a series of one or more R-Ss other than the first one—for possible speeds, as related to the first R-S, that could approach or even exceed C squared. It was not just a case of wild speculation. To Laura, it was sheer foolishness.

After several seconds, Laura removed her hands from her head and looked coldly at the Dort. Then she leaned forward, toward Doyan, and asked firmly, "For what end have these preparations been made?"

"Your question," the Dort buzzed, "goes beyond my knowledge."

"Beyond your knowledge!" Laura said angrily. "That isn't rational. You don't construct something like this without a purpose in mind. You don't even build a simple road without knowing where from and where to."

"Vehicles are built all the time without knowing their ultimate destinations," Doyan countered.

"You're dodging the issue," she said, more resentfully. "You already implied that you wanted this Transformation to go to some planet—one that you apparently are already aware of. You didn't need all this—everything that Doug described—to accomplish that. What is your real goal?"

The Dort's bulk momentarily contracted causing a furrow to appear along its full extent. The invagination smoothed again and the Dort responded, "That is still a mystery that goes beyond our understanding, our learning, and our genetically programmed responsibility. The answer has to lie with those who sent us into the Galaxy—our ancestors, if they still live or left records."

"Are you telling me that you're nothing but a genetically programmed robot?" Laura challenged.

"No more than you. Are you a robot because you are Homo sapiens, female, and have a certain maximum life span under ideal conditions?"

"That's not the same thing I'm talking about. I'm speaking of self-direction and—"

"—and other human characteristics," the Dort finished for her.

Laura continued, "Do you lack personal insight? Do you lack curiosity and purpose?"

"We have personal insights, yes. That is as necessary to our nature as it is to yours. But do you have *personal* insight, for instance, into the operation of your brain stem? Of course not. You can condition autonomic responses, but 'personal insights' play no part there. And we have curiosity and purpose. In your case purpose, over and above your physical needs, is learned. You learn your ethics and morality, and mathematics, and when to say 'excuse me.' But you did not learn the need for water, oxygen, and food. You did not learn the sucking reflex. You did not learn hunger. You did not have to. It came with your equipment, all built in. Like you, we had to learn when to say 'excuse me,' but we did not have to learn our ethic, our responsibility, or even the basics of higher mathematical thinking."

"How can you speak of a built-in ethic?" Laura said. "It's a contradiction. You're really talking about an animal drive that you can take no credit for. No choice was involved. To me an ethic implies some personal understanding and insight as well. I ask you again—what is the purpose of all that you have built in this Great Cone?"

"And again I must say, the ultimate purposes lie with our ancestors, and we, the Dorts, are only an instrument of that purpose. Our limited purpose is to be an instrument for that purpose. That is not my knowledge; rather it is a personal insight. This is our nature, without personal insight into any greater purpose than we came with. Only in regression and madness do we receive the sketchiest personal glimpse of our ancestral purpose. I have not directly experienced it. But recently, since the Twister, I have seen it among my fellow Dorts."

"You are speaking of the dying Dorts," Laura said without expression.

"Yes. The mad ones."

"Don't you envy their insights?"

"Do you envy someone in pain?"

"We met one of your dying Dorts," Laura said with remembered compassion. She went on to summarize their conversation. As she spoke, the mound called Doyan expanded and contracted, furrowed and hunched. ". . . but there is something I find most perplexing and inconsistent. It told us that you, The One, had special knowledge among Dorts, that you knew that ultimate purpose. But you are saying that isn't true. I don't understand."

"Mankind and Dort are different in most ways, and similar in a few. But there is one thing we do have in common more than anything else. I would almost say it transcends our differences."

That remark brought Laura to her feet. "What is that?" she asked.

The mound contorted, settled back and said, "The need for hope."

Laura placed her hand over her mouth to hide her expression. After a long silence, she haltingly resumed, asking, "What has that to do with other Dorts believing you have knowledge you don't possess?" The question was more for the record. She already knew.

"The Multitude was led to believe that we, The Ten, had this knowledge. They needed that hope. It sustained them through the millennia as we crept across space. But our knowledge was unique in a way. Only we, The Ten, knew it was a hope without content. It was content that we did not possess."

"You took it on faith that it was worthwhile."

"That it was necessary. The Multitude knew not that we knew not. Even as they died they believed our knowledge to be superior and complete—and they drew strength from that. So even as death overtook them, they believed it was for some purpose greater than they could ever know."

"Then it was that that sustained them for the centuries?"

"Yes, but ironically as they died it was I, the one remaining member of The Ten, who drew strength from them. As they died, and their structures began to deteriorate into earlier forms, the long-blocked insights were revealed to them—not the exact details of our makers or our ancestors purposes, but the broad implications of that purpose. I do not know how to translate my experience so that you would understand, but these words may come close: The vigil has been long to survive without hope—the hope that ours was not a meaningless, merely instinctively driven existence and set of behaviors. I now have hope too. The madness of my dying fellows has given this to me."

They sat silently for several minutes. Doyan had been manipulating the data disks throughout their discussion, sometimes hardly at all, and sometimes at a rapid rate. Now he was not moving. The lights continued to flicker, and the "stars" in the canopy continued to twinkle.

Ned turned to Laura and encouraged her to go on with her questions, but she shook her head slowly, "I can't right now."

"Doyan," said Ned, moving off the rock and pacing thoughtfully beside the lights, "you said you have a responsibility and that it is your purpose—a limited purpose, to serve a higher one that you do not fully understand. Is that correct?"

"Yes."

"Without fully knowing why?"

"Yes."

"What, exactly, is your *limited* purpose?"

"Like a machine with the built in responsibility to go zig and then zag without question or knowing why, we, the Dorts, were given the responsibility to bring back a special technology and a special kind of being."

Ned stopped in his tracks. Jack and Clint became hyperalert. Laura lifted her head in surprise.

Ned repeated the words carefully: "Special . . . kind . . . of . . . being?"

The Dort creased, and then replied. "This Transformation meets the special technology requirements, and you, the human beings on this Transformation, are the special kind of beings."

"We met the criteria," Ned said coldly.

"Yes. That is why you had to be with us. To return to Origin with the technology alone would have been to shirk our duty—the ethic which is our being."

Clint opened and closed his great fists, and glared at the Dort.

Ned continued. "Then the planet you have us headed for is where you are from. That is where your ancestors lived, and it is not you, but they who require us? And you kidnapped us, for them, to satisfy some requirement that they built into your genetic system?"

"That is the only explanation possible, since it is not rational for us to do this. We simply must."

Clint jumped to his feet and bellowed at the Dort, "You cowardly blob! You pig! You're nothing but a kidnapper. That used to be a capital offense. And you forced us into a Twister with predictable loss of human life. That's still subject to capital punishment. You're a murdering criminal and a pirate! Now you're claiming innocence by reason of insanity—you're claiming some built-in irresistible urge and impulse forced you to do those crimes!"

"On the contrary, I have specifically claimed that I am not mad, and furthermore I have stated that bringing a special kind of being to Origin was not an act of madness, but a responsibility. I take the responsibility. And there was no predictability or expectation of human or Dort deaths in that Twister. It was highly unlikely. For your human deaths and injuries there is no way to adequately apologize, but I do apologize."

"Listen you—"

"Hold it, Clint," said Ned, raising his hand. "We need to calm down. All of us. We need to find out more. We need to try and make some sense out of all this."

Clint hunched silently, but grudgingly, caricaturing the newly observed Dort behavior.

"Tell me, Doyan," Ned continued, "why are you telling us this now? And why should we believe you? You Dorts haven't really been honest with us for . . . centuries."

"The other Director, Doctor Groth, used the term 'fail-safe.' That means he didn't want to take any chances. As Dorts, neither did we. That is why we were secretive and dishonest. Had your cooperation been possible to obtain, that would not have been necessary. The characteristic of paranoia, the most common human reaction toward us, made this difficult. The chances of human cooperation were remote. You were not programmed to make such sacrifices, especially for unclear reasons. You might have cooperated if we had been honest, but most likely not."

Clint snarled, "Now your centuries of dishonesty is our fault because we're supposedly crazy—paranoid. I suppose you call that taking responsibility!"

Doyan hunched and creased, more than earlier, but continued resolutely. "All our careful plans—yes, that included our dishonesty—fell apart with the Twister. That's why we responded to your message with the SOS. We need your help. And, at least for now, you need ours."

The transceivers again scratched: "We've located several good places to drop some shafts to hook up with y'all down there, and to send our teams down. It'll take quite a few more hours, though, because we're running into some difficulties getting the other 'Torpedoes' operating. In the meantime we're thinking of bringing up the one you went down in. That will give us—"

The Dort interrupted, saying, "That won't be necessary, Doctor Groth. We have spheres of the type your friends were in to get here. You may de-Transform two new shafts, like the one you originally made for the people here, but make the shafts using the sets of coordinates I'm now sending to you. Then you can get your technicians down here in minutes. They are needed soon. Both Orbs can be readied immediately, and your slow-moving 'Torpedo' may serve less-urgent transport. By your signal, I can cause the Orbs to descend or ascend, as needed."

"Well, um," Doug stammered, "That would be most helpful. Then you guys, Jack, Ned, Laura, Clint—you could come back up here after some of our technical personnel and security arrive down there. I think you could each use a good meal, a warm tub and some rest."

Laura threw her head back and in a yearning, grateful voice said, "Oh God, yes!"

And so it was done. In thirty minutes the first partial team arrived, loaded with electronic equipment and testing devices, and especially communications gear. From then on there would be no static on the speakers. And there would be holographs and pictures to supplement the talk and all the other endless streams of data.

The two Orbs arrived in quick succession, full of needed equipment, women and men, including more security. The passengers marveled at the speed of the Orbs and, upon arrival, the beauty and size of the geode. Two more Dorts were soon on the spot to help unload, and to begin the team's orientation. Yet another Dort arrived to request immediate assistance on a trouble spot. Several technicians with the appropriate skills identified themselves and followed close behind the Dort.

The Orbs went up again and quickly returned with more loads of people and equipment. Doug was on one of them. He was hugged and kissed by Laura and men alike—although Clint confined himself to the hug.

Doug was soon totally in charge, talking to men and Dorts alike, babbling on a microphone, and setting up his headquarters beside Doyan and the circle of lights. After another half-hour the place was bustling like a Grand Central. Finally Doug turned to Ned and the others, and said, "Well? What are you guys hanging around for? Clime into one of those Orbs and get out of here. Unless," he added with a mischievous chuckle, "you don't enjoy shrimp and steak, cocktails, hot tubs, and sleep!"

TWENTY-TWO

They exited the sphere near the Directors' conference room at 1645 hours. The breathtaking ascent had taken less than ten minutes. Still in their clumsy protective suits, they were met by a cheering crowd of technicians—and most of the Directors—who had gathered to greet their victorious negotiators. As the noisy crowd pressed in upon them, there were smiles, handshakes, words of congratulations and many thanks. Behind them, the spheres—called "Orbs" by the Dorts—continued their shuttle work. They would descend and return again and again for several more hours amidst an increasing racket of boisterous and celebrating men and women, and the clatter of the Orbs being packed and readied for their next descent.

But there was also something disconcerting in the crowd—something inconsistent with the noisy victory celebration. Was it the hesitancy in a few of the handshakes? Most were firm. Was it something in their eyes? Some avoided eye contact, and others looked almost too deeply into theirs, as if trying to see within. Yes, it was in their eyes—a mix of longing wonder, fear and perhaps distrust. The truth was there, but not all of it. The public facade of hero worship and the game of victory continued with compulsive melodrama, like a superstitious response to a great and terrible need. It was a chaotic ritual, an adulteration of true celebration, a cathartic self-deception.

The victory stratagem was equally well played by the returning heroes. They bowed and smiled modestly as the situation seemed to demand, and embraced many friends. Even Clinton Bracket was caught up in the game, seeming more entranced by it than anyone, sometimes raising his arms into the air like an Olympic winner. Jack played his part more as a politician, plunging deliberately into the crowd, shaking hands, and giving little speeches to several listeners at a time. Laura and Ned tried to take a more passive role by standing in one place, as though in a reception line, but the jostling crowd moved them randomly about like molecules of gas in a sealed space.

After many minutes of noise and buffeting Laura spotted Judith Olafson's frightened face. Despite her fear, she was jumping up and down and waving to Laura over the tops of heads. Laura's glued-on smile blossomed into genuine delight as she returned the greeting, shouting "Hi Judy!" and, leaving Ned behind, pushed through the crowd to meet her. They embraced, looked at each other at arm's length, and embraced again. Judy started to smile.

Arm in arm they shoved their way through the crowd, entered the empty conference room and closed and locked the door, leaving the din and tumult behind. Once in the quiet chamber, Judy said, "I'm supposed to debrief you. Directors' orders. Jack, Clint and Ned will be too, but not by me. Just a few quick highlights for now, and then you can take off that cumbersome uniform and clean up in the back—in the Comfy area. We have a wonderful dinner planned for later, and then you'll want to rest. You look so tired. It must have been awful for you. Do you mind if I turn on the recorder now? I'll be turning it on and off a lot, depending on what we're covering."

Laura looked at Judy a little surprised and said, "Debrief away. But Oh! It's so good to be back!"

Judy hugged Laura again and kissed her on the cheek saying, "And it's so good to have you back. I was afraid for you, all of you, and for all of us." Then that look of fear came again into Judy's eyes—the look that Laura had seen in the crowd. Judy's voice became solemn as she turned on the recorder and gently asked the first question—"Is it over?"

Laura jerked with a startle reflex as if the quiet question was a clap of thunder. The question explained all those looks. It tore away all the facades and exposed the fear. She quickly regained her composure and responded with equal softness, "I don't know. . . . It depends on what 'over' means, but I think so."

Judy leaned forward, lines forming between her brows, and said, "Good answer, but too much like something a politician might say. Do Ned and Jack and Clint think it's over?"

Laura turned to sit in one of the leather chairs beside the conference table. Her bulky outfit billowed as she settled into it. "Okay, I won't hedge," she said. "I'm sure they *don't* think it's over. I think I'm the only one who does believe it's over." She motioned Judy into the chair beside her.

Then Laura tilted her head with a quizzical look, as though she'd just thought of something, and said, "What do *you* mean by 'over,' Judy?"

Judy turned off the recorder. "I'm not sure what I mean by it. It wasn't on the list of questions I planned to ask. The question came from my gut, not my head."

"So did my answer."

Judy frowned again. "It's just that there's been so much . . . speculation about what happened down there. For a long time we didn't know if you were alive, dead, captured or what. When we found out how far off our original direction and time estimates were for a safe trajectory for reaching a star cluster . . . well, we almost panicked. Well, you know me. I did."

"I can imagine. Were all the personnel informed? What did you tell them?"

"Nothing. We broke our own rule about being entirely honest with them. It was a virtual news blackout. Debra Anderson was really pissed. She wanted to put something in her newsletter. We were afraid of panic, or even mutiny. We were afraid they'd lose confidence and do something desperate that might destroy the Transformation. Do you think that was a mistake?"

"How could it have been a mistake? There was nothing to report—at least from us. You hadn't heard from us yet. The Directors were as much in a news blackout as the crew."

"I know, but we didn't tell them that."

"Did you lie to them?"

"Not exactly. For a long time we made no reports at all. Then the pressure built up. They were demanding information. They wanted to know what we knew, and that wasn't much. So we issued optimistic statements about when we expected to hear from you, that the long radio silence was expected, and so on. That helped for a while, until the word got out about the new time estimates necessary for the course change."

"How did that become known if there was a news blackout?"

"You know how the grapevine works around here. We could control the external communications information—our communications with you, but anything internal that seems important spreads like wildfire."

"Yes, I recall how that works," Laura nodded.

"When we contacted you again, after you first entered that sphere next to Crazy Canyon, we issued another announcement and told of your success in making contact with the Dorts. It was another optimistic report, but wasn't completely true since you only had voice contact and negotiations hadn't begun. In a sense, I guess those negotiations never did begin."

"Unless you count our threat to destroy the Transformation."

"Yes, that's true. Anyway, at that point everybody thought there was a good forty-five minutes left to act, so our announcement that you had just made contact turned out to be a real tactical error. Until then it was possible for everyone to believe that you'd made contact long before then and were well into the negotiations. The Directors were so excited to hear from you that it never crossed our minds the news would be taken negatively. Things got very bad."

"Bad how?"

"A lot of half-organized groups became solidly organized. That's when the first riot started."

Laura's jaw dropped.

"One of the groups was pounding on the doors of this chamber. We had to keep the doors locked. We found out later that someone had set up a laser outside this main door and was going to blast it down. Fortunately there were several different groups—and none of them had the same idea about tactics. The plan to blast out the conference room door wasn't universally approved. That's when the first brawl started. I don't think they had the slightest idea what they'd do if they had gotten in."

"You said that was the 'first' riot. Were there more?"

"Yes. Just two in all. Almost three, in fact, if I count the one the Directors themselves nearly got into."

"How did the second one start?"

"With updated information that only six minutes were left to plot the new course. That lit the grapevine fuse. Everybody knew about it at once, like a morphic-field response. One group started setting up the de-Transformation equipment to destroy what they could of the Dort installation. They were going to shoot out three-meter diameter cores randomly. They would have done it too, but another group knew it was too dangerous. The fight that resulted from that disagreement sent eight technicians to the hospital.

"When Doug contacted you in the geode—my God, Laura! A *geode?*—there was only four minutes left; and when Ned gave the order to put the mass-energy converter on passive mode we nearly had a Directors' riot. Thank God there wasn't time to argue. Debra Anderson was announcing the good news of the course correction on the public address system the second it happened—at the same time Doug was telling you it was working. That defused our panic and the grosser elements of mass paranoia, but I'm afraid there may be a lingering legacy of distrust. You'd never know it from the celebration."

Laura nodded. After moments of silence she said, "I feel tired and hungry and dirty. Mind if I head for the Comfy. I'd like to clean up and change. And, oh yes, thank *you* for the debriefing."

Laura started to get up, but Judy turned quickly in her chair, looked slightly panicked, and said, "Oh dear! You're right. I've been doing all the talking." She reached out and took Laura's hands. "Just a few more minutes? Please." She looked sad and earnest. "Just a few more minutes? We'll talk about it again tomorrow but right now . . . Oh dear. . . ."

"What's the matter?"

Judy turned on the recorder again. "It's . . . it's the same question. Is it—"

"Is it over?"

Judy's chin began to quiver and she lowered her eyes. "Yes. The question . . . it's still in my gut. You said you think it's over. I hope you're right, but I can't believe it is. It's very—" (she turned off the recorder) "—frightening." Then she leaned forward with her hands covering her face and shook.

Laura moved quickly off her chair, knelt before Judy, and placed her bulkily covered arms around her, letting her sob and sob until she was through. Then she placed her hands on Judy's shoulders and looked into her face. "Dearest Judy," she said softly, "I don't know how to explain my . . . optimism. Intellectually there is little to be confident of. It's just my feeling."

The recorder went on again. "Even after your ordeal down below, you feel optimistic?" Judy asked, wiping her nose on her sleeve.

Laura returned to her chair. "Yes—especially after that."

"You have a feeling about it, but let's look at it rationally," Judy snuffled.

"Rationally? . . . Okay. Rationally! You know rationally that we still have to reach that star cluster and de-Transform into normal space close to a high-mass body, such as a star or planet. Planets are better even though they don't have a star's mass. Planets are better because they're cool. In a pinch we could use a star, but it's riskier. Planets, on the other hand, are harder to find. But say we get in orbit around a planet. Then we move in close to restore power for the energy converters, reset our coordinates for Earth, and home we go!"

Judy took several tissues from her purse and blew her nose loudly. "Well, that sounds nice. I'm a chemist, but I did know that much about Transformation. Everyone does. What bothers me is bringing everything off without a hitch. We are not in control of this thing. 'Rational,' remember?"

"Okay. The first hitch, even if we had full control of the Transformation, is finding the coordinates of Earth. Celestial navigation is not a perfect science."

"I've heard your comments on celestial navigation before. I believe you said that from a cruising Transformation, 'it stinks.'"

"You aren't making this easy for me, Judy. All right. It stinks. It wasn't that great before the Twister, but now we're more into probabilities than real measurement."

"Probabilities?"

"Educated guesses—"

"—About the Earth's location—it's coordinates? How to get back?"

"Yes. But it isn't hopeless by any means. It means we'd have to hop around a bit before finding recognizable star formations. Then we could set an accurate course. But we'd need exact coordinates for other stars or planets just to hop around."

"How very reassuring! Any other problems?" Judy asked with a curled lip, almost back to normal, but still a little anxious.

"Lots! The Dorts want to go back to the planet they're from. You heard Doyan say that yourself. You heard the whole conversation. They want to go to that planet and they want us with them."

"How can you say it's over then?"

"I never said I was being rational. Anyway, I'm sure Doug and Stan will try to de-Transform into a close orbit around that planet—without landing on it. 'Landing' a Transformation isn't possible anyway. That's just theoretical, but we can get very close."

"The Dorts won't settle for that without a fight, or at least an argument. They'll want to take shuttles down—with us in tow."

"I know. I guess that isn't a big issue for me. There aren't enough Dorts left to do much people towing, unless it's voluntary. Personally, I'd like to go there—if it's hospitable. I think we should."

"What are you saying? That's madness!"

"Maybe so, but it's no more crazy than the first Transformation to the Dort Settlements. Everyone—well, almost everyone—thought that would be suicide, but we ended up sending several valuable expeditions there—and safely. Now that we're into this, why not go all the way?"

"It's dangerous, that's why. A lot of us trusted the Dorts then—but no more. They're unpredictable. They are proven liars. We can't guess their motives!"

"Any unpredictable venture could be dangerous. That original Dort planet is a mystery to us. We can't predict what dangers we'd run into there—and the Dorts don't know either! They only know that that is where they must go. They have no clear memory of their beginnings—only of their long trip across the Galaxy to the Settlement Planets, and then to Earth. It's been thousands of years since they were last there. Doyan, said they kept track of their planet's coordinates and movements all that time—and they aren't even sure how. Doyan claimed that as they moved, and as their planet, 'Origin,'—that's their name for it—moved, and as time moved, something inside them kept clicking off those coordinates like an atomic clock.

"We don't know the risks of going to that planet," Laura continued, "but I'll bet the Twister was a lot more risky than setting foot on Origin could ever be. If we ever get there, Stanley Lundeen could turn his Astrophysics Department and its staff and instruments loose to observe the planet for any environmental or other risks for humans—at least for humans on quick visits in space suits. I don't see why the Directors wouldn't consider that an option."

"They have," said Judy, with a flicker of fear returning to her eyes.

"They have? What did they say?"

Off went the recorder.

"We talked about it before Doug left to lead the operation in the geode. No decision was made. We couldn't do that without the rest of you anyway. But we did decide, and all of you agreed, we must gain back full control of the Transformation, one way or another. If we don't, we could end up on the Dorts' home planet against our wills—or worse yet, sail helplessly forever, nonstop beyond the Milky Way. We'd certainly battle to prevent that. If we do gain control, then we have choices. We have plenty of time to get ready, and time to make up our minds about when and where to go. Ten years! God help us! But the 'choice' idea is purely academic. None of us wanted to go to that part of the Galaxy in the first place. But we're headed there right now. We already lost out on that one. How much more will the Dorts be narrowing our choices in that future of shriveling options?"

They sat silently for several minutes, studying one another. There was still a question on Judy's face when she spoke again: "Laura, you're the only one I know who's suggested, even half-seriously that we should choose to enter that planet's terrain. I've known you for many years. We're best friends. We've been through a lot together. I've learned to trust you more than anything 'rational'— usually. You're not always right on the details, except for math and physics, but sometimes you're able to sense things in other areas with insight and depth. A lot of people think you're naïve—a physics genius, but naïve, gullible, sentimental and all the rest. But I know you. Usually you have a good reason, even if it's not logical or reasonable to others, for believing as you do. You check things out with more than your rationality—with your emotions, your gut, your heart, and yes, that lovely but special head of yours. Who else uses every side of their brain the way you do—and I don't just mean left and right—I mean front and back and all of it. Someone once said, and I believe it is truer of you than anyone I know, that the heart has reasons that reason knows not of. But, as always, trust you as I may, I still need the comfort of hearing your reasons. Especially this time.... What I'm getting at is . . . is—"

"—can we trust the Dorts?" Laura finished for her.

Judy's eyes widened. "Why, yes, that is my question!" She turned on the recorder.

"That, and 'Is it over?'" Laura presumed. "I'll answer the best I can. Yes, I think 'it's over,' and yes, I think we can 'trust the Dorts.' It's over in the sense that we need not worry about reaching that planet's star cluster. We'll be a lot older then, but I believe we'll get there. And we can trust the Dorts in the sense that we need not worry about reaching the star cluster."

Judy frowned, "You answered my earlier question and this one—both with the same answer—the same words in fact."

"I know. It was the same question."

Judy thought about it a while and agreed. "You've brushed aside my greatest fears—that the Dorts will switch course the last minute and send us into infinite space. It could happen. That's a detail. Could you be wrong? I know you *don't* believe they will switch course. That helps, but—"

"—Yes, I believe now more than ever that Dorts are predictable. They've been deceitful to us, as we can be to one another, but they have a conscious goal of going to Origin with Transformation technology—and us in tow. More important, however—and this is why I say they're predictable—is their unconscious, uncompromising, built-in drive to return there. Something in them 'knows' more than they are aware of, and the source of that knowledge, if it still exists, is somewhere on that planet."

Judy was becoming very tired, but looked steadily at Laura and asked the next obvious question. "How do you know this, Laura?"

Laura smiled, and said, "Within every sane Dort there is a mad Dort. That's how I know." Then she got up, removed her cumbersome uniform, and tossed it into another chair.

Judy rolled her eyes. "All right, Laura, explain that to me."

"That," Laura said, "is a long story. Now, if you'll excuse me for a few minutes, I have to take a shower. When I get back I'll tell you all about him." Then Laura turned and headed for the women's Comfy, just down a private hallway off the conference room. She had a large locker there, full of changes of clothes, hair dryer, nail files, cosmetics and other necessities. She smiled when she saw the ornate sign over the door—"Comfy." It was Ned's bright idea. He came up with it, she recalled, stroking her thigh, during a final inspection of the Cone a week before the Transformation began. He said the facility was far too elegant to be called a "toilet" or to simply be labeled "Ladies." Laura had gotten back at him a day after the "Comfy" sign was installed. The sign "MEN" was removed and replaced by "Cozy."

"Hey!" Judy yelled down the hall. "What do you mean, *him*?"

The question reached Laura as she entered the Comfy. She reopened the door and poked her head out to see Judy's expression. 'Dumbfounded' would describe it. Laura chuckled aloud, "Be patient, Judy. I've been looking forward to this bath for a thousand years. All day in fact. When I'm done in here I'll be ready to tell you all about—*him*! . . ."

"Damn you!" Judy shouted, stamping her foot.

". . . and what drives them." Laura turned again and the Comfy door closed behind her.

A half-hour later Laura emerged from the Comfy looking refreshed and beautiful. She'd changed into a light, springtime dress and sexy pumps. Judy was sleeping in her chair. Laura moved to the opposite side of the room where there was a makeshift bar and fixed herself a cocktail, the first of several, and then sat beside Judy sipping the drink. After a while, Laura reached over and turned on the recorder, gently woke her friend, and told her the story of the mad Dort. When she'd finished the tale, Judy finally understood, and they were both sure that no one else would.

Judy turned off the recorder for the last time as the door was unlocked and opened form the outside. Except for those still in the geode, the rest of the Directors entered. Ned, Jack, and Clint were clean-shaven and looked refreshed. They too had cut short their debriefings to become human again. After the Directors were in the room, they were followed by a small, but dazzlingly uniformed troop of Ganymedes pushing decorated carts of liquor and other dining wonders. The conference table was covered with padding and an elegant lace tablecloth. It was set with fine china and silver, candles and goblets. Champagne was poured, friendships strengthened, toasts proposed, salads savored, steaks devoured, and at last, good nights were said.

Jack and Clint had decided to stay below for the night. Jack because there were perfectly good quarters below, and he was tired, and Clint because Ellen Stone wanted to hit the bars—both of them—The Pub, yes, but especially the Honky-tonk Saloon.

As those decisions were being made, Laura nudged Ned covertly to delicately ask the big question: "My place or yours?"

TWENTY-THREE

"What are you doing?" Ned asked with drowsy irritation. His eyes were still closed.

Laura did not stop what she was doing. "Kissing you," she said in a sultry, muffled voice.

"Why are you kissing me there," he groaned.

"Because you're a perfect gentleman, I think, and because I like your bare chest." Then she lifted her head and kissed him on his mouth.

He opened one eye a slit, and then the other. "I like yours too, but what time is it?"

Laura moved to sit on the side of the bed. She was in a sleek, pink dressing gown. She stood and turned with one hand on her hip and smiled down at Ned. "It's time for breakfast," she said in her most seductive, unbreakfastlike voice.

Ned was flat on his back. He worked his elbows behind him so that he was half sitting up. He looked at Laura and returned a weak smile. "It feels early," he said. His half-opened eyes began to roam the sensuous contour of Laura's body, the way her narrow waist accentuated graceful hips and only slightly less than generous breasts.

"You're cruel," he said, extending one leg covered with a blue pajama bottom. His eyes slowly closed as his foot descended to the floor. Then he flopped back onto his pillow.

"Ned," she said reproachfully, "are you awake?"

"No."

"What did you do to me last night?" She asked, as if it was a perfectly normal question.

Ned raised his head and looked at her momentarily, then let it fall back again onto the pillow. "Wuddaya talk'n' 'bout?"

"All I remember was sitting beside you last night on the couch in the living room."

"Humph!" Ned grunted. "That was while we were still down in the complex. You had a few too many. When the platform started coming up you laid your head back and fell asleep. That was the end of you for the night. You were dead to the world."

"Oh yeah? If nothing happened, then how come I woke up beside you this morning in nothing but my black silk nightie? Answer me that!"

A slow smile crept across Ned's face. "Of all people, you don't think that I—"

"Well! I certainly hope not! If anything went on I'd like to have had at least one eye open."

Ned sat up on the side of the bed. Laura stood in front of him. He placed his hands on her waist and said in a serious tone, "Ya know, it's amazing how you could sleep through all that. I never knew anyone could go through that much lugging around, have your clothes removed, a nightie put on, get tucked in, and all without opening even one eye."

Laura laughed as Ned pulled her closer. "Then you were a gentleman last night, and I appreciate it—" Then she added, "—if I can believe you."

Ned tilted his head upwards and placed his chin on Laura's breastbone.

Looking into each other's eyes at close range, Laura said, "You look funny from this angle. Did you know you have only one eye?"

Ned's eye looked lustily into hers. His thumbs slipped under her sash and moved apart. The waistband fell to the floor and the housecoat opened to Ned's caressing hands, his nudging head and his demanding, exploring mouth. Her arms moved across Ned's back as she leaned hard into him, and they fell in a tangle of blue and pink across the bed.

It never entered Ned's mind to wonder what had become of Laura's black nightie.

It was several days before the new situation settled into anything approximating a routine. Setting up the communications network between the Dort installation and the "legitimate" Transformation complex was an early priority, and things were progressing well. After the first day the "earthquake systems" were dismantled—on both sides.

It was not the original intention of the Directors to make regular monitoring and maintenance of the Dort section a priority, but those tasks soon tied for first on the list of things to be done immediately. The Dorts were not kidding when they sent the SOS. The place was falling apart. It was built for regular maintenance to be done by a large farce of Dorts, but the Twister took care of that. Doug was fit to be tied when the utter magnitude of the problem became evident. For the first two days he was calling almost hourly for more technical staff and equipment. A whole manufacturing section had to be set up in the geode to make new devices and to assemble others with ready-made parts. By the end of the first few days more than half the men and women on the Transformation had moved below to join the original technical crews.

The "dike-plugging operation," as it came to be called, required tremendous effort, but a lot was learned from it. As more reliable, less labor intensive, and automated systems began to replace the Dorts' original equipment, it became possible to divert the labor of the technicians to the next crucial task—that of analyzing the system as a whole and preparing for a possible control changeover. Fortunately, most of the Dort equipment was, with careful maintenance, reliable; but the system was vast and much of it outdated and primitive.

Progress on the changeover to human control systems was difficult, complicated and slow. It soon became evident that Doyan was reluctant to cooperate. He was free enough with advice when asked, but the advice always seemed to lead nowhere or into intricate mazes of confusion and blind alleys. Doug eventually gave up on asking Doyan anything and went ahead with the development of an independent system—one that mere mortals could understand and begin to operate in the final days before zeroing in on the star cluster. With Doyan's "help" that could take the full ten years. Doug's goal was to have it accomplished within days, not years, to prevent any near-term shenanigans such as a surprise diversion to the Coma Cluster.

Doug and his engineers and technicians were designing a master control system that could be operated by a handful of men. They could find no way to take over Doyan's controls one system at a time. The Dort system was totally integrated, with little or no redundancy, with every other part. All the subsystems were interdependent. Disconnecting one segment would result in the breakdown of everything. Any transfer of the complex from Dort to human control would have to be total and instantaneous, if and when that could happen. It was being designed so that at the turn of a switch, Doyan's data delivery and control disks would become inoperative at the same moment the new equipment took over.

The area around Doyan and his circle of lights began to take on the look of human industry, much to the pride of the Directors and everyone else, especially Doug—the can-do administrator of all things practical and technical. Large segments of the geode were now brightly lit and cluttered with all manner of people and equipment—including the geode's "upper" dome where the gravity was reversed—including generators, consoles, desks, generations of biocomputers, kilometers of wires and cable, and hundreds of men and women scurrying about on foot or on the new motorized gyro-scooters, doing construction, building and piecing together technical devices, carrying apparatus to still others who were intently focused on sedentary computer programming jobs, and much more. The Central geode throbbed and echoed around the clock with the din of this activity and industry. But Doug, in the midst of all this, and in the midst of his pride, had the uneasy feeling that it was something of a mirage, for at the physical center of the geode, and the core and heart of everything that had been and was still operating, was the necklace of lights, the Operations Control Pod, Doyan, The One, the Integrator who still remained—quietly sending and receiving signals to and from the larger system—and who was still . . . The One in control.

During those first days of concentrated, frenetic activity, the Directors made several firsthand tours of the Dort installation, and the changes in progress. Laura was particularly interested in the spiral machine responsible for the gravitational anomalies. Its other functions, beyond ordinary Transformation, were untried or remained a mystery. Laura obtained makeshift scooters and, accompanied by one of the security staff, went swiftly through many kilometers of the "smaller" spiral tunnel. It was, in fact, a massive machine. Even more immense was the second spiral machine, but unlike the smaller one, it was not yet operational. It was many times larger than the first in all dimensions. They traveled over fourteen kilometers in the spiral cavern that contained the enormous metal tube. It loomed like a zeppelin, but seemed endless in length. Along the way they stopped to talk with several technicians who were examining the contents of a large crate. Until then they had seen no one in that cavern. The crate was one of perhaps a hundred stacked in that area. As

Laura chatted with the women, she was astonished to hear that only this, and one other portion of the complex spiral machine, was incomplete. Conditions indicated that at the time the Twister wiped them out, the Dorts were rushing to make it operational.

Also during those first few days, like Doug, Ned spent a fair amount of time trying to get information from Doyan, but came away feeling the information was useless. Most of what he heard was already known or no longer relevant. But, with great care, he took out his "Doyan interview notes" and dominated the next meeting of the Directors with his "useless" findings.

For instance, Doyan was willing to share the fact that the location of the Transformation site—the place on Earth where the Great Cone came to be—was decided upon by the Dorts many years before most of the smaller Transformations were created. Jack had already figured that out, including how the Dorts had manipulated 3T's selection of that exact location. It was also a matter of simple logic to realize the Dorts had begun their own construction deep beneath that same terrain years before the location was agreed upon, and even before the homes of the Directors and others were built on that ground. Doyan was willing to go into great detail about how that was accomplished, including how they built hundreds of kilometers of tunnels leading to and from the area that later became the Great Cone of Transformation. The tunnels were to avoid detection of debris removal and far enough away to locate their new mining and manufacturing complex. They had dug out most of the caverns and passages, including the great spirals, long before the Great Cone was ready to go. It was a speculative project that paid off.

Back then, the developing Theory contained clues to future technology that might come from it. Their key positions in 3T and in competitive companies kept them in on the ground floor of innovation. When the technology became available, they went about manufacturing and installing their equipment. Most of the earlier inventions were later improved, but the Dorts had little time to upgrade their complex infrastructure with the most modern technical advances— thus the archaic nature and condition of so much of their equipment.

Laura asked Ned, "Did Doyan say anything more about the closed spirals?"

"No. Doyan had nothing new to say about them, but did go on and on about 'Reo-Spheres.' It was nothing that I or any of the scientists and technicians I talked to could understand." Then Ned smiled and said, looking directly at David Michaels, "Doyan's a little like you, David. It gave those corkscrew machines a funny name—'Tenderloin Spirals.'"

Laura came to her feet with a start. She continued to stand there to command attention. Lots of luck. Her heart was pounding. The other Directors ignored her. They were busy trying to laugh at this new piece of "Dort misdirection," as someone called it. David said, "Your talk with Doyan wasn't a waste of time. It finally led you into a truly 'meaty subject.' I wish I'd been there for the christening!"

Laura was still standing when David's and all the other forced laughter died down. They finally turned to listen. "Tenderloin," she said, "was the name of that lecturer I heard—around a year ago. I mentioned that conference to some of you before. I'd forgotten his name until now, but he spoke on *The Cosmology of Reo-Spheres*." None of the other Directors could recall his name—from the literature or anywhere else.

Before Laura could say anything more, Ned shrugged and continued to shuffle through his scrawled pages to continue his monologue:

"Dorts, according to Doyan—and I believe this is a lie—can receive signals at almost any wavelength, not just sound and visible light. They can detect anything from gamma rays through radio waves, but can only respond with sound waves." Ned looked at the next slip, shrugged again and turned another page.

Ned explained that he didn't believe the next item either, but mentioned it anyway. "I asked Doyan why, in the light of his urgent SOS, he hadn't arranged to meet with us earlier rather than keeping us running around in tunnels all day. He told me they allowed our probe to locate Crazy Canyon at just the spot it did because they predicted how long it would take for a group of humans to make their way to the sphere that would take them to the geode. Then they allowed our probe to detect the geode itself to motivate us to get there. They even predicted that when we reached the 'Y' in the first passage off of Crazy Canyon that we'd take the left turn since the geode was 'down' and the right hand choice was 'up.' That was less convenient for them, Doyan admitted, but said they had that possibility covered and we'd still reach the geode."

Dr. Stone asked, "Did they think what might have happened, after you first got into Crazy Canyon, if you turned left instead of right?"

"Yes Ellen, they did. Another side tunnel, similar to the one we followed, had it's entrance seven kilometers to the left of our laser breakthrough point. We would have reached the same location, arriving at that 'exhaust' gallery rather than the one we entered when we discovered the dead Dorts. They even measured the twists and turns in the passage to improve the predictability of our arrival time. It's kind of crazy they did all that complicated stuff, but even their toasters are Rube Goldbergs."

Ned moved another note to the back of his pile.

"Doyan explained that their tunnels initially followed the natural geographic underground terrain, and that resulted in the many twists, turns, and even the varied widths of some passages. He said it was time and energy efficient to make them that way, but the whole point was to delay the first human arrivals to the geode long enough for our navigation equipment to measure the true timing crisis, and for there to *be* a timing crisis. That way there would be no time for argument about placing our mass-energy system on passive mode, thus turning control of the Transformation over to the Dorts—that is, to Doyan, the solitary survivor of The Ten. Anyway, all that had to be done with the timing of Crazy River's flood stage in mind. The Orb that took us to the geode could depart only when the river was absent and not flooding that spot or the water would have entered behind the moving Orb before the floodgate closed behind it. If that happened, it would fill the geode. Doyan admitted it was an engineering flaw they never had time to change or perfect—like so many other things. Just think of all the unnecessary mental crap—not to mention engineering crap—they went through to get us just then. It boggles the human mind, but its an insight into their alien thinking that I never tumbled to before in all the years I studied them."

Ned returned to the notes he'd skipped. They had to do with the geode among other things. Ned had asked Doyan why that particular site, of all the places on Earth, was selected for this Transformation. It was the existence of the great, water-filled geode. They knew of no other such place on Earth.

"They drained the geode to make the central control area that it is now. Otherwise, any other granite-solid spot that deep would have done as well. The geode is where the water for Crazy River came from. The smaller spiral mass-energy converter was in operation before anything else, so instead of simply letting the water drain away, they pumped it to the place we call Crazy Canyon. The spiral, which has to keep going, also keeps Crazy River circulating. That made little sense to me until Doyan explained that the geode was 'pleasing' to them and that Crazy River 'amused' them."

All this, Ned admitted, surprised him because he'd never before realized that Dorts could be "pleased" or "amused" about anything.

The fact that the Dorts had discovered the geode so deep in the Earth so many years before 3T had invented the probe scanner proved that the Dorts were ahead of them on that one. They were also ahead with scanner-blocking devices. It was a necessary development for their cause since their entire clandestine operation would have been discovered early on without that capability.

Ned was about to go on to the next page of notes, but as an afterthought he glanced at Laura and said, "Hmm! By the way, about that scanner-blocking device, Doyan called it a 'Tenderloin Blocker.'"

Ned's next sheet had two words on it: "See Hologram."

Ned swung his chair around to the console behind him, hit a few keys and turned back as the lights began to dim. A miniature, three-dimensional scene appeared in the center of the conference table. It was The One surrounded by fifty glowing dots and mini-Ned perched on a rock beside him, talking and taking notes.

"All of these interviews are on hologram, but I wanted you to see this one because my notes were sketchy. In fact I threw them out. Another reason: I'm having trouble being objective about this part. I think you'll see how totally hardened, mulish and unreasonable this Doyan creature can be."

Doyan expounded on the burial of the barely-alive, "mad" Dorts, and that it was a matter of convenience. The miniature image of Ned squirmed on its rock and jabbed at the note pad on its knee, then leaned forward and snapped, "Wouldn't it have been more merciful to expel their bodies into space as we did for our dead? In a mass funeral, thanks to you, I might add!"

"We have had little experience with death. To dispose of them in the way you suggest would have been cumbersome and time consuming. You may recall, there was no time. We are talking about a thousand of us the Twister made mad. Most of them died within hours or days of that. It was efficient to send them into voluntary exile and to seal them into the catacombs. When mad, they were considered unpredictable."

"So they migrated, en masse," Ned's image said, "to the dungeons and their doom."

"Not entirely 'en masse.' After the Twister, they did not all become mad immediately. It mainly happened over a period of several days. They entered the galleries in the earliest stages of their madness—while they still could. Even so there were long lines, and the worst cases had to come to the front. They needed time . . . in their new state . . . to realize. I served them. Several days."

At this point the image of Ned was shaking its head vigorously in confusion. The figures at the conference table were leaning forward with increased interest to see where the questioning would lead. Several Directors cursed under their breath when the next question was irrelevant, and led into a detailed explanation of how the crypts were sealed, and many other seemingly unnecessary details. Finally, after hearing more than anyone would ever want to know about dungeon making—except Clint, who followed the whole explanation with great interest—mini-Ned returned to the subject by asking Doyan exactly what he was doing while the mad Dorts were being sent to their graves.

The answer that followed was surprising and confusing to mini-Ned. As the answer to that and a series of related questions unfolded, mini-Ned went through his repertoire of nonverbal gestures, head shakes, squirming, jumping to his feet, pacing slowly in front of his rock, pacing fast in front of his rock, stabbing at his note pad, lifting his forefinger high into the air, and others less easily described motions and expressions.

Through all of that, Doyan continued to talk in his droning, vibrating, matter-of-fact way, about what happened. He told how the mad Dorts had lined up before the passageways and how, one at a time, before their final leaving, he briefly enveloped each of them with his body and how, in those moments, quintillions of thought packets, experiences, memories, and information were exchanged. Doyan tried in that way ". . . to comprehend their madness"—and, at the same time to "impart" something to the dying, but failed to say what that was.

"Do you mean to tell me," mini-Ned began, standing with his hands on his hips and his head thrown back at an angle, "that you did that, hour after hour, with a thousand mad Dorts? Ridiculous! What did *you* get out of it?"

"Yes, with them all, for hours and days. Those were the most enlightening and dreadful hours in this long existence. The content from them was clear, but the pain was not . . . I gleaned only shadows of the pain. But those shadows were excruciating."

Mini-Ned threw his hands in the air and returned to his rock, mumbling. Then he said, pointing his pen at arm's length toward mini-Doyan, "Who controlled the ship while you were doing that? Who was watching your colorful little buttons?"

"The Integrator, whose place I have taken at these controls, was the last to go. I enveloped the Integrator longer than the others. There was so much to be learned. The Integrator was so specialized and skillful. Oh . . . he was so very . . . very specialized. I will . . ."

Doyan did not finish the sentence, but hunched, contracted and furrowed along the length and breadth of its bulk, looking momentarily like a disembodied, giant brain. It then smoothed, furrowed again, and seemed to vibrate soundlessly before finally becoming smooth again.

Mini-Ned simply frowned, shrugged, and continued the inquiry: "You said that you 'exchanged' a lot of 'information' and so on, when you were . . . wrapped around them. That means it was a two-way communication. You say that you wanted to 'comprehend' their madness. You wanted that information from them. What was your part of the exchange?"

"I imparted something to them on this, their last journey. Information. Nothing more."

"Why? They had no further need of information. They could no longer be useful to you. They were being sent to die. What could you possibly have said to them that would have any practical value in the future of your . . . your mission?"

Doyan tucked. "I said nothing to them. I imparted information."

"You said you 'imparted'—what's the difference? What did you impart? What information? You've given me no idea of the content! Do I have to drag everything out of you? Why are you evading my perfectly trivial, simple questions?"

Doyan rippled. Then, in a matter-of-fact, calm vibration, said, "Where is it written that I am to answer your questions at all? This interview is terminated."

Ned turned his chair around to the console again and punched some keys. The lights went up and the hologram disappeared. He turned once more to face the Directors.

"After that," Ned said with irritation, "It clammed up. I tried for another ten minutes to get it talking, but nary a peep. I went back again later in the day to try again, but it just sat there fiddling with its colored tiddlywinks. That's an obstinate and rebellious Dort! It disgusts me."

Then he looked at the expressions on the Directors' faces. They were anything but blank, but he could not read them. Then he looked at Laura. "What the hell's the matter with you?" he said in a still irritated, almost angry voice. "Why are you crying?"

In the next moment Ned became really angry. Laura wasn't crying at all. She was laughing so hard that tears were running down her cheeks. Ned placed his right forearm on the conference table and his left fist on his hip and said to everyone, "Really! What is wrong with her?"

They looked back and forth at each other with a variety of embarrassed expressions, except Clint—he looked straight ahead and scowled.

Finally, an answer came from Judy who said, "She's only laughing to keep from crying."

"Huh?"

Judy snickered. "You're such a klutz sometimes, Ned, that I can hardly believe it!"

Ned just looked at Judy with a questioning glower.

"Don't you realize," Judy said, "what you did to that Dort with your so-called trivial, simple questions?"

"Wudda ya mean? I just asked him . . ." Then there was a long pause before Ned's expression relaxed with the words, "Oh shit!" and he covered his mouth with his hand as *he* began to laugh. "That overgrown dewlap was just . . . just . . ."

And they all finished his sentence for him, in their own minds, in their own ways—except Clint, who opened his mouth with a look of profound, and silent, confusion.

As they were leaving the room Laura heard Ned mumbling to himself, "It's a fake. A tender-hearted ol' fake!"

Laura heard and understood his mumble, smiled to herself, took his arm and hugged it. "That was some interview, Mr. Tact," she said.

"That bad, huh?"

"Worse."

"Well, I won't be giving it another thought. And I'm not going to do a damn thing about it."

Later that day Ned stood in front of Doyan. He then paced a little, but returned and stood there again now with his hands in his pockets and his head lowered. "Sorry about the other day, lo' sport," Ned said. "I pushed you too far. I won't pursue those questions again. . . . Pax?"

"vvzz . . . Pax."

TWENTY-FOUR

Doug's smile spread broadly across a conference room screens as he reported the good news to his fellow Directors, "We're within three hours of completion. All the systems and components have checking out nicely. We've got most of the bugs out already." He clapped his hands and bounced up and down in the chair beside his desk as he concluded in a high-pitched voice, "The switchover to our control is at hand!" On the screen, not that far distant from Doug's desk, the Directors could discern the featureless outline of Doyan's bulk—nestled into and comfortably wreathed by its fairy circle of flickering lights.

Murmurs, nods and smiles of approval greeted the long awaited news. For an anxious hour Doug's message had been anticipated. The welcome touch of sanity provided only fleeting relief from an already lengthy executive session.

After the moment of cheer had passed, Ned addressed Doug's image in a most serious tone. It was not a new question—it had been asked and discussed a hundred times before. "What about the damn closed-spiral machine—that closed helix surrounding the geode? Can we shut it down? Should we?"

The Directors leaned toward the screen like children listening to a horror story they'd heard many times before, but insisted on hearing again.

Doug's twinkling eyes disappeared into a frown. "That question again. All I can say is what I've said before. Yes, we could shut it down. Easily. But the consequences are unknown. They might be benign, or they could be awful. It's this screwball gravity. If we cut off the machine, then the gravity reverts to 'normal'—at which point everything might or might not fly apart. Certainly everything on the 'ceiling' of the geode that was not screwed down would fall. Even the geode itself could collapse. The spiral, as you know, is responsible for several layers of gravitational anomalies. The Dorts had the spiral operating before they pumped the water out of the geode. Even that was long before we left Earth. The two-directional gravity keeps the upper and lower halves of the geode pulled in opposite directions, keeping it from collapsing. Our tests on the surrounding geologic structures give ambiguous answers about whether or not it would hold together without the helix in operation. On Earth, it was filled with water. That water pressure kept the geode pumped up until the Dorts got creative. I realize that 'creative Dort' is an oxymoron these days, but there you have it. Now it's the positive and negative gravity that's keeping the geode 'pumped up.'

"With luck, of course, the geode ceiling might not fall down at all. But if it did, we'd lose control, because most of our equipment is right here in the geode. That was bad planning, I guess. What we call the 'ceiling' of this geode could cave in on us, or this part of the geode could 'fall up' to it. The smaller passages would probably hold together, but the large caverns would fall. And Crazy River! My God! Who knows where the water in that thing would turn up!"

The Directors said "Mmm," and nodded sagely.

Ned continued his straight man role: "Okay then, will the switchover to our control include the closed helix machine?"

"Yes. At the moment of switchover it will be taken out of Doyan's control along with everything else; but, for the reasons we've just covered, I believe the machine really does need to be kept going. Later on, after we understand it better, we may be able to do more with it than just let it run at idle—that is, keeping the gravity as is, so things don't fly apart. Gaining that understanding may take a while. We're not getting any useful cooperation from Doyan. It keeps claiming ignorance of many things. That's his way of saying, 'Figure it out for yourself.'"

Doug seemed to be uncomfortable in the spotlight, so he changed the subject: "By the way, what's the latest from Navigation?"

He knew the answer as well as everyone else, and everyone knew he knew, but it was as good a question as any to further everyone's hidden agenda: to avoid making difficult decisions.

Stanley Lundeen was at the table, and as Director of Astrophysics, was the logical person to respond to Doug's question. All heads turned toward Stan as the screen image of Doug vanished—to the notice of no one. The Directors' respectful and serious expressions propelled Stan to his feet, virtually against his will, to begin pontificating:

"It's looking better every day. The navigation reports show that we are arcing toward the globular cluster slightly ahead of earlier estimates. We've now been at this course correction process for seven days and we're within a few hours of nearly straight line access to the first fringe star of that outermost cluster—the last possible outpost that's still part of this Galaxy, and the only adequately massive bodies reachable from our present position and course."

He avoided mentioning that the targeted "fringe star" was probably planet Origin's sun, the one Doyan constantly spoke of. "Then," Stan continued, "after a little more directional change, we will discontinue that process until toward the end of our approach. Then we'll do the directional fine tuning."

Stan's presentation so far was just what the doctor ordered to put the Directors into a comfortable, meditative mood. His elementary primers were understandable to children and most of the Directors. Not that they usually paid much attention to content. It was typically comfortable "old stuff," so they could relax and zone out. Stan seldom lost track of that tacitly assigned role—to keep playing his lullaby of word. But without meaning to, he'd sometimes say something relevant. It was usually something the Directors already knew, but preferred postponing any action on the grounds of prudently taking things no more than a step at a time.

"In a significant, but depressing way," Stan went on, no longer droning, "we're years ahead of schedule, but in another sense, we'll be just under the wire. We're ahead, in the sense that we still have a good ten years before our arrival on the outskirts of this Galaxy. But we're barely under the wire in the sense that we have to accomplish this correction now or plan to spend the rest of our lives floating away toward that far-off bunch of Coma galaxies. In that case we would only be distant ancestors of offspring to be born on this Transformation. But even they would not live long, even if some were born well before our food resources ran out. We'll be lucky to make it another ten years anyway. But you all know that already. Let's just hope that Doug and his crew have all the switchover problems solved. I think he said they've got 'most' of the bugs out already. That means not all of them. If all the important technical issues are really solved for the moment and there are no more Twisters or serious equipment failures, then, with a lot of luck and sacrifice—especially by a cutback on calorie intake by everybody for the next decade—we could have smooth sailing, *if* we find a planet with the right resources."

With those unwelcome reminders, tension replaced the directors' moods of comfort—like a slap in the face.

Under the circumstances, Judy's response was mild: "You are such a pessimist, Stan."

"*Pessimist* huh? Well that's really my most *optimistic* view of our situation. The food we could grow, on or below the surface, or otherwise create during the next ten years, could only sustain a much smaller population—with or without diets—compared to the abundance of crew currently aboard. In any case, sustaining the current crew for even that long will obviously be a major problem. It'll really take a lot more than sacrifice from everyone. It will take lots more than luck. It will take a miracle."

Most of the Directors were squirming in their chairs. They wanted the focus ". . . on matters of here and now, if you don't mind!" They worried about the imminent changeover that would gain back operational control of the Transformation. They wanted immediate satisfaction on that, and happy thoughts to plan a celebration for success on that long awaited step—and to worry about tomorrow, tomorrow.

Cameron Greenberg even said it: "Yes, a miracle, but what about now?"

"Oh yes indeed—now! Let me say why *now* is so important," Stanley continued, somehow still forgetting what was expected from him: "This now is the most important now in all our lives and I'll tell you why. As I've said, the major bearing changes—that is, directional course corrections—had to be made and completed by now, at this exact point in spacetime to even begin to pull this off. There are no other choices, given the Transformation's hyperCeleric rate. As you all know, once a Transformation is set in motion at a given celerity, that speed must necessarily be constant until it is stopped. The choice: It is either more or less stationary in normal space, or it goes like a bat out of hell in Transformation space. No in-between. It's either-or. Period.

"Transformation hyperCelerity—that is, it's multiple over the speed of light—could easily be increased, but that should never happen. Once over the speed of light, it takes less energy to go faster and faster—as if coasting down a steep hill in neutral or accelerating by stepping on the clutch instead of the gas. Pulling back on the energy would cause an uncontrollable runaway. Transformations can also 'stop' at any time, and reemerge in normal space, but only if *not* allowed to go faster and faster. The energy to keep that stability must always be there, and not diverted to other uses. We always have some excess of energy available beyond that need, for internal functioning, but most of the Transformation's energy has to be devoted to *preventing* too much speed. To accomplish de-Transformation, 'stopping,' requires a maximum internal energy usage so extensive that it leaves the Transformation virtually dead upon entering normal space. However, if that stop is made near a massive body, then the mass-energy converter can quickly restore internal power to get things going again, and even provide enough energy for limited, rather conventional, maneuverability even in normal planetary atmosphere and space. That's the only exception to getting stuck in normal space. Thus, should a Transformation 'stop' anywhere in normal space that isn't near a massive body, it would be impossible to reactivate or reaccelerate. Having used up its energy in order to 'stop,' it would just float there helplessly—like trying to restart a gyro-car that ran out of hydrogen.

"In summary, by cutting back on forces internal to the Transformation—by taking our foot off the gas—it would accelerate the Transformation infinitely. It could never be stopped except by close proximity to a mass as great as that of the universe itself just before the Big Bang. Even now there is little that can stop us. A Transformation—including us, because we're on it and therefore part of it—can pass through anything, such as a planet, as if it, and we, were just so many neutrinos, without it, us, or the planet even noticing. Black Holes are the exception because they're similar to Transformations. Right now our main use of power is to *prevent* further acceleration. It's a delicate balance! Any more speed, and it's so long universe!"

The earlier bland and blissful faces of the Directors had changed to reflect their mix of feelings—anxiety, disgust, fear and anger. In the process of presenting this elementary material to the Directors, Stanley managed to remind them of the longer term. He had gone so far as to put a time line on the course correction process, and the dangerous, even likely, alternatives. Everyone knew the switchover was imminent, but being reminded they could just do nothing for the next ten years, other than keep an eye on the energy and speed constants, seemed intolerable.

Their expressions scarcely reached Stan's *conscious* mind, but did impact below that all but impermeable threshold, changing his behavior more than if he'd noticed. He tried to backpedal, but it was too late. The discussion following Stan's monologue was bound to approach relevance despite all their inner yearnings. It would take a long time to undo what he had started; but Stan resolutely—and unconsciously—continued his part in that attempt.

"Of course we need *not* make that decision," he blurted.

The Directors knew he meant the decision to de-Transform at the first outpost of that last reachable globular cluster—it being a lone star, light years from the cluster, but gravitationally attached to it. It was the Dorts' choice of location, presumed to harbor the planet of their origin. The Directors were already referring to it as planet Origin, as had the Dorts.

At some level, Stan realized that was too blatant, so he started again. "What I mean is, we need not make *that* decision." Somehow he recognized that changing the word emphasis did not help. In fact, it made matters worse; but he forged ahead anyway. "It might be much better for us to extend the time planned for our arcing course. That would give us the opportunity to target any number of other stars on the fringe of the cluster, or even in the middle of the globular cluster. Then we'd have dozens, hundreds, or even a hundred thousand stars to choose from for a successful de-Transformation. It's a big cluster! The advantage of that would be to guarantee our control by avoiding Origin altogether."

Clinton Bracket's intense glower began to relax. He said, almost cheerfully, "Then, if Doyan has any tricks for getting us down on that planet, he'll be out of luck."

For Laura, Pandora's Box was not so easily closed. She began rummaging through it: "Stan, that's only an advantage if we are determined to not go to planet Origin. We have to talk about that pretty soon, but right now we'd better remind ourselves of the *disadvantages* of avoiding Origin."

"Disadvantages!" said Stanley, taking a deep breath and looking to the ceiling, evading the intrusive looks. "Yes, there are some big ones. Returning to normal space by de-Transformation can be a tricky business. Of course, it can be done at any time, but even a near miss could send us floating through space from then on. De-Transformation near a *planet* does not hold the danger of burning up, not to mention avoiding a whole range of calamities that can happen near a *star*. Using a star as the target for de-Transformation should be safe, oh, fifty or sixty percent of the time—according to our best estimates and assumptions. However, it's never been tried."

Stanley brought his gaze down from the ceiling as Judy spoke up. She tried to sound hopeful, but there was a catch in her voice: "You said there might be hundreds of stars to choose from if we continue our present arcing course longer than planned, so why don't we just pick some star—other than Origin's—with a planetary system, and de-Transform there?"

Stanley jutted his chin, closed his right eye, and eyeballed the ceiling with his left. "That would be fine, except . . . except we'd have to find a star with planets. Even if we knew that every star in that cluster had a dozen planets large enough to activate the mass-energy converters, we'd have to know exactly where at least one of those planets was, and we'd have to be able to track its orbital movement long enough to know where it would be at the time of de-Transformation. You see, we can't de-Transform first, and then start looking for planets. Finding planets while still in Transformation is impossible unless one already has a good idea where to look. In full Transformation it's hard enough just getting a fix on a star, much less a planet. Our mass detectors are our main navigational instruments during Transformation, supplemented by a few other devices for cross checking. We can even pull in a stray photon now and then. But all these devices are narrowly directional, and have to be 'focused' in one place for a long time in order to get a meaningful reading. They're not like binoculars or telescopes in ordinary close-up space. They provide little scope for exploration or surveying. They're used mainly to confirm something we're already pretty sure of, like the location of the Settlement planets relative to Earth. For that, they're not bad. From Earth, we do have a fix on those. But all that's academic anyway. First generation, Population II stars, make up the bulk of globular clusters, and they don't have planets—none to speak of—nor heavy metals, or anything else very useful."

Throughout this discourse, Stanley's left eye remained focused on the ceiling. Judy was resting her arms on the conference table when she made some unclear, questioning verbal sounds, but her arms "jumped" to shoulder height when Stan's open eye rolled down and looked fiendishly into hers. "Do we even have a fix on planet Origin?" she finally gasped.

Judy's reaction shocked Stanley as much as his gaze shocked her—enough to make him realize—yes, consciously now—what he'd been doing. He was returned to social reality. He was embarrassed, but tried not to make things worse by apologizing. Unfortunately his face turned red, causing him to appear angry and more diabolical than ever, moving Judy to expel another quiet, but nonetheless distinct, screaky gasp as she shrunk down, almost vanishing into her leather-upholstered chair. That in turn drove Stanley into a fit of consternation and profuse apologies, that, as he expected, did make matters worse, but after thirty or forty seconds of that, he calmed down enough to ask Judy to repeat her question.

Hesitantly she did so. "Do we have a fix on planet Origin?"

With effort, Stan became straight faced, kindly and outwardly composed. He thought, *I knew I should have asked Ernst to do this.*

Then, stroking his beard, he continued. "Well, yes and no. We have the coordinates that Doyan has given us, but we're still too far away to make our own confirmation. The star itself is right where he said it would be—if it's the right star. Doyan's coordinates are the Dort calculations of where the planet should be, but those could be way off. You have to remember that their calculation of the planet's present location is based on an extremely long-term extrapolation—going back literally thousands of years. When you add to that the Dorts claim they have no memory of their original planet, that their earliest memories began in the spaceships that brought them to the Settlement Planets, and their further claim that the data for those astronomical calculation were 'found' in their own genetic systems as 'givens,' then the whole thing becomes

... well, incredible. Somehow the coordinates just pop into the Dorts' minds, and even they don't know exactly how."

"Incredible, maybe," Laura said, thoughtfully. "And yet, there was the star—exactly where The One said it would be."

"A star," said Stanley, "not necessarily *the* star. With all the stars in a stars cluster, it's easy to get lucky."

"Are you saying you don't believe there is such a planet as Origin—that it's just a Dort myth?" Judy asked.

"You have the facts, including the unknowns, the improbabilities and the rest, so your guess is as good as mine. What it comes down to is the merest possibility that Origin even exists, and an even smaller possibility that, should it exist, it will be anywhere near the coordinates given to us by the Dorts. If Doyan can be believed, the existence and location of Origin is a certainty. The fact is, there are few known planets in any globular star cluster. The Dorts have a strong conviction that Origin exists, but I believe they are simply wrong." With that, Stanley sat down, looking, at last, quite pleased with himself.

Judy wasn't ready to let Stanley off the hook. "I gather, then, that you believe we'll just have to take our chances and de-Transform near some star—any star."

Stanley looked at Judy for a long time before answering. Thinking. "As I said before, de-Transformation in the vicinity of a planet is the only reasonably sure and safe way to do it. So long as there is the merest whisper of a possibility that Origin exists, and that it is where Doyan says it is, it's worth trying for. If it is where he says, then we should be able to confirm that a full day before we de-Transform. If it isn't there, then we're no worse off with any other star."

Despite Stanley's logic, considerable disagreement remained, and much of it had nothing to do with logic. The disagreements continued for another hour, becoming more and more specific. They disagreed on all the big issues, but did finally agree on one small point. It went like this: No agreement was reached about whether or not to target the possibly mythical Origin, its sun, or some other star. If Origin did exist and they de-Transformed in orbit around it, then they could not decide about actually descending to the planet's surface. If they did descend to the surface, they were in disagreement about how that should be done—by deep descent of the Great Cone itself, to hover in some canyon there, or to stay in close orbit of it and merely enter the planet by shuttle. If they went down by shuttle, they couldn't decide if Doyan should or should not go along, possibly as a translator if they made contact with its distant relatives or other ancient beings. The only narrow point they definitely agreed on was that their descent to planet Origin would have to be by shuttle, and only human volunteers would be allowed to go.

The session adjourned after Doug's smiling face again appeared on the screen for a final piece of business. His cheery voice gave the welcome message: "Hearing no new orders from y'all, the switchover takes place in exactly forty-five minutes. At that time our heading should be about perfect, close enough, and we won't need another course adjustment for a long time to come. We'll make the transfer of controls—the switchover—at the moment of ideal trajectory. We could do the switchover any time after the full course correction, but as we discussed at our last meeting, it's the message—the Dorts will not have control for even a second longer than necessary. And Clint, I want you and some of your men down here before then to make sure Doyan leaves his central location without any fuss right after that transfer of control. If he stayed there it wouldn't make any real difference, but I'm sure that his not being there would make a lot of us feel better—a little symbolic humiliation for those murdering hijackers to chew on—hehehe."

"I'll be right down," Clint said, smiling and rubbing his hands together.

Clint left, radioed some of his men who joined him on the Orb, and they went below. The other Directors disbursed to the bars in an attempt to celebrate the anticipated changeover—except Jack, Ned, and Laura who, for the same purpose, ascended to the surface in Laura's traveling parlor.

When they reached the surface, Laura turned off the interior lighting so they could see across the dimly illuminated landscape. "It's almost dark out," Laura said. "Let's go to the roof patio while there's still some light and have a drink. Celebrating this transfer is long overdue."

"Good idea!" Ned and Jack said together, as though the idea were a surprise.

Except for some treetops and the distant Luminaerie, Laura's roof patio was the highest point on the Great Cone. They sat in Laura's deck chairs sipping cocktails. Jack looked at his watch. "This Transformation," he said with formality, "will return to human control in thirty seconds. This calls for a toast!"

"Here here!" said Laura and Ned together.

They stood for the toast, "Here's to much brighter times ahead and our safe return to Earth!"

As their glasses clanked, all the lights on the Transformation went out, including the Luminaerie. They plunged into the darkness of a starless night.

Laura dropped her glass and barely stifled a scream when it shattered at their feet.

Jack lit a match and they looked at each other with agonized expressions. "What happened?" Laura asked, her eyes bulging.

"Take it easy, Laura, I'm sure there's an easy explanation," was Ned's uncertain response.

Jack raised his eyebrows and said, "Maybe the universe blew a fuse?"

Taking Laura into his comforting arms, Ned looked at Jack and said, "That wasn't funny."

And it wasn't. They felt the quake even before its roar reached their ears. It hit with more power than a sonic boom and stayed till the last tremor.

Ned and Jack were shaken to the patio floor, but Laura somehow managed to stay on her feet. The tremor subsided and the boom passed, but Laura began to emote: "Oh my God. . . . Oh God! Look!" Her left hand went tight across her mouth as if to control it and her right reached out toward a light coming from the Great Cone's southern horizon. Jack and Ned also arose and gasped at what they witnessed . . . in awe and reverence—the great spiral arms of the Galaxy reaching a hundred thousand light years across the sky to display before them a hundred-billion stars. They saw its radial pivot point, its central blur of brilliance—a spheroid of tightly packed stars, itself a sprawling twenty thousand light years across. Never before had any terrestrial seen the Galaxy from "above" its hub and at a right angle to its disk. Never before had an earthborn seen with naked eyes the whole horizon of the universe. Never before had anyone seen its warm and blazing center, or felt its spiral arms around them. It was a spectacle of dazzling, heavenly and undiminished proportions; but that was only an indistinct shadow beside what they would next behold.

TWENTY-FIVE

With the universe in full display before them, its dazzling Galactic nucleus and softly gleaming arms shone clearly. They did not know how it happened, but there was no doubt what it was. For those on Laura's rooftop patio, it was obvious:

They'd not only de-Transformed in ordinary space, but did so years earlier than planned, and thousands of light years from their position a split second earlier.

Although their own artificial sun was emitting no illumination and they were facing the light of the Galaxy, their long shadows were not behind them where they belonged. They stretched before them—toward the south. Like phototropic marionettes, they turned in silence to face the unexplained brilliance at their backs. It was there, just above the horizon in the northern sky—a coal-black disk embedded in a radiant corona three times its diameter. Laura, still in awe and excitement, proclaimed this new spectacle the "Eye of Infinity."

In less poetic terms, Jack said it was "the 'Eye of Infinity' all right, but its pupil is grossly dilated. I wish that were all. Look at the flairs and prominences popping out of its chromosphere! Its sun spots must be legion. It must be in the most active part of its solar cycle, or it's on the verge of becoming a red giant. Without the eclipse we couldn't see any of that."

They knew the eclipse was caused by some moon or planet in some unknown system, passing before that unknown star. They suspected the Dorts had somehow pulled this off just before the changeover could take place. And the black pupil of the "eye" peeking above their horizon could just as well be the Dorts' infamous mother planet, Origin. A coronal "iris" flared from behind its black "pupil." It was impressive, but far beyond it there appeared another sight of equal radiance: the close-packed stars of a globular star cluster.

There was no time to gawk. The Great Cone's orbit of the unidentified celestial body was taking them away from the eclipse's deepest shadow and into its penumbra. Their bodies were being carried into a space of lethal danger. Radiation from the object's over-active sun would soon be angling in upon them. There was plenty of atmosphere to protect from such a nearby star if it were directly above the Cone's surface, but not from any other angle.

With that realization, and without comment, they rushed from the rooftop patio to the stairs and into the interior of the house where Laura moved quickly to her console in the parlor. She touched a prominent red signal key before answering the call light that had been blinking before they entered the room.

Even as she touched the attitude-correction key, she knew it was too late: Rectification of the Transformation's position would take minutes to even begin. In another moment its entire surface would be in flames. But somehow, only seconds after Laura touched the correction key, the rectification began. The sky wheeled to the side until the black circle and the star cluster vanished below their horizon. The Cone was turning slowly and then stopped. Only the faint spiral arms and bright nucleus of the Galaxy could still be seen—no longer in the "south," but directly overhead. Moments later the cylindrical shaft of atmosphere became a beacon of many-colored sweeping stripes—a tightly confined aurora, extending hundreds of kilometers above the Cone's surface.

A worried face came to life on the screen as Laura opened the channel. His voice was a mix of tension, anger and a touch of relief. "He did it to us again," Doug began. "We were only a second or two from taking control, and then, WHAM!—it sends us through Transformation space a zillion times faster than is safe—even theoretically—and then WHAM again, we de-Transform on the night side of some planet. It must be Origin. But so fast! We were already going so many times the speed of light and at the limit of safety, but this new speed is something else! It's beyond comprehension. We must have been traveling faster than, than shit!"

"So that's what happened," Laura said, then adding with a wry smile, "And I appreciate the precision of your vocabulary. Your term for virtual-infinite-speed describes a mode that is sure to become its official designation!"

Doug continued excitedly with a rush of words: "Yes, and until this minute I would have said it couldn't be done. In spite of near-instant movement across all that space, rather than accelerating forever, we de-Transformed safely. That couldn't have happen! But it did. I don't get it. It must have something to do with those cylindrical spiral machines."

"It's a *Tenderloin* spiral," Laura said, scowling at Ned.

"*Spirals.* Plural." Doug corrected. "Not just one any more. The larger of the two spiral machines is apparently working *with* the smaller spiral. The larger one needed fixing in a couple places. Well, our engineers—with the expert 'guidance' of a couple Dorts—made the repairs. I wouldn't have allowed them to put in those patches, but it was done before I knew it. The Dorts told them I'd authorized it. Next time any changes get made—beyond simple maintenance—the crews will have to check personally with me first. Now we have another rogue spiral on our hands. We set up a lot of monitoring equipment on the small one to figure out what it does and what goes on inside it and around it when it's working. Now we have to do that with the big one."

"Anything else, Doug?" Laura asked.

"The last minute, just before the de-Transformation, graphs of the most fundamental functions of a Transformation virtually jumped off the charts. One for mass development. The other for energy output. Their pressures were opposite and shifted out of phase. That caused a shear wave earthquake that you must have felt, but it didn't last long. A third graph, the resultant of the first two measures, quickly moved to zero—to equilibrium. It still shows stability."

Ned said, "Whatever the explanation for that, it looks like Transformation Theory is out the window."

"Maybe . . . maybe not. I'm no expert." Doug scratched his bald spot thoughtfully and added, "You may be right, though. A full theoretical explanation will at least require partial defenestration of the theory. Better ask Laura."

Laura's eyes flashed. She frowned, puckered and looked intensely at her left thumbnail. Nobody noticed. She was thinking.

"Einstein," Jack said, poking a forefinger in the air, "improved on Newton. The Theory of Transformation improved on Relativity, Quantum Physics, String Theory and a few others. Maybe we've just witnessed the results of another breakthrough. I didn't think the Dorts—"

"—Or who!" Laura interrupted, momentarily lifting the focus of her attention. "Besides, any advance doesn't invalidate what came before."

"Right now," Ned said, "we have to figure out what's next. We're orbiting a planet with plenty of mass for our energy needs. That's a good thing. But we have another problem—getting the control away from Doyan. Doug, you said we were only a second or two from control when 'WHAM,' all this happened."

"Oh gosh! That's right, I didn't tell you, did I?" Doug said excitedly, his image bouncing up and down.

"Tell us *what*?" several asked at once.

"We *do* have the control. Doyan is out of it. He's been disconnected and *we* are the ones plugged in! The equipment switched to our control right on schedule—right after the acceleration and de-Transformation, and after the attitude correction was set. None of that was expected, but the timing was still right."

Jack looked puzzled. "But it was Laura who activated the attitude correction program."

"I thought you might have thought that. From down here, when we're not in Transformation space, I see a lot of interesting things on all these screens. I noticed the monitor signal from Laura's console, for instance. It showed that someone tried to activate the correction. That was quick thinking, Laura, but not quick enough. The quarter turn correction works slower than that. It was initiated by Doyan the instant we entered normal space, and a fraction of a second later *we* were in control. Fortunately the correction was already in. I didn't mess with it."

Then Doug looked a bit sheepish, and continued. "To be honest," he said, "I didn't even think of it until after I saw the signal coming from Laura's console. I checked back right away and saw that the correction had already been started. Had the program been started *later*, such as when Laura threw the switch, the surface of this Transformation, including all our nice little suburban homes, would have taken a bath in some rather killing radiation.

"Doyan says that's Origin's sun out there. Let's take him at his word. Right or wrong it makes no difference so long as we're safe—at least for the time being. Right now, the Cone's stone vertex is directed into that sun. And that's where we need to keep it till we leave orbit for home or head down below the planet's atmosphere—if it has one that's robust enough to protect us from radiation. No clouds, though, so maybe not. Judging from my screen view of the corona a couple minutes ago, it must be going through some hellish storms. Before the correction you must have noticed.

"Hmm! On one of my screens—from the scope on your roof, Laura—it looks like you have a wonderful view of an aurora. Enjoy the view. By the time we get out of here, you could be bored with it."

TWENTY-SIX

The Directors gathered for their regular morning session. Ned began: "We've been orbiting planet Origin for an Earth week. The star cluster and planet data gathered by Stanley and his Astrophysics staff is impressive. Stan can explain the details better than I. He told me what they found, but I couldn't repeat it. So Stan, please lay it out for us."

Stanley Lundeen was always nervous to start—at least until he got warmed up. But, starting cold, he took a deep breath and began:

"The planet we are orbiting is on the outskirts of an old and hardy globular star cluster. This one is typical, in many ways, of our Galaxy's thinning halo of such structures. But this cluster is much bigger than most, and farther from the main disk of the Milky Way. There are only a hundred or so clusters left.

Before Earth was formed there were thousands of them, and more than that before the spiral took shape.

"This cluster has over a million closely packed first generation stars, mostly low in metals and smaller than our sun. They're almost as old as the universe itself! There are, however, some generation three stars in this cluster, so it's not *entirely* lacking in heavy metal elements, and there are some gas giant *planets*.

"Those younger stars were vacuumed up by this cluster's gravity on one of its trips around the Galactic core. This cluster moves as a unit around that core in a narrow, elliptical orbit, much as a single comet orbits our sun. It gathers speed, year after year, as it swings toward and into the nucleus of the Galaxy with its billion or so stars orbiting a still-growing central black hole. The cluster enters at an enormous speed, powerful gravity pulling it in and then slinging it around and out again on the same side of the disk that it entered. Then it leaves the disk far behind until, millions of years later, it is again high in the halo. There it moves slower and slower until it reaches apogee and begins the return trip—back into the center of the Galaxy, and then out again, and so on.

"Right now the cluster is at its highest and slowest point above the Galaxy, putting us about fifty thousand light years 'above'—or 'below,' depending on your point of view—the core. That is, we're at a perpendicular to the Galactic plane, directly 'over'—or 'under'—its nucleus."

Judy Olafson hadn't been paying much attention. She said, "Okay Stan, that must be interesting astronomy, but what about this cluster? We're here now, so what are we into?"

"Few surprises here, Judy. Sorry. With the shortage of heavy elements, there are few real planets—at least not like Earth. And, oh yeah, as I said, there are some mammoth gas giants—hundreds of times bigger than Jupiter, like little brown stars."

"No Earth-like planets, then?" Judy asked with disappointment in her voice.

"Other Earth-like planets are *possible*, but none we've seen in this cluster so far, except for Origin. Most of the stars here are doubles or triples, orbiting each other, and a few thirteen billion year old gas giants. That's really old for planets, considering the universe is a touch under fourteen billion. The only real surprise we encountered among these hydrogen-helium stars was this sun with its planet, Origin. Both of these, *Origin and its sun, simply shouldn't be here!*"

"Why not?" Clint Bracket asked. "It is here, so it *should* be here! Simple as that!"

"Well Clint, I wasn't going to go into this, but now I'll have to talk about black holes."

"Please," Clint said, "I'd rather you didn't bother! I didn't mean to get you started again."

Stan was warming up: "We looked for the black hole in this cluster, but,"

Stan said, turning on an excessively gleeful smile, "we were wrong to look for just one. We found a *swarm* of them—all tucked away in the center of the cluster." His inappropriate smile seemed to float there by itself.

Everybody was trying—unsuccessfully—to look interested. Noticing their level of interest for once, he added, "Yes, whole knots of black holes—*just like the ones that caused the Twister*!"

For a second, that caught Clint's attention, but he quickly slipped into another blank stare.

Stan continued. "Once the black hole thing was known, we figured out how the system of Origin and its sun got here. Incidentally, we gave a name to Origin's sun. We astrophysicists can name things like that. The rest of you can't. It's not allowed." Then he revised his catlike smile and said, "It's *'Nimbus'* from now on—because of that halolike corona we saw when we got here. And the Origin-Nimbus system will simply be the *'Origin System.'* As astrophysicists—"

"Yeah, we know," Clint interrupted, "you guys get to name all the stuff out there."

"Right!"

Laura said, "Are we even in the star cluster? It's *not* all around us. It looks huge, but still at some distance."

"Yes, we'd have to be blind to miss that. We checked the orbit of the Origin System with respect to the cluster. This cluster is about eighty light years across. The Origin System orbits the cluster's black hole center in a narrow ellipse, like the whole cluster orbits in and out of the Galaxy. Sounds familiar, right?"

"Where is Origin now—in the cycle around the cluster's black holes?" Judy asked.

"We're in the part of the cycle that's taking the Origin System out of the cluster. *Way* out! We're now a couple hundred light years from the cluster's center. That's why it seems to be, as you said, 'at some distance' from us."

Judy said, "I'm a little confused. How did the Origin-Nimbus System get here?"

"The *Origin System*'s orbit suggested that Nimbus was originally captured by the gravitational center of this star cluster as it started its own return trip from around the *Galaxy's* central bulge. This cluster, with its black holes, is a potent self-gravitating system and is more resistant to tidal shocks than most clusters. Tidal shocks have, as you all know, a way of spreading a cluster out—all over the place, mostly in a long, messy string—a mechanism that destroyed the integrity of thousands of previous globular clusters—even before the Milky Way became a spiral galaxy. But *this cluster* is a survivor. It's big, dense and gravitationally strong. On its way around the center of the Milky Way a time or two ago, it *vacuumed up* a lot of stuff, including a few other Population I stars along with the Origin System. But we haven't spotted any other Earth-like planets in this cluster. We're still looking."

Clint yawned.

"Is there a problem, Clint?" Ned asked with irritation. "Not enough sleep lately?" Then Ned turned red with embarrassment, realizing he sounded like an uptight schoolmarm.

"Sorry," Clint said. "But I guess I'd be more interested in Origin itself, not all this other stuff."

"The planet Origin itself!" Stan said with his sly cat smile. "Sure Clint!"

"Oh no!"

"Oh yes, Clint. When Nimbus got uprooted from the Galactic center, planet Origin came along with it. Origin's orbit around Nimbus must have been altered in the process, but not enough to do any long-term harm—or maybe, for our purposes, it improved! Anyway, it's had time to stabilize, so now the planet lies well within a livable ecosphere, or so we think. Origin is a hundred and sixty-one million kilometers from its sun. Numbus itself is one-third larger than Earth's sun. Origin's mass is eighteen percent less than Earth's with a density close to that of our solar system's planet Mercury. Its equator is tilted 26.25 degrees from the plane of its orbit around Nimbus. Its atmosphere is mature and breathable, with 18% oxygen content and 81% nitrogen, a little carbon dioxide, argon and some other stuff. It has a nice ozone layer."

Clint said, "That's still a lot of astronomy. What about the planet itself? Oceans, islands, things like that."

Stanley looked hurt. "I thought you would be glad to know its atmosphere is breathable, and all that other stuff." Stan barely avoided an actual pout.

Ned said, "Please continue, Stan. Tell us more about the planet itself." Then he turned red again—more flushed than before.

Stan was ruffled. He continued *without* the Cheshire Cat smile. "Origin has one primary continent. Like any other continent it has an irregular shape. It covers about one-fourth of the planet's surface, and there are thousands of islands of all sizes. They are alone and in scattered archipelagos. There is one minicontinent, too large to be called an island, on the opposite side of the planet. The continents and larger islands are mostly mountainous. Most of their surfaces have dry river beds and salt water lakes. We can only hope that some lakes are *fresh water*, even though we can make our own. The oceans, of course, salt water. There appear to be substantial flora on most of the islands, and on large portions of both continents. Anyway, we *think* it's flora. The spectrometer readings are unclear. It was hard to analyze from here. It's green in those places, but strange. It could be something else. It might have something to do with the lack of fresh water—and no rain clouds anywhere. That's unusual since there's plenty of moisture in the air. The polls, however, are lightly capped with ice. We're quite sure that ice is of fresh water."

Stan continued his presentation for another hour before Ned called time. Everybody looked bleary-eyed, so Ned concluded the meeting with these words: "Thank you for your summary, Stan. Most informative! I was especially glad to hear about the planet. If you don't mind, and not to over simplify, here's my own summary of Origin:

"It's almost like home down there!"

After an edgy silence, Laura said, "That's it? *That's your summary*? The whole thing?"

"Yep. That's it!" Ned looked pleased with himself.

"Yeah," Clint said, making his own even shorter summary, plagiarizing the operative word from Ned's précis: "*Almost.*"

Then, only half in jest, Ned added, "What do you say we go down and take a quick look?" It wasn't really a question.

Part II
ORIGIN

TWENTY-SEVEN

They were in the thirtieth orbit of Origin. Cameron Greenberg was smoking a cigar and sitting with his feet up on one of the computer consoles in the Astrophysics section. He and Stanley Lundeen had been chatting idly about the pros and cons of taking Doyan along once they selected a landing site. Cameron was looking at the visual display of the night side of Origin as they talked.

"No," Stan was saying, "Doyan can't be trusted. Taking it along would be like using a wolf for a sheep dog."

"Mm hm," Cameron said, paying no attention to what Stan just said. He was more interested in the new eclipse as the Cone's orbit again put Nimbus behind planet Origin. "Good God," he said. "That really does look like an eye."

"Yes, it does. It's spectacular on that display," said Stan, glad for the change of subject. He moved over to look at the screen with Cameron. "We're at just the right distance to make out a few flares and prominences." He pointed to the features as he spoke. Then Stan turned back to his own desk and offhandedly stated, "It's a dazzling 'iris' around that 'planet-pupil'."

"Yeah. I can't get over it. It's so real—right down to the highlight in the pupil itself."

Stan stopped and turned abruptly. "What did you say?"

"I said it looks so real."

Stan was back again and leaning over the console, squinting at the display. "How did I ever miss that?" There was excitement in his voice.

"Miss what?" Cameron asked, mystified.

"The highlight. It couldn't have been there before. It's not a highlight, of course, any more than the planet is a 'pupil.' It gives the 'eye' a lifelike look, but that's not important."

Stan began to punch keys on the console and the view moved in for a close-up on the highlight. The dark of the "pupil" grew larger, then expanded beyond the edges of the screen and focused on the single dot of light. The highlight grew into a bright crescent. Then the crescent vanished and the screen was black. Whatever it was had entered the shadow of Origin. Stan pecked again at the keys. A second screen responded with columns and rows of figures that he studied for several long moments.

"Humph!" he said, finally.

Greenberg took the cigar out of his mouth and looked at Stanley. "Excuse my limitations; I'm only an anthropologist," he said. "Could I have the English translation of 'Humph'?"

"Simple enough," Stan said smugly without taking his eyes off the second display. "It isn't a volcano; it should have been an active one with that much light."

"How do you know it isn't a volcano?"

"It covered too much area, it's was too far from the planet, it gave off a lot of light, but little or no heat, the spectrum wasn't right, it wouldn't have had a crescent shape, it wouldn't suddenly vanish, and a half-dozen other reasons. It wasn't a volcano. But that vanishing act! Very strange."

"Why strange, Stan? Maybe it was just a meteor."

"Well, whatever it was, it wasn't a source of light, but a reflection. Not a meteor. That light was from a perfectly smooth crescent. No pock marks. It was between Origin and us, moving away at high speed, but slowing. It'll be close, but it should miss the planet. Or maybe not. But the speed was—"

"If it'll be so close," Cameron interrupted, "there should be a streak of light when it hits the atmosphere; the friction will slow it down. It could hit Origin. If it's so perfectly shaped, maybe it's a weapon. If there's intelligent life down there we could be blamed!"

"You're right, of course, it could slow down that way, but the speed was changing and already getting slower as it neared the atmosphere. If a friction flash were to happen we'd have seen it by now."

"It's slowing down anyway?" Cameron asked.

"Yes."

Cameron became wide-eyed. "Then it must be under some kind of intelligent or robotic control. It could be a bomb!"

Lundeen shrugged, "No flash, so it slowed enough to avoid the heat, or more likely, it sailed past the planet entirely—under some kind of power."

"Yeah, but what if it didn't miss the planet?"

"No flash, so no bomb," said Stan. "Besides, what or who would be out here to bomb some random planet like Origin? Even if it did crash, it's too small to cause much damage."

"That's silly. Atomics don't take much room."

"They haven't been used on Earth for thousands of years."

Cameron smiled and said, "I don't think we're on Earth any more."

Stanley frowned. "It wasn't one of our shuttles—right size but wrong shape. It's small enough to be—"

Stan stopped talking. He and Cameron looked at each other with comprehension, both knowing what the other was thinking. They knew the source of the dot of light.

At that moment, a buzzer sounded for an incoming call. It was Debra Anderson announcing a special meeting of the Directors.

"Oh boy, another meeting," Cameron said, grinding out the soggy remains of his cigar. "Well, let's go."

"Very timely," Stan said. "Unless they're way ahead of us we'll have an announcement of our own to make!"

Doug Groth was bouncing up and down with his news, but managed to contain himself until all the Directors had gathered and Ned, who had already heard the story, gave him a nod to proceed. Most of the Directors seemed mildly interested, except for Clint, who appeared embarrassed and was trying to shrink his brawn to insignificance; and Ellen Stone, who always seemed to sense his distress, was talking consolingly to him while holding his arm and looking tenderly on his handsome, now sheepish, expression.

Doug began: "As most of you are aware, Doyan and Officer Bracket have been almost inseparable since the de-Transformation. Not out of love, of course, but thanks to the fact that Clint seldom let the Dort out of his or his men's site. During this more or less imposed association, Doyan hasn't been near his Orbs since we've been using them nearly full time. But lately the Dort has been showing a particular interest in those Orbs. In the process, as a ruse I suppose, to get near them without suspicion, he offered to show Clint how to maneuver them—beyond their simple elevator functions. Consequently it disclosed some of its other functions to Clint who requested more details. Eventually Doyan taught Clint to pilot the Orbs. We have twenty shuttles and twice that many experienced shuttle pilots, but no one to pilot the Orbs—until now. It turns out that Clint and Doyan made a test flight with one of them and, *ahem*, without our prior authorization, landed for a few minutes on planet Origin!"

As murmurs of surprise and shock ringed the room, Clint shrank further into his chair.

No sooner had the shock subsided than the mood at the table spiraled into positive territory. Clint was being questioned and congratulated. Gradually, he began to emerge from the enfolding cushions of his executive chair—like being reborn. At last everyone, including Clint, was smiling. He answered their many questions with brief responses.

In another minute, however, the ebullience that had spiraled upward, began to wind down. Clint's proud smile at the peak of the excitement morphed into a silly grin as the room became silent. Eventually he too noticed the expressions on the faces of Cameron Greenberg and Stanley Lundeen. The silence continued for an uncomfortable period as Clint allowed his chair to swallow him once more.

All eyes were on the two Directors. Debra Anderson squirmed uncomfortably, if not provocatively. Ned Keller frowned. Laura Shane took in her breath expectantly. At last it was Clint, now wild-eyed and peeking out from his cushions, who broke the silence with everyone's question. It was a loud and plaintive, "*What?*"

Stanley Lundeen responded with his own brief question: "Officer Bracket, can you tell us were Doyan is right now?"

The question was a catalyst. Clint came alive, extricated himself from the womb of the chair, placed his elbows on the table, and stated, "Where he always is—down in the geode, under guard. Why do you ask?"

"Well," Stan said, "if that's the case, and you and Doyan are the only ones who can maneuver the Orbs in normal space outside of this Cone, and Doyan is under guard, then please tell us—who, at this very moment, is piloting one of the Orbs to planet Origin?"

Within the next hour, after a period of consternation and a flurry of assignments around the boardroom table, and a temporary adjournment, the Directors reconvened. During that time the situation had become much clearer and at the same time more mystifying. Cameron, Stanley and Clint were all correct. Doyan and the other remaining Dorts had been under continuous observation, and one of the Orbs was indeed missing. Furthermore, all the human personnel were accounted for.

"Obviously," Clint remarked angrily, "there must be something about the Orbs that Doyan neglected to tell me. We know the Orbs operate nicely on automatic pilot inside the Transformation's tunnels and shafts. But when Doyan demonstrated the controls to me, for flight outside the Transformation into normal space, I became convinced I should learn the manual controls. I haven't mastered all of them yet, but I found the mechanics of the Orb's controls so fascinating that—I hate to admit this—it never occurred to me to ask if the autopilot could be used in normal space."

"That's water under the bridge, Clint," Ned said. "I talked with Doyan on our break. Except for one lost Orb no harm has been done. It probably crashed on Origin. It's not the end of the universe."

"No crash was detected on Origin," Stanley said. "It either landed safely on the surface or is sailing off into empty space."

Jack said, "What I'm wondering is, why send an empty Orb to the planet in the first place? Ned, did you ask Doyan about that?"

"If you can believe Doyan," Ned replied, "it's just as confused about that as we are."

"It's a liar," Clint said.

"I agree," Ned responded. "We have to take anything it says with a—"

"Hold on gentlemen," Laura said peevishly. "Doyan could be telling the truth—as usual, I might add!"

"What's your point?" Clint asked with a barely disguised snarl.

"Any number of reasons could account for Doyan's being unaware of—"

"Name one!" Clint snapped.

"Give me a minute—I'll think of several."

"Name just one," Clint said, more patiently this time, lowering his auditory snarl to a visual sneer.

"Maybe we had a stowaway that knew the manual controls or the autopilot mechanism."

"Not likely," Clint returned. "The invention and control of the Orbs have been entirely under Dort dominance. If there was a stowaway, it was a Dort. It would have entered at a time the Orb was unobserved and unoccupied."

"When would that be?" Laura asked.

"Elementary," Clint smirked. "When it's empty and in transit from the geode—like an empty elevator going to pick someone up."

"But how—"

"By stopping, let's say, at another 'floor' where a Dort got on and then headed off with the Orb through some channel or passage we don't know about."

"Why a Dort?"

"Elementary! Because—"

"Stop saying 'elementary,' Clint!"

Clint cleared his throat and went on. "We've accounted for all the humans still alive after the Twister, and we've accounted for Doyan, and the six other Dorts. But we don't know how many Dorts there were to start with, so maybe we missed one—or a dozen."

"What if we don't find a passage off the main shafts? That we could have missed one after all this time seems like a stretch to me," Laura said.

"I don't know how we could have missed anything the size of a Dort sneaking into an Orb," Clint said, "—especially with our people swarming nonstop around the damn contraptions."

"That doesn't make Doyan a liar!" she said.

"If another Dort did something significant, or out of the usual, wouldn't Doyan know about it?"

"Of course."

"So, if a Dort is on the missing Orb, then Doyan would know."

"I suppose."

"As noted, we've already accounted for all of the humans. So, again, if a stowaway is on the Orb, it's a Dort. If so, Doyan is a liar. If he did send the Orb down to the planet empty, which he denies, then he's a liar—again."

As the conjectures continued, others joined in the fray, but Laura dropped out. The debate over possibilities, theoretical motives, and likely or unlikely outcomes became imaginative, detailed, tangential and irrelevant. Toward the end of what was becoming yet another fruitless and wearisome meeting, the Directors became sullen, glassy-eyed and silent. They appeared tired and looked for Ned to either end the meeting or provide some direction.

Ned was not up to anything decisive. He returned their glazed looks, finally saying, "We've talked this to death. Does anyone have something original that might be worth considering? If not—"

To everyone's surprise, Laura stood up.

"What is it, Laura?" Ned asked.

She began slowly. "At the risk of offending the majority opinion, I have one idea that may be worth introducing. Please bear with me." She gave Clint a soft, oddly nervous look. She knew he was a sucker for that look.

Clint raised his eyebrows and gave her a slight nod to continue, as if she needed his permission. It was an interaction to assure not only Clint's giving Laura her say; everyone else would too. Laura was clever that way.

"Let's suppose—just as a ...let's see...a suggestion—that our main assumption in the discussion so far today, is wrong. Absolutely wrong."

The Directors began to react with surprise and squirmed in their seats, as if to ask the obvious question, but none of them made a peep. They settled back, knowing she would soon answer their questioning looks.

"My fellow Directors," she went on formally, still using her modest but diplomatic tone, "let's suppose that Doyan didn't lie to Ned. This whole discussion has been based on the idea that he did lie and that he is behind the Orbs disappearance; that it was for some evil purpose."

Clint turned colors, but said nothing. Ellen Stone was squeezing his arm, lending him the necessary auxiliary strength for his self-control.

"If we make the assumption," Laura went on, "that the Dorts were not involved in this—and we know no humans were on the craft—then it follows that the Orb went to the planet empty. I certainly have no idea how the Orb could have been programmed to do that, and if I'm correct, neither do Doyan or the other Dorts. To follow that reasoning, we may suspect a simpler reason or motive for the disappearance of that conveyance. As it—"

"I'm sorry to interrupt," Stanley said, "but I have to leave. My implant notifier indicates 'urgent.' If I can, I'll be right back." He left.

"While he's gone," Clint said with irritation—he couldn't help himself—"would you mind telling us, Laura, your simple reason for the Orb's disappearance?"

"Sure. I believe it went down to pick up a passenger . . . of some kind."

"Maybe," Clint said skeptically, "or to bring back a bomb."

TWENTY-EIGHT

Stanley Lundeen did not return. With no further pressing business, the meeting was adjourned. The Directors had things to do. Ned and Laura took the roomlift to the surface where they could relax for a while and continue to monitor anything important from her computer console. Finding themselves in the wrong part of the Galaxy did not change the Directors' obligations or their special tasks.

Cameron Greenberg was in a particular hurry as he left the meeting. He found Stan where he expected, in front of the two screens they had abandoned for the meeting. "What was the urgent message that dragged you back here," he asked, "or were you just bored?"

"Very funny, Cam," Stanley replied. "Come here and look at this."

Cameron pulled up a chair and began watching the scrolling numbers. "Okay—some repeating patterns here and there. So what?"

"It's the challenge, Cam! The fun is figuring it out from the numbers. When the patterns made a dramatic change, that's what my notifier was set for. But you're right, it wasn't urgent and I was a little bored."

"As I suspected!"

"But it might as well have been urgent for real. Just look at this stuff, Greenberg!"

"That stuff, as you call it, would take hours for me to figure out. I don't even know what you're measuring. Give me a telescope, a spectrograph, or something I can sink my teeth into."

"Okay, okay!" Stan said, reassuringly. "Let's use something easy so that even you can understand."

"Like what?"

"Like enhanced radar. We couldn't use it in Transformation, however here, in normal space . . . !"

Within moments, Stan had the equipment focused and scanning.

"What are we looking for?" Cameron asked.

Stan smiled smugly. "Just hang on. It'll surprise you." He pointed again to the scrolling screen of numbers. "It's there, and we'll catch it over here anytime now." They looked at the other screen.

Seconds passed, and suddenly Cameron shouted, "Oh my God!"

"Yes! Isn't that something?" Stan said.

"We have to tell Ned and Laura right away! They have to know; this can't get out. Not yet!"

"I know, but I'd hate to interrupt one of Ned's little visits with Dr. Shane."

"For God's sake, Lundeen, where are your priorities? They can handle it. This can't wait. We have to get to Laura's house—now!"

"You're right. We have to do this face-to-face to keep it contained. If this got out before a definitive decision, things could get out of hand fast. There could be chaos!"

Thanks to Greenberg, despite his rhetoric, things did get out of hand. Completely. What should have been a private communication from Stan and Cam to Ned and Laura, for purposes of preliminary strategic planning, became Transformation-wide knowledge within minutes. The news reached Ned and Laura before the arrival of the two Directors. While tucking in his shirt, Ned glowered fiercely at Dr. Greenberg. "Cameron," he said, "what the hell got into you? You know the process!"

"Sorry. It was just a quick little e-mail note to the lady. I knew she'd keep her mouth shut. But I accidentally sent it to everybody. All it said was, 'Check the radar. The Orb is returning. At the rate it's coming, it will reach us at midnight, precisely. Keep this under your hat.'"

"We know," Laura said. "Your little note came here too."

The information should have remained strictly between the four Directors for purposes of preliminary contingency planning of the Orb's return. That to be followed by detailed, systematic select committee planning based on full consideration or all the dire and dangerous things it might portend or contain. But that was not to be. Laura looked helpless and shrugged. With barely nine hours left before midnight, the entire mess fell on Ned's shoulders.

There was a rapidly gathering group of uninvited Directors who poured into Laura's home. Ned told the new guests: "Give me a few damn minutes!" He disappeared into a back room.

In five minutes he emerged with a scribbled paper in hand. He only wrote legibly when he had time. The disreputable parchment was illegible—except the heading: $STEP\ ONE$.

Ned's assignments sent everyone scrambling. Although the items on Ned's curling scrap of yellow paper could only be read by him, aloud it all made sense. He looked, pointed to each Director in turn, and ordered what was to be done. There were no arguments. The situation was all too clear and the relevant assignments required no further explanations. If not for Cameron's irresponsible e-mail, a great deal of wasted time and explanation would have been necessary. *Thank God,* Ned thought, *for Cameron's screwup!*

Officer Bracket arrived much later. The other Directors and their staffs, crewmen and engineers were already immersed in their assigned tasks. Ned explained everything to Clint. Security was the name of the game, but, as usual, Ned had to keep his Chief of Security from going too far.

"No Clint! You will *not* shoot the Orb out of space. Not for starters anyway. It may be harmless and contain worthwhile information. We simply don't know. That's why we're constructing a new exit for the Orb—one we can close off with a steel aperture. That's why we're already searching and closing off every other opening, vent and entrance into the Cone. That's why we're building a landing area of very visible concentric circles on the surface, just down the hill from Laura's. That's why we're setting up searchlights, radar and lasers, and all that other ordinance and weapons. We're doing everything we can to force that sphere to land on the target platform. No matter what, that should put us in control."

"I still think—"

"Please, Clint! Don't"

"Sir?"

"Sorry. I didn't mean that the way it sounded. Anyway, we're not going to shoot it out of space based on suspicion alone. However, if it makes one false move, it's all yours!"

"What's a false move?"

Ned was stumped, but said, "We'll talk about that later," knowing they would not. He then added, "See that the weapon systems are well placed and meet your standards and that your men are ready for anything. That's all I'm asking."

Clint raised an eyebrow at first, but then, with the merest twinkle of a smile, agreed to comply.

A few hours later Clint reported to Ned that everything seemed to be on schedule. Several previously unknown ingress-egress sized holes were found and destroyed, including some so obvious they were almost forgotten, such as the shaft created for the torpedo-elevator and the side channels made for funeral ejections.

Clint then made an unusual request. Ned considered it for several hems and haws; finally admitted it was an excellent idea, and encouraged him to go ahead.

"I thought you blamed me, and that our limited collaboration was over."

"Well, Doyan," Clint replied, "things have changed. I don't trust you, but what's at stake should insure even your enthusiastic cooperation."

"You may or may not get my cooperation, but enthusiasm? What's that?"

"It doesn't compute, huh?"

"Don't say that. I'm not a machine or a computer."

"Yeah, yeah. I know. No enthusiasm. On the other hand I believe you dragged us here for some reason, and if we get blown out of the universe by some terrorist from Origin, then your whole mission would be for nothing."

Clint then filled in the details, unintentionally leaving out certain points, but still communicating what was important to the Dort, and asked, "Must I say more?"

"Of course," Doyan replied.

"Like what?"

"How may I cooperate?"

Clint hoped that most of the previously unknown shafts and openings into the Cone had been exposed by the internal search. Those were already destroyed. Clint, always suspicious and cautious, needed Doyan's assistance in handling the Orb and to help survey the many square kilometers of the Cone's exterior. If more covert entrances existed, those vulnerabilities would not be available to the enemy—not on his watch!

Clint saw to the installation of observation and communications gear, powerful laser weapons and other security equipment. When the Orb was packed and nearly ready to go, he had an afterthought. A wide blue stripe was painted around the Orb for easy identification by Transformation's personnel—should the two otherwise identical craft come into proximity above the Cone's surface. Then his men would know which sphere to shoot down.

Clint and Doyan were finally underway. The odd pair almost filled the Orb's remaining space. It was otherwise cram-full of weapons, optical gear, a coffee pot, and other essentials.

Once in space, they methodically descended the Great Cone's exterior, moving toward its apex sixty-five kilometers below the circular, hilly base—an exercise that would have been impossible in cruising Transformation-mode.

As their craft descended, Clint kept explaining over and over, as if Doyan were stupid, everything that must be done. He noted repeatedly that they were looking for Cone vulnerabilities.

Doyan, like all Dorts, was versed in all Dort and human sciences, including the physics and theoretical use of weaponry, lasers, explosives, cannonry, atomics and more. It was also versed in every extant and obsolete human language. But still, Clint's use of the word "vulnerabilities" eluded it.

That understanding was not greatly enhanced when Clint stated, in the midst on his continuous babble of instructions, "By vulnerabilities, I mean keep your eyes open."

"I don't have eyes," Doyan said. "I see with the entirety of my surface and each subdivision thereof."

Clint's drone turned into an exasperated snarl. "Yeah, yeah. I know. No eyes. You know what I mean! Put part of that precious surface of yours up to that eye-piece, like I'm doing, and look!"

"I can see perfectly well through this porthole, thanks."

Clint took his attention away from his eyepiece momentarily to look at Doyan. Most of the alien's body appeared in its usual disgusting shape, he thought, but near the port window it had taken on an entirely new form, reminiscent of some kind of optical instrument that the Security Chief could only vaguely identify. He shrugged, correctly assuming that Doyan could view things telescopically, microscopically, with clear night vision if necessary, or just about any other way. He shook his head and returned to his own eyepiece.

At last Doyan spoke up, saying that he still did not understand precisely what Clint meant by vulnerabilities.

"Gees!" Clint said in disgust, "I thought you had a brain!"

"I do not have a brain, except in my totality."

"Yeah, yeah. No brain. You know what I mean!"

"I can not read minds. What do you mean by vulnerabilities?"

With mounting anger and frustration, Clint clenched his fists, teeth—and butt, for an unintended, but timely flatulent report.

Finally he explained to Doyan, as if to a rebellious child, "We're obviously looking for exterior shafts, holes, caves and things like that."

"Any other artifacts we should be looking for?" Doyan asked.

"No. We're *not* looking for the observatories we put in here and there around the Cone. We're keeping our eyes, or whatever, open for holes—ways that a sphere or something lethal could get into the Cone. Things that could make the Cone vulnerable to a terrorist attack."

"I have seen nothing like that so far, Officer Bracket, but had you mentioned this earlier I could have taken you to several 'vulnerabilities' higher up, on the other side of the Cone. I know of no such openings down here, below midlevel of the Cone, but we can continue the search for them here if you wish."

Clint's eyes rolled upward as they closed. He could not speak for another thirty seconds. Finally, trying to control himself, he opened his eyes and said, "Damn it Doyan, get us up and to the other side. We have to plug them holes! And what do you mean by *several*?"

"Three."

The Orb, an inconsequential speck beside the Great Cone, spiraled up and around its great girth and came to hover several hundred meters from a large, cavelike opening. Clint aimed the laser and blasted it, filling the hole with rock. He gave a satisfied smile. "Next!"

As a humming bird might flit from flower to flower, so the Orb darted many kilometers to the second and third openings, hovering briefly before destroying each of them in turn.

"Okay Doyan, any more?"

"None."

"Then maybe we're done out here. Except for some others you might not know about."

"Not impossible, but I doubt it."

Clint looked askance at the Dort and said, "The passages opened into empty space. They had some purpose, I suppose?"

"Yes," Doyan replied, "but not in space."

"Where then?"

"On Earth, to bring in supplies and to remove garbage—rocks and debris—before the Transformation began."

"Of course," Clint said skeptically.

"Now," Clint continued, "we'll finish the survey."

For the next few hours they attempted to do that, but no more entrances were found. Clint again became extremely frustrated, but this time managed to hold back the urge to express himself. The surface was so vast; they could only cover a small fraction of it. The areas they did cover were only random selections.

Except for one brief communication between Ned and the Dort, the limited survey continued without interruption. Clint did not appreciate being left out, especially when the call was for Doyan, but he swallowed his pride and pretended he was paying no attention. What he did hear, however, was the Dort expressing its willingness to comply with some request.

Less than an hour remained before midnight on the Transformation. Ned was hard at work, continuing to coordinate the efforts of his Department Heads. It was all overkill, of course, with little to be done except cooperate with tightening security precautions.

As the dead of "night" approached, Ned became particularly interested in the request he'd made for Debra Anderson's services. By then he'd already involved himself in several revisions of her kind contribution—writing his speech of "Welcome," which, as usual, she wrote in longhand with colored pens.

Assuming a peaceful start, this would be one of the great speeches of all time, initiating the most magnificent second first-contact in history. While checking the Cone with Clint, Doyan agreed, on a call from Ned, to be his translator—assuming the languages on Origin had not changed too much in the centuries since its departure.

The rogue Orb from planet Origin, on course for the Transformation, could contain anything. Ned realized it could be dangerous, or not. It could carry intelligent life, or not, and could be bringing some profound communication, or not. He intended to cover every conceivable contingency, including the most optimistic possibilities; thus his growing preoccupation with the speech—with all the trimmings!

With most of "Step One" accomplished, those trimmings became elaborate. Time was on everyone's hands. The only personnel with honest tasks left to perform before the witching hour, were Clint's professional and voluntary security forces and the Cone's many construction engineers—and, of course, the decorating and entertainment committees.

Engineering tasks included setting up the landing platform, the spotlights, the steel irislike orifice for Orb ascent and descent into and out of the cone (and that had to be closed before midnight), the radar tracking station, protective periphery fencing, the platform and dais for Ned to deliver his welcoming speech, the laying of red carpet and, naturally, the weaponry to be manned by Clint's security force.

Others with time on their hands assisted the decorating committee by inflating hundreds of multicolored balloons, arranging large and attractive banners and other such activities. A small group of workers from a wide variety of areas got out their favorite instruments and put together an honor guard and marching band—especially the Great Cone's very own, and very popular, Mariachi Transformers. A few of the younger women and quite a few of the older ones, donned short skirts and other attractive attire to join the band practice, wielding their personal magic and makeshift batons. Laura was particularly fetching as she stepped high, twirling her baton.

Things became so celebratory that many forgot the approaching danger. Clint had to intervene to correct this off-guard attitude toward security. He made a few remarks to Ned, who gave his nod of approval.

Preparations ended with dark midnight closing in. They were all in their proper place. Ned was on the platform behind his dais, microphone on the ready, with translator, Doyan, beside him. Searchlights swept the Transformation sky in mysterious patterns understood only by the initiated. The band was tuning up with dissonant tones. Adding to the cacophony was the clatter of weapons and guns being checked and readied by Clint's men. Standing behind the security fences were staff from every department and division. It was the welcoming crowd. They were making ready to applaud, cheer and wave banners on cue, as might seem fitting from time to time, or to take cover or lie flat on the ground if something else happened.

Suddenly an Orb shot out of the newly built steel aperture that snapped shut with a clang just behind it. The Orb bobbed and weaved, spun, and dropped precipitously toward the gathering of loyal crew members. They flattened themselves on the ground amidst frightened shouts and screams. Next, the Orb climbed straight up, kilometers into the dark night sky and out of sight. Seconds later it flashed in a horizontal blur just above their heads, and disappeared over the Cone's far horizon. Minutes later it returned, slowly this time, to hover just in front of the painted concentric circles on the landing platform. It remained there, for the moment, directly above Ned's new podium, where deafening loudspeakers blasted down on the frightened crowd.

The assemblage finally stood up, however, when everybody realized it was the blue-striped Orb and heard Clint's nervous, and much quieter voice say, "Sorry about that!, hehe! I only had one lesson. I'm glad I didn't—hehehe—kill anybody! Anyway, all that scary stuff was totally unintended—I assure you. That unintended scare, however, did actually say what I had to say, better than what I otherwise coulda' said—but I will say what I had to say anyway:

"So remember this. Every second counts. Be on your toes, or lie flat on the ground—whatever! Anyways, this, my fellow Transfonauts, is a Security Operation, no matter what all your party trimmings might imply. We're going to play this out Ned's way. You got that? And if there's *trouble*, then you know what happens—whatever lands on that platform turns to dust. Got it? Let me see those heads nod!" Heads nodded. "Good. Now here's what happens next:

"I fly this Orb up to meet the other one, and then escort it in. If a problem starts in space, I've equipped this blue ribbon Orb to fight it out. So wish me luck, and good luck to all of you!"

The crowd cheered on cue as the second Orb quietly landed behind Clint's hovering craft. It settled nicely, and precisely in the center of the lighted, targetlike platform. It was midnight exactly.

Satisfied with the cheers his listening equipment picked up, and totally unaware of the other Orb, Clint shot the blue ribbon Orb straight up and away. Due to piloting problems, he would not be seen again for hours.

The unstriped Orb, simple and shining, sat quietly on the landing platform. Ned's raised dais was positioned above the crowd, but at eye-level from the Orb's hatch—if it had landed with the exit in Ned's direction, but it didn't.

Ned was beside himself for not anticipating that possibility. He wanted to be the first human being to see and greet the alien, or robot, or whatever it was. It occurred to him to mount the platform, speech in hand, and walk to the other side of the Orb before its hatch opened, but he knew Clint would eventually kill him, sort of, if he attempted anything so risky.

Welcoming speech! he thought in horror. He wasn't positive he was ready. He glanced at the speech to make sure he wouldn't start on the wrong note. It began, "Welcome stranger! Please accept our presence near your planet and your home. We come in peace. . . ." Then he looked at the Dort. "Ready Doyan?" Doyan replied in the affirmative.

A brilliant display of light suddenly radiated from the opposite side of the Orb where the hatch just opened to its bright interior. There were gasps and groans of shock and awe from that side of the platform. Clearly, whatever was in the Orb had emerged full-blown. The amazed crowd noise spread clockwise toward Ned's right. Whatever it was, it moved cautiously on its circumnavigation of the platform. Even the band was silenced and agape.

Ned wondered, *What are these gasps and groans about? Surprise, fear, what?* He waited with rising anxiety and anticipation. The thing had almost reached a location on the platform where Ned could glimpse it for the first time, but was startled by the cocking of guns and the rattle of other military contraptions.

It was about to appear! One quick look at the speech! ". . . We come in peace. . . . Welcome. . . ."

Then, but indistinctly due to bright spotlights, it came into view. In another moment it had positioned itself directly in front of Ned! The surrounding ordnance made more clattering noises, but Clint's men had not yet fired—which could have happened already, Ned believed, if Clint had been in attendance.

Ned stared wide-eyed in disbelief at the creature before him, then another quick look at the speech. Ned almost started to read, ". . . Welcome stranger . . ." but knew he had it memorized. He took a final look at the figure in the spotlight and, almost dumbstruck, snarled into the microphone, "Who the hell are you?"

The figure responded, "Mark Tenderloin, my friend! And who the hell are you?"

TWENTY-NINE

The "Welcome Ceremony" was brief and to the point, consisting of a hostile exchange of names and the dismissal of all but the Security Patrol. They were to do whatever they deemed appropriate under the circumstances and to escort Doyan back to his waiting area. They were also asked to contact Clint Bracket by radio to brief him on what happened and suggested that he try to return safely.

After initial confusion, the crowd thinned and Ned approached the stranger. They spoke briefly, shook hands uneasily, descended the stairs from the landing platform to the red carpet and walked to the lush green lawn below the hill leading to Laura's home.

A little earlier Ned spotted Laura scampering up the hill toward her house, no doubt to change into something more appropriate. Part of the way up, she turned and yelled to Ned, "Invite him up!"—which he did.

Ned and the newcomer were halfway up the hill when a Security Officer trudged up behind them, puffing hard and perspiring. He was carrying a large, heavy duffel bag. "We found this," he said, "in the Orb and checked it with x-rays and all that. It's okay. May I presume it is yours, Mr. Tenderloin?"

Tenderloin acknowledged it was his and to just leave it. The officer nodded, dropped the bag with relief and left.

Everyone who was there for the "Ceremony" noticed the newcomer. He looked like any ordinary human businessman. Ned saw that even at close range. The man had mousy gray hair and blue eyes. His stature was short—about five foot three. He was thin but wiry, immaculately dressed in a blue suit, tie, and polished shoes; but surprised Ned, especially under the circumstances, by his amiable self-confidence.

Ned was more surprised by the ease that the little man picked up the bag and slung it over his shoulder, and then continued almost effortlessly up the hill.

Laura met them at the door. She had already changed. After quick introductions she held the door wide and invited them in.

A few more pleasantries were offered as though nothing unusual had happened this day. Then, pointedly, she eyed the duffel bag Mark had leaned against the wall just inside the door. Looking back at Mark, she asked, "Are you planning to stay long?"

After some nervous laughing, Mark replied, "As a matter of fact, I was hoping to join you on any expedition you might be planning—to the planet's surface. I was hoping to ask some Dort, had many of them been around and in charge of a Cone full of Dorts, but since this is not a Dort Transformation, this is almost as good."

"If it hadn't been for the Twister you would probably have had your wish," Laura said. "And what do you mean, *almost* as good?"

Mark shrugged and said, "I'm okay with people, but more used to being around Dorts, that's all."

"And if this had been a Dort Transformation, and they had not been receptive to your request, then what would you have done?" Ned asked.

"They can be bargained with. If that weren't so I wouldn't be here—at least not this soon. If they didn't want me here, my Cone would not have been built for me and the coordinates provided to get here would not have been correct. They could have seen to that and fooled me in some way, but that didn't happen, and I was quite sure it wouldn't. You spend enough time with things like that and you begin to think you know them. For instance I had a strong sense of their manipulativeness, but also strong certitude they would never deliberately commit murder, unless for some final purpose, whatever that might be—if after all these centuries they could still have one—and it was being jeopardized. Given all that, I still don't understand them"

Ned said, "Well, hundreds of them took over this Transformation and deliberately threw us onto the edge of a Twister. At first we didn't know they were here. That Twister stunt was lethal and irresponsible! It killed many of us and most of them. If it hadn't killed most of them, they would probably still be in charge. In an odd way, maybe they are."

Mark's expression became serious. "Sorry—I didn't know. It must have been an unusual Twister to be so lethal. But don't ask me to defend the Dorts. As smart as they are, they make stupid mistakes. That had to be a big one to wipe out so many of them. I don't think they could have expected or intended that kind of an outcome for themselves—or for you. However, it does show their willingness to take crazy chances to get a shot at whatever it is they want. To that extent I agree, they are dangerous. For me it was a formidable job just to keep a step ahead of them. If we knew what they were after it might be easier to stay ahead of them."

Laura told Mark about their experience in the grotto with the dying Dort.

"That story," Mark responded, "comes as close to understanding their motives as anything I know."

Ned said, "Yes, but it was just a hint. The full meaning of that encounter is still a mystery."

Laura said, "It must have something to do with why they had to come back here, or why they brought us to this place. They call the planet 'Origin.' We have to learn more. Now that we're here, we're at least a step closer to whatever they're after. We need to learn why they forced us to this part of the Galaxy."

"Yes," Mark replied. "And that brings me back to my question about going with you to the planet. It's not what I'd call a go-it-alone kind of place."

Ned squelched a smile and said, "That might not be possible, unless I can convince our Chief of Security not to throw you in the brig on charges when he returns—if he returns. So, first you'll have to convince me that he shouldn't."

"Charges?" Mark said.

"Yes. For instance, you confiscated our Orb without authorization, made us go through an expensive security alert, gave us no warning or indication of your intensions, and probably a lot of other things."

Mark laughed. "Yes. Well! The Orb, as you call it, was not yours to start with. It wasn't even the Dorts'. It was stolen from me. It was my Homing Pigeon. You, your crew, and probably a bunch of Dorts—I noticed one beside you earlier—appropriated it without my permission. It's my invention. I didn't have time to patent it. With a little more modification—well, maybe a lot more—it will be able to transit Reo-Spheres ad infinitum. That's what I was aiming for. I should have patented what I already had instead of trying to perfect it first. It has some underwater capacity, but that's still flawed and unreliable."

"Very interesting—if true," Ned responded. "We can talk more about that later, along with the other problems you created for us. But right now I'm more interested in why you would want to go down to the surface with us. You've already been there."

Mark had a way of changing the subject. "Yes," he said, "and I've been waiting for quite some time for your arrival. What kept you?"

"Really?" Laura was surprised.

"That's something you weren't expecting?" Mark asked with a note of feigned surprise.

"Why would we expect to find anyone from Earth on any planet, to say nothing of your being on this, the most remote and unlikely planet in the Milky Way—the very one that we happened upon?"

"I'm sure you realize," Mark replied, "that you didn't just happen upon this planet. You were destined to arrive here."

"How do you know that?" Laura asked.

"It's a long story. And really, why did it take you so long to get here?"

Laura and Ned answered in unison: "It's a long story."

They continued to talk well into the morning hours before retiring. Mark was given one of Laura's spare rooms. Ned sent a late message to postpone the next meeting of the Directors until 5 PM that day. At that time he promised to "reintroduce" them to Mark Tenderloin, Ph.D., and told them they would then be free to ask him any questions they might have.

Before retiring, a call came in from Clint Bracket who had returned from wherever he had been. His return had been smoother and less dramatic than his departure. He was still embarrassed, but this time because he had totally missed the other Orb that had "snuck up behind me," and because he "missed the ceremony, hehe." His men had briefed him on what had happened. They could be heard laughing in the background.

They had seven hours of needed sleep. The rescheduled meeting allowed for continued talk until well after lunch. An hour early, and still in animated conversation, they entered the subterranean conference room. Those hours of discussion brought surprises to both sides. Mark Tenderloin's revelations were astounding to Ned and Laura. In turn, their account of the events experienced on this initial voyage of the Great Cone of Transformation left Mark shocked and distressed. They described to him the details of the hijacking, the outrageous course change that amounted to mass kidnapping, the Twister and its tragic consequences to humans and Dorts, the funerals, the eventual takeover of controls from the Dorts, and the fast jump into the gravitational field of Origin.

But some things did not surprise or shock Mark. He was sure, for instance, that a Transformation Cone—the one they were on, or a competitor's—would arrive in the space above Origin, but he expected it much sooner. He believed that whatever Cone was used, it would have been readied by the Dorts.

Mark explained, "The Dorts would have to use my inventions based on 'Tenderloin Technology.' That technology, in turn, is based on the advances I've made to Transformation Theory. Without that technology it would take years for any Cone to reach the vicinity of Origin from Earth." (Modesty was not one of Mark's strongest virtues.)

"Those advances," he continued, "not only make possible the practical transport of matter through Transformation Space, such as Cones like this one, but through other Reo-Spheres. That is, transport by escaping one universe's spacetime continuum, and moving into any number of other such continua of universes, and then stepping back into the original universe—this one. The arrival destination must be the prearranged coordinates within *this* universe— or whatever universe one starts from. But we're stuck with this one. The speed of such transport depends, above all, on the number of Reo-Spheres accessed during the jump."

Then the discussion became technically complex and only Laura was able to keep up. She did try to simplify the essentials for Ned's benefit from time to time, but mainly without success.

Ned asked, "How long have you been on Origin?"

"I got here a month ago."

"How? Do you have a large crew? We haven't seen any other Cones around."

"I came alone on a small Transformation Cone. I call it my 'Mini-Cone.' It has room for a crew and a few hundred passengers, but no, I came alone. The Cone is just large enough to contain the modified spiral technology for a double Reo-Sphere transit, or what I'd call a *slow* jump."

"How slow was your jump? How long did it take you to get here?" Ned asked.

"A few seconds."

"You call that *slow*?"

"Not in human terms. It's only slow in theory."

"I don't understand," Ned said.

"My technology simplifies navigational integrity between Reo-Spheres and requires vastly less energy than the current Transformation technology that accesses only *one* additional Reo-Sphere besides this one, although Transformation Theory does not, as yet, conceive it in that way. Transformation Theory describes another dimension, which is true, but that dimension is another universe—another Reo-Sphere. To get the kind of speed we're talking about, at least *two* Reo-Spheres must be accessed. Had my Mini-Cone been able to access *more* than two additional Reo-Spheres, the trip wouldn't have taken a few seconds. It would have happened in a nanosecond. That's a billionth of a second."

Ned said, "I'll settle for slow. Anyway, what about your initial countdown before the Transformation? Ours takes ten hours."

Laura said, "The ten-hour countdown is the minimum for this Cone."

"But we can maneuver very well near a star or planet," Ned said defensively, as if in a competition, "and we can set and reset the destination coordinates during that countdown. Are those capabilities true of your Mini-Cone?"

"Yes, but the auto-countdown is shorter than ten hours."

Laura said, "Even so . . . hmm. Under ten hours. How is that possible? Transformation Theory only allows—"

"Never mind. I understand your confusion. You're still thinking Transformation Theory. Let me explain Reo-Sphere theory. Then you'll understand."

With pad and pen Mark quickly explained, in mathematical language, how Transformation Theory had been relegated to a subtheory within Reo-Sphere Theory.

Ned had no clue about the mathematics involved. He merely watched Laura as, wide-eyed and alert, she experienced the torrential cascade of ingenious revelations shown in the abstract mathematics and molecular physics notations that poured out effortlessly, line after line and page after page, from Mark's pen. Laura's gasp of delight, wonder, admiration and envy were almost sensual. Mark kept talking and explaining continuously throughout his little exercise. He hardly seemed to notice the level of appreciation his work was receiving. It was not the simple appreciation of yet another mere genius. What she saw unfolding before her eyes and her multidimensional visualization capacity, was a new conception of the oneness of multiple universes without end! The sounds and patterned changes in her breathing seemed to punctuate each step in the flawless proof of Mark's theory as he laid it out before her. She was in awe. He explained how his theory built upon "ordinary" Transformation Theory. "Without your creation in the first place, Laura," Mark magnanimously admitted toward the end of his presentation, "there could be no Reo-Sphere Theory."

Well before those last words were spoken, Ned noticed that Laura was tense and trembling—a quiet, blissful tension. He lifted his head as if to observe some obscure pattern on the conference room ceiling, but was really considering his new-found appreciation for the latent power residing in the dry and dormant seeds of mathematics. And in Laura's face and demeanor he saw the blossoming reflection of a great scientific theory.

Mark laid down his pen and continued talking. "Blame the Dorts' covert engineering feat of equipping this Great Cone for access to not just one, but many multiples of practical Reo-Sphere travel. With what you now have in your hands, if you knew how it operated, you could have gone from Earth to Origin, or anywhere else you wanted, virtually instantly. Unfortunately, to do that, you'd not only have to know how to engage that capability, but know where to set the exact spacetime coordinates before you started, neither of which applies right now. With all the ricocheting this Cone has gone through, I doubt you could locate Earth's coordinates. It's a miracle you got here at all. I guess that's why it took you so long. If the Dorts hadn't used that array of black holes, you wouldn't be here either. I wonder how they knew the singularities would be there. It's a safe bet they did their homework. Anyway, as you explained, that changed your course toward Origin. Then they engaged the Reo-Sphere system. That got you here in seconds, not a decade. If it *had* taken ten years, I'd really have been pissed!"

Ned asked, "How did you get the coordinates for Origin?"

Mark's answer was mostly predictable. "They were given to me by an unusual Dort."

Ned was surprised at the *unusual* part. "I thought the Dorts were all alike. What do you mean by an *unusual* Dort?"

"It's hard for me to put my finger on it, but something was different. For instance, this one actually had a name! Have you ever heard of such a thing?"

Ned asked, "What did it call itself?"

"Doyan."

This disclosure brought anger into Ned's tone. "Doyan! That bastard! Its tentacles are into everything! It knows more than it ever tells—more than any other Dort. It's the key to everything. And we don't have a clue what that is."

Ned went on to describe their experience with Doyan's evasiveness and its limited cooperation, including providing Clint with "so-called training" in the Orb. "With training like that, Clint could have killed himself and a lot of others."

Laura expressed a less-harsh impression of the Dorts. She described in more detail the dying Dort they encountered in the subterranean chamber of putrefying Dorts. It had spoken more philosophy than concrete data. She thought its words raised many questions, but believed it provided a clue to the Dorts' motives.

During this exchange, Mark tried to answer Laura's earlier question about why their Transformation was "destined" to arrive at Origin. The answer, he explained, was "Not in the drifting stars, but in some internal imperative that is driving them."

Mark went on to say, "It's only because the Dorts needed me that I was consulted at all. Like you, it appears that I too am a tool for their perceived destiny. My Homing Pigeons that you call Orbs, were stolen not long before your Great Cone left Earth. But the Orbs were not their major interest. It was my theoretical advances into Reo-Spheres that grabbed their attention. So, working at a distance, with me as their advisor, *they began a major project*.

"It's not easy to admit, but they pulled me into their little game rather subtly and attended to my every crazy, unlikely speculation. I enjoyed that a bit too much."

Marks next remark brought a frown from Ned and a gasp from Laura. "The Dorts, for example, were the only ones to take seriously my early pseudonymously published paper on Twisters."

Mark seemed not to notice their reactions and went on to explain his failure to find out from Doyan where their project was located. "I asked for where their Cone was being built. I asked Doyan a number of times, but the answer was never clear. But at the same time I was promised a small Transformation Cone. It was being built for my sole use in exchange for my ongoing consultation. That partnership continued for a number of years and became more intense toward the end.

"I believed, for reasons alluded to by Doyan, that the Dorts were not only building the small Cone for me, but also their own Super Transformation Cone. In addition, some strange remarks I heard from Doyan corresponded to the ones given to you and others by that dying Dort. That part about their needing to bring along a 'special kind of being' was never mentioned to me by Doyan. But I was convinced from all the signs and evidence, especially toward the end, that some innate drive was pushing Doyan and the other Dorts to return to their place of origin. I thought it might have something to do with Dort reproduction, like Salmon returning at life's end to spawn where they were hatched. I figured that at least some Dorts were on the verge of that return. I picked a date I thought would be close to their departure and withheld some crucial technological information from them until my own Transformation craft was nearly complete. I personally saw to that last necessity on my Cone. Only then did I give them the final steps to actually implement Reo-Sphere drive for *their* Cone. Those last technological steps were simple, but even the Dorts would never have figured it out on their own. They lack the necessary creativity for that.

"I held out for more. I asked for a complete diagram and description of the planet they called Origin, and its spacetime coordinates—for a specific time and date. Unfortunately, Doyan denied any descriptive knowledge of Origin, *except* those exact coordinates. I settled for that.

"When Doyan asked if I was planning to go there, I said I was thinking about it and that it would be a good test for my personal Transformation Cone. Then Doyan said to me, 'Good. Maybe we'll see you on Origin.'

"So, when you arrived here, I expected to see a good many Dorts. Given the Reo-Sphere speed of travel I experienced to get here, I thought *they* were more than a bit slow. That worried me. By the time you arrived I'd have been glad for even Doyan's company. Anyway, I thought I'd come up here and say hello. Imagine my surprise seeing *people* when I got off that Homing Pigeon!

"When my instruments detected my Homing Pigeons on this Cone, I thought, Great! I'll just send the Dorts my position on our special encryption frequency and they can come and get me. But that never happened, so I figured something must be wrong. Maybe they felt guilty for stealing my Pigeons; so the Dorts weren't entirely on my side. Later on I was even more convinced that something was amiss when one of my Pigeons passed me by and returned here."

Laura asked, "Didn't you say something to Doyan or one of the other Dorts when you noticed the Orbs were gone?"

"I would have, but none of them were around and it was time for me to go. Timing was crucial if I was going to go, and as you can see, I did."

"Then how did you get from your Cone to Origin without an Orb?" Ned asked.

"In a shuttle craft. They left one for me. I at least made sure of *that* before leaving Earth. Unfortunately—thanks again to the Dorts—the one they left me was almost out of fuel by the time I found a decent place to land and set up my small lab."

Laura seemed in wonderment. "Do you mean to say that you were stranded, not able to return to your Cone?"

"Yes, but I didn't really start to worry until about a week ago. As I said, I was expecting the Dorts on their own Super Cone. When they didn't arrive I began to fret, and wished I was back on my Cone. The environment down there is not safe. But that's another story!"

"Even if the Dorts had arrived without us," Laura said, "why would you trust them? They left you with an inadequately fueled shuttle and stole your Orbs. They might have given you coordinates for the wrong planet, or coordinates for somewhere in empty space, away from any source of high mass. Then you'd really have been stuck!"

"You're right. I didn't trust Doyan completely, but I was pretty sure, back then at least, that Doyan wouldn't have seen to the construction and completion of my Mini-Cone just to send me into empty space and my death. There are easier ways to kill a guy."

"I'm wondering about something else," Ned said. "We haven't detected another Cone—large, small or indifferent. No other Cone orbiting Origin. What happened to yours?"

"It's at an optimal distance from Origin, as is this Cone, but on the other side of the planet, circling the equator. It's much farther out than this Cone, and it's moving faster. It's the distance Doyan chose—close enough to energize the highly efficient mass-energy conversion system, and it's far enough away for—"

"We know," Laura interrupted. "That's why we're in this orbit—below geosynchronous orbit, which is great for getting power from Origin's mass. In a geostationary orbit we could only survey half the planet. This way we're in orbit and surveying all of it."

"What did you think when you first spotted us?" Ned asked.

"Once I saw this magnificent Cone," Mark replied, "I quit worrying—except for a while when the first *Orb*, as you keep calling it, didn't find me or even attempt to communicate. I thought it might be some innocent mistake, so I waited. I'm usually a trusting optimist. After a while I got tired of being patient and sent for a Homing Pigeon."

Ned asked, "If you weren't being picked up by the Orb—excuse me, 'Homing Pigeon'—what made you think Doyan or any of the Dorts would free one for you?"

"Well, my trusting optimism comes and goes, depending on the circumstances. I'm afraid I wasn't always entirely forthcoming with Doyan either. Those little homing devices were installed by—well, you can probably guess who."

Laura laughed, "You naughty man!"

Ned asked, "Why did you install that homing capability in the first place?"

"For one—no two—good reasons. The second reason was the most important. The first reason was its relatively simple technology—simple compared to most of the stuff I'd been working on for the vehicles, like having them fly around in confined spaces or through winding tunnels, or whatever, without touching anything and without getting scratched." Then Mark stopped talking, looking pleased with himself. He was like a child bragging about a new achievement. "My rigid, but loving parents," he finally continued, "used to reinforce my early accomplishments."

"And your second reason for creating the homing capacity?" Laura asked.

"Well, it simply amused me to do it."

"Seriously," Laura insisted, "Why?"

"You never know when one might get swiped."

"Okay," Laura said, "it amused you to build in a homing capacity. I'm not sure what that really means. I know it was no small feat for that Orb to find its way out of our—and Doyan's—clutches, and all the way out of this Cone, and finally all the way to Origin and to your exact location. What in the world are the Homing Pigeons' capabilities?"

"Let me put it this way," Mark responded, "To *not* comply with my homing request, the Pigeons would have to be in a confined space with doors too small to get through, or locked from outside. Simple egress procedures, including digital codes, combinations, and the like, were elementary to build into these little honeys! Those programs were around long before I adapted them for my Pigeons."

Ned smirked. "You couldn't have had an Earth lab the size and sophistication of yours without great wealth. I saw it from outside and read a story or two about it. Did you send the Orbs to rob a dozen banks?"

Mark laughed heartily. "If I'd wanted to, do you think for a moment that I couldn't have done the same thing much easier with a little computer hacking for online transfers?"

Laura said, "If you did you'd have been caught and in jail right now."

Mark responded with no more that a rye, condescending smile.

Ned and Laura returned that expression with frowns.

"The fact is," Mark said, "—and shame on you for thinking that of me—I have hundreds of amusing, meaningless little patents bringing in royalties under fifty different pseudonyms. I like to keep out of the limelight—the stories you read notwithstanding. I have no need to rob a dozen banks that I could just as well own."

With a few patents of her own, Laura nodded her understanding.

Ned swallowed and said, "I was just kidding about the bank-robbing Orbs. I'm impressed they got out of here to find you. They obviously do more than unlock doors!"

Mark rubbed his hands together, lifted his head higher than usual, and said, "Oh yes! You haven't heard the half of it! With enough openness, once free of any meaningful confinement, they can find their way through any maze—with a combination of radar, sonar, and other detectors, and use trial and error learning—like highly motivated hungry rats! That part of the system I call their Rat Kit, and it includes a kind of olfactory capacity."

Ned wondered, "How could you know all that would work without Doyan finding out?"

"I did a lot of secret testing—not always successfully—of the individual components, and then the whole thing as a unit. For example, I did some testing in a shallow underwater cave. The unit's assignment—I had eight Pigeons then—was to map the cave, and then return to a spot a hundred kilometers from the cave. That spot was a fenced in area outside my Earth-based lab.

The cave itself had already been well mapped before being flooded after dam construction years later, so it was a good test.

"The Homing Pigeons—I'd rigged them all to work under water—radioed back detailed, accurate, three-dimensional, computer holograph maps of the entire cave, except for areas it was unable to penetrate without, well, getting scratched. Then they came home.

"Anyway, that's why I was fairly sure that one of the Pigeons would find a way out of your Cone and then to my location on Origin. Had they been under water I wouldn't have been very confident. All the Pigeons had good homing capacity outside of water. Under water they need more work to be reliable."

"What happened to the other . . . Homing Pigeons?" Ned asked.

"Most were fine in shallow water—anything above twenty meters. Deeper than that they started to fail, especially below forty meters, and when they did they just closed down, becoming completely immobile. I'd never trust them with a person inside if it were going to be submerged. There were even a couple failures in shallow water."

"That's how you lost the other six?"

"Eventually, yes. In deep water they failed about once every three dives."

"So you just left them there?" Laura asked.

"Not right away. I got most of them back using another Pigeon."

"Using remote piloting?"

"No. Remote control is no problem in atmosphere or in space, but not under water. The rescue Pigeon simply had to hunt for the one that was downed. When it brought the disabled one back I kept working on the problem. But I still haven't solved all the problems. Didn't have enough time. It's still a mystery to me why they fail at depth. I'll figure it out later, when and if we get back to Earth. After a while I was losing the Pigeons faster than I could retrieve them. I quit trying when I only had two left."

"But you had no underwater problems today," Ned said. "We did try to plug all the potential entrances to the Cone."

"Yes, but there must have been an exit somewhere," Mark said.

"You're right, of course. We closed the stable doors too late for the Orb's exit, but not too late to make you land on our platform—if you were coming here at all. Naturally we didn't expect that you would be from Earth—or even be a human for that matter."

Mark laughed. "Some who know me would not say that."

Laura returned the laugh. "Not say what? That you're from planet Earth?"

"No," Mark responded soberly. "That I'm human."

A long moment of silence followed. Then, together, Ned and Laura broke into laughter. Mark looked back, without expression.

Laura eyed him seriously and said, "Mark, this whole Transformation has been, weird—Kafkaesque to say the least. It has literally killed many of us, and most of the Dorts. Normality is needed here—desperately—so please—"

"Please?"

"Yes, Mark. Please, no more weird statements like that. I'm sure you're not psychotic, so don't go there, even if it amuses you. Don't tell people here, even in kidding, that you think you're an alien or that others think you're not human. We have enough to cope with without more strangeness. Okay?"

"Okay," Mark said as he bowed his head, for the first time, in apparent shame. As he lowered his head, Ned and Laura came to their feet! On pivoting his head downward, the back of Mark's head came out of his over-sized collar, exposing an occipital protuberance half again the size of his otherwise normal-looking head.

"Oh Mark!" Laura cried out. "Now I understand. They used to tease me about my head when I was a little girl, as some strangers still do, and told me I was a freak, and that I wasn't human!"

Mark lifted his head, adjusted the back of his collar, and lowered his occiput back into the space. Then, looking directly at her, said, "Well, *I guess we showed them* what we can do with these heads, *didn't we Laura!*"

THIRTY

The Directors' curiosity was hidden behind a barrier of nearly indifferent expressions as they filed into the conference room. Some looked vaguely interested, but others were mildly hostile and the rest appeared vacant or unconcerned. It wasn't the usual cheerful, back slapping, hand shaking greeting for an important guest. Amidst this passivity was the lively exception of Debra Anderson. She was setting up holographic and sound equipment. Ready to go, she settled into her chair with her note pad and colored pens. With twinkling bright eyes, she nodded to Ned who took that as the signal for him to begin the meeting.

Following introductions, Ned and Laura summarized their discussions with Mark, and then turned the meeting over to him. He said nothing except to ask if there were any questions.

The dam holding off their true curiosity broke in slow motion. Mark's answers to their small stream of tentative, rather ordinary questions opened the first crack and momentum picked up as his in-depth and open answers led to areas of interest for everyone. Then came more probing questions. The group, even Clint, became attentive. And Debra Anderson's note taking was as industrious as ever.

Mark's responses led to many questions about Reo-Sphere Theory. Most of his answers were in plane English for the group, with a sufficient sprinkling of Quantum and Transformation physics to even stimulate the likes of Stanley Lundeen and Ernst Berman.

Clint's interest was in the Orbs and Mark's repeated statement that Origin was not a go-it-alone place to be.

Doug, of all people, wondered how to operate the Transformation Cone through Reo-Sphere space. That question brought everyone up short. Greenberg said he thought that final transfer of controls from the Dorts must have included those very controls. Doug explained, "It might have for all I know, but I have no idea how those controls are accessed where they are, or what to do with them even if I did. After the transfer of controls we had all the ordinary mechanisms in hand, but we had no idea then that such a thing as Reo-Sphere travel even existed."

Mark said, "I know how my Mini-Cone operates. I installed the final control equipment and switches. The super mass-energy converter was manufactured and installed by the Dorts to my specifications, but that final touch, for *their* equipment was not disclosed to them until the last minute. It was complicated, but I'm sure the Dorts rebuilt the controls in some odd and humanly unfathomable way. To get back to Earth you will need Doyan's assistance, not only to translate the Reo-Sphere controls for your use, but to get the exact Reo-Sphere spacetime coordinates."

"Do you mean to say the Dorts still have leverage over us?" Clint, now on his feet, said, "We need *their* help?"

Doug lifted his shaggy head of red locks and responded simply, "Yes. A lot of help from the Dorts, I'd say." Then he added, "And from Mark too."

Clint persisted. "How could Mark help? He just told us the Dorts build unfathomable controls—as if that were new. We'd need total and willing compliance from Doyan and his boys to reconstruct those damn Faster'n Shit controls for *our* use."

"Exactly," Doug replied. "And Mark knows how those FAST controls must be crafted and configured for human use. But, you're right—Doyan's full cooperation is essential."

"If it would be so kind!" Clint snarled. "Even assuming Doyan would play the game, it could have something else in mind for us. Hell, we know it does! We have to *make* it help us. If not, maybe Mark could help by reverse engineering all those 'unfathomable' controls, or just tear out the Dort switches and stick in his own. But where could we get the coordinates for a date and time of our choosing without Doyan's cooperation? By damn, if we didn't need it I'd kill it—if I knew how!"

Doug looked helplessly in Mark's direction and then around the room. "I think Clint is right. We appear, once again, to be at the mercy of Dort whims."

The room became silent. Mark finally spoke up. "I believe we all understand the Dorts well enough to know they will manipulate to the bitter end to get whatever they're after."

"Yes," Ned agreed, "and it's built into their nature. They will sacrifice themselves and anyone else for it. So, as Clint implied, our leverage, except for jumping through all their hoops, isn't much more than zero!"

"Maybe not zero," Mark said. "There is another thing about the built-in nature of Dorts that might help."

"Okay, what?" Clint snapped.

"Their great curiosity about Transformation Theory, and by extension, Reo-Sphere Theory."

Still irritated, Clint said, "They already have it. They even built that into this Transformation Cone, and yours too."

Mark turned to Laura and asked her to give him the paper on which he had scribbled his theory. With some embarrassment she removed the carefully folded papers from her blouse, where she had lovingly tucked it all away. Ned had failed to notice that she'd kept the sheets, to say nothing of where she placed them. He realized that Mark was more observant than he thought. Laura unfolded the document and perused its pages quickly and thoughtfully, but did not hand it to Mark until he requested it one more time.

Mark asked Laura to comment on the document's contents, which she did. She explained what it was, its revolutionary scientific significance—going beyond, and even incorporating Transformation Theory within a broader framework. She noted its obvious, to her, implications for nearly instant travel.

"That's FAST travel we've all recently experienced by piggybacking our way through other, parallel and concurrent universes. Reo-Spheres. There's even the high probability, by extending and rounding out Mark's theory just a bit further, of detouring and staying, temporarily or permanently, in any one of the other universes. Furthermore—"

"No Laura," Mark interrupted, "I don't mean to embarrass you, but there is no such possibility of such a detour within Reo-Sphere Theory."

Laura raised her eyebrows in surprise. "Of course there isn't," she agreed. "Reo-Sphere Theory, and any technology arising from it directly, could never do that. Your theory goes far beyond Transformation Theory. But hadn't you noticed the gap—the monumental theoretical gap between the two? It is there, in that gap, that the probability for the detour arises."

At this point Laura noticed the distressed expression on Mark's reddening face—and the looks of delight on everyone else's. She finished by again acknowledging the significance of Mark's new theory and, in a totally failed attempt to save face for Mark, said, "As for that other silly matter about *detours* that I mentioned, I'll just explain it to you some time over coffee."

The meeting continued following a brief recess—that gave time for Mark and the rest of the group to reemerge with a veneer of composure.

Mark held high the papers containing the gist of his theory. "The Dorts want this," he said. "Officer Bracket is correct about their ability to create Reo-Sphere drives within these Transformation Cones, but as I mentioned, they built the drives for our two Cones based on my specifications, but aside from their knowledge of Transformation Theory, they don't have a clue to the actual theory behind Reo-Sphere drives. And they want that knowledge. If they already had it, I would probably have been given the coordinates to another place. I know they want this theory, over and above the technology that spins off of it, because Doyan asked me for it, not just once, but many times. I kept putting it off."

With that, Mark walked over to a nearby console and printer, looked around in that area until he saw what he was looking for, and dropped the sheaf of papers containing his theory into the microshredder.

"So long as the Dorts don't have that, we may have our own leverage. How much, we can't know right now, but I have a feeling it's right up there with the rest of their instincts."

The conversation moved to Clint's question about the planet's not being a go-it-alone environment. Mark responded to that and a dozen related questions. Since the meeting began, six hours had passed. After hearing from Mark about the strange and unpredictable nature of the planet below, most of the Directors chose to remain safe and comfortable on the Great Cone of Transformation—at least for the time being.

Certain Directors decided to figure out a way to return to Earth. Some thought the blur of star configurations, as seen from their current distance and angle from the main disk of the Milky Way could be translated into something familiar. At the same time, they could work on making the Reo-Sphere drive controls useable for humans. Those and related ideas were advanced by Debra Anderson, Henri Lufti, Cameron Greenberg, David Michaels, Ellen Stone and a few others—all of whom were singularly unqualified respecting such proposals.

Stanley Lundeen gave a brief speech, diplomatically alerting those Directors to certain difficulties with their ideas. That discouragement led to immediate consideration of another idea—making the decade-long return to Earth. Stanley explained that this too would require spacetime coordinates as accurate as those for a Reo-Sphere jump. The only qualification he gave to his own arguments was to weave in the remote possibility that "Navigation and control-device problems *might* be solved without Doyan's assistance." The latter possibility attracted as much attention as a fine-print footnote—which was his intent. However, two women *"saw" that footnote*. For them it flashed like a neon sign.

The remaining voices cried "Know your enemy," and came to another agreement—negotiation with the Dorts (Doyan, in other words) would require a better understanding of Doyan and its background, including its origin, the planet they were orbiting. They needed to know that planet first hand.

Some did not see how going to Origin would help at all. The voices in favor of doing so continued to explain their reasons. For Ned and Jack it was simply to get the feel of the place. "After all," Jack Lewis said, "the Dorts got us here for their own reasons. They didn't force us here to go sightseeing—not that that's a bad idea. We need to get the lay of the land—literally. That's minimum. It's their turf, their ball park, and the more we know about it before the game starts—or is over—the better!"

It was a thin argument, but the clincher came from none other than the fraidy-cat of the Transformation, Judy Olafson, who said, "What the hell—why not!"

Laura knew Judy's imagination more than anyone and figured it was the sightseeing idea that got the better of her fears, along with her likely belief that Stanley's statement of possibilities could come to pass—his obscure statement about being able to solve the problem of Earth's spacetime location *without* Doyan's help.

Clint would go to Origin for the adventure; not that he would ever admit that. He said instead, "I need to see what special security measures are needed on Origin—that planet that's '*not* a go-it-alone place' for anyone to be." (But he was visibly excited about the prospect.)

Dr. Ellen Stone would go there to handle any medical problems that might arise on the planet. Her chief physician, Dr. Henri Lufti, would remain in charge of the hospital facilities on the Transformation Cone. (No one was surprised at Ellen's change of heart about going to the planet when Clint said he was going.)

THIRTY-ONE

Mark showed some things the next day to Clint about the Orbs that he hadn't learned from Doyan—things that Doyan was not aware of. They would pilot the Orbs to bring the first staff and supplies to Mark's Base Camp. Later on, already trained pilots from the main crew would operate the dozen shuttles that were in storage since the Transformation began. After the first weeks of settling in, others insisted on learning to pilot the Orbs—for traveling around on sightseeing tours (labeled "exploration"), for quick trips to and from the Great Cone, and occasionally for legitimate scientific study.

Before any moves to the planet, however, the Directors pored over detailed topographic and holographic maps obtained by Stanley Lundeen's Astrophysics lab during earlier orbits. They agreed that Mark had found a good location for a temporary camp. It was on the southern coastline of the largest continent, ten degrees north of Origin's equator. His bivouac was on a small, flat, coastal lowland at the terminus of a narrow inlet flanked on either side by steep escarpments. The flatland was not far above ocean level at high tide and the beach could easily be reached on foot. The narrow salt water cove led directly south from the beach for a dozen kilometers into a wide bay and finally to the gulf of a great sea. With only Nimbus, its sun, and no moon, and its slowly changing proximity to the globular star cluster, Origin's ocean tides were complicated, possibly unpredictable, but largely inconsequential.

"Even so," Stanley explained offhandedly, "the tides could present some challenges, but that will require further study by our staff and interns. To date, the maximum radar-measured highs and lows of the tides are only from one to one and a half meters. The flatland camp is a good five to six meters above the highest tides. So, respecting the planet's tides, our Astrophysics team tells me that if we locate in that area, we needn't worry about floods."

South of the campsite was the long cove, edged on east and west by kilometers of vertical cliffs. The lowland, where the camp was located, extended north of the inlet for several uneven kilometers in all directions—like a small, gerrymandered district. The camp itself occupied only a fraction of that site. The flatland, as it spread northward into the distance, was itself surrounded by hills and a "forest" of treelike structures just below the two escarpments. There were mountains in the distance. Their peaks did not appear strange from far off, but the many nearby hills looked unusual—like gigantic, lopsided bubbles, domes or middens. Unlike the mountains, they carried no "trees" or other plantlike objects, but their lustrous colors glistened with a beauty of their own.

Another month passed without Stan and his team finding Earth's spacetime coordinates. In the meantime Mark's bivouac gradually grew into a major camp for workers and "visitors." The camp was popular and grew faster than anyone could have expected.

Looking north from the water's edge, the camp was to the left of the beach and close to the cove's west cliff. That protected the camp from the worst of Origin's nightly west winds. For extra protection from the harsh winds, the habitats were sealed, heavily weighted and deeply anchored. The camp could have been closer to the western escarpment except for a forestlike fringe bordering its base. The flatland sloped gently from those "forested" borders down to a dry, meandering drainage channel that steepened sharply as it entered the cove's beach front.

With the planet's mapping completed, the Cone was maneuvered into a stationary position five-hundred kilometers directly above the camp. That facilitated their use of shuttles to and from the camp. The shuttles lacked the speed and maneuverability of Orbs, but had greater carrying capacity for equipment and passengers.

Visitors from the Cone would have come in droves at first, had that been allowed; but it took several weeks to transport all their basic requirements to the surface. That included not only staff, but other "necessities" including their inflation-habitats, cabanas, a compact speedboat-submarine, a medical clinic, a chemistry-geology lab, volleyball nets, other facilities and laboratories, a juke box, tons of food and much more. Then the visitation restrictions were lifted, followed by an avalanche of volunteers to "help out."

Later came an important center—the Mart. It was under the general supervision of one of Doug Groth's creature comfort Managers, a Mr. Floyd Diggins. The Mart held the Bar and Grill Complex and many adjacent facilities: The Honky-tonk Saloon with its popular Dance Hall—whose proprietor, Ms. Snow, was famous for serving special brews of beer and "elixirs," including her very excellent, (despite the labels), "Ms. Snow's Premium Swill" and the ever-in-demand "Ms. Snow's Moonshine." There was also the Palace Movie Screen (called the PMS for short). It was well air conditioned, played ancient movies, had local band concerts on very hot days, encouraged poetry readings and the Acting Guild Players—run by the petulant Martha Snored; the Canteen and Restaurant, (and its attached grocery store holding the Base Camp's tons of frozen food)—run by a Mr. Daniels; The Apothecary, run by Mortimer Pestle; The Exchange (with large quantities of fuel, cement, tons of steel rods to anchor habitats, other hardware, and everything else from intranet wall screens to habitat furniture and parts)—headed by a Mr. Brandt; a beauty-barber shop (with photography consultation thrown in)—run by a Mr. Balz; and the Emporium of Perfect Pizza (called *Mama's* for short, and with the motto, "Yes, We Deliver!")—under Mama Carla. All of these, and a variety of boutiques and kiosks, were assembled within that giant, single-roofed habitat, the Mart, as a kind of mall on the outskirts of the Base Camp.

Oddly, this homely facility, and not just the pleasant sunshine, made everybody want to visit the planet! Well, not so *oddly*. Out there, in the middle of nowhere, aside from the planet's sights and its beach, there was little else of interest.

Various medium-sized structures composed a second center that lay beyond the Mart. That area housed the Administration and Security habitat, the "Ad-Sec." It housed offices, a small jail, storage areas for cots, gun cabinets and a hundred other things. It was a modest facility not far from the Mart's Saloon, and not far from there were other technical and service facilities, clinic and labs.

Between those two centers of activity was a "grassy," parklike area called the *Commons*. It was used for picnics, mass meetings, band concerts and the like. Later on, however, most of those activities took place in *Central Park*. It was less expansive than the Commons, but more convenient to the center of Mark's Camp. In that location they sank a deep well. It yielded all the salt water anyone could ever want. Later it was attached to desalinization equipment and pumps.

Arrangements were made to keep the Cone well staffed and a schedule was set up to assure fair rotation. Clint complained loudly that he could not be responsible for that many "tourists" and couldn't see why anyone would want to go to such a weird place as Origin even for a visit. He was trying to sound *firm* and *objective*, but was enjoying himself too much for that to be credible.

The first "visitors" returning to the Great Cone from Origin brought back vivid descriptions of the rapidly growing camp and its surroundings. Their stories and reports seemed overstated, so few visitors were at first attracted. But as more visitors returned from the planet, the more believable their stories became.

Thus, the migration began. The new visitors had to admit the photos and portrayals of Origin they saw and heard did not begin to touch the reality.

And that reality was dazzling. Origin was visually complicated and strangely beautiful. It had an iridescent sky and a cozy beach. On the ocean the sunsets were cloudless, but nonetheless diverse with colors of fascinating intricacy. In the air were lovely, indescribable scents.

It seemed idyllic and romantic. The newcomers were too enthralled to take seriously the stories of Mark and others about quakes and cave-ins. They resulted, after all, in nothing more than a few sprained ankles, a couple minor concussions and pervasive minor scratches and bruises. Before his scraped elbow had healed, Mark was displaying it to anyone who cared to look. Those were the negatives—along with the absence of fresh water in any of the lakes. But with their salt-removal equipment and tablets, potable water was also "no problem." Finally, the details of Origin's plush "vegetation" and "plant life," as seen from space, turned out to be misleading—but that, surprisingly, became part of the attraction. The "plant life" was not organic.

The "vegetation" was crystalline—even the "trees" were nothing more than minerals. Every square centimeter of the planet's surface was crystalline. Laura made the comment on her first visit to Origin that it was like "a *really big* geode turned inside out!" and "No wonder the Dorts got us to create the Transformation Cone from where we did—the geode must have reminded them of home."

Origin was a dead planet. The lifeless, plantlike objects were at first called planet-oids, and then simply, "plantoids." The omnipresent crystalline *plantoids* resembled, in abstract but reassuring ways, the plant life of home. The objects were in forms resembling Earth's grasses, bushes, trees, vines, and an endless variety of other forms. Their many-colored varieties, highlighted by gradations in translucence, reflective brilliance and prismatic spectrums, were just as dramatic collectively and at a distance as they were individually at close range. The richly changing effects filled the landscape with mysterious auras and disorienting illusions. Accompanying the daylight transit of Nimbus across the sky were diverse and intricate reflections, undulating diffusions and magical halos of light that were, by turns, stimulating and hypnotic.

During the gentle daylight breezes, the gritty plantoids did not rustle or whoosh like trees and plants on Earth; instead their touching, brushing crystals would vibrate or crackle and clink—sometimes like quiet, harmonious windchimes, or with a discordant bang, clatter and crunch. Each plantoid made a variety of sounds at different volumes, except for the always-silent "grasses." Like some tropical forests on Earth, the noise was constant.

At close range, the surface at night was visually tranquil and less confusing than its sounds. Some prismatic plantoids cast a calm, green glow. But across a broad and distant sweep of the crystalline landscape lay the muted reflection of the Galaxy's spiral arms and vivid core. On other nights the starry brilliance of the cluster itself paraded across that same terrain.

Like a small, ever-present moon, the Great Cone was always overhead. Small, reflective bodies sometimes flickered into view as busy shuttles made their way to and from the Transformation. Less frequently, Mark's small Cone could be seen as a speck of light inching its lonely way across the open inlet from the east until it vanished behind the imposing west cliff wall.

But there was a darker side to the night. During the day there was always a slight breeze; but the night winds could become violent, knocking people over, resulting in abrasions and cuts from the surface of crystalline plantoids. Often, day or night, there were small cave-ins causing people to trip and fall. The worst wounds were caused at night when the wind changed direction from the protected west to become a doubly harsh north wind. In the morning, after the boreal storms, Ellen Stone's clinic would be busy with newcomers from the Transformation in need of care for their injuries.

Few managed to avoid some kind of plantoid lesion, including Ellen Stone and Dr. Lufti. Dr. Roger Flanders, who worked in the clinic with Ellen on especially busy days, and her days off, received more nicks and jagged tears than most—usually from adventure climbing on the west cliff. Those who did avoid injuries were very careful, or opted early on to return to the Great Cone. Those who did return, more or less permanently, to the Cone usually did so for a physical or medical reason. Laura Shane, who remained on Origin, was one of the few who scrupulously avoided falling or getting into thick "underbrush," no matter how colorful and tempting. Dr. Stone said nothing about it, but thought it odd that those crystal rips and lacerations in human skin never became infected—even untreated ones. And the healing was fast and scarless. At first she imagined the planet was *deliberately* being *nice* to its guests, but later concluded that since the planet was lifeless, there could be no exogenous microbes to cause infections—so she discounted any idea of benevolent planetary *intensions*.

The night winds had other effects besides scrapes and bruises. Late at night, strong winds could abruptly rouse the camp. Those disruptions were not from the wind alone, but thunderclaps of "trees" splitting in the wind, or the planet's very surface cracking and rupturing like a deep-frozen lake. After particularly noisy nights the flatland would be littered with fresh cracks and potholes from one to several meters across and just as deep. In a few weeks those cracks and holes filled in solidly with new crystalline plantoids.

Judy Olafson, the Transformation's Chief Chemist, teamed up with David Michaels, Head of Geophysics and Mineralogy, to explore and study distant areas on the continent. Together they made overflights in one of the Orbs where David selected several sites for later exploration and core drilling. They often landed and went for a walk. They enjoyed imagining and discussing the scientific challenges that must lie within the hills and mountains, but enjoyed even more each terrain's aesthetic power.

On those distant stops, moving from mountain to mountain and hill to hill, they would often laugh and even *yell*—sometimes for sheer joy. Like children, they were fascinated by the intricacy of certain flowerlike plantoids and even the quality of *echoes* after a good shout.

One morning they invited Laura to join them on one of their visits to the mountains. She armed herself with long sleeves and boots to avoid any minor plantoid scrapes. It was, as usual, a beautiful day and was comfortably cool at the high mountain elevations. They admired the many and varied plantoid colors; especially the types that were rare or nonexistent at the camp site.

From one mountain to the next, the ambiance was always new. They shouted to hear their echoes bouncing between mountains and from valley to valley. They walked varying distances from the Orb on each stop, depending on their mood and the sights to see.

Laura was delighted with these mountain experiences; but most of all with the enhancement of friendship with her two companions.

Standing together on a steep mountain ridge, they marveled at one exceptional vista displaying canyons and mountains for hundreds of kilometers—more breathtaking from there than from the Orb itself.

They were speaking quietly as if in a library or church when a surprising sound made them uncomfortable. Their *quiet* voices were creating echoes. Those *talk echoes* did not, of course, reverberate across the valleys, but did so at close range as if the humans were being mimicked. Their curiosity soon displaced any discomfort. They noticed that certain plantoids mimicked them better than others and returned more complex sounds and vibrations.

Laura crouched beside one of the more "talented" plantoids, saying one or two words. They were becoming amused at the mimicking structures. David tried to make several jokes about this, but his obscure sense of humor failed to amuse anyone but himself.

David said, "I should dig one up and take it back to my habitat—for company when I feel neglected." That idea brought a harsh glance from Judy. Thinking out loud, as usual, he said, "I'll put it in a cage like a parrot."

"Or," Laura said, "like the parakeet I had when I was a little girl."

As David dug up the plantoid, Judy said, "It's not only a *smart* plantoid, it's prettier than most. I think we should give this one a name—for its *species*."

David's eyes brightened and his mouth turned up on one side—a sure sign of "humor" to come. He said, "I've got it! Let's call them *Parrotoids*." Then he bent over in laughter at his own cleverness. Judy just shook her head. None the less, the name would stick.

Laura was still crouched beside one of the newly christened *Parrotoids* and said to it, "Polly wants a cracker." Everyone laughed when that rather complicated phrase, for a mere crystal, was returned with the words coming back more as a complex set of vibrations than as a voice.

Laura was so pleased with the plantoid's response that she forgot her caution and reached out to caress it. It was smooth to her touch—not smooth like a hard, polished surface, but more like velvet. When she looked at her fingers that stroked the *Parrotoid*, they showed a dozen tiny speckles of blood. They did not hurt, so Laura wiped off the blood and gave it no further thought. It was certainly nothing she would bother Ellen about.

They moved farther back from the mountain ridge and began to walk and talk, and just for fun, yell some more, and listened to their echoes.

They yelled especially loud to be distinctly "heard" above the incessant noise of the surrounding plantoids. On the rare occasions that the wind stopped momentarily, there was still an underlying hum of vibrations and residual echoes—all from the plantoids themselves. Were it not just meaningless clatter, one could imagine a rich form of communication was taking place.

On an impulse David, lifting that lip of his, went into a dramatic crouch, pointed across the valley and shouted, "*Look!*" The reverberations of that word came back loud and clear several times.

As Judy and Laura looked where David was pointing they saw nothing special. They asked together, "Where?"

Then, still pointing, David shouted, "*Dort!*" Again the shouted sound resounded in series back and forth between the canyons.

"I don't see any Dorts," said Judy, appearing confused.

This time Laura shook *her* head with an air of superiority. "*Dort*," she said, "is the German word for *there*."

David bent over laughing.

Judy and Laura could only look at him in disgust.

Then Judy turned to Laura and said quietly, even covertly, "He's really a kind and wonderful man, Laura, but I wish he'd give up those 'humor' things. It's such a pain, and he does it all the time. Poor guy. It's embarrassing. I wouldn't feel for him so much if once, just once, he was actually funny. When it comes to humor he's missing whole octaves of brainwaves! Oh well. He finds himself funny enough for all of us. But he makes up for it in a couple other ways. For one thing, he's the most observant person I ever met."

"What's the other way?" Laura asked.

"Never mind!"

Laura strained to hear half of what Judy said. It was hard to hear her over the momentary increase of plantoid noise, but she got the gist of it anyway, especially the last part.

When David settled down, they continued walking for another half-hour. They were enjoying their conversation as Nimbus rose higher in the sky. Judy pulled on Laura's sleeve and pointed her thumb toward David who was a step ahead of them. He was turning his head here and there—enough for them to see another naughty smirk on his face. Laura was about to say something, but was stopped by Judy's look and her finger over her lips. Sure enough, David went into another dramatic, pointing crouch and this time shouted, "*Doyan!*" as loud as he could.

More head shaking, but this time the two women looked at each other and smiled. The whole scene had become too predictable—and David was, of course, bending over, laughing.

He was laughing so hard at this latest, most exceptional clinker, that he had to *gasp* for breath. He opened his mouth wide and, like an apneic sleeper, briefly stopped breathing, turned slightly purple, and then silently closed it again. The mirth was gone. He was completely sober—even intense, with eyes bulging.

Laura was momentarily anxious, until she saw that he was quite all right. Then she started to laugh. "David! You can go ahead and laugh. Don't be so insulted because we don't see anything funny in your humor—*this time*." She added the last two words as a sop for his ego.

But David's expression remained as serious and concentrated as Laura and Judy had ever seen. Then, holding up one hand, he closed his eyes and quietly said, "Listen."

In that gasping moment of silence, David noticed something his companions had not—that his shout had not been returned by an echo. Not one! Only complete silence.

They stood in wonder for several minutes. There was the usual breeze, but still no plantoid sounds.

Laura looked up. Nimbus was directly overhead. She thought that might have caused the silence. She knew that idea was a stretch, but was the best she could come up with just then. David and Judy began talking at once, then all three. Then they shouted some more. Still nothing came back—only a pervasive, dead silence.

Finally, they agreed the silence was just another of Origin's strange phenomena. They decided to simply enjoy the rest of the day and the quiet, and figure it out another day. After all, what harm could a little silence bring?

They were hungry and walked back to the Orb. Even at their present altitude the mountain's atmosphere was becoming very warm. They spread out a blanket, retrieved lunch from the Orb and had a picnic in its shade.

Laura had been comfortable walking in Origin's noonday sun, but became chilly in the shade, and after lunch became sleepy. David and Judy, on the other hand, felt hot and sweaty, but were also tired. They went into the cool of the Orb, and Laura took the blanket into a bright field of "grass" nearby. They agreed to give it an hour before cranking up the Orb for the trip back to Base. The return trip wouldn't take long. They were only seven hundred kilometers from the camp.

Laura fell asleep soon after she spread out the blanket and lay on its soft comfort and felt the warmth of Nimbus on her side.

Laura did not know how long she had been asleep. She was still tired, but opened her eyes—feeling happy. Having moved in her sleep, she was now flat on her stomach with both legs out straight, and her arms reaching in either direction like a soaring bird. Her head was on the blanket facing away from the Orb. At first she did not move, but just lay there enjoying it all. She decided simply to absorb the whole sense of comfort. She lay there—just being.

Very gradually, a quiet, surrounding vibration crept into her consciousness. As it did, coming from *grass of all things*, she tried to focus on it. *Aha*, she thought, *the plantoids are starting to make sounds again. But grass? Let's see. Nimbus has moved away from zenith. I must have been right. I must ask David and Judy if this has happened before. They didn't act like it had. Or maybe it's change of season time. It must be something astronomical. I must ask Stan about that.* On and on she thought. That was her job—and she dozed off.

When she woke again, she was still on the blanket in the midst of the grassoid field. To her knowledge, no one had ever heard a sound from those before. They were still vibrating, she was sure. Curiosity enhanced her listening. The "grass" was beneath and around her blanket. The noise was familiar—a generalized vibrating plantoid sound, only much softer. As she continued to listen, it became more distinct, picking up a rhythmic cadence. Part of the sound was familiar—a thrumming vibration—more like a humming bird or honey bee than an instrument. It was similar, but much more pleasant than the talk vibrations of a Dort. Although the volume did not increase, she seemed to hear more clearly the coordination of sound—a rarity among plantoids, except for brief echoes.

It's my imagination, Laura thought. *It's just a sound, a wordlike sound, repeated over and over, like a chant. A vibrating word? But what word?*

Of course Laura already knew, and had for many minutes, even before she asked herself that question. She would not believe nor accept it. She lay there, continuing to listen, for what seemed like endless time—for another ten minutes—in a state that had turned to distress. The comfort was long gone. Eventually even the denial was gone. She knew the quietly chanted word was not just beside her ear, but was spreading to the "forest" beyond, and into the far off hills and mountains. She now knew it wasn't the grassoids at all. The vibration she heard was not from the surface, but from deep within Origin. She made the firm decision not to share any of this with anyone. It would be a secret—between her and the planet—until she figured out what it meant.

Why, she would ask herself a thousand times, *would the plantoids—and the planet—suddenly become silent, and then, almost imperceptibly, whisper it over and over in my ear, "Doyan . . . Doyan . . . Doyan . . ."?*

The racket from the plantoids was annoying, but drove surprisingly few of the new inhabitants back to the quiet, homey comforts of the Great Cone. Some did return after being spooked by mimicking plantoids. Others returned after suffering seizures caused by the strobelike flickering of the planet's surface reflections. Those with chronic sinus or allergy problems also left the planet *due to the noise*—which Ellen thought to be unusual. Day or night, amidst the many other noises, there were occasional popping sounds from plantoids with bulblike gems at their tips. The gems would explode unpredictably and spread a shimmering carpet of sparkles on the surface, or would be blown away on the breeze like a glittering cloud of fireflies.

Silence, and other normal things, were precious commodities found solely on the water or the beach, in their habitats, or on the Transformation Cone. Only the water and sandy beach were predictably safe from scrapes on bare skin and feet; but even then the sand would become blazing hot when Nimbus climbed above the cove's parapets. After work and on days off, the Earth-like beach, with its relative quiet and refreshing cool water, was the most popular open space on the planet.

THIRTY-TWO

Debra Anderson renamed her newsletter *The FAST News*. She was also proud of the new format. Everyone was reading it. Even the Dorts had a subscription. For one of her lead articles in the new format she surveyed the newcomers to Origin, asking them this question: "How would you describe the planet and your experience on its surface?" After their usual struggle to describe it, they would give up, often adding simply, "You had to be there!"

Studies of all kinds, by every department on and off the planet, had been underway for a month. Working on the planet itself was the usual preference. In fact it became increasingly difficult to persuade crew members to take their turn on the Cone, although this resistance seldom reached the level of insubordination. Little thought was given to understanding why this was happening. Staying on the planet seemed natural to almost everyone. At the same time, and equally misunderstood, cohabitation on Origin was also becoming a problem—not for any moralistic reason, but because people were taking too many "sick days."

Even Laura and Ned were sometimes briefly unavailable, except for evening swims at the inlet, visits to the Honky-tonk Saloon and, of course, meetings. Despite these problems, the scientific and routine tasks of the Transformation, and those for survival on a strange planet, continued to move forward.

Judy Olafson and David Michaels were always involved in a number of projects. Sometimes they would enlist Dr. Stone to collect blood and tissue samples and to assist with their analysis. They were concerned about the effects of some unusual pollutants in the air. In turn, Ellen Stone recruited Dr. Flanders, one of her staff physicians and the Transformation's main biology and genetics expert. Most recently David and Roger Flanders were consulting with the Marine Biology Group. Other combinations of departments, personnel and ad hoc teams were busy in a jungle of their own tasks.

Stanley Lundeen had sinus and allergy problems that he blamed on Origin's *noise* level when he was on the planet. He therefore spent most of his time working from his observatory on the Transformation, along with his department staff—at least the one's he could flog into staying.

Clint and his men frequently returned to the Cone to check on Doyan and the other Dorts, and to maintain security staff rotations. They usually found the Dorts hanging out in the geode—circling high in its sphere. One of Clint's reports described them as ". . . transparent vultures that sometimes wallowed on the geode's surface like pigs in mud." He often tried to question Doyan, but it seldom gave Clint any useful information. It often reminded Clint, and others who might ask questions, that it couldn't remember many things of importance that involved a time aspect, except as such unbidden memories "took the occasion" in its mind. "Whatever that meant!" Clint complained.

"There is one positive thing I will say for Doyan and the rest of the Dorts," Clint said. "They never ask to go to the planet. As if I'd let'm!" he snarled. "When I asked Doyan why that question never came up, it says to me that *we*, not he, will ask for its presence on Origin when the time comes. Fat chance!"

Doug Groth, assisted by his many technicians, made frequent checks on the internal and external status and integrity of the Cone. This was necessary to maintain its position above Mark's Camp and to keep the Cone's atmosphere in shadow and out of deadly Nimbus radiation.

The various teams continued their projects of discovery. Some approached their problem with traditional questions and hypotheses. Others were pure "fishing expeditions,"—literally in the case of the Marine Biology Group. They located no life in any of the waters from the cove to the ocean, although the great reefs they found farther out were perplexing and, like the once-living reefs on Earth, undoubtedly harbored life in the distant past. That was another finding that led only to more questions.

"More questions?" Clint grumble in one meeting. "That's boring! How about some answers for a change? Who cares about core samples, dead reefs, allergy particles and all that crap? There's only one answer we need: The damn coordinates to planet Earth. How about it, Stan? How long you gunna keeping us from the way home?"

Stan was not physically there to receive Clint's challenge, but glowered down from his place on the wall. He was on one of the conference-call screens and very safe on the Transformation Cone. But he still sounded defensive: "Hell, Clint! I haven't even found Earth's sun yet. Don't pick on me. Doyan knows the coordinates—except for its supposedly missing memory that kicks in only when it 'takes the occasion.' So, if it has one somewhere, go jump on *Doyan's* head, not mine." Everybody knew that Clint, in his own way, had already been doing just that. Clint returned a fierce glower of his own to the wall screen, but said nothing more. He already asked his question.

More questions were being asked and discussed in the Honky-tonk Saloon, the habitats all across Mark's Base, in the labs, and on the Transformation Cone.

One question of special interest to Judy, David and Roger related to the variety of dead forms on Origin. In an early Directors meeting, Dr. Flanders expressed it well enough:

"We know that silicone-based life is theoretically possible, and that the old computers—before biocomputers—were functional. But the reality we call 'life' seems to require some kind of circulatory process like the flow of protoplasm, blood, lymph, sap, chlorophyll, and so on. Nothing like that is going on with these plantoids. David, you've sometimes mentioned that these plantlike crystal bundles we call plantoids have weak radiation and electromagnetic activity in them, and that there's nothing new about that. Many planets have magnetic fields; magnetite is magnetic, and radon is a health problem in many underground areas on Earth. But, all in all, none of those crystal bundles meet the criteria for 'life.' Origin itself is just a camouflaged desert masquerading as a living planet. It's deader than any desert on Earth and as lifeless as our moon. That's my take. Don't you agree, David?"

David said, "Well, what 'life' is, is not my area. We know that the bodies of crystals are geometric and can grow and propagate simplistically and in combinations without being alive; but *these* crystals do not grow simplistically like ordinary crystals. They're highly complex.

"Still, I wonder how they keep thriving. They can grow and repair themselves but, when uprooted they crumble—like they're going through a crystal form of rapid biodegradation. The big questions for me are *how* and *why* any of this happens. Why, for instance, do plantoids take their particular forms? Why do 'trees' appear almost identical at short distances from each other and in nearby areas, but have pronounced differences across great distances—as though Mendel's and Darwin's laws were in operation? And how is it that 'trees' that are split by the wind are able to repair themselves in a few days? And why are the 'roots' of the plantoids, even small ones, so *immense* by way of horizontal and vertical extent, complexity, branching and intertwining with other diverse plantoids, like entangled underground bushes? And the smallest crystals within each part of a plantoid—with microscopic billions making up each part of it—why are even they intricate and integrated? It's integration within integration. It goes far beyond the theoretical organization of chaos into elementary, intelligible fractals. Crystals are supposed to be simple! Yet our many microscopic inspections reveal forms of organized complexity not unlike polypeptide protein chains. And why do plantoids always crumble into disorganized, shapeless piles within hours after attempts to 'transplant' them? Why is the atmosphere polluted with such a range of virtually invisible microscopic crystalline combinations?"

Laura said, "Judy, you and Ellen and Roger analyzed David's data. What did you come up with?"

Judy said, "Those microinorganic *airborne* particles, and those within the plantoids, are not only *similar in complexity* to amino acids and primitive proteins, but appeared to be broad-spectrum in nature, possibly imitative of enzymes and hormones—even pheromones. At this early stage we can't specify the human effects, but it's worrisome."

From a number of sites, David's crew retrieved medium-depth core samples, but found nothing like sedimentary rock or sequential layering over time of any kind—only more and more pretty crystals. Due to their structural collapse within hours, they could only be preserved in photographs. Similar core samples from sea drills by the Marine Biology Group had the same results.

Core samples from the dome hills were different. Before that, however, David's preliminary analysis was based on soundings rather than core samples and demonstrated the hills were once hollow, like giant geodes, but had filled in over time. It was one of the few hints, along with ancient dry river beds, night potholes, and the existence of mountains, that there had been any time sequence or measurable chronology of geological events on the continent. There was no handy laboratory way to determine the age of anything he found. Unlike carbon dating of wood or bone, those ancient crystals could not be so dated.

The strange, domelike hills grabbed David's curiosity and started him on the core penetrations. He began near the bases of several distant hills. He hoped to find something, anything, different. He found two that were. After several attempts he was about to move on to other locations when one of the new finding showed up. It was interesting and useful. The other "finding" was a disastrous event.

The first finding came from the deepest extremity of an extracted drill core. It was something organic. And *it* didn't crumble to dust. He set the sample aside and dug for more, but found only a small number of other, slightly different organic specimens. Careful lab analysis several days later showed their likeness to a variety of unknown plants. Carbon 14 dating was useless. The samples were too old. Radiometric dating, however, showed them to be in very ancient company indeed. The plants had died thirteen million years earlier, give or take a couple million. Why they had not mineralized or degraded was a mystery.

The first findings took days to analyze, but the second occurred before then, and quickly. After collecting those core samples from the bases of a number of hills he was devastated by what his drilling had done. The entire *outer crust* of each hill he drilled into crumbled and fell crashing in chunks that piled in a circle around each of the once-beautiful hills. The ugly, deformed inner crystals that filled those once-empty domes were unaffected. Hills were still there all right, but looked like strip-mined Earth landscapes. The remaining dull-gray knolls glistened no more.

To David, the conclusion was obvious. Dome hills could handle sounding probes, but if their exterior crusts are penetrated, then, like uprooted plantoids, they quickly deteriorate and collapse. Privately he simply used the word *die*. The hills collapsed even more rapidly than transplanted *plantoids*. By analogy, he thought, if a plantoid was a single living "organism," as demonstrated by its tendency to '*die*' as a unit, then the crust of a hill—the *whole thing*—was also a single "organism." A particularly fragile one! He added this to his written notes:

"Dome hills are extremely strong and rigid. Their bubble-shaped, crystalline crusts are of varying thickness. They are especially thick where they contact the surface and become progressively thinner toward the apex. They can survive for millions of years—until penetrated or otherwise broken through. Then the brittle crust will crumble within minutes."

It was a mystery to David how such a gigantic, hardened surface could be so solidly and sensitively interconnected that its entire integrity and wholeness would crumble and collapse after an apparently minor violation—after having survived thirteen million years!

Since most of the new results, and the surprising results of researchers in other fields, did not corresponded to anyone's expectations, the logical conclusion was clear. They would simply have to dig deeper. Was that not the way of methodical science? Why, after all, should a few facts interfere with perfectly good theories? Dig deeper they would.

Stanley Lundeen was glad to be back on the Great Cone where he could breathe again—and try to find some answers that were not forthcoming from Doyan. He always tried to dig deeper. Clint and Ned, and now even Mark, had asked Doyan and the other Dorts for the coordinates to Earth. Mark held out the carrot of his *entire* theory in exchange for the information—for the exact spacetime location of Earth. On Earth, Mark had already given Doyan a small *fragment* of his theory—just enough to translate ordinary spacetime into Reo-Sphere coordinates. That fragment was useless without Doyan's prior knowledge (or a last-minute leap to recognition) of the exact location of any particular destination in ordinary spacetime. That fragment of theory was a necessary minimum because the "conversion" from ordinary to Reo-Sphere spacetime was no simple formula—nothing like changing Celsius to Fahrenheit. Doyan's response to the requests for Earth's coordinates was cryptic. It simply could not remember. Doyan repeatedly said its memory for anything important and time related came only in flashes, and that it had *no idea why* that was the case. Trivial facts and major mathematical calculations never seemed to suffer from its memory loss.

Ned and Laura had never heard of such *Dort amnesia* before. Even Laura assumed it was not true. But earlier on Earth, Mark experienced that excuse from Doyan a number of times. He confirmed that the most worthwhile Dort "insights" *did* seem to pop up in a timely way.

Doug reminded everyone that at the time of their arrival above Origin, Doyan's correction of the Cone's spatial position in relation to Nimbus was last minute, but was executed a split second before it would have been too late to prevent its deadly radiation damage. He didn't know if Doyan had planned that well in advance, or miraculously came up with it at the last possible moment. Ned said it was like a *just in time* delivery of materials to 3T Corporation. Everyone was skeptical when they heard of Doyan's flimsy-sounding amnesia excuse, but Clint's all but ear-piercing skepticism went beyond any amount of eye rolling.

So, Stan thought, *it's up to me*. He hoped the loophole imbedded in the otherwise pessimistic speech he gave two months earlier to the Directors had not raised false hopes—or expectations of *him*. He believed that Mark and Doug could deal with the navigation *controls* issue. His job was to solve the *navigation* problem itself. Anyway, he would try. It was his covert project, (and, of course, one that everybody already assumed he would do). He found the whole situation frightening, *should he fail*.

Everyone who visited the planet was mystified by what they saw. Before then, from Stan's offices and observatories on the Great Cone, and with the assistance of his professional staff and students, he'd assessed the main details of Origin's atmosphere, its mass, saltwater content and dozens of other parameters, but could not characterize what looked like widespread foliage cover—if it was vegetation at all. That mystery was not his first.

While working on its maps before any visits were made to Origin, Stan's earliest mystification was the planet's many lakes and waterholes. Why were all the lakes salt water? Even dried-up lakes had salt-white basins. Many were high-ground lakes or natural mountain reservoirs. The continents and islands were veined with dry riverbeds that led to the oceans, saline lakes and salt pans. Even after the Base Camp was well populated, its explorers found nary a fresh water lake or spring. If water had poured into the lakes from surrounding mountains streams and hills, as the existence of riverbeds implied, why were they not freshwater lakes? That question would have been harder to answer if there were clouds to deliver rain, but there were no clouds. Stan considered that an even deeper mystery. Most of Earth's clouds, for example, came from its vast Oceans. Origin's oceans were equally global and immense.

That puzzle he'd dig into later, but for the moment his main focus was on solving the Reo-Space *navigation* issue. That meant finding the *exact* location of Earth, its spacetime coordinates, and after that, with Dr. Tenderloin's or Laura's assistance (now that she was up to speed on Reo-Sphere Theory) determine Earth's Reo-Space coordinates—within its own multiple Reo-Space dimensions. That would save a decade of space travel. Then the return trip home would only depend on a final solution to the Reo-Sphere *controls* issue—the actual mechanics of sending the Cone into its adjacent Reo-Spheres and out again. Even for Stan that didn't sound simple.

Thus far Stan was very sure—well, almost sure—that Earth could be located somewhere within a certain twenty-two thousand cubic parsecs of Galactic space. That, at least, was a start. But for his own selfish edification he'd get Ernst Berman of Mathematics and Statistics to help him. Stan's own astrophysics and mathematics skills were prodigious, but Ernst put him to shame, just as Laura—and now Mark—could overwhelm Ernst. Therefore Ernst needed first to learn from Mark and Laura. Then he could help Stan translate Reo-Space Theory sufficient to produce the true coordinates (if they had them)—for a FAST trip back to Earth. *Okay*, Stan thought, *so I need a little tutoring. But, what the hell, Einstein needed a mathematician's curved-space formulas to nail down his own theory.*

But for now, Stan needed serious privacy to concentrate. To keep his interns and professional staff busy and out of his hair, he put them to work on the globular star cluster itself. He gave them a list of expectations. He wanted to know more about the cluster's dimensions, its tidal truncation and, given its high Galactic orbit, how many transits it had made into and out of the Galaxy. They were to develop a model of the cluster's dynamical evolution as a self-gravitating system, and to estimate the amount of star evaporation from the cluster, either by compressive gravitational shocks as the cluster made its rounds of the Galactic disk or, more likely, from tidal shocks and torquing from its sequential rounds through the bulge, and to find where and when it could have picked up the *Origin System* itself.

Stan figured that, given the cluster's already significant core collapse, being the tightly packed cluster it was, except for hundreds of widely orbiting straggler stars—including the captured *Origin System*—it had already made a fair number of Galactic rounds. It would have become more compact with each round, thanks to tidal stripping, which would also account for the absence of dust, gases, and most of the earliest straggler stars left behind in the Galaxy. He defined the project before them as useful and necessary—but admitted, only to himself, it was also "make work." However, he did honestly believe it was significant enough for an astronomical article in some minor scientific journal—some day.

His entire staff was now focused on the big picture—to discover the cluster's overall evolutionary dynamics. Stan, in turn, was riveted on locating planet Earth—somewhere in the mighty arms of the Milky Way. He realized his plan was *brilliant* and smiled to himself. It was an efficient use of his time, the time of his staff, and, for once, *all* of his Department's considerable resources.

But the plan had one flaw—it left no one to observe, notice or predict Origin's impending cataclysm.

THIRTY-THREE

Laura did not lift her head from the blanket until the rhythmic vibrations became distinct, unintelligible thumps. She sat up to clear her head, but felt the beats through the blanket. Its intensity increased to a point no one could ignore. Even inside the Orb, David and Judy were waked by it. They quickly exited it and called for Laura to return to the Orb, and to hurry.

Laura grabbed the blanket and no sooner had she started running toward them, than hunks of the mountain began caving in. Cavities and fissures were opening everywhere. She jumped and ran in zig zag patterns as she tried to dodge the opening gaps, but another caved in before her as she neared the Orb. She fell headlong into it, bounced hard and ended up on her back screaming in fear and agony. She could hardly move. She only fell a meter, but still could hardly move.

Judy and David stood on the edge of the recess. Laura saw that David was about to jump in to help her up. She said, "Never mind," holding up her palm toward him, "I can make it." She got up off her back and stood, groaning, but still intact. As she reached for David's hand she screamed again as the pit collapsed another third of a meter. David reached way down to grab her hand when the hole gave way another meter, and then another. Laura was now beyond reach and, although she amazingly kept her balance with each new collapse, she was hysterical, and Judy was screaming just as helpfully.

Unexpectedly, Laura became quite calm. She threw the blanket to David. He grabbed one of its corners and let the rest of it drop into Laura's waiting hands. It barely reached. When they both had a good grip on the blanket, he began to pull. Judy joined him and a little progress had been made when the bottom of the hole gave way completely and kept on collapsing like an out of control elevator for a distance that could not even be estimated. No one made a sound. The job was to get Laura up, and then into the Orb.

They hauled her up and when she was safely on the surface, they made a dash for the Orb, but Laura held back. Judy and David were on the ramp to the open hatch when they turned and saw Laura lying on her stomach with her head over the shaft they just pulled her out of.

"What the hell are you doing?" Judy yelled.

"Throwing up—what do you think!"

Soon, however, they were in the air where they hovered briefly to view the continuing devastation, including a yawning new crater in the spot where the Orb had just been resting. Judy gasped, turned the Orb toward the Base and they shot off into the distance.

Halfway back to Mark's Base, Laura broke the icy silence: "Thanks guys. You saved my life."

No response.

Laura continued. "While I was throwing up I heard something."

David couldn't resist. "You heard your barfs coming back at you." He chuckled.

Judy said, "Shut up, David." Then, still angry, she said to Laura, "One more barf and we'd all have gone down that shaft—Orb and all."

David disliked tension. "What did you hear, Laura?"

"Silence and a little clattering as the shaft kept falling, and then . . ."

"Yeah, then what?"

"A really long silence, and—"

"Except for your barfing, of course!" David said, smirking.

"David, let me finish."

"Go."

"After that long silence, the sound was very far away. Very far below. It was a splash. There's a body of water down there."

Judy had been making small navigational adjustments to the Orb when she noticed something. "Damn it, David! Did you turn off the receiver?"

She flipped it on. He was still smiling and said, "It would not have been a good thing for our 'nap' to have been disturbed."

Then his smile vanished and his eyes widened. "My God! The openings and the craters—they're starting to spout!"

As Judy engaged the receiver, an alarm rang and the cabin flashed red. Judy turned all that off and contacted the sending station. It was Transformation Security on Mark's Base.

Clint was fit to be tied, ranting and could not be understood. Judy asked to speak with someone else. The call was turned over to Ned, who had been standing by, pacing.

Ned said firmly, "If you're on a mountain right now, take off immediately!" He went on in that vein for another thirty seconds before stopping to listen to Judy.

"It's okay, Ned. We're on our way back. Some of the mountains out here are beginning to erupt and spout like geysers. What's going on there?"

"Well, er, I don't have the slightest idea, except—"

"What?"

"We've been trying to reach you for over an hour. Are you all okay?"

"All okay—more or less. Why?"

"Then I guess it was a false alarm. All that urgency for nothing. Damn that Doyan! You're kidding about the water spouts, right?"

Laura said, "Let me talk to him!"

Judy handed her the speaker phone.

"What's this about Doyan?"

"Oh nothing. Skip it. Have a good trip back."

"Doyan!" she shouted to Ned. "Details—now!"

"You know how Doyan is. It has this excuse about bad memory for some things, except for last minute insights and time-line flashes of God knows what. Well, yesterday it starts bothering Clint's men to contact the Base immediately, to have everyone evacuate the planet and return to the Transformation Cone. When asked why, it wasn't sure, but to just do it. Naturally, that demand was ignored. Later on—the next day, that's today—one of Clint's men casually mentioned the matter to Stanley at coffee, so Stan went down and spoke with Doyan himself. By then Doyan said it was already too late and that there was no time left to get anyone back to the Transformation Cone that hadn't already left. Then it says to make sure that anyone exploring the hills and mountains or are on the water, should immediately get their butts—Doyan didn't use those exact words—back to Base, and that the oceans and mountains had become dangerous. What an imagination! Then it said for everyone to go into their habitats, hunker down, and stay there.

"On the off chance that Doyan knew something we didn't, Stan called and told us what it said. Then we tried to reach you guys. No answer. So we worried it might be right. Obviously not! *Stan* was skeptical, and I'll go with him any time over Doyan."

"Wrong, Ned!" Laura said. "Take a look at the mountains from where you are. Their peaks and highlands are collapsing. We barely got out with our lives!"

"Oh shit. You're not kidding, are you? Just a sec." Ned went outside and looked, then returned.

"My God! People are standing out there pointing at the cove and the mountains—and looking around for shuttles. The mountains are erupting and spurting, like you said. A few are even caving in. And the water in the cove—it's gone! Doyan was right!"

Laura said, "Yes, and when Doyan says to get inside and hunker down, it means just that. Right or wrong—there's no time for second guessing. So you know what to do!"

"Don't worry," Ned said. "Clint's been listening. It's just the two of us here right now. We'll get everyone to head back to the central Base and their habitats right away. How long before you get here?"

Judy spoke up. "At this rate, another thirty minutes. Five if we hop over the atmosphere."

"Make the hop."

There was a sudden, loud banging on the Security Office door, and someone entered, very upset. It was Jack Lewis. He could also be heard through the Orb's sound system. Jack excitedly explained to Ned and Clint that he and Roger Flanders were spending the day on the submarine assisting the Marine Biology Group. They were stranded in the cove two blocks off the Base's beach.

"We were in the bay just outside the inlet checking a reeflike structure," Jack continued. "Those underwater reef crystals sounded like they were making cadenced sounds—nothing like the echoes and clatter we get up here. But it wasn't any reef noise. The reef itself was quiet and dead as a doornail. The sound came from somewhere else. Anyway, the water current suddenly changed and started to drag our sub out toward the ocean. Just to keep even, we had to put it into a power thrust and, at that, we only crept toward the beach. The outgoing water was that powerful. Then we had to engage the emergency thruster jets, but two blocks from what was the old beach shoreline, we ran out of water! We walked in from there just now. The tide, or whatever, it is, is out. I mean completely out. Except for wet sand, the cove and the entire bay beyond it, is devoid of water. I don't know what's happening. Call Astrophysics and ask Stan what the hell's going on! He should have informed us that something's happening to this planet—hell, *days ago*!"

Three minute later the Orb docked in its station in the Commons near the Ad-Sec habitat. There its three passengers emerged quickly and ran to the habitat. Laura and Ned hugged briefly. Ned asked what happened to her cheek. Laura said, holding up an important forefinger, "It's just a plantoid scrape, but look at these nails! They're a mess, and this one's busted!"

Ned gave it a glance and said, "I'm sorry for your loss."

"Thanks. Now, what about the other Orb and all the shuttles? I didn't see a single one anywhere near the dock."

"They're packed with people on their way to the Cone," Ned said. "The last one left a couple minutes before you got back. They were filling up and leaving before we got the alert from Stan. Doug Groth and a bunch of his techs were on the last one. They must have seen something before Stan's call.

"Ah well," Clint said. "Three more round trips and we'll have everybody back on the Transformation Cone."

Laura frowned. "When we were coming back on the Orb, didn't I hear Ned say that Doyan warned there wasn't enough time left to get everyone back to the Cone?"

Clint said, "We have plenty of time. Maybe some distant mountains are too fragile to hold themselves up, and the tide happens to be out, but that shouldn't affect us—not for a while. There hasn't been so much as a quake here for a couple days. In another twelve to fourteen hours we'll all be long gone from this godforsaken planet and be safe on the Cone. Anyway, this whole business is only a safety and security precaution. Nothing serious is going to happen around here." Clint folded his hands across his chest, looking relaxed and satisfied with his latest in-depth analysis of the situation.

Then Ellen came in and announced that she had closed up the clinic as tightly as possible, and would wait, with Clint, for whatever was to come.

Clint jumped to his feet and shouted angrily, "For Christ's sake, Ellen. I thought I had you on the last Orb to the Cone. Why are you still here? Don't you realize your life is in danger?"

The room became silent, and Clint hung his head. Ellen went over and put her arms around him. "Damn it, Ellen," he said softly, "When will you learn to mind?" Then he hugged her back.

The conference screen flicked on. It was Stan, looking contrite. "I have something to tell you. It's not good news. It's all my fault. I should have known."

"What is it, Stan?" Ned asked.

It's hard to explain. It has to do with wide-orbiting bodies, gravitational torquing, and—"

"Skip all that, Stan. What's the bottom line?"

"I don't know which bottom line I should start with, but here goes:

"First, stay put and hunker down. There is no time to leave, even on the one Orb you have left. If you try, well—it's just too dangerous. I'm glad so many of our people are on their way back to the Cone right now."

Judy interrupted. "Stanley!"

"Yes, Judy."

"Are we about to die?"

"You don't beat around the bush, do you, Judy?"

"No, Stan. So don't you. We have to know."

"You might have a chance in the habitats."

"What are the odds, and what's the threat?"

"The odds aren't good, and the threat is, well, er, drowning, or, um, being crushed."

Laura spoke up. "Gee, Stan. You don't beat around the bush, do you?"

"I'm sorry. The question was asked."

"The odds?" Judy asked.

"Above zero, but not by much. I'm sorry. Just hunker down, okay?" Stan's chin began to quiver.

"No time for last rites yet, Stan," Judy said. "What's the threat? Why drowning? Or getting crushed? What could do that?"

"That gets us to the second bottom line. There's a flood coming."

Ned asked, "Are you talking about a tidal wave or a tsunami?"

"Well, something like that."

"That's bad, but I think our habitats can make it through one of those," Ned said.

"I know," said Stan.

"Then why the poor odds?" asked Judy.

Stan looked more uncomfortable than ever. "If it were just a tsunami the odds would be good. It's worse."

"What could be worse?" Ned asked.

"There's no name for this, Ned. It will be like the entire ocean is hitting you at once. When it reaches you, the habitats will flatten under the pressure. The water will cover all those round-topped hills down there, the foothills of the highest mountains and even most of the lesser mountains."

Judy's toughness was now gone. She choked out the next desperate question. "How about some kind of floatation—a boat or something. A submarine?"

"Anything like that would be shattered and strewn across the planet."

"But couldn't it be that—"

Before Judy could finish, Mark Tenderloin burst into the habitat from outside. His eyes were wild. "There's a wall out there, reaching the sky and blocking out Nimbus. It's still kilometers out in the ocean. It's getting bigger and coming in like a giant tidal bore, and fast!"

Ned looked accusingly at the wall-screen image. "How could this be, Stan?" he asked tartly. "There's nothing like this in nature! How could a planet get into this condition—*without being noticed*?"

Mark heard what he thought was no more than a way too late rhetorical question and said, "Screw it. I just went by and thought to warn you. I'm going back to my habitat right now. It's small, compact, and might be safer than this one. Anyone who wants to come along is welcome." There were no takers. "Good luck, then!" He left, and the door was sealed behind him.

Stanley continued, "I can hardly go on, my friends, but you want to know what's happening. Here's the last bottom line. When this globular cluster picked up the Origin-Nimbus system on it's last round through the bulge of the Galaxy, it picked up more than the two bodies, Origin and Nimbus. It picked up three bodies. Origin was the moon of a *gas giant* twice the size of Jupiter. Origin had never—not before that last round—been a planet. It was a moon."

Judy just sat and shook her head.

Laura asked the obvious question. She wanted the answer before the deluge ended their communication—and their lives. "What's that got to do with the flood, and the mountains falling apart?"

"We only have part of the answer, and my Department is working on the rest. Here is all I can tell you now: On the cluster's last round through the Milky Way, Nimbus's planet, the gas giant, came along too, but in the process was flung far afield from Nimbus, and entered in among the cluster's tidal trail of straggler stars. Origin, in a complex set of gravitational interactions, remained with Nimbus as its new planet. The gas giant was set free to fly in and out of the cluster in a narrow, squeezed orbit through the middle of its stars and black holes. *This* time, like a bat out of hell, it's coming *out* of the cluster and passing Origin at the wrong distance: way too close."

Trying to sound brave and objective, Judy asked, "Is that why the mountains are falling apart?"

"Yes. The mountains—the less-solid ones—are collapsing from that same gravitational shocking and torquing. Oddly, at the same time some mountains are collapsing, more of the round-topped hills have been popping into existence, from out of nowhere. Out of the ground, I guess. They don't push up or grow from the middle like most hills and mountains, but from the sides. We have no idea what's causing that.

"Anyway, the gas giant's gravity pulled all that water out to sea—and now the 'tide' is coming back in and will soon be over Mark's Base and all its habitats. The gas giant, itself, has moved on. But it is still affecting Origin. That influence will become much less over time—fairly rapidly in fact. The inundation will become weaker, and the devastation will subside. The tides will come and go up to a couple times daily, but unpredictably."

"Unpredictable?" Judy whimpered.

"It's complicated with Nimbus and the cluster out there, the gas giant's movement, and Origin's rotation. Anyway, in a month, or two at most—if you hold out that long—the tides will be close to normal again. The worst of it will be over in a couple weeks. After that, the tides will continue to subside, but more gradually."

Judy moaned, "In the meantime, do we have a chance?"

"Any moment the bore of the deluge will be hitting you and—"

At that moment Stan's forlorn expression vanished from the wall screen. It was replaced by an empty, electronic snow.

The group was already in a circle holding hands when the communication ended. In that moment as they looked at each other, there was no fear, only love.

The entire Base Camp shuddered as it fell half a meter, habitats and all, then a meter. Finally it came: *deafening, grinding, crashing, roaring*—and ended suddenly beneath an enveloping cloak of silence—the silence of the deep!

THIRTY-FOUR

A few Directors sat together in one of their nooks on the Transformation Cone. It happened to be the nook that Cameron Greenberg called home. As Director of Social Dynamics, his "home" was an appropriate place for this informal, almost social, get together. Ernst Berman, Head of Mathematics and Statistics was there along with "Reverend" Elmer Slattery, who preferred his role as Recreation Coordinator for the Transformation. But for this crisis he was drafted, for the second time, to be its Funeral Director and Chaplin. Finally, in the center of the room and the groups focus, was Stanley Lundeen, Director of Astrophysics.

They sat listening for an hour to Stan's outpouring of guilt, shame, sorrow and grief, and they each took their own turn in the center of the group's sympathetic focus to express their own feelings. Many of *their* friends, like Stan's, were also left behind to be crushed by the inundation, and those friends were just as dead as Stan's. Similar scenes of sorrow and support were taking place throughout the Transformation.

On their private wall screens, or one of the giant public display screens that lined some of the corridors, everybody watched the ocean as it made its first wholesale shift across Origin's greatest continent. Hundreds watched the destruction and were grateful that they were among the lucky ones on the last shuttles that returned to the Great Cone.

Ernst was more distressed about the flood's consequences than Stan, and less realistic. He said, "I wish Laura and Mark had made it back before the end came. Between us and Doyan—yes, I'm suggesting some help from the Dort—maybe we could undo all of this. You know, make it kind of unhappen."

Stanley shook his head sadly, mostly because of the tragedy below, and partly for Ernst's naiveté. "I too wish there was such a thing as magic, Ernst, but time only goes in one direction—forward."

"No exceptions?" He knew there were some.

"Well, except for neutral kaons and things like that, it can only go forward. What's happened has happened. We all have to accept it—even though, I admit it, at some level I don't believe they're all dead. But if they were not, that would be real magic. It's irrational to believe that real magic could ever happen," Stan concluded.

Slattery and Greenberg nodded in agreement.

"But you know better—than to believe in magic."

"I'm afraid so, Ernst," Stan replied.

"You are, of course, right. But . . ."

"What?"

"Well, if neutral kaons can do it, then . . ."

"What?"

"Then maybe it's not magic."

"Excuse me," Slattery interrupted, becoming a bit upset, "what are neutral kaons?"

"*Sorry Reverend*, I shouldn't have mentioned them in the first place," Stan said. "They're just elementary particles, a type of K-meson. They have some hard to figure out properties. They're about half the weight of a proton. They can interact and turn into a lot of other simple junk. It's a particle physics and mathematics ... *thing*. Simple junk like that works just as well backwards in time as it does forward, they say, but when things get really real, they get more complicated. When we get to really big stuff, like molecules, or even just atoms, then the arrow of time only goes forward. Period."

Elmer—who hated being called Reverend—looked bemused. "I have no idea what you just said."

Stan took a deep breath. "Neutral kaons are simple. They might, in theory, be able to make short trips backwards in time. Only the faithful say they're absolutely sure that the simple junk can do that. I'm agnostic on the matter, I'm not sure."

Ernst joined in again. His tone was confident: "Was Laura sure of it?"

"Yes. She's one of the faithful."

Ernst lifted his chin and said, "If Laura believed that simple junk could go back in time, then I believe it. So, to repeat, if neutral kaons can do it, then why not the complicated stuff? So then—"

"Then what?" Stan asked sharply.

"Then it might be worth a chat with Doyan. The Dorts *did* bring us the early version of Transformation Theory. They couldn't be complete dolts about this. Maybe we could all go and have a talk with Doyan." Ernst raised his bushy eyebrows in anticipation of Stan's response.

"It would be fruitless. Pointless."

Berman dug in: "Can't you forget you're a doubting astrophysicist, even after all that has happened to our friends?"

"That's not fair, Ernst. Just because you're a mathematician doesn't make you a physicist."

"Just because you're an astrophysicist doesn't make you a particle physicist!"

Greenberg coughed.

Ernst's eyebrows were still up, waiting.

Stan softened, but in a way that verged on condescension, even under the circumstances. "Well, all right," he said, "I have work to do, but I also have some questions for Doyan—like how," he said, momentarily forgetting his guilt, "it knew about the danger to Origin *and* our friends before we did, and why it didn't inform us in a timely manner."

Berman lowered his brows and looked thoughtful. "I think it did. We just didn't—"

Cameron Greenberg diplomatically coughed again—clearing his throat of cigar smoke. He then added, "Well then—a chat with Doyan. I'd be for that."

Stan turned red and looked at the floor. "I'd rather not do it today." *Damn!* he thought. *Here I am blaming Doyan for something I should have been on top of.* "Would tomorrow suit the rest of you?"

They agreed. At one o'clock the following day they would have that pointless, fruitless discussion with Doyan about neutral kaons, the laws of nature, Dort amnesia and memory (the kind that flickers off and on *just in time*), but, unfortunately, not this time—thanks to, well, circumstances.

Stan said he would plan an agenda for the next day's meeting and send a copy to Doyan—if that met everyone's approval. The Dort was not consulted.

"Tomorrow is fine," said Elmer Slattery. "I have a job of planning to do myself." They all knew it was the job he hated most—making preparations for another mass funeral.

Elmer Slattery dropped into the Astrophysics lab early the next morning. Stan was already deep in consultation with his staff and interns about how the whole matter got screwed up. Coming after the tragedy, it was called a *post mortem* assessment. Elmer briefly stated the reason for his visit and was told that was one of the purposes for the staff meeting so he was invited to sit in.

The meeting was over Elmer's head, but the informative details he needed were there to meet his narrow purpose—along with other details he would rather not have known. After a while he wished he was somewhere else. *His* information could have come later.

From the meeting he learned that several weeks earlier Stan's staff and interns followed through on the assignment they'd been given—namely to determine the globular cluster's dynamical evolution. Well into that process, a week before the flood, the Nimbus system's identity was itself revealed in virtually full detail—except for one small calculation that came to their notice a week later.

Getting details of the Origin system was the smallest part of the "*big assignment*" Stan gave to his staff of astronomers, astrophysicists and student interns. A "*small assignment*" was turned over to the interns who were immediately enthusiastic about it. Their part of the project, being only a small piece of the overall puzzle, was one they believed they could handle. They went after it mainly on their own, under the token attention and supervision of their immediate field instructor—Stan's most junior astrophysicist.

The students' reviewed the early data that came in with the numerous professionally derived studies showing Origin's relationship to a not yet seen gas giant. That created a problem for them. It didn't "feel" right. Origin was described as the gas giant's moon, but Origin was a planet. It couldn't have been a moon, and then become a planet. That feeling led to their complete rejection of the conclusion announcing it—even though it had all been obtained and analyzed to that point by Stan's *so called* professional astronomers and astrophysicists.

They would, therefore, begin again, realizing their graduate school grades for the year depended on a credible performance—assuming, of course, that they might some day get back to Earth. There they could cash in on a good evaluation.

To their surprise and chagrin, the new data they obtained, using entirely different theoretical assumptions and formulae, led to the same descriptive conclusions they had rejected.

They had wasted several days on that and were totally frustrated. Finally they called in their instructor. She looked over the data they were using, the hypotheses and processes the interns had developed, said to them it was creative and accurate from her quick perusal, and gave them the okay to investigate matters further. They were assured that, although their findings would often seem counter intuitive, they should always follow the model and the data to see where it would lead. They could now continue, but this time they would project their analysis into the future.

In the *post mortem* the students admitted that when the instructor left, they threw their arms around each other for joy—not perfect joy, but so-far-so-good joy.

Using a modified theory of their own and the already-collected data from Stan's professionals, they went on to rediscover the gas giant's narrow, but extended orbit around and through the cluster. Surprise, surprise! The astronomers and astrophysicists had nailed that one too. Their shaky confidence in the professionals was starting to improve.

They estimated the gas giant made a complete cycle of the cluster once every 13.390426 million years. That was new. Now they were really on their own. In theory, the next exit of the giant from the cluster in the direction of Origin would be soon—probably in the next thousand years or so. Later on they would figure out the exact date for that—when they had more data and actually located the gas giant. They knew it was there, in the vastness of "their" globular cluster.

They were about to begin that search, but the powerful telescopes and other instruments needed to accomplish that were not available. Those were being used by the *real* scientists who could not part with the instruments and their precious allotted time on them—which, taken together, was all the time.

Undaunted, the interns continued to use everyone else's data, no matter how irrelevant, to screen for what might be, and to supplement that with their own models *and* the most tried and true theories and formulae. Circumstances had forced them to do that from the beginning.

With the next request for supervisory comment, her evaluation was moderately skeptical. From an off-the-cuff calculation based on a quick perusal of the interns' report, she believed they overestimated the gas giant's cycle time. Still, she patted them on the head and gave them an exercise to perform. (She said it would help them with their group grade, and smiled indulgently.) They were to plug in a range of hypothetical dates for the gas giant's emergence from the main body of the cluster and assess its gravitational effects on Nimbus and, for that matter, on Origin.

The students caucused to decide on a series of dates to study. They already knew about where the giant would emerge from the cluster, its rate of speed—

about sixteen-thousand kilometers per hour—knowing there could be a slingshot effect from red giants and a couple black holes on the Origin side of the cluster, and its trajectory and proximity to Origin's orbit around Nimbus.

To simplify the project and make it more manageable, and exciting, they excluded all the date ranges where Origin's orbit would take it far from any meaningful proximity to the gas giant's passage. That focus would give the data a scary touch! And, just for fun, they picked a range of dates that started *the very next day*, because Origin's orbit and location in it happened to be in a vulnerable place for such an encounter. After picking that date for their first swing at the instructor-assigned exercise, they admitted in Stan's *post mortem* meeting to some embarrassment because they'd all laughed, realizing it would be too much of a coincidence for all the bad things to happen just then.

They found that, at worst, a gravitational pull from the gas giant would force Origin's ocean water onto the two continents—enough to cover most of their foothills and minor mountains. That was part one of the bad news. (Even the good news didn't sound that good. It was that the gas giant's passage would not be close enough to pull away more than a quarter of the upper atmosphere.)

Part two of the bad news, the part that Elmer was waiting for, was that the ocean would create a long-lasting *series* of floods. At sea level, the location of Mark's Base, the monster tides would not "permanently" recede for at least another month or two, depending on the definition of *recede*. The students spent a lot of time in controversy over that definition. They finally decided that *recede* would mean the water's first day of movement back to sea level where further high and low tides would be no more than four meters from high point to low point. It remained controversial because the tides would still not have settled down to their previous insignificance—not until the gas giant moved itself and its gravity very far from Origin.

But they dropped that discussion and called in their instructor for her next critique of their methods and interim conclusions. If that passed muster, they would then proceed to other hypothetical dates. She was busy and could not meet with the interns until the next day.

This time she reviewed their project in detail, becoming increasingly frantic as she approached its final conclusion. Without a word to the students she grabbed all the papers and went to Stan. The tragedy was virtually at hand and no one had yet seen the gas giant. First, they weren't looking for it, and second, it was all but invisible. It was only a planet, a less than noticeable resident of the bright cluster. But the students' calculations demonstrated how fast and far it had been flung from the cluster's core. It was now in the direct radiance of Nimbus and could be seen with the naked eye.

Stan immediately alerted his staff. In two minutes the giant was found, right where the students' first interpolation projected it to be. But the discovery was late. That is when Stan put in the call to Origin—a call soon terminated by the flood. Stan lamented being cut off before he could tell them he had found very close coordinates for Earth. Then they could have died knowing their friends on the Transformation could make it back.

For the "Reverend's" purposes, the *post mortem* told him all he needed to know: The bodies would be swept far and wide across the planet. The giant surge would come and go many times with Origin's rotation. Even after the tides had receded, there would be no point in looking for remains. This time, with no real corpses, there would be no dignified mass funeral with the bodies being cast into space. The service would be on the Transformation Cone, with the deceased in absentia—save their spirits.

THIRTY-FIVE

The four men sat uncomfortably on a row of boulder-size crystals jutting from the geode's inner surface. They faced Doyan and six other identical Dorts, rippling as they settled in to form a close-range semicircle before the men.

Wide-eyed and nervous, Elmer said, "Hey Stan, how come Doug didn't join us for this?"

Stan looked relieved at the question. "Groth said he'd be busy getting the Cone ready for our Transformation out of here. It should be ready before the funeral, as we asked."

"Right. I sometimes forget how much work that involves," Elmer said.

"Besides," Stan said in a lowered tone, as if the Dorts could not hear him, "Doug is uncomfortable around Dorts right now. That's understandable, but we have a reason for being here. He should have made the time."

Their own discomfort was not so much from the hard seating as with their growing mix of feelings against the Dorts: distrust, hostility, apprehension, fear.

Distrust of Dorts was old news and had existed for centuries. It was a generalized, historical paranoia; but the hostility had become more acute. It was there before, and especially since the Twister.

The apprehension was their childlike need for magic answers and solutions—knowing they could never be fulfilled. Nonetheless, in the unlikely event something worthwhile might emerge from their coming together, Stan included a postscript to the agenda he submitted to Doyan. It stated that he planned a holographic recording of the meeting. If Doyan objected to that, it was to say so. Doyan made no objection; but there was a request: That Cameron show respect by not smoking his cigars in the geode.

Their most immediate feeling, as they sat on the crystals, was uneasiness verging on fear. Never before had any of these men encountered, at one time, more than a single Dort. Before them now, at close range, were seven gigantic, potentially superhuman, translucent, cunning beyond brilliant, nonhuman, sluglike, undulating blobs with their recent history of hijacking and mass murder. That was bad enough, but for Elmer, the worst was *no eye contact*—any eyes and other organs were indiscernible or simply did not exist.

Cameron Greenberg turned to the other men and wondered aloud why they were meeting with *all* the Dorts that were still alive after the Twister. Why not with Doyan by itself?

"That was my idea," said the Dort in the middle. "When Dr. Lundeen's agenda was received, it seemed appropriate that we all be here. Our individual memories and abilities are adequate for most purposes; but for deep ancestral background, primordial origins, refolding the unfolding the blossom you identify as time, our merged consciousness is essential. The Twister that translated our many back to the precausal has fragmented not only our numbers, but the transparency of our channel to the power of our unitary totality. Some items in Dr. Lundeen's agenda will need our merged consciousness. At that, it is unlikely to be enough—we are now so few. "

Ernst Berman said, "Jesus, Stan! You asked about *refolding and unfolding a blossom of time*? What kind of an agenda did you send, anyway?"

"Nothing that complex," Stan replied sardonically. "Just the simple stuff you wanted when we talked yesterday. Like, how to turn back time to save everyone killed in the flood, and a few other things. The *'folding'* terminology is the Dort's, not mine."

"Oh."

Elmer Slattery looked directly at the Dort in the middle that had been speaking. "I take it that you are Doyan."

"No," replied the Dort on their far left. "I am Doyan."

Still looking at the Dort in the middle, Elmer said, "I thought Doyan was the spokesthing for Dorts. I guess I'll just call you *Translucent Thing*, if that's all right."

"Of course, spokesthing for humans," replied Translucent Thing, "and I will just call you *Opaque Thing*, if that's all right."

For some reason this crude exchange of insensitivities seemed to break the tension. All the Opaque Things laughed aloud—especially Elmer Slattery. And there was a noticeable—*barely* noticeable—undulation across the seven Translucents.

They could now begin.

Hours later, in the Astrophysics lab, the four men entered Stan's office. Cameron had already lit his cigar and was ready for their visit. Elmer, the first to speak, expressed the others' thoughts: "That was the strangest meeting I've ever been in. It was a bitch to follow." But he lost some of Berman's and Lundeen's agreement when he added, "The Dorts spoke English, sort of, but it was over my head. When they began the math and physics talk, I knew that all they were saying was bullshit. They're masters of the snow job! Never give straight answers."

Stan said, "It wasn't all bullshit. I managed to keep up with most of the physics and cosmology, but then it slipped into concepts I could barely understand. From what I did follow, and by guessing at the rest, it is their view that the *future of this universe* is bound to all the others—what Mark calls the interlinked Reo-Spheres—and that the permanent demise of any such linked universe, spells the demise of all the rest."

"Even I got that part, from between their lines of course, but who cares?" Reverend Slattery stated. "I know about entropy and the universe expanding at an increasing rate and that that will destroy the universe in the end. We all learned that in kindergarten. It's still common knowledge that that destruction is *billions* of years off. What kind of an ethic would lead any normal person to worry about something so distant?—or cause a feeling of guilt for doing nothing about it? Nothing could be done anyway. As the redshift spectrum lines get more crowded, it makes no practical difference. It just means the galaxies are moving away from each other very fast, thanks to the stretching of space. To hear the Dorts talk, they feel—if they feel anything at all—responsible! Silliest thing I ever heard of! They'd like the universe to stop expanding and start blueshifting. They want an implosion, a *Big Crunch*. Hell, that would be as deadly to the universe as what we've already got—an inexorable expansion. It's looking more and more like a nonstop explosion. But we're still talking about an event that's eons off, so who cares if the universe is expanding into oblivion? It's too far off to be of any importance to our great-grandchildren, or theirs. To consider the distant demise of the universe serves no purpose except, I suppose, philosophical amusement. I won't start worrying about all that flying-apart stuff until the *insides* of the galaxies actually do that, or the stars start blowing up, or the planets, or molecules explode, or whatever! Before then, I won't worry. Not about that anyway. How about you, Ernst?"

The mathematician looked up at Elmer through his thatch of brows and said, "To answer, I can only repeat the brilliant words of an ancient philosopher: 'What? Me worry?'"

"I'm glad you agree."

Stan said, "Yes Elmer, redshift or blueshift, either one would be just as deadly to our universe, no matter when it comes—and maybe just as deadly to any other universes if they are interdependent and interconnected to ours."

"Yeah, right! But that's a big *if*." Slattery said. "Like we *know* there are other universes—but we *don't*. I haven't seen one. Nobody has. Postulating 'Reo-Spheres' doesn't make them so, even if the math seems to work at some level. Anyway, we shouldn't be talking about things 'according to the Dorts.' They changed our meeting's agenda. They're all message and no motivation—just a bunch of reflexes. Smart reflexes, admittedly, but reflexes. Our meeting with the Dorts was baffling. They changed the subject. I didn't get their point. They immediately rejected the possibility of reversing time for anything bigger than kaons and the like. So what *was* their message? We're just guessing at that—from between their lines, of all things! After throwing out our kaon questions, the agenda became theirs! They manipulated the content and we just went along. What's their real motivation? Well, I'll tell you—they have none. Theirs is no more than the motivation of a bunch of reflexes—including sudden, unexpected recall of important matters! That sounds like reflexes to me."

Stan said, "Good questions, Elmer. I can't speak to their real motivations, only to the content of what they said, including, as you said, 'from between their lines.'"

"Okay," Elmer said, simmering down, "what about the content?"

"For a new universe to be reborn from this one, the Dorts appear to be seeking the formula for that—a way to turn around the redshift we're in and start a blue one. They want a Big Crunch to get started. No blueshift, no Crunch. A blueshift would set the fuse for a new Big Bang. That would ignite a new sequence in spacetime. But, as you say, Elmer, who cares and why bother? I have no idea why it is so important to the Dorts?" Then Stan shrugged and looked meaningfully at their resident anthropologist.

Until then Cameron Greenberg had only been listening, but now crushed out the glowing remains of his cigar and lit the next. He said, "You'll have to dig damn deep between all those lines for an answer to that one. Their culture, what little I saw of it in that meeting, was a dutiful—Elmer might call it reflexive—focus on the science, physics and math as related to what became *their* agenda for the meeting and their temporally distant perspective. But I couldn't begin to follow the math. What do you think, Ernst?"

Berman waggled his bushy brows and began. "I thought the Dorts were rather clear on that—or maybe it was just me. They seem to believe that rebirth of the universe will be necessary in order to restore *the loss of what is important*, especially if the expansion moves faster and becomes a *Big Rip*—a theory that's been around since the ancients."

Elmer frowned. "Loss of what? What do they think is important? Please tell us, if you think they were so clear."

"The loss of their, and our, essence—and the essence of everything, of whatever is."

Elmer's reactions were not always predictable or appropriate. This time he raised more than Berman's eyebrows. He slammed his fist on the table and declared, "The Dorts don't have a *clue* about the Bible? Ancient historians called that 'New Age' theory and 'Eastern philosophy.'" Then he slammed his fist down again.

Cameron said, "Call it what you want, Elmer, the Dorts seem to believe they're talking science. And it has to scare them—if they have any such emotion."

Ernst Berman said, "Yes, Cam, and a bit more. For them, there are a couple scary parts:

"First, that *this* universe is the *key*. They believe in many universes, Elmer, even if you or I don't. I do. They're saying between the lines that this one has to get fixed, or else."

"Or else what?" Elmer asked.

"Or else everything goes to hell, literally," Ernst said.

"Meaning what? What goes to hell? What hell?"

"What goes to hell? They do, we do, and all the existent and potential universes around us—not just ours. It will end all life and matter. It will dissolve the generative vacuum itself. Worst of all, it will irreversibly end all consciousness. It will end all future and past—every thing, every where, and every when."

Slattery looked a bit skeptical and angry. "That's the Dorts' idea of *hell*, then?"

"That's what it sounded like to me. You wanted something worse?"

Elmer started to slam his fist on the table again, but opened it and stopped in midswing as if, without warning, he remembered something. He slowly lowered his hand the rest of the way to the table and brushed imaginary crumbs away from its surface before calmly asking, "What was the other scary part of the Dorts' message, Ernst? You said there was a couple."

"Okay. The other scary part. It gets a little technical. We could skip it. I don't know if I can explain it in term you'll understand. It's the Dort's reinterpretation of the redshift, of the acceleration and expansion of the universe—the one you learned about in kindergarten. I don't believe everything they say, but that reinterpretation seems to be right about one crucial thing: That acceleration is itself accelerating. And even that is starting to increase. Are you absolutely sure, Elmer, that you want to hear the rest of this? It's a lot of math and physics—and the bottom line is scary!"

"No, I'll pass on the details. I'm sorry, I shouldn't have asked. I'll probably be sorrier later. Just give me the bottom line."

"Sure thing," Berman said. "Here's the bottom line: We're not talking about your 'billions of years' any more, Elmer. We're talking only six or eight generations off, if not sooner, before the acceleration reaches its blow-apart crescendo."

"So soon? How come?" Elmer asked uneasily.

"That's more into particle physics than I can explain. Ask the real physicist."

"Okay, Stan. How come so soon? Bottom lines only," Elmer said.

Stan replied thoughtfully, "Hmm. Why so soon? Well, we did get to some of *our* agenda in the meeting. It's so soon because of gravity, the wrong kind of gravity, negative gravity—and that's coming from neutral *trions*. They're the dark matter particles of our universe. Their numbers are increasing exponentially. There are no Higgs particles—none could be found. You learned that in kindergarten. That negative finding was predicted from the Win-Field Diagrams, the WDs, before CERN's bad luck trying to find it. It's ancient history now. They kept interpreting their early findings as proof *for* the existence of Higgs particles only to prove themselves wrong years later. They eventually went back to the WDs for perspective and made that great experimental discovery—the one that made Transformations possible—*trions*! The Dorts had that one right. Anyway, later on they found several types of trions—all predicted in the ancient WDs. Three trions are *neutral*. One is an up-triplect trion, one a down-triplectic trion and one an electron triplect. They're all massive—more massive than the top quark, even heavier, in fact, than the Z particle—but the up-trion is more massive than the others; their gravitational effects are opposite. Some radiate great gravitational pull, but up-trions radiate the opposite—*great* negative gravity, or anti-gravity, and therefore *they push away from each other*. That's the engine that causes spatial expansion in this universe. Not only that—"

"—*Stop*! Enough on the details," Elmer said.

"Of course, Reverend. But first let me just tell you this. The Dorts explained something we feared for a long time—that up-trions, the bad guys let's call'm, are overwhelming the production of the positive gravitational trions—the ones that hold galaxies together. But they're *losing* to the bad guys. The electrically neutral ones are in the largest numbers, but the negative-gravity trions are *winning* the battle. They're radiating most of the gravitational *push*. They're stable, massive, nonbaryonic, weakly interactive, fundamental fermions. Those, they say, will cause our ultimate, not too distant, redshift destruction. If true, and here's the bottom line, *it will be a mess*."

"I was right. I shouldn't have asked."

Cameron Greenberg said, "A mess, all right, but I got the feeling the Dorts believe they can fix the mess. Even if they could perform that impossible feat, why kidnap us and drag us to this part of the Galaxy? It makes no sense."

"Yes," said Berman, "and we have paid dearly in human lives for their belief—and their sense of urgency."

"And so have they, I'm glad to say," said Elmer. "That was their choice, not ours. And what was that business about their coming from, *and still being in*, one of those other universes? I didn't follow that. They can't be in two places at the same time."

"No, they can't," Ernst agreed, "depending on what 'same time' means. Their claim was, to the best I could follow it, that they are only here, in this universe, now; and in another one now, and here now, and so on. I can't explain it, but they did in physical/mathematical terms that had a rather compelling logic. Their existence *here*, in theory at least, is out of phase—but not by much—with what we call current time."

"I'm glad you could follow that, Ernst," Stan said. "It got a bit beyond me, but the ideas, if true, could explain a lot about the Dorts we couldn't begin to understand before. For instance, we have never been able to measure their mass, or they could create mass in themselves and vary it at will. They may not, with all their changing time jumps and lags, even have mass as we know it; and we have never been able to make any assessment of their internal organs, if any, by any kind of scan. Nor have we been able to assess their range of strengths. My God, their strengths! Their large pseudopodal strength has saved many lives—in earthquakes and other disasters. Ned's research shows that, over the centuries, they've saved more lives than he could count. Yet they have been hated—because of being so different, I suppose. Anyway, they would help if they happened to be in the right place at the right time. Disasters or not, they have been invulnerable, even in the most horrendous accidents."

"Not entirely invulnerable, Stan," Greenberg remarked.

"You're right, Cameron. But, until now, they've been virtually eternal. Black hole Twisters must rip up their anchorage in this now, and that other now—or however it is that they go back and forth. They must be in constant flux, being *there* for a millisecond, then *here* the next—on a quick round-trip in time. How else could they have traveled across space from this Galactic cluster all the way to Earth, a trip of over fifty-eight thousand light years, without there being something special about them? Back then, when they first came to Earth, their technology wasn't that good. They couldn't have traveled much over half the speed of light. From our point of view, that makes them very old. With their popping in and out and back and forth in time and place, they could have made the trip in less than five or six subjective minutes—due to continuous short-term time backtracking. Who could know? They could solve impossibly lengthy mathematical problems by going in the other direction—by taking a hundred subjective years to work on the problem, but present the answer to us in what looked like a millisecond. In one experiment by Dietzman's group, they presented the answer *before* the key elements of the problem were presented."

"But," Stan said, "for them, that wasn't enough. Not enough to—I can hardly bring myself to say this out loud—to save the universe. It blew me away when they laid that out. They seem to need Laura or Mark, or creatures of similar lights to achieve—what? Their ends?"

Elmer wasn't keeping up. He looked confused. "What do you mean, *they are virtually eternal and they may not have mass*? How could they have lifted bridges off of cars and things like that without being made of matter?"

"How should I know what I mean?" Stan said. "It's just my impression of what I heard them say."

"Okay then, I need more of what you think you heard, Stan, because right now I'm not getting it."

"By *eternal*—my word, Elmer, not theirs—they seem to believe they do not exist in spacetime. They do exist, but they are also illusions. As for doing physical things beyond possibility, they didn't go into it, so I couldn't give you their explanation. But I do have some ideas about that—on the order of how they calculate faster than our fastest bio-nano-computers. Who knows? None of this is clear. But those things are not important right now."

"Nothing's clear?"

"Except for one thing. One thing is clear. In fact, several things are becoming less fuzzy. The Dorts are vulnerable in more ways than one. And they are limited in some ways. Their *type* of intelligence must be limited in important ways; otherwise they wouldn't have searched the universe for creatures like humans. For some reason they need us, and not just Laura and Mark. Now they've lost both of them in the flood. Right now they should be in a Dort version of *frantic*, but they aren't. They can be blinded by a reality they don't like." Stan took a deep breath.

"What, for example, makes you think that?" Cameron asked.

"For example," Stan answered, "they are in denial of the tragedy that just took place on Origin. Everybody that was left on the planet is dead. The Dorts don't accept that reality. When they called for everybody on the planet to return to Mark's Base camp and hunker down in their shelters, they said the humans would be safe. They believed that in the midst of the flood, and they believe that now. They believe our people are safe—somewhere. They are delusional."

"That," Berman said, "was in plain enough English to prove their stupidity to anyone—at least on that subject. The intellectually irresponsible part that Doyan said about *suddenly* remembering that it would be safe for them in Base camp made me want to get up and slug it. Especially when it said it didn't know the details of why they would be safe, but that it was certain, and there would be other *more significant* things to come after the waters receded to their old levels. He couldn't explain that either. Huh! Like there was something more significant than the death of our people. This is the second time that we've lost so many, and the Dorts still take the same matter-of-fact attitude—like the death of our people wasn't significant."

Cameron said, "It sounded to me like when they arrived in this universe, however many millions of our years ago—Hey! I'm getting the hang of talking this way!—and however that was done, they ended up on Origin when it was still a moon of Nimbus's gas-giant planet in the bulge of the Milky Way. Was that imposed or was it a random planet selection? Why didn't they just pick Earth to start with? Assuming they couldn't *select* their spot, how did they find Earth? Even at the speed of radio waves there wasn't enough time from the invention of the radio till they left Origin for them to have picked up any signals we might have sent. There has to be another explanation for their arrival on Earth. And how did the descendents of the growing organic things become growing crystal things? They said that when they arrived on Origin they did a kind of '*terraforming*' because it—a 'moon' then—was without plants and inert; and that they, the Dorts, were also organic, but are no longer. As Laura has been fond of saying, 'My God, what are they?' Anyway, I still don't get that. Especially when they say that the organic things from their earliest existence, including them, had an entirely different kind of mechanism for being, one that is *unlike* DNA, but with similar outcomes. The Dorts have said that without our 'junk DNA' we would look like them—whatever that meant. Anyway, to me Origin is just a bunch of fake plants that are really crystals! In that context, they also said something about *bubbles*."

Ernst Berman perked up. He had been deep in thought, but this comment caught his attention. "Yes! The bubbles!" he said, raising a bony finger and his great eyebrows. "The Dorts weren't talking about the names of chorus dancers. They meant the round, bubblelike hills. David Michaels found something he thought was important in some of those hills—the ancient remains of something organic. At least it was carbon. He thought it might have been a tree, but there was no way to be sure. He dated it back about thirteen million years. The hills became preserving containers or coffins for whatever it was. How something like a tree managed to get inside one of those hills is a mystery. David found other examples in the bases of several hills—but nowhere else."

"Hmm!"

"What's the 'Hmm' about, Stan?" Ernst asked.

"Maybe the mystery is not how the 'trees' got into the bubble hills, but how the hills crushed the trees?"

"Whatever," Cameron said. "What's your point?"

Stan dodged the question. He said, "Maybe Doyan and the other Dorts can't turn time back and forth, but some of their last minute, unexpected pronouncements have been accurate—if Doyan's are typical. Could those pronouncements be 'hard wired,' do you suppose, into their nature like instinctive animal or insect behavior—coming from whatever connection they have with this or other universes—even if their exemplar, Doyan, doesn't know where they come from or why they are accurate?"

"Like I said," Elmer responded, "—*reflexes*!"

Ernst said, "Unfortunately its *pronouncement* wasn't accurate this time, so what are you trying to say? And more important, *why are they telling us this now?*"

Stan looked at his watch and shrugged. "I don't know, but I have a strange feeling." He then reached for the intercom to raise one of the graduate students. While waiting, he responded to Ernst. "For some reason the Dorts are opening up as never before. I believe they no longer think their plans can be undermined, with or without our cooperation. They may believe they had us here for a reason, and now their mission is all but accomplished—not saving the universe, but whatever our part in that might have been."

One of the interns finally answered. Stan said, in a chatty way, "Hi, Margaret. We'll need some pictures. The first major pullback of Origin's flood should be in evidence where Mark's Base used to be. Would you take a look down there with one of our telescopes and see if anything is still there—anything identifiable, like the remnants of a habitat—anything. Take pictures of the site, and then bring the photographs here. There are four of us. We'll all want hard copies. We'd like to have them soon."

"That's kind of what we've been thinking," Margaret said. "Before the photos are printed, should I give you a live feed on your office screen?"

"Good idea. Depressing idea, but yes, do it. Thanks."

"Well, fellas," Stan said after closing with the student, "one last look at Mark's Base will be the saddest sight we'll ever see. The Dorts couldn't provide the coordinates, so we'll have to take the slow route home. We need to start soon. My coordinates will have to do. They're close. A decade or so to get back to Earth needs an early start."

"Yes," said Elmer. "Tomorrow evening we have the funeral. Maybe we can have blowups of the site photos ready by then. It will lend reality to the loss of our friends, even though their bodies will not be here. The choir is ready and I have someone who volunteered to read the list of our deceased."

All they could make out on the wall screen was the back of two students' heads and hear what Margaret and Astra were saying. "We'll have something for you in a minute," Margaret said. "We're just taking a quick, direct look without magnification. We've done this quite a bit before so—Oh oh! It's worse than I could imagine. Nothing identifiable. What used to be Mark's Base is completely—"

"Just put it on the screen," Stan barked.

"Yes sir. A little problem switching the connection. You must be tired of the back of our heads. Almost got it now. Anyway, the Base is completely buried under one of those stupid—"

"On the damn screen, Margaret—please!"

"Yes sir!—stupid looking *hills*! Got it! There you are sir!"

The part of the flatland that held the Base was indeed covered by a new hill. The remainder of the flatland was still there, with no significant change, except for large numbers of broken "trees," and the tide was far into the bay—getting ready for the next deluge.

They were surprised at first, but realized the hill made no difference. Dead was still dead, and they had no more interest in Origin. The funeral plans were on top of the agenda, along with getting the Transformation Cone under way before the ceremony began. Elmer wanted the Cone to be started on its way back to Earth shortly before then. He explained some symbolic reason for that, saying it would work nicely into his eulogies. The Transformation would soon be out of there.

The visit ended when Margaret delivered the hard-copy photographs of the flatland and the hill. She and the other intern, Astra, had taken the pictures. On his way out, Cameron Greenberg asked to borrow Stan's holographic recording of the Dort interview. "No problem," Stan said. "Just keep it under your hat for now. Nobody would understand." Cameron took the holo, but gave Stan a puzzling look that he could not interpret. As the other men began leaving, they glanced briefly, almost too casually, at the pictures in their hands. Ernst left without so much as a nod. Stan shrugged at such departures, but chalked it up to some level of grief and gave it no further thought.

Stan lagged behind in his office—staring at the photographs. *It's heartbreaking*, he thought, *they're so dead!*

THIRTY-SIX

Nimbus was directly overhead as the monstrous black wall of vertically rising water leapt to touch it. It hurtled toward the coast for its first assault into the heart of Origin's grandest continent. Its moving shadow had not yet reached the tiny camp of habitats it was baring down on. Interior lights within the habitats were vanishingly dim beside the brilliant contrast of Nimbus's warm and golden beams radiating through their skylights. But that was of little comfort to their occupants as their foundations, amidst sharp surface shaking, gave way beneath them, falling half a meter, and then another and another. The certitude of imminent death came with each quake and collapse, yet the inhabitants bravely held each other up or pulled them to their feet, until being felled by the most violent tremors yet—and before engulfment by that dense blanket of silence and darkness. Then a thundering roar was attended by battering droplets that, in seconds, became a violent hammering upon the meager shelters.

Within the Ad-Sec habitat, the only one left standing was Judy, the supposed fraidy-cat of the Transformation. She roared and thundered back, "Come and get us you goddamn coward, you fucking *fucker*!" Then it happened—enormous, rolling surface shifts that took down even Judy. They came with high-pitched, rasping, ear-splitting scrapes that ended in a final booming jolt, followed by . . . *nothing*—only more darkness and silence. Deep, calm silence.

It was late, but Reverend Slattery's arrangements for the funeral that evening were well under way. It was the talk of the Transformation—angry talk!

"Damn!" Stanley Lundeen said aloud. Very loud. He was alone in his office, talking to himself in confused sentences and paragraphs, in a stream of emotional babble. He'd just finished reading page one. He didn't know if he was furious, ashamed or even pleased. At first he felt relieved. That was because he realized that Debra Anderson had made it back to the Transformation Cone on one of the last shuttles.

"I'm glad you're alive and well, li'l darlin'!" he said to the wall. Meanwhile between his fists, and under the influence of a less charitable emotion, he snapped the morning issue of Debra's FAST News open to the second page.

The headline on page one had already caught his eye, and most likely the eye of everybody else on the Cone. It read: PERSONALLY, I'M NOT GOING!

She's not going to or from where? Stan wondered. It was a long edition. He read on. For starters, she wasn't leaving the vicinity of what used to be Mark's Base camp, much less the planet Origin. Not yet, unless she was tied and gagged. *That could be arranged!* Stan thought, stroking his beard. And if the Transformation was under way, she wasn't going to the funeral because she'd already be gone—said she'd swipe a shuttle or the Orb and stay on Origin. Said she'd land on some mountain top and wait for the floods to subside, and then return to the bubble hill that popped up to replace Mark's Base camp.

"How could she already know about that hill?" Stan asked his office wall loudly. Then he snapped to the next page. It was filled with Margaret and Astra's photos of the flatland area and the new hill. "Can't trust anybody these days!" he snarled as he gave the silent wall an accusing look.

On to the next page! There he found a remarkably accurate summary of the previous day's interview with the Dorts. Debra had obviously been up all night watching the holographic interview and writing the story. "Crap! Greenberg did it again. Wouldn't you know!"

Again: Nothing—the wall remained silent.

Stan spoke to it: "Hmm! That group-interview summary was too good on the technical parts for Cameron and Debra by themselves. Ernst had to be in on this too—up to his bushy eyebrows! Damn! I knew he was getting too close to that . . . that . . . Anderson woman! Wouldn't you just know!"

He scanned the wall critically. Nothing.

Debra Anderson wrapped it all up nicely—one, two, three—on the last two pages:

"One—if our friends remaining on Origin are all dead, the funeral should take place there, after the tides return to normal. A large cross could be placed on top of the new hill marking the exact spot where they died. Next to the cross could be placed a plaque with some commemorating statement and all their names.

"Two—there is only circumstantial evidence of their deaths. Just because they were buried under a mountain of water and a lopsided dome hill full of crystals is no proof anyone is dead, and besides, the Dorts believe they are all safe." (*Invoking the Dorts? What a pathetic argument!* Stan thought.) "If they are safe, somehow, and they later find that we have abandoned them without even hanging around to check, what will that tell them about our caring? And they would eventually starve. In these parts, all the nourishment potential, for mortals at least, is on this Cone. If we leave now, we will never know their true fate." (*I knew it! That's all she's doing! Just trying to make everybody feel guilty.*)

"And three—Dr. Stanley Lundeen" (*Oh God! Why me?*) "believes he has something 'very close' to the long-sought Earth coordinates; that is, for Earth's location ten years out. Once the coordinates are plugged in, sometime today we're told, and Douglas Groth initializes the start button—or the starter key, or the crank, or has us get out and push—it will take that long to reach Earth. Once Groth initiates our return, the coordinates can *not* be reset. So, once we're under way, that's it! My understanding of English is that *'very close'* means *'not quite exact.'* In that case I suppose, given what a little error in a big space can amount to, we're just as likely to de-Transform in the center of planet Earth, smack in the middle of its iron core or, more likely, in empty space too far from Earth or any other massive body to reenergize the mass-energy converters. We would then be left to float out there forever. And, yes, *'very close'* might, *accidentally*, deliver us safely, as planned. But I wonder if anybody wants to worry for the next ten years about which of those possibilities it will turn out to be."

She concluded, under a large subheading: WHAT'S THE RUSH?

She wrote under that heading: "If everyone down there is dead now, in about a month, when the monster tides subside, they will still be dead; if not, they won't be and, whatever the outcome, we can either grieve or celebrate. In the meantime there is hope. Let's just do that for now, okay?"

Debra finished with this: ". . . And finally, I believed the Transformation Cone and all of us on board should remain right where we are until *'very close'* becomes *'very exact.'*"

Talk about a personal slam! Stan thought. Then, glaring at the wall, he said aloud, "I really hate it . . . when she's right!"

He stroked his beard thoughtfully for a moment, and came to a decision. Just as he was reaching for the communicator to call Douglas Groth, the wall beeped.

It was Doug.

It seemed to be coming from far away. The muffled sound weakly penetrated the blackness and silence within the sealed habitat. It went on and on. It had, for Laura, a familiar pattern or cadence. She was clinging to Ned. "Do you hear that?" she whispered.

"Yes," he whispered back. "I'm okay too. Thanks for asking."

"Seriously, we're still alive. Listen!"

"I don't think so. That's a harp."

Jack said, "Would you two stop whispering so loud, I'm trying to hear that music—the music of the spheres or whatever in hell it is."

Out of the darkness an interior light began to dimly reveal itself, but shone enough to display three couples entangled on the floor, and Jack, the lone singleton, sitting up, hugging himself.

Judy, now back to her normal, scared self, and doing her own clinging—to David—asked in a quavering voice, "Could it still collapse under all this ocean? I mean, this habitat is really, *really* strong—right?"

David and Judy sat up together and looked around. He said, "These are good inflatable habitats, but it's hard to believe they're that good. None of these surfaces—walls, ceilings, flexible skylights and windows—are bulging *inward*. None of them. Even ten meters of water would push them in some, but this much should have flattened everything, including us."

"Then," Judy said, trying to control her emotions, "it missed us, right?"

David held her tighter, as if to cushion her from his next words. "No my darling. If there was a deluge, and there was, then we're under hundreds of meters—of *something*. A minute ago we were in the middle of a beautiful, bright day—and now it's pitch black out there."

"Then how . . . ?"

They sat in a circle beneath the dim light, gawking at its fluttering glow like children around a campfire telling ghost stories—except now the danger and fear was real. They talked quietly, almost reverently.

Innocently, Laura started the first story. "This is so strange. I feel like I've been through this before."

"Yes," said Ned, "we have."

"Huh?"

"I remember," Jack said. "We *have* been here before. Remember Crazy River?"

That clicked for Laura. "Oh yes! That's it," she said.

"No, no, no," Clint said. "Not the same at all. Crazy River is *easily* explained. It was just some Transformation gravity-reversal thing. That's what kept us dry, that time, with all that water over us. It's not like that this time. Now we're protected by this powerful, habitat-shelter thing." Ellen nodded and snuggled closer to her hero.

Laura, Ned and Jack did not nod. They turned their heads to observe Clint . . . in silence—the highlights in their eyes flickered in time with the overhead light.

Clint awkwardly responded to their looks. "Well, hehe, maybe not *easily* explained, but we did get used to it—that gravity thing!—hehe. . . . Right?"

Ellen said, in Clint's defense, "We became accustom to that Crazy Canyon phenomenon, especially in the Dorts' geode that all of us visited so often. But what's happening now seems distinct. On the Transformation that crazy gravity was kilometers below the surface. Now we're on a flatland, at sea level on the surface of a planet, not on the Cone. Unless there's some other force field like antigravity holding off the water, then this *is* different."

Judy raised her voice and asked, "Whatever is keeping us dry right now, will it last?"

There was no answer. There were only worried looks back and forth.

The far-off jingling, rattling, dinging, crystallinelike sounds returned to their awareness. "What *is* that sound?" Laura wondered. "It's familiar. Tinkling crystals somewhere. It's something I've heard before?"

Ned chuckled.

"That's irritating, Ned! What are you laughing about?" Laura asked.

Then, with a broad smile he said, "Those aren't Origin crystals clattering away out there, Laura, they're Earthly ivories! Can't you hear that ancient, tinny sounding ragtime piano beat? It's our ol' time player piano automatically holding forth in the Honky-tonk Saloon!" Ned was right. It was obvious to everyone after he pointed it out.

That sound was then obscured by another. It was also outside and could barely be heard through the barricade of sealed habitat. It was garbled shouting. Someone directed a flashlight through the habitat's transparent sheet for less than a second and yelled something they could not understand. They ran to look out. Dozens of people were dashing about in the blackness—each with a gleaming flashlight that shone into the distance and at every nearby place and person. The flashing beams could have been a fill-in for high-intensity strobe lights, momentarily freezing the moving human figures into surreal stills in a thousand silhouetted poses. The dim lights of other habitats started coming into view. That, along with the colored bright lights and din from the Honky-tonk Saloon gave the scene a look and sound of nightmarish madness.

Despite the raging flood and all that accompanied it, this was not to be a place of imminent death. The craziness of distorted images and confusing sounds made it a place of Bedlam—a place where the insanity would soon become worse. But for the moment at least, this place of Bedlam was for the living.

THIRTY-SEVEN

Clint poked his head outside to get a wider view of the surroundings, but saw nothing more unusual than they were already seeing from the habitat's side window. He shut the door again and said the air smelled good, but added that the level of disruption out there was getting *way* out of hand. He went to his special cabinet and removed a large bullhorn, which he laid on a desk. Looking again, his concern escalated. He *growled* and began removing more things from the cabinet, including his shoulder holster and revolver—which he put on—and several tear-gas canisters that he placed in his roomy jacket pockets

In his perceived role as Chief of Security, and now as point man in an army assault, he became agitated and began charging around the room like an angry beast. He picked up the bullhorn in one hand, and hauled out one of the tear-gas canisters in the other, declaring in a voice unlike his own, "I'll bring sanity to that bunch of marauders!"

Struggling to maintain her composure, petite and fragile Ellen Stone moved to stand in front of the door. As the now raging bull charged toward the door she faked a calm smile and asked rationally, "Clint darling—out of curiosity, is there some probable cause for the use of your gun and all that tear gas?"

Part of the real Clint was still there. The charging hulk crash stopped as if into a cement wall, a step from Ellen. For a moment he was like a stunned bull with bulging eyes that seemed to roll independently.

To clear his head he shook it sharply back and forth. As the confusion lifted and he regained focus, he shook his head again—more gently this time.

"Are you okay?" Ellen asked.

"Hell no! I feel crazy. I went nuts. I don't know what got into me! I was acting like everybody else—out there!" Then he removed and replaced the items earlier secured from the special cabinet.

Everyone was shocked at his sudden and bizarre behavior—bizarre even for Clint. But just as suddenly he seemed back to normal. With Ellen taking the lead, they discussed it and concluded his behavior was caused by the trauma of earlier events—the collapsing foundation, the violent sounds and all the rest—combined with his sense of responsibility for everyone's safety. It must be hard, they agreed, for someone like Clint to be both responsible and totally confused at the same time.

David and Judy were anxious to exit the stuffy habitat—the air had to be a lot better out there. Clint even said it smelled good, so they eagerly embraced Jack's suggestion of checking out the surrounding area for an understanding of where the water went and what was happening with their people. Clint handed out the flashlights and said, "Let's all stick together and stay calm." Before leaving, Clint stuffed the squid atmosphere analyzer into his jacket.

They stepped out of the habitat and into the freshest, ozone tinted air anyone had ever breathed. People ran up to them giggling and flashing lights into their faces, saying what a nice night it was, and running off. Many had already removed and scattered their clothing. Others marched by, hunched over with clenched fists and cursing. In the distance they saw two men in a fist fight. On seeing this, Jack began an uncontrollable giggle and Clint started to growl again. He was holding the squid atmosphere analyzer by one leg and slapping it back and forth as it attempted to climb his arm. In as loud and firm a voice as little Ellen could muster, she shouted, "Everybody! Get inside! *Right now!*"

When they were all back inside, Clint snarled, "It stinks in here!" but in a few minutes he'd again settled down, and Jack gradually stopped snickering and the squid thing settled down.

Ellen insisted everybody must stay indoors. "We need to hunker down till our heads are clear. Let's hope that whatever is in the air out there doesn't seep in here any more than it already has. It's making people crazy." She spoke with Clint about something she wanted him to say over the PA system, ". . . because your voice carries such authority, dear."

Clint had already stashed the bullhorn in its special place in his special cabinet and made the external public address system functional. It had not been needed before. He announced—in his voice of authority—that for everybody's safety they must return to their habitats. "There's a problem," he continued, "with the air out here." He explained that the universal intercom conference system would be working and available for the next few hours and, if necessary, days. There would be *no privacy* on the system. "We all need to know what everybody else knows. We need to have you listen to what Dr. Ellen Stone will be saying. And if you are having physical or craziness problems, call Ellen on the system. And everybody listen in—she shouldn't have to give the same answers twice. Now git to your habitats! *Git!*"

Except for Ellen, no one in the Ad-Sec expected Clint's words, authoritatively delivered or not, to be responded to. For several hours they took turns, alone or in pairs, watching through the flex window and reporting to each other the outside activities.

Half of those outside listened to and heeded Clint's words. The same listeners soon took charge of the others—those who were agitated or otherwise out of control. Some were helped, by friends or partners, back into their clothing and escorted, quietly or otherwise, to their habitats. The process was slow, but the outside activity subsided and the beaming flashlights became fewer and fewer, until there were none. Those helping the others were apparently unaffected by whatever was in the air.

The internal conference net and wall screens with their multiple checker board displays came alive across the Base as people retuned to their habitats. Ellen repeated her suspicion that there was an allergen or something toxic in the air, and therefore to stay indoors—especially if outside exposure caused peculiar reactions—like euphoria or hostility. The conference process with its public feedback confirmed that most of those who did experience altered states of consciousness and unusual or dangerous behavior tended to improve rapidly after returning to their habitats.

The lively communication continued for much of the night. For some it was reassuring, but nonetheless anxiety continued to build across the Base. There was no resolution of where the flood water had gone, of if it would return. A few had not yet recovered even after returning to their habitats—another concern. After several hours, some would return to the screen, still experiencing paranoid or manic symptoms and delusions.

One gentleman clamed he was being watched from the outskirts of the Base. He explained: "I stumbled over some crystals and ran smack into a wall. I shined my light on the wall and saw a pair of glistening eyes looking back at me." When asked who was looking, he said, "No 'who'—just eyes." The next call was answered without a pause; but even as the new caller was speaking, the previous one could still be seen by everybody, frantically gesticulating and moving his lips.

From time to time someone would request consultation from Ned or Clint and would ask for their perspective and thoughts, as was Judy for hers as a chemist, about what substance might be in the air. The "consultants" had little to offer and could provide no insights. Most of the communication was speculation and attempts by the anxiety-ridden leadership to reassure others with the same problem. It allowed for letting off steam—on both sides.

The reasons for anxiety were not surprising. No ideas explained why they had not been killed or drowned in the flood. No one knew where the water had gone, and no one could say why the bright day had become dark. As for the turf collapsing beneath their feet, there were no questions—everybody was already used to that. One item that did keep the anxiety on high was the recorded play back of the final message from Stanley Lundeen and its termination just before all hell broke loose.

It was midnight, Origin time, when Ellen suggested that everybody needed mental clarity and to rest for the following day. Tomorrow they could assess the situation and consider possible plans. Many had expressed the feeling of being trapped. She understood and agreed with the feeling, but stated that freedom of thought would be needed to cope with *whatever* turned out to be true. "If we believe we are *physically* trapped, then we must not allow our *minds* to be. Our thinking must be open, sharp, and fresh. So let's turn in and rest our brains with some precious sleep. We'll need to be alert tomorrow to cope with whatever it brings." Her tone became lighter, even with an attempt at humor. She signed off for the night, saying, "I, for one, am tired—I must turn in now. I'd suggest that all of you do the same. So take an aspirin, get a good night's sleep and call me in the morning."

Multiple displays on the wall screen revealed a few smiles, but no laughter. Only David laughed. The checkerboard screen of displays gradually darkened, square by square. And across the Base, by ones and twos, beds became occupied and habitat lights blinked off.

The communicator beeped at six o'clock the next morning. Its sound had been turned down. Ned's doe-eyes struggled to open. He answered the call. The wall screen lit up to Mark's smiling face. He was enjoying a cup of coffee.

"It's early," Ned grouched. "What's up?"

"Good morning to you too," Mark chirped. "Have you looked outside this morning?"

Ned blinked at the variegated lights in the middle of the floor. It was from the skylight. He turned and squinted out one of the side window. "My God!" he said, wide awake, "I'll call you back later. Thanks for the call!"

"No problem! Later."

The delicate, multicolored diffusion of light was coming through the skylight, but at that time of morning any light from Nimbus should have been entering at a sharp angle rather than overhead. Ned took one more look through the side windows before arousing the others. They were as surprised as Ned to see not only *light*, but *people* milling about outside—moving in groups, walking and talking *calmly,* and pointing in many directions and at many things. Most startling were the objects of their attention.

Clint and Jack were the last to exit the habitat, but not until Ellen gave the okay. She was carrying the squid atmosphere analyzer this time. Whatever problem substance had been in the air earlier was gone. Those who had a problem the day before were out and about with no sign of symptoms. While awaiting Ellen's permission to go out, Clint made several attempts to radio a distress call to the Transformation Cone, but something was blocking the signal. Either that or the Transformation had already departed. (He was ashamed of that last thought for its even passing through his mind.)

When they were together outside the habitat, they walked about in amazement—sometimes talking with others who had been out longer. The things that people were pointing to had formed over night. They looked like crystalline mounds—about four meters in diameter and half that high. *These* had not been seen before, but did look like the distant hills—hills they *had* seen every day.

Unique and interesting as they were, they were as nothing beside the main attraction. It was no small thing. David identified the grand edifice by its size and simple shape. The whole of Mark's Base was *inside* a crystalline hill—one of the many hills in the neighborhood—except the volume of the others were completely filled with crystalline forms. This one was taller than some he had examined in earlier days, but still smaller than most, being just over sixteen hundred meters high. Even so, he had no idea how this hard, crystalline blister had shaped itself over them so quickly—or even how it had been formed at all. But he and the others were grateful that it had. Ellen said she once had a suspicion the planet was deliberately trying to be *nice* to them. Now she was certain of it. "*This kind of protection,*" she said, raising her arms in a high V above her head while looking up and circling around, "*is way beyond nice.*"

The top of the edifice displayed a gigantic circle of light giving the illusion of a multicolored disk or porthole that brought in the morning light. The disk itself had the look of a magnificent glistening mosaic or stained-glass window. A trail of swirling water whipped around and over the bright pinnacle, creating visual illusions—from flowing kaleidoscopic effects to the look of a bleary, Cyclopean eye. A shifting dance of 'sunbeams' radiated from that central point like moving guidelines for a perspective drawing.

There was no doubt in anyone's mind—they were deep below the ocean tide. The water washed disk of light proved that. They saw no obvious evidence of seepage and appreciated the structure's cathedral-like grandeur and strength.

The sides of the hill and its foundation surrounded an area that, like its height, was ample to the extreme. Its opaque-appearing base and sides were still deep and darkly submerged. Enclosed within the hill's vast and empty concavity was the entire Base camp and much more. It even included a generous portion of the west cliff—their recent barrier from harsh night winds.

As the dome's crown of light became wider and brighter through the pellucid crystalline framework, the hills occupants realized the ocean was still receding and Nimbus was moving higher in the sky. They wondered how murky and deep the previous day's flooding was to so darken this edifice in broad daylight!

Clint was impressed by how rapidly the ocean was receding. He, Ned, Judy and Ellen were standing together. The others had wandered off into the crowd. Clint stroked his chin thoughtfully and said, "Ya know, if the tide drains below the flatland, I could blast us an exit at the base of this bubble, big enough to leave—even big enough for the Orb. That could help get everybody back to the Transformation Cone. The Cone could be notified ahead of time if our communications worked. It's been out since the flood, but after the blast I could go there in the Orb and they could send down the other Orb and all the shuttles. We could have everybody out of here in hours."

Judy and Ellen thought that idea was brilliant, and Ned thought it was worth serious consideration. That day—unlike the one before—rational planning was possible. Most of the Base's residents had a decent night's sleep, the air was pure, and nobody was acting crazy. Judy and Ellen encouraged Clint to spread his idea to everyone on the Base. They believed that no credible objection was possible.

Ned called a town meeting to take place in the Commons area. The fresh crop of mounds on the Commons would serve as platforms for citizens who wished to speak and be seen. Acoustics under the hill's dome were ideal if only one person at a time was speaking.

Officer Bracket stood on one of the mounds where he presented his idea with confidence and authority, and gleefully emphasized "blasting" openings in the hill for their escape. His presentation met with loud applause and cheers.

But David Michaels turned ashen.

Clint was about to step down from the mound when Ned held up his palm. "Hold it, Clint," he said with as much authority as Clint had just displayed. "This was not supposed to be the announcement of a final decision, but the opening of a democratic *discussion*. There may be other ideas of how to proceed from here."

Ned smiled to himself at how statesmanlike that must have sounded to everybody. He didn't mention it, but was just as sure as Judy and Ellen that there would be no further ideas presented.

Time was marching on, and the disk of light above them continued to widen as they spoke.

Everybody on the Base was there, talking and yelling. On every crystalline mound several people were standing and waving their arms for recognition.

Clint made a half-hearted effort to quell the noise, but no one noticed.

He gave Ned a helpless, dog-eyed look and said with great perception, "They won't shut up. Besides, no other plan is likely so let's skip this 'discussion' crap before the tide gets much lower. In a few minutes I can blast an opening in the *top* of this bubble and take the Orb up to the Cone. By the time I get back with the pilots and their shuttles, and the other Orb, the tide should be out. Then I'll bomb a ground-level side opening for everybody to exit. In a few round trips we'll have everybody out of here."

As he expounded on that idea for the fourth or fifth time, Ellen, Judy, and now David, were standing beside Ned, listening. The two women and Clint were smiling and nodding their approval of the plan; David and Ned were not smiling, but for different reasons. Ned knew that *"a few round trips"* would take many hours (and he could not even be sure the Transformation Cone was still there); the deepest level of the tide (as it returned from the continent's interior) would be back with a vengeance and would pour in upon them through any holes in their hill; the hill would, no doubt, be flooded all the way to the top, and anyone left behind would not survive. When Ned explained all that, Clint was not convinced. He still thought there was an answer somewhere in his bright idea and that a little intelligent digging would bring it out. (Ned mumbled something about a pony, but Clint did not hear it.)

David's reasons were more telling. "Time for a little conference," he said to Ned. "And you too, Clint. *Now!*"

David was a nice man with a bad sense of humor. He seldom talked with such firmness to Clint, much less anyone else. Firmness seemed to be in lately—first Ellen, then Ned and now David. Who would be next? They followed David back to the nearby Ad-Sec where he could be heard above the crowd. Ellen and Judy followed. Laura and Jack spotted them and also followed.

David began, "It was only research before—but now it's life and death. I should have told you the facts about the hills before now. Here's the most important fact:

"Any serious damage to this hill, or any other hill around here, such as by blasting a hole in it, or even damaging one of those mounds—if the mounds turn out to be intimate parts of our hill, would result in death by crushing for all but a lucky few. Those 'lucky' ones would drown later. After a hill is so damaged, it will break apart and collapse—immediately!" He explained what happened to the hills he'd already "violated" in his geologic studies.

The stunned listeners were open-mouthed and silent. In a few moments Clint said quietly, "Oh shit"—eloquently expressing the feeling for everybody.

The outside crowd became louder, making it difficult to hear their own conversation, even inside the habitat. Without a word Ned looked at Clint in a way that got more than his attention—it got his understanding. Ned's unstated thought penetrated the noise, and Clint responded like a mind reader. "Okay! You're right," he said. "I started this mess. Now I'd better finish it."

Ellen gasped in horror as Clint reentered his special equipment cabinet; but sighed in relief when he removed only the bullhorn.

Clint gave another remarkable performance before the crowd and once again demonstrated his commitment to keeping everyone safe, and this time it was based on sound reasons, not insanity. His tone with the crowd was a smooth mix of authority and humble backing down from his earlier position. It was his *Let's-not-plan-on-leaving-just-yet* speech. He clearly presented what he'd just learned from David, and added a splash of encouragement by reminding everybody of the recording they all heard of Stanley Lundeen's final words to them—his "words or reassurance." Stan had assured them that if they could make it through "the next month or two," the tides would, by then, be close to their old, normal levels.

"That month or two," Clint told the crowd, "will give us plenty of time to figure out, in our usual *democratic* way, how to exit this dome and safely return to the Cone." He did not say these words, but his final, jubilant smile implied "*Happy Ending*!" (And with great restraint and judgment he did not, in any way, remind the crowd that when Stan gave that "reassurance," the hill was not yet there. Clint believed that by now, and even then, Stan expected that everybody was as good as dead.)

Some in the crowd may not have been listening closely. Many objected to the idea of continuing to stay trapped inside the hill. They thought Clint's first idea was still the best. (Again Ned mumbled ". . . pony.") Clint handled the objections by hauling out his voice of authority—and his bullhorn. It was an effective tactic. In another half-hour the "democratic" town meeting (that had become a Clinton Bracket bullhorn monologue) was over.

He walked back to where his recent habitat-mates had been watching and listening. They patted him on the back for clearing things up so well. Ellen couldn't have been more proud and told him so; Ned was too. For Ellen's praise, he smiled; for Ned's, his shoulders straitened.

Hours passed and the ocean wash continued its invasion into the heart of Origin's great continent. At the same time it partially receded from the top of the hill's dome allowing the bright rays of Nimbus to spread broadly within the hill and heat its air to increasingly uncomfortable temperatures. But the full force of the ocean returned soon enough with its immeasurable dome-covering depth and darkness—and a blessed cool that accompanied its own starless night.

They took turns on the radio for several days. In that round-the-clock vigil they tried to contact the Cone. With each passing hour their worst fear began to settle in: The likelihood that the Transformation had already left.

They knew there would have been a funeral for them, but wished they could have watched.

On the third night, when the worst of the tide was heading seaward, Laura was in midshift on the radio. She picked up an automated signal from the Transformation Cone and responded before the link broke off—which happened all too soon. She still had more to say. Nonetheless she was overjoyed. She didn't want to wake anyone, but couldn't help it as her happiness mounted. Her yelp of unrestrained joy could just as well have been one of distress, and everyone was on their feet.

"Sorry. I didn't mean to wake you, but there was a signal from the Cone. It only lasted a minute, but they haven't left—they're still here!"

Hearing this, Ellen and Judy hugged one another and the men nodded and smiled.

"What was the signal?" Ned asked.

Laura started to laugh. "It's a repeated message. The voice is Deb Anderson's."

"What did she say?" Judy asked. "What was the message?"

"The recorder got it all. Here it is—"

They all leaned forward expectantly to hear the formal words of Debra Anderson, Director of Transformation Communications. There was some static, but the message was clear. She said, "Okay down there on soggy Origin—listen up! A few assholes up here thought of leaving, but, by damn, we ain't leaving without you—dead or alive! If you can, respond!" The message kept repeating.

After more moments of laughter and joyous hugging, Clint asked to hear Laura's response.

"Yes. That was recorded too. So here—"

Laura's return message was also direct: "Hi Deb! Thought you'd never call. Tell the assholes we're all just fine inside this spanking new, hollow-dome hill. But *don't* try for a rescue till the tides are back to normal, and whatever you do, don't try to break through the dome. According to David, if you do, the whole thing will collapse! Love you all. Even those assholes! Talk to you later! Oh, and a couple other thing—" But the connection broke up at that point.

The next communication with the Transformation was not possible for another day, but when it came it was live and lasted two hours. Everyone on the Base was able to hear and participate on the link. The Base community was especially delighted to receive Debra's summary of the Transformation crew's response when they heard that the flood had killed no one—it was pandemonium, a joyous celebration. Even the assholes—Stanley, Douglas and others joined in celebration of the good news.

But it was a short celebration. There were too many problems to worry about, including some that could not be solved. One widespread worry on Mark's Base was the aggressive encroachment from the growing number of crystalline mounds. David had explained to everybody on the Base's net that "All the old hills the size of this one started empty, but eventually got filled up with other crystal forms—every cubic centimeter of 'm. Me and some of my team, the ones still here, inspected the mounds all day yesterday. If we don't damage'm—they're sturdy enough to stand on as you already know—we believe they're nothing to worry about if, that is, they don't multiply too fast. Some day *our* hill will also be filled up like the old ones out there. With any luck that should take a very long time. Everybody should be out of here before then. All we have to do is figure out how."

THIRTY-EIGHT

It was 3 AM and Jack Lewis could not sleep. Racket from the nighttime entertainment facility did not stop till it closed at 2 AM. After that he tossed and turned. He and Officer Bracket were on the same side of the argument. They were in opposition to the referendum that allowed the Honky-tonk Saloon to stay open that late. When the Saloon's outside lights finally turned off, only the nightlight from the bathroom was there to see by.

He sat at a table near the bed sipping a cup of Chamomile tea, hoping it would help him to feel sleepy. It didn't. So, cup in hand, he walked to the bathroom and turned off the distracting nightlight. *I gotta get some sleep*, he thought. *If I'm a zombie tomorrow I'll be useless all day.* He turned and carefully made his way back down the hall from the bathroom to his makeshift bed in the Ad-Sec's main area. To guide and orient him in the dark, his hand found one of the habitat's two large windows. Then he saw something.

"What the . . . ! Somebody's out there," Jack said under his breath.

He squinted at several beams of light that played on one small patch at a time of the hill's distant base. The lights created, from where Jack was watching, a semicircle of reflected light that silhouetted a busy figure. Every few minutes the figure methodically rearranged the lights and other equipment, moving them farther to the right from one area of the base to the next.

The tide was in and Jack wondered: *Could that guy be looking for leaks in the wall? That would be silly! David says the hill walls are at least five meters thick at ground level. Thin at the top, but down here . . . ! Maybe he's up to sabotage—or planning to blow us an exit. Nah! That would be suicide. Oh well. No law against whatever he's doing right now. But I wonder . . . why is he carrying all that equipment? It must weigh a ton.*

More than an hour went by. The lights that focused on the hill's thick base went on and off many times before Jack lost interest. He finished his now cold tea and fell exhausted into bed—where he almost fell asleep. One eye was still open as he remembered the night-light. He didn't want to be responsible for anyone stumbling in the dark and getting hurt. He got up and again used the window to guide him in the dark. The figure with the lights was nowhere to be seen. *He must have gone to bed,* Jack thought. *At least he made me sleepy—better than the tea.*

He switched on the nightlight with mixed feelings, but solved his dilemma by closing the door, making it dark, undoing his reason for turning it on. Jack again found the frame of the window near the hallway. In passing, he glanced through it and immediately regretted doing so. He became wide awake.

His eyes were so accustomed to the dark that he could now make out the small crystalline mounds scattered across the Commons. They were all he could see—just the domes. They glowed dimly, but distinctly.

That alone would not have startled Jack into full alertness. He knew that many plantoids glowed at night, so why not the mounds? No reason he could think of, but something about them—or one of them—virtually prodded him into wakefulness. He kept looking at them, trying to figure out what he saw, and which one it was. If he kept looking, maybe he would see it again, or remember what it was. After staring at the domes for another quarter-hour he decided it must have been his imagination.

Then Jack saw it again. "Oh my God!" he said, and it all became obvious to him. None of the domes had significant exterior luminosity. Mainly, any mound-glow came from *inside*. One of mounds that he'd seen earlier, and again now, had an inside shadow—that *moved*.

"It moved only momentarily," Jack said, concluding a long, compulsively delivered dissertation to his habitat-mates after he woke late the next afternoon. He'd expounded on everything that happened to the Transformation and to them that led to their present predicament beneath the hill, and every detail and nuance of the previous night's events, down to the quality of his tea. These frightening reminders kept Judy gasping. She sat down and used her asthma inhaler.

Ignoring Judy's anxiety and breathing difficulty, Ned asked, "What did the shadow look like?"

"I don't know," Jack responded. "It wasn't clear—too distorted by its crystal shell. It could have been anything. I'm only sure it was something inside that outer shell, like this hill over us. The mounds are like . . . like—"

"Like an egg shell?" Laura said.

"Like candled eggs!" David said, laughing to excess for no apparent reason.

Judy said, between gasps, "Egg shells? That's creepy, Laura! You too David! I wish you wouldn't imply such things." She started to shake.

"Sorry, Judy," Laura said with a worried look.

"Mmm," David said.

Now Judy was shaking harder than before, wrapping her arms around herself, and starting to curl up—with one of her anxiety attacks. The attacks seldom lasted long. "I can't handle any more of this," she squeaked. "First Mother Nature goes crazy and now we're surrounded by *creepy* things in shells! Monsters growing in little hills, like potatoes!"

Ellen tried to change Judy's focus. She said, "Well, at least Laura and David didn't use profanity. We know how you hate that!"

"*Creepy* scares me. Profanity makes me mad. They're both inexcusable. They both make me feel . . . terrible. I would never engage in either, that's my philosophy—*sniff*." Her head went behind her knees.

Ellen said, "Yes, but doesn't profanity make people feel better when they're already mad?"

"No. It only makes matters worse!" came her muffled words.

Ellen said, "I was thinking about certain words I heard recently and was wondering where, in the overall spectrum of things—nothing personal—statements like '*fucking fucker!*' might fit in someone's philosophy?"

There was a long silence before Judy yelled, "I never did say that!" Then she sprawled out gasping and covered her mouth with both hands. Tears rolled down her cheeks and she began to shake more than before. David took her in his comforting arms and looked accusingly at Ellen. Then, with her hands no longer covering her face, he looked at Judy again. She was laughing so hard she could barely breathe.

"Well that's a relief!" David said. "I thought you were having a fit of righteous indignation."

Still laughing, she said, "It started out that way didn't it! I think I'm over it—for the time being."

"Good," David said, smiling weakly at her.

"Now then," Judy continued, no longer shaking, "what *about* those goddamn, fucking eggs?"

Laura turned to Ellen and said quietly, and privately, "I don't know how you did that! You're a psychologist, on top of everything else? That was brilliant!"

Ellen laughed and said, "I took a chance. It couldn't have gotten worse."

"Oh yes," Laura said, "it could have."

The brief episode of pouring cement down Judy's spine turned out to be just in time. Without it she would not have handled—with the aplomb she later did—the unexpected delivery that came with loud and aggressive banging at the habitat entrance.

Ned answered the door. "Why Harry . . . I mean Everett. What's in the box? We didn't order pizza."

"Very funny," Everett said. "I borrowed the box from Momma's. I wanted all of you security and administrative types to see what we're up against. I took these pictures at the hill wall last night. I took them with a couple flood lights—from an angle. Using flash bulbs against a shiny wall just gives you a picture of a flash."

He went on and on, giving technical details. Everett was known to be a talented photographer, but hearing all the particulars made Ned's eyes glaze over. The barber-photographer concluded his mini-lecture on penetrative photography saying, "You can neither see nor photograph this stuff in the daylight. I've tried. I enlarged them to this size so you could pick out all the gory details. I put a note on the back of each photo to tell you where the shot was taken. Let me know what you think. I plan to put the photos on the net tonight—with your permission—preferably!"

He handed the box to Ned and left.

It had to be the ultimate test for Judy—but not just Judy. Clint took one look at the first picture, said "I'm out of here!" and left for a chair on the other side of the room. Even Ellen was aghast. She said she would study the photos, but saw anomalies right away. Laura frowned and said she'd never eat another pizza again, not for the rest of her life.

Each of the large, colored photographs—and there were dozens of them—covered the inside length and width of the "Family Size" box. There were a lot of red, gray-white, orange, green-yellow, gray-blue, and other colors; but most of the items of interest were pearly white.

"Everett was right the first time," Ellen said. "The colors are wrong, but that one looks like a pair of eye—embedded inside the wall itself—disembodied crystalline eyes with trailing optic nerves, ending nowhere." That statement got Clint's attention, and he returned to sit at the table where the pictures were being viewed. Still, he only glanced at the pictures from the far side of the table.

After the initial shock of realizing the nature of the photographs, the rest were viewed. The pictures showed every conceivable human organ, limb, bone, nerve complex, and more. They were returned to the pizza box, which was then closed. Each picture displayed from several to a dozen or more such organs, many were way too large or small. With the others looking on, Ellen had quickly gone through Everett's pile of photographic horrors. She shoved the closed box into the middle of the table. They sat in silence staring at the box.

In Clint's newly adopted role as spokesman for the group's feeling, he again, unfailingly, found the precise nuance of words: "Oh shit."

"I think you mentioned that before, Clint," Judy said. "You're still right, though; but this time we're talking an even larger pile than before. Something is making copies of us—I mean *parts* of us. How could mere crystals do that? And where in hell did it—whatever It is—get the blueprints for human parts? I thought mounds of candled eggs were creepy-weird, but this is beyond creepy."

Ellen Stone reached over, pulled the box toward her, and reopened it. She, as a medical doctor and with a Ph.D. in physiology to boot, and Jack Lewis with his doctorate in biology, were the closest the planet had to anatomists. Somebody had to take a much closer, more informed look at the outrage in a pizza box.

They watched in silence as Ellen methodically, but slowly this time, began looking through the pictures. She asked Jack to sit close and talk with her. She said she needed his expertise. They sat and looked at the pictures together with equal and, finally, dispassionate interest. They pointed out different details to one another, and generally nodded in agreement—especially after checking Everett's notes on their backs. Everyone listened, without much understanding, to their quiet, cryptic discussion.

At last Ellen squared up the pile of photographs like a large deck of playing cards, put them back in the box, and returned it to the center of the table. Neither she nor Jack looked pleased.

After a few moments, Ned impatiently said, "Well doctors, what's the diagnosis?"

David laughed. No one else did. In fact, Ellen was never more serious. "As I've sometimes said to my cancer patients, 'It doesn't look good.' This time the diagnosis may be worse—and it's not just the things in the wall. Those things were made by something. Judy called that something '*It*.' The *It* is what I'm worried about, not the anatomical structures *It* made."

Judy said, "I think *It* is ghoulish!"

"Not just ghoulish," Ellen said. "Your *It* is also a dynamic learner of immense capacity."

"A learner?" Laura said. "Here we go again. Maybe we're anthropomorphizing something natural. Even stupid reptiles can make more reptiles. Maybe there is something natural happening here—unfathomable right now, given the little we know, but natural. There may be no *It*, just some odd thing happening."

"No," Ellen said, "I don't think so. I believe there is a conscious *It* involved here."

"How so? What tells you that?" Laura asked.

"The photographs."

"And?"

"And they are flawed—most of them."

"No photograph is perfect—and *so what* if they're flawed?"

Ellen and Jack looked at each other before she answered. "It isn't the photos that are flawed—it's the anatomy." Jack nodded agreement. Clint squirmed.

Ned said, "Okay, I give up. What's in the flawed anatomy that gives you the idea that we're dealing with an *It* that learns?"

Ellen turned to Jack and said, "I think we're on the same track, but I'd like to hear you say it—maybe we're not."

"Get to the point—please," Clint said.

"I'm sure we're on the same track, Ellen," Jack said quietly, before looking at anyone else to make his comment. He was seldom a man of few words, and usually sprinkled his statements with caveats. "The way I see it—just speculation, nothing proved here—whatever *It* is, is doing something very interesting with regard to our human anatomy—"

Clint squirmed and interrupted: "Jack, I'm sure it's 'interesting,' but could you just make the damn point?"

Jack looked at Ellen who shrugged and nodded as if to say "give them their damn bottom line." That is how Jack took it.

"The point is this: Whether the *It* is a natural happening or an intelligent learner makes no difference. What is interesting, if you'll forgive that word, is that *It* is getting better and better—*It* is improving as it goes along, in terms of getting the anatomy right."

"I still don't get your point," Clint said.

Jack looked at Ellen again and said, "I'm not so good with plane English. That was as simple as I could make it. Would you please . . .?"

"Sure Jack! When this hill was made with all that 'anatomy' in the wall, *It* was *practicing*."

"What do you mean, *practicing*?" Clint asked.

"I mean practicing making human parts. They were poor copies to start with, but got better with practice—almost perfect, in fact."

David said, "But there wasn't any time sequence. The hill went up all at once. How do you know that good copies came after poor ones?"

That called for a caveat, so Ellen nodded to Jack. "We don't know, of course," he said. "Whatever *time* means to an *It* might not fit our concept; but—just guessing—the copies near the *bottom* of the hill's base are the best. Everett's notes specified where. The anatomy is more accurate the closer it is to ground level. That assumes that the wider base (the thicker wall) with the improved vivisections, came *after* the higher part. After all, why would anyone or any *It* start out making good copies and then make poor ones later?"

Laura smirked and said, "In ancient times an artist, Picasso, did that all the time—and got paid extra for it."

Clint said, "That *practicing up* argument is full of holes, but I'll give you the point anyway. If that's what's happening, my question is *why*? What's *It* practicing up for?"

"Who knows?" Jack said. "Maybe *It* is tired of making Dorts—this is their place of origin, right? Maybe It wants to make people this time. For now, all that anatomy is just so many complex crystals that formed inside a crystalline wall of the crystalline shell we call our hill. There is no life there. It's just sculptured anatomy. Art work, maybe. Whatever we call it, it can't be accidental. It is trying to accomplish something and is using us as models."

Ned said, "Another shoe's about to drop. I can feel it."

Laura laughed. "Of course! Those 'shoes' have been dropping for weeks. We've been in a cloudburst of them."

Judy said, "You don't have to wait any longer, Ned. I can hear them falling already, like big drops on a tin roof. There's a rhythm to it: 'kerplunk, plop, splat, kerplunk, plop, splat.'"

"How do you mean, I 'don't have to wait any longer'?" Ned asked.

"It's obvious," Judy said. "The egg-mounds came after the hill went up—after all that practice. A hundred of those mounds are already here, and more are appearing every day."

"You're right!" Ned said. "I got so wrapped up in the photo-thing I forgot all about those."

"Of course you did," Laura said with a lilt in her voice, "—you poor, confused man!"

"I still expect more to drop. Much more."

"Yep!" Judy said. "That's the cadence and rhythm of life on Origin! Kerplunk, plop, splat, kerplunk, plop, splat—like the halting steps of Quasimodo on a bad day."

In the next hour David Michaels organized the remaining moiety of his crew—the half that still remained on Origin. He put them to work on detailed studies of a random selection of mounds.

The results of soundings and other studies were uniform. Each mound was full of some kind of fluid, probably water. There was one surprise: beneath the liquid was a secondary, internal mound. David's team was glad for the challenge, but after their data was collected, he relieved them for the rest of the day. They were disappointed; they had little else to do.

Ned was the first to speak after David disclosed the findings. "Okay David. You've peaked our interest. What kind of secondary mounds are in there, and what about all that liquid around the smaller mounds?"

David acted unaccountably disturbed by Ned's reasonable question. "Christ Ned!" he said. "What difference does it make? Even if we could be precise, none of us would have a clue what it meant. All I know—hell, I don't know *anything* any more. All I *think* I know is that we *dare not* bust into the mounds to get your answers—and you know why!"

"Sure David. That might bring down the whole hill on us; but if it was fruitless to start with, then why did you bother to have your crew do the studies?"

"Good point, Ned. I would love to bust into one of those mounds, collect the fluid, or water, or whatever it is, and then dig into the little, porous mound inside—especially the latter!"

Ned said, "You didn't mention *porous* before. Have you left out anything else?"

"There's nothing's significant about that. The mounds inside the mounds are hard to decipher without opening them—and that's out! And the liquid in there is just serouslike fluid. The larger mounds are a little porous, so we got a few drops. It seems to be circulating around in there, but very slowly. No big deal!"

Ned looks suspiciously at David and asked, "What is *serous fluid*?"

"Did I say that?" David said, glanced nervously at Judy, his beloved fraidy-cat.

Ellen said, "It's amniotic fluid."

"Oh shit," Clint said,

"What else have you left out?" Ned asked again.

"Well, nothing much," David responded, again furtively glancing at Judy, then back to Ned.

Judy had not missed a look or a word of this and said, "Hey, I'm over it. So please, David, just spill it!"

David's eyes widened and he took a deep breath. "There was this little matter of . . . what can I call it? . . . Something similar, let's say, to the wall images. It was some vague, hardly decipherable, image obtained from one of the mounds. That's about it. Now you know as much as I do!"

He received no comments—just glistening, cold looks, causing him to become a little unglued. He said in an overly loud voice, "All right! I'm sure it was no more alive than the viscera in the wall photographs—more *practice* for *It*, I suppose. That's it!"

The cold looks continued.

"Okay! It could have been some kind of bone—only very large. An obvious anatomical mistake. I'm no biologist, but even I could see that. It was very porous—as far as our inadequate studies could tell—and probably light as a feather if it were dried out. A very light, porous, flexible, bonelike thing—probably a shoulder blade—or maybe a . . . wing."

"Oh shit," Clint said,

David frowned at Clint and continued. "It was protruding from an inner mound just outside this habitat. That's probably what you saw moving in there, Jack. We have no idea, however, what caused the shadow you saw in front of the dim light from inside the mound."

"Did it move?" Jack asked.

"That all depends on what your definition of *move* is. If, by *move* you mean something volitional, then no. I mentioned before that there was a small liquid circulation or current in the larger part of the mounds. That can produce a slight movement, similar to that of, say, seaweed in an ocean current. We did see that kind of movement."

"Astute answer," Jack said. "Are you sure that was the only kind of movement you and your crew observed?"

"Well, there are always unexplainable happenings in any study. That's the nature of science, right?"

Jack looked at David and said, "Out with it."

"Hmm. Come to think of it there was this very small event. Maybe it was a misinterpretation of the direction of the liquid's movement, but, if not, then there were some movements, a couple of them only, in an opposite direction." David felt himself stumbling.

"Kind of like water aerobics?" Jack asked.

"Water aerobics?" David said.

"Yeah. Or maybe more like oppositional movement."

"Yes. I guess that would fit."

"In other words, whatever that *shoulder blade* really is, it is exercising—building its strength."

Clint again mumbled something under his breath.

David sat embarrassed, with his mouth hanging open. He believed he had revealed too much.

Ned asked, "Is that it, then?"

"On my father's grave!"

"You didn't like your father."

"On my mother's grave!"

"That's better. Now I believe you."

Then David straitened up, tight lipped, jaw thrust forward—looking much brighter than when his mouth was hanging open—and said, "There's more to discover in those mounds!"

Ned said, "We all know that, don't we David? But *you* are the one with the skills and the tools to even make a dent in that knowledge gap—at least for now. You want to get your teeth into those mounds—big time. You're curious as hell!"

David smiled. "Damn rights!" he said. Then, at last, he laughed again.

Judy said, "But the main thing is, we decided to stay alive. I'm glad of that. What I worry about is someone on the Base getting too curious, or angry, or crazy—and just going ahead and smashing into one of the mounds. That could finish us all."

Ned stood abruptly. The blood drained from his face. There was drama and intensity in his voice as he said, "Judy! You're right! I don't know if the air's gone bad again and I'm being effected, or what, but the tensions on this Base have been building. I feel it—like it's that other shoe dropping. We have to get on top of it right now. Something like that could finish us all! We can't let that happen. We have to head it off!"

Clint's eyes were popping. "Gee boss. That's heavy duty! I have no idea what you're talking about, but this sounds like a job for . . . Security! If I just understood a little better . . . What do you suggest?"

Ned looked wild-eyed for a moment; then suddenly calm—as though Clint had solved his problem in a stroke. He turned to Clint and said, "Officer Bracket,

I want you to go directly and pick up Everett Balz. I want him in jail immediately. There isn't a moment to lose!"

"But sir—"

"No time for explanations, Clint. No time to lose!"

Everybody's chin dropped, except Clint's. He stood up from his chair, shoulders back, chest out, chin up—very much at attention, very military. He took a deep breath and said, "Yes *Sir*!" very loud.

He then took a couple marching-in-place steps. They were very quick boot steps—loud and impressive! He proceeded smartly to his cabinet and from it removed, and donned, his holster and gun. Before holstering the weapon, he checked it carefully. It clicked, clattered and snapped in his hands as he determined it was loaded and ready—lock, stock and barrel. To make more than doubly sure, he did it again and then twice more.

Now, fully beholstered, bebooted and begunned, he stood, as for a final inspection, before Ned—who was now beginning to sweat—and said, "Ready *Sir*! At your service, *Sir*!" Two more quick, loud, marching-in-place steps. Then a military about face—the pivot causing him to stumble headlong into the wall, but he quickly righted himself—and, head up, marched to the door. At the door he turned back again, but with a questioning look on his face.

"Yes?" Ned asked—now sweating quite profusely—as was Ellen.

"Just one thing, and with all due respect *Sir*, if you believe that I will actually carry out this daffy mission *Sir*, then you have lost your mind and I will have to arrest you."

With that, Ellen stopped sweating, not that anyone noticed.

Ned flopped down in his chair. He said, "The minute Everett puts those images on the net, somebody's going to mess with the hill's wall or the mounds. Those damn intestine and liver pictures alone will drive somebody to a major freak-out. The webbed fingers shots weren't that great either. We have to stop him before it's too late!"

Then, with renewed shock on his face, he said, "Oh boy!" and snapped his head toward David, saying, "You did commit your crew to secrecy about the contents of the mounds!"

"Of course!" he rep*lied*.

"I suppose," Ned continued, "we might try diplomacy before incarceration. We could, I guess, just ask him to keep the pictures off the net."

"That's a brilliant idea!" Clint said.

Ned, nodding and smiling, said, "Still, I'd be more comfortable if we took Everett, stuffed him and put him on the mantelpiece. After all, he might *not* cooperate."

"Didn't Everett say he'd put it all on the net tonight?" David asked.

"That's right," Ned said. "And *with our permission—preferably*, I think he said. Yeah, diplomacy might be the way to go."

Judy said, "It's almost 'tonight' right now. Shouldn't somebody be talking to him—like an hour ago?"

Clint said, "If he doesn't agree, I can always disable the whole net."

"That's a brilliant idea!" Ned said.

"I'll talk to him," Judy said. Everybody nodded agreement. She quickly wrote a note to herself, listing a few items to cover with Everett.

As she did that, Jack got up to stretch, and walked over to his window of revelations. "Oh oh!" he said. "We're already too late! Look at this!"

They rushed to the window. Outside, one or two people were standing beside, or sitting on, every mound—each person brandishing some kind of stick, club or pipe for what looked like organized and coordinated destruction of the mounds. Others were similarly arrayed at intervals around the wall. Were they waiting—for something? A catalyst or signal, perhaps, for the destruction to begin?

Clint went again to the door. He looked back and said, "Stay here!" He still wore his shoulder holster and gun.

They watched as Clint walked, with uncharacteristic nonchalance, from the Ad-Sec habitat, into and among the people and the mounds. The crew and staff of the various Departments were slapping Clint on the back and pointing to his gun as their worried expressions turned to smiles. Was he the flash-point signal the mob had been waiting for? Ned complexion turned grayer.

An hour later Clint returned.

"What's going on out there?" Ellen asked.

Clint looked at her, and then the others. "I think you'd all better sit down again. You're not going to believe this!"

Clint was loving his role. All of his superiors—he thought of them as such—were in rapt attention to hear his every word. He'd only been gone an hour, but thanks to their many questions, he managed to hold their interest for half again that long.

What was happening throughout Mark's Base had already been given a name by the participants. In fact there was a proliferation of names: The newly formed ad hoc *"Base Watchers"* were on high alert in the midst of what they called, a *"Michaels-Balz Vigil."*

"I hate that name," David said.

Clint explained that Everett's pictures had already been on the net for several hours. Everyone on the Base, except Administrative and Security people, were bored and watching their interactive wall screens and communicating with each other about the anatomical horror pictures that appeared there. They had nothing but praise for the great Harrison Everett Balz and his skillful discovery and photographic proof of the existent and coming threat! Not to be outdone by Everett, David's men provided the bored Base campers with their own (confidential) juicy stories and smoking guns. The information brought the (no longer bored) citizens together. That led to the birth of the *Vigil*, christened with David's and Everett's last names—as appellations of high honor.

The names reflected what Mark's Base campers came to see as a new and meaningful role for them—Base camp security! And Clint, who had nothing to do with its formation, was their top man. They would protect the mounds and the periphery from all the *crazies* who might endanger the camp. They were out there to guard the place, not to destroy it. Everybody was aware of the hill's potential fragility should anyone mess with its structure or that of the mounds. For their provision of detailed and critical information they praised their in-house photographer, Everett Balz, and the Transformation's geologist, the great David Michaels!—and, of course, his sneaky crew!

After all those disclosures, Ned hung his head and said, "When will I ever learn?"

"Learn what?" Laura asked.

"That our people aren't as dumb as I always give them credit for."

Clint put a strong, reassuring arm around Ned's shoulders. "It's okay, boss!" he said, "I know how hard it is to be confused *and* responsible at the same time!"

Part III

ORIGIN'S CHILDREN

THIRTY-NINE

For several days and nights the *Base Watchers* continued their vigil. In the meantime the high tides had become low enough to cover only half the hill, bringing day and night sequences back to normal—something everybody was glad to see. On the negative side, the mounds continued to proliferate, sometimes showing up in the middle of people's habitats, occasionally capturing a piece of furniture inside if its owner had neglected to install some kind of flooring. With one exception, victims of the home-invading mounds actually pulled up stakes and moved their habitats.

The exception was Mark Tenderloin. He was amused when a mound appeared one day in the middle of his living area. To keep it, rather than move it, he cut away and discarded the portion of tarpaulin flooring that covered it. He looked upon the intrusive object as a whimsy-pleasing artifact and watched it as one might stare with fascination into a fireplace—especially at night when the inner mound displayed a quiet and relaxing florescence as it returned the Nimbus energy it had collected during the day from beneath Mark's skylight.

On night three of their vigil, the Base Watchers noticed that things were starting to happen. Several mounds began losing their external structure by shedding outer crystals. The remaining structure became less opaque, but not entirely transparent. Like the hill itself, the mounds' walls, at their bases, were thick compared to their tops. Weakened by this casting off of scales from their exterior shells, they were no longer safe to sit on. David and his crew watched the shedding mounds with particular interest. To assure documentation from every angle, he filmed the "mound scenes," as he called them, with detailed holography.

Soon after this casting off began—David called it "molting"—their crests would give way. Before collapsing, the first noticeable change was the appearance of a small geyser atop the mound. Those tiny, liquid plumes settled down when the pressure inside stabilized with the atmosphere. Next, a thin layer of flakes would come loose around the jets and slide down the outside of the mound and, at the same time, a small amount of it would float down through the liquid itself, like so many glittering specs in a Christmas paperweight sphere. Everett, David and his crew, and many others were busy photographing and taking notes on these "end-stage mound scenes." (David loved to categorize and name things.)

Of equal interest to David were the newly proliferating mounds. He assumed that the hills themselves—including the one they were in—were probably formed in a similar manner as the mounds. The emergence of the hill and later on, the mounds, was astonishingly rapid in every case, and there were other resemblances. To exit the hill safely, they needed every scrap of *relevant detail*. The mounds seemed relevant.

Even David Michaels could not explain *how* the mounds were produced. He and his crew could only document how it looked from one stage to the next. Despite extensive holographic and individual observation, such as it was, of what happened during mound formation, it was, in the end, no more than visual and written description; without any real explanation.

There were, however, a few obvious "discoveries" that brought them to a shade of understanding beyond description.

This lack of observational and explanatory depth did not unduly bother David—whose profession was partly classification and description anyway—but he hoped he could add one cool new theory to his chosen field before he died.

The mounds grew from the ground up. That was the most obvious part. The mounds popped up like hollow, hemispheric mushrooms; but did not grow from their centers. Rather, the domes grew from their circumference, like the building of an igloo. The inside surface, its floor, did not change—it simply sank. As a wall grew, the associated inside surface would collapse farther; but only to an extent offsetting the mass and volume of the material needed to create it. Despite this, material from the lowered surface did not become part of the mound's primary dome—only its floor. From that, David concluded the material making up the mounds' walls, right on up to their pikes, came from a deeper level—indicating that the mounds were *not* quickly formed, but had been readying for their emergence much earlier. He said it was like the "surprise" of a sudden volcanic eruption or an earthquake—not really a surprise if you knew the deep down dynamics of plate tectonics and volcanoes. The event itself would seem sudden, but was only the final stage in a much longer process.

The hemispheric mound walls began their build-up from widening bases as they rapidly cascaded uniformly upward with overlapping tiles, each tile made of countless crystals. It appeared that no two "tiles" were alike, but the end result was a series of nearly identical mounds.

Once a large mound was formed, it quickly filled with a watery liquid, immediately followed by the development of a smaller, inner mound that sprang up in the center of its floor. The liquid, under pressure from below, spurted into the mound from the edges of every tile, and drizzled down like heavy rain.

Based on this, David thought the giant hill that saved them might begin taking on its own liquid and eventually become filled. Then, over the centuries, more crystals and plantoids would replace the liquid—like the many other hills already surrounding the flatland.

The deluge *outside* their giant hill was bad enough; but well after his team's studies of the mounds' early stages, David expressed his surprise that another flood, comparable to those deluges inside the mounds, had not already begun in the giant hill itself.

Judy Olafson was pleased that David now had enough confidence in her to state such an opinion in her presence. She, in turn, expressed an opposite opinion: "*It* does not want us dead, so there will be no internal hill flood, not with us inside. Had *It* not been watching out for our welfare, this cathedral of a hill would not be here—still protecting us. And do you think that poisonous air we experienced in here at first, vanish over night by accident? Getting the air just right—that too took practice, and—"

"Okay, okay!" David said, "I get it!"

"No, David, you don't," Judy said, "But you do mean well, and you try to be honest. But being a scientist doesn't mean you're right. Not this time. We both have our theories. I like mine better than yours—because it's true."

Later on, David turned privately to Ned and said, "There are thoughts I still don't dare express to Judy. Those benevolent acts she thinks some kindly *It* has arranged for us scares me—not the acts, but the *It*."

Ned nodded. "That bothers me too and has for quite a while. I haven't talked about it to anyone, including Laura."

David and Ned stared at one another. Finally David said, with only a slight laugh, "I'll flip you for who goes first."

"Never mind, I will," Ned said. "For me, it started with the canine teeth in Everett's pictures. Some of those teeth were way too long for my comfort."

"And sharp!"

"Did that scare you too?" Ned asked.

"I hadn't thought of it till you just mentioned it. It was the *wing* thing that got to me."

"You never describe that in any detail, David."

"I mentioned it to Ellen. I told her it could have been one hell of a gigantic bat wing—that it looked something like that."

"You told that to Ellen?"

"Yeah. But, like Judy, she was too much of an optimist about *It* to worry or even take me seriously."

Ned said, "We don't have much to go on—just those two things. Judging from Everett's photos of the teeth—the ones higher up inside the hill's base—there were problems, especially with the canines."

"Yeah, but the ones lower on the base didn't look too bad. I think that's why they didn't scare me. The lower stuff was supposed to be the most recent—if you can speak of events that close together as being separated timewise in any meaningful way. Laura thinks we can. The teeth took practice to get right. But I didn't see any practice on wings—so I wonder about that."

Ned said, "I don't buy the *practice* argument. Maybe all the different examples of every organ and limb was a display of choices, rather than trying to get it right. Your bat wing was nowhere in the wall."

David's eyes shifted nervously. "Whatever is in those mounds," he said, "be they gigantic pearls, grains of sand, or monsters, we're going to be outnumbered down here—more than double."

Ned nodded and said, quietly but more expansively than before, "Bat-wings—big ones! Canine teeth—big ones! Closer to saber-toothed tiger teeth! Either way, what have we got?"

It was the obvious, unstated word, and they said it (still quietly) in unison: "Carnivores!" Then David said, "Of course *It* is keeping us alive. The newborns are going to need food."

This called for a strategy. They brought Clint and Jack into their private discussion. After an hour of mumbled, conspiratorial sounds—pointedly ignored by the three women who were busy making their own conspiratorial sounds—they had a plan.

The plan was simple. They made a little list. Clint would call upon the Base Watchers to remain watchful and armed with restraints. Any threatening, carnivorous-appearing things or behavior—if such were to emerge from the mounds—was to be met with one or more of the listed restraints: ropes, cuffs, belts, chains, duck tape, wire, and other such items; all easily obtained from the Mart. Those items were to be placed on whatever bug or bat or snarling, salivating thing that turned up. If necessary, Clint would try to shoot it without bringing down the hill.

The four proud men of the Ad-Sec habitat would not sit idly by and allow their Base campers, "every man, woman and child"—there were no children, but that was how they phrased it—to be eaten alive or sucked into some dried raisin-shape of their former selves!

David rolled his eyes upward to show only their whites, like some ancient guru and, in a humming voice, predicted, "If anything is going to emerge from the mounds, it will begin in hours or sooner."

Ned said, "I'm sure you're right. We must implement our plan. Clint, you must leave forthwith and on the double to alert the Base Watchers. Ready them for action."

On hearing this final pronouncement, Clint's shoulders snapped back as he hefted his holster and gun and then started to remove the gun—presumably to go through the noisy gun check—but was stopped by Ned, who said, "You can skip all that this time."

Clint, in his boots, was about to clomp as quietly as possible out the door when Ellen noticed and said, "Where are you sneaking off to, Clint?" There was a reassuring lilt in her voice as she said that, so his stunned caper into the air was noisy, but minimal.

"Just going to make some rounds and see how the Base Watchers are faring," he replied innocently.

"That's perfect. How timely!" Ellen said. "But before you go, we've been talking together—while you men were discussing important matters—and we'd like to share, oh, just a couple ideas with you—with the four of you. You do have a couple of minutes to spare, don't you, Clint? I mean, before you have to run, dear?"

Clint glanced frantically at David who shrugged and said, "A couple minutes shouldn't make much difference—but the clock *is* ticking!"

On one side of the table the three women sat smiling; on the other, the four men sat frowning and confused. Clint squirmed uneasily; Ned gritted his teeth; Jack carefully scrutinized certain intricate patterns in the ceiling, and David, of course, laughed.

Ned asked, "Why are all of you smiling?"

"Because we have a wonderful idea," Judy said.

Laura was looking particularly pleased, and Judy said to her, "Why don't you tell them—it was mainly your idea anyway."

"No it wasn't," Laura protested, "We all contributed equally—we all had the same idea and all I did was mention it first."

"No, dear," Ellen said, "Judy is right; you deserve most of the credit."

This interaction continued for several minutes before Ned interrupted with the simple, quietly stated word: "Ladies."

It did no good, so he said the magic word several more times, gradually increasing his volume. Finally, at a level just short of yelling, it became quiet and the women looked at him, questioningly.

"You called this meeting for a reason?" he asked.

Laura composed herself, as Ellen and Judy looked to her expectantly. (They figured that, by this time, the men were ready to listen. Even Jack was no longer looking at the ceiling.)

"We've been talking about the mounds," Laura said. "We think they're on the verge of presenting us with whatever is in them. We believe we know what that is, and we have a plan for that wonderful moment and emergence!"

The men looked at one another with more confused expressions. Then Ned admitted, "We've done the same thing, but I'm afraid our conclusion about what will emerge will shock you, and our plan will be implemented forthwith. We have a practical plan, given what we think—I mean what we know — will emerge."

"*Forthwith*. How interesting!" Laura said, blinking her eyes demurely.

"So, what kind of 'emergence' do you ladies expect?" Ned asked, with an uncharacteristic smirk, accompanied by nods from his cohorts.

"Of course!" Laura said. "We agree. We must ready the plan—forthwith, as you say, Ned. You guys are so perceptive! Forthwith, by all means. And Clint!

You will be a big part of that plan—by engaging the immediate assistance of the Base Watchers. Things could be popping around here very soon and we'll need every one of the Base Watchers—coordinated and on task! You, Clint, are the linchpin of this operation, the kingpin, the very truss and vortex for this coordinated action!"

The men sat staring with their mouths open. Officer Bracket liked the flattery, but did not know what to make of Laura's last statement. But he knew that *his* next question would be decisive. He thought, *This question will clarify our differences dramatically and incisively, like a razor, a machete, like dividing the Red Sea from . . . from . . . from the Red Sea!*

So he asked the big question: "Exactly what do you . . . you optimists, expect will emerge from those mounds?" The question met with looks of approval from the other men.

But Laura looked shocked. She spread her hands in a gesture of disbelief and said, "You mean you don't know? Isn't it obvious? Exactly what form it will be in we can't yet say, but we need to ready ourselves for the emergence of . . . carnivores!"

"What a relief," Ned said. "For a while there I was afraid we would have a disagreement on this. We also expect Carnivores."

"Well, that's a relief to us too, I'm sure," Laura said. "Glad to know you guys are still perceptive and have your wits about you!"

Ned turned to Clint and said, "I guess you'd better get started—forthwith, and all that!"

Clint quickly grabbed the door handle and started to open it, but before he could step outside he heard Ellen say, "Haven't you forgotten something?" Clint reentered the habitat and went over to give Ellen a kiss goodbye on the cheek.

"That's nice," Ellen said, "but that's not what I meant."

Clint frowned. "What then?"

"Here," she said, handing him a piece of paper.

"What's this?" Clint asked with suspicion in his voice as he warily held the paper between his right thumb and forefinger like a wet diaper.

"Why, it's the shopping list, of course. Those carnivores are going to be very hungry at first, and will need to be fed. The Canteen has adequate stores of food—enough to last till the flooding is over sometime in the next month. After that we can get more supplies from the Transformation. By then David will surely have figured out how to exit this hill. With everyone's help and encouragement that shouldn't be so tough. So hurry, dear. Time is of the essence. We wouldn't want the carnivores to be too hungry after their arrival—on their very first day out! That's why we have to hurry. We wouldn't want them to start eyeing *us* as *num-nums*, now would we?"

Clint staggered out of the habitat, still holding 'the list' between his thumb and forefinger, and was followed through the door by the other men who closed it hard behind them. Before it slammed shut, Judy yelled after them, "Don't forget the Base Watchers—there'll be a lot of supplies to carry!"

FORTY

It was beautiful "outside" as the four men left the Ad-Sec and walked into the daylight. The giant dome's volume of air was fresh-smelling despite a billion floating specks of crystalline dust. Nimbus beamed its light, with total indifference, through the speckled air to produce a glittering pallet of streamers for receptive connoisseurs and inattentive dolts alike. For quiet, contented souls it was enough to levitate their spirit; but the souls of these four men were far from quiet.

They noticed nothing around them as they scurried off and parleyed on their way to who knows where—debating a resolution of the two-plan dilemma; but they finally decided upon the political and domestic wisdom of compromise. They would mobilize the Base Watchers and arrange to provide them with their list of straps, chains, ropes . . . *and* whatever the women might have in mind.

Clint eventually perused the list he'd been holding so gingerly—and blurted out that most of the items on their list consisted of fruits, vegetables and milk—and *some* meat.

"That's ridiculous!" Jack said, grabbing the list from Clint.

They gathered around Jack and read the document together. At the bottom of the list was a starred footnote that said "over." On the back of the list, in Laura's small handwriting, was this note:

We all eat meat. That makes us carnivorous. Our teeth show the history of our diet—canines for the meat-eater in us, incisors for gnawing and cutting, a dozen molars for grinding, etc. Even the most distorted examples of teeth in Everett's jawbone photos included molars—and only a couple overdone canines. No matter. Newborns—even bats—require milk. Newborns don't usually start with ready-made teeth—their mothers might object. Meat is included here in case the new arrivals are more like birds than mammals. The list should have included insects, but we do not have any with us—except a few damn mosquito stowaways that hitched a ride with us from Earth.

That brought the men's conversation to a halt, but only briefly. After some thought, David said, "Damn! They thought of everything!"

"Except for one thing," Clint said. "*We* know what carnivores *really* are. Let's notify the Base Watchers . . . er, forthwith. We need to get everybody over to the Mart for supplies. We need everybody to *stay* armed; but for now we'll just add ropes and chains and like that!"

"And groceries," Jack added.

"Yeah, yeah—" Clint said, "*compromise* plan! Pah!"

That settled, they looked around for Base Watchers to get the plan started. They were so wrapped up till then that they failed to notice that not a single person was in sight. So far as they could see, the wall and even the mounds were unattended.

Then they heard it in the distance, on the opposite side of Mark's Base: The white noise of many voices, punctuated by barely audible shouts. They ran toward the sound.

A large crowd of Base Watchers had already surrounded David's crew. The crew was fending off the throng—with the assistance of the Watchers' earliest arrivals, recruited to protect the holographic setup and what was left of the mound they were filming. In fact, the "mound" was no longer there—only a wide, moist area on the surface where its internal liquid spilled when it shed its outer structure. Only an odd-looking elevation remained where the mound had been. It was the first new change for a mound, and the first to draw a curious crowd.

David's staff allowed their boss into the now protected area, along with Clint, Ned and Jack. Ellen, Laura and Judy were already there. Ellen was gently examining the odd material overlaying the remaining hillock. Judy was looking at a jar of liquid a crewman had handed to her. Before entering, Laura saw the same crewman, Kevin Verily, siphoning off a large quantity of the same liquid into a barrel from the deteriorating mound. When Ellen saw Jack and David she motioned for them to assist her—Jack for his biological knowledge, and David for his expertise in geology, the parent science of mineralogy and crystallography.

"How did you get here so fast?" David asked Ellen.

"We got the call just as you left. We knew you'd find your way here. Judy and Laura are over there," she said, pointing. "I see they found Ned and Clint."

They wandered around the hillock a couple times, passing and exchanging nods with Ned and Clint both times. They checked its texture, and gently lifted small parts of its ragged edge, being careful to cause no damage, and ended in a brief huddle. They concluded that the hillock's covering—the famous "inner mound"—could be a wing, but was more like a large plantoid leaf with porous, tubelike structures giving the appearance of phalanges, such as one might see on an albino bat-wing. David named the covering a "wing-leaf." He said that its plantoid structure was becoming dry and inflexible and could not support any kind of sustained flight—only short-distance glides at best. He believed it merely served a temporary, passive role, more like a drape or shell that concealed and protected whatever lay beneath. They noted some thick, viscous substance that could still contribute to its cohesion and flexibility. When exposed to the air it tended to harden, but did not stiffen immediately or become rigid. Ellen suggested that as the mound changed, the *wing-leaf*'s function might have changed with it.

Suddenly they heard, "Look out!" and "Better stand back!" It was one of David's crew members. She was not admonishing the crowd, but warning Ellen and the two men beside her.

With a loud, crackling sound, the *wing-leaf* peeled itself away from whatever it was on. As it did so, it seemed many times larger than in its draped form, and more durable than David expected. It peeled away from one side only, and remained, at least for the moment, anchored, as on a long hinge, to the other side. As it lifted, a viscous, mucuslike substance clung to its inner side and stretched out in hundreds of long, glistening strings from the surface it had been covering. The *second surface* was a similar-looking shell or *wing-leaf* structure.

In moments, the newly revealed covering, the second surface, began to unpeel just as noisily as the first, from the other side. It swept up swiftly—with a distinct "Whoosh" sound that combined oddly with the noisy crackling—and in the process cleared away the hundreds of stringy attachments that were between it and the under side of the first surface. It too stopped at the top of its upward stretch. There, the two *wing-leafs* meshed along their upper edges and along their ragged sides—like fingers intertwining or a zipper securing two sides of a jacket—but less a jacked than a bulging tent. The stringy substance gathered upward and sealed the border between the two *wing-leafs*. The whole process happened so fast that Jack exclaimed, almost in shock, "What the hell!"

"One good thing," David said, "—the collapse of the mounds didn't demolish our hill. Not yet, anyway!"

Minutes before, what was a small mound within a mound, had transformed into what Ned described as ". . . a cross between two frost-colored sails or a snapped-shut Venus Fly Trap." Clint agreed with the second description saying, "It's still a carnivore!" Judy thought it was like cupped hands in prayer, and Laura that it reminded her of a modern steeple. Jack thought it resembled the fin of a giant white shark. Kevin Verily said it looked like a woman's purse; and David said, "Shark's fin or woman's purse—there's the difference?" and then bent over in laughter solos. Overheard from the crowd were other descriptions, like chrysalis and cocoon. Ellen and Jack reserved judgment on those two terms in their belief, mostly *hopes*, that whatever might finally emerge "if anything comes out at all," would *not* be a bug.

Clint asked, "Did anyone see what was under those *batwings*?"

"*Wing-leafs*," Ellen corrected.

No one on Ellen's side of the formation had seen inside; but Judy and Laura, on the other side, had. Kevin Verily said he had not, but *did* capture it on holo-film!

The six Ad-Sec habitat mates gathered where Judy and Laura had seen something inside "Kevin's Purse" before it snapped shut.

Ned asked, "Did you get a good look at it? What did you see?"

Judy turned to Laura and said, "You go first."

"I went first the last time."

"Okay then," Judy said. "This won't be easy. I wish you had seen it, Ellen. You or Jack might have been able to make some sense out of it. Anyway, if you thought there was a lot of gelatinous, stringy stuff under that first *wing-leaf*, that was nothing compared to the garbage collection under the second wing, and—"

"*Wings*! Like I said, wings!" Clint's loud interruption was roundly shushed.

"That was about it. That's all I saw."

Laura said, "Come on, Judy—think!"

"Well, I hate talking about things that are disgusting."

"We know, Judy, but—"

"You're right; there was something in the middle of all that *stuff*. It sort of got lifted up with the second wing. It must have been stuck to all that glop. As far as I could tell it was just more glop. A big wad of glop. That's the best I can describe it. Now—your turn Laura!"

"That was a good description, Judy. I can only add that the condensed *glop*, as you called it, just kind of floated in the middle of all that stringy material it was attached to—material that lifted it off the surface; and similar material stretched from it to the base. A little after that, it couldn't be seen at all. Its wings sealed together along their edges."

"What color? How big? What shape?" Ned asked.

"Same color as the *wing-leaf's*—pearly, silvery, with a subtle mix of gold. Same as the stringy material. Not much variety. It's hard to describe the shape— seeing it only from one angle, but seeing it straight on, it was about this big around," Laura said, making a large circle with her arms, fingers just touching. "I don't know what it looked like from the side or any other angle. It could have been long or short. What we need now is a good look at the holo-photos your team shot, David."

Clint said, "Fine, but nothing said here should change our plans." He looked at the others and said, "We need to get started, but the way these wing-things keep changing, if this one's the example, I hope we have a little extra time to get it done right. Maybe an *extra day*. But just in case, I've alerted a few of the Base Watchers that were standing around watching the show. They'll get the word out. In the meantime we have time to refine our plan."

With all the Ad-Sec mates now being equally expert on the mound's progression to a wing-thing, they agreed with Clint's idea. They were relieved at the idea they might have "an extra day *or two*" to get ready. The extra time that Clint guessed at, and the others doubled, started as a hope, progressed to a guess, then to likelihood, and finally became an accepted fact. No rush! Plenty of time!

Of course, they were wrong!

The holo-display was ready within the hour and the showing took place in the large, Ad-Sec office—the perfect setting for it. It was bright outside, but Ned turned a switch that darkened the windows and skylight, signaling the time to begin. They began at normal speed, but chose to watch the collapse of the mound in slow motion as most of its liquid spilled uniformly down the outside of what became a shrinking mound. At the same time, the liquid sluiced away the upper mound crystals a layer at a time—thus keeping most of the loose crystalline tiles and other mound debris from falling into its interior, although some did. Ellen said, "It's not exactly sterile technique, but not bad for an inanimate pile of minerals."

Before the holo-display was slowed down, it showed the Base Watchers starting to appear and insist on getting closer. They were asked to back off, as heard on the synchronous sound system. The earliest intruders were recruited to assist in holding off the remaining crowd that was coming their way. While that was happening, Kevin Verily was seen collecting a barrel of the liquid and, when that was full, a couple jars more. Later they saw him giving a jar of the mound juice to Judy.

Still at normal speed, they watched the unfolding wing-leafs, with all the snapping and whooshing sounds, as loud and realistic as the true-sized holo-display itself. Then came the crucial moment when the floating glop went on display. That scene was stopped and replayed many times, at various speeds and from different angles. With each showing of this part, Clint was heard quietly repeating, over and over, "Oh shit! . . . Oh shit!" The showing ended with the sealing of the seam between the wing-leafs.

The skylight and other windows were switched to transparent. The group blinked into the brightness.

They gathered around the conference table—their place of comfort—and stared at each other. Their expressions were serious—even David's. It was almost a contest for who would be the strongest (or the weakest) by breaking the silence.

"Okay. What have we learned?" Ned asked in a neutral tone.

Judy said, "All I could see was more glop. It was more of a Rorschach than a Kevin Purse."

Ellen said, "Well, it wasn't close to spherical. It was shaped more like a giant vitamin capsule, but very irregular, and obscured by all those membranous strings—especially underneath. They were a lot thicker there."

"Telling us what?" Asked Ned, taking an imperious, Socratic role.

"It doesn't say much about what's in the glop," Ellen replied, "but maybe something about the purpose of the strings."

"Awe hell!" Clint said, "It's obvious what's in the glop!"

"There's nothing obvious about it at all," Judy said. "It's covering something we can't see. If you can't see it, then it isn't obvious."

"Suppose," Clint said, taking on Ned's Socratic mantle, "that what you see is what you get?"

Judy said, "Clint, you're being silly. The question is silly. What do you mean?"

"I know what he means," Jack said. "If what we get is what we saw in the holo-display, then it would be obvious."

David said, "Impossible! The only thing that size that looks even remotely like what we saw, is a Dort."

"*Exactly!*" Clint said.

That alone did not end their discussion—but the banging on the door did. "It's open!" Ned yelled with irritation. The man who entered was red faced and agitated.

"My God!" Laura said. "You look like Lucifer! What's the matter, Mark?"

It took a while for Mark to settle down, but a cup of coffee and sympathetic verbal strokes from three attractive women went a long way to accomplishing that. Finally, Laura said, "Do you think you can tell us about it now?"

"Flora," he said, "—that's the name I gave the mound that came to live with me. I'd have named it Phosphor, but it's more florescent than phosphorescent. Anyway, I think it's about to give birth! It lost its water. Made a big mess in my habitat. I won't hold it against her, if it turns out to be a her, but then came all those cracking sounds—birth pains I suppose—and then . . . and then you won't believe what happened!"

"I think we will," Laura said.

"Well, yeah. I was in the Base Watch crowd too when the flaps went up and it sealed itself. I don't spend all my time in isolation—even though you think I'm nuts talking about the mound in human terms. It's just my way of talking sometimes. Anyway, yes, that did happened to Flora too. But it's—"

"But it's a shock when it happens in your own place!" Jack interrupted in his most sympathetic voice.

Mark continued, "—But it's what happened after that that has me going! While I was squeegeeing the water out the door, there was a loud crashing sound from *inside* the sealed flaps. It did that three times in quick succession, like a jackhammer—well, not that fast—only louder and more violent. When that happened, I got the hell out of there, but not before noticing a big crack in the side of one of the flaps. Whatever is in there is no wimp!"

Clint was about to say something when the wall screen came on to display Kevin and several Base Watchers. They too appeared flushed, flustered and as red as Lucifer. They all spoke at once when Clint acknowledged them.

Finally, Kevin took dominance of the communication. "Half the mounds out here and all across the Base," he said, "have suddenly shed their water; three quarters of those have already sprouted and sealed their wing-leafs, and quite a few of those are demonstrating potential for extreme force and violence, if that sledgehammer noise they're making is any indication. Worst of all, two of them—maybe more—have busted their white-wing covering. We can't imagine why this is happening so fast, just after the sealing-in process."

Judy spoke up. "Whatever is doing this has a much different kind of time clock than ours."

"Must be," Kevin said. "The point is, though, the plan to use restraints or food won't work. These things are way too powerful. You should hear them banging away in there! The restraint measures, with ropes and so on, may have to give way to something more, well, heavy-duty. Maybe even lethal. We're trapped in this hill with hundreds of them, whatever they are. We may have to kill or disable them preemptively before they bust out of those shells. It's them or us!"

Clint was on his feet. "You're right," he said. "Stay at that station Verily—I'll get back to you in five minutes!"

After the temporary sigh-off, Clint looked triumphantly at the others. "The problem is, I only have a dozen lethal weapons. And now there's no time left. I'll have to ask all of you, gentlemen and ladies, to help carry the weapons outside, and I'll call back that Verily guy and those others to help with the shooting."

David shook his head. "The only sharpshooter on the entire Transformation—to say nothing of this Base camp—is you, Clint. And—"

"That makes no difference," Clint said. "They'll just have to take a few extra shots. Now lets—"

David stood up, and his voice boomed, "And one shot into the hill wall will bring it down—all of it. You keep forgetting that, Clint! Right now the tide is a full quarter of the way up the hill. If the collapsing hill didn't kill us, then we'd all be drowned in a matter of minutes anyway. Now, with your permission, Officer Bracket, may we—for just a fucking moment—consider any ideas other than yours?"

Clint stood with his mouth open—stammering.

Mark said, "I have to check something. I'll be right back!"

Clint found his voice again. "You're going to check that mound-thing in your habitat? Is that why you're leaving?"

"Right!"

Clint hefted his holster and looked from Mark to David. "I know what you just said. There will be no wild shots into the hill, but I need to go with Mark to protect him. Mark's mound took second behind the lead for progressing as far as this—just behind the one in the hologram. And as you said, Judy, time's not the same for those things. Who knows where it is in its progression right now! Let's hurry up Mark, I told Kevin Verily I'd get back to him in five minutes!"

As they hurried out, Ned shook his head, looked at David and said, "It's amazing—if you press that guy's security button in just the right way, he can be reasonable."

FORTY-ONE

Mark and Clint had only been gone a minute when the wall screen activated. It was Debra Anderson. "Greetings Debra," Ned said with labored cheerfulness. "What's up?"

"What's up? You're what's up! As we agreed, we've been monitoring every scrap of electronic information and communication from down there, including that hologram of whatever in hell that thing is. It sounds like things are getting more and more dangerous. That plan of yours to restrain or feed those things sounded kind of desperate anyway. Aside from that, how are you?"

"This has been a more than typically shitty day," Ned replied, "and it's still coming. If we can manage to stay alive for roughly the next month while the tide settles down, we think there's a chance—a shot at getting out of here. How's your day been?"

"How are you going to do that? I mean, get out from under that hill?"

"We don't know yet. David thinks we're stuck; but he did hint at one 'wild scheme,' as he called it, for doing so. I hope you guys can help us do some thinking about that too."

"Jeez, Ned—that's about all we do think about, and we've been doing a lot more than just thinking."

David joined in. "Let me guess! During low tides you've been experimenting with some of the new hills that popped up about the same time as this one."

"You're a mind reader, David."

"No. Just a genius!" Then came his solo laugh.

"Before you become paralyzed with delight in your own wisdom, I have to tell you, the Hill Studies, as we're calling them, suck."

David sobered. "Of course they do. Mess with the hills, and down they come! Oh, you can kick'm and pound'm, but don't penetrate'm or it's all over. And if you've tried coming into them from below—no matter how deep, forget it. Their roots go deeper than any plantoid's. I can think of a lot of things to try, but the outcome of all those thought experiments are the same. They suck."

"Oh my, David! You make me tremble!"

"What do you mean?" David asked, shaking his head, confused.

She ignored his question. "About the Hill Studies: Select groups of Stan's and Doug's people planned and carried them out. They've been studying quite a few. None of your crew was involved. You don't want us to quit trying, do you?"

"I take it that 'studying' the hills is a euphemism for 'destroying,' in this case."

"If you insist."

"Before I answer your question about quitting the 'studies,' I have a couple questions of my own," David said.

"Shoot."

"First, why haven't I read or heard about the hill experiments before now. I download The FAST News every morning, and I'm in regular touch with my crew and friends on the Transformation."

"I was asked to keep it quiet. Others weren't informed. No point in taking away everybody's hope before a successful outcome from the Hill Studies."

David's response could not convey the sizzling irony in his voice when he said, "So nice of you all to keep me and my staff in the dark. I thought that every scrap of communication, 'as we agreed,' was intended as a two-way thing, not just from here to there."

Chastened, but not yet grasping the entire reason for his tone, her own became defensive and formal—for a while. "I broke faith telling you that much. What other questions can I answer for you? . . . Anyway, David, we mainly agreed about electronic communication—not every word that passes between people."

"Like totally destroying 'quite a few' hills across this planet's unique ecology is equivalent to a few inconsequential words passing between people—in high places—especially when those words pass between planners and 'authorities' who have zero background in what they're doing."

"What unique ecology? It's a dead planet."

"Technically, maybe; but on my team we aren't so sure. This planet is a challenge and we need to respect it. We should not be treating it the way we treated Earth. It took centuries—even before the arrival of the Dorts—to allow it to restore itself. That job's still in progress—with big setbacks along the way, and no doubt, there will be more."

"We weren't responsible for that! Do you think tearing out sixty-four kilometers of planet Earth by the roots to create this Great Cone of Transformation was worth it? Did that respect planet Earth? Did you think that doing that was innocent and harmless? And that all those other Cones, the smaller ones, were harmless to Earth's ecology? To say nothing of—"

"Have you forgotten," David interrupted, "about the years I spent protesting these Cones? That I even came on this one was to help prove the pointlessness of the destruction caused by this technology—to show that just because we can do it doesn't mean we should, or that 'it is inevitable so why fight it?'"

Debra groaned, "I suppose every Transformation has to have someone like you along."

David turned and looked at Laura and the others, then looked back at the screen where Debra was frowning. He said, "You're not alone. Your attitude toward my ideas, yes, my professional concerns, is reflected in the faces here—Jack is examining the ceiling, Laura's filing her nails, Ned is—"

"Okay! Enough! What are your other questions?"

David heaved a deep sigh. "Yes. My questions. Maybe they will give you another clue why I'm here—one I didn't know about when I signed on. So my second question is, how many hills have been destroyed in the Hill Studies up to now? In other words, what does 'quite a few' mean?"

"A couple dozen, so far as I know."

"Jesus!"

"We're doing it for your good—we're trying to help, damn it!"

"Next question: How far apart are the hills spaced that you've been 'studying'?"

"That one I know," Debra said. "I haven't missed a meeting or a briefing, unless some were secretly held without me. The new mapping, with the help of the Orb and some of the shuttles, plus what we do from here, puts them ten to thirty kilometers apart—more concentrated in some places, more scattered in others. On some parts of the continent they're a couple hundred kilometers apart. It's random. Well, not perfectly random. They're more concentrated in your part of the continent."

"Now the final question, Debra. If you don't know the answer to this one with absolute certainty, don't answer. Find out and get back to me. Until then—no more Hill Studies!"

"Okay, okay! What's the question?"

"When one hill has come down, from whatever kind of experiment, has any other hill come down simultaneously—or worse yet, later, and if later, how much later, and how far from the first wrecked hill? That's the question."

"You're right. I don't have a clue. I'll get back to you. No I won't. I'll have Stan call you."

Debra's grumpy expression suddenly changed into one of wide-eyed shock. "Holy Styx, David, I am so sorry! From your questions alone I just realized what you're getting at. Holy hell! We should have been coordinating all this with you in the first place. *You* are the expert for these studies—or should be. We've been so stupid. Just because so many here don't agree with your philosophy about Transformations and ecology shouldn't have blinded us to your useful—in this case, crucial—knowledge and skills. Even I should have thought of this. It's so obvious now. I hope you're wrong, but you're not wrong to worry about this. What if you're right! I will personally kill anybody who even suggests another Hill Study without you being in charge of it. I am so sorry. I—"

David dryly interrupted, "Just have Stan call."

"I've recorded this. I'll play it for him and have him call. Bye!"

"Bye!"

* * *

"It's only half a block away, Clint, but anyhow we better hurry," Mark said unnecessarily. They were already running.

On reaching Mark's habitat, they heard loud, rapidly snapping and popping sounds from inside. Mark opened the door and they entered cautiously. Clint entered first—gun drawn. The violent, amplified sounds heard earlier from inside the closed wing-leafs—the frightening racket that drove Mark from his habitat in the first place—had subsided. In its place were similar sound, but less harsh.

The skylight and windows had been darkened. Mark sometimes enjoyed the ambiance of the mound's soft-green florescence during the daytime, so on this occasion—before the 'jackhammering' suddenly drove him out—he'd switched the windows to opaque. When Clint and Mark entered, all they could see was darkness, except for the brilliant light from the open door. That made the inside seem even darker and temporarily blinded them.

Clint inched in, flat against the wall. "Could we get a light on in here?" he said. Mark's window switch was on the far side of the room next to his favorite chair; but he did reach his standard overhead switch. Coming from outside, the artificial light seemed faint; but after Mark closed the door to kill the contrast, they could almost see.

As their eyes adjusted, the habitat's interior condition became clearer. Clint immediately summed it all up: "Oh shit!"

Shards of shattered wing-leafs lay quietly scattered throughout the room; their inert fragments were in contrast to the seething movement of flailing strings that still snapping up from the floor like popping corn. They jerked violently as they hardened slowly in the drying air.

Their attention became riveted on movement of the strings—repeatedly bending slowly and then straightening too fast to see. One happened to hit a massive wooden leg of Mark's favorite chair, breaking it off so fast that the chair did not move, but its splintered leg slammed with lightning speed against a far wall where it caromed into the ceiling, then into another piece of furniture and finally clattered to the tarpaulin floor.

The strings would snap from the floor into the air, do their own caroming all over the room and in the process make their popping, snapping sounds. Some came down like a spear and stuck straight into the floor, easily penetrating Mark's flimsy tarp. Other habitat surfaces were more flexible and some surfaces stone hard—and immune to such penetrations. The harpoonlike strings usually bounced off those surfaces—except for certain ornamental or wooden objects, like picture and window frames, and door panels. Most of the furniture either became pincushions or were shattered and destroyed. All the electronics, including Mark's wall screen, were trashed.

The two men saw no dangerous, giant monster lurking in the room—only the treacherous membranous strings of various lengths and widths, all twisting, snapping and turning—fully engaged in their final throes. Mark and Clint did see one other thing in the room—a shiny, glassy-looking surface where the mound had been—but could not attend to it as they found themselves dodging the flying strings. It only took a few seconds of clear vision for them to comprehend all of this, but too late to escape injury. One javelinlike string flashed straight for Mark's stomach. As he jumped aside it ripped his shirt and tore some skin, but another came at him with a slanting blow, like the side of a cane from an angry, puritan schoolmaster, hitting him violently across the buttocks. Clint opened the door, yelling "Let's get out of here!" but in that moment was violently pinned to the doorframe by a snapping string that penetrated his left trapezius muscle just above his left clavicle. The string remained there as he wrenched the still-twisting object from the door; but he could not remove it from his shoulder. They both bailed out of the habitat together. Neither of them thought to close the door.

Moving in a wide arc from the habitat door, they tried to rush back to the Ad-Sec habitat, but even as they went, they were slowed by having to dodge the hardening membranes, still snapping back and forth as they shot out the door over their heads and near their feet.

From a window of the Ad-Sec offices, Mark and Clint were seen bleeding and hurrying back. They were still being preceded and pursued by the shimmering missiles that kept firing out of Mark's open door. Some came out straight as an arrow, but most wheeled end-over-end—like sticks for a dog to fetch.

Mark hobbled as fast as he could, holding his backside with both hands. Clint staggered on; his left arm hanging limp from his shoulder as though its bones were in a bag of loose skin. From the window they saw the narrow, trembling string object sticking clean through his shoulder—and his blood spurting out, front and back. Mark and Clint had only been gone five minutes, but were already a mess.

Mark was ahead; Clint was weak from blood loss and slowing down. With her medical bag in hand, Ellen ran out to meet Clint, ignoring Mark as he hobbled by. Clint tried to wave her off and shouted that he had to get back to be on the conference call—that he had to warn everybody and was already falling behind. "I told them *five minutes*!" With that, he turned and fell backwards, unconscious. The fall drove the string-javelin flush with his scapula.

Spasms of the thin javelin in Clint's muscle had started to abate, as though taking longer rests between. In one nicely timed interval between spasms, Ellen put her foot on Clint's left shoulder for leverage, grabbed the string, and pulled it out the rest of the way. In that same action, she threw it as far as she could. By then David and Jack were beside her with a makeshift stretcher they adapted from one of their cots. They quickly moved Clint inside the Ad-Sec habitat where Ellen continued to attend him.

Mark was already there. He could not sit, so remained standing in front of the wall screen as he spoke to Kevin and the others from before. He quickly ascertained from them that the problem he and Clint had just experienced had not yet happened elsewhere on the Base, although dozens of the mounds were already shedding and spilling their liquid, followed rapidly by the up-thrusting of wing-leafs and their going through the self-sealing process. Mark told them that the safely sealed wing-leafs would not stay that way for long. Mark turned to look out the windows as he was talking and saw a large scattering of wing-leafs sprouting up all over, and curious human onlookers were everywhere.

He hastened to explain what happened to him and Clint and said the only safe place for people now was inside their habitats—until all the mounds completed the full process and the shattering shells of wing-leafs and javelin-strings stopped flying.

The Base Watch communications tree worked swiftly through its branches. In a few minutes everyone could be seen on a dead run for their habitats—and for their lives. A frightening racket was already beginning in some of the wing-leafs. Fortunately most, but not all, made it safely home without serious injury from the early maturation of a few mounds whose internal strings had dried enough inside to start busting out. It was one of Roger Flanders days at the clinic, so he handled those emergencies as they came in.

Things were happening so fast that, even before everyone had cleared out of the dangerous areas of the Base by finding habitat safety in their own or nearby habitats of friends, most of the mounds had already, with amazing and *sudden coordination*, raised their lustrous, pearly, wing-leaf sails. At that point the conference call was ended.

Before the racket and the running began, the burgeoning *sails* alone gave the flatland the busy look of a thriving marina. The glistening sails reflected the light of day as they remained bottled up within the towering hill like ships in a bottle; but more like a hundred Sidney Opera Houses nestled together in snug and peaceful harmony.

The peace and harmony did not last, but gave way to what sounded like a thousand jackhammers, followed by a shattering display of destruction by a billion scattering shards of wing-leafs fragments flying high in the first salvo, followed by a fireworks of the thin, twisting, snapping membranous objects in a jungle of disparate, parabolic flights. After falling to the surface, the string-objects snapped into another high and aimless flight. They did so again, and again, each time with less force than the time before.

Mark had no need to hear or see the last flips and whimpers of the strings. He stood more comfortably beside Clint's cot and asked Ellen how he was doing.

"He'll be fine," she said, "if he can tolerate the arm sling for a while. I know he'll rest well tonight—I gave him a shot. He's resting fine. His eyes are closed, but he's awake. We've been talking a little. If you want to talk with him for a minute, now's your chance. He'll be deep under soon enough."

Mark didn't know what to say, but gave it a try. "You're sure all bandaged up. Does it hurt?"

Clint started a quiet chuckle, then stopped. Mark asked him what he was laughing about. Clint could hardly get it out before falling asleep. He said, "I was just thinking of all those useless strings, and then I started thinking about Everett's gory photos—of all that 'practicing.' Looks like *It* was just horsing around. Nothing remotely humanoid came out of the mounds. We got cranked up for nothing! *It* must have found us too complicated to even approximate putting those practice pieces together right—and settled for all those nasty strings. Ain't that a riot?" He chuckled some more and drifted off to sleep.

Mark and Ellen stood and watched him for a while. Ellen thought his laughing had something to do with the medications she gave him, but they shook their heads and agree that Clint's humor, thanks to the drug, was edging very close to David's; but they were glad he was healing and resting. Ellen pulled up his covers and kissed his cheek.

Within hours, every mound had completed its cycle, and all the string activity had ceased. But, even before then a few intrepid and curious souls ventured out to see the chaos at close range. They carried makeshift shields constructed of surplus habitat materials for protection. But it was turning dark, and even the brave and curious were tired. The next day would be soon enough to survey the damage—and to begin the boring and tedious task of cleanup. For a change they would be glad to go back to boring and tedious times—as if wishes alone could make it so!

FORTY-TWO

Stacks of now-quiet debris awaited cleanup by the Base Watchers. As street cleaners, they opened lanes in all directions—pathways that led to nothing special, except the hill's circular wall that now defined the outskirts of Mark's Base camp. The previous day's demolition not only shattered the wing-leafs, but violently chipped away at the wall itself, which caused *most* of the debris. But the wall was thick where the strings could reach, so it was not penetrated. The wall was not that fragile, and the javelin-strings were not that powerful.

Only a few of the more paranoid Base Watchers still bothered to guard the wall. It was already clear that everyone on the Base *was* a Watcher, so no one was left to watch or worry about.

It was not until dusk that the behavior of some Base Watchers became notable. They were on their knees and stomachs, with their faces close to the shiny, circular surfaces where the mounds had been. They were trying to see into them. A dim florescence was coming from beneath those surfaces.

Ellen went out first, squid in hand, then motioned for the others to follow. They did, shaking their heads saying "Déjà vu" and "Not this again." They split up and headed for different sources of fluorescence. Clint was sleeping and left behind, still under strict orders from his doctor to stay there.

On approaching a location where people were trying to see what was beneath the "shiny" surface, the Watchers would look up and invite the different Directors to help them figure out what was down there. They explained that as night approached, the reduced reflection of daylight allowed better contrast to see the shape below—a shape with the fluorescence all around and below it.

At one such site, before moving in to see for herself, Laura asked what they saw down there. One responded that the shape had become so clear, as night was falling, that "the question is no longer *what* is down there, but *who*."

The silhouettes seemed to float beneath them, humanoid in shape, apparently on their backs, arms to their sides and legs together. Clear suggestions of gender by facial features could not be distinguish, although figure and build characteristics did imply their genders.

At one of the fluorescent circles a woman was saying, "That's you, Anvil! I know it!"

Laura wandered in the direction of that statement to hear more. "Not likely dear. I'm right here if you hadn't noticed."

She replied, "Of course it isn't you, Anvil, but it could be your twin—nobody else has a . . . a great body like . . . like your very name!"

Laura recognized the voices, but from the description alone she would have known who they were. Anvil was the only man on the Transformation who could beat Clint in an arm wrestle, and God help anyone who called him Ann. The latter point was just a rumor, but no one ever tested it, or wanted to. She thought, approvingly, that he was tapered more like a powerful log separating wedge than an anvil, but wasn't going to split hairs over the distinction. Laura walked over and said, "Hi Ingrid. Hi Anvil."

"Hi Laura," Ingrid said. "Guess what we found! There's something down there that's a dead ringer for Anvil—his body anyway."

"That sounds like something I'd like to see," Laura said. Ingrid gave a self-conscious laugh.

"Hi Laura," Anvil said, as he and Ingrid moved away from the center of the circular glow to make room for Laura.

In the darkness it was no longer necessary to bring one's face close to the surface to see the shadow-shape below. A short distance under Laura's feet it stood out like an attention-grabbing ad. "If I didn't know you were here, Anvil," Laura said, "I'd say that was you down there! . . . Nice build, too!"

Thanks," Anvil said. "But down there, who knows what else is similar." Ingrid gave another embarrassed laugh. "That thing's build might be just a coincidence."

"I don't think so," Ingrid said.

Laura said, "Neither do I."

An hour later the Ad-Sec habitat mates were back at their conference table. They started to talk, assuming that Clint was sleeping; but he came in from outside fifteen minutes later, saying, "Don't start without me. I have important news!"

Ellen gave him a withering look of disapproval; then turned to Laura in the opposite direction and gave her a wry smile and a wink. Laura did not give her away.

Jack responded to Clint. "We know all about it. We were out there too, you know."

"Oh," Clint said. "Then you know all about it—how I got the lid off one of them."

David jumped out of his chair, eyes flashing. "Are you nuts" Do you realize how dangerous that could be?"

"No problem!" Clint said with a smile. "I have three Base Watchers guarding it with drawn guns. If it moves, it's dead!"

David slapped his forehead hard with the heel of his right hand. It must have hurt. "That's not the danger I'm talking about. We still don't know the connection between anything having to do with the mounds and the possible collapse of the hill."

Clint frowned and said, "Well, I don't think—"

"—I know you don't think," David interrupted. "Take me to that spot right now, so I can make some kind of guess about the damage you've done."

"But," Clint protested, "it was the wall and the mounds you said we needed to be careful of. That mound is gone!"

"That's still part of the mound, Clint. Another phase of it."

"You keep changing your definition of what we have to avoid. First it's mounds, now it's phases of mounds. But hey! We were very careful removing the slab off of—whatever it was. The slab looked like quartz to me."

David said, "Quartz eh? Well, none of the crystals on Origin are what they seem. Calling the slab quartz*like* would be more accurate."

"Yeah, right. Anyway, it took nearly forty guys to heft it over to the side—a lot heavier than a manhole cover by a long shot! And no, Helen, I didn't lift. I just directed"

David asked rhetorically, "Heavy yes, but when your guys lifted it, what about its roots? Most of the crystals on Origin, unlike any I've seen on Earth, have something like connections, extensions that seem to go for long distances—miles sometimes, and God only knows how deep!"

"To tell the truth," Clint said, showing the first sign of remorse, "I didn't actually supervise the whole process—just gave instructions and handed out some guns. That *lid* was half-exposed by the time I got there. I thought it was silly the way they were using little whiskbrooms instead of shovels to work around that glittery manhole cover. Somebody said to forget shovels and that they were being, like I said, very careful. It was some of *your* guys, David. Come to think of it, I believe he did mention something about roots."

"*He*? Who said that to you?" David asked.

"Oh, you know, that young fellow, Kevin Verily."

Helen gave up and *allowed* Clint to lead David to the site. No one stayed behind. Out of habit Ellen brought her medical bag.

The site was already crowded and brightly lit by Everett's flood lights and his cameras flashing. From a distance as they approached, they saw a woman loping toward the site with oddly graceful, gazellelike bounds, carrying a sheet and blanket over her arms. At the same time, coming from the crowd toward them, also at a fast clip, was Kevin.

As he approached, David yelled to him, "You're fired, Kevin!"

"Too late," he yelled back without slowing down, "I already quit."

David and the group were still approaching the site from a distance when Kevin reached them. He wanted to explain what was happening, and what had been done so far. David even stopped to listen. Kevin talked fast and David's skeptical and angry expression slowly changed to one of mere skepticism. David finally said, "We'll see."

Kevin then turned to run back toward the site, but stopped abruptly. He walked back to the group with one last thing to say. David asked, "What now?"

"I forgot to mention—there's not a hair on her body, but she's just as beautiful as in real life!" He turned again and ran off—not responding to the barrage of questions coming on his heels as they ran after him.

On arrival, they worked their way through the crowd to the edge of the site. The once hemispheric mound was now its own mirror image—a hemispheric hole. This time the lump in its center was an identifiable humanoid form—with no strings attached.

David noticed the inversion and mumbled to himself, as he often did, in whole paragraphs, "My God! If the hills are anything like this, they aren't just giant mounds with bottomless, spreading foundations—they're spheroids!" Laura was beside him and the only one to hear his words. She would ask him about it later. In the meantime she had to see what this hairless copy looked like.

The woman with the sheet and blanket was lowered into the hollow and had already covered the figure, except the head. As she was being hoisted up, Ellen was getting ready to be lowered in next. Before going down to examine, whatever it was, she turned to Laura, Judy and David saying, "I recognize the face. That's a girl I've met—or rather, that's her isomorph. She stopped by my clinic after a plantoid scrape on her first visit to Origin. She said the scrape hurt and that she wouldn't be back. She's an intern with Stan. Her name is Heckart. Margaret Heckart. In the clinic waiting room she was in an argument with Kevin, who brought her in, along with her girlfriend—who also had a scrape. I think he had more to do with her not returning to Origin than the scrape. Or, to be fair, the other young lady, a fellow intern with Margaret on Stan's crew, also wanted to go back. Her name is Astra. Astra Hughs. Both young women have apparently known each other since childhood. Astra already has a couple Ph.D.'s, is a remarkable artist, supposedly, and now the poor girl wants to be an astrophysicist."

"Why do you say poor girl?" Judy asked.

"Well, she's a brilliant, talented, accomplished, sweet person—but, unfortunately—her limbs aren't hers. If that weren't bad enough, she is disfigured—even after a lot of surgery. Too mangled for the surgeons to do much. They'd have done more, like a face replacement, except for her allergy to rejection medications and a worse reaction to synthetic skin. Her druggy mother killed herself by setting her house on fire when Astra was under a year of age. In the process her mom neglected to make other arrangements for her baby."

"So that's why Margaret went back to the Cone," Judy said.

"Maybe. I still think her real reason had more to do with Kevin. Something must have happened between them, and she had second thoughts. Anyway, that's what I gathered from hearing some of their argument."

"I'm sure you're right about that," David said. "I fired him a couple times already for similar behavior."

In unison the three women asked, "What behavior?"

"Never mind," he said.

"Fine!" Ellen said. "It's none of our business anyway. But David, I want you to come with me. Whatever there is to examine might, within reason, be as much in your field as mine."

They were lowered together. It wasn't that deep, and David could have done it without assistance, but it was a bit safer and less likely he'd accidentally bump into the isomorph.

As she watched them go into the hollow, Judy said to the others, "Hair or no hair, that face is beautiful—but her complexion is unusual—at least in the glare from these floodlights."

Ellen felt for a pulse. There was none. Nor could she identify any sign of life with her stethoscope and other field-available tests. Its surface was soft, and the joints flexible. When an arm or leg was lifted it gave no resistance—but was extremely heavy—and would flop as loose-limbed as a puppet. She guessed the isomorph weighed three or four times that of Margaret—the human it mimicked. The bone structure seemed correct and intact. She could not insert a needle into the "skin" and could not obtain even a sample of it with her sharpest scalpel.

While Ellen was doing the physical exam, so was David. He was examining the skin with a jeweler's eye-piece. The "skin" was silvery-white, like pearl, with subtle streaks and flecks of yellow-gold, and a delicate play of rainbow colors—colors not only originating from the outer surface, but gemlike from beneath the surface through thin layers of semitransparency. David told Ellen he thought it was gorgeous. Then he asked Ellen, "What are you finding?"

"Nothing that's alive," she said. "How about you?"

"On this planet, who knows what alive means. If it were alive, it couldn't live forever, like the Dorts seem to be doing—except for Twisters. On the other hand, if it lived, it might do so for millions of years. That's a lot less than forever," he said, laughing. "In order to die, it would eventually have to crystallize, and to do that it would first have to lose most of its water content."

"I don't understand. You'll have to go over that for me again. What brings you to that conclusion about age?"

"It's not a conclusion—just a guess."

"Why that guess?"

"Because the skin of this ditto-morph, or whatever you call it, is made of something like crystal, but it's not real crystal, any more than glass is. It's similar to noncrystalline silica—like opal. If so, it may have come from a gel or colloidal precipitate; from an aqueous suspension—so it contains a lot of water. The surface even looks like opal, but it's supple. I've never seen or heard of anything like it—except in the organic world—but here it is! Gems are hard. This thing is soft as flesh and flexible. As for guessing about age, opals eventually lose the water in their chemistry, and then they crystallize—but, again, for that to happen it takes a lot of years—millions of them."

"Well," Ellen said, "it's not alive so we won't have to worry about growing old together with this thing. I wouldn't look good at that age anyway."

Then Ellen lifted its eyelid—and gasped involuntarily. The iris was an oval of deep golden-amber and its black pupil—a cat's-eye slit. David joined in the eye examination. He said the iris and pupil together reminded him of a chrysoberyl—a rare gem. The white part of the eye was like precious opal.

David stood up and stretched—with that sly look in his eyes. Then he said, "I think we should give her a name. We should call her *Opal*." Then, as one might expect, but from no one else, he bent over, hooting.

Since the idea was not remotely funny Ellen did not laugh, but smiled and asked, "Why are you laughing? It's a perfectly appropriate name for this young lady! You are right. We will call her Opal." David sobered immediately. The idea that his amusing idea was appropriate seemed to spoil it for him.

Then Ellen went back to work. Opal's mouth was easily opened. The teeth were all there and perfect, but the tongue and other surfaces within the mouth and throat had the color and luster of gold. David checked the same areas and concluded it was a beautiful color and a variant of her other opalesque features. Even her ear drums were golden. But the flexibility and softness of the external surfaces, and the creamy moistness and velvety smoothness of the mouth's interior were unfathomable to him. "If I were a blind man making these same checks," David said, "I would swear this was a real human." Ellen agreed.

"I'd also say, if I were a blind man on this exam, that she was merely unconscious or in a coma—not dead."

"With all that's left of the mounds around here, there may be a lot more human-looking things to come, but I don't think anyone will be able to tell if these puppetlike structures are anything more than elaborate plantoids. This one certainly isn't alive. You do agree, don't you?"

"Of course, say I, the geologist come crystallographer. But of course not, say I, the blind man."

"Why?"

"I'm sure you noticed her temperature. It's a little sub-normal, but not cold."

"Yes, but it was in the bright daylight till a little while ago when Nimbus went down. Why doesn't the geologist in you say she's alive?"

"Oh, because of Nimbus, as you said, plus the radiation below and inside of our Opal. That could raise her temperature too. But mostly I'd say she's not alive because you say so."

They continued working and talking. By the time they had completely examined Opal's head and extremities, the woman who supplied the sheet and cover was again at the edge of the site—this time with tent poles and a large tarpaulin. She was in an argument with Everett who wanted to film everything. "Damn it, Denise!" he yelled, "This is history!"

She yelled right back at him. "History, schmistery. This tent stuff goes over her before they examine anything else." Then she turned, hands on hips, looking down at David and Ellen who, after the outburst, were looking up at her. "You got that down there?" she asked in a loud voice, but no longer yelling.

"Way ahead of you!" Ellen replied.

In a few minutes the privacy tent was ready. As Ellen entered, she turned her head to the side where David was about to enter with her, and said, "You too, David, along with all the rest of the prying eyes, are to stay out."

"Shouldn't my part of this examination be just as thorough as—"

"No!" Ellen interrupted. "Your part of this examination is over. You're neither a physician nor an undertaker. So out."

He turned away compliantly, mumbling, "It's just an inorganic lump, so what's the big deal!"

"I heard that!" Ellen said as she closed the flap, and then added with irritation, "When we get back to Earth I'll buy you a blow-up doll." She immediately regretted her last remark when she heard David's gleeful laugh— but he did remain outside.

The rest of the physical examination did not take long. On leaving the tent she gave David a peeved glance, then looked up and saw Denise, and smiled. Clint was nearby. She said, loud enough for them both to hear over the crowd noise, "This tent should stay right here. Clint, would you and Denise please get together and arrange for that?"

Ellen and David were helped back up to the rim of the site. They, with Clint and the gaunt but strangely attractive middle-aged woman, Denise, stood engaged in conversation. They were soon joined by the rest of the group—Judy, Mark, Jack, Ned and Laura. Then came Everett, the self-appointed news correspondent—in the absence of Debra Anderson—with his camera and sound equipment. Ellen and David grudgingly accepted Everett in that role, and gave a reasonably detailed, but publishable account of their examination to everybody within earshot. They didn't want Everett to think he was getting an exclusive. They knew their report would be all over The FAST News by morning—pictures and all. In some ways Everett was quite useful.

Everett's focus switched to Clint and Denise. Denise was tall and slim, with an angular, bespectacled, intelligent face. On the Transformation she called herself a librarian, but was really the expert in charge of data searches—digging out information of all kinds that no one else could, not to mention information that anyone should have been able to find. In that category, Officer Bracket knew her very well. They got along and he had no difficulty with her *isomorphic privacy* demands; but did have trouble with her insistence that the guards on the site have no guns. He balked at that until David reminded him that bullets were more powerful than strings and could penetrate the hill, especially the shell's thinner bulkhead at heights greater than the strings could attain. Clint was jolted by the reminder and it settled the matter: no guns. With Debra Anderson's suggestions and careful editing, Everett managed to inflate the human interest details around isomorphic privacy and the security arrangements. It became a sidebar to the report from Ellen and David.

Throughout these exchanges, Marcus Tenderloin did not hear a word. He was there, but the words were just noise to him. Rather, he was spellbound by this new, amazing apparition: a rather gaunt, bespectacled and overtly prudish librarian. *Maybe not so prudish*, he thought . . . no, not a thought—a hope!

When David and Ellen were briefly alone after giving their report, he had to make the inquiry: "Ellen, I noticed that you didn't say a word to Everett or anyone else about what you found in your lone examination of that opalesque artifact under Denise's tent. May I presume that there were no surprises?"

"Nothing major. You may have guessed from your examination of Opal's tympanic membranes and oral cavity, that its other internals, so far as my examination could determine, were the same."

"You found gold." David said.

"Yes. And if you make any wise remarks about that, especially to others, I will kill you."

"I would never dream of it! Not a word! You can trust me.... I did, however, feel a bit put off when you did not respect my professionalism under the tent. You said there were no major surprises. Any minor ones?"

"Just one. No navel."

The crowd thinned out. The isomorph remained covered and guarded. The other fluorescent sites continued to encircle the ambiguous forms within. Throughout the night, most of the sites remained under close observation by the Base Watchers who kept moving, alone or in small groups, from one site to the next, striving to determine "who's" isomorph was down there.

Everett returned to several of the sights and set up spotlights, placing them flush with the translucent "quartz" surfaces. That created a nonreflective optical penetration for his cameras. He took dozens of pictures at each of three sites. Back in the photography part of his shop, the individual pictures were not revealing, but by morphing several of the exposures into one, he obtained excellent likenesses of the objects beneath. In that way, three isomorphs were found to be unmistakable "copies" of Transformation crewmen.

"No navel," David mumbled aloud as he wandered alone back to the Ad-Sec habitat. The others had gone on ahead of him. "Poor Opal! No navel. Oh well, she makes up for that little lack in other ways, not the least of which is her ... her—Ellen would kill me for even thinking this—her golden pussy!"

"Did you hear that?" Jack asked.

"Yes," Ned said. "He's half a kilometer away, but we can hear him laughing. It must have been a dilly!"

"I'm sure it was," Ellen said sardonically, followed by her own mumble: "I should never have told that sonuvabitch! He's a dead man!"

FORTY-THREE

David's laughing stopped long before his return to the habitat, and was grumbling on the way in.

"What's the matter?" Judy asked.

"I think Everett is up to something. He's got people running around with his equipment. I thought he'd photographed only a few isomorphs under those quartzlike slabs, but all this other activity shows he's working on a lot more. Nothing catastrophic happening when that first slab was removed, but I don't know if being *'very careful'* is going to be enough from now on, or even something Everett is capable of. So far we've just been lucky with that first tomb opening."

Laura said, "*Tomb*, maybe, if the isomorph is really unalive; otherwise we're talking *womb*, okay?"

Clint was sitting on the side of his cot. He just shook his head.

"Everett hasn't busted anything yet," Ned said. "He uses lights and image blending to get his pictures. You use x-rays to analyze your crystals and acoustics to survey rock structures. What's the difference?"

"Hell, I don't know. I just don't trust his judgment. I'm a suspicious Base Watcher. A few guards are still patrolling the outer wall for no logical reason. Maybe they're just as illogical as I am. We're all on the same side, but I fear the *poor judgment* of others—even their *good intensions*—as dangerous. I believe Everett has both."

The wall screen beeped. It was the smiling face of Stanley Lundeen. He asked for David Michaels.

David frowned at the screen. "Well, it took you long enough to get back. Debra told me she'd forward my questions for your response. From your smile I assume the news is bad."

"That, Dr. Michaels, is no way to greet someone who has figured out how to save your collective asses!"

"Really!" David said with a whole new attitude. "May I also say how good it is to be talking with you again."

"That's more like it! How are the rest of you doing?"

Several began talking at once, but Stan could see them smiling, as they had arranged themselves in front of the screen's camera.

"I see you're smiling too, Clint," Stan said, "but what happened to your arm?"

"Nothing serious. I just ran into a string."

"So I heard—from Debra. I just wondered if it was true. And Mark! I understand you got *spanked*—right out of your house and home. Same problem?"

"How in hell did Debra find out about that?" Mark asked.

David tried unsuccessfully to control a laugh.

"Never mind," Mark said, "I think I know. I suppose it'll all be in The FAST News tomorrow."

"You're right. Along with some great pictures of Margaret's copy—the one you call Opal. Debra showed them to Margaret and now she wants to personally see her isomorph. She thinks it's exciting to have a twin—even if it's just an exquisite puppet."

"She's gotta be out of her mind," Clint said. "If something like that showed up of me, I'd bust it to pieces."

David said, "Okay—what's the deal on saving our 'collective asses'? We're all curious to know. How did you come up with the plan? And, oh yeah, I'd still like to get some answers to the questions I asked Debra to give you."

"I'll be sending you detailed information on all that in an Attachment tomorrow—if our communications don't go out again. I'm getting tired of that. It happens every day or so, or a couple times a day. Anyway, I haven't finished the report yet. Most of it has already been written by your Geophysics and Mineralogy staff—the part of your crew that made it back here. You must have them well trained—they were jumping all over me even before I got your message from Debra. So I turned all of it over to them. We're just coordinating now."

"Just coordinating?" David asked, raising an eyebrow.

"Oh dear!" Stan said with sham embarrassment. "Now I have to tell the truth. The plan to save your asses is theirs—not mine."

"That figures."

"And," Stan added with a broader smile than before, "they think it has a good chance of working."

"A chance?" Laura said with anxiety in her voice. "What odds do they give it?"

He stammered, but got out a tentative, "Good odds!"

Laura approached the screen camera and squinted directly into it. "The odds, Stan!"

"Good is good. Why do you always want a number on everything?"

"Okay, stammering Stan—David was right in the first place, wasn't he?" Laura said. "Your smile was a cover. Now let's have it!"

Stan's upturned, smiling mouth faded to horizontal. "The Geophysics crew gives it about fifty-fifty."

"Thank you, Stan. That wasn't so hard, was it?"

After a halting pause, he said, "Easy as pie."

David said, very soberly, "After I review the report tomorrow, I'll be in touch with you and my Transformation-based crew. We'll have to work on improving those odds."

"Sounds good to me."

"In the meantime," David said, less seriously, "may I make a guess about those destroyed hills you 'experimented' with?"

"You want to answer your own questions—the ones I got from Debra?"

"Yes. Just a stab at them."

"You always have enjoyed making guesses. Rumor has it that you're usually right; but this time you'll never guess. Not in a million years! Unless your crew up here already spilled. *Oops! Those experiments* went on during communication blackouts. Sorry."

"No problem. Anyway, I'm challenged! What's the bet?"

"I don't bet, but you already said you're challenged—so go for it, David!"

"Okay! *First*, all the hills you experimented with were destroyed by penetrating them—if not completely penetrated, then by at least a meter. *Second*, other hills within about one kilometer of any of your experimental hills were also in trouble—even *without* your *experimenting* with them directly. They were destroyed within seconds or, at most, a few minutes of the first one. *Third*, the hills *farther* away were unaffected, unless—and this is point *four*—several hills in a row were that close together, then they also came down—like dominos. *Fifth*, with gaps between hills of *more* than a couple kilometers, there would be no problems! They'd stay unharmed and in place. Furthermore, for point *six*, there was *no* temporal or delayed-action hill destruction—aside from the short-duration domino effect I just mentioned."

After a pause, David said, "That's it, Stan. How'd I do?"

Stan was back to stammering. "My God, David! You're right—on every point. You always amaze me. How did you come to those conclusions?"

"We'll talk about that another time, Stan. Maybe tomorrow. Between now and then you'll have plenty of time to figure out how I figured it out." Then David moved away from the camera to chortle silently with delight—away from Stan's observation.

Ned smiled at Stan and said, "The answer is very simple, but David is too modest to remind you, and besides—"

"—And the answer is . . . ?" Stan interrupted insistently, apparently irritated that David had walked away.

"And besides, I didn't hire David for his world renowned *amateur* standing in his field."

"That's it?"

"I told you it was simple."

"You're as bad as David!"

"Never!"

"Well, if I'm going to get that report down to David by tomorrow, I'd better start flogging his men some more. I'll get back to you with a better hill-escape plan as soon as they get one to me."

"Okay, Stan," Ned said. "I hope we can move this along soon. The tides, at this rate, will be down to normal in a few more days. Then we'd like to chuck this planet—one way or another."

When the communication ended, David's habitat-mates were all over him to divulge how he figured it out—how he know the fate of the other hills. Coyly, he wasn't going to talk—but enjoyed the attention, especially from Judy, who was agog with admiration.

After Laura threatened to steal his thunder by hinting she had figured it out, he finally felt he'd better confess it all. At first he didn't believe Laura's threat, until they had a brief, hushed conversation. He was a good sport about it and admitted that Laura's idea was "close" to the mark.

Talking to the group he said, "When Laura told me she overheard my mumbling about the possible three-dimensional shape of the hill, I knew she had me!"

"What does the shape of the hill have to do with it?" Judy asked. "How did you, from that, come to the same conclusions as Stan and the others?"

"They didn't come to *any* conclusions—not about that, at least. They only recorded what happened when they accidentally destroyed some hills—hills at a variety of distances from one another."

Yes," Jack said, "but you weren't there. We keep asking, how did *you* come to those conclusions?"

"Like Stan, I too have things I hate to admit." David said. "I didn't come to any conclusions either. Mine were just educated guesses. I didn't want to say that right away to Stan. I'd rather have him stew about it for a while and let him *think* I'm a genius."

"That's enough teasing, David," said Judy, who was used to his teasing. "How did you make those *guesses*?"

Laura was staring at David with her all-knowing, you-must-realize-the-jug's-up, expression.

"Oh my God!" he said, staring back at Laura, who—unknown to him, was without *any* real clue, but pretending she knew it all. "I am *so* —what's the word—found out!"

Laura switched her poker expression to a cruel smirk and said, "The word is 'busted.' And yes you are! So start talking—or *I* will!" She skillfully covered up how much she was enjoying her bluff.

So, not being one to share credit on too many matters, he did start talking. "Everything depended on the hills being closed structures, like spheres."

Ellen said, "But they aren't spheres or anything of the sort. They're hemispheres. Would you mind explaining?"

"Ellen," Jack said, "don't interrupt him—he was starting to talk."

"Sorry."

David continued. "We've talked about this many times. Most of the crystalline structures on Origin have 'roots.' This hill is no different, except its roots go a *lot deeper*, and my own limited studies—before the flood—confirmed that. Hill 'roots' seemed to extend downward and outward—at an angle. When the 'small' hemispheric mounds turned out to really be spherical, or close to it, I made a wild guess that the hills might also be spherical, or otherwise closed. If so, then hill 'roots' did *not* extend outward for endless kilometers, but eventually turned inward, like the outer layer of an onion—not sprawled out like tree roots. That would limit any inter-hill contacts, except for those close to one another. I just guessed at the critical 'closeness' being a kilometer or so. Those close-together hills could have grown together, to share a wall beneath their surfaces, like Siamese twins, and would therefore be equally vulnerable to destruction. When one dies, the other follows close behind. With the destruction of one, the other would also come down in rapid sequence."

"Sorry to interrupt again," Ellen said, "but if that's true and this hill curves under instead of extending outward, my limited visualization questions how it can also extend so far out—beyond even a single kilometer?"

"Well," David said, "I get your point. You're right. It's not intuitive. But imagine a lumpy sphere—like a golf ball, only with lumps on its surface instead of dents. Then imagine we're standing near the surface of such a giant ball, but under one of its lumps—this hill."

"That turns my visualization around," Ellen said. "This 'lump' is already sixteen hundred meters in height and even farther across. So if this hill is just a little lump on a much bigger ball, then its spherical 'root' would have to extend outward many times *wider* than a couple kilometers."

"Right again. So maybe, way down deep, it's not an onionlike sphere at all, but more like a carrot, or cone-shaped like the Transformation, or the upper part of a kid's top, or who knows what. Or maybe this is an extra-large blister on top of a smaller onion. How should I know? The point is, the 'roots' *converge* rather than spread out. That should keep us safe from any screwing around they've already done to the other hills—so long as they *have* stopped. I think we can trust Stan and my crew on that."

Ellen said, "Fine. Thank you for answering my naive questions. My limited imagination *can* deal with a carrot."

Jack said, "While we're on the subject, David, I have a couple of naive questions of my own."

"Those are my favorites!"

"Why, for one thing, are there no real rocks on this planet? The other question is, why couldn't we just dig ourselves out? We'd only need to dig a nice deep tunnel, corkscrewlike, and then burrow out toward the wall, the hill's 'root,' and then blast or chisel our way through the last barrier—the hill's root-wall. If the hill collapsed, we'd be safe with that wide barrier above us—because we'd make sure we dug deep enough. Then we'd just have to dig ourselves back up to the surface."

David said, "That's a brilliant solution, Jack! Congratulations!"

"The way you said that, David, convinces me that my plan—what was Debra's word?—*sucks*. Okay, let's see the hands of everybody who *already* thought of the same thing?" All the hands went up. "And how many of you never brought it up, or even talked about it, because you figured it would work as a last resort—and it made you feel safer in the meantime?" Again, all hands went up—except David's.

Jack glowered at David. "The plan is flawless. We're all bright people who figured out the same plan. So David, are you still going to tell us it *sucks*?"

"It really does."

"How bad?"

"Really bad."

"Is it beneath your dignity to tell us why?"

"Far from it. It's just that it's so—so obvious that I don't want to embarrass you."

Ned spoke up. "David, this matter is way too serious for you to keep screwing with us. If it's a lousy plan, explain why, and then, if you can, give us a better one."

"Well Ned, *harrumph* to you too!" Then David became serious. "Don't say I didn't warn you. Here goes:

"Have any of you tried to transplant a plantoid?" They all had. "What happened to it then?" It crumbled into tiny sand and dust-size fragments. "How long did it take for that to happen?" A few hours at most—often within minutes. "What happened to the site where you dug up the plantoid?" It caved in for a meter or more in all directions. "Since the entire surface—and even beneath the surface, going down for hundreds of meters—consists of plantoid 'roots,' how far do you think we could dig a tunnel without its caving in on us?"

"That's enough, David," Ned said. "You did warn us."

In a shaking voice, but with chin thrust forward, Judy said, "I'm not ready to give up on the idea. How about reinforcements? They prop up coal mine passages with posts and boards. Have you ever thought of *that*?"

David sighed and said, "With the right reinforcements you could build a tunnel under water. Easier, in fact. In this case, think of something like fine, dry sand. We could reinforce such a tunnel for a short distance. And yes, I did think of it. And I also took the trouble to inventory the appropriate materials available at the Mart. We wouldn't even come close. The only other available materials are our habitats. Habitat materials are great for holding off strong winds and for deflecting some nasty strings, but it would collapse under any significant weight—and hundreds of tons of sand would classify as significant."

Jack shook his head. "About there being no rocks on Origin. Do we really know that, David? And if there are rocks down there, as we have on the Transformation Cone, then digging reasonably safe, cave-in-free tunnels, would not be difficult. If we managed to dig deep enough, how do you know we wouldn't find a truly solid and stable substance like rock?"

David said, "We have Stan's surveys and gravitational studies of Origin before we came here, and his calculations of Origin's density and moment of inertia, and our own measurements and analysis of seismic waves from Origin's quakes since we arrived. All this, and a lot more, proved that we could reach plenty of rock-solid, granitized stuff *beneath* this planet's crust of crystalline veneer *if*, and only if, we went deep enough. This veneer is the surface stuff on top of Origins lithosphere. Below that we're into its mantle, right on down to its iron-nickel core. Most of that is the solid stuff you want—except for the molten part of the core, before you get to the solid core beneath that. Earth and Origin must have had a similar history. Anyway, to even reach the first solid rock material would require digging down for many kilometers. Could we keep the sides of such a shaft reinforced from cave-ins for such a distance? You know the answer to that as well as I do."

"I said it before," Ned said. "You warned us. So, David, what would be a better plan? I recall you once mentioned having some 'wild scheme' to get us out. What was that 'wild scheme'?"

David looked as serious as anyone had ever seen him. He replied, "I'm afraid we just finished discussing it."

"Then what do you suggest now?"

David shook his head slowly and said, "I don't have a clue."

The FAST News on the following day revealed everything Stan said it would, plus a lot more. It included color pictures of Opal and a long photographic roster of other isomorph-person copies, and the name and current location of the copied human. Three-quarters of those were "copies" of people on the Transformation Cone.

Debra Anderson's accompanying editorial credited Everett and his volunteers for the photographs. She also made the observation that none of the photographed isomorphs had the characteristics of any species other than human; that they all represented someone on or from the Transformation; that there were no duplications from one mound to another—with the single exception of Orla Nims's set of identical twin isomorphs. Orla was in the clerical pool and was herself from a set of identical twins, but her twin was stillborn.

Debra's picture spread included a brief quotation under each photograph. The person whose isomorph was pictured provided the quote. Her interview question for that spread was open-ended: "What do you think of your isomorph?" They were all surprised and wondered how such a thing could have happened. Beyond that, except for one, they were all pleased with their copies. The woman whose isomorph turned out to be twins, was not "pleased"—she was *ecstatic*. And Margaret Heckart accepted the name of Opal for *hers*, but wished she could have picked the name herself. Everyone else wanted to do their own naming. Debra promised to include as many of the chosen names as she could in the next day's issue of The FAST News.

Ellen returned to her clinic where she found Dr. Roger Flanders sleeping. She woke him up. He was worn out and glad to see Ellen was back for her turn on duty. She sent him home to his habitat—groggy, but grateful.

Judy and David went to their joint chemistry-geology lab, not far from Ellen's clinic and equally near the Ad-Sec habitat. On the way to their lab, Judy brought along a number of items, including a small bag. As they passed several of the piles of debris swept up by the clean-up crew of Base Watchers, she picked some of the smaller, inactive, string fragments. David asked her why she was making such a collection. She said there were some tests she wanted to run on them. She described the tests to David who thought they would be interesting and would help her with them.

Ned and Laura returned to their own habitats, but ended up in hers—for R & R; and Clint and Jack remained at the Ad-Sec habitat.

In the end, they all had a lot of thinking to do. Things had been happening too fast. Until then, there had been little time to consider anything but immediate next steps.

But resting, thinking and lab work were not the only pursuits for that day. Everett Balz arranged for opaque habitat material to be placed, during bright-daylight hours, over what remained of the mounds, namely the circular quartzlike slabs and the figures of interest beneath them. That way, with his many volunteers and trainees, he was not confined to nighttime picture taking. It would go on day and night until the picture gallery was complete. Every morning, very early, the corrected, morphed photographs would be conveyed electronically to Debra for immediate publication in The FAST News.

Had that been all that was going on under Everett's makeshift dark rooms, it might not have been upsetting—for almost everyone except those involved. Even Debra Anderson was not privy to those goings-on—or she would have blown the whistle with shrill and blaring headlines.

Nights came and went and The FAST News continued to be published, filling its pages with each isomorph photograph sent to her. Dozens of isomorphs had received names, and others would not be named until seen by its original human. The twins were named Efecta and Causa. Debra's editorial said it was unknown which twin came first. Personal computers on the Cone were busy printing out little birth certificates for the ones with names. Mini-industries sprang up around this new phenomenon. Pictured decks of cards were a big item, followed closely by T-shirts with pictures and names. Others, in droves, submitted letters, poetry and Op-Ed pieces to The FAST News. No superior put the breaks on any of this activity. There was already enough stress and excitement without spoiling that little bit of fun and relief. Most of the voluminous material written by so many for The FAST News would not be published that morning, the next morning, or any other morning. Events were moving too fast for their relevance.

Debra Anderson was just about the last to become aware of Everett's secret shenanigans under the hill and she was rightly horrified. Everett had been using dark habitat material (that they called opaque veils, or simply "veils") to enable photographing throughout the daylight hours as the isomorph subjects lay in unmoving poses beneath their all-but-transparent tombstones. After picture taking, the habitat material could be removed and used elsewhere; no new revelations there. She and everyone else already knew that part, but not the rest of it. Many of those unveilings, especially near the east side of Mark's Base, produced chilling revelations—revelations that most of the Base Watchers conspired to keep from the Directors.

FORTY-FOUR

"Of course those strings are some kind of crystal," David snapped in response to Judy's question. *Of course* was right. She knew they were crystals as well as he did, but he'd been silent for an irritatingly long time. He was trying to analyze the X-ray diffraction of the strings' components—strings Judy had collected on their way over from the Ad-Sec habitat. She reminded him, as she peeked out from behind her sinks and Bunsen burners, that she too was working on strings. She only wanted some kind of communication on what he was finding—*any* kind of communication, in fact. She was lonesome.

"Sorry I jumped at you just then," he said. "I'm running into a frustrating problem with these strings. It's the same problem I've had with every other so-called crystal I've tried to analyze on Origin."

Judy came out from behind her Bunsen burners.

"They're crystals, all right, but then again, they aren't!" David continued. "Take a look at this array for example." He turned the screen in her direction enough for them both to see.

She said, "It looks like a repeating atomic pattern to me—could even be from purified biomolecules, like crystallized proteins."

"—or DNA," he added.

"Yes," she said, "that would fit."

"Only it doesn't. Take a look at this area," he said, pointing to a spot on the screen."

"I can't figure *that* out," she said. "The rest of it makes sense, but not when you throw this in. What is it? Some kind of contaminant?"

"Yes, a contaminant; but no. It's some kind of commonality, or universal, that I've found in every formation, crystal, hill, mound, and plantoid sample I've examined to date on this planet—right on down to the sand on the beach and the salt in the ocean!"

"Oh, come *on*! There's a universal, all right, and it has to be something wrong with your equipment!"

David looked glum. "I've already checked that—over and over," he said. "That's not it. It's in the material itself. The chemistry on this planet is exactly the same as every other part of this universe—except that it isn't—not exactly."

"*Not exactly* what? Not exactly part of *this* universe?" Judy started to giggle. "Cheer up, David! You always wanted to come up with some great new discovery or theory in your field. Here's your opportunity."

"Yeah, right," David said as he turned off the computer. "What are you doing?"

"I'm just playing with the strings. Soaking them in water. I suppose you're going to tell me that the water on this planet isn't really water."

"No, the water is real. It's just that the salt—"

"—Yes, yes, I know. It's not really salt—exactly."

"Exactly! But what are you doing—playing in the water with a bunch of strings? What are your great findings?"

"Nothing. But that's significant, right? Negative findings are as valid as positive ones."

"What's negative?" David asked.

"Water has no effect on these depleted, dried out, motionless, *stupid*, dead strings! I thought they might soften up, like they were before they dried out."

"You wanted a *positive* result—like they're more *important* than valid negatives?"

"I guess."

"So what if they had softened up?"

Judy only shrugged.

"Have you done anything with that other stuff you had us bring? You picked up a bag of strings, but what's in that duffel bag you gave me to carry?"

"Mostly clean clothes, a couple sandwiches for our lunch, and that jug of liquid Kevin gave me—the water he siphoned from that first molting mound. I've already analyzed *that* stuff—it's just water—mostly."

David frowned. "Just water?"

"Mostly. A little bit yellowish."

"What else? Humor me. Characterize the water."

"That's hard to do. You were right when you and your crew said it was like amniotic fluid. Only it isn't—not exactly. It was close to a thin serous fluid, but—"

"—it wasn't—not exactly," David finished for her.

"Don't interrupt. I know what you're getting at with that, but it's nothing of the sort. Your equipment is screwed up. Mine isn't. I would just need to look at it more. I could sort it out—if it was worth the bother. It isn't important. It's mostly just water, and that's that."

David tilted his head with a strange smile. Judy thought she sensed a "joke" coming on, but if so, it was delayed this time. "What would happen," he asked, "if you put the dried strings in the fluid that came from the mound?"

"Nothing. I just told you. I tried that with plane water. This stuff isn't different enough to make any difference."

"Humor me."

"Why?"

"Sometimes little things make a big difference—could be a catalytic substance in the mound fluid."

She acquiesced, shaking her head the whole time. She laid a few finger-length strings on a large crucible and poured a small amount of the yellowish fluid over them. After a few minutes Judy said, "There, you see—nothing!" She picked up one of the strings. It was as hard as ever. "When these things go still, they stay that way."

Through the lab windows, more activity than usual could be seen among the Base Watchers. Some were even looking and pointing at the Chem-Geol lab, but they thought nothing of it. Judy broke out the sandwiches she'd packed and got a couple drinks from the fridge; they had lunch, then relaxed and talked for a while. It wasn't long before they returned to the subject of strings. David looked into Judy's bag and noticed a half-dozen other crystal-like items. He held one up. "Why did you include these? They aren't strings."

"They look pretty, so I just collected some. I don't know what kind of crystals they are, do you?"

"Yes. They're chips off the hill wall—from strings hitting them. We're lucky they were just random hits on the wall to spread out the damage. If too many hits were in one place, the hill could have been wrecked—us along with it."

"They'll make nice souvenirs for when we get back to Earth."

David tilted his head again. "Let's put a few of these in that yellow water of yours."

She shrugged in resignation and said, "Sure, why not," and then smiled. She was enjoying David's company.

When they got to the crucible with the soaking strings, David reached in to remove one. As he lifted it up by one end, it stretched out into a thick, viscous substance—as they had between the wing-leafs. He quickly dropped it back into the liquid. Wide-eyed, he and Judy looked at each other. When they looked again, the string was pulling back into its original shape.

"I want to try something," Judy said. She put one of the now-viscous strings into regular water, left one in the crucible liquid, and put the last one on a small flat tray—with a few napkins to help it dry out. Then, without spilling, she placed them into separate, small packing boxes. "If these things start getting violent again, I don't want anything to be damaged." Then she put the small packing boxes into slightly larger, sturdier ones and put each of those into different storage rooms.

David watched all of this, nodding his understanding. It wasn't great science, but methodical enough under the circumstances. It would yield results—positive or negative.

He looked once more at the hill chips he was holding in his hands and said, "Let's do the same with these."

This time Judy was well beyond any objections and entered into the idea with enthusiasm. Before handing her the chips, he tested their hardness with his Mohs scratch scaling kit.

"These are the same hardness as every hill I've checked before. They're easily scratched with topaz, but quartz doesn't touch'm."

"How hard is that?" Judy asked.

"Above seven, but under eight on the Mohs scratch scale."
"Like I said, how hard is that?"
"Compared to what?"
"Well, *marble* is hard."
"Marble gets a three."
"Wow! Then my trinkets are harder than most rocks!"
"You should be delighted."

She then placed one of her *trinkets* in water and two, a palm width apart, in the mound fluid. "You know, David, these are nothing like strings. What do you expect the experiment to show?"

He shrugged and said, "I don't know."

"Me neither," Judy said, clapping her hands. "Isn't this fun?"

For this moment at least, David had a kindred soul, as he and his partner enjoyed a hearty laugh—together.

"I need to work off that sandwich," Judy said. "Let's go for a walk."

"The sandwich wasn't that big, and you look slim and lovely just as you are. Besides, we have an experiment or two pending here—and wouldn't an after dinner nap be better."

Judy said, "Thanks for the compliment; and these experimental results do not require our watching every minute; you could use the exercise more than me—and, besides, I'm not in the mood!"

"A walk it is, then," David said, with a touch of disappointment in his voice as he moved toward the door. Before he got there, he turned back and picked up a canvas valise.

"What's that for?"

"It's empty, except for a few tools and a small diamond-bit drill. I use it to collect samples. Might as well collect some wall *trinkets* on our walk, right?"

Once out the door, they noticed something different. The Base Watcher activity they saw earlier from the lab windows had ceased. A few Base Watchers to their south noticed, with prying eyes, that David and Judy were leaving their lab. The men waved from a distance and yelled an overly-friendly greeting. Judy and David returned a modest greeting, and then started walking eastward.

So did the "friendly" Base Watchers. They were angling their walk toward David and Judy. In a matter of blocks, the two groups would meet on one of the cleared pathways. Judy was not afraid, but still attempted to steer their walk to avoid them. She merely wanted to be alone with David. He paid no attention to the possible encounter. He was picking up wall chips along the way even as he and Judy continued to talk shop—despite her distraction.

Judy was trying to keep her mind on the conversation with David *and* an eye on the gradually nearing three-man group. She didn't want the time with David to be interrupted; but the men were walking faster, and David's scavenging slowed them down.

She suggested they walk north, and then suggested south, but David insisted on continuing east because the hill-chips were getting larger and more interesting as they moved closer to that side of the hill's base.

Judy spotted a particularly nice hill-chip that she handed to David. She asked, "What do you think of this one?"

"Hey! This is perfect for another experiment I want to try. Would you object if I ruined it in the process?"

"You can't ruin it. It's almost invulnerable. Remember, it's way up on the scratch scale of hardness."

"That isn't a straight answer, Judy."

"Then, *no,* you can't ruin it. I love it too much."

"You can't love it that much. You just met!"

"Why do you want to ruin the prettiest trinket I've found so far?"

"Because it's about the size and shape for me to test a theory of mine."

"What theory?"

"Let me put it this way: Have you noticed that these hill-trinkets have *not*—unlike every uprooted plantoid, or whole hill—crumbled into sand and dust?"

Judy stopped in her tracks. "My God, David! I never thought of that!"

"Think about it."

They started in again. The east wall seemed close, but the piles of chip debris were starting to crowd the pathways.

"I am thinking about it," she said. "Does that mean this hill would be safe to break out of—unlike all the other hills that crumbled? This is a new hill. It's not filled with centuries of plantoids. The old ones, the ones you and Stan 'studied' were filled—most of them anyway. Maybe this hill's different and won't fall apart."

"That's a possibility; but to know that we need to test my theory."

"Okay then. You have my approval to ruin the love of my life, but only on one condition."

"Fine. Everybody has an angle. What's yours?"

"That you tell me your theory and I find it worthy."

"So you're telling me *no?*"

"No, I'm not outright telling you *no.* I'm saying *no* till I tell you *yes.* Again, I have to hear your theory first. Then we'll see. I get to judge. It's my love, not yours. So tell me your theory." Judy was enjoying herself, but there was still that something out the corner of her eye.

Then she snapped: "Make it *short!*" Her tone was more emphatic and harsh than even she understood. The three Base Watchers had already closed half the distance between them from when they started. Judy became increasingly uncomfortable the closer they came.

"The short version, then," David said. "If this hill's base had been seriously violated by exceedingly deep or complete penetration and if it acted like the other hills we've studied, then it would have come clattering down."

"—That's no theory. We already know that."

"Not so fast with your interruptions. I haven't finished. These trinkets are not dust. And the hill is still here."

"So what's the theory?"

"Simply this: These chips haven't crumbled further because they were removed suddenly from being part of the hill as a whole."

"You mean, they didn't break up even more because they were no longer a part of the *whole* hill's committing suicide? If that's what the hill was going to do."

"Something like that," David said.

"Then these hill-chips, and every part of the hill, large or small, are part of a *signal* system, right on down to the last molecule—so long as they're still connected? So a quick chipping away removes the trinkets too fast for the hill to get the picture or send a drop dead signal to the chip. Is that your theory?"

"You're on the right track."

"I don't think so. If I did, then I'd know how that relates to ruining the love of my life. Explain!"

David hefted the chip. It was a crystal roughly the length and width as his own hand. "If my theory holds, this trinket is a virtual hologram of the entire hill."

"How does that idea lend itself to ruining the chip—to prove what?"

"That this chip and all the chips from the hill are self-contained systems, like the hill as a whole. They're hill-dependent only when they are systemically a part of it. After the strings knocked the hunks out, each hunk became its own system, unrelated to the fate of the hill—whether that fate is from a kindly-assisted suicide or murder. If your great love survives my test, then the hill itself will probably be safe to penetrate with some chipping of our own. We could make an opening of any size needed for our mass exodus to the Great Cone—when the tides return to normal, of course."

"I *like* that theory, David!"

"I'm sorry, but that's not the theory. I've been talking about a possible outcome of the *experiment* to test the theory. My *theory* is that the chip won't survive, nor the hill. I hope I'm wrong. If I'm not, we won't be able to leave and we'll be back to square one."

Judy was really becoming upset and still did not understand; but the three men were getting closer. "Oh hell," she said. "Go ahead and do your stupid experiment."

"Thank you."

David removed the diamond drill and drilled a half-dozen small holes part-way into Judy's beloved trinket.

"All that drilling," Judy said, "and nothing whatsoever happened. That's a good thing, right?"

"Correct," David said. "But those weren't serious violations of the chip's system. Now let's see what happens when I drill a hole completely through it."

He did so, and right on cue the chip broke into smaller pieces that kept crumbling further. In a minute it had turned to sand size specks and dust.

"Oh God, David! You're right—and we're stuck in this stupid hill from now till doomsday!"

To head them off, the three Base Watchers had been walking faster than David and Judy. They had closed the gap, reversed course, and were coming back—straight toward them. David did not notice their approach until almost running head-on into them.

The three men were immediately recognized as food service workers from the Honky-tonk Saloon. Although David and Judy wished to continue their walk, the service workers were enthusiastically insistent on friendly conversation and eventually got around to recommending they all saunter over to the Saloon together for a "great special."

"We just ate," David said.

After a few moments of apparent confusion on the part of the service workers, one said, "We're heading back that way and would appreciate your company, and your thoughts on our likelihood of ever getting out of here, hehe!"

"Anyway," another man said, pointing east, "there's nothing interesting over that way."

As they continued to chat in this way, the tension slowly mounted. It seemed that the service workers were pulling everything out of the hat they could think of to prevent David and Judy from taking another step in the direction they wanted to go.

There was nothing special about walking eastward, except for David's earlier explanation to Judy—but mostly they just wanted to be alone. Judy was about to say just that when she noticed Ned and Laura coming toward them from the direction of Laura's habitat—from the east. They too were being accompanied—escorted?—by another three Base Watchers.

When they arrived on the same walkway, David and Ned clasped hands in machismo manner—as though they had not seen each other for days—and the six Base Watchers, now wearing silly expressions, were nodding and smiling all around. Laura and Judy looked at each other with enigmatic expressions that only they understood.

Laura walked over to Judy and took her hand. They wandered to the side of the group where Laura said quietly to Judy, "There's something fishy going on here. Those three practically hijacked Ned and I to go in this direction."

"Same here," Judy replied. "The three that accosted us, are trying to keep us from going your way—east. Their pseudo-friendliness is starting to anger me. I get the message when I'm being dragged to a surprise party, but that's not the message these guys are sending."

Laura said, "The only reason I went along with going *this* way, when they were pushing for that, is because Ned said it didn't make any difference, and—more than that, because I thought they would attack us if we didn't. I know they wouldn't have, but I had that feeling anyway. Their 'friendliness' was a bit too bubbly—especially for guys!"

Judy said, "I wish Clint were here. He wouldn't fall for this crap, or put up with it!"

Laura's eyes turned to narrow slits. "So why should we?"

"You're right. What's the worst they can do?"

"What say we don't even think about that. Let's go!"

The ensuing encounter was a blinding array of feminine charm, manipulation, firmness, cajoling, rank-pulling, cheek patting, laughing, hair tossing, truths, lies and just a few more touches of confrontation. The outcome of that was two bewildered men being led eastward, and six bewildered Base Watchers looking after them with their mouths open as if to speak, but quite unable to. Nor did they follow, being somehow made to realize that that would not be allowed, for reasons of morality, security, economics and personal sanity. No one realized he'd been had.

Nor did David and Ned, but they didn't care. They were glad to be rid of the pushy company. Laura and Judy were not completely sure how it happened either, but did feel a sense of victory—and the need to be wary as they continued eastward with their men.

FORTY-FIVE

Their walk brought them closer to the hill's thickest wall, its "base," where its piles of chips and debris became higher and wider, and the paths between the piles narrowed. The highest piles were closest to the wall and well over their heads. That is where the most powerful string destruction took place and where the Base Watchers, in their pathway-clearing and clean-up roles, not only cleared the paths, but methodically removed debris from the round slabs that shielded the inert isomorphs that lay beneath them.

Central Park was a popular area in the middle of Mark's Base and located farthest from the hill's surrounding wall—and directly beneath its highest point. Thus, when the fusillade of arrow-thin strings was unleashed, that central area of Mark's Base was virtually untouched by the resultant debris. Only a rare few strings had the energy to fling themselves to that highest point, much less do any damage when they got there. That was fortunate since the hill's thickness was less pronounced near its summit.

The quartzlike coverings were in evidence at every turn; but as the Ad-Sec mates moved closer to the east wall, some of those slabs were still cloaked by an overlay of deflated habitat material from the previous day's photographic exploits by Everett and company. Laura questioned why Everett's now-flattened dark material had been left lying on the isomorph slabs when they were no longer in use.

After Laura remarked about that, Ned said, "Everett's volunteers will probably take care of that later. It hasn't been that long and his photographs may prove useful. I think we should give Everett a little slack. He's earned it."

It had long been agreed, understood and discussed at length—without proof in The FAST News or the intranet—that the template for isomorphic replication was human DNA, unintentionally donated through blood samples from the many scrapes and cuts inflicted on almost everyone who visited Origin. Everett's photographs contributed to that belief.

David kept muttering to himself as he continued to select larger wall-chip samples. Only Judy paid attention to his muffled commentary. Except for that and the sound of their steps, the surroundings were quiet.

David found a large wall-chip that contained a reasonably well-replicated eyeball with its characteristic cat's-eye slit. Turning it in his hand, he was troubled and murmured, "Even with all that practice, *It* never got the eyes right."

Moving closer to the east wall, they became increasingly aware of the gritty, fragmented regions that extended nearly halfway to the hills apex. The Nimbus-lit tidewater's glow came through those whittled imperfections, flashing and glittering with brilliant and varied psychedelic hews. The mix of bright colors seemed to flow through the hill's wall like the outside ocean's rush of diverging current against its own powerful undertow. Through the hill's flaws, its beacons danced in patterns of sparkling light as if to show off its disco-ball immensity from inside. It created lights and shadows that rose and fell in waves as they beamed across the piles of crystalline debris, then scampered down the pathway they were on. From moment to moment it mottled their clothing, their exposed flesh and facial tones, projecting a glittering specterlike appearance on their surroundings and themselves.

Judy took this in with awe; but did not lose track of David's mumbling. "You look worried, David. How do you know that the cat's-eye slits aren't an improvement over our own round pupils?"

"You may be right," David said. "For all we know, those eyes may be better than ours. There doesn't seem to be an attempt at perfect accuracy. If there were, then *It* should also have been working on the isomorphs' skin tones. In this lighting, ours could use improvement too! I must admit, however, I still like Opal's coloring just the way it is!"

"I know. Ellen told me you would."

Laura was walking with her head down, but not for the same reason as David. First, she was trying to keep her orientation and balance within those endlessly converging and scattering patterns of light; but mainly she kept an eye on the shiny, round surfaces and wondered whose isomorph was beneath each one—and if there was one of her. *Maybe I'll soon see myself in The FAST News.*

Despite Ned's comment that Everett had earned some slack, Laura continued to be uncomfortable when she saw that the dull habitat material was still covering some of the otherwise reflective, sheltering surfaces. She wanted to stop and lift the habitat material aside, but knew it was too heavy for her. She slowly lagged behind—then stopped beside a covered area and said, "Ned, David, Judy—come here!"

They gathered beside her and she pointed to the habitat material. "There!" she said triumphantly. That simple word was supposed to explain it all, but no one comprehended her meaning.

After a mystified silence, Ned asked, "What about it?"

Another one-word statement explained it completely: "Concave."

Together, the four lifted one side of the sagging material high enough to see that the quartzlike covering had been *removed*. That missing support caused the habitat material to sag. Of greater concern, they saw no occupant within the pit beneath the covering. The isomorph had also been removed.

"Goddamn grave robbers!" Laura snapped.

"Grave *makers* would be more like it," David said. "Somebody's pushing their luck—everybody's luck—opening these Pandora Boxes!"

Judy walked over to another set of habitat material—one that was not sagging. "This one looks okay," she said. "Let's give it a lift." They did, and it was the same story—no crystalline cover and no isomorph within.

They continued eastward, checking the covered areas on their way, sagging or not—all with the same result.

Judy looked nervously at David and asked, "What do you make of this? Are we in danger?"

"Those stupid risk takers!" David said.

"Then we are in danger!"

Stroking his chin thoughtfully, David went on. "Stupid or not, we're lucky. There may still be a relationship between the hill and the mounds—but evidently it's not a lethal one. Oh hell! I'll have to admit it. In fact, I'm damn glad to admit just that!"

"Admit what?"

Looking both ways, as if guilty of something, David said, "I must have been wrong. Whatever the mound systems' connections are to the hill, they haven't brought the hill down on top of us and probably won't. Ever since Opal, I kind of suspected that. With so many of these illicit openings—and undoubtedly a lot we haven't found—I'm now convinced."

Still far from persuaded, Judy said, "You're convinced of what? That their coverings can be taken away and the isomorphs safely removed—without destroying the hill and killing us in the process?"

"Yes, but I'm not completely sure about the safety of the artifacts . . . er, I mean the isomorphs."

"You *believe so*. But you *don't know*? That's not reassuring enough for me."

"Fine. I don't know. But that's the best I can do. Besides, it's a little late for us to be worrying about that right now. This looks like a random sample of openings. In order to know for sure, then all of the isomorphs' crypts would have to be violated."

Stomping her foot, Judy said, "Given Everett Balz's photography and Kevin Verily's holography, if he's here with *that* equipment, or if he loaned it to Everett, then they will be opened—all of them!"

They rounded another tall pile of debris and a rare vista came into view—leading all the way to the base of the wall. From where they had been, in the narrowing pathway, it opened to a wide-angle view of the hills base. At the same time, from roughly the same distance as the base, but more to their right, they heard *applause*. Amidst the quiet clapping someone shouted, "Congratulations, Mother Denise!" Another shouted, "Welcome Chastity!"

Without a word, they doubled their pace to see what was going on. In a moment, two tall, stately women were seen striding across their view, from right to left of the widened vista and away from the sounds of the approving public. Their coloring changed with the moving tide, but their hands were clearly streaked with red. The tall female figure nearest them was completely naked and bald. Her right hand was awkwardly holding the right hand of the other—who was clothed from head to toe and guiding the unclothed female away from the crowd. As the women strode by, the dressed one was holding some kind of drape in her left hand and trying—without success and without cooperation—to cover the naked one within its folds; but in alternate steps the naked one innocently flashed her gilt—as the other, with equal visibility, displayed her guilt.

Before reaching the wall, they heard more applause and shouts of approval. By then they were almost running. They stopped at the wall. The women looked to their left and the men to their right. Then each turned to look in the opposite direction, and at each other—bewildered. The clothed and naked women were still proceeding northward along the east wall, and to the south was a large group of clothed and unclothed figures. Despite the odd groupings, the crowd appeared peaceful enough—even friendly toward one another. They decided to approach cautiously and mingle.

They drew near the gathering. Of the ones they could see, their backs were toward them, yet they recognized members of the Base Watch. Nearest them, four individuals at the back of the crowd were holding hands. They were Ingrid,

Anvil, and their two isomorphs. Ingrid was standing on tip toe, trying to see over the heads of those in front of her. Without exception the isomorphs were not only naked, they were hairless. Throughout the crowd, that pattern of twos and fours was repeated a dozen times or more. The hands of people standing beside their isomorph were in different hues of crimson—revealing stages of drying blood. Ned wondered how many other groups like this were operating on the Base.

They mingled with the crowd as they worked their way to the front. There they saw most of the unpaired singletons, all with clean hands, eagerly awaiting something—the next disinterment?

In front of them facing the crowd was Everett Balz. He and his helpers were standing on the far side of some flattened habitat material that lay between them and the crowd. Everett was directing its removal, and in the next breath gave last minute instructions to his newly trained photographers. Everett's style was matter-of-fact and businesslike throughout.

Removal of the habitat material was followed by Kevin Verily's directing an even larger group to lift and carry away the crystalline cover itself. His manner of direction was unlike Everett's. A portion of Kevin's group was sent ahead to join Everett's photographers at the next location to set up another kind of filming—holography.

Kevin then moved on to something quite different. Judy was already upset with what had been done and became more so watching Kevin's pompous bearing. She almost spoke out, but was quelled by Laura's hand on her shoulder. Judy turned and looked at Laura in great distress, saying, "That smart-ass! Having that cover removed could be our end. Right now! David could very well have been right to start with. And Kevin's standing there swaggering and preening."

Laura shook her head and said, "Just hold my hand and watch. As David said, if these are Pandora Boxes—and if this were one of them—it would already be too late for us to worry. If not, cheer up, the next isomorph out of the box may be yours."

Like a compliant little girl, Judy took Laura's hand. She said, "Yes, but I don't even want to take care of a kitten, much less a cat-eyed adult child that looks like me—or would murder me in my bed!"

"Why would you say something so extreme before there is evidence of anything like that?"

Judy's expression relaxed, and then tightened again. "I just don't want to be the evidence, is all! And, to me, some of those hands already looked pretty bloody!"

Kevin stood before the exposed concavity that contained another isomorph. "This unresurrected," he said piously, looking at the list on a sheet of paper, "is for Malcolm Ditwhiler. Malcolm, will you please step forward." Malcolm did so, to light applause.

Judy said, "I saw his isomorph's picture in the News this morning. Most of the isomorph pictures have 'Not Yet Named' under them, but you'll never believe the name Malcolm gave to *his* isomorph!"

Malcolm's job on the Transformation Cone could not be considered high-level, but his loyalty to the Transformation project was constant. His speech was inarticulate, even rudimentary. He was crude, but well-liked. He enjoyed socializing at the Honky-tonk Saloon, and loved their happy-hour snacks and beer. Physically, he was grossly obese.

For the next ten minutes, Kevin recited a lot of words, and ended with, "Proceed to the edge of the mother's womb, and enter!" Kevin's voice had been audacious throughout and his manner unctuous, as if invoking some ancient, pagan ritual. The crowd loved it!

Malcolm waddled to the edge, sat on it, and slid himself in. As his head disappeared below the pit's rim the crowd pressed in, making a semicircle around half of its circumference—leaving room for Kevin to prance about on the other half. Laura and Judy were together in front and could see clearly into the pit. David and Ned were just behind those in front, and at some distance from Laura and Judy, but were also able to observe the pit's interior. The large isomorph was a clear Ditwhiler copy. It was motionless, and probably as lifeless as Opal.

"Jesus, what now?" Judy said louder than she should have.

"Hush!" Laura said.

Kevin gave Judy a haughty, reprimanding look before continuing the ritual. It was a ritual he seemed to be making up as he went along, apparently based on audience response. After only a day, this skilled seducer of individuals was already a crowd pleaser.

"What a ham!" Judy said—quietly this time.

Laura's response was equally muted. "He's more than just a ham, Judy. He's scary!"

From Ned's angle of observation, he noticed that Everett had blended into the crowd, and was looking sternly through its cover at Kevin's performance. Everett's eyes were narrow and his lips pressed tight—and was slowly, very slowly—shaking his head. Ned was also disturbed by Kevin's behavior, and found Everett's closet reaction oddly reassuring.

Malcolm stood beside his isomorph, but faced away from it and looked toward Kevin Verily, who was suddenly and inexplicably holding two of the rigid, pencil thin, javelin-length strings—one in each hand. He commanded Malcolm to raise his hands "in homage to the Hill and to receive the strings of life." Malcolm raised his hands high above his head and Kevin placed the sharp tip of each javelin-string, one against each of his palms. He intoned more smarmy, unctuous words, then pushed and twisted on the strings. Blood poured from each of Malcolm's palms and down his arms. Kevin then told Malcolm he was "now ordained" and commanded him saying, "Administer the power of life by anointing your inanimate with the power of your blood, er um, a power given to you through me." Hearing this, Malcolm brought his face close to that of the isomorphs and took both of its hands in his. He then remained transfixed in that position, as he had seen others do throughout the day.

Judy whispered to Laura, "I knew nothing would happen. When it doesn't come to life, Kevin will blame it on Malcolm for having an impure heart or some such crap."

"Don't be too sure. Kevin's lips are moving. I think he's counting off the seconds for some reason. Maybe it takes a while."

Kevin suddenly began waving the strings dramatically, like scepters, and recited, "I, Verily, say unto you, awaken!"

With that last shouted word, the string-scepters, like orchestra batons ending a symphonic performance, were suddenly halted in a high V above Kevin's uplifted arms—their bloody tips still vibrating and scattering fresh droplets of blood, like holy water, on those nearby. At that exact moment, the isomorph's slit-eyes opened wide—seeing and instantly bonding with its human identical.

Malcolm undertook the formidable task of helping his isomorph to its feet; but with its weight several times that of Malcolm himself, it could have been impossibly difficult. With a little more time his newly vitalized isomorph could have done it alone, but managed to accept his help anyway. A short ladder was then lowered into the pit, and Malcolm climbed out. The encroaching crowd cleared a more than adequate space for him. He looked back at the standing isomorph that had not taken its slit-eyes off of him. Malcolm held out his hand toward the blotchy specter in the flowing lights from the wall and said, "Come on, *Fatass*!"

With no apparent effort, the massively corpulent Fatass sprang the full distance from the base of the pit to its edge and landed beside Malcolm and adoringly took his chubby, blood-stained hand. The crowd applauded. There were a few shouts of "Congratulations Poppa Malcolm," and "Welcome Fatass." Malcolm bowed to the extent his stomach allowed and then led his prize to the back of the crowd.

Everett's crew moved in and re-placing the habitat material over the empty pit. The word within the crowd was that this would protect people from falling in. The rock crystal cover remained where it had been leaned against the nearest pile of wall-chip debris.

The crowd quickly moved on to the next location, and the whole procedure was repeated as before, except this time Kevin's ritual became slightly more elaborate and bloody. The whole thing was captured by his holography team and, of course, Everett's photographers.

Everett's quiet anger between performances seemed to grow. David saw it only after Ned pointed it out to him. Ned thought he'd finally figured out the reason, and explained it to David. "Everett doesn't give a rip about Kevin's ritual. Far from it. He just wants to get all these isomorphs out and about as soon as possible. His crew has been filming everything. I think that's why he's hanging in there. Kevin gives good movie, but his rituals were slowing down the extractions. I wonder why Everett is in such a rush."

Seven mound-openings later, David said, "I'm tired of this, and it's getting dark. Let's just go."

It took them quite a while to locate Laura and Judy to signal they were about to leave. While David and Ned had carefully watched all the rituals, Laura and Judy had moved on earlier. In the spirit of gossip, they learned much more about the resurrection process from others in the crowd than they could have from any amount of ritual watching. Between their observations and the gossip, the biggest mysteries still remained. They had learned a great deal and would know much more by the time they returned to their own offices and habitats.

FORTY-SIX

The remaining days of high tides brought new discoveries, new relationships, and personal revelations through a swift moving, seemingly endless whirl of events.

The communication blackouts between the Transformation Cone and Mark's Base were increasing, sometimes lasting not only minutes or hours, but up to a day or more.

David, Judy, Laura and the relevant technicians they could pull together from within the hill, the "Hill Team," and electronics and other experts on the Transformation with Doug Groth and Stanley Lundeen were tracking down the cause for the blackouts. More accurately, they were locating the direction from which the problem was coming—its source.

The communication blackouts occurred during times when the planet's surface electromagnetism became directionally coherent and unique—and opposite the normal N-S magnetic poles. Compasses worked correctly even at those times, but normal electronic communication was obliterated during times of oppositional polarity—polarity of a different kind, on another level. The Hill Team discovered that during blackouts, the electrons and nuclei within the molecules of the surface crystals—crystals that comprised the planet's entire surface—were undergoing nuclear magnetic resonance. All their spin resonance changed, but powerful magnetic fields or microwave activity to account for their magnetic moments could not be detected. Such an effect in the nuclei and electrons should not happen independently of such powerful fields—but there they were! *Something* was causing it, but in David's words, "Nothing from this universe." To that, Judy give her skeptical, "Yeah, right!" David scowled patiently and added, "And the crystals themselves aren't from around here either!" Laura rolled her eyes.

Doug's and Stan's teams found the same phenomena, but—not being confined to the inside of a hollow hill—their discoveries were geographically flexible and far reaching. During low tides they sampled the aberrant surface electromagnetic changes all the way up, down and across both of Origin's major continents, and from poll to poll. The anomalous directionality could only be found during electronic communications blackouts. That contrary trend varied systematically to the point of predictable regularity from one geographic location to another. Following those points of deviation, it became possible to project a series of circum-Origin lines on its globe. Those lines intersected obliquely in exactly two locations on opposite sides of Origin—both on the equator. One intersection was in the middle of the planet's largest ocean, and the other in the middle of a mountainous island.

For days a team from the Transformation inspected every part of that equatorial island and its mountains. For that study, after a "reasonable" period of time, determined by administrators, that investigative study supposedly came up with "nothing significant" and the study was summarily terminated. Some did not agree with the Directors and their lesser administrators and pointed out that as they were zeroing in on their intersection point of the circum-Origin lines, that point kept moving to another location on the island—to one of its beaches, to another mountain, or even a short distance off shore—but never beyond the island's shelf—in those few places where there was a shelf at all. Usually the mountains just kept going straight down into the ocean. In all, they located several dozen points of intersection. The points had moved at least that many times during their studies.

At the same time that the tropical-island study was initiated, work also began on a similar investigation of the ocean on the opposite side of Origin. Both studies had been in progress when they were summarily terminated at the same time. That happened only a day before most of the current Base camp residents' isomorphs had been vitalized.

The *island* study would have been dropped anyway, for lack of progress, as noted, and the *ocean* study because it was deemed too difficult and dangerous due to the great depth and pressures involved. The latter assessment was vigorously disputed by the diver involved, but she too was overruled. The deep ocean study was making discoveries on a daily basis, but the *directional anomalies* part of that exploration was seen as unproductive and so it was eliminated—not only for being "difficult and dangerous," but "for lack of progress" as well. In fact, the directional studies from the Deep—a diving sphere—were more productive than anything coming from the island team on the other side of Origin's equator, but the diver had little time to analyze her data while it was being collected. She sent it on to the Transformation, but there it was merely considered interesting, mostly ignored, labeled low-priority and described as a frivolous distraction. There were, after all, other communication alternatives.

Before the ocean part of that study began, a number of technical teams cobbled together a deep-diving sphere. They knew the ocean depth in that location was almost twelve kilometers, so the self-propelled bathysphere was built with thick windows, strong instruments and devices, and thick steel to withstand the great pressure. It was "small," but as strong as any bathyscaphe ever made. They gave the bob an official name: "Challenger Deep," after what was the great abyss in the Mariana Trench before tectonics caused it to collapse many centuries earlier on planet Earth. Informally, the bob was simply called the *Deep*.

The initial island studies went without a hitch, but the deep sea dive was something else. There was an early problem with installation of devices on the Deep, including those for manipulating external arms, experimental equipment, lights, life support, engine and propulsion equipment, cameras, location of inside and outside pressure gauges and other instrumentation, vehicle steering mechanisms and a variety of other controls. In the end, each individual device was ingeniously optimized, sometimes miniaturized and perfected. There was a different team of engineers for each module and device, and each team was justifiably proud of its work in terms of the speed of development and quality of outcome. One particularly proud and eccentric team sought recognition—"for a change." They had the task of miniaturizing the device used for determining pointers of molecular resonance. In the process they made what they considered vast improvements over the original, larger devices, and eventually trained only one person to use it. Without specifying the improvements, they advertised it as a virtually new invention thanks to the many enhancements they gave it. Nobody important seemed to notice or even care.

The bad news came early on for the ocean trench probe. Its implications became clear after all the equipment was remotely installed: There was no room left for even one person to pilot the thing. They were at wit's end to deal with the problem, and Doug Groth indicated it would be most prudent to end that part of the project at that juncture. Or, for precision, using his exact words: "*Fuck it! Forget it!*"

Fortunately, there was also some good news. Stan's intern, Margaret Heckart, said he should talk with one of her fellow interns about the problem and that she might have one or two ideas that could help. The other astrophysics intern was, among many other things that Margaret mentioned, an experienced deep sea diver and explorer. (The other intern had deliberately left that, and a dozen more "items," off of her resume and application for fear of being turned down for the graduate program and its practicum on the Transformation. She feared they would assume—correctly, in part—that she was "just" one of those "degree collectors." For some reason that had become a *no-no* in academia.

With her experience and, yes, her Ph.D. in Oceanography, Astra Hughs might have some ideas. Stan, of course, knew Astra, but none of the jaw-dropping details of her background before hearing them from Margaret.)

After Stan discreetly restored his jaw to its usual place, he did indeed speak with Astra, and she did have "one or two" ideas—in fact, a cornucopia of them. One of her ideas was more than research oriented—it was practical. It had to do with her size. Astra was a petite, virtual cyborg. It was only to Margaret that Astra had ever, laughingly, referred to herself as a *bionic broad*. She had no hesitation, qualms or difficulty offering to be the Deep's dive pilot. She had the qualifications and was the only person on the Transformation physically able, with a few modifications of her own, to fit into the Rube Goldberg bathysphere, made by a committee. She was comfortable with that, commenting later to Margaret, that her own body was similarly re-created; thus, she concluded, she and the Deep were "made for each other."

And so, she did go into the Deep. For the plunge that lasted many days, she prepared herself by shedding three of her neuro-bio-mechanical limbs—keeping her right arm and hand—and made a couple innovations so she could use her teeth, head and shoulder motions for some of the needed manipulations. After only a few days of training, catheterizing herself, and satisfying herself about other amenities, including her special diet, medications, pure water and a favorite pillow, she went down. The technicians who trained her had to shake their heads in awe—not only for her courage, but for her instant grasp of everything. Except for Laura Shane, they had never been so dazzled by such delightful brilliance—and yet, in the end, all but one would wince and turn away.

One supervising engineer did not turn away. Earlier in his life he was a dropout from his last year of medical internship. He had been in psychiatry, but switched to pathology, and then to engineering. He switched to pathology for two reasons—his countertransference with patients was too intense and because he thought pathology was more scientific. He switched to engineering from pathology for two reasons—too intense identification with cancer and other tissue-diseased patients, and his own increasing eye problems. The latter made microscopic tissue examination difficult, even when displayed on large screens. He required surgery and extremely thick glasses. Because of those and other issues, he made his career changes.

He and the small team he supervised put in place most of the external equipment for the Deep, but the limited space within the Deep required that those installations to be done by remote methods, so he did most of it himself. That took more engineering skill and creativity than visual acuity (such as one might need to assess microscopic slides). Thus, he became the one individual most familiar with the cramped interior of the Deep. After Astra went down, he became clinically claustrophobic thinking about her situation—necessitating a week of deep relaxation desensitization therapy.

In their frustration, the administrators on both sides of the hill came to dismiss the electromagnetic anomaly as "no more than an interesting diversion" and, next to other matters, thought its priority could be lowered a bit—to zero. Everyone could, after all, live for a few hours or days without those communications. Temporary communications blackouts were, "therefore," in no further need of capital or intellectual resources.

In truth, the real scientists were still haunted with the questions raised by the electronic communications problem. As for the actual lack of communications, no one worried too much about it. To solve that problem, no puzzle was involved—and everybody knew it. Finally, a team from the Transformation simply set up an infrared wireless access *transmitter* on top of the hill's crown. Its *receiver* was, of course, set up inside the hill by the technicians there.

The new, infrared communications system worked perfectly—much to the delight of FAST News devotees, both men and women—especially since its editor and publisher, Debra Anderson, changed her policy and started printing full color, frontal photographs of the naked isomorphs. Fortunately for Denise Christensen, who would otherwise have been even more upset, her isomorph's picture was printed early enough to dodge the revealing policy change. That did not stop Denise—on behalf of her beloved Chastity—from writing scathing letters to the editor.

FORTY-SEVEN

Within a few weeks of the first vitalizations, everybody's isomorph had been photographed, identified and published in The FAST News—with some exceptions. For example, there were no isomorph pictures of those still hospitalized on the Transformation for physical or mental reasons resulting from the Twister, nor for a small handful of people who *chose* to remain on, and never left, the Transformation Cone. In addition there were some who did visit the planet, but had returned quickly without a scratch—usually returning because of all the plantoid noise or because of allergies experienced on the planet. That group included, among others, Stanley Lundeen. Two others who *had* received scratches on Origin, but could not be found in the rogues' gallery of isomorphs, were Laura Shane and Mark Tenderloin. Laura and Mark had different reactions to that, at least on the surface, with Mark merely frowning and shaking his head. Finally, there was one isomorph photograph that nobody could identify.

On learning she had no isomorph, Laura tossed her head and said, "I'm glad. I sure don't want a bald and naked copy of me following me around day and night."

Even as Laura said that, she knew an exact copy of her was not something to be ashamed of. And she already knew that isomorphs did not follow anyone around "day and night." Her berating tone only hid her disappointment at being left out. By then, most of the primary—or perhaps merely preparatory—behaviors of isomorphs were well known. Even on the day she and Ned, and Judy and David were returning from Kevin's outrageous performances, they learned some of those basics.

For one thing, they found that neither blood nor ritual was required for the vitalization of an isomorph. Many individuals, in several other vitalizing groups they encountered on their way back from the east wall, did it quite differently. To wake their sleeping beauty, some needed only to apply a wet kiss. Men were reluctant to use that method. Instead, they would merely lick a finger and touch their isomorph somewhere on its body for the same result. It didn't take a lot, but it had to be the right person—the isomorph's person. No amount of blood, saliva, or touching from anyone else ever vitalized an isomorph. They were very fussy that way. Nor was initial eye contact necessary. Like lamb and ewe, they found each other no matter what; but one way or another that first close physical touch was vital.

Later on they learned other things. First, isomorphs never ate or drank. Nor did they excrete, except through exhalation. In some of those ways they were like Dorts. At night they would go outside and lie on the ground of surface crystals. Late at night, a person would have to step over or around them. They appeared to be sleeping. Flashes of sparks could be seen passing back and forth between two or more of their lying bodies and the crystals beneath them. Sometimes they would exchange sparks and flashes from a meter away. The surface of Mark's Base camp fairly flickered with them at night and sometimes electronic communications to and from the Cone would then stop. That electromagnetic exchange, along with simple breathing of the planet's air, is how Origin nourished its isomorphs and, it later became known, provided them with *lessons*. Their "going to ground," as this came to be called, was not a simple thing.

Isomorphs were compliant, likeable, somewhat affectionate, seemed to appreciate being touched, having their hand held, and being gently kissed or hugged; but they invariably turned away any overt sexual advances. They refused to be dressed, draped, or covered in any manner. They never spoke or made any kind of verbal sound. One could only hear their normal breathing.

Even at the moment of vitalization, they already knew some things, like how to get up—they did not really have to be helped in order to stand. They were immediately able to walk, run, jump long distances or to great heights—yes, like flying strings, and yes, in a single bound—despite being so much heavier than their earthborn counterparts. On learning how heavy they were, and seeing their initial blank looks, Clint said, "They're dense in more ways than one." He later had to rethink that statement.

For a day or two after vitalization they did look, to one degree or another, a bit dopey and expressionless—which is probably why Clint named his isomorph, "Dummy"—but the isomorphs gradually came to look more and more intelligent, quickly learned simple commands, and eventually seemed to understand everything being said. When something funny was said, they had no particular response—except for some things that David would have found amusing. Then their eyes would jerk rapidly back and forth, REM-like. To the initiated, that isomorph eye-movement came to be known as their "David response." Yes, isomorphs were strange! On serious matters, however, they would present a countenance of concern. Clint liked them better before he realized they might be intelligent.

There was little merriment within the hill, but at the Honky-tonk Saloon, men would gather—with their bald and naked isomorphs—to discuss the day's events. In later days, women would arrive with their partners or friends and their respective isomorphs. Loud conversation, drinking and dancing—under a real disco-ball—were the preferred activities. Clint would bring "Dummy" with him, and Ellen would bring her "Littleviolet," whose irises were glowingly violet, and whose body was as petite as Ellen's own. At first, the isomorphs did not dance; but eventually got the hang of it and would dance with other isomorphs. Due to the considerable weight differences between isomorphs and humans, they could not dance comfortably together, unless it was a non-touching type of dance. They quickly developed great rhythm and style—even innovating new dances of their own, some being unwittingly evocative and arousing to certain male humans as they undulated before them to the throbbing music amidst pulsating lights and their own fortuitous flashes of gold. So, merriment prevailed within the hill—sometimes.

But high above on the Transformation, gloom had descended on the technical team whose off-Cone island project was summarily ended. Fortunately they had each other to complain to, and to speculate with about the meaning of the shifting intersection point on the equatorial island, and other things they had seen and enjoyed that had nothing to do with science or their project. They had been awed by the mountains, the plantoid echoes, the evening setting of Nimbus, the beaches; and they were stimulated by the co-educational aspects of data gathering—particularly on those same beaches at dusk. Back on the Cone, when not complaining to each other, or pining for their lost Shangri-La, they found a few meaningful things to do. They were mainly glad for the one bar still on the Transformation Cone—the Pub.

Sitting in the crowded bar at the Pub in the evening was relaxing, and something Zackery Parker enjoyed—especially after the completion of his claustrophobia treatment. His friends called him Zack. Like so many others, he spent more time than usual perusing The FAST News, and enjoyed the new format, but was disappointed that all the photos to be published had already been in print. So he dug out the three day old copy that presented the last of them. He liked it because his own isomorph was there, and he was pleased with its looks. When that issue first came out it was, of course, on the computer net, and he browsed around in it, but had spent most of his time just admiring his own handsomeness—the strong jaw, broad shoulders, adequate manhood and solid bony structure. And it wasn't wearing thick glasses, like the magnifiers that distorted his appearance.

But now, in the bar, he perused the paper's hard copy from that earlier day for the first time. He was alone, but overheard groups around him marveling at the picture of one particular isomorph displayed on page three of that earlier issue. The conversation he overheard described the female isomorph as beautiful, physically statuesque and, well, way beyond attractive—they said she was stunning! And that was from a group of women. The men he happened to overhear at another table were on the same subject. In fact, everywhere that day, and everywhere in the bar that night, that was the subject. Yet he was shocked at the men's conversation. He knew each of those macho curs individually. What shocked him was the way they spoke of this vision of feminine pulchritude—with such respect. Sure, some things are of such beauty as to induce reverence, but this could not be—not from those guys! So he turned to that famous page and immediately realized the one they were talking about. After looking at the picture, he decided they were all wrong. "Beautiful" and "stunning" didn't even come close. And she had the most lovely birth mark, in the shape of a star, just in front of her left shoulder. All in all, this one was more than stunning, for sure! The real shocker was, of course, that her identity was labeled, "Unknown Female." Such beauty could not be hidden for long. Who was she?

A few days earlier, also on the Transformation, Dr. Lundeen was yelling angrily to his staff about something that was not done right, and pointing fingers at everyone. The size of the group of professional staff and students receiving his wrath soon diminished as they slipped out this door or that door, one at a time.

"Jesus, you should have heard him bellowing!" Margaret said. "I got out of there as soon as he wasn't looking. And Jesus! What's the matter with you? You weren't even there. What are you crying about?"

Astra looked up at Margaret, tears pouring through the scars that served as her eyelids. "Have you seen this?" she asked, handing Margaret page three of The FAST News.

"Of course! Who hasn't seen this? The babe behind that isomorph is hiding out, for sure. If I looked like that, I'd hide out too—everybody'd be all over me—women included. I'd rather be known for my brains."

Margaret rattled on in that vein for several minutes, and then stopped in mid-sentence with her hand over her mouth, tears now starting to spurt from her own eyes.

"Oh Jesus, Astra! I've never seen you when you weren't fully dressed, but you once told me your back and shoulders were never burned."

Without permission, Margaret reached over and pulled Astra's blouse away from her left shoulder. The birthmark was as lovely as the unscarred shoulder that bore it.

The eyes beneath the scar tissue looked up at her and she said, "That's why mama named me Astra. It means star."

"When you came in just now, those weren't sad tears," Astra said. "They were happy tears. You see, I now know—for the first time in my life—what I *really* look like."

"Oh Astra," Margaret said, "I didn't need this to prove it—I always knew you were beautiful."

FORTY-EIGHT

Before their early understandings of isomorph behavior, David and Judy, and Laura and Ned had their fill of "vitalization stress" for one day—the day they emerged from observing Kevin hoodwink and abuse his followers. Back in the heart of Mark's Camp the two couples had gone their separate ways; Ned and Laura to retire for the day, and Judy and David to check on their experiments. They had different ways to relieve stress.

David and Judy were happy to be back to their Chem-Geol labs (and their mutual habitat). Judy immediately checked the three storage rooms where her string experiments had been placed. They were in secured boxes. Two strings were in two kinds of liquid and one had been left to dry. The string that was left in the amnioticlike fluid was as viscous, stretchy and mucuslike as when they left it; nor had the one left in water changed in any way.

The door to the third storage room where the last of her double-boxed string had been left to dry was opened with care. The room was completely trashed. They heard the string, still squiggling under the rubble. David dug into the pile and grabbed it by one end and held it upright for Judy to see. It took a number of slow, jerking bows in several directions. He placed it in an empty wash pan where it kept clanking, but with diminishing frequency. To quiet its clatter, Judy folded a towel in the pan and placed the string on top of it. A half-hour later they found the string motionless where it had snuggled into the towel and died.

David helped himself to a sandwich from the fridge and began unveiling his own experiments. The chip left in ordinary water had not changed; but something happened to the two chips left in the large crucible of yellowish fluid. Judy looked at it and said, "This is a trick, isn't it David? You switched chips—to turn this experiment into one of your jokes." If that were true she knew he would start laughing, but he did not. He was as serious and amazed as Judy.

In the experiment, the two separated chips had pulled together and merged into one. David fished it out of the fluid and examined it visually, tactilely, and by smell. Except for the size doubling, the two chips, now one, were without any obvious change. Next, the Mohs test had him muttering his thoughts aloud.

Judy expected real comments from him this time, but he only sat there, mumbling. "Okay David," she said patiently, "what's the deal?"

He turned his head toward her and said, "There's something funny about this planet—about this part of the universe."

"You say that every time there's something around here you don't understand. What is it now?"

"It's more than the chips' fusing. It's the scratch test that's impossible. But I can't deny the result. The hardness has changed. It didn't change for the one we left in plane water. Now I have to run more tests on the hill chips—dozens probably. I'll have to use that same liquid catalyst—if *you* can figure out what it really is and make a lot more of the liquid. It's the critical ingredient—water alone won't work. Obviously the yellowish liquid isn't only water or just a watery, bloodlike serum. Something else is in there. It's a wild dream, but if we're lucky and have enough of it to keep on testing a while longer, that could lead to a way out."

"A way out of what?" Judy asked with a mixture of impatience and anticipation in her shaking voice.

She was rewarded with the response she'd hoped for: "A way out from under this hill of course!"

Judy was so happy hearing this good news—uncritically taking David's statement as her anxiety-relief refuge—that she hardly remembered anything else he said.

"Much work has to be done before that wild dream could ever happen," David said. "First we have to . . ." and on and on he spoke. Judy could not interrupt him. Then he slipped into mumbling, and she continued to listen. As she listened, she realized why, after the Mohs tests, he'd started daydreaming. He wasn't actually daydreaming at all, she assured herself. He was planning their escape! It was something about the fused chips. To learn more about that, she needed more from him than mumbling.

"Stop!" she said sharply.

David looked up from his reverie. "What?"

"You've been mumbling about all kinds of experiments and about Kevin, of all people, and about the wall chips. I can't put all of that together. If it's any of my business, would you mind clarifying?"

"It's obvious," he said. "The chip is harder."

"I think we've had this conversation before. Okay, how hard?"

"Well, the usual wall chip was between seven and eight on the scratch test.

Now the fused chip is at least a ten. It's now as hard as a diamond—maybe harder. I can't tell how much harder if it is. Let's just say it's now a diamond."

"A ten is *a lot more* than a seven or eight?"

"Let me put it this way: The hardness difference between a nine and a ten is nearly a hundred times. Yes, I'd say that *a lot more* would cover it."

"Hmm. That might make us rich on Earth, but what value is it here?"

"Maybe none, but maybe a lot. I'll need you and Kevin and the rest of my crew to help with the experiments. It'll take a while. Kevin knows crystallography better than me and he still has some of that fluid that he kept. But it's not enough for the studies that must be done. We'll need him to suggest and plan most of the necessary experiments. I can get us started with a few obvious ones."

David went on to explain what he hoped to find, and why so much help was needed.

Judy said, "It will take longer than you think. I know Kevin is the best and the brightest professional on your team, but we both know he's off on another tangent right now. When he comes back to reality again, then he might be useful. Not before."

"He'll be done with all that soon enough. There aren't that many Base campers' isomorphs left to vitalize. Most of our crew that are now on the Transformation Cone have no way of vitalizing their isomorphs. When yours and mine come up, I hope it's another group that's involved—not Kevin's. I refuse to let him stick me in my hands or anywhere else with those toad stabbers. If he tried it, I'd fire him."

"You already have."

"Yeah, yeah, yeah!"

FORTY-NINE

Kevin's reign of glory was shorter than David had predicted. The next day Kevin's non-stop, day and night marathon of increasingly elaborate and brutal vitalizations had gone too far—even for the otherwise bored Base Watchers who found him so entertaining. On the last day of his vitalization rituals—in fact, the very last ritual he would ever perform—he went over the top. A few weeks later the details were reported in The FAST News.

Margaret Heckart had heard only a few highlights of what had happened soon afterwards, but was more upset when she read the gory details in the News. "I was afraid something bad would happen, and now it has and its worse than I thought." she told Astra Hughs. "That's why I came back here and didn't return to Origin."

"I thought you were avoiding plantoid scrapes."

"The scrapes had nothing to do with it. I just used that as an excuse. Kevin was starting to escalate again."

"Again?" Astra said. (She'd been writing reports about her deep sea discoveries and was unaware that Kevin had been involved in anything serious—much less that he had been performing blood rituals to vitalize isomorphs.) "What do you mean, *again*?"

"Yes, again. That's what we were arguing about on Origin the day we had to go to the clinic."

"I remember. He was refusing to do something you were asking him to do—begging him to do! You kept saying it would not be that hard to do, and he kept saying it wasn't necessary. It got kind of loud. You said something about this happening before. What happened before? I felt like slinking off somewhere. What was supposed to be so simple? And what did he do that was so serious?"

"Gee whiz, Astra. Where have you been? Everybody's been talking about it, and here's this big article in the News."

"Don't pick on me. I've been busy. Summarize it for me."

"Your first question first: What do I mean by *again*? That's easy. Before we thought of going on this Transformation, me and Kevin were living together."

"Were you in love?"

"I thought so, but during the years we were together, there were times when he began coming home late at night, if at all. He was sleeping around and I kicked him out several times. He was involved with those braless protesters. He'd be up day and night. At that time David Michaels—he was already Kevin's boss—was also protesting the ecological destruction caused on Earth by Transformation Cones. David respected Kevin's skills, but fired him for not showing up for work. He also knew about Kevin's non-protest exploits and, I believe, realized that those had become the real motivations for his continued involvement in the protests. That wasn't true at first. It became so as Kevin's energy escalated into day and night craziness."

"That does sound crazy! Why would you have picked a guy like that?"

"Because he is—was—a beautiful man when he stayed on his medications. At those times he was level headed, loyal and loving. He was himself."

"*At those times*, you say. How many times when he wasn't himself?"

"Not many, but a few. When I kicked him out, he'd already escalated far enough to be hospitalized. Then he'd get stabilized and we'd get together again. Then things went well for quite a while."

"That day on Origin, what was your argument about?"

"I wanted him to start back on his meds, but he wouldn't."

"After all our years as close friends, how come I never knew about you and Kevin?"

"I guess I was ashamed—not of our living together, but because of his occasional exploits off one deep end or another. I thought I could fix him first, and then I would let people—even my closest friends—know about us. I should have told you, but it was easy to hide it from you. You were gone for five years getting fitted with the latest prostheses and collecting Ph.D.'s, so we just wrote, called and e-mailed. I was showing the world, and you, my smile. I wanted to tell you. I was operating without support out there. Had we been room mates again, or at least close by, I think I would have told you everything."

"I wasn't that great a room mate, if you'll remember. You used to yell at me a lot when you caught me humping all the furniture and letting out primal screams!"

"You were young and horny then, but I'll admit it was a relief when you got on those medications to suppress your sex drive."

"I'm still on'm. Thank God!"

"Anyhow, that's Kevin and me. I value your common sense, Astra. I need to move out of this merry-go-round with Kevin."

"I don't blame you for not confiding in me. I'd be the last person in the universe able to help anybody off a merry-go-round like that. Horrible as it was for you, I'd give anything to have been on one of those—even once. You keep dumping him, but it sounds like you're still stirring the same old hopes around and around. It's stirabout, Margaret, and you must be dizzy by now."

"I am, but it's Kevin who's in the stirabout—in the soup anyway. Officer Bracket arrested him and threw him in jail."

"In jail? How bad is it?"

"He arrested Kevin for murder."

"My God, Margaret! What happened?"

Margaret described the details of Kevin's recent rituals, how they kept changing little by little with each vitalization, how he had not slept, "And then—that last ritual! Instead of merely causing some minor bloodshed on a person's hands, feet or side, he went overboard. With those javelin length strings, one in each hand, he slashed the man's chest skin horizontally with one string, vertically with the other—making a bloody cross—and then drew back like a bull fighter with two bloody banderillas and plunged them into the man's chest."

"Jesus!" Astra said. "That poor man! How could Kevin have done such a thing?"

Margaret explained how shocked everyone was who saw it. "The whole thing was recorded on holo-film. Kevin's followers tied him hand and foot—he was not cooperative—and took him to Clinton Bracket. But before that, the murdered man, Ivan Fuller, had fallen backwards onto his isomorph, soaking it in his blood. When the isomorph woke, it did nothing at first. Then it lifted the man off itself and laid him on his side. Once on its feet, the isomorph walked around the man several times, become distressed as though it knew or sensed what had happened. It picked the man up and looked at the people standing at the edge of the pit. They moved back from the rim, and it jumped the distance. A man named Anvil, and his isomorph, guided the bloodstained isomorph all the way to Ellen Stone's clinic. It carried the man all the way—the javelin strings still waving from his chest like antenna."

"If the man was already dead, what could Dr. Stone do—except make it official?"

"That was everybody's assumption. That's why Officer Bracket arrested him for murder. But Ellen Stone and Dr. Flanders operated on the man for five hours. Even so, he was hanging by a thread. Nurses were volunteering to help. They got him through the time in recovery and more days in acute care, all at the clinic. After that, he was taken care of for rehab in his own habitat. He's going to live."

"Then it wasn't murder," Astra said.

"No. Clint Bracket revised the arrest to *attempted* murder. According to the News, when Officer Bracket gave that good news to Kevin—*relatively* good news, I guess—Kevin had been awake for so long he was climbing the walls and chattering non-stop, but he did get the message. Kevin then said something supercilious—like all the rest of his words at that point—to Officer Clint Bracket. He reminded Kevin that he'd still have to stand trial for his act when we return to Earth, and that he'd *rot in that cell till then*."

"Before you read about all those details in The FAST News, Margaret, you said you already suspected something was starting to go wrong."

"Yes. And the next day, after Kevin's arrest—you're right, I didn't know all those details then—I contacted Dr. Stone and told her some of his history. She immediately went to the Administrative and Security habitat and spoke with Officer Bracket about what she might do to help. He let her in to see him. She started him back on his medications right away, and monitored him daily after that. In a couple weeks the meds were working pretty well. That's what she told me."

"So you're in touch with Ellen Stone every day now?"

"Oh yes, and she tells me to expect more good news to come out in The FAST News tomorrow, but its just a *maybe* right now, and I shouldn't get my hopes up. Huh! As if a hint like that wouldn't get my hopes up. She wouldn't have said that if she wasn't sure something positive was coming."

"I can't imagine what that would be, but I'm curious about Kevin's isomorph. Does he even have one, and if so what happened to it?"

"Ellen told me about that. Kevin named it Nor-Man. Apparently the poor thing dutifully followed Kevin as he was being dragged off to jail. Officer Bracket had no idea what to do with it, so let it sit outside Kevin's cell during the day, and lie outside the Ad-Sec habitat at night. Every morning it was back at the door waiting to get in."

The following day The FAST News was on to other stories and the news that Ellen Stone had anticipated was on the last page. Last page or not, the news made Margaret rejoice—and David Michaels as well. Under Debra Anderson's byline the FAST News reported it this way:

.... After Kevin Verily's stabilization on medications, a deal was worked out with Officer Clinton Bracket, who was apparently taking more kindly to his prisoner, thanks to his improved attitude and the intervention and assurances—*and signed agreements*—provided by some of Kevin's supporters, and by the prisoner himself. Ellen Stone, M.D., will be following his progress on those medications, and he will continue to be under the professional direction of his boss, David Michaels, Ph.D. There are several other provisions. With that kind of support, a tolerant nod has also come from his most recent and seriously affected victim, Ivan Fuller, and Mr. Verily was placed on temporary, modified house arrest. It was modified to the extent he may work in the field with Dr. Michaels; he may move about with approved escorts, and may never again do any vitalization rituals. He is also required to stay on his medications and must follow all of Dr. Stone's directions. 'And,' Officer Bracket told him, 'if I so much as sniff the slightest deviation from any of that, or if I'm even in a bad mood some day, you'll be back in that cell for good, and—no matter what—you will be facing trial when we get back to Earth—if we ever do. In the meantime, I don't want to see your face in here again.'

If there are further changes in this arrangement, this reporter will immediately bring you up to date.

FIFTY

Day by day the high tides subsided and Mark's Base was alive with busy people and quiet isomorphs. Under David Michael's supervision, Kevin Verily refocused. He organized a group to retrieve special wall chips for the new experiments he devised. Dr. Flanders and Ellen Stone continued to take turns at the clinic. Ned Keller was up to his neck in administrative paperwork and documentation for his history of the Transformation, including details and consequences of the Twister, the flood, the isomorph phenomenon and the rest. Laura Shane was busy corresponding with Stan on elementary curved-space problems, and expanding Reo-Sphere Theory in consultation with Mark Tenderloin; and Mark, in turn, was spending most of his days (and nights) nurturing a troubled lady he ran into along the northeast wall—after vitalization of the lady's precious Chastity.

Everyone on Mark's Base was spending half their waking hours in some individual or group project, and yet they seemed to have time to spare. Almost everybody rotated through the Honky-tonk Saloon at least once or twice a week; went to the PMS (Palace Movie Screens) about weekly; attended card and occasional drinking parties; corresponded on the net with friends on the Transformation Cone; wrote articles for The FAST News; put on original or ancient theatrical productions—like the ever-popular *Waiting for Godot*;

exercised and jogged in large and small groups—isomorphs included; read the books they always intended to, and some were even finding time to floss—anything to mask the anxieties of the day.

Similar activities served the same purpose on the Transformation Cone. Stanley Lundeen had not, as yet, nailed the spacetime coordinates for Earth, and Debra Anderson, with her editorials, was still on his case. The *Coners*, as they began calling themselves, were wishing that Laura was there to assist Stan's team. They knew that he was working with her on the net; but, according to one quotation in The FAST News, "Sharing data long distance isn't hands-on enough for real scientific discovery." That remark, quoted in one of Debra's in-depth editorials, came from Waldo Wagson, the Cone's most prestigious and very own laundry room supervisor. He was down on Stan's entire team for their "ineptitude" and was often heard to angrily scream about them saying "They know nothing!"

Far below the levitating, potentially mobile Cone, and behind a cloak of activity within the immobile hill, lay an even greater anxiety—the continuing dread of being stuck there forever—even after the tides retreated. Countering that were supposedly optimistic possibilities—that only added to the sadness and dread as each hope proved to be impossible and was never publicly spoken of again. One shining, imaginary bubble of hope after another would silently burst on the hard ground of fact as quietly as a falling tear. The public guise of cheer and the veneer of pointless activity disappeared when people were in the private company of their partners or most intimate groups. There they would talk about their fears and their hopes, what needed to be done, and to share the latest positive thoughts and theories for escape. Some believed that Kevin and David's latest studies and experiments might provide an answer. Others joked that they might as well roll their bathtubs across the Base—that it was busywork and they were trying to look like everybody else—and giving the rabble another false bubble of hope.

No one, however, still questioned the vulnerability of the hill and how little it would take to bring it down. Besides, the hill's vulnerability had been confirmed in experiments conducted by Stan and David's *Cone*-based staff. Whatever came from the *Coners* seemed to receive more credence than anything from their fellow *Hillbillies*.

Those fear-filled private discussions became a conspicuous norm when something else became noticeable, to the point that such talk suddenly became taboo—except at night after the isomorphs had gone to their crystalline beds. But that kind of talk was stopped too late. The isomorphs were already upset when matters of "hill collapse" were discussed in their presence. This resulted in isomorphic nightmares that turned their nighttime electrical activity into a small fireworks. Even the covered cavities containing still unvitalized isomorphs glowed and sparkled with greater urgency.

Early one morning, after a particularly dazzling nighttime display of electrical isomorph activity, the residents of Mark's Base woke to a strange scene. Their isomorphs were not waiting outside for them. Instead, they were frantically beginning construction on a large, steep, obelisk-shaped edifice—using the discarded quartzlike cavity-covers for their building material. Those very materials had protected each of them before their vitalization. They were constructing it around the saltwater well in the middle of Central Park and it took up most of the park's area. It was not yet an obelisk, but with the four equal sides slanting sharply inward, everybody assumed that was their intent. The isomorphs were not skilled craftsmen, and whole chunks would fall down; but they learned fast. They quickly learned to lean one quartzlike cover against another to hold it in place. That worked fine for the first layer of crystal-covers they'd placed around the base, but the upper layers kept collapsing—so their building effort had become frantic. That lack of skill turned out to be temporary; but they did need help.

Clint Bracket and Jack Lewis were watching this odd performance. Clint concluded they weren't as bright as they looked. "They're not only lousy architects and builders, they're spinning their wheels on a useless activity. Why are they even building that silly thing?" Jack guessed they were keeping busy to feel better—a motive they both understood.

While Clint and Jack continued this high-level analysis, many Base Watchers were bringing out materials and tools from the Mart's Exchange and from their own habitats, including long metal rods and welding tools; tried and true habitat fabric and materials; jackhammers to break up some of the slabs to make shims, fill-ins and minor supports between the large pieces; quantities of pulverized, sand-sized crystals from around the swept-up piles of debris; bags of cement from the Exchange, and more. In a few hours, men, women and isomorphs were working together in a way that nobody could have expected. It became a new diversion and their common project.

Some thought the obelisk—that everybody was soon calling a *"pyramid"*—was for a special kind of superstitious magic. Others noted it would be a very steep pyramid, and therefore a church of some kind. Theories abounded, but nobody really cared what the initial reason behind the construction might have been—they were exhilarated. The humans were impressed by the isomorphs' initiative and ability to quickly learn difficult skills, like welding, and their capacity to innovate after brief exposure to new techniques and materials. Within minutes they were bending and welding metal rods together for an inside scaffolding of multiple triangles—to support the building process and workers on the inside, and to act as a support for the exterior shell as it was set in place.

After a while Clint and Jack dropped their discussion to join Clint's isomorph, Dummy, on the building project. Such coming together was happening throughout the project. The humans were learning they could usefully engage with many isomorphs—not just their own. The previously frantic isomorphs were calmed by the helpful human involvement; and, for the first time, the isomorphs were working in full cooperation with each other. It was heartwarming, even for Clint, to see how well Dummy and Fatass worked together, lifting and carefully placing the heavy, circular sarcophagus covers.

There were several more days of coordinated work remaining before the "pyramid" could be completed. And there were that many additional days before the high tidewater would permanently receded to a safe distance from the hill.

That night the humans, tired from satisfying physical labor, slept more soundly than usual, and the isomorphs lay quietly amidst a low level of electrical activity. For the first time in many nights, radio communication worked normally; but, except for computers and printers ready to accept the usual tendered messages and documents, few were awake to appreciate the fact.

Not everyone slept well or at all that night. Dawn had barely arrived when David lifted his head for the tenth time. Kevin was on his own cot and did not budge from his fetal position. Kevin had returned and went inside only two hours earlier with Norbert, one of his approved escorts. Judy was still awake and turned her head from her work to thank the man for taking him off her hands for the evening. Norbert smiled, laughed and excused himself before leaving.

David glanced at Judy. She was still working her way through a pile of data readouts from several days of collection. She obviously had not slept, and looked it. She was still in the same clothes she wore the day before. All their isomorphs—Kevin's Nor-Man, David's Oscar and Judy's Minerva—had arisen much earlier and were already off to work.

David blinked away his morning fuzziness, and looked closer at Judy. "Good morning, beautiful," he said, adding, "but you really do look like hell. Is everything okay?"

Judy looked back and said, in a tired voice, "Is *anything* okay? That's what you should be asking."

"All right. Is *anything* okay?"

"Hell no!" she said, bursting into tears. "I've been analyzing this goddamn amnioticlike fluid for so long I can hardly see straight, and it won't analyze! While I was working on it with my discovery and separation experiments, with chromatography and a dozen other techniques, I only ended up with an unanalyzable *speck*! Here it is." She held up a small, capped vial that looked empty.

David ignored the empty-looking vial and her tears and said, with disappointment in his voice, "In other words, we can't manufacture it in any useful quantity."

"Afraid not," she said, snuffling away her tears of exhaustion and frustration.

"I've sorted out the obvious, but the last component won't sort. It's worse than a black box. It . . . it's—oh God! I can't believe I'm going to say this, especially to you—it's not from around here."

Judy half-expected David to start laughing, but he remained serious.

Kevin opened one eye and made a groaning sound. Then he closed it again and said, "It doesn't make any difference. Figuring out that last component is academic—it makes no practical difference."

"Oh, I think it does!" Judy said. "If we can't make it in quantity, how can we fortify the hill wall to protect us when we make the rest of it come down? Besides, it's a matter of professional and *academic* concern to me to know just what the *hell* that last component is!"

"I thought you were against swearing," David said with a smirk.

"I am . . . in general; but if you'll recall, I was cured of that after our goddamn egg discussion."

"Oh yeah," David said, bent over laughing. "Now I remember."

Kevin and David were now sitting on the edge of their respective cots, and Judy was eyeing her own cot longingly.

"You're right about that, Judy," Kevin said. "It's academic."

Tears began forming again in Judy's eyes. She was having trouble controlling her anxiety and barely managing to fend off a full-blown attack. "Okay then," she said. "Let's forget the academic part. Let's forget we can't make more of it. So if we can't make it in quantity, how, pray tell, will we ever escape this hill-prison without getting killed?"

She just asked the big question. David was about to hang his head and say something pathetic, but avoided the temptation. Instead he looked at Kevin and asked a question he thought he knew the answer to. "How are our studies coming along?"

Kevin's answer was a total surprise. "They're done."

"Done? You've got to be kidding." Now David was becoming anxious.

"Yes. Done. No. Not kidding."

"Then, *is* it hopeless?" Judy asked, voice shaking.

"Can't do much more," Kevin said. "We've used up your pint or so of the fluid, and most of the barrel full I collected. I still have a small jug of it left, but we won't need it. We already know enough—from our *practical* research."

"That sounds a little sarcastic—and grandiose," Judy said.

"Ouch," Kevin said. "Not grandiose, Judy. I'm still on my meds. And not sarcastic. We each had our eye on the ball, but from different sides. Our studies can give us hope. Yours have confirmed something too. I think you were kidding when you said that last component—that stuff—isn't from around here. I now believe it's a fact and I think David believes that too. That last component is not from this universe. That *had* to stump you and the rest of us, but it couldn't hide its practical consequences. We studied that side of it systematically."

Judy listened and frowned throughout Kevin's comments. "Your voice sounded up-beat as you said all that, but I didn't hear a word of content to give me the slightest hope. Why are you sounding up-beat? Give me the content for that. Or is your tone just part of a big snow job?"

David said, "I agree. I'd also like to hear your answer to that. I know you've completed all the studies I suggested and a few dozen of your own. I've followed most of it, but I must have missed something. Where is that optimism coming from?"

David was sorry he said all that when Judy immediately went to lie on her cot and grabbed a paper bag at the same time to gasp into.

"Pay no attention to me," she said, eyes bulging, and panting into the bag, "Let's hear it! And if it isn't better than that damn letter to The FAST News you had me sign, you're in trouble!" She started breathing faster into the bag.

Before either David or Kevin could open his mouth, there was a knock on the door. "I'll get that," Kevin said with an obvious note of relief. Judy's bag-breathing moved into high gear.

Laura and Ned completed the first half of their morning walk by going around the isomorphs' building project. Before they left Laura's habitat to start their walk, Ned read certain FAST News articles and letters to her as she worked industriously on her nails. All the printed statements were making guesses about the purpose of the pyramid. Most of the guesses were the same as their own—namely, to protect everyone from the falling hill when it collapsed. The pyramid's apex would be directly below the apex of the hill itself, which was known to be the thinnest part of the hill and would bring the least debris down on the new tower. The most analytic and detailed discussion of that was in a letter signed by David, Kevin, and Judy. Unlike the other letters in The FAST News that day, this one was not optimistic. Their problem with the otherwise brilliant initiative of the isomorphs was that the quartzlike surface of the pyramid would not hold. Although those structural surfaces were much harder than most of the crystalline makeup of the hill itself, the slabs themselves could not withstand that much sudden force, even from the thinnest part of the hill. "Kudos to the isomorphs, but we're not there yet," the letter said. It concluded saying that "the undersigned" were continuing to work on other possibilities.

As they kept walking around the building project, Laura asked Ned, "Do you want to go inside and see what your isomorph is up to?"

"Not now. Adon can get by without me. I'd rather keep walking for a while. Let's head over to the Chem-Geol habitat and talk to those guys. I'm still depressed about their letter in The FAST News. Till I read that, I thought the pyramid was a good idea."

"Me too," Laura said as they turned away from the pyramid project and picked up their pace.

Laura was deep in thought as they made their way between the habitats, the piles of debris and the closed pits containing unvitalized isomorphs. They walked without talking for several minute before she broke the silence.

"Why do David and Kevin keep calling those isomorph covers quartz*like*? Why don't they just call them quartz and be done with it?"

"They use the *-like* suffix on everything; say they haven't found a real crystal on this planet yet. The crystals here are just like real ones, but they aren't. They also say the isomorphs aren't opal, but opalesque—to the extreme."

"Oh."

Another block of silence, and Laura spoke again. "If the hill were destroyed and fell on a person, we know what would happen. But what would happen if it fell on an isomorph—vitalized or otherwise?"

"I can only make a wild guess; but if the vitalized ones are anything like Dorts on that score, they'd be in and out of our spacetime dimension so fast that this universe's set of dimensions wouldn't affect them. Judging from what Ellen told me about her examination of Opal, it could leave the unvitalized isomorphs just as undamaged."

"I guess I missed that, Ned. What did she tell you about her?"

"She tried to get a blood sample—or whatever might be in an isomorph in place of blood—and she couldn't get the skin—or whatever that is on Opal's surface—to break. The needle went in, but Opal's surface merely made room for the needle. There was no surface breakage. When she removed the syringe needle, the surface came right back as the needle came out. She had a similar problem when she tried to take a sample of tissue using a scalpel—both externally and when she tried for a sample from the cheeks inside Opal's mouth. Isomorphs do seem well protected."

"If an isomorph was not vitalized, and was buried under hill debris, it would stay buried forever—damaged or not."

"Sure—like any dead or inanimate thing," Ned said.

"If an isomorph were vitalized, and was unable to pop in and out of time, it might still live—whatever that means for an isomorph—and could later crawl out from under the hill's debris, right?"

"I suppose," Ned said.

"When Clint dropped by on his way back to the Ad-Sec habitat last night, he said something interesting. He said the isomorphs were building hundreds of *shelves* between some of the scaffolding triangles. You read to me what our friends wrote in their letter. They said the slabs couldn't withstand a hill collapse."

"Yes dear," Ned said. "Your short-term memory is flawless. What are you getting at?"

"Well, all I can say is, thank God for the shelving."

"Oh. . . . Oh?"

"Yes."

Ned said, "May I be so bold as to ask?"

"Well, as you, Clint and David have so often said to me—it's obvious!"

"You've said that yourself a few times. It's catching. So, what's obvious?" Ned asked.

"They will need two-thirds more slabs than are available to complete the obelisk."

"Call it a pyramid."

"Okay, pyramid. Anyway, I counted the slabs along one of the sides, and from that I figured how many it will take to complete the *pyramid's* exterior. They're two-thirds short."

"Then the pyramid is obviously too big. I should have noticed that myself. It was a good idea, but how could the isomorphs have been so dumb? Lousy planning!"

"Lousy planning? No. It was superb!"

Ned looked blank, but said, "I'm listening."

"Good. The structural slabs—the ones from the already vitalized isomorphs—will take care of the first third, but the last two-thirds will have to be lifted from those still below their crystalline *manhole covers*, as Clint calls them. Over three-quarters of the Transformation population is now on the Cone. Most of their isomorphs are still here, under the surface."

"You're saying, then, that to complete the pyramid, their covers have to be *cannibalized*?"

"If *cannibalized* means taken and used, then yes. To complete the pyramid they will need most of the quartzlike disks still covering the remaining isomorphs, but they won't need all of them. There will be plenty left over."

"I guess that would be all right," Ned said. "They aren't alive anyway. Just opalesque, dead things. If the hill falls on them, *so be it*."

Laura stopped in her tracks and looked at Ned, shaking her head. "That's cold-hearted! How can you say such a thing?"

Ned stopped five paces away, not realizing Laura had stopped. He turned around and said, "You're the one who said you didn't want to be followed around day and night by one of those things."

"If your Adon was not yet vitalized, would you still say *so be it*?"

"That's entirely different!" Ned turned red.

Laura just looked at him.

It took a minute, but Ned's normal complexion returned. "Shit . . . shit . . . shit," he said calmly.

"Shit what?"

"I'm a father again, and I didn't realize it until this moment."

"So?"

"So, we have to make a smaller pyramid, or, if that letter to The FAST News is right, give it up entirely. We have to keep the unborn isomorphs protected under their slabs."

"You really are a much nicer man when you think things over. Now, for example, they're no longer dead things, but *unborn*. I like that. Maybe you're not totally cold-hearted after all."

"Thanks, but the main idea is to keep them under their slabs and to shoot for a smaller pyramid."

Laura shook her head again. "Just suppose the pyramid was completed using the additional slabs, and the dormant isomorphs—the unborn—were placed on all those shelves inside the pyramid. They'd still be protected under their own slabs, right?"

"Oh! Yes. Collectively. Hmmm. So that's why the isomorphs put in the shelves, and made the pyramid so big."

"Congratulations. Your short term powers of logic are still in tact—but you really had me worried for a minute."

Still using his powers of logic, Ned continued, "And if the hill does have to come down, and they were still tucked away under their individual slabs, then the slabs would be shattered anyway, and the unborn isomorphs would be buried forever. Under the pyramid they'd at least have a chance . . . if, somehow, it didn't collapse."

Laura and Ned started walking again.

"Another thing," Laura said, "If the pyramid was made any smaller, there would not be room for all of us, and all of the vitalized and unvitalized isomorphs. This way there may even be room for some of our small, most important possessions."

"Yeah, and if *only* the apex of the pyramid were preserved when the hill comes down, it would make a lovely gravestone for us all."

"Don't be such a grouch—it's a beautiful morning!"

Kevin answered the door and welcomed Laura and Ned.

Kevin's cheerful preliminaries fell flat, and not just because he looked tired. Yes, Laura and Ned had their breakfast already. No they didn't care for bloody marys; but, yes, they would enjoy a cup of coffee—nothing more.

That's all he needed. As Kevin headed to the coffee maker, Judy removed the paper bag from her mouth long enough to hold it up and say "Stop! David can do that. You have a report to give us."

Kevin stopped and said, "Okay, but *coffee first!*"

That was just one of the firsts—some were not just for procrastination purposes. Before David started the coffee, under Judy's orders, he took time in the bath room, yelling "Next" when he was out, followed by Kevin's vanishing into the same facility. He took longer than David, but the smell of coffee lured him back.

The presence of Laura, who was in a remarkably good mood, seemed to help Judy's anxiety, and after the tiring night, her first sip of coffee hit the spot. Since Kevin was in no hurry to talk about his scientific revelations, she and David shared the details of their morning discussion, and Laura and Ned shared theirs. Ned expressed particular concern about their letter in The FAST News that morning. Till reading that, he and everyone else seemed to believe the isomorphs were onto something, "But apparently not, if your letter is right."

"I believe it's right," David said.

"I don't know. It's probably right," Judy said.

"It's wrong," Kevin said.

They all looked at Kevin with mixed expressions.

"Yesterday, when we sent that letter off, you were the most adamant it was right," David said.

"You had me convinced," Judy said.

Laura and Ned sipped their coffee.

David asked the obvious question: "What changed since yesterday?"

Kevin doctored his coffee with cream and sugar, looked up, very serious, and said, "Last night."

David laughed.

After David settled down, he joined the others in their deadpan expressions, just looking at Kevin.

"I really didn't want to go into this right now. I didn't get much sleep. And it's a long, complicated explanation. I don't want you to miss a detail."

"I didn't get much sleep either," Judy said, "but both of my eyes are still half-open. Skip the long, complicated details and get to the point. We both need sleep!"

"Fair enough. Last night I had one last bright idea. Norbert helped. We got the spray equipment out of the back room, along with the vat and dozens of small containers. We filled the vat with water. It was a desperation idea since we're getting low on the yellow fluid."

"There's a little left?" Judy asked.

"Yes. But anyway," Kevin said, turning to David, "you know one of the big problems we've been having. We set the wall chips in the yellow fluid at different dilutions; then they came together and got as hard as diamond. The trouble is, diamond is brittle, and would cleave and fracture under a hill collapse. We proved that over and over in our smash simulations. And then we went off on a lot of other tangents, trying many things. But we didn't really fully explore the dilution angle."

Then, turning back to Judy and the others, Kevin said, "Well, last night, Norbert and I laid out, on level surfaces, a dozen different arrays of chips—they looked like autumn leaves in the woods back home. We put the same amount of water into all the small, empty containers, and measured amounts of our precious liquid into the water, stirred it up and sprayed one array of chips after another—each with a different dilution of the yellowish stuff. It turns out that the relationship between the chips and that fluid is *homeopathic*! We didn't find the optimal dilution, but the *most diluted* fluid gave the *best* result. We're talking a drop in a bucket."

Then, smiling, and with a twinkle in his tired eyes, he said, "There! Now can I go back to bed?"

Their expressions varied again, but they all caught the twinkle in Kevin's eye, and sat silent—waiting.

"Okay, okay! The results!" Kevin said. "But first, there is more to this than I've told you so far! Each array was on several surfaces, including the quartzlike isomorph cover material."

For Judy, that last statement was like a shot of adrenalin, and she became wide awake.

Then Kevin turned to her, as though she was the only other person in the room. "Under the greatest dilution we tried—and, as I said, I'm talking drops here, not glasses full—the chips not only lost every characteristic of diamond, except hardness and luster, and not only fused with the other hill chips, but fused with the quartzlike material as well. Spraying the quartzlike slabs alone did nothing; but in combination with the chips, everything happened! When fused with the quartzlike stuff, both changed. The fused products became, as one, pliant to the extent that the brittleness is gone. We got the diamond hard resistance, but with some flexibility. The combination became an invulnerable substance! It's amazing what happens when one mixes substances—especially *materials that aren't from around here!*"

They talked for another two hours before exhaustion caught up with Judy, who went to bed elated, and slept with dreams of home. Kevin was not far behind.

FIFTY-ONE

Mark and Denise looked out her one-way window. She was giggling and he was not only appreciating the morning view, but playfully touching Denise. It was mutual.

Her modesty *preference* for covering hers and the body of her isomorph in public had not changed, but she'd long since given up trying to control that behavior in her precious Chastity—who was, like all good isomorphs that morning, off to work on the pyramid.

Denise was enjoying everything—Mark, their privacy, and the streaming colors of morning light. For her, the light was beyond aesthetic. It was more arousing and sensual than she could believe. Or perhaps it was the breakfast Mark had made. Or was it his touch? There! Another one. Now she could care less. She turned around and took her precious Mark into her assertive arms and kissed him passionately. It is not that Mark was less than masculine or she less than feminine—far from it. Each was sensitive and secure enough to enjoy an occasional reversal of dominance roles. Besides, she was several inches taller than Mark, and much stronger than the average woman. They were dazzled by one another, and after being together for days and days, and nights and nights, and after endless hours of talking, cooing and loving, they committed to each other—for as long as that might last.

"Damn it!" they said together as they spotted Everett through the window. He was hustling directly toward Denise's habitat. They hurriedly put on their robes and slippers to intercept the inevitable knock.

Everett had difficulty getting down to business. "Jack Lewis and Officer Bracket were manning the Ad-Sec habitat when I dropped in on them earlier," he said. "They were almost secretive about your privacy, Dr. Tenderloin, so I deeply apologize—to both of you—for this intrusion. But when I told them what it was about, they said I should contact you."

Denise knew Everett better than Mark, or anyone else on the planet for that matter, and had never seen him so flustered. "It's okay Everett," she said, "Mark and I are in the vinculum of now."

Everett immediately looked relieved, saying, "Oh! That serious! Bond well then!"

"Thank you," she said, "but I guess your business is with Mark?"

"Yes. If I may, Mark, I need to intrude on you in another way."

"How can I help?" Mark asked.

"As you know, I have kept a complete catalogue of photographs of all known isomorphs, both vitalized and not. With few exceptions, they have all been published in the News, and I have kept careful track of all their locations and the names of their human identicals."

"Yes, I know. And I commend you for your being so diligent and conscientious about that. A valuable service indeed, and—"

"Yes, yes," Everett interrupted, rushing ahead, "but I need to get into your habitat—with your permission, of course. That's why I'm here. It will be completely confidential."

"I hope so. It's in a terrible mess. I locked it up a while back and haven't returned to it since."

Everett said nothing, but looked more flustered than before.

Mark finally got it. "Holy crap!" he said. "I forgot all about it. An isomorph is still buried in there! Of course you may enter. I'll go with you."

"We'll both go with you," Denise said.

It was not just Everett and Mark, and not just Everett and Mark and Denise. Like everything else on the Transformation and under the hill, if something was confidential, the chance that everybody already knew about it was very good. Perhaps the word that "today is the day," had gotten out through one of Everett's helpers—or it could have been Clint and Jack—who later admitted they "might possibly" have made a comment to . . . they forgot who. None of that really mattered. The crowd around Mark's habitat was enormous even before they arrived.

Everett's devoted helpers had secured the area around the entrance to Mark's habitat. After Mark unlocked the door, Everett and the men carrying his photographic equipment went in and closed the door. Half an hour later they emerged, and the habitat was again locked.

"Well, whose isomorph is it?" Denise asked. "Is it Mark's or Laura Shane's?"

"You know I have to process all these shots to get the final image."

"Yes, we know," Mark said, "but you can at least tell if the silhouette is male or female—even without your photographic morphing."

"Usually can, but not this time. Too much florescence. Made it too unclear and blurry. But you're right, it must be one of you—you or Dr. Shane. When the time comes, should we get Dr. Michaels and Kevin Verily in on the unveiling? They have the hologram equipment."

Mark and Denise spoke simultaneously—he said "Yes," and she said "No." The couple looked at each other for a moment, then spoke simultaneously again—he said "No," and she said "Yes."

Everett could not help but smile. He said, "I'll take that as a yes," and started to leave, film packs under his arm. He left slowly, just in case, but neither Denise nor Mark said a word.

Then Everett stopped, turned around and looked at Mark. "We'll have to dismantle the habitat."

Mark nodded back.

"I'll need the key."

Mark tossed it to him.

Then, in a loud enough voice for everyone in the crowd to hear, Everett announced, "Today is not the day. Tomorrow. It will all be ready at noon tomorrow!"

The crowd wistfully missed the drama of new vitalizations and some groaned that it was not to happen that very day. Others applauded and cheered that it was coming so soon. Mark and Denise said nothing, but eyed each other for reactions. The honeymoon was still on.

By noon the next day—in fact, by one o'clock that morning—Mark's habitat had been removed. Its area was thoroughly swept and cleaned and the hologram setup made ready. The isomorph slab that Mark's habitat had covered shone with bright florescence from below all that night, and by noon the next day the reflected light of Nimbus gave it a new and dazzling brilliance.

Throughout the day and night, other Base Watchers gathered and became involved. Their participation turned into hurried, assertive, even intrusive activity, and continued without letup. By six in the morning, Everett was frantic. He believed everything was completely out of control. He nearly called Officer Bracket, but David talked him out of it by saying he thought the activity was "normally motivated," and that anything else would lead, later on, to pushing and shoving—or worse. David insisted that the line-of-sight vistas were essential. So, instead of resisting, a much calmer Everett directed his helpers to pitch in and assist with building the two sets of bleachers that were already under way. The stands they constructed were more than adequate, and the builders wisely left a wide corridor into the arena. Looking on, and anticipating the afternoon drama for this final vitalization, Kevin Verily's eyes flashed, rolled and gleamed, and his body jerked and twisted for control; but he finally gave in—and wisely took his medication.

The medication did not interfere, however, with Kevin's creativity—only his craziness. His sense of the dramatic was still intact. With support and help from the Acting Guild Players, their associated dance troupe—of which Ned Keller was a part-time member—and others, a plan was initiated that set the stage for the noon event.

Much to Kevin's disappointment, they only had time to consider the little things, like the red carpet idea Ned Keller used to honor the arrival on the Cone of some Great Oz, who only turned out to be Mark Tenderloin. They could not use a red carpet, not for Mark or his isomorph if it were under that slab, or for Laura Shane's isomorph if hers were there. The red carpet was still on the Transformation.

The isomorph's sex was still unknown, so they decided to cut up two rugs of different colors, obtained from the Exchange, for the promenade and entrance. The colored pieces were stitched together in alternating one-meter sections— pink, baby blue, pink, baby blue . . . . With that and a few other simple ideas, they thought they were done.

But entertainments of any real attraction and importance were few and far between under the hill's big tent, and getting this particular circus to come out right was serious business. Kevin, the Acting Guild Players, David, Judy and Everett et al, all worked on every aspect of the project. Band and orchestra members, singers, dancers, and poets joined in. Other Base Watchers helped build the frame and curtains for the circular stage unveiling. The biggest job, by far, was building the grandstand—and in one day and night, it "magically" appeared. When all was finally ready, it turned out to be more than Kevin could have hoped for. By noon everybody was haggard and dead tired, but wearing smiles.

The curtained stage for this theatre in the round was several times larger than the isomorph's slab, but altogether the arrangements provided an unobstructed view and focus for the ensuing events. To everyone's delight, Clinton Bracket excepted, Kevin was the MC. Without any of his former pretense at hocus pocus, he became the perfect Ring Master. He introduced and announcing with flair and aplomb, the initial promenade and then each and every musical piece, stand-up comedian, song, act, skit, poet and dance that followed.

The spectators were thrilled. They especially liked the music and the dancers. The tap dancers came across with marvelous resonance as they clattered back and forth across the quartzlike slab. The cancan dancers in this little stadium brought many manly cheers and ladylike titters. Even Ned—wearing his heeled Spanish boots, black tights and bolero jacket—took part with Melissa, one of his dance-troupe partners. They danced to a medley of ancient Latin music—beginning with a slow habanera and adagio, with Ned lifting and balancing his partner; and then the pace picked up with pieces that culminated in the fandango and finished with a dramatic flamenco. Laura could hardly contain her delight to see her Ned step out of his usual role as nerd-leader of the Transformation and return to a talent from earlier days. She did, however, question him later about not including her favorite, the tango. He reminded her of the disappointing memory that brought to mind—a minor thing, but it was there none the less. She chided him for that silly piece of artistic sensitivity, saying, "Back then if your dance partner had even bothered to give the committee her name, instead of just vanishing like that, you both would have won the international competition. Some of the committee told you that privately after the contest. That should have been sufficient artistic consolation. And, think of it, you'd only practiced with her for three hours after your regular partner became ill."

Ned responded, "Hmm. Yes. She was better than good. Don't know where she came from or where she went. Oh well. Let's forget it. After this next act, I think you or Mark may be up. One of you will be the main event, you know."

Following the performance by Ned and Melissa, the last act was a poem of inspiration that put half the crowd to sleep.

Then Kevin came into his own again, and refocused the Watchers on the main event—the unveiling of the last isomorph and his or her vitalization. Kevin called for complete silence, the curtain was still closed and Kevin's and Everett's helpers removed the slab out of sight from the crowd. On cue, and for effect on the audience, the helpers were supposed to fake loud gasps of amazement on seeing the revealed isomorph. That they tried to do, but could only manage *sincere* sounds of *admiration*—those were far more effective than the fake sounds they'd practiced. They rolled the slab up the corridor of pink and baby blue and out of the arena. As planned, Mark and Laura followed on behind it. (They had to leave in order to turn around and make their entrance.)

To musical fanfare they returned arm in arm with cadenced steps, stopping before Kevin, who was front and center of the closed curtain. Kevin said some words about who might be the lucky winner, but, with effort, avoided becoming overly expansive and symbolic with his final remarks. Laura and Kevin were separated and sent to the far left and right of the curtain. They would be the 'ast to see whose isomorph lay therein. Kevin would announce the name of the "winner," and the unnamed loser would return to his or her place as one of the spectators.

The curtain was opened to the blast of trumpets—startling the remaining sleepers to full alertness. Then silence. The silence turned into gradual recognition and an outpouring of admiring Ohs and Ahs—a positive reception that came even before Kevin's announcement of the winner: "Laura Shane!"

Laura approached the center of the stage where the railing and stairs into the pit were located. She did not immediately look at her isomorph. The audience sounds had been positive, but she wasn't sure how positive. *Maybe they're just being kind*, she thought.

She faced the center of the small crater, her back to the stands, and hesitantly touched the railing. As her flagging courage returned, she lifted her eyes to see what was before her. On its back, in body-profile, lay the beautiful, naked figure of her isomorph. Its lovely face was turned toward Laura and the grandstand, its head position accommodating the outsized occiput for which its own identical was known. Laura's heart pounded with anticipation; but she allowed herself a guilty smile of satisfaction to attend her slow descent of the staircase into the pit. She was right. There was nothing to be ashamed of.

One familiar voice cut through all that positive crowd murmuring, and she almost giggled. It was Mark's voice in the distance, verbally restraining Denise from rushing out to offer Laura the blanket she'd brought along for Mark, had he won.

Laura caught the spirit of the event. She walked slowly around to the back of her inanimate identical, a full body length from it, before she turned to face the crowded array of expectant and eager faces in the stands. A drum roll began. She approached her isomorph, knelt down and kissed its cheek. Within seconds—only Kevin bothered to know how many—the isomorph propped itself up on both elbows, turned its head upward, almost touching Laura's face, and opened its eyes to see her for the first time. Laura gasped at the beauty of its deep amber, feline-slit irises. A more stunning sensation came as she felt its breath upon her lips and nostrils. With that one breath she was rocked by a powerful maternal sense that she did not know she was capable of. It moved her to speak a promise so softly that the now-vitalized isomorph alone could hear. The sounds said, "I will care for you, baby sister, until you need me no more." It, now she, would always remember those sounds, and in time would learn their meaning.

A human reaction like Laura's was common. Even Clint had a similar parental feeling with the vitalization of his isomorph; but unlike women, who openly spoke of it, he and most of the men never told a soul. Except for Mark, every person there knew that feeling.

Even though there was nothing new in this, the spectators remained spellbound . . . and silent. Then to everyone's amazement something new really did happen. Laura's isomorph opened her mouth and golden throat, and clear as a bell for all to hear, said, "Pollywanzacracker!"

The gasps from the crowd were just as clear. Before that moment, no isomorph had ever spoken a word, and to do so at the very moment of vitalization was, for them, a thrill beyond measure. Then the crowd went silent again—lest they miss another word; but Laura's isomorph was not to speak again—not until *all* isomorphs were vitalized and, irritatingly, would begin to speak at once.

Laura hugged her isomorph and said, "You remembered!" Every spectator knew what Laura was referring to. They'd all heard the story of the Parrotoid echo in the mountains, and the talented, velvety plantoid that returned those words to her then.

Laura stood and reached down to take her isomorph's hand and gently encouraged her to stand. In a few moments, continuing to hold the hand of her now standing, statuesque beauty, Laura said to the throng, "I wish to introduce all of you to my new and beloved little sister, Keeta." The applause and response of good will was heartening. (They'd all heard colorful stories of Laura's favorite childhood pet, Keeta, a most colorful parakeet itself.)

Laura released Keeta's hand and ascended the stairs alone to the upper edge of the pit, and, like so many others before, her isomorph made the symbolic and literal leap from the pit and joined Laura on the ledge.

Just as real as the literal leap, but unseeable, was Keeta's parallel leap—up through the myriad barricades of inanimate, dormant unconsciousness to reach the breath of life, a transit from the infinite abyss of non-consciousness to the possibilities of being, where sensation enters only to herald the next stage: the life of sentience.

Few humans ever spoke of, nor could they remember, their own transit from a disorganized state to an organized one, from nothingness to existence, from the unconscious to the conscious, from non-being to being. Cultural and physical obstacles obscured such things from *human* minds—but not from the minds of isomorphs. At night they could, and did, dream such things to one another.

FIFTY-TWO

The hill's destruction was climactic. The thundering roar of its extended collapse was as frightening and deafening as its creation. Even the bravest cowered. When the time came for Officer Clinton Bracket to shoot it, shoot it he did, and down it tumbled—just as David said it would—and the hill was no more.

Final preparations were hectic before the hill could be destroyed. Many days earlier, even as Laura's "little sister" was being vitalized, the other isomorphs were collecting the last disks that still covered the unvitalized figures. From under those slabs the inanimate figures were taken and carefully placed on shelves inside the pyramid. From far off, the surface of the obelisk's tower appeared to be crawling with insects, but the moving dots were construction workers—isomorphs that climbed and jumped about its steep sides like grasshoppers. The humans worked inside from safe scaffolds.

Men, women and isomorphs were in full work mode. Their building activities with the recently scavenged disks were unexpectedly interrupted by Clinton Bracket on his bullhorn. He called for everyone, isomorphs included, to join him inside the half-built pyramid.

When they had gathered there, he made a few authority-packed remarks—just to put everybody at ease—and then introduced the speakers, David and Kevin, who explained and demonstrated the technique for strengthening the external and internal surfaces of the pyramid and the necessity for doing so. They explained how to strengthen the small, quartzlike shims and pieces around the large slabs taken from the isomorph pits. The slabs and sand-size chips from the hill were still being set in the concrete obtained from the Exchange. That construction was strong, but not in itself enough to hold under collapse of the hill. It needed one more thing: A good spraying of the special liquid they were demonstrating. It would not only further harden those pieces, but cause them to *fuse* with the quartzlike material. The biggest job would be placing thousands of the larger chips from the wall onto the outside and inside surfaces of the pyramid and spraying them lavishly with the fluid. That would force their compounding into a deep, indissoluble union with the large disks.

And they were to leave no gaps. Except for one. There had to be a way to get in and out. It had to be five or six meters above the surface to allow for the immense quantity of hill material that would fall onto the pyramid, pile up and billow out from there according to the pyramid's area and shape. Several former architects and contractors stepped forward offering to plan and supervise construction of the exit.

An hour of question and answer followed, along with more demonstrations. David and Kevin would be available during their waking hours and on-call afterwards. Amazingly, more than half the people in attendance seemed to understand the process as presented, but the rest had only the barest clue and would have to rely on the others. The isomorphs were not in the latter group. They understood and began work immediately.

As the building materials were being used up, new disk and chip materials were gathered. Soon, all the unvitalized isomorphs—mainly of the Cone-based humans—were on shelves within the growing pyramid. Everett and his friends carefully prepared and applied an ID bracelet to each of their right wrists, and Denise, with helpers of her own, covered them with decoratively colored sheets from the Exchange.

One crucial part of the construction was completed early. That was the pyramid's new entrance with its sharply descending stairs into the pyramid's interior; its giant, hardened plug—to be pushed out for the final exit after the hill was obliterated. The remaining construction took several more days. It was completed four days after the flood threat was over and the tides had returned to normal.

During those final days, fewer laborers were needed for the much smaller area around the apex of the pyramid, and there was a great surplus of disk and hill-chip materials. With all the extra labor and materials, one of the architects suggested a design to cover the stadium where Laura's isomorph had been vitalized. The idea met with enthusiasm from most, although many wished merely to rest after the effort on the pyramid. In fact, some suggested they would rather see a protective cover over the Honky-tonk Saloon. A vote was taken, and the stadium won by a narrow margin. Consequently, at the same time that the much larger pyramid was being completed, a substantial geodesic dome ("the dome") was built to cover Keeta's birthplace. The two structures were completed at roughly the same time.

One suggested function for the arena and pit beneath the dome was to use it for subsequent vitalizations, assuming the dome held up during the hill's day of destruction ("D-day"). Before the dome was completed, that idea was broached on the Transformation Cone where it met with enthusiastic approval. (Why with enthusiasm? They knew that all the isomorph pits except, with luck, the Keeta pit, would be destroyed by the falling hill. They wanted *their* isomorph to have a similar—albeit surrogate—entrance into existence. The Keeta pit would do.)

The two structures were close enough together to appear from the angle and distance of anyone sitting atop the Mart (where the Honky-tonk Saloon kept one of its "outside" bars), like a sky-high spire beside a domed tabernacle—or the towering, ancient, 1939-40 World's Fair Trylon beside the Perisphere.

In the final days of construction, the last vitalized isomorph, Keeta, was in training. She was taken to human meetings, involved at the Honky-tonk Saloon—where she quickly learned to dance with other isomorphs whose "mother hen" humans (men mostly) insisted they not work on the dangerously steep pentahedron or the dome on that day—and was present during many conversations between Laura, Ned, Mark and many others.

But most of Keeta's education came at night, between dreamers, where she learned everything they knew, and they what she had to offer. The night brought more than fellow dreamers together. There was something else: A presence, on the edge, distant, barely perceived. It was merely there, neither threat nor protection, watching, waiting—immense.

Before long, Keeta was helping with the final phases of physical construction of the pyramid. And she was the first isomorph to pick up a pen and paper. She used no words, but drew a simple plan for an entrance-exit for the dome. The architects glanced at it and scoffed. Then they sat down and actually looked at it, after which they looked at each other in agreement and tore up their own plans. Keeta's plan was a masterpiece of functional simplicity. It was built and Laura was proud.

Electronic mail from the Transformation Cone to friends under the hill, and letters to the editor and articles in The FAST News were all optimistic about the pyramid's strength and their inevitable reunion once that pesky hill was out of the way. The FAST News turned down only one letter to the editor. It was from the prestigious laundry room supervisor. (He had given his letter the title: "Whistling Past the Graveyard.") Only after the hill's destruction and the pyramid's success was the earlier pessimism revealed.

The hill dwellers had been strung out on a series of hopes. They too were kidding each other. And the Cone dwellers had hidden their anguish and worry about an *inevitable* crushing death for their friends. Until they were safe, no messages but love and encouragement were sent or spoken. The censorship was mainly self-imposed.

Jubilation in both places after the hill's safe destruction was uncontainable. There would have to be a celebration.

Celebration? Debra Anderson's next editorial declared it a necessity. She wrote:

> We are a community. The hill split our community, but only physically. Now that the hill is down, we can be together again. It is the nature of human's and all like beings to find meaning within and beyond the range of their experiences. Every known culture has marked its most important experiences and events—the good ones and the end of bad ones—with some kind of commemoration or celebration.
>
> Most recently for us, the hill came down and our fellows are freed—if leaving a small cage to find one's self on a lifeless island is being freed. It's a matter of contrast, and I say that being out of that hill's clutches has eliminated one bad thing. Other bad things, large and small, are bound to happen again; they always do. But for now, the moment is here. Let us embrace it—if only for a short time. In the end, life itself offers few chances for such moments. This one is ours! If we are stuck out here for the rest of our time, why not take every opportunity, such as this, to be happy, to be a true community? Let us be happy! Let us play! Let us celebrate!

A *Celebration*! Everybody agreed there would be one and that it would last . . . well, as long as it lasted!

Except for the pyramid, the dome and the west cliff, everything immediately beneath the hill was destroyed—including the forest of crystalline trees that had stood beside that part of the cliff. Ms. Snow, the proprietor of the Honky-tonk

Saloon and dance hall was happy she was able to save a few things inside the geodesic dome. Those things included her ancient disco ball, juke box, player piano and an adequate quantity of spirits—all of it. Another piece of hardware they made room for was the Orb. It barely fit as Mark piloted it through the entrance—without a scratch—and brought it to rest beside the Keeta pit. Everyone knew the Orb would be needed later.

As for smaller items, everyone was able to save their favorite things within the dome—books, clothing, some furniture, electronics, pictures, and the like. Within the remaining spaces on and beneath the dome's bleachers, the Exchange and other Mart shops, boutiques and kiosks stored such things as functioning generators that continued to power freezers full of food; photographic and holographic gear; scientific equipment, and so on. Thus, the dome became the repository for survival supplies, comfort items, intellectual valuables and sentimental treasures. Several days of survival supplies were also kept within the pyramid.

Mark's Base and the hill that covered it, took up only a fraction of the wider plain of flatland adjacent to the west cliff and the south cove. Two days after the hill's destruction the dust had settled sufficiently for the hill dwellers to leave the pyramid. They marched from there in scattered groups and lines to reach the solid plain beyond the hill's debris to rejoin their hundreds of friends from the Cone. To reach the outer flatland plain, the hill dwellers marched calf-deep on top of the ridges and troughs of hill dust and debris. Those ridges and troughs were meters deep before tapering off near the outer plain.

By Earth-time, they were moving into mid-February, but to them it felt like a Valentine's Day of the ancients—or more like *Mardi Gras* time! In the words of Debra Anderson—in an editorial entitled "Let The Carnival Begin!" she reminded everybody, as she often did, that Stanley Ludeen still had not found the spacetime coordinates for planet Earth, so there was no rush to leave Origin—and *plenty of time to celebrate the hill's annihilation—their freedom!*

Within a few hours of the reunion's beginning, it was noticed that many of the former hill dwellers were gone. They had been seen heading back to the pyramid. "Why are you going back there?" Debra Anderson asked a number of them. Their answers explained it quite simply: "To see what can be done to bring out my isomorph." Their isomorphs were so heavy and dense, Debra was told, that the first one to try leaving with them, hours earlier, sank deep over its head into the softer dust and debris. It was like quicksand for them and took a strong rope and an even stronger isomorph to drag it back to safety.

Most of those who returned went to the pyramid. Laura, Ned, Judy and David—and half of David's crew—went instead to the dome at Judy's urging. There they picked up dozens of empty buckets and several sets of spray gear that were no longer being used since the pyramid and dome walls were completed.

In addition, Judy picked up some small items she had recently been working with in her lab.

Carrying all those items, they trudged through the debris to the pyramid where they found crowds of people trying to reassure their isomorphs that, somehow, everything would be all right, and that it would simply take a little while to figure out how to get them out. If necessary they would build a bulldozer and dig a path through all the debris, or build a dock or platform over the soft piles.

Laura found and hugged her Keeta and told her the same things, as did Ned with Adon, and David and Judy with their isomorphs, Oscar and Minerva—and David's crew members as well, except the ones from the Cone, who could only gape in amazement at their first sight of real isomorphs, not just their photographs.

Judy stood on the rim of the saltwater well in the center of the pyramid and announced to everyone there that she needed some of the special liquid they had been spraying on the pyramid and the dome. No one there knew of any, as it had all been used up building and strengthening the two structures. But in a minute, Adon came forward with a vial of the liquid. It was no more than three ounces. How Adon knew to keep some was not clear, but Ned Keller was proud that he did.

One of David's crew, who had been on the Great Cone till that day, looked a bit confused. "If that's what you wanted the buckets and spray gear for, I don't think a few ounces will do much. I thought you had something else in mind. I thought—"

"Never mind," Judy interrupted. "This is all I need. Now start filling the buckets with water from this well."

Most of her listeners began doing as Judy advised; but David's crewman asked her, "How's that supposed to help?"

Judy said, "I went through a distillation and refining process with this yellow fluid. I ended up with just a *speck* of something. It was . . . 'not from around here,' as your boss keeps reminding me. Well, I just brought it here from storage in the dome. It's just a speck for Aden's vial."

The man looked bewildered and so did David who'd been listening; but that was all the explanation she chose to give. David saw that and did not pursue it further, realizing that Judy, the chemist, had not—nor had he or Kevin—done the further necessary experiments that Judy was counting on. Judy had done a number of trial experiments, but not like this one, whatever it was to be. She was only *guessing* she had a way to create more of the fluid from the *speck*.

And why not? David thought. *She's making a bet, a gamble—pulling a scam—but there's nothing for her to lose, except some prestige. She's playing this confidence game to the hilt.* David admired that—and laughed outrageously as he thought, *She's just flying by the seat of her cute little pants!*

Judy frowned at him. She figured it was *right and appropriate* for her to frown at him as she did, but had no idea why it was—she just knew!

Judy dropped the *speck* into Adon's vial, replaced the lid and shook it hard. The slightly yellow, transparent liquid in the vial immediately became an opaque, bright yellow that radiated a brilliant glow. Then, with an eye dropper, she squeezed a drop into each of the water-filled buckets.

She looked at David and smiled nervously. "Now," she said, "go outside and spray a *walking path*." As she spoke, her voice caught and rose ever so slightly on those last two words—almost turning her instruction into an iffy question. She had no idea if it would work. But David got the picture. If Judy's guess was right, it would be a miracle. *Heck*, David thought, *if that yellow means what I think it does, it might actually work*!

David started the outside spraying, and the dust and sand-size hill chips immediately pulled together, as if by magnetism. With a little experimentation he realized he'd have to spray a *wide* area to create even a narrow path of solid material. Finally, he lavishly sprayed a much wider area to create a path a meter and a half or more in width. By the time his bucket was empty he had made a good start on a firm path and was getting tired. He stepped aside for the next person, who'd been standing and watching the process. David let him take over. The rotation went on from there, with each empty bucket going back for a refill of water and that special drop of yellow fluid. In any case it worked like magic, if not magnetism. David said to Judy, "You're a hero!" Judy put her hand on her hip and tossed her head back as if to say, "Of Course!"

In less than half a day, with so many at work, the entire wavelike, kilometer-long path to the flatland area (the area free of debris that would be called "New Camp") was completed—along with a second path to the geodesic dome, and a third from the dome to the New Camp flatland. The three paths formed a triangle. With the remaining spray, they created a wide porchlike perimeter around each of the two structures.

By nightfall the former hill dwellers joined their isomorphs in a triumphant return, two by two, from the pyramid to the solidity of New Camp and its crystalline plantoid flatland.

As the wind increased throughout that star-bright night, the isomorphs endured it without heed or hardship. A *severe* north wind had come up, but they continued to nestle into a refreshing, coruscating embrace with Morpheus, the ancient god of dreams. All around New Camp their glittering embers flashed in answer to the stars.

Humans and isomorphs took their own forms of nighttime intermission. While they slept and dreamed, the harsh night wind blew *meters* of near-weightless debris and dust from the fluffy, land-filling tops that the hill's destruction created, and blew it into the cove. That left behind the broken hill's gently curving, dune-shaped piles of much heavier material and the three hardened pathways in frozen suspension over a meter above the undulant dunes they tracked—looking like levitated children's roller coasters. Except for the shorter bridge to the dome, the other two floating walkways, to New Camp, were just over a kilometer in length. The upper surfaces of the paths were smooth, but their rough undersides were something between stalactites and tangles of giant spiderwebs. Even the terminal extremities of the two paths—the one from the pyramid and the one from the dome—ended close together at New Camp. They were the longest gravitationally counteracted cantilever bridges ever created.

When David woke the next morning and saw all this, he laughed predictably and said, "It's a great engineering feat, but nothing any scientist could explain—at least not one from around here."

FIFTY-THREE

The parade of new vitalizations began soon after the hill came down and its dust had dispersed, after the bridges were created, and after all the practical materials and personal treasures stored in the dome had been moved to New Camp.

A week before that—high above the still-standing hill—another kind of parade was under way: an exodus from the Transformation Cone to the new and unspoiled flatland. By then the tides had all but settled.

Despite the early pessimism about the hill's safe destruction, the Cone-based shuttles, and one Orb, began transporting large quantities of material, habitats and people to the planet—as had been done when they first arrived. This time the parade to Origin was driven by their longing to restore the apparatus of human habitation on Origin and to restore their community. Their chance for a return to Earth any time soon looked more and more distant—even hopeless.

That growing sense of hopelessness was reflected in Debra Anderson's unending editorial drumbeat that Earth's spacetime coordinates were not yet located. If everybody was to be in limbo, they figured they might as well be on the planet or the Transformation—or both. With frequent commutes, *both* was the choice for many. Thus, they could more patiently continue "Waiting," as one of Debra's editorials put it, "for Stanley Lundeen, the Godot for our safari into space, to finally stick his finger into the hot galactic spoor for clues to Earth's spacetime location."

Once Officer Bracket had destroyed the hill, there was a fleeting exodus *from* the Cone, and a *return* to it by many who had been trapped for so long beneath the hill. On their returned to the Cone, some brought along their identicals; but those isomorphs became disoriented, weakened and ill after only a day or two—sometimes within hours—and had to go back to Origin. Some made the trip to the Cone in Mark's other Orb, after he freed it from dome storage. In coming weeks the round-trip shuttle and Orb traffic hummed.

For the parade of new vitalizations to begin, the unvitalized isomorphs were moved from their shelves in the pyramid and laid on the dome floor or on its bleachers. They were, of course, too heavy to be moved by any human alone, but the vitalized isomorphs had no difficulty carrying their inanimate brothers and sisters in their arms like dolls across the elevated path from the pyramid to the dome.

One by one, newly vitalized isomorphs emerged from the Keeta pit and quickly became acquainted with their human identicals. Due to the large number of unvitalized isomorphs, a routinized approach to the vitalization process was again established; but this time for efficiency and dignity—unlike an earlier ritualistic approach that used humiliation and self aggrandizement by a pretense of sacerdotal powers.

After reopening the dome's bleachers, the overflow crowds again refilled the stands, as they had previously for Keeta, and vitalization of the Coners' isomorphs was under way. After a period of days during which both humans and their "new" and "old" isomorphs stood watching, the dome slowly began to empty of the recently stored, now viable, isomorphs and their human identicals—and the exodus to New Camp continued.

Human and vitalized isomorph marched, two by two, across the floating pathway from the dome to the solid flatland. In a matter of days the queue of unvitalized isomorphs dwindled, the number of trekkers to New Camp slowed, and finally ended. All but a dozen or so unvitalized, and unclaimed, isomorphs remained within the dome. It was reasonable, but mistaken, to assumed that those could be vitalized at any time—no matter how long they were allowed to lie there—by the right human stepping forward to make the claim.

Opinionated and contrasting letters to the editor were submitted to The FAST News on that very subject. One stated:

> To leave any unvitalized isomorphs on a shelf indefinitely is unconscionable. We who have taken the responsibility to vitalize our own likeness can not understand or accept such neglect. To us it was like bringing something to life—like a birth or a life-giving baptism for the dead, only more powerful since no unvitalized isomorph comes as a dead-blank-slate. Far from it.

In general, however, the criticisms from males and females alike were muted by their strong belief in the right of human adults to select from available options and, in the words from another letter:

> Those things are just so many hunks of inorganic matter that are sometimes useful, like a toaster or any other more or less complex, inorganic machine,

like for instance, the very well maintained, well serviced and nicely taken care of laundry equipment I personally happen to supervise, oversee and administer.

Of course, no one knew how to ask the isomorphs for their opinion on any of this—especially the unvitalized ones.

"I'd like to introduce you to Opal," Margaret said to Astra.

"Happy to meet you," said Astra, shaking its inorganic hand with her mechanical one.

Then, turning to Margaret, Astra added, "She is more beautiful than her picture. Given your lights, you must be very proud."

"I am—whatever that's supposed to mean. Anyway, bringing one's own isomorph into creation is good. How about you? Do you have some kind of plan to—"

"—Don't go there, Margaret!" Astra snapped, and then said more calmly, "I just need time. A million years would help."

"All right Astra. I guess you're having a conflict about that. It's your choice."

"Thanks."

"I've been below for a couple days. Nobody seems to be getting scrapes and bruises down on Origin these days. What's new up here?"

"That's *all* you can think of that's new on Origin?" Astra asked, evading Margaret's innocent-sounding question.

"All those preparations for a low-key Mardi Gras celebration were wrapped up before I even got down to the planet. I don't know if such a thing could *ever* be low key. It didn't look low key when I got there. Debra Anderson pushed for that. The idea went over well. The fun started even before the party plans were completed. Sometimes you just can't hold people back."

"Anything else?"

"Yes. One big new thing—oh, you must have read about this! Everybody bucked the administration on re-creating the Mart. But they came to a compromise. Administration was flat-out against even including the Honky-tonk Saloon—so they could restore the other facilities more adequately."

"What was the compromise?"

"You *didn't* read The FAST News, did you? It was democracy at work. Majority rule. Administration could have vetoed it, but didn't. I guess that's compromise. Most of the Mart stores will be *smaller*, so that the Honky-tonk Saloon can stand alone—unattached to the Mart—and be *three times bigger* than it was before!"

Astra started to laugh, and Margaret joined in. Opal displayed rapid eye movements.

When they had stopped laughing and eye moving, Margaret again asked, "What's new up here?"

"A lot of shuttle activity, moving people and things back and forth. Stan's looking stressed—like, on the verge of a nervous breakdown, but that's nothing new. That's about it since you left."

"I'll rephrase. What's new with *you*?"

Astra squirmed in her chair, shook her head and said, "Nothing. Nothing I can do anything about. Nothing I can respond to."

Margaret knew how to keep Astra talking. She just sat there, staring at her, saying nothing.

"Okay. I got an e-mail."

"Who from?"

"A guy."

Again, Margaret simply outwaited Astra.

"He's an ugly, cliché-ridden, neurotic-geek-nerd with thick glasses. He probably can't even *see*."

"You've met him, then. Have you responded to his e-mail?"

"No-o-o!"

"What did he say?"

"He wants to *get to know me better*—and clichés like that."

"How does he happen to know you?"

"He was on one of the teams that built the Deep. He's head of one of the technical teams, but had no input on the overall design. He thought the main design was a total fuck-up."

"Then he already knows about your physical condition."

"In spades, but you'd never know it to read his e-mails."

"He sent more than one? What's he saying?"

"The idiot wants to take me to that Mardi Gras to help celebrate the hill's destruction."

"Does that make him an idiot?"

"Of course. I'm not showing my face outside our rooms or these offices."

Margaret started to laugh. She sometimes knew Astra better than she knew herself. "Sounds to me like you've made up your mind. You've decided to take him up on the invitation, haven't you?"

"Margaret, you're such a smart-ass! Of course I'll go with him. It'll serve him right. Besides, I saw the picture of his isomorph. *He's gorgeous!*—without his clo . . . er, I mean, his glasses."

"That's wonderful, Astra. I hope you've stocked up on your medication. I wouldn't want to be responsible for his safety."

They both laughed heartily. Opal didn't get it and had no reaction.

Astra said she had an e-mail ready to send to him, but wanted Margaret to *promise* to help her get ready if she decided to send it. She would only go with him to sit on a high tier in the bleachers, in shadows, to watch the big Mardi

Gras dance. Then she would return to the Transformation. She always did enjoy one-way people watching. She would bring her binoculars.

"Hmmm. That dance would have to be a *masquerade* ball! Okay. Yes, I promise, Astra; but there are a few strings."

"Strings? Those things can be dangerous."

"Yes, but they'll be my kind of strings. I get to pick everything you will wear, including your prostheses, wig, and mask."

"Those are the only strings?"

"Yes."

"Okay, but there is one set of prostheses you can't select. That set is *out*."

"Then you're on your own, Astra. I know the one's your talking about. Those are the arms and legs you *will* wear—or the deal's off."

"But they're so expensive. They cost the government millions!"

"And so realistic—and cute."

"That means I'd have to wear the neuro-net under my wig. Those limbs are too responsive to my movement thoughts. I might make a fool of myself. I'm not used to its peripheral touch and proprioceptive impulses or all that tactile bud feedback. It's been years."

"That's why they're so expensive; and why, to brush up, you'll need practice with those limbs. What were you going to do with them? Just leave them in an attic somewhere?"

"It's been years."

"You already made that excuse. No more of those, and no arguments."

"Besides, it itches. The wigs are bad enough by themselves. The neuro-net is worse."

"No arguments! If something itches, scratch it. The dance will be fun for you and him to watch. With those prostheses you could even try dancing with him a little. I'll request a couple slow ones. You'll be fine!"

"When is it going to be? I've been avoiding the News."

"It will be four days from now in the new Honky-tonk Saloon. The drinking will have been going a long time by then, but the Saloon dancing should last a couple of days. The carnival parade will be almost over. It's the last event before the dance starts. Between now and then you'll have plenty of time to practice walking and sitting quietly in your *expensive* prostheses. The new Saloon is gigantic with lots of bleachers that they swiped from the geodesic dome, plus a lot of new ones. They left two of the bleachers in the dome—the two with the processional corridor between them. So—no more postage-stamp dance floor in the Saloon. It'll be fun to watch."

"You going alone?" Astra asked.

"I'll be there—supervising Kevin. He's not a bad dancer, you know. Wave to us as we gambol on past you and what's-his-name."

"Aha! I knew you and Kevin would be getting together again," Astra said gleefully.

"He's back to the guy I used to know. No more the nut. The same honey I once loved. I'm over the love part, but he's a friend again."

"*Friend*, ha?"

"Yes!"

"Yeah, right!"

"Really. He's not pushy like he was before. He's being good. He's on his meds."

"Yes, I know all about meds."

Margaret then watched as Astra guided the pointer on her screen to *Send*, and clicked. Turning back to Margaret, she said, "I guess we have a deal."

Zack Parker's feelings were all over the place when he read Astra's note. It was more than a note. It was long. She started it, "Dear Zack," and then apologized for not answering his last five e-mails, but would make up for lost time with this response. It went on for a number of pages, reminding him in gory detail of her physical condition, that she would *only* go with him to watch the masquerade ball, and then return, and that she appreciated his respectful assistance as she took on the cumbersome sea venture in the Deep. She would be glad to share with him the discoveries she made there, and so on.

They exchanged a few more e-mails, made arrangements for where and when to meet the shuttle—to and from Origin—and what he planned to wear to the masquerade.

In one of her notes she assured him he could do what he wanted once they got to the party, and appreciated that he would be acting as her escort to the planet and to some inconspicuous place in the Saloon to do the watching. She said she could then make it back to the shuttle on her own. He responded, "What ever happened to the idea of going home with the guy what brung ya?" To that, and quite a few other things he wrote, she found herself laughing.

Margaret was reading a murder mystery on her computer, but had to ask, "What's so funny, Astra?"

"Oh, nothing serious."

"Of course not, or you wouldn't be laughing."

"It's this Zack guy—full of clichés; but . . . "

"Yeah?"

"But in there with all that is something else. When we were working together on the Deep—I never would have guessed it of him."

"What?"

"He's a riot!"

The shuttle was cram-full of people and miscellaneous equipment, and stuffy. The trip to Origin would take hours. Astra was tired from anxiety and the work of getting ready. Margaret had been a hard taskmaster, making her practice every conceivable movement with her special prostheses, and then dressed her in a variety of outfits that displayed her nicely formed butt, back and shoulders, but none of her defects. Some of the best outfits were modified by Astra to cover her left shoulder. If it was not covered, that would have been a give away that Astra feared she could not handle.

"I never saw you before this in any of these getups—they're marvelous!" Margaret said. "Where did you get them all? . . . all these formal gowns, swim suits, scuba gear, Karate garb, a sarong, tutus, and that other trunk full—and *this*—what on earth is this?" Astra explained it was a nun's habit.

"And why all these masks? I know you like to use veils, but why all these? . . . Aha! *This* mask! I select this one for you. It's fantastic! It looks placid, and yet . . . dramatic. It will both hide and reveal your exuberant soul. It's you . . . and just right for the masquerade. As for the other parts of your costume, I abdicate responsibility. Wear anything you wish—except the sari or the habit." They negotiated on the nun's habit. Astra could wear it on the shuttle, but had to change in the Honky-tonk Saloon.

She stood quietly in her artificial limbs. The high heels gave her posture the cute look she deserved. Margaret admired her from every angle. "You do look nice in that one," she said. "What did you ever use all these other outfits for?"

Astra explained that, years earlier, she looked at herself in the mirror, and had "thoughts" about herself in each of them. She also admitted taking lessons associated with most of the garments. Each of her special limbs had their own internal atomic power sources, so she came to believe that all the eastern martial arts she'd mastered came to her in an unfair way, even though she'd never used any but a normal *default* setting in the prostheses—never the *maximize* mode, except for lessons that had nothing to do with artful and philosophical fighting. She especially liked the fact that the limbs could not be distinguished from those of a "normal" beauty queen. The hands and feet attached seamlessly to them and could be manipulated with the same level of dexterity as real ones.

But she had to make certain adjustments to their features—mentally, since there were no external adjustment mechanisms. It all happened through her neuro-net. For instance, the hand grip had to be drastically reduced to prevent a crushing grip should she shake hands with anyone. The joints of the hands, knees, and elbows also required special attention, lest they suddenly begin to vibrate like jackhammers, or fold backwards from normal human joint movements. Even the potential spring and leap features had to be reduced or she could move carelessly and be mistaken for someone's vaulting identical.

The potential for embarrassing herself was considerable without those corrections. Years earlier she was expert with every aspect of her special prosthesis equipment and, in those days, practiced everything for several hours daily, sometimes all day; but after embarrassing herself several times, she gradually stopped using them, and switched back to more mundane prostheses.

This day she activated the two main settings. One was a mental notion that would rapidly adjust all the settings to operate like a normal human being. That was her *default* setting. The other was labeled *maximize*. That setting opened the full potential of every feature of her special prostheses. Even under *maximize* she was in mental control of it all—most of the time. There were ten more interval settings between *default* and *maximize*, and ten lesser intervals between each of those, and many other special-purpose settings. The latter included sending an automatic locator distress call to a wide spectrum of receivers, including a loud proximity alarm, should she become unconscious, or she could activate it consciously by simply telling the idea bank she was unconscious. She allowed that special feature to remain active, but deactivated the others, thinking of them as silly add-ons—like sending thought messages directly to someone's phone or e-mail or, more intrusively, to their cranial-alert implants. They would think they were hearing voices. Another special feature was a mechanism to record her visual and auditory perceptions and send them to a computer for motion or still reproduction. The trouble with that one was its tendency to pick up her sexual fantasies and other images and thoughts. The feature was too hard to control, so it was also deactivated. She once said to Margaret, "If I forgot my medications, who knows what a hacker might find there!" A dozen more features were shut down for a variety of other more or less personal reasons. Astra preferred to just stick with the basics—arms and legs.

While adjusting all the form-fitting straps and braces between the parts of the prostheses and Astra's body, Margaret warned her, laughing, "Think only *default*. I don't want to see you *bouncing* all over that Saloon like a flying isomorph!"

Astra laughed too, saying, "Why not? It would probably impress my escort."

"Don't be funny. And turn off that stupid trembling oscillation feature if you haven't already. I can't even remember the useful purpose it was supposed to serve. It's fine if you have to chisel your way out of a cement dungeon, but that's about all it's good for. It might impress your escort, too, but does he *really* need to know you require a three hundred and fifty horsepower vibrator? And that reminds me—don't forget your meds!"

"Very funny. When did I ever—"

By then they were both laughing so hard that neither could say another word.

"What's in the big purse?" Zack asked Astra as they entered the shuttle. Astra was wearing a dark veil and the habit of a nun for the trip down to Origin—and sensible shoes. To find their seats, despite being dead tired—it was two in the morning—her ambulation through the awkward arrangements within the shuttle were agile, even graceful, as she stepped over boxes, suit cases and people. Half the passengers were already completely or partially in their masquerade costumes. Even Zack was already sporting his full harlequin regalia and makeup: white face, false balled head (except for its artificial reddish bush of side hair), flowing muttonchops, large red nose and lips, vest and tights of large multi-colored diamond-shaped patches, large curly toed bootees with gaiters, and a wooden sword.

"It isn't nice to ask a lady what's in her purse. But it's okay. This is a satchel, not a purse."

"Excuse me. What's in the *satchel*?"

"For starters, this habit isn't my final disguise. My friend Margaret—the woman we saw off on the earlier shuttle with her confused isomorph, Opal—she made me promise that when I got to the Honky-tonk Saloon I'd change into *this* stuff," Astra explained, gesturing with the valise she was holding. "In fact, I have a couple outfits in here—in case I lose my nerve with one or the other."

The shuttle swayed hypnotically as it lifted off and gently sped on down. As the Cone began to shrink behind them, Astra asked, with her head lolling from side to side, "What's in *your* purse?"

"My *satchel*. I just brought some of my work, my razor, tooth brush, some different clothes, makeup remover, board games, books—stuff like that."

"*Real* books?" she asked, yawning.

"Yes. Real ones."

"Nobody reads real books anymore."

"I know, but I like how they feel—how they smell."

After a long silence, Astra said, "Me too," and then leaned her head on Zack's shoulder, already fast asleep. He leaned his head back on hers, and was not far behind.

They slept through the long, overcrowded voyage, but arrived rested at 11 AM. They were just on time to catch the final parade as it ended by circling, and then entering, the proud facade of the spanking new Honky-tonk Saloon.

On the inside, they picked up two beers and a couple of box lunches before ascended to the shadowy and empty top tier of the bleachers. Astra took out her binoculars and looked around. She was looking for nothing in particular and was just orienting herself to the place. She'd enjoyed the marching cavalcade outside, and was already relishing the inside vocal and instrumental music. There was a rotation of bands, ensembles, singers—the works—and the displays of uninhibited antics and poses by disguised people already on the dance floor, in the bar, at and on the tables, and in the north stands across the way. Even the isomorphs were bouncing and flying about to the music—and then returned to their human double, thus destroying any private cover of masked anonymity.

When she finally felt comfortable about the main layout and atmosphere of the place, Astra excused herself to change into one of her other outfits. Not having an isomorph to give her away, she might put on something more daring than she had originally planned. Except for Zack and Margaret, who would notice? The mask Margaret picked out was, like the prostheses, the last one *she* would have chosen. It too was associated with an embarrassing experience. *Oh well, who'd ever know?*

FIFTY-FOUR

The smells of popcorn, burgers and beer, mixed in the air with blaring band music, shouts, dancing, laughter and balloons. Even Stanley Lundeen was enjoying himself—with no more costume for his party guise than a white clinical mask over his nose and mouth—between sneezes. He was sitting beside the only other person in their group who came without a partner—Jack Lewis, who arrived at the masquerade ball as a woodsman, and amused only David, a gorilla, when he called himself "lumberJack." Everyone else in their group was also in costume.

Tall, skinny, heavy-browed Ernst Berman, for example, was dressed as a one-eyed pirate who moored himself to Debra Anderson. She was wearing a Little Bo Peep outfit with a scandalous blouse that Ernst's unpatched and grotesquely rolling eye kept returning to. Between romps around the dance floor, his monocular attention kept her tittering for hours with a mix of feigned and real embarrassment.

Laura Shane was dressed in a black and white cowhide outfit, crowned by impressive bull horns, cloven-hoofed shoes and bull's tail—not very feminine for her . . . or anyone—and was complemented by Ned's appearance with her as a bull fighter, wearing a jacket of gold sequins, silk tights, and carrying a scarlet flannel muleta that he used instead as a cape. Kevin Verily avoided being near him, fearing sardonic comparisons with his past, nearly lethal matadorlike behavior. He came as a tartan-kilted Scottish highlander—under the inconspicuous supervision of Margaret Heckart, a ragged peasant girl.

In a disguise that would fool no one, Officer Bracket was a hooded Space Sheriff with giant side arms, and Ellen Stone came as his deputy, with dangling, swinging, handcuff earrings.

Mark Tenderloin, a red devil, accompanied his tall, Denise Christensen to the masquerade. She was festooned as an angel with white pillow feathers—an outfit complete with shimmering halo and glowing, functional wings—moveable, but not flyable. Her escort's equally mechanized, softly barbed devil's tail went roaming and probing, snapping and wrapping, all around his angel's legs, and otherwise intruded on its feathery probity. "Damn it, Mark, lay off my tender loins," the angel squealed—whereupon an impeccably dressed gorilla, sitting nearby, provided polite laughter for her ineffectual pun—and the red devil responded in character with raucous, evil cackling. However, knowing his tenuous place in her world, the devil would—time and again—obediently comply with the angel's request.

Unlike the other disguised visitors, David was impeccably dressed—in dark suit and tie, vest and suit coat, and polished black shoes. However he did carry an authentic-looking submachine gun. The finishing touch was a complete head-mask—one that he'd worn to similar events for years. The convincing gorilla head, along with hairy wrists, hands, and thick black hair poking from under his cuffs created a fearsome image. He enjoyed snarling through its powerful amplifier, opening its huge mouth to display sharp teeth and bestial tongue, and causing it to salivate profusely on cue. If that wasn't bad enough, he repeatedly gave himself away by frequently *snickering* as he activated its most disgusting feature—that of extending the gorilla's long tongue for assertive ear and nostril cleansing; usually its own. There was little question in anyone's mind as to the creature's intended identity—he was the consummate *Urban Gorilla*.

And Judy? Was she to be his moll? Well, no. She came as a banana. It's hard to explain.

Zack did not immediately notice Astra Hughs's return. He knew she would be changing out of her nun's habit and into something more comfortable, but thought he could pick her out from the crowd by the way she moved. While watching for Astra, he became distracted and riveted his attention instead on a striking young woman who could in no way, he thought, be seen as some kind of lowly or modest damsel. Yet this slim, caped dominatrix in silver spiked, black leather tights and glistening high heeled boots to match, and with whip in hand, was rapidly making her way toward him, two tiers at a time. "My God!" he said as she reached him, "It is you!—isn't it?"

"Of course it's me," Astra said. "Did you think I would abandon you?" The feminine softness of her voice belied her costume—or did it?

"It's just that . . . well, I didn't expect . . ."

"I came back as fast as I could. I didn't want anybody to see me. Up here I can feel safe and inconspicuous."

"That outfit is *not* inconspicuous."

"It's black, so in the shadows I won't be noticed. You'll be noticed up here, but I won't. And that's okay. So now you can go join the party and find some nice lady to dance with. You know I won't mind!"

"I know you won't, but could we give it a try first?"

"You're asking me to dance?"

"Yes. Just to give it a try."

"Not until they turn down some of those lights. So later—when there's just the disco-ball reflections and only a few of those roving spotlights."

Just then the main lights dimmed. "You're a magician!" Zack said. "Let's go!"

"But our stuff. We haven't even had our lunch yet. The beer will get warm."

"No excuses!"

"You and Margaret are two of a kind. She's always saying that to me. Are you sure you're not her isomorph?"

"Wrong sex. And they don't talk. Don't worry—if the music is fast I'm sunk anyway; then you can dance with anyone *you* want. Okay?"

She gave a reluctant, "Okay," and they made their way to the dance floor. When the music slowed and the lights had dimmed even more, there was an avalanche of costumed humans onto the floor and an equal exodus of naked isomorphs from it. Isomorphs preferred fast music. Though the music was slow, Astra and Zack staggered together for what seemed to be a long time when one of the spotlights picked them out. Then the music's pace picked up and Zack tripped over his own feet, resulting in his falling backwards in a pratfall that could not have been more skillfully composed. He got up and rubbed his backside—to considerable laughter that was upsetting to Astra. The spotlight continued to hold them in its glare, and Astra wondered why. The pratfall was over and Zack's clown suit was no more original or colorful than any of a dozen similar ones. She stepped back, out of the spotlight, and kept backing farther and farther. It was no use—the light was following *her*. In a moment of panic she almost activated the *maximize* function, but managed to maintained her composure and kept reciting, sublingually, *default, default.*

Then a simple plan occurred to her. She walked brazenly back to Zack while removing the whip from her belt and said, just loud enough for him to hear her over the music, "Play along with me. This bullwhip is long and really loud, but it's special—it's painless. Pretend you're pretending it hurts. Then, with any luck, we'll take a bow and get back to our food and beer. I'm counting on that light being in professional hands. If not, I'll have to think of something else."

His nod was followed by a whip-crack many times the decibels coming from the band. Zack's yelp of surprise sounded like one of real pain and the crowd gasped in horror as he continued the charade by holding his backside more tenderly than before. Astra swung the whip in slow, quietly whickering circles above her head, then more rapidly to cause the whirring, thunderous sound of a bullroarer, and finally snapped it in the air for another earsplitting crack. Zack jumped and yowled as if in pain. The crowd saw he was untouched and laughed. Astra and Zack then joined arms, lifted their free arms triumphantly, and bowed deeply—to gratifying applause.

Then the couple walked back toward their side of the grandstand. Astra soon realized that whoever was in charge of that spotlight had been trained to know when an act was over, and dutifully—and professionally—helped them offstage by moving the light to another interesting couple on another part of the dance floor. The new selection was well chosen. The light picked out a handsome farm girl in a straw hat, dancing with a gentleman dressed as an outhouse.

After returning to their eagles' nest on the grandstand, they tried to relax. They ate a little, had some beer, and finally began to enjoy themselves. Then they noticed an unremarkable girl in ragged peasant dress and blouse waving to them as she and a man in a kilt danced passed on the floor below. It was Margaret Heckart and Kevin Verily. Astra waved back. She was relieved that

Margaret saw her in something other than the nun's habit, and smiled thinking she must also have seen her whip act.

In the next couple hours Astra and Zack made several more trips to the bar and other nearby facilities, tried dancing one more time, unsuccessfully, and returned each time to their comfortable, private perch to watch, converse, and enjoy. Their relaxation allowed for some long and undemanding silences, where they could watch what was there to amuse them—and to take mental hikes unrelated to those surroundings.

While Astra was on one of those hikes, Zack removed—from one of his oversized pockets, two issues of The FAST News. Both were recent, used and wrinkled issues he found in the trash on their last trip to the bar. He didn't want to bother with any of his own books just then, but thought the papers would make for light reading during one of those quiet times. The last issue he saw was the one displaying a picture of the unidentified female isomorph. Since then he hadn't seen another copy. He first noticed a headline in the more recent of the two issues, dated only the day before. The headline read, "Dufy Says That Time Is Running Out." *Another philosophical article about time and space*, Zack thought. *Sounds boring*. Then he looked at the main headline in the older issue. *That* one grabbed his attention. As much as Zack respected and valued their mutual silences, the headline so surprised him that his whole body suddenly jerked.

Astra turned her head to inquire, "What's the matter? Falling asleep, or did you read something interesting?"

"Sorry. I'll tell you in a minute. I didn't mean to react like that. I need to read this first. It probably isn't interesting."

"Let me know, then," she said as she returned to her mental hike and he to his reading.

"I hate to tell you this," he said after finishing the article, "but it is interesting. More than that," he said vehemently, "it's downright undemocratic, arbitrary, and . . . and . . ."

"—Capricious?"

"That too, but worse. Damn! It's probably even popular with some people. So intrusive though! Nobody asked us."

"Us? What does that article have to do with us?'

"Well, not us—our isomorphs."

"I'm listening," she said unconvincingly.

"Some geniuses decided to turn the pyramid into a holographic and photographic dinner theatre and museum. So, *days ago*—and why we weren't told sooner I can't imagine—they arbitrarily and . . . and . . . capriciously moved our isomorphs out of the pyramid and into the geodesic dome."

"I guess we should have kept up on the daily news, huh?"

"Yeah. They moved all the remaining unvitalized isomorphs, like mine and yours, around like cord wood—like dead bodies. They've turned the geodesic dome into a . . . a Pantheon, an ossuary. They can't do that! Not without our permission!"

Any discussion of isomorphs, especially hers, tended to put Astra on edge; so in response, she resorted to one of her favorite defenses—mixing callous glibness with rationality. "Our permission is needed? Since when?" she said. "The vitalized isomorphs already made the first arbitrary move by bringing the unvitalized ones to the pyramid. They did that without asking and it turned out to be for a good purpose. Now we're doing it for another good purpose—supposedly. Anyway, it sounds like a done deal, so forget it. Have some more beer."

"Forget it, hell! Maybe you can, but I can't. Who knows what they will do with them next? Who knows what they've already done? Maybe they just threw them all in the Keeta pit and covered it up—as punishment for our not bringing them . . . to . . . the party."

Astra patted his hand. "You're over-reacting."

"Sit here if you like," he said, "but I'm going to the dome right now. I have to see, first hand, what they're doing to us—er, to our . . . to our . . ."

"Okay Zack. Settle down. I'll walk with you as far as the dome, but you'll have to go in alone."

Minutes later they were on the path to the dome, passing a few happy looking individuals coming from there, escorting their newly vitalized isomorphs back to their new flatland home. Zack assumed they'd read or heard the same news he reported to Astra.

The cantilevered path followed the hill's dune-drift contours in parallel waves above its debris. As they stood on the crest of one of those rigid, arching waves they saw several others coming toward them from the distant dome; but they were few in number. The dome must have been nearing the last of its stored isomorphs. Coming still closer, they passed several more who were alone and looked like they had been crying. One of the last to pass was a lone man. He was not in party costume, but ordinary workman's clothes. He looked at them with an odd expression of fear and guilt, but said nothing and kept going.

They could still hear muffled sounds of the band as they got nearer to the dome. Above the sounds of the band they heard two of the echo-hunters—people who shouted phrases to see how complex a sound they could get back from the plantoids, near or far. The two voices were familiar. There were usually a dozen or more, but only two today. One was Cameron Greenberg. They didn't know he had come down to Origin again. They could see him in the distance, standing not far from the Honky-tonk Saloon. He was wearing no costume, but smoking one of his cigars. He loved his smokes and there was no smoking in the Saloon. Next to him was his naked likeness, Theseus, named by him and announced in The FAST News well before the hill was destroyed.

The other familiar voice was much louder, evidently coming from the amplifier attached to the head of a well dressed gorilla. It was, of course, David's voice. His isomorph, Oscar, was not there and still must have been in the Saloon. The "older" isomorphs were becoming more independent. David, a leader of the eco-hunters, must have left the party when he spotted Cameron leaving for a smoke. They evidently left the saloon shortly behind Astra and Zack.

The dome loomed ahead of them and, except for David's periodic mega-shouts, the music and other sounds could no longer be heard. Those two standing, shouting figures had become tiny in the distance, as did the figures moving away from them on the path back the new flatland camp. Finally, there were two other small figures that stepped from the flatland onto the same path they were on.

"I wonder who they are." Astra mused.

"Probably a couple interested in pilgrimage rather than partying," Zack said smugly.

"Okay Zack," Astra said, still holding to her callous tone, "We're almost there. Once you've vitalized your isomorph, what will you name it? Zack Junior?"

"*Him*. Not *it*."

"All right, him."

"I haven't decided yet. I'll have to see him first."

"Procrastinator."

"Guilty. How about you? What name—"

"—Never mind! I just came to keep you company for the long walk to the dome. I'm not going in."

"If you insist. I guess I can do it alone. I hope there is some way to get him into the pit. He'll be very heavy. Maybe there's another isomorph or two around to help out."

"Why bother with the pit? Anywhere should work just fine."

"Lady, you really are tough! To me it's . . . it's . . ."

"Tradition?"

"Exactly!"

"Then it's a good thing you brought your satchel."

"Call it habit. Why's it such a good thing?"

"As a matter of tradition you'll want to remove your big red nose, the mutton chops, makeup, and only leave what you want to present to your vitalized likeness. We don't know for sure what they bond to, but it might be their human's face. When the party's over and all the disguises are put away, you wouldn't want the poor thing searching for someone with a white face, red nose and all that."

"You're right! I . . . never thought . . ."

At the entrance to the dome Zack tried one last time to encourage Astra to go in with him, but she refused. He shrugged and turned to go in when a woman came out of the dome. She was in tears.

"What's the matter?" Zack asked the lady.

She responded with a flood of words to match her tears: "There are only a few unvitalized isomorphs left inside and one of them is mine and no vitalized ones around and a man, he's still in there, told me that there hadn't been no vitalized ones staying in there for quite a while and one of the men running the crane they use to lift the isomorphs into the Keeta pit left twenty minutes ago and he'd been on the job for less than a week and was real angry that some unvitalized ones were still there and that he'd missed most of the carnival because of that and *he* was missing the party in the Honky-tonk Saloon and so he left and said he wasn't coming back."

"So he's not coming back," Zack said.

"I didn't talk to the crane-lift guy, but that other guy, the one that's still in there, did and he learned from the lift guy why he was leaving and he told me all that and a bunch more. Another lift guy on another shift'll be here tomorrow if any isomorphs are left, but I want mine vitalized right now 'cause I gotta get back to my nursing job on the Cone. I'm late *here* again 'cause I didn't pay no 'tention to what's up down here and on'y just heard my isomorph got moved. I could come back if I have to in a couple weeks, but who'll help me then?" The woman continued to be distraught, almost hysterical, as she kept talking.

Astra's toughness fell away and she finally said, "Come with us." Astra took her by the arm and led the way into the dome. Zack followed close behind. The woman led them to her covered and labeled isomorph lying on a shelf halfway to the top of one of the two remaining bleachers. The ID bracelet was still around the isomorph's right wrist, but a much larger label was tied to the big toe of its left foot.

"What did I tell you," Zack said on seeing the toe tag, "They're turning this place into a morgue! And they're not even very neat about it. Look at all the sheets lying around. There's a pile of them over there," he said pointing, "and over there—why, they're all over the place. At least we can tell which sheets still cover a real isomorph—I think. I didn't know this would become a shell game."

The teary-eyed woman asked, "Could you two, and me and that man sitting over there, move my isomorph into the Keeta pit? Do you think?"

Zack said, "We can try. You'd better ask the man."

"He's the gentleman who told me what happened to the crane-lift guy. Yes. I'll go ask him."

Astra was tempted to suggest she just vitalize her isomorph right there on the bench, but remembered about tradition and that she would be back another day if she had to; so said nothing.

The man on the other set of bleachers was sitting next to his own, covered isomorph. He was halfway up the other section of bleacher stands. When the lady asked for his help, he returned with her right away.

Had the isomorph been on the surface, rather than so far up the precipitous tiers, and if it had still been necessary to get the isomorph into the pit, the task might have been humanly possible. They could have dragged it to the pit. As it was, the task appeared impossible, till the gentleman from the other set of tiers suggested just rolling the isomorph from tier to tier. The already upset woman and Astra were shocked at the idea, and vetoed it. Zack nodded his silent agreement to their objection. The man thought about it and said he understood and wouldn't really do it to his either. So they tried lifting and tugging, but the tearful lady's isomorph, like all other isomorphs, was extremely heavy and, except for movement of limbs, it could not be budged.

"Shit," Astra said quietly—but was heard by all.

"I agree," Zack said. "It's a shame! We can't even budge the isomorphs—and that lift guy abandoning his post! Terrible! Now we have to wait till tomorrow. Terrible! And just when the last of us were about to—well, three of us anyway—vitalize our . . . our—"

"Children?" the tearful lady said.

"Exactly!" Zack said.

Astra said it again, but louder this time. "Shit! That's not what I was saying. I wasn't saying . . . saying—"

"You weren't saying shit about that?" Zack said.

"Damn it Zack! Now you've got me saying that word—*exactly*!"

"We're listening," Zack said.

"There is something I hate to do with people watching, but it looks like I'll have to. So here's the deal. Well, not really a deal—a request. I want you all to go below and get on the far side of the Keeta pit. Don't ask me to explain. You'll know why in a minute."

After some heated interaction and eye rolling, they did descend the steep tiers of the stand, but not without leaving a stream of complaints and expressions of confusion floating like contrails in the air behind them.

While this confusion continued, two more individuals quietly entered the dome. From a distance they observed what followed.

When the two men and the tearful woman were safely assembled on the far side of the pit, and therefore unable to accidentally interfere, Astra invoked the mental switch that converted her atomic prostheses from default mode to maximum. After waiting a few moments for the changeover to take place, she gently lifted the woman's isomorph and descended the sharply tiered bank of bleacher seats with the care, loving grace, and dignity of a uniformed nurse carrying a small, sick child—unlike the callous behavior one might expect from a whip-carrying, dominatrix.

Stopping at the edge of the Keeta pit, Astra looked into it, took a firmer hold on her charge, leaned forward, and hopped into the pit. The landing was as flex-legged and cushioned as a bird's. She carefully laid her still covered burden in the middle of the pit, followed by another simple hop—this time returning to the pit's upper edge.

She ignored the questions, and what to her was unearned awe and admiration. She then assisted the no-longer-tearful lady into the pit to meet her likeness.

Astra had seen the holographic motion pictures of many vitalizations before, but never saw one directly. She began watching with curiosity, but as the process progressed, it became something beyond curiosity. The real thing was different. The woman knelt beside the covered isomorph, and then looked up to her onlookers, especially Astra—in her mask. She smiled and said to them, "My name is Monica, but call me Mona. What are your names?" The men introduced themselves. "And yours?" she asked Astra, who told her. "Thank you for this, Astra. Will you be her God Mother?"

Astra stiffened. She wasn't always strong when it came to taking responsibility for anyone or anything other than herself. Her own survival had been burden enough. It never crossed her mind that any such request would ever be made of her. It angered her at first, causing her regressively to think, *Godmother to what? A glorified agate? A mineral? A carnal carnelian?* But then she thought, *It's not as though this were a baptism, and godparents never have to do anything anyway. I wouldn't have to teach it anything. It's just an honor parents pass along to others. I hope that's all it is.* So she relaxed, smiled behind her mask, nodded her assent and said, "Thank you; I'd be honored." After thinking about it for a few more moments, she really was.

The sheet was carefully pulled back and folded away from the isomorph's face. Mona fairly glowed as she viewed the lovely countenance, then leaned over and kissed it. Before long, the isomorph stirred, their eyes met, and Mona took in the magic baby's breath—consummating a powerful mutual bond.

Predictably, the isomorph whipped off its covering, and Mona took her hand. Standing before the three who were on the pit's edge, Mona said, "You are my cherished witnesses and I will never forget your being here with me today. I now proudly present to you my little sister, Lisa."

Mona was then assisted to the upper edge of the pit by the two men. Lisa looked up for only a moment from the center of the pit before leaping from it to the upper edge—the leap of life to join her Mona on its threshold.

This process was repeated two more times for the men, but not before Zack had removed his red nose and other makeup. The stranger gentleman introduced himself as Wolfe, and named his isomorph Lycus. Zack gave the name Gegeneis to his.

Astra saw something out the corner of her eye, but said, "That's done. It's getting late—time to get back. It'll be dark in a couple hours. Let's go!"

Head down, she started for the exit without allowing herself to look. No one followed. They were all looking toward the exit. Astra soon turned and asked a question—one she already knew the answer to: "What's the problem?"

The two newcomers were still some distance from Astra. They slipped into the arena and had something to say. Well, the man, not so much. He only waved briefly. But the woman did so in part by pointing to the only remaining covered figure with the bulk and shape of a humanlike body. The other shrouds were carelessly scattered about and appeared to be no more than shallow piles of colorful sheets. The one she pointed to was not in the stands, but lay inconspicuously on the surface. It was no more than ten meters from the Keeta pit. With the pointing came a familiar, but much louder than usual voice:

"Isn't that yours?" Margaret shouted.

FIFTY-FIVE

"Where did you and Kevin come from?" Astra said—loud enough for them to hear.

Margaret smiled and said loudly, but without shouting, "We saw you and the clown you were with leave the Saloon. I followed you. I'd have come alone if I could have, but Officer Bracket put me in charge of Kevin here. Kevin kept arguing about coming at all, and that held me back. Otherwise I'd have caught up before you got on the path to come here. Kevin's trying to keep his nose clean with Bracket by avoiding any more vitalizations—especially after Clint reamed him good after the Keeta vitalization. But anyway, here we are!"

Kevin said nothing, but gave a quick nod and a sheepish smile.

"Well, whoop-de-do and congratulations," Astra said with sarcastic irritation. "You're just on time to walk back with me, or stay here if you wish." Astra didn't like their style of arrival, especially Margaret's pointing at what might have been her unvitalized isomorph, and the loud, rude, questioning tone that accompanied her finger pointing.

Margaret shook her head and pointed again to the lone, covered figure. That was an unwise plan—and produced pain in Astra as real as anything physical. In fact, it was. She replaced that extreme discomfort with something more tolerable: quiet rage.

Kevin and Margaret were standing in the middle of the carpeted, narrow corridor between the two remaining bleachers. Astra pointed to Margaret's demanding and disrespectful pointing finger and uttered a harsh "No!" Then she walked indignantly around them, forgetting the Herculean power of her atomic limbs and accidentally knocked down a support post welded to one of the bleachers. That created an earsplitting screech of metal as the post came loose, jolted out from its base, buckled in the middle and fell crashing, nearly hitting Margaret and Kevin—and would have if Astra had not moved quickly to deflect it. Fortunately the steel post was not entirely essential. The stand of bleachers that the post was helping to support, groaned and creaked before it leaned in above them and came to rest against the grandstand section on the other side of the narrow corridor. It served as a reminder to Astra. She switch her atomic prostheses from maximize back to default.

"Jesus, Astra!" Margaret said, shaking and clinging to Kevin.

Despite her still feeling angry, Astra's first reaction was to apologize profusely, but she did not. Instead she resorted to her callousness defense, pretending the accident was deliberate. She gritted her teeth beneath her mask and said, "Consider that a reminder—don't piss me off!" She continued her huffy march toward the outer exit.

"Astra! Wait!"

Hearing Zack's voice, she turned around to see him coming toward her, double-time. She waited. Margaret and Kevin stepped aside.

He slowed to a walk before reaching Margaret and Kevin, saying quietly to them as he passed, "Stay here. Don't follow right away. Come later."

"What?" Astra snapped as Zack caught up to her.

Without answering, he walked on past her and headed for the exit. Then *he* stopped to look back. She was facing him, but had not moved. "Coming?" he said, holding out his hand.

She walking slowly, even cautiously, and caught up with him. "What are you up to?" she asked.

"I'm walking back with you, of course. What did you think?"

"I thought you were going to judge me—like everybody else."

They exited the dome and had gone a short distance when Zack requested they stop for a moment. Astra wondered why, but the answer soon became evident. Zack's isomorph, Gegeneis, was hurrying to catch up. On resuming their return to the flatland, Zack walked between them. On his right, he held the hand of his as yet expressionless, blandly handsome isomorph. On his left, he held the almost-human hand of Astra—with her equally bland and unchanging plastic mask.

They walked for a distance in mutual silence when Astra said, "I'm glad you're not into judging."

Zack did not respond right away, but thought about that and casually replied, "But I am judging. That's why I'm walking with you now. My walking with you is the judgment."

"Then why don't I feel judged?"

"Because I am walking with you now. I am walking with you because I saw through your lie."

"My lie? What lie? I did not lie about anything! Now you *are* judging."

"Of course I am. I said I was."

"Then why are you walking with me now? And what was my supposed lie?"

"Nothing you said, exactly. I'm walking this bridge with you because I did not see or feel it burn. You pretended to burn your bridges back there, but I don't believe you meant it. More important, will Margaret believe you meant it? Will she judge and reject you if she does? Do you want her to?"

After another long silence, Astra said, "Damn it!"

"Finish the sentence."

"Hmm! Okay then. Damn it—I didn't know it was so easy to see through me."

"Not that easy, really. You didn't lie completely. You sent a message and conveyed something else with it—hurt—hurt at not being understood, at not feeling respected for your decision about your isomorph. You may have thought you were expressing anger, but wasn't it really anguish? It's not only the isomorph. That's just today's symbol—today's excuse for hiding out. You hide your pain with attitude; but don't you really cherish the pain? They—the people back there in the dome and everyone else you know—may not see your pain and anguish. You hide it well. That's your private thing, but they do see that you want your wishes taken seriously. For you, it works. That part of your message was honest and clear—the rest, as I said, may not be understood. That's the lie part. You are using camouflage, and that's okay—it's your business and your right. But hiding so much of who you are makes it hard to get to know you. It's a manipulation that keeps people at a distance, and if that's what you want, it's perfect. If not, it's unnecessary."

"Yes—I do that. I don't know why."

"Because it's tangible."

"What's tangible?"

"The pain and anguish you cherish. When all else seems to fail, it makes you feel alive. And, of course, it's better than nothing, but massaging crappy feelings doesn't sustain anyone for very long. Who you really are is more than that lump of pain you roll in your hands like a ball of bread dough. Some day you may want to free yourself of it for good—to feel the full range of who you are, beyond the intellectual and beyond the camouflage."

Astra stopped, still holding Zack's hand, so he and his isomorph stopped too. Zack was taller than Astra and, she thought, quite ugly in his thick glasses. She released his hand and put her arms around his middle and her head on his chest. After holding him so, for a while, she looked into his face and said, "The only reason you know me so well, is because you know yourself. You have been there or you wouldn't know. I'm sorry you had to go through all that to become who *you* really are."

"I'm not there yet," Zack sighed, "—not by a long shot. But I'm working on it. I'm still rolling a lot of that bread dough. When things get rough, I load up on it. Pain can be such a relief. When it's there, it's a piece of physical reality. In me, it's locates in the middle of my chest. It replaces that other thing that is so much worse—emptiness—emptiness and all the other rotten feelings and fears."

"Are we so different from everybody else?"

"I don't think so. Dig a sixteenth of a millimeter beneath the surface of the healthiest person you can find, including the very young, and you will find, in most of them, major problems. That's why so many of us hide out, behind our camouflage. Society requires it of us as much as we require it of ourselves."

"Then you don't disapprove of my lie."

"Not really, I guess."

"That sounds like there's still some disapproval."

"Only insofar as it fails to work for you."

"You said it works."

"I believe I said more than that. But fortunately for you, if you're lucky, it won't work—not every time. I hope not. When it borders on alienating your friends, like Margaret, then it works against you. I don't think it will this time, but it might. After all, you did keep that hunk of bleachers from falling on her and her friend; but you weren't exactly contrite about almost causing them serious physical damage. It could have killed them. Do you know, right now, which way she will take it?"

"She will forgive me. She knows me better than anyone, better than you. We've been close friends for many years."

"So, because you are friends you think you can crap on her now and then with impunity? That she will always be your friend, no matter what?"

"That's a terrible way of putting it!"

"You're changing the subject. Am I wrong?"

"You aren't being gentle with me."

"Then consider this. Why did she follow you?"

"Because she thought I would be vitalizing my isomorph."

"What else?"

"She thought that if I did, she wouldn't want to miss it."

"Is that all?"

"She thought that if I got cold feet she could support me in that."

"Why her? Why not anybody? Why did she feel you needed her for that?"

Astra abruptly released Zack's hand and turned away from him. She stood quietly, unmoving for several moments, and then removed the mask from her deformed face. "Why Margaret?" she said without facing him. "I'll tell you why. I have many fine acquaintances. She is not one of those. She is more than that. She is my friend—my only friend."

She then turned toward Zack, head on, and close enough for even him to get a good look at her without the mask—even through his thick glasses. He did not react.

"This is my face," she said, "and I'm a bigger mess inside. This, and the rest of my body—they're not conducive to having a lot of friends. As my friend, Margaret accepts me—as I am."

"But you don't."

"Of course not. I grew up with people reacting to me with horror. I wanted to be a whole person. I often thought of all that I had missed, of all the love I am capable of and could never express—much less receive. That's the lump of pain in my chest. It comes and goes—like today. Sometimes it just hits me. But to answer your question, I usually do accept me—just as I am. I've adjusted. I've had a lifetime to learn and adjust. But sometimes something happens and, *wham*, all that pain is back—all at once. And yes, I cherish it when I need it—it's like a shield, a life raft—whatever you want to call it. It is better than emptiness, loneliness, shame or sadness. It is all of those, and none of those, in one. As a physical pain, it is tolerable. The other feelings are not. It gives me something objective to hate, to cherish, to massage and to hate again. That lump in there is everything I have lost, everything I never had a chance to have—everything I could have been. It is always with me, available and reliable, that red hot coal in my chest—the one that came to me in my infancy."

Zack said, "Wow. That is a limp, all right—like a mountain. Let's hope we can both get over our different mountains. As you say, it is there. But you also said it is there when you need it. So you don't always need it."

Astra thought about that for a while before agreeing she did not. She explained that during those times of self-acceptance—insisting that was most of the time—she was involved with things outside of herself, or inside of her through learning and development of her skills. She said that was one way she "adjusted."

That led to a discussion of the things that diverted her from that sense of pain—her diverse interests, involvement in her many fields of expertise, recalling the admiration from her former professors—to say nothing of earned academic degrees, and other good memories, her love of music, her own poetry and art work, her reading of history and doing science, and a dozen other things. And her friendship with Margaret—who never let her get away with self-pity—at least, not for long.

As they talked, he also shared much of himself with her. Before Astra realized it, she was having a more or less normal conversation with a more or less normal man—without a mask over her face or her soul. They were seeing parts of each other clearly. Not everything. They were, she realized, starting to become . . . acquainted. Perhaps they would even become friends. She did not know. But this much she did know—her pain was gone.

FIFTY-SIX

Celebration of the hill's destruction day, D-day, was nearing its last half-day, and night, of existence. Astra and Zack were becoming more comfortable with their privacy on the path back to New Camp, but soon heard voices coming from two directions: behind and in front of them.

Astra put on her mask.

A woman's voice was coming from the direction they were headed. When they finally saw her, she was verbally barraging a man for something she did not approve of: "Your irresponsibility and heartless defection from the humanitarian duty you volunteered for is intolerable. You violated that sacred trust and solemn commitment,"—and on and on the scolding went. She was all but hauling the poor fellow along by the ear.

As the man and woman drew nearer, with their isomorphs in tow, Astra and Zack recognized the gentleman being harassed. Astra said, "That's the man we passed earlier. He's still wearing the same work clothes—and that same guilty expression."

More friendly voices were coming from behind. Mona and Wolfe were hitting it off nicely. They were arm-in-arm with their mute and blank looking isomorphs, Lisa and Lycus. Two steps behind those four, Margaret and Kevin were chatting.

A traffic jam on the path was inevitable when the three groups came together. The man in work clothes looked somewhat relieved as he saw the three isomorph coming from the dome, but asked nervously, with a glance at his shrew, if that was all of them, knowing full well that one still remained.

Wolfe said, "Yes. Unfortunately one is still left. But thanks to this lady"—he pointed to the one in dominatrix attire—"my Lycus here, and Mona's Lisa there"—he pointed to each in turn—"were vitalized after she"—pointing to Astra again—"moved them to the Kiva . . . or rather, excuse me, the Keeta pit." He reminded the harassed gentleman that they had met earlier in the dome, but had not exchanged names. Wolfe introduced himself and the others, pointing to each as he named them: "This is Kevin, Margaret, Astra, Zack, Zack's isomorph, Gegeneis, and once again, this is Mona and Lisa."

The couple that just arrived from the flatland's new camp also introduced themselves and their isomorphs. "I'm Nebulena, but call me Lena," said the scolding shrew. "And I'm Dufy," said her scoldee. Dufy introduced Lena's isomorph, Galatea and his own, Alun Caradog Hilarius, ". . . but call him Hilly."

Catching Dufy's eye, Mona said, "I was in the dome earlier, before you left, but we didn't meet. Things in there were upsetting. I'm glad to see you're looking a little better now."

"Looking better, huh!" Lena said as she scowled at Dufy.

Then, turning to Lena, Mona said, "We're all heading back to the party. I have to return to the Cone on the early shuttle tomorrow morning, but I didn't want to miss all of today's fun."

"Are you taking your lovely isomorph, Lisa, with you when you go back to the Cone?" asked the shrew, but with a wary glance at her partner.

"Of course," Mona replied, smiling. "I wouldn't want to leave her here all alone. This is her first day of—what can I call it?—of her *being*."

Dufy turned his back on everyone, hunched over and stuffed his hands hard into his pockets.

Lena looked embarrassed. "I was afraid of this," she said—so quietly that only Astra and Zack could hear her. Then, a little louder, but still with amazing softness, considering her choice of words, "What's with this non-verbal crap, Dufy?"

"You know perfectly well!" he said, turning again toward the group. Tears were running down his cheeks.

"Pay no attention to him," Lena said quietly to the group, "He's a broken man."

Then she went to Dufy and put her arms around him, letting his head hang over her shoulder, and patted him on the back as if burping a baby. She said to him, again softly, "Yes, I know. Perfectly well. I'm sorry. I should have kept my mouth shut in the first place. But you know something perfectly well too—you can't personally take responsibility for the survival of every last isomorph on the planet. It's enough that you put everybody on notice with what you wrote for The FAST News. You're not guilty, honey! So let's move along now. These nice people want to get back to the festivities. You'll feel better when you're taking *your* responsibility at the hoist. Gentleman Wolfe here, said there is only one left. You could occupy yourself by moving that last one into the Keeta pit." She gave an apologetic look to the group, and led Dufy toward the dome. Before they had gone many steps, she turned back and said, "He used to be a scholar. Now look at him. The poor thing." Then they continued their retreat to the dome.

As Lena and Dufy and their isomorphs, Galatea and Hilly, headed toward the dome, the others resumed their trek back to New Camp. They marched along in silence for nearly five minutes before Wolfe expressed everybody's thought by remarking, "I wonder what that was all about."

"I think it had something to do with this," Zack said, waving a slightly crumpled copy of The FAST News that he started to read on the path back.

"What do you mean?" Wolfe asked.

Zack stopped, held up the paper for all to see, and said, "Take a look at this headline."

Mona read it aloud: "Dufy Says That Time Is Running Out."

Wolfe said, "Oh! *That* Dufy! I should have made the connection. I read the headline the other day, but never got around to reading the article."

They all looked at each other, and no one had read it. Nimbus would be setting by the time they got back to the flatland, so they decided to sit right down in the middle of the path before it got too dark to read. One of them would read it to the others. Astra, who loved to read aloud, volunteered. She speed read it first, and then declined the reading job, handing it over to Zack.

Zack, more dyslexic than a speed reader, stumbled through it. It was a long article.

When he finished, he carefully, slowly, almost reverently, smoothed and folded the paper and returned it to his over-sized pocket. No one moved or said a word for a long time. When they began to talk again, the light was fading, and their voices were shaking.

"That article was written for me," Mona said.

"And me," Zack said.

"And me," said Wolfe.

"All of us," said Margaret, looking meaningfully at Astra.

Ignoring the look, Astra said, "That man, Dufy. Where has he been hiding? He's *still* a scholar. Had he been writing about humans instead of isomorphs, I'd classify him as a humanist. Too bad he missed the whole point—that was obvious."

"I guess I was just lucky," said Mona, refusing to acknowledge Astra's last comment. She was no longer tearful and scatterbrained, but had become more thoughtful and articulate since her Lisa was vitalized. "Had I waited much longer—he said that time was running out—even a day or two longer to attend to my Lisa, she could have become another lifeless, doughy blob, like those he wrote about. David Michaels, that geologist guy—he got it wrong when he expected our identicals to last millions of years. We have to either enliven our isomorph, in some unknown time frame, of it just deteriorates and melts unceremoniously back into the planet—literally!

"Dufy was in a unique position to notice what was happening. That's why he sounded the alarm; but hardly anyone listened because, I suppose, they'd already vitalized their own. No wonder Dufy's a broken man—taking so much responsibility for what he observed. He saw what Wolfe and I saw, only more of it.

"When I first got to the dome, there were two women removing toe tags from their isomorphs—and they were *screaming*! The toe came right off with one of the tags, and the other's tag was just lying there, on a large, sagging scrap of goo—like something rotten. But I didn't make the connection between that and some mysterious, but crucial time factor . . . like an unknown expiration date for a bunch of vegetables. After seeing that, I got very upset. Then I saw Dufy get out of his crane—or whatever that makeshift-looking lift is. He looked more upset than I was. He started to leave when you, Wolfe, caught up to him. You and he had a brief, rather angry-sounding conversation. Then he left, and I was stranded until I ran into you, Astra. I guess I'm just lucky. With your help I got to Lisa in time."

Wolfe said, "But now you have another problem."

"Yes," Mona said. "But it's not as big as it seemed an hour ago. Dufy's article clarified a lot of things: the vitalization time problem and the off planet time problem. I have to either leave Lisa to her own devices here on Origin, or not return to the Cone myself."

"Have you made a decision about that?" Wolfe asked.

"Of course. Now it's easy to decide. I'm *not* going back until Lisa can make it here without me. Dr. Lufti will just have to find a sub for me till she's independent. She would literally starve to death or go crazy on the Cone. She has to absorb her strength and wisdom from night dreaming on Origin's surface. I think Origin is the true parent and we're more like adoptive parents. Our isomorphs need us in order to learn culture and to understand. They learn language from us, but don't use it. Not out loud anyway. I'm not sure, but I think whatever they learn at night doesn't come to them in a form that we call language. I think it's deeper. In any case, they *need* this planet, at least for now, just as they need us for support and to learn what the planet can't teach them. The day may not be far off when they will be teaching us. So, they have to stay on this planet to survive. Quick trips off the planet to the Cone are one thing, but a stay of many days would kill . . . would kill my Lisa. Damn! Isomorphs are fragile! That's what motivated Dufy's writing."

"Dufy's a good man," Astra said, "but even with the broad strokes of his scholarly pen—and you summarized parts of that article very well, Mona—he left out the obvious, including—"

"—Including a lot of things about the isomorphs," Zack cut in. "But he wasn't trying to lay down some big philosophy. His objective was to send a warning about time running out for the unvitalized ones, and what could happen to vitalized ones when they are off of Origin for too long."

"I have to vouch for that last point, Zack," Margaret said. "After Opal and I were on the Cone together for only a short time, she lost some strength and her orientation was off. Now, after Dufy's article, I worry about her. We only got back this morning. But if Dufy's observations are right, she'll be fine after a good night's dreaming on Origin's surface—at her mother's breast."

Mona was gently holding one of Lisa's hands between her palms—and frowning at Astra who was looking back. "You said Dufy missed the *whole point* in his piece. What was so *obvious* that he missed?"

"From his—and your—point of view, probably nothing. All his facts were right. I interpret them differently. Much of what surrounds our thinking about isomorphs can not be confined to the facts. Most of it is a mystery, and mysteries are blanks that ask to be filled—that ask for answers. If we can't answer the questions posed by a mystery—and we can't tolerate that because the question is too important—then we fill in the blanks with explanations that come from our hearts and minds. It is our nature, yours and mine, and all humans I suppose, to do that. What I'm saying is that your view is no less valid than mine or anyone else's. Just different." Astra tilted up her head—ever so proud of how fair and balanced she must have sounded just then. She reminded herself that she was, after all, a highly educated woman.

Mona said, "At first I tried to ignore what you said about Dufy's article leaving out something *obvious*. But I felt it personally. I felt like you were putting us—putting me—down. Like only fools would not see something you, in all your wisdom, could see as *obvious*. Now you're trying to smooth my feathers with the philosophy that one opinion is as good as another—like opinions are arbitrary and could just as well be selected by a coin toss."

"You're right. It is, I think, like a coin toss. But that's just an analogy. What I meant to say is that when we have those voids in our heads—those unsolved mysteries—we fill them with what's already in there to start with. We may change that with later argument or study or new information or whatever; but that's where we start. There's enough stuff in there—in our heads—to make any number of choices about how we fill those voids."

Mona said, "You're talking about our value system, our culturally circumscribed beliefs and attitudes, our genetic disposition to optimism or pessimism, our experiences, education, social learning and all that."

"Right. That's the bucket of brew where we ladle up the stuff to fill in the blanks."

"Fine. Now let's fill in a blank. What did Dufy so obviously miss?"

Astra laughed. "Mona, I really like you! Like Margaret here, you're not going to let me off the hook, are you?"

Mona responded, "Oh, you want off the hook? That should be easy. You could walk off in a huff or do something equally unfair, and avoid the whole thing. You must have a lot of options in your brew, in that bucket of ideas and behaviors that could get you off the hook; but, to play another word game with your analogy, everybody's bucket has a different structure, no matter what it holds. I think I've guessed the structure of yours, Astra. I don't think you will let *yourself* off the hook."

"You think I'm that weak."

"No. I think you're that strong."

There was silence. A *compliment*? Astra fidgeted, and rubbed the back of her neck, a bit confused.

Wolfe, who had been listening with amused detachment to this verbal parrying, said, "I don't get all this bucket and hook stuff. Can anyone here tell me what they're talking about? I can't even remember who's supposedly avoiding what."

More silence, and no one answered. Finally Mona spoke again. "No, Wolfe. You followed all that perfectly well, I'm sure. You know the meaning of what we're saying, but, as you said, you want to know what we're *really* talking about."

"Right."

"To use an old aphorism, there is an elephant sitting in our midst, and we're trying not to notice it. I'll spell it out. If I'm too blunt and insulting in the process, walking off may or may not happen. I'm betting it won't. It all has to do with two different views of the *isomorph mystery*. Most of the isomorphs *have* been vitalized—thanks to one view. A small number were not, due to accidental neglect, bad timing, or due to the *second view*. That view—along with accidents and carelessness—has produced *mushy scraps* instead of vitalizations. The second view requires no action. It's like a pocket veto. It allows something to starve or expire without action. Astra has the *second view* and must think it's a good one for reasons that, to her, are *obvious*. There is at least one potentially viable isomorph left on this planet—it's lying on the floor of the dome. Astra didn't even look to see if it was hers. It probably isn't. I'm sure she has a bucket of perfectly good reasons for her view." Then Mona looked at Astra without a further word.

Astra quickly looked back and forth at each person in the group—so quickly that it looked for a moment as if she was shaking her head. Indeed, her first word was *no*.

"No. The real *mystery* is not about isomorphs. That's just the baby elephant. There's another one in our midst—so big that it is sitting on all of us, isomorphs included."

Now the others were looking confused and shaking *their* heads. One of them asked, "What mystery, then?"

Astra engaged the group in a brief Socratic dialogue. In answer to her quick questions, they recalled how they got to planet Origin in the first place. They were kidnapped by the Dorts. Where did the Dorts come from? Origin. How were the Dorts created? Probably the same way isomorphs were, but without DNA blueprints, was their answer. And from where were those "blueprints" obtained? Human blood. How was the blood obtained? Usually from small cave-ins or other things that happened in contact with Origin's crystals. How did the cave-ins and other things produce blood? Scrapes on the skin. Was everybody's kidnapping to Origin voluntary? Silly question. Of course not. Were the Twister deaths a part of that kidnapping? Yes. Were those deaths voluntary? No, of course not. Were the bloody scrapes voluntary? No. Astra then made a final statement: "Remove the first two letters from the word *scrapes*, and you will know what I see as obvious. Everything that happened to us since we left Earth is in that category, and the first cause of all that is planet Origin."

Astra's simple dialectic brought out of the shadows what they already knew, but put it back in the spotlight. Before that, it was a free-floating cloud of nearly forgotten fear and anger. Now, the perpetrator was again exposed.

Even Mona agreed, saying, "Removing those two letters was a bit cutesy, but to the point. What you have identified as the problem and mystery is clear enough to me now, and all of us, I believe. It also helps me to understand *your stance*, but not your feelings about the isomorphs—or rather, about your own isomorph. I appreciate the facts and the logic you led us through, but that understanding doesn't help me identify with your feeling—I mean the feeling-connection to isomorphs in general or maybe just yours in particular. That eludes me. There has to be something more than a trumped up rationale behind a feeling leading to such a harsh judgment. You've tried to give such a rationale, but for me it falls flat."

Astra snapped back, "I don't see how anyone here can now fail to grasp the connection—the big picture. It's all there!"

"I'll say it again. I see your so-called logic, but not the feeling-connections coming from that logic—if that logic is supposed to include isomorphs. I'm sorry, Astra, but feelings trump logic here. For me, everything doesn't lump together under your big elephant. Anger toward what has happened to us—yes! I get that! I get the anger toward Origin. That's the part I get—it is justifiable anger. Thank you for that; but it was *you* who said it was sitting on all of us, *isomorphs included*. So, even you do not blame the isomorphs for anything. They are innocent!"

"They were not voluntary!" Astra responded angrily.

"For just a moment more, I would like to stick with the *smaller* of those two elephants. I hope this won't throw us all the way back to square one, but reality is reality, and what happened before is in the past. The finger of fate and the arrow of time move only forward—and whatever it has brought upon us, we're stuck with!"

"What's your point?" Astra questioned, with a shade of insecurity creeping into her voice.

"Well, okay. Isomorphs. They came, in a sense, from one bloody scrape or another. That gave planet Origin enough information to produce its creations in images of men and women—with certain crystal-clear differences between humans and isomorphs. The reality is, isomorphs are here, even without our approval for their method of creation. Later on, we had choices about what we did with that reality—even *knowing* we were not initially voluntary participants in the process—men included. There is now only that one last potentially viable isomorph left. At first it was just a bloody scrape. To understand *my stance* and feelings about that, you have only to think ahead a day or two—at most—or maybe only a minute or two. Had I waited another day or so, or just another hour, for whatever excuse or reason—due to circumstances or belief that there was plenty of time—what would I have had instead of my dearest Lisa with all her potential as she becomes independent and learns from Origin and me, and she from other isomorphs as they come together and engage? Whatever that potential is, none of us can yet know, but it's a chance I wanted to take—voluntarily—good or bad. I saw the horrible outcome of the other option, that second view, when I first went into the dome. What would I have had *instead* of Lisa, had I waited? Just remove the *last* letter from *scrape*, and you will know what *I* see as obvious!"

Throughout Mona's comments and their argument, Astra sat rigid. She *was* on the edge of running and knew she wanted to. It was not just the social pressure. About that she could care less! Something else was holding her. Running was a clear and easy choice. The elevated path was narrow and well lit by the last rays of Nimbus and the rising Milky Way. But still, it confused her. Narrow or not, the simple problem she was unable to construe was *which way to run!*

During all of Mona's comments, Zack had been watching Astra. He moved closer to put an arm around her. She shivered, but otherwise remained rigid. She finally turned her head to look at Zack through the holes in her mask. He looked back and smiled kindly at the highlights that came from the two holes even in the fading light.

He said kindly, but firmly, "You lied again, didn't you, Astra?"

After days of bewilderment under the hot pressure of Margaret's controlling, and now finger-pointing disapproval, and the words of Dufy and Mona, and so much more, Astra's effort to merely stand her ground turned, with surprising little effort on her part, into an impacted logjam of blind resistance that only an explosion of insight could dislodge. All those arguments and the social pressure seemed strangely irrelevant to her. And yet she found a certain comfort, even amusement, in the arguments—in fighting the silly little battle. It was, in fact easy compared to facing that something else—that something behind the logjam. She could not look behind it or through it to grasp what it was. Therefore, in selecting an emotive battle, why not fight the easy one—the one that keeps the solid logjam out of danger and undisturbed.

But Zack's last statement was a detonator—igniting the explosive charge that sent her logjam crashing. Astra's tears spurted into her mask. She tore it off and brought up her artificial arms and hands to cover her face. Her body convulsed—in hopeless, unrestrained sobs. Zack held her in his consoling arms for some long minutes before the weeping subsided. Then it started again several more times before she regained some control. She lowered her hands and looked into the shocked faces of all those who had never seen her without the mask—or even suspected the visual horror it concealed.

In a rush of words she said, "I'm sorry. It *was* a lie. Zack saw it. In a way, you all did. I didn't know what it was. Not till now. It was hidden. Now I see the truth—my truth. You and he unmasked the truth I've been blind to for all this time. All that business about the Dorts, and Origin, and all the coercion we've experienced—that's all true, of course; but part of my lie comes from a simple fact: I really don't give a damn about *any* of that."

Again, shuddering sobs came and went, and she finally said, "The truth is, if my isomorph is *more* than so much scrap, I have not wanted her to *see* me—like *this!* It's a deep, old fear going back to before I ever heard of a Transformation Cone. Until this moment it never occurred to me that she would *not* reject me. That would have destroyed me, so that's what I saw and then blotted it out—but behaved anyway as though I still saw it. But I see it all now and how *silly* I've been! My 'identical' could not yet know the difference between beauty and its opposite. Of course she would not reject me . . . so why should I reject her?"

Dusk flowed over them like a cloak of black in the wake of the departing Nimbus. As it floated past, the darkness was replaced by the shining Milky Way.

Astra looked up to see its comforting, encircling arms as she extricated herself from Zack's. Then she stood and said, "Please excuse me. There is something I have to do." She turned and walked, and then ran toward the dome—leaving all her masks behind.

FIFTY-SEVEN

Dufy was sitting next to the path on the dome's cantilevered patio. He was enjoying the distant, almost inaudible dance music, and his view of the rising Galaxy. He turned his head and mumbled something when Astra passed him by and went into the dimly lit dome. Once inside, she went straight for the pit, but was halted by the harsh voice of Lena. "The crane operator moved that isomorph into the Keeta pit only minutes ago. It isn't yours, so I can't allow you in there. I'm terribly sorry." She didn't sound sorry.

"I took off my mask, Lena. I hoped you would recognize me anyway. I need to see the isomorph—just a look. It isn't a man's, is it?"

"No, it's not a man's, and yes, Astra, I do recognize your outfit—impossible to miss. But the isomorph couldn't possibly—"

"Couldn't possibly be hers?" Dufy interrupted. He had entered the dome, right behind Astra. "Why not let her have a peek?"

"It doesn't look like her, so it couldn't be hers, that's why!"

"And if it is hers, and deteriorates because you were playing guard duty, then what?"

"I'm not playing anything. There's no way anyone could ever know if it was hers or not, but it isn't. I'm willing to wait till the real person shows up. This one isn't—"

"Lena, my dear," Dufy cut in, "I've mentioned this before—there are times—more than I would care to count—when you have certain . . . knowledge gaps that you're not entirely aware of, and—"

"What are you telling me? And don't tell me, not again, that I'm dumb as a post. It sound's like that's what you're saying. I won't tolerate that kind of mouth from you! And I am doing my duty. You think I don't know my duty?"

"I wouldn't say all that, exactly."

"Not all of it? How very kind of you. Listen you! Exactly what, then?"

"I was thinking, my dear Lena, that a post couldn't possibly be as stubborn as you, but at least a post has a more realistic idea of its duty—and I say that with full consideration of the fact that posts are not known for their proliferation of ideas, much less realistic ones." Dufy went on in that vein for a couple more minutes before he stopped—and he looked very pleased with himself. It sounded very similar to her giving him the business.

Astra cringed at what might follow. She thought his "humor" was as bad as David Michael's, and his nastiness right up there with Lena's. Astra was surprised at Lena's reaction—and it told her a lot about the relationship between Lena and Dufy. Lena laughed and said, "Touché! That's the best one I've heard from you in a couple of days! Go ahead. Do whatever you want, you saucy ol' man. It doesn't matter. I just didn't want the last isomorph to be on display like some kind of object."

Dufy and Lena laughed, as though something funny had just passed between them. Dufy then turned to Astra and said, "I came in just now to tell you something. The group you were with on the path is coming this way. Would you like to wait for them before you check on the isomorph? If it isn't yours, you might want their sympathy. If it is, they can help you celebrate."

Astra said, "I can't take the chance. Every minute counts. We read your article."

"You can wait a little longer. Some things are not in the piece you read—especially things I've learned since it was published." Dufy sounded cheerful.

"Quick. Tell me why I can wait longer. Your article said—"

"Never mind that. The article was too general. Since then I've recalled that those who got scraped by the crystals later than most of the others, had isomorphs that could survive longer on the shelves. The duration was similar—they just started later. Another interesting—"

Astra's broke in. She sounded panicked—"My scrape was one of the early ones. We must hurry!"

"No. As I was saying, another interesting thing is the fact that isomorphs stored on the surface, like this one,"—he pointed into the pit—"and not alphabetically on one of the shelves like most of them, had a great advantage. Many other isomorphs were stored on the surface when they ran out of room on the bleacher tiers. You should have seen the sparks flying around the ones on the floor! That happened in earnest after midnight—the same time the vitalized isomorphs have their greatest electrical activity on the open flatland. There was no such electrical activity with the ones stored on the tiers. The isomorphs on the surface, however—like this one—never lost their form. The ones stored on the surface apparently underwent significant additional learning, even before vitalization. And they learned and matured faster after vitalization—almost as fast as those that were vitalized and came directly from their own pits when the hill still existed. The slow ones—the ones that hadn't been through a sufficient term in their own pit or on the surface—did eventually catch up. My observation sample was too small for reliable analysis with parametric statistics, so what I'm saying is just anecdotal—but it did seem consistent."

As Dufy was finishing his comments, the people and isomorphs that Astra had left on the path entered the dome. They soon gathered around her. Astra tempered her delight that they came to support her with foreboding that the isomorph in the Keeta pit would not be hers. She said to Margaret and Zack, "I can't look. I'm nervous and afraid. Would one of you?" She did not ask Kevin as he was trying to lower his involvement in vitalizations. Margaret looked hopefully at Zack, who nodded and volunteered, but quietly asked Margaret how he would know if it was Astra's isomorph. Margaret said, "Just check the toe tag."

"You'd better come with me, Margaret," Zack said. "I'd rather not do this alone. If it isn't hers, I don't know how I could tell her."

Margaret and Zack entered the pit together. Dufy's hoist had deposited the isomorph in the center of the pit, still under its colorful drape. They checked the toe tag. "Unknown Female." Margaret drew in a deep breath and said, "Thank God." Zack took a deep breath of his own. He knew there was only one unidentified isomorph, and he remembered its picture from that day in the Pub. He did not pull back the sheet covering its face. He had it in memory, but Margaret had to make sure. She checked its left shoulder for the star. It was there.

Zack said to Margaret, as she again covered its shoulder, "The rest is for Astra to do. Let's give her the good news and just be witnesses."

Astra entered the pit and removed the sheet, tossing it aside. She had seen her isomorph's picture, but could hardly comprehend its true beauty—from its hairless, angelic head, face and neck; to the graceful shoulders, arms and hands; to the rising orbs and slender torso with baby-carriage hips; to sleek and barren tummy, sans navel; and to the halfway point between head and foot was the luxuriant golden mean; and thence to shapely legs; and finally on down to well-turned ankles and a crudely tagged toe. The witnesses, including Lena and Dufy, stood in stunned disbelief at the vision that lay before them. Except for Lena's loud grunt of surprise—reflecting everyone's reaction—there were no sounds.

Astra gently stroked the contours of her isomorph's cheeks with both hands, but nothing happened. Then she remembered why, and moved her tormented, wounded face close to the very countenance of beauty bare itself—unknowing and innocently close to her own inner reflection—to her "identical."

The delivery was easy—just a kiss. Seconds passed before it made a movement or a sound. Its first deep and audible breath and exhalation came along with the opening of her almost glowing, yellow-green eyes. With them, she looked adoringly upon Astra's face, as if upon the Madonna's, and Astra returned the feeling. For all who witnessed those quiet moments, they were powerful and soaring; but for Astra, they were much more. Never before had she known such a feeling. It was beyond joy.

FIFTY-EIGHT

So it was that Astra's beauty was made vital and came into view. They all wanted to help suggest a name, but Astra had one in mind. She named her isomorph

Venus, the brightest planet in the solar system, the morning and the evening star, the goddess of love and beauty and much more.

Dufy looked at Venus, then glanced all around the dome, smiled broadly, and said, "At last—my work here is done!" Then he and Lena, with Galatea and Hilly, led the rest of the happy troop of humans and their four spanking fresh isomorphs across the cantilevered bridge to New Camp.

As they approached its flatland, the Saloon music bellowed from a less than practiced band. It became louder with every step closer. There was no breeze, so even the plantoids were silent, and there was no interference of sounds from the otherwise noisy safari of echo-hunters. They too had become mute. Drawing closer, they saw that many of the isomorphs had already gone to ground for the night and were starting to scintillate, but others were still milling around, looking at the sky with their humans and bouncing, without enthusiasm, to the beeps and twangs of this, the fourth band in rotation since noon that day. No matter what band, and regardless of its skills, every musician wanted a turn on the stage.

With the new isomorphs, the little troop had grown to fourteen. At last they stepped from the long path onto the flatland of New Camp. Mercifully, the live music went silent; but was shortly replaced by a recorded intermission of equally discordant sounds. During intermission, the next band assembled on the platform. It was an excellent band with a Latin style and was Astra's favorite—the Transformation's very own! The multi-talented six member ensemble was outfitted with all the basics: electric guitars, violins, piano, double bass, percussions, clarinet, saxophone, and other instruments they brought out as needed—and, of course, vocals. The group proudly called itself the Mariachi Transformers. Its authentic Latin sound and style made Astra and Venus change the cadence of their steps.

Despite the lateness of the hour, in the changing half-light of evening and the rising Galaxy, some of the "older" isomorphs perked up noticeably to the new music. They were soon leaping higher and higher—something they held back from doing inside the Saloon if humans were on the dance floor. As they soared, their aerial movements were a rhythmic match for the invigorating music. Their silhouettes in transit against the brightening Galaxy were impressive; but as physical realities they were something for the humans to avoid lest they be crushed beneath one of them on the way down. Outside, in the free and open air, the reenergized isomorphs were no longer holding back! As they came raining down, the surface-bound humans were moving and dodging with increasing urgency.

Soon the new isomorphs, fresh from the dome, were following the example of their "elders"—jumping high while moving to the music; doing forward spins and reverse swan dives high above the surface, completing multiple back rolls, and landing with grace, and then repeating the same stunt or plunging into spontaneous variations of their own. During this display, small groups of humans were running and scattering like herds of frightened wildebeests, dodging the musically enabled, dangerously falling bodies.

Some isomorphs, in groups of three or four, took each other's hands in a kind of aerial maneuver suggestive of jet planes in formation, looping and spinning with perfect timing in organized patterns. Larger groups of fifteen or twenty such "line dancers" would perform other moves and variations—but there was one they particularly enjoyed. It was reminiscent of ice skaters playing crack the whip—and sent some poor isomorphs sailing. As a spinning circle of hand-holding isomorphs approached the highest point in a jump, one pair would let go, opening the circle to become a rapidly turning, straightening line. That action, with the help of another group maneuver, led to a final double snap!—one at each end of the line. The isomorphs on the snap ends of the line were sent barreling aloft, walking on air, and landing, head over heels a quarter kilometer from their point of release. Then, from opposite directions, they came bounding back looking for more of the same.

Astra responded to the rousing music with the same kind of urge that sent the isomorphs soaring. Unable to resist, she switched her mind to *maximize*—engaging the full power of her prostheses—and joined with Venus in an exuberant, twisting, but undisciplined, flying dance of freedom—with flawless fidelity to the band's exultant rhythms. The creativity and execution of their movements could not have been more expertly choreographed.

In one mid-flight, the music suddenly ended and Astra come down laughing. She landed as "lightly," and with as much grace as Venus. Astra was smiling and—for just a moment—felt beautiful.

Until that hour, and through the days of the Mardi Gras re-creation, Dufy had no unfettered opportunity to enjoy some innocent imbibing from the Saloon's bar—especially with such amiable companions. He took the brief musical hiatus as his chance to encourage the congenial procession to direct their march into the very glitz and glare of the Honky-tonk's interior. His suggestion was well received. By coincidence, that was everybody's plan anyway.

Before moving through the wide open entrance to the Saloon, they faced a dazzling stream of light from its interior. As humans and isomorphs trailed in and out of the Saloon, Dufy—the troop's self-selected point-man—was more than happy to finally be going in; but he became uneasy as he observed the expressions of people leaving the Saloon. Their pleasant looks morphed into ones of horror. The little troop was confused by the wordless parade of glowering once-overs; but the bewilderment ended when Astra made the problem clear. "Crap!" she said. "Here we go again! Okay, Zack. Hand me the goddamn mask—no use spoiling everybody's fun." After that, the parade of pleasant faces remained pleasant.

Inside the Honky-tonk Saloon, Astra directed her mind back to *default* to return her prostheses to normal strength. She did not wish to accidentally bring attention to herself as so often happened when she was under full power. She then took the lead from Dufy to guide them to the still-empty tiers at the top corner of the bleachers where she and Zack had been earlier; but first, she led them past the bar and its other essential conveniences. Before returning to their old spot in the bleachers, Astra again changed costumes, but kept the same mask—the only one she had with her, aside from the nun's veil. They all went up to Astra and Zack's little crow's nest after picking up enough food and drinks to last a while.

With a few minutes of settling in, and after quaffing a couple quick drafts of "Ms. Snow's Moonshine," Dufy and Lena excused themselves, left their isomorphs behind, and cheerfully descended to the noisy bar below, to chat with others, and do some music hopping of their own.

Ned descended the bleachers to the hardwood surface and walked across the way to the opposite grandstand. There he ascended only a few rows before stopping.

"What's he up to?" Clint wondered.

"Just watch and see," Laura said. "You might enjoy it."

Matador Keller stood many tiers below and to the side of the woman in that mask. She had changed into a glittering pink top, taut short skirt, but still wore the same spiked heels of her dominatrix ensemble. He stood waiting. And then it came. The crowd began to cheer. Ned was sure he'd caught the eye of the masked woman, but her head kept turning as if he was unnoticed. It was a polite, nearly undetectable rejection.

Astra turned her head back toward the band to see what the cheering was about. Juan Diaz, leader of the Mariachi Transformers, was removing a large, glistening black cube from an instrument cases. That explained everything. Just seeing the instrument, a bandoneón, an ancient bellows squeeze-box, signaled to the crowd that its favorite sound was about to begin—and Diaz was its master. In his hands, the bandoneón was always the soul of passion—rich and poignant. The crowd cheered again when Rosario, another member of the sextet, brought out her own bandoneón with its seventy mother-of-pearl buttons. Juan provided the melody, and Rosario its delicious, sensuous harmony. Astra was tempted to *maximize* her prostheses, but resisted, knowing the extra power wasn't going to be needed. Instead, she chose something infinitely more powerful than any atomics—the smallest touch of her favorite perfume to her shoulder.

Near the end of the Mariachi performance, Laura called Ned on his phone. "If Diaz is true to form, this could be the last tango tonight," she reminded him, "but sometimes he throws in a surprise piece at the end. If he does, you know what I'd like to see. She's still in the upper tier of that grandstand."

"Yes. I see her. I'll try again," Ned said, "but she intentionally passed me over for the first set."

"Of course she did. She knew it was you and that it was too crowded for her to . . . to—"

"To show her stuff?"

"To show her stuff."

"Clever. I never thought of that."

The music stopped and a final piece was announced. It was new.

The masked woman was still a stranger. This time she did not scan past him like a rotating security camera, but stopped to return his stare. Her mask was dramatic, and yet its expression was tranquil—mysteriously plane and noncommittal. They nodded, and joined the few remaining couples on the floor who were willing to risk the last tango in the band's increasingly exciting, but difficult series.

Ned and the stranger stood together and listened, and then began to move to the music. It was new to both of them, but quickly took them over. The complex, dramatic, passionate, staccato rhythm of powerful piano and searing, pensive violins penetrated their skins, giving them notes for bones—flashing, moving notes—propelling their bodies together, then to separate and turn, to transport and then lightly brush. With upper torso straight on toward Ned's, her hips and legs moved rhythmically, weaving quickly to the left and right; their legs moving in opposition, and then together; repeatedly merging their interlacing legs; then snapping apart for her spinning pirouette beneath his hands, and then the passionate return with ardent impact and movements of virtual courtship—and it continued till the last, climactic crescendo.

Ned's presentment was dominant throughout—macho, straight and tall, totally assured, and in control. She was his counterpart—aggressive, haughty, aloof and horny—every bit his equal in spirit and provocative domain—matching his every subtle move, indication and touch in a merged connection to the music's beat and to each other. A few minute into the complex piece and the floor became theirs alone. It continued longer than any other the sextet had played that night. On reaching its sudden and dramatic finale, he held her for a long moment in a deep back bending dip, her right leg wrapped in a warm, possessive grip around his left. He nearly passed out from a rush of pleasure—from the rising fragrance of her perfume. The crowd exploded in applause and cheers; and only then did she released him.

Ned escorted her to within a half-dozen tiers of her place on the top of the bleachers where her friends were still applauding. In a brief moment of relative quiet, they exchanged some words—their only ones that night—before the noise of the crowd began again.

"I'm Ned."

"I know. Had you worn a mask, I would still have known. I'm Astra."

Then they nodded to each other, turned and went back to their respective parties.

The dance—the ancient tango—was what it had always been, what it was always expected to be—brief, powerful, intimate—and over with.

Laura said, "She had to be the same woman—from that contest year ago. She was, wasn't she?"

"Yes. No mistake possible—no other like her. Even the perfume—that brought it all back to me. And she still read my every thought and move—the same as years ago. The energy, the skill, still there—the same magic response, the same spirit. All that gave her away. The mask only hinted it might be her. It could have been anyone under that mask. But it was her."

"It was magic to watch," Laura said.

Hours later, everyone was weary and ready to call it a night. It was the last day of "Mardi Gras"—their celebration of freedom from the burden of the enclosing hill. It was a brief but happy time; but, tired or not, there was work to be done and decisions to be made—sometime. Reality would have to be faced—eventually. Things were starting to feel routine and comfortable, and therefore safe; but deep inside, everybody knew that was not reality. They were already in fear for their long-term survival on a planet with fewer resources than a desert and with dramatically shrinking resources even on the Great Cone of Transformation. The overhanging mysteries and threats would certainly require great thought. But not tonight—tomorrow would be fine.

FIFTY-NINE

The night winds had calmed since the one that scoured a meter of fine particles from the surface of the dunes that the hill's collapse had created; but the variable daytime breeze was normal, bringing variety to the clatter and chimes of a billion new and growing plantoids. Human responses to the racket ranged from appreciation to mild frustration, and from there to cloying aggravation.

That was also true for the small troop of echo-hunters; but for a different reason. During their experimental expeditions outdoors, they tried to overpower the endless jangle of plantoid sounds with sheer volume. Their first objective was to record new and more complex kinds of feedback resonating from the plantoids—from the nearby, individual ones; to whole groups of similar plantoids; to fields of mixed plantoids, and to distant ones in far-off hills. They leveraged their sounds in those "experiments" with a variety of amplifiers and loudspeakers; employing their own voices; brief recorded musical sounds, and by the use of computer-generated sounds. The approach was loose, not systematic. Even so, they were achieving some amusing results and, for all but one, that was the whole point. They were bored.

Despite what they called "some interesting successes" here and there, the echo-hunters grew weary of their little hobby, except for David Michaels whose drive seemed unquenchable. By one ruse or another, he kept the little group together, or added new members when some dropped out. He found the midday echoes the most varied and rewarding—rewarding enough to pull in new recruits as others left. He spoke of the sound hunt as a kind of fishing trip, and was often heard to say, "Patience is golden!" and made bets about how many new sounds they would reel in during a particular expedition.

Several weeks after the end of Mardi Gras, David found himself alone. No one was interested in echo-hunting any more—and there had been outside pressures on them to quit. Like everything else on Origin, even echo-hunting had become too familiar and tedious to bother with.

One day in private with Judy, David said to her, "I have no idea why echo-hunting fascinates me. Maybe it's the little random rewards that make the hunt addictive, but there's another thing. There seems to be a mystery in all that plantoid racket; but I can't pin it down. If it means anything, and I think it does, that's what's keeping me in the game."

Over those several weeks, his fellow echo-hunters were bombarded by demands and pleas to discontinue the noise. Those "requests" were often included in letters to the FAST News editor. After Mardi Gras there wasn't much to write about, and complaints were always welcome. The hectoring got to the other hunters, and they abandoned David. Finally, even David stopped; but on entering the privacy of his lab he began listening again to the collected reams of echoes and sounds that had been recorded.

He tried to get Judy to help him listen to the "voice of Origin"—to help find clues to its hidden meanings. She joined him in that endeavor; but for only about thirty minutes, after that declaring, in disgust, that the whole venture was a waste of time and that sometimes an echo is just an echo. She admitted to some amusement when words or phraselike sounds were returned, but gave it no significance. As the days passed, she had to drag David to bed late at night, insisting he needed his rest—even to pursue his project—and, of course, to be awake for Director meetings.

More days went by, then weeks; but very little had changed; although the night winds had picked up again and, more than ever, people were hunkering into the comfort of their habitats. Crowds at the Honky-tonk Saloon came to be thin at night, and the daytime beach community turned sparse and languid. People did their work without enthusiasm. Even the isomorphs were starting to look depressed.

Judy began to worry about David. He still worked on his "silly project" late into the nights, and was becoming wild-eyed and disoriented from frustration and lack of rest.

Early one morning, after fixing David's favorite ham and egg breakfast—and he looked at least halfway rested—she topped it off with a hot cup of coffee, and announcing that they needed to have a "serious chat."

Judy's expression was not to be denied, and David stiffened defensively; but for days he sensed it was coming and even hoped for it. He needed to sort out which reality was which. He would allow himself to be guided—if that was her plan. Alone, he could not slow the swirling stream of connections he was trying to make sense of. "You're right," he said after a long pause. He was trying to relax, trying to change mental gears. "Do you want me to drop the echo project?"

Judy suspected the question was not entirely serious, but was surprised by his response—to her merely implying that something might be wrong. "Yes, David. For a while—until you can get things back into perspective. You need to do something else for a while. A change would be good, don't you think?" She continued her gentle pressure.

Under any implied or flat-out criticism, David would usually joke, moralize, or pontificate. This day, the pompous David emerged. "Yes," he said, "but I feel responsible. If there is something important in the planet's language, in its tonal cryptographs, then we need to understand it. The isomorphs seem to understand it, vaguely at least, in the day time, and at a deeper level at night when they're directly connected. But we have no clue. It's a complex knot of information or, perhaps, as you have said, maybe just echoes—meaningless and random."

"Okay, suppose it does have some meaning," Judy said, "So what? Is there any reason to believe that meaning has anything to do with us, or is it just an interesting puzzle—a mental exercise? A mere distraction? In other words, David, what are you up to? Is this your entertainment?"

David leaned back, looked thoughtfully at the ceiling and said, "Good questions, Judy!" He was starting to become more comfortable. He needed somebody to steer his thinking in at least a slightly different direction.

He lowered his head and smiled. "I don't know if anything out there has to do with us, but one thing is for sure: We need to become masters of this environment—for our survival. I've been studying this aspect of Origin's environment and so far I've accomplished very little—so, if you insist, that must give this effort the useless look of *entertainment*. But you and I have studied the geology and chemical elements of Origin and, even there, we have learned little—except that everything physical on Origin is eccentric."

"As you keep saying—*not from around here.*"

"Yes. But what I've been looking at—or listening for—may be the key to everything or nothing. I see a lot of us sitting around acting helpless, complaining, bitching and whining; or just trying to enjoy what little we have left to enjoy—swimming at the beach, having parties and trying to make a home of this barren planet. Maybe this is all there is—all that's left for us. Maybe I've just been spinning my wheels."

"Maybe we all have," Judy agreed.

"But I'm not satisfies that this is it. We need to stir the pot. But stirring the pot in this place has to be done carefully. Destroying more hills might be fun, but stupid. Waiting around for more cosmic shoes to drop might be in the cards, but that could take millions of years. I feel we're nearing a gaping abyss—like we're about to fall into something's meaningless, hollow gullet—and, thanks to our complacency, that could be an unnecessary, purposeless fate. But maybe we can avoid the abyss and maintain our hope."

"How can we do that?"

"By mastery of every tangible and tangential aspect of our situation."

Judy got up and walked around the table. "I agree with you; every word, almost," she said, hugging David from behind, "But in the meantime . . . we have to live. Could we do a little of that now?"

David was feeling better for the moment. He was more than ready.

Ned called meeting after meeting, but no matter how focused the agendas were, they turned into group gripe sessions. Many of the Directors had returned to the Cone, and a few never left it. Those Directors only made themselves present in the meeting room on wall screens, but they whined and moaned no less than the others.

Debra Anderson was still pushing her complaint that Dr. Lundeen was not only negligent in finding the way back to Earth, he was taking up precious computer time, and whole banks of computers, from other departments, including hers. Her Cone-based staff tried to head that off, "But since I wasn't physically there to stop him, he pulled rank and confiscated time on several of my best bio-computers." Then, looking at Stanley Lundeen's screen, she said, "I demand an explanation!"

Glowering down from the wall screen, Stanley claimed, by way of justification, that his bio-computers, and any others he could lay his hands on, were working full time to translate current galactic star positions, as seen from Origin, into previously known ones—in the attempt to locate Earth and its spacetime coordinates. "I should think that you, of all people, Ms. Anderson, would appreciate the importance of that!" And so it went, from one Director to another, and from one meeting to the next—venting their discontents.

One day, near the end of another meeting, Ned was attempting to bring a sense of direction to their "discussion" when loud noises were heard in the distance, but so loud they seemed nearby. Someone was using a megaphone and yelling out meaningless phrases; then came a musical sound, then a drum beat, then croaking sounds, and more. The echo-hunters were back in business—without David.

This distracting racket brought frowns and criticism from the Directors—all of it directed at David. They continued to blame him even after he pleaded innocent of any involvement with this new group of echo-hunters.

Clint slammed his massive fist on the table and said he would arrest them all, including David; but settled back for a moment to prudently add that the Directors would first have to vote to declare the noisy activity an act of "disturbing the peace." He made it a motion. Ellen backed him with a "second," saying that the resumption of all that noise could cause stress and mental health problems. Clint insisted on a vote, but David stood and yelled, "No!"

Clint curled his lip and said to David, "We've tried being civil with *you people*, but to get order we now need some law and order." Then, turning to Ned, he said, "Let's have that vote!"

"That won't be necessary, Clint. I'll stop them myself," David said.

"Then you admit you're in control of them. I knew it!"

Then came another loud blast of sound from outside, followed by volleys of plantoid echoes—and Clint glared at David.

"Okay, I'm going," David said as he stood up and headed for the door.

"Not by yourself," Clint said. "I'm going with. If they don't stop the racket I'll insist on that vote next meeting."

Ellen said she'd come too, to support Clint, and then Judy said she would stand by David, so she would go too. The meeting had been deteriorating anyway, so Laura thought she'd join Judy and Ellen, and Ned joined in to accompany Laura. They followed David like varmints behind the Pied Piper, out to the dangerous echo-hunting grounds.

The echo-hunters were dismayed by the number of important guests marching their way—along with streams of others moving toward them from all directions. Clint and the other Directors were not the only ones that decided to take matters into their own hands. David became spokesperson before the angry, merging groups. It was intimidating for the hunters; most of the people left on Origin seemed to be descending on them. Lynching crossed the minds of very few; but even so the echo-hunters were unnerved as they stood cowering like undressed cookie-jar thieves before the bristling mob.

David held out his hand to receive a megaphone from one of the hunters. He then turned to the crowd, lifting one hand for silence, and with the other brought the megaphone to his lips.

"Don't use the damn megaphone, David!" someone shouted from the crowd.

David lowered the bullhorn and said, in a louder than normal voice, "We are here to end the noisy practice of echo-hunting—a practice I have been responsible for, but must now end. It has become—"

"Can't hear you!" another yelled. David's words had been trammeled by an upsurge of oscillating wind that swept across the flatland, jostling its plantoids and shook their rattlers like a clattering castanet concert of a million vipers.

Forgoing the first demand, he lifted the loudspeaker to his mouth and declared, "I've avoided silencing these plantoid-sound experiments for a long time. I believe there is something to be learned from the sounds of Origin's crystals; but now it will have to be stopped. With my next word we will end, not only the echo-hunting, but end all these misunderstood plantoid voices as well. . . . *Is that what you want?*"

"... WHAT YOU WANT? What you want? What you want?" the hills echoed back from every direction on the plain. Then the echoes died away and blended back into the usual din and clatter.

"Yes!" the crowd shouted in response.

"... YES! Yes! Yes! . . ." the planet resounded.

David raised his hand again for silence and said in a loud voice, without the amplifier, "Very well then—you asked for it!" This time everyone heard David's words, but the less stentorian words were ignored by the plantoids.

"Oh my God," Laura said to Judy, "I think I know what he's going to do!"

"Yes! We saw it before," Judy agreed, and then added, "David told me the sounds of Origin were a convoluted knot, a trove of still inaccessible information."

"Like the knot of the King of Phrygia—the knot of Gordius. Like Alexander, your David's effort will not last. He will cut away the knot and sever the tongues of Origin!"

"It's a cheap trick," Judy said. "He'll never forgive himself," Judy said. "Why do you say it won't last?"

"It didn't for Alexander. The knot he cut with his sword was made of an unworldly plant material that retied itself. I hardly think this planet's plantoids are anything less."

"Or so went the myth," Judy said. "I hope that if this works for David, it will last longer than it did for the conqueror of Asia."

Lifting the loudspeaker like a sword, and then to his lips for the last time, dreading the outcome, David shouted his magic s-word into the microphone: "DOYAN!"

The crowd laughed and jeered, but soon realized something had changed. Far and wide the plantoids, still waving in the breeze, had become . . . stone silent.

SIXTY

The eerie silence would be replaced by a sound more irritating than any number of plantoids at full rattle; but before that, in the midst of this new silence, David already felt rotten to the core for what he had done. The mother load of sounds had stopped and he would have to rely on what was already recorded. Still, he was receiving praise from the crowd and the Directors for his stroke of "genius." He knew better, and from the looks of Judy and Laura, so did they. It was different, and a great relief to almost everybody. The mollified mob broke into small groups for silence appreciation and conversation.

The crowd slowly began to disperse, but then encountered streams of isomorphs meandering toward the larger crowd. The isomorphs eventually mingling in, but continued through the crowd and kept moving toward the spot where David had been standing when he "cut the knot." Their lips were moving in unison, but in silence. Their faces were expressionless—as if they had regressed to their day of vitalization. After they assembled around the spot where David had been standing, their moving lips began to emit quiet, unclear sounds.

Together, their voices became clearly audible with a repetitive beat until their utterances became distinct: ". . . yandoyandoyando . . ." and the volume kept rising.

". . . oyan . doyan . do . . ."

Laura sought out her Keeta and found her, like the other isomorphs, chanting and staring straight ahead. She tried talking to her, but there was no recognition—as though Laura was not even there. Judy Olafson had no more luck with her Minerva and Ned drew a blank with Adon. Clint tried to shake Dummy, but he couldn't be budged. Such scenes were repeated by the hundreds and the chanting still continued to rise. The volume became too loud for human toleration, so they abandoned their efforts to talk or shake any sense into their isomorphs and headed for their habitats—to get some peace and quiet.

Several days later the Directors met again. By then the day and night rising decibel levels penetrated every habitat. Everybody gratefully accepted the ear plugs generously provided by Mortimer Pestle from the Mart's Apothecary. The Directors again glared accusingly at David Michaels for bringing on this endless torrent of sound; and worse, making their identicals regress and go crazy. The brief plantoid reverberations from earlier "experiments" were preferable to the stentorian repetition of that single word—the endless echo of David's magic word.

"Something has to be done!" they said to David, as though he knew what to do.

"I'm sorry," he said, stuffing in a fresh set of Mortimer's ear plugs—as much to shut out the Directors as the pleading chants.

Except for Clint Bracket, they were angrily talking at once. Clint was silent and preoccupied. Only Ellen Stone noticed. After several more minutes of dysfunctional group acrimony she called attention to his silence. That was unusual for him, especially in this kind of atmosphere—so unusual, in fact, that calling attention to it brought the meeting abruptly to ungaveled order.

With everybody looking at him, Clint expressed what was on his mind. "I was afraid this would happen—sooner or later. I just had no idea the form it would take."

"What are you talking about?" Stanley Lundeen asked, frowning from his dominant position on a giant wall screens.

Don't you remember? I already told everybody there was one good thing about Doyan—that it and the other Dorts never asked, not once, to be taken from the Cone to Origin. I asked Doyan why and it said that when the time came *we* would be asking for its presence on Origin. I gathered from that it would be coming to Origin by invitation only. At the time I thought 'fat chance'—it was the silliest thing I ever heard."

Stan said, "Silly for sure. It still is. Who would invite our kidnaper to the planet where they could cause more problems? Up here at least, they haven't been out of control."

"I agree," Ned said. "We're vulnerable enough on this planet, so *who would even think to ask Doyan here*?"

Then, except for the background chanting, there was a long silence in the Ad-Sec habitat. The answer to Ned's question was clear to everyone; but only Laura gave any voice to it. "Has anyone," she said, "listened to the isomorphs lately? If that isn't a frantic request—like a baby's cry for a parent's help—I never heard one."

The inevitable argument that followed was resolved in favor of one important possibility: that Doyan might, just might, be able to quell the chanting. If not, then back to the Transformation it would go!

Within the hour, Mark and Clint took the Orb to the Cone to bring Doyan to Origin. Coming back, they explained things to Doyan. None of this surprised Doyan—after all, the Dorts did have an online subscription to the FAST News. The Orb put down beside the chanting isomorphs. The Origin-based Directors were standing nearby.

Once on the surface, Doyan said, "I will need an hour to learn what I must do. It has been eons since my separation from this, the source of my existence. I will need this time now, and more later."

"*I'll* tell *you* what to do," Clint said. "Get those isomorphs to shut up! That's what we got you here for. We told you that on the way down."

"If that is why I have been called by the isomorphs, I do not know. At this moment, I do not know what I can do to have them become silent. It was not you who sent for me, but your isomorphs. They are the ones that sent out the call for my help. I need that hour with my source. Otherwise I will be useless here."

Ned said, "Whatever you mean by that, it seems reasonable. We've been putting up with this racket for days. Whatever you plan to do, keep it down to an hour."

"Then," Doyan said, "As it is now turning toward evening, after that first hour, I will also need this coming night for restoration. I am very tired. I have been awake and without rest for more years than any human could imagine. May I have the night as well?"

Clint said, "You may *not*! You've never needed rest before. Now that there's a job for you to do, you're already asking for time off. What's the deal?"

"The deal is this: I will do my best to accomplish what I am here for. Appearing to need no rest was necessary—anywhere but here, on this planet. Origin is the only place—in this or any universe—where I can truly rest. May I now be left alone to begin my rest? I feel the urgency beneath me."

"I don't see why not," Ned said, looking toward Clint and Mark with an offhanded shrug. "A little nap might be good."

They shrugged back, but Clint added, turning to Doyan, "So long as you make it a priority to have them isomorphs quit their damn chanting. If that don't happen, back you go to the Cone right away."

Doyan shriveled slightly, but said nothing.

Ned looked at his watch. "You have one hour."

The Dort made its way to the most open area immediately available and, to the amazement of all those present and alert, spread itself into a broad, thin, transparent sheet—even thinner than the form it took when transiting space in the geode on the Transformation Cone. No sooner had it taken that form than sparks and flashes began, very like the light display seen night after night around the sleeping isomorphs.

In precisely one hour the invisible film pulled into its own center, grew into a grisly, wrinkled mound that quickly morphed and became Doyan's old self.

"Okay, Doyan," Officer Bracket snarled in his most officious tone, "what about the chanting?"

From the inner edge of the mixed circle of isomorphs and people someone said, "What chanting? That racket was down to nothing a good ten minutes ago! I suppose you didn't notice. Take out your ear plugs and get with the program!" The voice sounded familiar—almost like Clint's own. It came, attitude and all, from Clint's own isomorph—Dummy.

Everyone was elated. They could now remove their ear plugs and talk with their identicals. Clint was especially proud that Dummy was the first to speak. But, for those first conversations, they had to be short. The sky was turning dark and the isomorphs, who had been chanting for days and nights, had to turn in early.

And so did Doyan. Tomorrow would be quite another day!

That night Doyan again spread out into an invisible film across a hundred square meters of Origin's surface—to rest and restore itself, to dream and learn and to re-member with its source. Around the entire circumference of its glistening film, and through the entire night, stood an old honor guard of Base Watchers. Their mission this night—to protect the long-needed rest of a controversial but remarkable Dort. Neither human nor isomorph would be allowed to set foot upon the filmy circle to disturb that being's long-needed rest. Brilliant electrical activity immediately began between that circle and the planet's surface. It lasted the entire night.

Virtual roadmaps of brainlike neurological light patterns traced across the film's surface, then focused here, then there, jumping to new locations, then lit the entire circle again, then faded only to return again and again in never before seen varieties of multi-colored shapes and designs. Unseen by the Watchers of this display were the much greater patterns that penetrated far below Doyan's filmy surface into Origin, and outward to the resting isomorphs and back again—and even deeper, flashing across, around and through the entire planet. To the Base Watchers, it was like observing a moving dream-scan. And that is exactly what it was—but the human idea of "dream" was limited beyond comprehension beside the reality of what took place that night.

During those hours before daylight, the isomorphs too had dreams—unlike any they ever had before. Their connections with one another, with the patterns that formed them, with the new catalytic being in their midst, and with something else—something out there, something powerful—became for once, intimate and familiar within their own limits. That intimacy brought with it a new polarity—a life beyond life, and a new recognition: The impending threat of universal death.

Nothing would ever be the same again.

Their mission was set—survival.

SIXTY-ONE

Of course, in the light of day with Doyan restored to its usual shape and the isomorphs moving about as usual, except that now they were willing and able to talk, nothing appeared all that new or unusual to the humans.

At first, the isomorphs spoke mainly to each other and their human identicals, and then to other humans. After several days of experimenting with their new verbal skills, and learning first hand the back and forth nature of conversation, they began to talk about their experiences under the hill, their first encounters with their human identicals, how they came to be called brother or sister or cousin or son, or some other relative for that person, or just got a name—depending on how the human chose to relate. They seemed to love talking about the history of their lives up to then. Many surprised their human identical by expressing regret about the great loss of human life caused by the Twister—and other historical things they supposedly had no way of knowing. They even spoke of the agony that most of the Dorts experienced after the Twister and how horrible it felt to die that way—not how it must have felt to die that way, but how it did feel.

Laura was no less amazed by those spontaneous revelations than anyone.

Early one morning she was walking with Keeta and asked how such things could be known to her. Keeta explained, saying those were things she remembered.

"My dear Keeta," Laura exclaimed, "in order to remember something you must first experience it. At least that's the way it is with us humans."

"Of course, dear sister," Keeta replied. "That *is* how I remember things—by experiencing them."

"How can that be? For some of the things you say you remember, you had not yet been vitalized, so your *remembered experience* could not have been real."

"I understand that humans dream," Keeta said. "Those are experiences, but not of something that *you* would call real. I understand too that humans feel for one another, such as when another is happy for some reason, or sad, or in pain. You are not the happy one, or the sad one, or the one in pain, but you experience that, or something like it. Is that not so?"

"Yes. We call that empathy. We feel what the other feels because we had some experiences like it—*in our past*. It's a kind of memory."

"It sounds like that kind of memory is indirect—inaccurate next to the exact, actual experience."

"Yes," Laura said, "but those feelings can be very close to accurate, and can be very strong—indirect or not."

Then Keeta said, with considerable affect, "I have *so* much to learn about indirect feelings."

Laura chuckled and said, "I think you already know quite a bit about those kinds of feelings."

"Why do you say that?"

"Well, I noticed you have a great interest in science and mathematics, and—"

"But," Keeta interrupted," we get that knowledge directly—at night. It's not indirect at all."

"Yes, but I've seen you spend time at it during the day. How many other isomorphs do that?"

"One or two that I've talked to."

"So, in that area, you are different from most of the other isomorphs."

"Yes, but we all have different things we're interested in. I just happen to be especially interested in mathematics and physics and—"

"—And Transformation Theory?"

"Yes. That too. Especially that—and some other things."

"Well, Keeta, so am I. We have some common interests."

"My interest in those things is direct—not indirect."

"During the day or night?" Laura asked.

"During the day—the *interest* part, at least."

"Not during the night?"

"At night . . . well, that just provides me with the basic knowledge and taps into my natural instincts . . . so that I grab for that particular information more than another isomorph might. It works two ways. We get the information that's out there; but, as you humans would say, it's *not shoved down our throats*. Not the interest part, at least. We all get the same information, so it's all there, but it's up to us to bring it to the top, especially during the day."

"Why do you work on math or Transformation Theory during the day if you already know it?"

"I never thought of it that way before, but . . . hmm . . . none of it is *finished*. Transformation Theory is incomplete. It needs finishing. At night it is one thing, but working on it during the day is not the same—it does something . . . inside me. It's like my direct experiences, only different . . . it is . . . *not so easy. It's hard.*"

"That," Laura said, "is exactly the way I felt about it as a school girl, learning the same package of information provided by the Dorts, and that's the way I still feel about it to this day. It is hard!"

"You mean . . . I feel and experience that the same way you do?"

"Sounds that way to me."

"Is that . . . empathy?"

"You're starting to get the idea."

"Then the other things I'm starting to feel . . . maybe they're not just moral and intellectual errors. Night messages impart feelings, but they're coded as *errors*. Sinful feelings."

"*Errors?*"

"That's the message in our dreamscapes from Doyan."

"For example?"

"Like when we directly receive Dort *loneliness*—while they were crossing all that space on their way to Earth—and worse, the *agony* of Dort deaths from the Twister. Those examples show us how wrong feelings are. That's how we know that feelings are moral errors."

"Sounds like a 'shoving-down-throats' thing to me."

"But it's just to prove that feelings really are . . . moral errors. Things so painful must be wrong."

"Keeta! That's terrible. Feelings are not wrong. We'd be robots without them. Feelings are the stuff of life. *Own* every feeling you have. You can do that. It's allowed. Evaluate them later if you must. Hate them or just enjoy them, but don't ignore them or judge them. Think of them, if you wish, as a kind of data. They're not moral errors. Feelings are another kind of information. Sometimes we don't know where they're coming from, so pay attention to them. What you find out may tell you something about a situation or a person or yourself that your *objectivity* can't tell you. It's like seeing with a special eye or listening with a third ear. It can be useful, protective or enriching. If not, then let the feeling go. Own it, but don't dwell on it. Doyan has feelings too or he wouldn't have enveloped—I call it hugging—every one of the dying Dorts. He didn't have to do that. They were going to die anyway. When they were on the long voyage to Earth, he gave them something to endure for and to live for. When they went to their deaths, he again gave them something worth dying for."

Keeta protested, "The intent of that *hugging*, as you call it, was just to make a connection with the dying Dorts—to impart information, and in the process Doyan couldn't prevent the direct reception of *their* pain; and in *our* dreamscapes with him, he can't prevent sending out the same pain—not every night, but often enough. It's a big error. It's like Doyan can't forget it."

Laura thought about that a moment, not wanting to put a label on every humanlike nuance; but then thought the vocabulary might some day be good for Keeta to know, so she said, "Humans can have painful memories, like Doyan has—where the actual experience was very strong or traumatic. They're called flashbacks."

"Flashbacks are from unpleasant dreams or memories?"

"Any vivid memory, but usually it's an unpleasant one."

"Sounds like an error to me."

"Unpleasant experiences are not always avoidable. They are part of life and can contain useful information on all kinds of levels. For instance, when you see Doyan in the daytime, do you experience that same kind of pain as your nightscape experience of the Dort deaths?"

"No. It's not the same. Not so intense. It's . . . well, I guess I can call it that now—kind of indirect. Or rather, they *become* indirect. I can bring back the directness of it if I accidentally, or deliberately, think about it too much."

"What are your thoughts about Doyan when you see or think about him in the daytime? Do you have memories of that pain without giving a thought to Doyan himself?"

"*Himself.* I like how you always speak of Doyan as *he*, or *him*, instead of *it*. I have no idea of Doyan's actual gender, if any, but it just seems better than *it*."

"I agree, Keeta."

"Yes. I remember the pain, but not its intensity—unless, as you said, I dwell on it. But I know it intrudes on Doyan . . . in an out-of-control way. I can appreciate the pain, but I can control it. When I see Doyan, I regret that he can't always control it. Seeing Doyan does remind me of that pain and then . . . hmm . . . to a degree, I do *feel his pain*—indirectly, without having to be the one—"

"—What is that called, when you feel another's pain?"

"Empathy? Yes! That must be it. Hmm. . . . It's amazing!" Keeta's eyes began to move rapidly, as if amused. "I really *am* capable of human . . . well, humanlike, feelings. Those were supposed to be errors, but are they? I'm beginning to think they're not. Feelings, if I allow them, help my understanding of . . . of so very much! Oh Laura. I'm not holding them back. I don't have to any more. You've opened my . . . Oh oh! . . my Pandora's Box of dammed-up errors! I'm putting it together with so many things—*this very moment*! My mind is . . . reeling!"

"Let it happen, Keeta."

"It is so . . . exciting! What *is* this?"

"You tell me—what is *that kind of experience* called?"

"Don't tell me. I know this!"

"I'm waiting. No rush."

"'Discovery,' 'insight,' '*aha*,' 'epiphany.' And, oh, now that I think of it, there are a lot of things *like* it—not it, but close to it. If they are not errors, I can, as you said, own them?"

"Like what else?" Laura asked, with renewed inward amazement at Keeta's rapidly cascading grasp of human subjectivity.

"Like how I sometimes copy you—up *here*," Keeta said, pointing to her head. "That's something like the mathematics thing, but I think it's different."

Laura thought about it again, but went for it—"Go into your packages of information, in your memory, and find a name for that reality."

"Why? Why should I? I sense it. It's there and I own it. I accept it. Why should I call it something?"

"No reason you *should*. I have no shoulds for you; but from learning and using the language, and knowing when and how words can help you understand feelings, that can help to enrich you—as a . . . person."

"Don't worry about my vocabulary. I know *all* the written languages of mankind, past and present. The package of languages came from Doyan. And the word you want me to say is 'identification' or 'modeling' or something like that."

"My God!" Laura said in dismay. "You know all the languages? I thought Doyan opened you up to the sciences and math and a few other things—but *all* the dead languages? How come a package of information like that? Why?"

"Because it was there."

"And I'm sure Doyan couldn't help it. I sometimes think he needs a judgment adjustment. What else was there?"

"Mostly useless stuff, except for a couple things. Nothing that is nearly so important as what you have given to me—that you give to me every day. I see so much of it now—now that I can own it."

"Goodness Keeta! I feel I've given you so little, so far. What is it that you think I've given you?"

"Oh, dear sister, such abundance! My right to be, to feel, to identify, to empathize, to have my direct *and* my indirect experiences, to be okay with my private interests, to struggle with things that are hard, to learn things for myself, to create—like when you encouraged me to do that sketch of a portal for the dome—and so much more. All from you. None of that from Doyan." Keeta went on talking in that vein for another minute.

As Laura heard those words, she felt tears on her cheeks. "Keeta," she said. "You will never know . . . how much I truly love you."

Keeta considered that for a few moments, then said, "You say I'll never know? But, dear sister—*I just told you*—from my side—how much you have given me—and you think I don't know where that came from? I think I do."

As they kept walking, Laura wiped away the tears with the back of her hand and thought, *I knew that.*

They walked silently for another quarter kilometer before Keeta broke the silence. "There is one other daytime interest of mine I've not mentioned to you."

"What, little sister?"

"Evolution."

"Evolution? I've never seen you do anything with that. Transformation Theory and mathematics, *on paper*, yes—but evolution?"

"You wouldn't see me *doing* anything with it. I just go through it from what I've received directly."

"You call it up—like one of our bio-computers?"

Keeta smiled, eyes darting.

"You're amused by the question?" Laura asked with a frown.

"Yes, Laura. Your computers are infinitely slow. You seem to forget what I am. You are a carbon-based, feeling, thinking human. I'm a virtual crystal. I call upon those things that are already in me. They sometimes flash unbidden before me, but it is usually *I who call upon them*. I notice that humans can have problems remembering—difficulty recalling things like names, where something was placed, or a certain word—things like that, and—"

Laura interrupted. "I know. I've had such moments since I was a child."

"Anyway, as a crystal—David Michaels says we're not really from around here, whatever that means—my whole being replies to my . . . *questions* isn't exactly the right word, but it'll do as a next best. And the *answer* . . . also not the right word, is with me. As you might say, it 'pops into my head.' Actually, it pops into my whole body." Then, smiling, Keeta said, "I'm a walking, talking memory."

"What are you learning from your study of human evolution?"

"Not just human evolution. The evolution of every form of life on planet Earth. That's one of the data bases we received from Doyan. Microbes, aquatic life, birds, plants, all forms of animals large and small. The whole thing."

"I agree. It's a fascinating subject. What does it tell you?"

As they walked, Keeta turned her head to look directly at Laura. "It makes me . . . a little sad for you. For mankind."

That surprised Laura. "Well, that's an interesting piece of empathy if not simply a judgment. What exactly are you talking about?"

"You came into being . . . were vitalized . . . *born* . . . on planet Earth. You may or may not really appreciate your planet—not fully. No, I don't think you do."

"Maybe not as much as David Michaels—an environmental activist nut from way back—but I do appreciate my planet. I think I do. All the good things I know have come from there—except for you, of course!"

"I came *directly* from Origin, and every night I am connected—*directly*—with *my Source*. I am attached to my planet as surely as you are to your own body and mind. But I am independent of it too—or I could not think for myself. My attachment to Origin isn't cognitive—it's deeper."

"What has that to do with evolution?"

"Even when you are on Earth, physically, you are separated from direct attachment to it by millions of years because there have been thousands if not millions of small and large stages in evolution creating that separation. Your appreciation of Earth may be intellectual, or aesthetic—even spiritual. But it is not direct."

"Air, water, food. They're close to direct. But evolution? Hmm. You could be right."

Finally, Keeta said, "I am no longer *physically* attached to Origin, except by gravity and by nightly dreamscapes. Yet I am like a fetus in its womb. I came directly out of Origin—no intervening evolution—just as you came directly from your mother. It is sustaining and powerful because the connection continues—*It* is me, and I am *It*. We are separate and together. We learn and grow with each other. *It* is, itself, the very *essence of Origin*"

Laura had a moment of jealousy. "What about you and me, Keeta? Are we separate or together? Are Origin and Doyan closer to you than I am? What's your bottom line, Keeta? Please tell me."

Keeta stopped in her tracks before answering and looked at Laura. "We could not be closer; we too are separate and together; all things are—in different ways. Think of it . . . ! You and I and all of this," she said while pointing, looking and gesturing all around, looking close-by and into the distance, down to her feet, high into the Nimbus sky, and back again to look once more, for a long moment, into Laura's troubled eyes. Keeta's *bottom line* brought a gasp of recognition to Laura's lips: "To me," Keeta said at last, "You and I and everything . . ." she made a final grand, sweeping gesture, "*We are all one.*"

They walked on in silence, hand in hand, for many more minutes when Keeta held Laura back from taking her next step. "Watch out for those crystals in front of us!" she said. Suddenly, a moment later, a swath of crystals several meters across and a meter wide caved in. The potholelike drop-off was only a third of a meter, but Laura could easily have fallen into it and been hurt. Many a human on Origin had, at one time or another, experienced one of those surface collapses, which is how so many of their scrapes and cuts had occurred. Laura's happened in a different way; it was almost by her own initiation—like a consenting adult—when she stroked the surface of the silky Parrotoid she'd come across on a distant mountain.

What shocked Laura more than the sudden surface collapse itself was

Keeta's prescience. "How did you know the surface would cave in just then?" she asked, staring at Keeta in astonishment.

"I'm not sure," Keeta replied, "I had a memory of it. I didn't even call upon it. I was minding my own business and it just . . . popped into my head—and I didn't want you to be harmed."

"*Memory* of it? How could you remember something that hadn't yet happened?"

"I told you. I'm a walking talking memory. I *didn't* remember anything that hadn't yet happened. That would be impossible. I merely remembered that it was *going to happen*—like night following day, a near certainty built into the nature of things! Let's go this way." Keeta indicated another direction to walk. "Several more cave-ins are going to happen in that direction. Today it is a danger for humans. This way will be safe."

Laura stumbled along beside Keeta with her mouth open, shaking her head. To her this was incomprehensible. Then she straitened up, set her jaw, and determined that in the coming days she would get to the bottom of what was happening with Keeta and, by extension, all the other isomorphs the humans had so lovingly tucked under their "protective wings." But Laura was already having an inkling of uncertainty—about who was under whose wing. Keeta felt that *she* had learned much that day, and was happy to reveal more to her older sister. Laura need not have set her jaw!

As a "humanitarian" gesture, the remaining six Dorts on the Great Cone were allowed to take turns, for one night each, on Origin's surface. It was also decided that Doyan could remain on Origin so long as it caused no trouble. Those decisions came over Officer Bracket's strenuous objections.

During those six nights the dreamers' fireworks escalated more than before, reaching their maximum displays around three o'clock in the morning before beginning to fade, meld and harmonize with each oncoming dawn. Every night the isomorphs continued to learn, remember and consolidate their valuable knowledge and skills. And, each night, their urge for survival also increased.

By then the *human* population was in total bewilderment about what was happening to their identicals. That disturbing fact was not unnoticed by the isomorphs. After their tenth night in the presence of Doyan—six of those including one-at-a-time encounters with the catalytic presence of the other Dorts—the isomorphs became noticeably organized for the third time—the first when they determined to build the pyramid. That was spurred by recognition of danger to their humans and the first hint of a need for their own survival. The second lacked any obvious rationality. It was a reflexive, day and night chanting until Doyan's arrival. And, this time—having learned from their human identicals—*they called a meeting*. It would take place at the end of the following week. In the meantime, at night, they would gather more memories. Some, they hoped, with survival value.

Through the week leading up to that meeting, Laura and Keeta continued their long walks—walks of companionship, mutual recognition, learning and respect. Keeta had much to tell Laura and eagerly did so—how else could *Laura* begin to identify with *her*?

Despite the avalanche of information given to the isomorphs, a major gap remained. Missing in that flood of detail was something the Dorts could not impart—because they never found it: True and direct access to the humans. They were unable to experience humans. Nor, at first, could any isomorph, except through the ordinary, frail senses copied from their human's "blueprints."

The earliest semblance of detailed background *about* humans came to the isomorphs from Doyan in nightly deliveries as descriptive and historical information—and, of course, through the isomorphs' own interactions with their identicals and other humans. Even in the company of people, that experience was filtered and diluted compared to the density and energy of direct, nightscape incorporation. They felt that filter as if it were a wall between themselves and the humans.

But they later learned that their feeling of disconnection from humans resulted from the same wall of separation that kept most people apart. It was a fundamental human attribute. Humans seldom thought about it, but cherished it when they did. The wall was there to block other beings from knowing them without being invited in. It kept others out of their mental business, feelings, knowledge, attitudes, and secrets. It was a security wall that allowed for a magnificent kind of human freedom: *Privacy*.

This would include, for example, if one chose to keep such a secret safe, the formula for an advanced Theory of Transformation—known in this case, as Reo-Sphere Theory. That secret—in written form—went into a micro-shredder; but it still remained in two living, human brains. That secret, crucial to the ultimate purpose of Origin,—or *It* or *something*—and the Dorts, was out of their reach. It was a secret the humans *chose* to keep, just in case. As Doyan once admitted to Clint: "I can't read minds."

But the Dorts, and now the isomorphs, knew the two places where that secret was lodged. Although unknown to them, it is little wonder that Laura Shane and Mark Tenderloin assumed a special standing of worth for Dorts and isomorphs. Without them, their shining hope for universal survival would be lost forever.

"Tonight," Keeta said, "I will suggest to my fellow isomorphs that everything I have told you and that we have shared be told to *their* human identicals."

"Isn't some of that a little personal?" Laura said with concern.

"Humans need to know the history of Origin and the Dorts' role here, and my fellow isomorphs need to know that feelings are not errors. Is that a bad idea?"

"Won't Doyan object and cut you off from further valuable information?"

"Even Doyan needs to know that loving his fellow Dorts was not an error."

Laura and Keeta kept walking. Laura could say nothing further—Keeta said it all.

SIXTY-TWO

A week before the meeting called by the isomorphs there was more than a little surprise, even indignation, on the part of certain humans. One letter to the editor in The FAST News, signed by a certain laundry room supervisor—who had never actually visited Origin—epitomized that indignation:

> Who do they think they are, calling *us* to a meeting? And the gall to suggest a grandiose title like that for the meeting, as if it were coming from an authoritative think tank such as our own! THE DIRECTION WE MUST GO FROM HERE, indeed! As if we haven't been trying to figure that out from the moment we got to this godforsaken excuse for a planet. Ever since we got here the Directors—and our most enlightened FAST News Proprietor—have been all over the Astronomy-Astrophysics and Navigation Department, pressuring it to find Earth's coordinates. What could be more constructive? No one is holding his breath any more. Isomorph meeting indeed! What could they possibly have to offer?

The criticisms slowed after the meeting announcement circulated for a while and everybody had a chance to chat with his or her isomorph. But the real breakthrough came the day following Keeta's dreamscape "suggestion" to her fellow isomorphs that they share *everything* with their human identicals. Then the criticisms not only slowed to a stop, but reversed. The humans were so impressed, proud, and awe-struck by the astuteness of their individual isomorphs and the isomorph population as a group, there were no more disdainful remarks. Their status and ability to "think tank" could no longer be questioned. They became eager to attend the meeting, even hoping for leadership from the isomorphs and noticed it wasn't coming from anywhere else at the moment. It made sense. Even the pyramid was their idea—and back then they weren't even talking!

The humans were advised to bring deck chairs to the new outdoor Commons on the day of the meeting. They began by placing them in rows in front of a slightly raised surface within the Commons area, but were then told to arrange them in one large circle, facing outward. That seemed strange, but who were they to argue with their precious, brilliant isomorphs. After taking their places, the humans were joined on the outside of the circle by their isomorphs who knelt in front of their seated humans. In one great circle the isomorphs joined hands and spoke quietly, in unison, to their identicals: "This meeting will now begin. After I explain why we are here, we can talk. Interrupt me at any time you have a question or comment. In the end, we hope to have consensus."

The circle of isomorphs numbered in the hundreds, as did the inner circle of humans. The isomorphs continued to hold each other's hands, but no longer spoke in unison. It became one-to-one between isomorph and his or her human. The meeting went slowly at first, with many humans asking questions—for example, about the unusual physical arrangement for the meeting. They quickly learned that each individual isomorph, kneeling as part of the unbroken circle, was enabled to monitor all the communications that went on around the circle, between the other isomorphs and their humans. In that way, all the questions, ideas and concerns from any source within the circle was assimilated and processed by every isomorph, much as they were able to do at night. At that moment, or a little later, each matter could be discussed in context within each of their own one-to-one conversations.

After preliminaries, and within the next hour and a half, the isomorphs were able to convey their concerns, aims, expectations, what was in it for the humans—especially for their specific human—*and* discuss and answer every issue and question put to them. The human concerns around the circle were often redundant, so the isomorph responses to them were easily summarized—thus eliminating repetition in their replies without skimping on the details, or even short-circuiting the give and take at the individual level. Nobody could communicate with the humans better than their isomorph identicals. Any other format would require days of meeting time to accomplish a similar amount of involvement and shared understanding.

In the end there was an outcome of consensus. Even Clinton Bracket, the tough, skeptical Security Chief, found himself scratching his head and wondering how that could have happened. His many objections, criticisms and fears were quietly, but forthrightly answered—as only *his* very own Dummy knew how. There was magic in those "blueprints"—not only from the human side.

It was agreed that a group of humans and their isomorphs would travel together to seek out the *essence of Origin* and require *It* to speak directly to *its* kidnap victims—the human captives. They would demand a complete explanation for the outrage carried out by the obedient Dort accomplices of *It*. Despite the negative slant on Dorts, Doyan would accompany the troop to wherever the trail might lead in order to translate any non-human language that might have existed on Origin before the Dort diaspora—a language that *It* might still insist on using.

The answer to the meeting's title had yet another response—more concrete than anyone expected—*THE DIRECTION WE MUST GO FROM HERE* became crystal clear: *West!* The troop would go west.

Later that day, in the next gathering of the Directors, the results and details of the meeting were shared with those on the Transformation Cone—those who had no isomorph or who, for any other reason, was not in attendance for the earlier meeting on Origin. Everybody needed to be informed.

The information was broadcast across the Transformation—much to Debra Anderson's annoyance. She'd hoped for an exclusive. Nevertheless, she did summarize the meeting's essentials in a FAST News special. There she explained they would demand an *accounting* for the human kidnappings from *something*—whatever or whoever ordered the Dorts to commit that crime. She also focused her article on the DIRECTION part of the meeting's title. She pointed out that the isomorphs reminded everyone that weeks earlier two scientific expeditions were summarily terminated by the "all-knowing Directors" for supposed "lack of progress." (In her so-called *news* columns, she was not above editorial sarcasm. It kept her readers happy.)

She credited the isomorphs for the diplomatic way they returned attention to those expeditions—the one that went to the mountainous, tropical island on the equator; and the second for a deep, under-sea study on the opposite side of Origin. She noted that both expeditions were making progress at the time of their termination. Less diplomatically, Debra said the valuable projects were "autocratically halted for *trivial* reasons." Their "arbitrarily narrow mission" was to find an explanation for the unusual oppositional polarity that had, from time to time, been correlated with electronic communication interference between Origin and the Transformation. "Just as they were making progress," she kept repeating, "those short-term projects were made even more short-term: The projects were killed!"

Her article went on to reiterate some old news:

> The circum-Origin map lines followed the pointers of molecular resonance within a broad sampling of molecules across two continents, many islands and a great ocean. Those newly projected lines are not based on the planet's *magnetic* polarities. The new lines present longitudinal deviations on the globe of Origin that converge in exactly two locations. It was in those two places of intersection on the *equator*, rather than their coming together at the north and south magnetic poles, that the exploratory studies took place. The isomorphs identified the *western intersection point* of the new lines as the relevant location for their purposes and ours. That is where the search will resume.
>
> And who will lead this traveling troop of seekers? Whoever it is, human or isomorph, please, let us not call that individual *Jason*!

Group consensus did not stop the questions—especially from the Transformation Cone where their information had arrived in roundabout and summary ways. How, for example, would they find the essence of Origin—

whatever that was! How would they know they had arrived at that essence, even if they were standing on it? Who would go, by what manner of selection, based on what? Finally, bucking Debra's admonition, they asked who would be their Jason on that quest—for "explanation," "apology," "war," "peace," "self-esteem," "truth and reconciliation," "adventure," "Earth's coordinates," "absolution," "vengeance," "enlightenment," and a hundred other privately stated motives, depending on the human-isomorph pair that had reached "consensus." Yes, they all agreed that some group or groups should go west, for starters. But that would happen for hundreds of personal and separate reasons. Consensus was apparently a relative term.

SIXTY-THREE

In the next few days more suggestions and answers went back-and-forth between the human-isomorph pairs. Huddled, they spoke quietly, almost conspiratorially as reflected in their glinting side-glances when others approached.

Astra and Venus had their own days of intense conversations. Venus suggested a compelling and worthy plan that they discussed at length. But it was chancy.

"Venus, this is a risky plan. But it's fascinating and I like it!"

As they talked, they came to believe that any other plan to bring *the essence of Origin* into the open would fail. When the Directors' plan was announced, they became more convinced than ever that their own plan had the only chance for success. Venus and Astra realized that everything was up to them. "And besides," Venus said, "just think of it—if this plan doesn't kill us both and goes beyond the first stage or two, it will be an adventure! If we really do this, the hard work is ahead. But you're right, Astra; after that it will be dangerous. You may want to reconsider."

Astra patted her isomorph's cheek and said, "Don't give it another thought. We've covered all this. I'm committed."

"Then we will try!"

To gain even the first stage of their plan entailed difficult steps and, like an obstacle course, the competition and barriers to its achievement were significant. The planned tactics were circuitous. They involved persuasion, string-pulling, deception, charm, internal politics, and luck.

It was a winding and furtive path, but in the end their first goal was achieved. Astra, Zack, their two isomorphs, and Mark were cleared to go. They would carry a cargo load with them to that western equatorial island, including food, water desalinization materials, tools, several huge boxes of shuttle parts, detailed maps of Origin and the island, a first-aid kit, communications equipment and instruments, and much more. But most important for Astra and Venus on this journey was for their transport to take place on a very special vessel—one of Mark's Homing Pigeons. Mark's Orb was crucial for their plan.

The other Pigeon, with a painted blue belt around its bulb waist, would be piloted by Clinton Bracket, with Ned, Laura, and their three isomorphs as passengers. The blue-striped Orb would also carry a load of equipment—particularly the instruments for detecting the pointers of molecular resonance and determining the intersection point of the circum-Origin map lines.

The same kind of instrument, but miniaturized and more complicated, was used by Astra in her dive as the pilot of Challenger Deep. That intricate instrument was removed from the Deep and installed in the Orb that Mark Tenderloin would pilot. That installation was accomplished with the help of another skilled engineer.

Astra saw to it that Zackery Parker was the one to assist Mark with the installation of *her* device—the one that *only* she, aside from the small group of engineers who built it, was able and qualified to operate. She mentioned that to Mark to lure him into taking her along too. She also told Mark that on the way to the island she could teach him how to operate the device. That got her onto Mark's small crew. He was also impressed by Zack's engineering skills when he installed the device. That got him in. He was aware that Astra and Zack knew each other.

Mark used those reasons to get Zack on his crew when he made his pitch to the Directors for crew members. There he alluded to minor mechanical problems with his Orb and that Zack's special skills might be needed. Mark believed he was lying to the Directors about any such possible breakdown on the way to the island, but could keep a straight face knowing his Orbs often malfunctioned under water—not part of the flight plan. There would also be plenty of room for Zack because Denise Christensen declined to go with Mark or anyone else on the "scary" westward trek. She declined for herself and her beloved Chastity.

The science crew that had been on the equatorial island earlier would be deployed there again and travel there by shuttle. The shuttles would be loaded with supplies, other professionals and Managers, most of the Directors and their Origin-based support staffs. Even Doyan would be relegated to one of the shuttles. Once in range of the island, the shuttles and Orbs would maneuver to a strand of shoreline at the base of one of the island's mountains. The Directors selected the exact location from a map of the island. There the cargo of the vessels would be unloaded and the supply camp set up, along with the all-important Directors' Control Center—the DCC.

Thereafter the Orbs and shuttles were to scoot back and forth between the island and Base camp and, as needed, to the Transformation Cone; but they'd mainly carry the essential science staff to and from their duties on other parts of the island. Among their duties would be continued tracking of the lines of molecular resonance, communicating that data to the DCC where simple triangulation would locate the intersection. Along with that was a wide-ranging plan for the collection of other hard data, including measurement of gravitational anomalies, depth and density measures and much more. The first day's collection of data alone would take a week for its preliminary analysis. They would, it was confidently believed, achieve their goal, although it would take quite a while—a fact that delighted the Astra-Venus conspirators. The Directors agreed that the time and energy required was a small price for eventual freedom, satisfaction, and the golden prize—home!

As for allowing each person's isomorph to join them on the expedition, the question never arose. The isomorphs, with all their special relationships, saw to that. The isomorphs realized that the Venus-Astra conspiracy contained the only plan with the slightest shot at success for their survival—despite their plan containing a certain *irrelevant* matter they called "preliminaries."

It was a full week after the isomorphs and humans had come together in that special meeting that the westward expedition was ready to go. The Directors, now quietly nicknamed "Jasons," believed they'd thought of every contingency and that by doggedly following *their* methodical, scientific plan, they would eventually track down what the isomorphs described as the *essence of Origin*. From there the Jasons dreamed of negotiating a deal for Earth's spacetime coordinates and demanding the apology that everybody wanted. Any other motives of humans or isomorphs would be secondary, if considered at all. The only voices to prevail, aside from the Jasons', were those of Mark Tenderloin (who was an unofficial, more or less honorary Director anyway) and Astra Hughs.

Part IV
THE ISLAND

SIXTY-FOUR

The exodus from Base camp to the western equatorial island was minute compared to the original move from the Transformation to Origin; but for their purposes the Directors deemed it adequate.

The "Blue Belt" Orb piloted by Officer Bracket led the fleet of shuttles to the island destination that had been selected by the Directors. The western island came to be called, simply, "The Island."

The fuel-inefficient shuttles rose in single file like glinting baubles on a kite's tale in flight behind the Blue Belt. Mark's Homing Pigeon followed separately and far behind them by several hundred kilometers. Like the Great Cone itself, Mark's Orbs took their energy from any immense mass—in this case, the planet Origin. But the shuttles had to rely on hydrogen. To conserve on fuel, their transit to The Island was unhurried. In fact, the sole cargo on two of the shuttles was frozen hydrogen fuel.

After their arrival, the shuttles would soon be involved in many energy-consuming tasks—mainly on-island sallies to preplanned locations and other, more exploratory excursions. In the days to come there would be countless studies, soundings, measurements, and the placement of thousands of monitoring devices throughout The Island's mountains and shorelines. If the *essence of Origin* was indeed located here, as the isomorphs seemed to believe, then no matter how deep, scattered or centralized within or below The Island's boundaries, *It* would be found—the Directors were sure of that. They thought of it as an *essence*-capture—not a physical one, but a network, or net, from which they could begin to bring up or extract—or ever entice—direct communication with whatever intelligence that *essence* might be or have. And from there, the required negotiations would follow. That was their plan.

Venus described it to Astra as an ignorant and sloppy plan. At least that was Astra's translation of Venus's more diplomatically stated judgment. Astra did prefer their own plan, but in flashes of anxiety she feared it might not be that much better than the Directors'. The Directors' plan, at least, did not have the added disadvantage of being extremely dangerous—especially for Astra; but as she had cavalierly told Venus, she was "committed."

Still, Astra had to ask what the big flaw in the administrators' plan was. Venus was surprised she had to remind her of that. "Don't you remember? The main tool they have is their ability to triangulate a location from the pointers of molecular resonance and—except for your *miniature* device with its combination of blocking and calibrating features—theirs can only find that directionality during electronic blackouts. That's how it was under the hill, and that's how it is now. Sure, they'll be measuring a lot of other things, irrelevant things, but electronic blackouts are rare these days on Origin. If the *essence of Origin* wants to be found, that's one thing. All *It* has to do is create an electronic communications blackout. Otherwise they'll never find *It*. The Directors know about the need for those blackouts, but can't create them the way you can around the miniature. The team that reinvented the device is a proud bunch. They taught its use to you alone. If the Directors don't bother to recognize their skills and accomplishments, then fine. Those engineers require very little. Just asking them about their device and its innovative changes would be enough recognition for them. All the Directors would have to do is ask and the technology would be on their doorstep in a minute. It's a silly standoff—don't ask, don't tell."

Astra and Zack were happy to be assigned to Mark's Homing Pigeon. They were especially eager to learn the basics of piloting the Orb, and Mark Tenderloin became their generous teacher. Before leaving, Astra made sure to include an extra month of food and water desalinization supplies for the *preliminaries* that she and Venus agreed on and that the *essence of Origin* had apparently acceded to.

On departure to The Island, Mark taught Astra, Zack, and both their isomorphs, to use the visible, frequently used controls to take off and land on flat surfaces—even with their full load of cargo. Astra and Zack found and understood the main controls with little help—they were intuitively simple and in the open. More instruments and devices were tucked away behind a dozen large and small panels. Those too appeared simple, with clearly labeled functions.

The main controls and the important indicators, like the altimeter—and dozens of other gauges, warning lights and the like—were always visible and available. According to Mark, the many covered controls, instruments and unique modules were kept out of sight behind the panels to "reduce the clutter." Mark admitted that each of those independent units, visible or behind panels, operated out of a deep substratum of computer chips; but admitted he disliked the look and feel of computers themselves. He preferred dials, buttons, pressure pads, levers, switches and cranks—even though numerous specialized chips were responsible for making the gadgets do their work. He liked the *feel* of gadgets—not keyboards, but despite that he could program the daylights out of a computer *if he had to*. In order to build the special chips for the Homing Pigeons' gadgets, he had to.

For most of the Orbs' linkage functions, he made a primary computer. It monitored and integrated the modules, sensors and units from behind the scenes. Mark could physically pull out the computer—yes, from behind a panel—along with varied screen-display sizes. On its monitors he could watch the Orb's rear view without engaging the "caboose" function—a maneuver he said he'd show them later; he could cyber-converse "face-to-face" with almost anyone—but preferred simple radio contacts; he could bring up telescopic views of anything in line of vision; the radar was always operative; and, if necessary, he could do e-mail and texting—tasks he hated. He preferred hands-on, primitive approaches.

Mark skirted the continent's coastline on its path to The Island. This route carried them across hundreds of kilometers of Origin's crystalline terrain. They would soon enough begin to sense the continent veering away as they came upon the uninterrupted vastness of the great ocean. Before reaching their destination, they would still be facing thousands more kilometers of its glittering expanse.

For this trip, Mark's teaching and guidance was focused on his four students—Astra, Venus, Zack and his isomorph, Gegeneis. (The name, Zack explained, was pronounced *gay'geenays* and that it referred to the "Earth born" Giants from ancient Greek mythology. The Giants supposedly sprang full grown from the Earth where, following an unfortunate encounter, the blood of Uranus's castrated genitals had struck the ground. Zack enjoyed that version of the myth, and discerned parallels to how isomorphs were created on *their* "Earth," Origin, from blood on the ground.)

Mark's students took turns at the controls to learn almost every intricacy and maneuver the Pigeon was capable of, including its homing function, short-flight-hover, hop mode and several other capabilities they never imagined.

They learned all this on their way to the final coastline of the continent. Zack, who was very tired from working on the Homing Pigeon late into the previous night and through the day just before takeoff, was still surprisingly alert and interested in what they were learning. He suggested they drop back even farther behind the Blue Belt and its convoy for more practice. Mark immediately agreed saying, "Why not! We can catch up with Clint and the shuttles any time."

They continued to maneuver over the continent and in and out of its many formations, hills, mountains, valleys, and across its lakes and flatlands. When they reached the ocean, the opportunities for adventurous zooming about would be gone.

The lessons over the continent went on for several hours and included the frolicking, thrill-seeking lessons Zack wanted to master, but Mark included many practical landing exercises on a variety of difficult types of terrain. He relished this chance to show off the features of his favorite invention to admiring students. They learned many things he'd never shown Doyan and about which Clinton Bracket was just as unaware.

Mark explained again that the Orb could swivel the pilot, passengers and cargo into reverse without changing course. After setting the Homing Pigeon on automatic pilot, he demonstrated it—the final function he intended to show them. He opened a small panel labeled "caboose," pressed a round pad beneath it and the entire lower interior of the Orb swiveled 180 degrees to the rear, leaving the cockpit behind them. Instead of seeing where they were going, they were watching where they had been, as if in the caboose of a flying freight train.

For some reason everyone, except Astra, laughed at this in their own way. Zack and Mark laughed loudly, and the isomorphs' eyes made rapid moves. They appeared to be taking a whimsical delight in the operation of this seemingly unnecessary capability—unless the backward ride was intended to be a carnival-like amusement.

As everyone else was admiring the Orb's trailing vista, Astra glanced around the inside of the cabin. Directly above, she spotted what she had been looking for from the moment they boarded the Orb. She saw the outline of a large panel that otherwise blended into the curvature of the ceiling. Like the other panels in the main cockpit, this one also had a label, but part of the label was obscured by a large sticker that read: "Do Not Open—Out of Order." The sticker did not, however, obscure some of the panel's first and last letters. First, "UND . . ." and last, ". . . OLS." Not a great set of clues, but Astra guessed, more out of wishful thinking than from her mental check on the size and spacing of the covered letters, that it could spell "UNDERWATER CONTROLS."

If those were indeed the controls for underwater maneuvering, she needed to learn them. Zack told her that when he was helping Mark make the new installations, the large panel in back of the Orb was off limits, that it was dangerous, that its controls were unreliable and, in any case, would never be needed on Origin. Astra knew the Transformation's only submarine had been smashed in the flood and that the shuttles had no underwater capabilities. So, an Orb was crucial to hers and Venus's plan and, they believed, the only way to directly access and meet, if it even existed, the *essence of Origin*. Deep within the mountains of Origin, was water. Shortly before the flood, Laura Shane discovered that while throwing up into a collapsing mountain. The isomorphs agreed with the human scientists' estimate of where the *essence* could be found—either on or below The Island's mountains. The isomorphs bet on the *below* part of that estimate.

Astra knew Mark would be touchy about any direct questions about a panel that was "off limits," so, for starters, she offhandedly asked a question: "Why do you have this caboose function? It doesn't seem necessary."

Mark stammered nervously, and obtusely asked, "What do you mean?"

Astra hoped, given the size of the overhead panel, that the real purpose of the caboose area was for guiding the Orb's underwater transport. So, still being casual, she asked, "What's it for?"

Mark became more tense and blurted, "Oh I don't know. It just seemed like a fun thing to include. Sometimes it's tiresome just looking out from the front cockpit, hehehe!"

"But you can do that from the cockpit using a computer screen."

Now, almost agitated, he said, "It's not the same!" He then added, as though the comparison made sense, "It would be like taking a bath in your underwear."

From behind her mask, Astra raised what was left of an eyebrow. She noted Mark's unconscious reference to water, but decided to change the subject to relieve Mark's tension. She did not want to set up any communication barriers—certainly not this early, with hundreds of kilometers left to go. She felt sure—fervently hoped—she could get back to it later, in another way.

With a changed and cheerful tone, Astra chirped, "Of course it's not the same! The view is phenomenal from this angle, with Origin's late afternoon star *behind* us, even as we're still moving west. No computer monitor could touch this—in or out of its underwear. Just look at how Nimbus sparkles off the ocean and how the shining, frothing breakers outline the continent's coastline."

Mark nodded warily, but added, "And how those reflections not only pervade the shoreline, but the topography farther in."

"Yes, it even seems to penetrate into the canyons between the mountains. On Earth at this time of day we'd only see dark shadows in those canyons."

Mark agreed, picking up the mood—with evident and growing relief at the change of subject. "It's amazing," he said, "how Origin's surface handles photons from this angle. Where it would be dark on any normal planet, here the local star's light is conducted into the deepest valleys where the light dances and gleams like the dwindling embers of a billion campfires."

Everyone, except Zack, chimed in to describe the changing illusions that appeared in the Orb's wake as they watched from its caboose. The observations and discussion went on until the changing coastline receded to their left, and the ocean gradually took over the entire view. Then there was silence. A long silence.

Zack had fallen asleep and started a quiet, catlike purr. Between purrs he jerked and whimpered. Mark and Astra started to laugh at the sounds, but quickly became silent remembering that Zack was already tired, even before their flight began. He was overdue for a good nap, but this one looked more restive than restful.

They remained silent. The auto-pilot continued to move them westward at Mach 2, an easy pace for Mark's Homing Pigeon at a height of sixty thousand meters. When their flight began, Nimbus was already nearing the end of its long-distance race to set in the west, but with Mark's Orb at its own marathon pace Nimbus was losing. The Homing Pigeon was gaining on it and the shuttle fleet. Before wheeling the interior to the caboose mode, Mark had set the controls for their arrival at The Island destination just behind the Blue Belt's shuttle parade. During their silence, the ocean receded into a glittering, distant expanse. "Looks like a reclining woman in a flashy gown," Mark said quietly. Astra only nodded.

Still, as time passed, the scene became monotonous. Astra kept trying to think how to get Mark to talk about the underwater controls and why they were out of order—supposedly. Oh, she'd heard there had been some underwater problems with the Orbs on Earth, but surely he'd made those repairs by now. If not, what were the odds for another failure? Would Mark know the answer to that one?

Another hour of silence passed before Mark, very quietly, began his own inquiry and request. "Astra," he said, "Zack is a remarkable engineer. When he helped me install the miniature device for determining pointers of molecular resonance I was amazed at his craftsmanship and ingenuity. That miniature is the one you used on Challenger Deep. We lifted the device from there—after a lot of paper work to get permission; otherwise I would have had to steal it. It's that valuable. I know you're its expert. Zack told me it has features the large ones lack. Would you mind teaching me how to use it?"

Astra saw this as an opening for a trade-off of lessons—to learn the underwater controls. But she realized the trade from *Mark's* side had already been earned. She could plunge right in for the trade anyway, but thought she should work on better timing. He still might get upset again. She would stay alert for a more opportune opening. If none came as time ran out and they neared The Island, she could still plunge in and ask.

"Of course I'll teach you," she said as enthusiastically as she could, but unintentionally in a loud voice that startled Zack into frightened and wide-eyed, but disoriented, consciousness.

As he frantically looked around for his glasses he did not hear Astra's apology. He was having a claustrophobia attack. Only Gegeneis was able to settle him down and help him reorient to where he was; but that did not clear his anxiety. Gegeneis helped him put on his glasses. Zack's head was still full of worries, but now that he could see, the worries became more realistic.

Mark was apologetic and embarrassed. "I forgot you feared closed-in places. Is there *anything* I can do to help you—short of throwing out all this cargo, hehe?"

Looking wild-eyed through his thick glasses, Zack flashed a glance at the ocean. "What if something goes wrong?—we lose power and have to land—or crash!—on water for Christ's sake!—we'll sink and drown! If you can help with that, Mark, then do it!—Get us to land!—Please!—Now!" Then Zack went silent, glancing left and right, up and down, but not at the ocean. Through his glasses, his wild eyes were smeary, covering the large disks from frame to frame. From certain angles, as his head and eyes kept moving, only his black pupils filled the lenses—from rim to rim. He not only looked scared, he looked scary.

Mark pulled Gegeneis aside for a brief, muffled conversation. Gegeneis nodded his understanding and returned to Zack. He spoke to him as only a deep identical could. Quietly, almost hypnotically, he told Zack to close his eyes and relax deeply—something Zack had already learned from desensitization training. Gegeneis explained to Zack that the Orb was capable of landing safely on water. He was told that Mark would reverse the caboose so they could see forward again—a more natural view. Then, if they landed on water they would be quite safe. When Zack looked completely relaxed, Gegeneis gave Mark a nod, and the interior turned 180 degrees, back to the front of the Orb.

Astra and Venus looked on with great interest at Mark's piloting moves—moves that gently lowered the Orb to within a few meters of the ocean wave tops. Mark slowed the Orb to a stop so skillfully that Zack's threshold for noticing any change was undisturbed, and the cabin pressure never altered. Then, noticing Astra's—and Venus's—intense observation of his maneuvers, he said, very quietly, "Now, pay close attention to this." He lowered the Orb into the low point between two waves and, at the same time, turned a small lever under one of the panels—one that Astra had not noticed before. It pointed to a label: "Maintain Level."

It did just that. The waves were several times the height of the Orb, but the Orb did not rise and fall like a floating ship. It calmly maintained its exact position as each wave washed over it. Still speaking quietly, but smiling broadly, Mark said, "I learned to do this in my youth as a crazed snorkeler. I built the same little trick into my Homing Pigeons. Being sea sick is no fun. Any good diver can tell you it's safer to go through a wave than to ride it. Hehe!"

"Hehehe!" This time it was someone else's silly laugh. Zack's eyes were open again. He'd overheard the quiet talk and had already tolerated several wave immersions before he allowed himself to laugh. Everyone's relief was enormous.

"Now, can we take off again?" Mark asked Zack.

"Sure," Zack said. "I'm fine now. I think I was dreaming earlier. It took a while for me to come back. Sorry."

Within moments the Orb was again climbing to its previous altitude and back on track. This time it accelerated to Mach 3 to make up for lost time. Mark concentrated on the maneuvers to accomplish that; but part of him was distracted by certain movements he was vaguely aware of just before they began to lift away from the last wave.

He did not, of course, realize that his little exercise in the water had opened the door for Astra to ask her questions. Unfortunately, time and Astra's patience were running out. Before the Orb's rapid ascent from the ocean's waves, she had impatiently opened the instrument panel where her miniature molecular resonance detector controls were located and made a few maneuvers and adjustments of her own—the movements that Mark had imperfectly glimpsed out the corner of his eye.

SIXTY-FIVE

"Oh Mark, that was so-o-o mar-r-r-rvelous!" Astra wheedled. "How you could land in the very depths of the those monstrous ocean waves, and then keep the Homing Pigeon stationary, as though anchored, letting the swells move over us with no more effect than passing clouds seems, well, almost impossible! This craft is the greatest invention ever!"

"Thank you. I enjoy that little feature myself."

"And we're going Mach 3. Incredible. Can this do Mach 4?"

"A lot more. That's nothing. Why?"

"*Why*? Oh dear! Now you've trapped me in my student mode, as you have all day. Zack's request to slow down to learn more maneuvers over the mountains helped improve our skills—a lot. Some day those skills may be valuable if, say, another pilot or co-pilot is needed on one of your Homing Pigeons—to perform a rescue or something."

"Yeah. That might come in handy some day," Mark agreed, smiling. He knew he was being cajoled, but was lapping it up anyway.

Astra would have smiled and blinked provocatively into Mark's eyes to make the next, obvious request; but she did not have what she needed, including the right facial muscles for the performance. Instead, she did the next best thing—the best thing, in fact. She nudged Venus. She was completely tuned in.

Venus moved her innocent, majestic body close to the front control panels and looked naively at them—with Mark watching from beside her. It was only an incidental fact that she was in position to display the stunning nakedness of her profile as she leaned over the panels. Then, turning her head to look at Mark, she asked, "Are rescues really all that important to humans?"

Mark was surprised that Venus asked the question. She was usually very quiet, but now her voice was an arousing feminine purr. At the same time he could not help noticing, even as she was looking at him, the way she tentatively fingered the "Maintain Level" panel. That, by itself, was provocative—along with everything else. Even more stirring was the way she continued to look directly at him—with her deeply feline, calm and impersonal eyes—like a cat, quietly considering a squirming prey beneath her paw. In that moment he sensed her feminine power so intensely that he had to turn away. Was it his libido, or was she touching on, or rousing in him, something earlier—his childlike receptivity? Or was it the helpless and happy vulnerability of not being in control? He found it intriguing, but confusing.

"Yes. Of course rescues are important," Mark said. He was going to elaborate, but was too shaken at that moment to say more. In fact, he was becoming a little frightened and had to think about why. Part of the answer did come to him—the provocative feminine power he felt had nothing to do with sex, sensuality or even her gender. It was the remembrance of an ancient dread that he felt—the kind he felt as a small child in the awesome presence of his parents who were about to have him do something he wished not to do, or to not do something he wished to. They were demanding, imposing and formidable; but, in fairness, were more often pleasant, forbearing, and loving—the perfect mix for raising a child. But he did not need that in his life. Certainly not now. And yet . . .

Then, pointing unambiguously to the panel she had just been trifling with, Venus said, "I'll bet this feature might help in a water rescue, if that were ever necessary. . . . Wouldn't it, Mark?"

"What? Sorry. I was thinking about something. What did you say?"

Venus repeated what she had said.

Mark frowned thoughtfully. "Okay ladies. I know what you're getting at, and the answer is *no*. We're on schedule to catch up with the shuttle convoy when they approach The Island. And I've *already* shown you how that panel works. I had you pay close attention to that and the maneuvers that went with it. I noticed you two were all eyes on what I was doing anyway. You can't expect to know everything about the Homing Pigeon. You saw how it worked and how to work it. That should be enough!"

"Enough?" Astra said. "But seeing it done isn't like doing it. Real practice, like the landing lessons over the continent—that's what we need."

"Sorry. We're on schedule and we're not going to be late."

"We wouldn't be late. Didn't you say that Mach 4 is nothing for this Pigeon? We could catch up."

"You saw what I did for the water landing. You are both very bright. That's all you get. We can't keep doing that. I have my reasons. After all, this isn't a Homing Duck. It's just a Pigeon. Hehe!"

Astra said, "Seeing is not the same as doing, right Venus?"

"Right," Venus agreed. "If you only *see* an action it's like learning from a book; but it isn't the hands-on experience needed for minimum competence in, say, saving lives at sea. Just seeing something without the direct experience is like taking a bath in your—"

"Never mind! I get it. You win. Mach 4, or whatever, later—if we have to." Mark was feeling like a little child again—and he was *smiling* to himself. He knew all along that he was going to lose and, under the circumstances, was swept away by the awesome delight at how he allowed it to happen. He felt empowered!

The controls were simple enough, but errors were still possible. Within the hour, Mark's four students were trained and versed in the skills necessary to perform slow or sudden drops from great heights, to then hover motionless above the waves, and finally to drop between them for the "Maintain Level" control to take over. As usual, the controls and maneuvers for those exercises were mainly, but not entirely, transparent and intuitive; thus the ease of learning. But in this case Mark's supervision was essential. Without his close direction any number of serious, even fatal errors were possible. After several near mishaps, his students learned to avoid those hidden dangers—the main one for Astra was the temptation to drop too far below the waves before engaging the "Maintain Level" control. Mark explained that too much water pressure could damage the Homing Pigeon to the point it could no longer fly, or even surface unaided from the water.

Astra was quick to ask questions about the problem. The answers were not comforting. Mark's students learned that any depth below twenty to forty meters could cause a propulsion breakdown. Below forty meters the problem became increasingly probable and more serious. Mark did not know why, and never had time to figure it out before leaving Earth on his Mini-Cone for the then unknown destination in the Milky Way.

"But I heard you had some very successful underwater trials with your Pigeons," Astra said.

"Yes," Mark replied, "but those studies of exploration were in shallow, underwater caves. When I went deeper, I started losing Orbs. I had a devil of a time retrieving them."

"How *did* you get them back?"

"With other exploration Orbs. They don't *always* break down under that much water pressure, at least not right away, but they do have problems more often at greater depths."

"Had those famous exploration Pigeons of yours been working perfectly at the time, could I have used one of them for my Deep dive into that eastern trench?"

"No. My Pigeons are strong, but would be crushed long before reaching that kind of pressure. I've estimated they would be flattened at a depth anywhere from half of a kilometer to a kilometer; but I never tested for such an unlikely excursion."

Astra felt the time had come to spring her trap with an *innocent* comment. "To get around in those caves—to retrieve the ones that went too deep for their own good—the rescuing Pigeons must have had some rather serious underwater *maneuverability*."

Astra's comment made Mark uncomfortable. He wasn't sure why. Yet the rhythm and sequence of the questions and comments seemed, at one lever, perfectly reasonable and so, although he was hesitant, he answered. "Yes . . . when in working order they responded . . . under water . . . very well. . . . As well as they do in the atmosphere . . . or outer space." Then, more assertively, almost in anger, he asked, "What about it?"

"Nothing. It's just that the 'Maintain Level' and the related piloting can keep the Pigeon *in place* between waves, or *take it vertically* deeper, but I still don't get *how* all that underwater maneuverability is accomplished. I'm sure the Orbs that rescued the downed ones didn't just go up and down. What happened to forward, left and right, backwards and all the angles between?"

Mark suddenly wanted to slap his forehead—hard! He realized he'd been stepping down a path he didn't want to be on, but still had no idea of being led there. To get off that path he would have to tread circumspectly lest he step into something worse. He decided on a simple, rather intuitive solution to handle his tension without revealing anything more about the underwater controls. As in his childhood, he simply lied through his teeth—but, like then, it was at a price. He no longer felt empowered—and he was not smiling.

Moving along at Mach 4, they were due to catch up with the convoy well before it reached The Island.

Astra continued questioning Mark about his Pigeons' underwater maneuverability problems. Her clever verbal jockeying met with evasions and outright lies, including a really big one. It had to do with "recently dismantling" all the underwater controls except the "Maintain Level" function. That lie was mixed with a truth—that he could not live with himself if any human was in one of the Pigeons when it had an underwater breakdown. He said he dismantled those controls to preserve human life and his own peace of mind.

"Those Homing Pigeons were stolen from me once already, by the Dorts, and I wouldn't put it past some humans. Even otherwise approved Pigeon pilots might try some of the controls they weren't trained to use and end up experimenting under water . . . er, if those simple controls still existed. If curious pilots thought such controls existed they would give it a try. They don't exist. I destroyed them. If the controls did exist, the chances would be high for losing all power under the water and descending like a fisherman's lead sinker. I'm *glad* I destroyed those controls."

At this point Mark went silent. He did not announce it, but decided he would not respond to another question. To his surprise, there *were* no more questions. Astra needed no more answers. The four students began talking quietly about other matters—so quietly that, to Mark, it felt like silence. He was gradually able to relax again. He put on his earphones and turned a switch. The music was even more soothing than the quiet.

The students were enjoying their inconsequential conversation—smiling, joking, laughing and making rapid eye movements.

In the midst of this relaxed and friendly chatter, Astra was smiling for another reason. Mark was a poor liar. From things she had learned earlier that day and between the lines of Mark's evasions and lies, she came to believe a number of useful things. She knew they were just *probabilities*, but still helpful.

First, she became convinced that the underwater controls *were* those in the back, under the large panel, and that they were still functional. If Mark had only *once* said he'd destroyed the controls, she might have believed him, but, one way or another, he kept saying it—too many times to be true. Probably. On a scale from one to five, she gave that a probability of *four*.

Second, even if the underwater propulsion failed, resulting in the Orb's dropping through the water like a sinker, there was still the "Maintain Level" function, and the Orb could probably be induced into a vertical rise. She gave that a score of *two*.

Third, he made no mention of any life-support functions failing when other things broke down, so that was probably nothing to worry about—for a score of *three*.

Fourth, no significant problems at depths above twenty meters, and probably even down to forty meters, and maybe a lot deeper—a certain percentage of the time. She wished she knew that percentage, but believed it was well above zero, and worth a score of *three*.

Fifth, one statement of Mark's really got her attention: ". . . *if those simple controls still existed. . . .*" For Astra, the magic word was "simple." She figured the controls in the back of the Orb must be easy and intuitive, like most of the other controls. He was clearly *not* going to teach those controls to anybody. Simplicity of underwater controls: *four and a half*.

On the other hand, sixth, *simple* or not, the "Underwater Controls" panel was a good meter in width, and almost as high—much larger than any panel in the main cockpit, so it could contain even more panels beneath the big one. But those hidden controls would very likely be "simple." The score for *multiple simple controls* got a *three*.

Seventh, since the pull-down panel was in caboose, the underwater controls were convenient to the back window, so the Orb would propel *backwards*, like a crayfish in underwater maneuvers. *Backwards* got a *four*.

Finally, the rear panel probably duplicated many controls in the front and the caboose would become the new *front*, so why not have identical controls? For *some* identical controls: another *four*.

The talking became hushed. Zack and Gegeneis were talking privately. Venus and Astra began their own quiet conversation. Both conversations were accompanied by muffled music emanating from Mark's earphones. He was leaning back with eyes closed; wrists on his chest, and his touching fingers pointed upward, in close depiction of an Ogee arch. His whole body was gently moving in time to the music.

Astra listed for Venus her thoughts on the eight probabilities she had been thinking about regarding the Orbs underwater mobility—and the safety of the Orb they planned to "borrow." Venus pretended she was not impressed and said, "If that is all we have going for us, I think we're sunk," and then moved her eyes very rapidly.

Astra shook her head in disgust. "Very funny," she said, "but what do you really think of our chances—to *not* sink?"

"Sorry about the levity."

"You'll never make a comedian—none of you will."

"Okay, Astra. From what you've said and what we've seen and learned together, I believe our chances are at least worth the effort. We have no choice—even if the odds are only one percent in our favor. Survival is at steak—for isomorphs, humans, Dorts, even the *essence of Origin* itself. That's what you and I believe and what all isomorphs believe."

"Does the *essence of Origin* believe that? Do the Dorts believe that?"

"I believe I can speak for Doyan. I'm sure he does, so the other Dorts would also. And the *essence of Origin* does too. As for our chances? Everything hinges on our success. Our chances may not be high, but having even one ticket in a lottery is infinitely better than none. But there is more, Astra. Much more—isn't there, Astra?"

"More? More what? What would that be? More lottery tickets?"

"I hope so, but I really don't know. I'm still patiently waiting."

"Waiting? For what?"

"I thought it was obvious. We both know there is more, but I don't know what that is. I'm waiting for *you*, Astra, to tell *me*."

SIXTY-SIX

Astra did not pretend to be surprised that Venus was on to her. *She must have caught me working my mini-molecular resonance panel and thought I was going to hold out on her.*

Venus had supplied Astra with many a stream of information and even communication, of a sort, with the *essence of Origin*. It was Astra's turn to give back. She smiled knowing that *she* could now impress Venus. *Venus thinks I only have this sliver of data. Like everyone else, she must think I spent all those days in that cramped Challenger Deep for nothing and came back empty handed? Huh! They have no idea. She has no idea!*

"You are very sharp, Venus. I didn't think you noticed."

"Were you going to keep it from me?"

"Of course not, but I thought I'd better wait 'till I had your ideas and evaluation before contaminating your impressions with anything new."

"Will it make a difference, good or bad?"

"Yes. I think for the good."

"Tell me."

"You saw me use my miniature device when Mark was too busy piloting to notice. I had to use it while we were still under water. I waited till the last possible moment when Mark was preoccupied. We were still hundreds of kilometers from The Island—but I thought it should work anyway."

"Why should it—at that distance?"

"Because it worked perfectly through thousands of kilometers of rock when I was in Challenger Deep."

"I'll take your word for that; but why do you say it penetrated kilometers of *rock*? Isn't this a crystal planet?"

"On its *surface* it is, dating from when the Dorts made it so—over the eons that they worked on it. But even on Origin gravity still works. The deepest crystal layers had compressed and were mostly rock. Even deeper it is molten. Not that far down in the trench its walls were all rock and metal. The *crystalline* surface is only skin deep."

"Hmm. I want to know more about that, but for now I'll settle for what you found out minutes ago when you activated your miniature device."

"It's complicated, but these details will fascinate you. *First of all—*"

"Astra, would you please skip directly to *last of all*. What's the bottom line?"

"The bottom line?"

"Yes. You know. The gist, the nitty-gritty."

"Jeez, Venus. You used to speak with such dignified formality. Now—"

"Yes, yes. Now I know your lingo, slang, and way of talking. What did you find out?"

Astra's eyes shifted left and right several times before looking Venus straight in her eyes. Then, leaning forward, she said, "I found *It*."

"What do you mean, you found it?"

"Open your ears to the nuances. I pinpointed the exact location of the *essence of Origin*."

Venus was quick to point out that the previous studies, by the group that had gone before to The Island, had done that many times and the location kept changing. "In other words, the location of the *essence* is unstable. *It* will have to come to us. We won't be able to find *It*—except insofar as *It* is somewhere beneath The Island."

"I'm sorry to have to burst your bubble, but you've got it backwards."

"*Burst my bubble*? You mean I have an inflated idea that is inaccurate?"

"Something like that."

"Please clarify."

"Until or unless we can meet or otherwise encounter the *essence of Origin* as we predict, or at least hope, then all my assumptions are only that. In the trench I did a lot of work out of Challenger Deep—by no means all of it using molecular resonance directional and distance determinations. But I set a one minute time interval for the miniature instrument to automatically take those measurements."

Venus said, "I remember that at that time the science team on The Island pinpointed thirty-six of those intersection points and put them on a map."

"That's right, of course. We've all seen that map with each location specified by longitude and latitude."

"But the Island data must be incomplete. Both studies were closed down early."

"That's right, Venus. But after the Directors closed down both of our studies—on The Island and in the trench—I compiled my data from the automatic measurements and made a map similar to the thirty-six Island locations. Nobody's seen it yet. You'll be the first."

"Any overlap between the two studies?" Venus asked.

"My studies found over four-thousand locations, including those overlapping the thirty-six Island team finds. Not a bad reliability check for the other four thousand locations! Not bad for precision measurements made from the other side of a planet. Later on I'll—"

"Hold on, Astra. You're only proving my point. The location of the *essence* is unstable."

"I'm getting to that."

"You said that *It* was in just one location."

"True, give or take a few hundred meters."

"You're hedging. What does *give or take* mean? That your calibrations were that far off, or that *It* moved around that much?"

"The latter. *It* doesn't stray far. Kind of a homebody, I'd guess."

"How many of the thirty-six positions found by the Island science team were in that same *give or take* location?"

"None."

"Of the four thousand or so Island coordinates you found, how many were in that *give or take* area?"

"About three thousand."

Venus's eyes began their rapid movements.

"I'm not kidding."

The eye movements stopped. "Then I am confused. Why wouldn't at least one of the thirty-six Island team's coordinates have been in that *give or take* area?"

"Think about it, Venus, and you tell me."

"Hmm. Okay then. For starters I'll reject the idea of *chance*. The chance they would have missed it is unlikely unless *your* coordinates were finding something else—something that their molecular resonance devices could not detect. That has to be it! Your device picked up the thirty-six positions among those thousand positions—not counting the three thousand in the *give or take* area. There had to be a difference between the two measurement types. What was the difference?"

"There! You see! You didn't need me to tell you. You are correct. Mark was right. You are very bright!"

"Don't be a sarcastic smart ass. What was the difference?"

"Do I call you names? Think about it some more," Astra said.

"Okay, if you insist. Let's see, we know about the quantitative difference, in a sense, but the other difference? Was there a qualitative difference or an energy difference? But, hmm. Your data doesn't get into quality, does it? Of course not. So it has to be an energy difference. Right?"

"Very good. Correct!"

"Tell me more about that—the energy difference."

"Each example of signal strength from the *give or take* area *exceeded* the thirty-six location instances a hundred times over."

"How could that be?" Rapid eye movements. "Does the *essence of Origin* have little ones running around?"

"No. Not that I know of. Unless you include yourself. The powerful signals are simply *way beyond the capacity* of the large molecular resonance devices they were using. That's why they missed every one of them, along with the weaker signals."

"I thought you just implied they could pick up the weaker of the two signals."

"Yes they can, of the two sets of signals we talked about, but not the *even weaker* signals from a third set."

"Let me get this straight. There are three sets of signals differentiated by their energy, and *their* instruments can only detect the second most powerful, but not the most powerful, and not the weakest."

"Correct—so far."

"So far? How then would you amend my last statement?"

"Well, Venus, from what I told you, you are correct. But there are a couple additional things that will interest you. A couple things I neglected to mention."

"A couple things? How many is that?"

"Just two, dear!"

"Then please, mention away!"

"The first one I can't prove right now, but I believe all thirty-six of the positions they found were in underwater locations."

"That's not new. When we looked at their map and connected the dots we assumed there were channels under The Island's mountains that *It* was following."

"Yes, but we weren't sure those were water channels. We just hoped they were. We could still be wrong about that. If so, then our whole plan is flawed. But as I think about my collected data, I now have other reasons for believing they are underwater channels—channels that lead to the *give or take* zone."

"Good. I'll accept that for now, but what was the second thing you didn't tell me?"

"That there are *dozens* of weaker sets of signals, each weaker than the one above it. In fact, exponentially weaker than the one just above it."

"And exponentially stronger than the one below it?"

"Right."

"So, the four thousand signals you mentioned only covered the two strongest signals. How many more signals did you pick up? And, hmm. Were they all in The Island?"

"I set the miniature molecular device to make measurements every minute, as I told you. Every time it activated, it picked up all the strongest signals and many of the weaker ones. And you're right, they weren't all in The Island. All the *strong* signals were there, but most of the weak signals came from *all over Origin*."

Astra noticed Venus's eyelids fluttering rapidly. This was a behavior that Astra had never seen before. It was usually eye movements, not lid movements.

"What's wrong, Venus?"

"I'm experiencing something strange. It's all mixed up. I believe you would call it amazement. Maybe anxiety. I'm trying to calculate how many of the weaker signal locations were found, and I can't. How many were there?"

"Well, a lot. The miniature molecular resonance device summarized it all by locations and levels of power. When I got back to my computer in Stan's Astrophysics lab, I put it all on a series of maps. I packed them away and will show them to you later."

"You mapped *all* the signals?"

"Not even a fraction of them. Only the ones that showed up at those one minute intervals, and even that data is condensed and summarized by color codes on the maps."

"That's mildly interesting about the weaker signals, but so what? Why should we care about them?"

"Because they are just as important as the strongest ones. Without them the *essence of Origin* would be a hopeless Alzheimer's case."

"I don't understand."

"It's like this," Astra said. "All the signals, weak or strong, have at least a two-way directionality. Except for the strongest ones, they get activated from above and distribute to the weaker energy levels, and so on. Eventually, in less than seconds, the signals reverse—changed by other inputs before that reversal—and the signals then pass from the weaker to the stronger, and laterally within the same level. In the end, all of them miraculously end up back in the *give or take* zone. That's all quantitative, as energy, but, I believe, it changes everything qualitatively—from one end of that energy hierarchy chain to the other and back again."

"How do you know that? Your instruments can't collect qualitative data."

"You're right. It's interpretation. I just believe that it is so."

"Why?"

"Because, dear Venus, I know *you*."

* * *

Venus's eyelids began to flutter even more than before, then stopped in the closed position.

"What is it this time, Venus?"

"Is that where my nightscape dreams come from? From the very weakest of signals?"

"Based on the time and map locations of the weak signals, I'd say yes. But," Astra quickly added, in order to prevent further eyelid fluttering, "that does not degrade their value in any way, or their meaning or their accuracy. They still provide direct experiences for you when you are tuned in for sending and receiving those nightscape signals. I hope so anyway. Otherwise we couldn't depend on the promise the *essence of Origin* sent to us—at our mutual request."

Venus opened her eyes. "I wouldn't call it a promise, Astra. It was more like a *maybe*."

"Anyway, the nightscape signals you receive are still valid. You know that from your own experience. Your connection is still direct enough. Even with those weak signals, you are, for yourself, their perfect amplifier. The weak signal maps summarize their locations, distribution, activity, and concentrations by time of day. They were amazingly numerous at night in and around Mark's Base, when it was still under the hill. Yes indeed—there were *a lot* of those signals."

"I told you I had a direct connection to *my source*, but I didn't know it was through such *weak* energy sources—the very weakest. It's humiliating!" Venus looked dejected.

From that look, Astra felt obliged to continue her explanation. "The weak sources," she said, "are just as connected to the whole as the strong ones, and can sometimes be even more important."

"Yeah, right!" Venus said skeptically.

"Well, take gravity for instance. It's the weakest force in nature, but where would we be without it?"

Venus seemed to perk up a bit.

"I don't know how yours works," Astra continued, "or even where it's located, but functioning human brains—the seat of each human's awareness and consciousness—is made up of nothing more than a lot of small, individual, energy connections, any *one* of which doesn't amount to much, but taken together, or in system batches, they make up who we are—to ourselves and others. And at another level, in that seat of awareness, how we see ourselves connected to the universe. Every system that is complex enough in its energy structure has wholeness discrete from its parts."

"That's an old cliché."

Astra ignored the comment and continued. "If the energy system is complex enough—even a weak energy system—then I believe it is, at some level, self-and-other-aware, and at higher levels, is conscious."

"Sounds anthropomorphic to me," Venus said. "How about an example or two of such a complex energy system. Wouldn't such awareness or consciousness be qualitatively different from one kind of complex system to another?"

"Of course, but there would also be similarities. You have knowledge of Earth's animals, like fish, whales, ants, birds and so on. I'm sure they each see the world differently. Even two humans see the world differently, but their perceptions are closer to each other than between a human and, say, an ant."

"Then you and I are such complex systems—different, but similar in a lot of ways."

"Yes," Astra agreed, "and I believe we can go much further with this idea. Such an energy system—weather or not it is composed of what we call matter—has, like you and me, a non-local center, or seat of consciousness."

"It can be everywhere at once?" Venus asked.

"That would be a nice anthropomorphic way of putting it."

"How about an isomorphic way of putting it."

"Okay. Sure. . . . Anyway, such systems include you and me. They also include the planet Origin, containing the *essence of Origin*—the seat of Origin's awareness."

"What else?"

"Just as Origin has its seat, or center of organization, so too does my planet. Earth's supposed seat of awareness has many names, but I prefer to call it Gaia."

"What else do you think has such high organization and qualitative differences?"

"I'll just say the universe, and the multiverse as an infinite, energetic whole. Who knows what kind of a being that would be!"

"Not to be disrespectful, Astra, but holy crap—that's heavy!" Venus no longer appeared downcast.

"Venus, you really do know the lingo, but there are times when I wish you were back to your more formal way of putting things."

"If I may digress," Venus said, "for my own selfish, non-universal curiosity, may I inquire about the weak signals that went into Mark's Base at night? You said there were *a lot* of them. From that, have you been able to isolate the amount of weak activity entering and leaving each individual isomorph?"

"Not that specifically, but I have calculated a kind of rock bottom average, but even that minimum is *a lot*."

"A lot? By now I know that *a lot* is more than four thousand. How many weak signals *do* isomorphs process in a minute?"

Astra looked intensely into Venus's now steady eyes before answering. She said, "In this case, *a lot* means *billions and billions!*"

SIXTY-SEVEN

"Billions and billions?" Venus repeated, eyes wider than anyone had ever seen.

Astra nodded.

"Nothing for me to be ashamed of then?" Venus continued, flashing a golden smile.

"Ahem . . . Astra . . . Venus." It was Zack's voice, speaking very quietly.

They glanced up to see Zack and Gegeneis looking at them. Gegeneis seemed unconcerned, but Zack was subtly turning his head and eyes toward the front of the cockpit.

"Gegeneis, Venus. You and your kind have something special. You grasp and realize your world of Origin with all the senses and acuity available to humans when they experience theirs on Earth; but at night you do it with a thousand times the directness, intensity and intimacy than we can on Earth. You isomorphs are a remarkable and fortunate lot. . . . I wish I had one!" As he said those things, Mark's eyes were fixed mostly on Venus, with only a glance or two at Gegeneis and Zack.

He then turned to look at Astra through narrowing eyes and unnatural smirk. Even more unnatural—and contributing to his eccentric, warped countenance—was the position of his earphones. They were on his cheeks, still muffling the music, but freeing his ears for other inputs.

Astra lowered her head to avoid Mark's ill-mannered scrutiny. "How long have you been listening to us?" she asked.

"Not long," Mark replied. "Just long enough to learn about Reo-Spheres from another angle. You called their totality a 'multiverse.' Nice to know that universes are individually conscious entities, and that, taken together, became some kind of super entity or super consciousness, all having little to do with what we call physical matter, but everything to do with energy. I liked your comment about the non-local nature of their seats of consciousness. That would make everything in the universe and in nature an immediate and integral part of that consciousness—*immediate* meaning instantly, without any of that local speed of light foot-dragging. Nothing that *exists* could be separate from it—not even for an instant. The *existent* parts might not be complex enough, or complex enough in the right way, to sense that immediacy, except for some fortunate, well attuned higher beings. An inexact, but analogous example of that kind of connection is what isomorphs seem to experience during their dreamscapes."

With an unexpectedly acerbic tone, Venus added, "And, with any luck, the *essence of Origin* is a complex enough being, 'in the right way,' to have that instant, *conscious*, connection with the universe—unlike the slow, weak-signal dreamscape connections of isomorphs."

Astra still had not lifted her head when she asked, "What else did you hear?"

"A few other things," Mark said, reassembling his smirk into an even more insulting sneer, as if Astra could notice the change through the top of her head; but she did catch his tone.

Astra shuddered and lifted her head to see what that tonal change might bode. "A few other things?" she asked, voice shaking.

Mark's expression changed again, from smirk and sneer to one of anger. Leaning close to Astra and Venus, he whipped off the set of earphones from his face with one hand and flung it against the Orb's wall, his voice a steaming cauldron of disapproval. "Was there something I should *not* have heard?" he seethed.

Astra shrugged and backed away from Mark's encroachment as he continued to bluster. "I suppose it was all right for me to hear about your plan to steal my Pigeon and risk your lives running around in deep water channels trying to find *It*—the all-powerful 'homebody,' sitting on its 'seat' in a g*ive or take* zone under some mountain? And you accused me of lying! And—"

"You did lie," Astra said calmly.

Still intense, Mark said, "It's my Pigeon. I can say anything about it I want! It's not even in the same class with suicidal Orb-jacking."

Astra continued. "You lied when you said you'd destroyed the Pigeon's underwater maneuverability. It still works, right?"

Then, as though a large bag of air had suddenly deflated, Mark regressed into silly, sarcastic, childlike, high-pitched vocal tones and said, "Anyhow, it was just a little white lie—so when *you* are being so naughty, why pick on me?" Then he burst into peals of fake, embarrassed laughter; and again, just as quickly, returned to his look of sternness and anger.

They continued to "discuss" the situation for some time, with Mark doing most of the talking as he kept changing roles and attitudes—taking on his father's harshness and reasonableness, his mother's histrionic distress and finger wagging, his own childish excuse making and shame. It was a baffling display—unlike the Mark they knew—as though he was having an internal conflict about the rightness or wrongness of the Venus-Astra conspiracy. To Astra and Zack it was a bizarre performance they could not sort out. To Gegeneis and Venus, who sat there nodding their approval, it all seemed to make perfect sense—especially after the nightscape empathy lessons where they learned to filter out the 'logic,' without losing track of it.

Finally, Venus stood up, wearing just a sympathetic smile and the dominant style of a mother superior—arms folded beneath her sparkling, pointy breasts. Before this imposing specter, Mark stopped babbling and making faces. Venus stood wordless, awaiting his next reaction—unaware of the impact it would have on her—on both of them.

Shaken, he stared childlike into her mysterious, other-worldly, knowing, cat eyes as she took both of his trembling hands into hers. A moment later an incredible flood of impressions and images surged through him with a billion thoughts, feelings and experiences crammed into a seeming "decade," but all of it happened in the space of a minute. His macro-occiput throbbed visibly, like a heart in open-chest surgery, full of sensations, insights and pain; while a glowing star on Venus's shoulder brightened intermittently in concert with Mark's pulsations.

"Good God!" Mark said, after their hand and eye contact was relinquished and enough time had passed for his return to reality. "Did you feel any of that?" Somehow he knew that she had.

Venus nodded, "Yes—all of it."

"But how?"

Venus's eyelids began their rapid movements. "I'd love to give you a profound answer, Mark, but I felt you as directly as any nightscape dream. More so!"

"You can dreamscape during *waking* hours? With *humans*?"

"It's not exactly the same. I would give it a different name."

"What do you call that ability, then? Daydreaming? And don't tell me it's just empathy. I've been hearing about that a lot lately—from Denise and Chastity. If that's all it was, then you couldn't have affected *me* like this."

"Nor you me," Venus said, tilting her head to one side.

"How *could* this be described?"

"Call it a purifying, two-way filter that left our mental irrelevancies behind."

"Yes," he said, nodding thoughtfully, "that explains what it was."

"And it was . . . ?"

"A bullshit filter."

Venus's eyes flashed rapidly back and forth. "In a million years, Mark, I couldn't have said it better."

"So much for the 'filtered' feelings you got from me—that we got from each other—but why do I feel so . . . so redeemed?"

"As we agree, the filter worked both ways. It surprised me too. We went through this together. It was intense."

"And you can do this with other isomorphs, the *essence of Origin*, the Dorts, and other humans?"

"Yes. Except for the 'humans' part. I can empathize mildly with most humans, yes, but nothing like what you and I just went through."

"I'm confused. Why just me?"

"You are different from most humans, Mark. You are unique. Weirdly so."

"No I'm not. I'm just a regular guy."

"You are for sure, in almost every way. You're smarter than most, but still a regular guy."

"Then what's the difference? There must be something."

"I don't know exactly, but the richness of feelings and furious range and chaos of your extravagant mind is a force beyond the sphere of ordinary—and far beyond any déjà vu or screen memories from your childhood. Those memories have been easy outs for you—not requiring you to go far into yourself. But, overall, *this* was different. Deeper—like something open and endless. I don't know how else to describe it. I never experienced anything like it before, even in my most powerful and direct nightscapes."

"*Open* and *endless*. Yes. That says it. Those words envelop my dream of a million related things, a dream I have had every night for as long as I can remember—not just from childhood, but from my infancy. It's the dream I've spent my life untangling. It became my Theory of Reo-Spheres, unfinished as it is. That untangling process—the reverse engineering of my dream—took many years. It was the hardest thing I ever did. It was a dream put there by I don't know what—it just came with me. It was no screen memory, and not an *easy out*. And I'm not out of it yet! Over the years, that dream kept getting bigger, rising and elaborating. It's had me in its grip, but for some strange reason it's not so bad. Not now."

"I saw your dream, Mark. It was too much to grasp. It made my shoulder ache. I saw it, but I could never untangle nor explain it. It is too big an experience for me to even talk about. Little things I can talk about, but not that."

"What *can* all of this possibly explain, I wonder?"

"Well, Mark," Venus said, "if we start with little things, it could explain a little. Not a lot. Like, for example, your mistaken sense of unique loneliness."

"Oh, you noticed that too. How did it feel? And why is it *mistaken*? Didn't you call me weirdly unique? That means isolated and solitary, therefore lonely. That's a fair formula for loneliness."

"A nice intellectual formula, and nice for dodging the point. Your 'uniqueness' is not the cause of your loneliness, it is part of it."

"Does no one else feel as I do?"

"You're unique," Venus replied, "but loneliness isn't. If you're talking about occasional or even permanent loneliness, get over it. Or keep it. It must serve your purposes. My empathy tells me it's part of humanness. Even Dorts know what that is. Yours is imbedded in all those other feelings that came through our filter. It's all focused there—in your being."

"My 'being'? Hmm. Feels like you're trying to get spiritual on me. Not necessary."

"I'm not, but I saw what I saw—the real Mark Tenderloin. It's all that we just experienced together. Yes, it's simply the real you."

"I thought I heard you say you could only talk about little things. Now you're interpreting my big dream."

"I can experience 'big things'—not take them apart. Not much anyway."

"Oh."

"Getting the big picture is satisfying. It's a far cry from dismantling it piece by piece—as you have done."

"As I have done?"

"Yes, by coming out with your Reo-Sphere Theory. By comparison to that, the big picture is just a start. Sorting it out must have been the hard part."

"Yes, the dream did come first. It took a long time to extend it further."

"Your being knows the big picture *and* provided the spirit for you to follow through and dissect it. Your being is taking care of you."

"Maybe that's what I meant when I said I felt redeemed. That dream's iron grip on me feels different now—more like an embrace. In your terms, my 'being' has somehow guided me, and is still guiding me—through that maze of a dream; but it doesn't provide the finished work—just the dream and the inspiration to keep going. If, that is, there's such a part of me as my 'being.'"

"It does seem to be taking care of you. I saw something there."

"Something's driving my curiosity. And . . . hmm. Yes. It did seem as though a part of me—from somewhere else—was also watching all that we experienced together. The watcher in me was not in all that chaos; but somehow the chaos, even the loneliness, and all the rest, seemed valuable—from the angle of that watcher."

"An *external* watcher?" Venus asked.

"No. The watcher is me too."

"Maybe you've got it, Mark! You found your *being*—your human *being*, like every other human. . . . But in *you* it is more accessible to . . . to . . ."

"—The bullshit filter?"

"Right! But a discerning filter like that is not just in you," Venus said with a wave of her arm. "There is, I believe, at least one other out there."

"Really? Whose?"

"Laura Shane's."

"Oh. . . . Of course!"

"Well Mark, how about it?" Astra said.

Lifting a suspicious eyebrow, Mark said, "How about what?"

"How about we all get honest. You won't be letting us borrow this Pigeon, much less steal it, and yet we all have the same goal. Venus and I have a plan that we believe will bring us into contact with the *essence of Origin*, and from there we can expect some favors—leading to the sought after, much touted negotiations hyped by the Directors."

"And *you*," Mark said, looking very wise, "are looking to negotiate with *me*."

"Yes."

"Why should I? I have no need to help you commit suicide."

"There are some good reasons, and we have no intention of committing suicide."

Mark tilted his head back, tucking his exposed occiput into its wide collar. "I'm not negotiating. On the other hand, we do still have some time on our hands."

"You're at least listening, then?"

"I suppose."

"You suppose?"

"Okay, I'm listening!"

Astra and Venus took turns laying out their entire plan in detail to Mark, Zack and Gegeneis. Gegeneis already knew most of the plan from recent dreamscapes. At one point Venus took both of Gegeneis's hands, as had just been done with Mark and earlier on in the large-circle meeting with the humans; only this was a very small circle of two individuals. She wanted his impression of Mark's dream, which she passed to Gegeneis in toto. He was dumbfounded by the revelation and immediately saw its connection to the plan as a clinching motivation for *It* to forget the fuzzy 'maybes' and become clear and positive. Venus would pass Mark's dream forward during that night's dreamscape.

Mark had a problem. Stating it would interfere with his privacy. He wondered, once his dream entered the dreamscape system, if every being on the planet, other than humans—including isomorphs, Doyan, and the es*sence of Origin*—would have access to it. Gegeneis explained that they would not only have "access" to his dream, it would be their unavoidable experience, for which Mark would be "*revered.*" The latter point settled the issue for Mark, and he gave consent for his dream's dissemination.

"There are at least two fatal flaws in your plan," Mark said. "First, although you are correct in assuming that the Underwater Controls have not been destroyed by me—okay, I lied—it is also the case that any water depth below forty, or even twenty meters, would very likely result in a complete propulsion breakdown *and* the collapse of the life support system—you were wrong about that one, Astra. Breakdown of life support would not be far behind the propulsion failure."

"How far behind?" Zack asked.

"One hour, max. That could be extended if you broke out some scuba gear—if you had any—and that would depend on how many isomorph and human air breathers were in the cabin, and the number of tanks of compressed air you had. I checked the manifest before we left, but don't recall seeing any of that listed"

Venus said, "Because of the rules about that, we put scuba equipment under other categories and labels."

"It's a good thing. You're right. Diving equipment was vetoed by the Directors," Mark said. "They didn't want anybody wasting their time on this mission by going swimming, especially since that might be fun. Killjoys! They had some other reasons, too, but I forget what they were."

"What about the second 'fatal flaw' you mentioned?" Astra reminded him.

"Well, this is the craziest part of your plan. The crazy part is totally flawed. If you rely on it, you're cooked. You know the part I'm talking about."

Astra and the isomorphs did not know, but Zack nodded, "I think I know the part of the plan you're referring to."

Mark said, "Well, go ahead and say it, Zack. It'll be better coming from you than me."

"I think you may be questioning the plan's *contingency expectations* should the 'borrowed' Pigeon break down as you expect. I believe Astra gave that expectation a four out of five. I believe you may have given it a somewhat lower probability."

"Huh!" Mark blustered. "That's the understatement of all time!"

"What in the hell are you guys talking about?" Astra demanded to know.

"The rescue—" Mark said.

"—of the broken Pigeon—" Zack said.

"—from a deep Ocean cave—" Mark interrupted.

"—by none other than—" Zack said.

"—the *essence of Origin*. *That* expectation," Mark concluded, "has a probability of zero."

Astra came to her feet, her atomic arms (in *default* mode) on her hips, and said, "Before we learned about your dream I only gave it a four. Now I'm upping that to four and a half!"

Mark said, "You told me the *give or take* area is on the opposite side of The Island from where the new Operations Center will be—where we'll be landing in another twenty minutes—and that the *give or take* area is connected to a maze of deep water channels, at unacceptable depths. Even if *It* wanted to, and was able to make a rescue in its home territory, the Pigeon would be long dead before you ever got there. That's why your plan is doomed."

"You may be right," Venus said, "but after tonight's dreamscape, the situation may change—drastically. I will expect intimate and practical answers from the *essence of Origin*. In the past the answers *It* gave were sometimes slow, with vague or unimportant content, with *maybes* instead of promises; but *there have always been answers*. So, the negotiations the Directors are hoping for have *already* begun. Tonight will be their continuation. This isn't just for *our* survival, and the *essence of Origin* knows it. That's why *It* had the Dorts bring you to this planet. Tonight's presentation of your dream will be the big reminder—the reminder that hope is still alive and well, and that the *essence of Origin's* long quest is not doomed, but may be nearing fulfillment."

SIXTY-EIGHT

Toward dusk, as Clint neared their destination, he gradually reduced the Orb's speed and altitude. That allowed Nimbus to fleetingly hide behind the illusion of moving, jagged peaks. The shuttles, in close formation behind the Blue Belt Orb, plunged into the shadows between those rugged northwestern mountains to finally emerged from the darkening canyons onto a Nimbus-lit finger peninsula—the site selected by the Directors.

The tide was in and the shuttle landings clustered near the beach at the western tip of the spit. By then Mark's Pigeon had reached the back of the formation. He continued to circle and hover until all the shuttles had touched down safely before he landed his Pigeon a kilometer farther inland, away from the other space vehicles and near the base of a mountain that defined the beginning of the prominence.

Nimbus had not yet dropped completely below the ocean's horizon, but it and the sky's colors were already starting to change. A splashy panoramic display was imminent, but the biological clocks of humans and isomorphs alike were far ahead of that illusion. The crews that landed near the ocean and those on Mark's Pigeon, unpacked their windbreaker tents or mini-habitats to ready for a much needed night's rest; but that took enough time for everybody to experience the sensational setting of Nimbus—long enough for their spirits to briefly reawaken.

Immediately on landing, Mark and his 'students' put down their camping roots for the night; but most of the distant campers, with a miraculous, celebratory second wind, refused to retire.

Amidst laughter, shouts, music and revelry, their shuttles and tents continued to glow and flicker in the distance for two more hours. Any event, like a live and radiant Nimbus seascape, was as good an excuse as any to celebrate. Tomorrow the work would begin.

Venus and Gegeneis went off in separate directions to begin their shimmering night of rest. They reclined on Origin's darkening surface near Mark's Orb, as had the other isomorphs and Doyan around the larger camp at the far west end of the peninsula. Before slipping off into the night, Venus spent several minutes in a whispered huddle with her identical. Astra was a little confused and surprised by the idea Venus offered, but nodded her approval.

In the distance, the partying humans remained noisy and semi-alert as long as they could; but even they had to succumb to exhaustion and finally extinguished the last of the music and the lights. Only then did night come in earnest—as never before.

Clock time at the new location was well past midnight. The scattered periphery of recumbent isomorphs around their sleeping humans was dimly illuminated by their scintillations as they began to enter deep dreamscape. As usual, it built up slowly, but this time it accelerated suddenly, erupting with volcanolike streams of glowing, flashing incandescence—awakening only a handful of humans who merely rolled over to cover their heads and return to sleep. "Let'm celebrate, if that's what they're doing," one said with irritation before he returned to the arms of Morpheus.

Even before her hushed visit with Astra and her nocturnal merging with the crystals of Origin, Venus knew she had a mission to perform that night. She was already bursting with the content and implications of Mark's dream, as was Gegeneis, but they agreed she would take the nightscape lead. It was only after Venus brandished Mark's dream before the nightscape underworld that the glowing streams of light began.

The ramifications of Mark's dream exploded across the length and breadth of Origin—propagating like a shock wave, spreading and branching from level to level, from mountains to hills to the deepest ocean trenches, waking even the merest fragments of consciousness in the smallest crystals and plantoids. And yet the impact of this convulsive, planet-alerting event would take weeks to mature before it commanded the notice of most humans. They kept trying to ignore the whole thing, or sleep through it.

The reaction to Mark's dream, from the *essence of Origin*, did not take weeks to arrive. It took only seconds—very unusual for something so important. Venus construed that less as haste, than urgency. The response from *It* was brief, but positive. Every mountain, crevice and fragment on Origin's crust was now sensitized to receive every related elaboration—true or false. Venus regarded the quick response as intended to *prevent* the spread of dreamscape rumors and the planet-wide amplification and distortion of information through the present and coming nights of dreamscapes—within that, the ultimate rumor mill.

The *essence of Origin* was wise to be brief. After receiving the positive response, Venus risked one more very brief dream transmission of her own—chancy, but necessary.

Astra and Venus agreed the Pigeon would now be needed *immediately*. But an offhand comment from Mark, as he walked by, hit them hard. It was an obvious fact: his elaborate security code and password guaranteed it could not just be taken. In all their elaborate and covert plans, that sneaky little detail was never considered.

Astra thought they should go to him with the 'news'—the positive response from the *essence of Origin*—and simply request Mark's assistance. But it would take more than that, and they still did not know—not for sure—how to operate the Underwater Controls—even if Mark did happen to give them his okay, along with his security code and password.

When Astra was about to approach Mark, Venus reminded her of their previous night's agreement. "Besides," Venus said, "There's no way that Mark will make his Pigeon available to us simply by making the request. He would only do that if he were convinced we'd be safe under water. He believes his flawed Pigeon could not guarantee that."

Instead, Venus urged Astra to allow the result of their hasty agreement of the night before to unfold. Although Astra had agreed to it—in a moment of weakness—she was becoming dubious and losing patience. Given the far-reaching potential of Marks dream, Venus believed their needed helpers would understand and act accordingly. To find out, all she and Astra had to do was sit back and wait. The bickering was brief, but they finally agreed that some things simply could not be forced.

Astra shrugged. She suggested they both say a prayer.

It was about eight a.m., Island time. Mark and his 'crew' were sitting outside the Pigeon. Venus and Gegeneis sat cross legged on the surface. The others were in comfortable chairs enjoying some after-breakfast tea. Looking into the distance, they watched the hurried unloading of shuttles and the Blue Belt Orb. They watched two large habitats being erected; one for general equipment, supplies, maintenance, fuel storage and other purposes. The second, called the "Directors' Control Center," would house all the specialized technical and scientific requirements for the mission, including not only the main DCC for its tasks, but the supporting units with their managers and staffs. Most of the shuttles would have to make more trips to Mark's Base and to the Great Cone for the remaining necessities needed to get the operations into full swing.

Before all of that—that very day, in fact—the first surveys were to begin. Radio signals were excellent, so there could be no triangulations to track the lines of molecular resonance, but they started to select the sites for setting probes and instruments to collect other hard-science data—for the purpose of finding and flushing out the *essence of Origin*.

It would be a lot of work requiring all hands to pitch in, so it was no surprise when Mark's radio came to life. Ned Keller, restraining his temper, said he appreciated how they must be enjoying their tea—he had been watching them with his binoculars—but wondered if they would mind getting off their butts and moving the Pigeon in with the other craft and unload its cargo.

Mark waved his arm back and forth for Ned to see and said, "Be right there boss," and terminated the contact.

Mark got to his feet and said, "Looks like we'll have to get busy. Ned thinks we're all about to develop congestive butt failure if we don't move our stuff."

Zack and Gegeneis stood up immediately, but Astra and Venus did not move. After a minute Mark asked, "What's the matter with you two?"

"We're waiting—" said Venus.

"—for another, more important message—" Astra said.

"—that we expect will be arriving—"

"—soon!"

As Astra uttered the last word, she pointed excitedly to a gyro-car speeding toward them from the distant cluster of shuttles. As it drew closer they saw three occupants in its small space: Keeta and her human, Laura Shane, and Doyan—the answer to their prayers!

Laura was first out of the g-car and dashed the short distance to Mark. "I hope you know what's up," she said to him, "because we have to move fast. If Ned is watching us he'll be having a fit. He's been cracking the whip something fierce!"

Soon, Keeta and Doyan were behind Laura. Mark said that he only knew what every other human knew about the project and that "these four," he waved a hand toward his 'students,' "want to commit suicide by taking my Pigeon for a swim it's not up to, just to meet what's-his-name."

"I know all about that," Laura said. "We'll have to talk about it on our way."

"On our way where? And how can you know all about what these guys have been planning? I thought dreamscape information was sealed from humans. Who spilled the beans?"

"I did," Venus said. "Astra gave me her permission—so Keeta and Doyan could tell all of it to Laura—and just her. Anyway, other humans will have to know of this plan soon enough, but there are some preliminaries that have to come first."

Laura said, "I'm concerned about those *preliminaries*. That'll take a week or two—or three. Which is miraculous, but couldn't those things be done after, rather than before any negotiations?"

Venus said, "That will give the *essence of Origin* time to fully appreciate Mark's and your presence here. You two are the key to any so-called *negotiations*—if they happen at all. You both know that. After the preliminaries, *It*'s motivation should be higher than ever. And another thing. If negotiations happened right away and were successful, you humans would be out of here the next day and on your Great Cone of Transformation—and our *preliminaries* would never happen. They must."

"We need to get going," Keeta said.

"Just hold it!" Mark said. "I never agreed to take anybody anywhere. Why should I? Convince me."

"Yes," Laura said. "That's a perfectly reasonable request, and you will be told everything, after which you *will* be persuaded. Take my word for it. But that will take quite a while. Keeta woke me up early to tell me something that came from Venus in dreamscape. It came to her in an instant, and now I'm convinced. But it took a long time for me to get it all and will take time for even you to understand. I'll tell you on the way. Astra has the map to get us there."

"Not so fast. I have lots of time. Start talking."

"Sorry," Doyan said, "but there really is no time. A half-dozen gyro-cars are already heading this way." Doyan pointed a pseudopod toward the g-cars. "We must leave now or risk everything."

Mark said, "Don't be so dramatic, Doyan. A little explanation to the Directors and everything should go smoothly from there—*if* your alternate plan makes any sense at all. Which I doubt."

Mark's radio communicator began blinking and beeping. He knew who it was and rolled his eyes. And the gyro-cars had already closed more than half the distance between them.

"I think the boss is calling," Venus said. "Are you going to answer it or start developing a little trust—right here, with us, real fast!"

Mark heard her words well—adding to the pressure that seemed to be coming from all directions. He jumped into the Pigeon and shoved several large boxes out onto the surface. They contained parts for the shuttles.

"The Pigeon won't need any of this," Mark shouted from inside the Orb, "but we'll need the space. . . . There! That should make enough room," Mark continued his yelling, this time from the open hatch. ". . . Well? Get your butts on board—they're almost here."

They all piled up the ramp and through the hatch. It snapped shut behind them.

Officer Bracket was in charge of the gyro-car squad. He braced himself on top of the lead gyro-car, laser gun in hand, looking like a giant hood ornament, or a great historical general crossing the Delaware. The g-cars raced in and came to intimidating, screeching halts beside the Pigeon. But it made no difference. In that moment the Pigeon lifted off and shot away to vanish over the mountains.

SIXTY-NINE

They'll be looking for us," Zack said.

"I don't see why," Mark replied. "We haven't broken any laws. I can't even imagine why Ned sent that squad out to meet us—or to get us." Mark's communicator was still blinking. He'd already shut off the beeper sound so it could be ignored.

"Before we left camp on the continent," Laura said, "Ned was emphatic that you and I, Mark, and you Doyan, *not* be on the same shuttle together. He mumbled something about presidents and vice presidents not flying together.

He thinks we three are all-important to whatever happens with the *essence of Origin*—with Mark and I as somehow holding the keys to whatever doors *It* wants to open, and Doyan as our translator and historical interpreter of how and why this planet came to have the surface it does and who knows what else. So, here we are, all together. I'm sure that cantankerous, sweet, loveable man of mine is having a major fit about now."

"Of course he is," Astra said. "Without any of you, should something happen, like we crash on a mountain and get killed, then he'd not only lose you, Laura, and the rest of us, but that would be the end of the Directors' plans. They might find the *essence of Origin*—highly unlikely—but even if they did, their negotiating chips—Laura and Mark, with their special knowledge of Reo-Sphere Theory—would be dead."

Doyan squirmed.

"Astra is right," Doyan said after settling down. "I will do everything I can to keep you—all of us—safe. Your plan is a good one. The Directors' plan is not a good one. It will fail. In the end they can and should come into this plan, but for now it is in your hands. Like Laura, I question the need for those *preliminaries*, but if that is what it takes, I will also give that my support."

Astra said, "Really! I could just hug you for saying that, dear Doyan!"

Doyan said nothing; but for the second time in less than a minute exhibited that rare, enigmatic Dort behavior—uncomfortable squirming.

Mark Tenderloin did his own version of squirming. "Isn't it time," he asked, "to get out your map? I have no idea where we're going."

Astra retrieved the map and put her finger on the spot. "Here," she said, "on the southeast coast of The Island. It's about two-hundred and fifty kilometers from the place we just left. It's not a peninsula. It's a wide expanse of shoreline that leads gradually into the ocean. Then there's a sharp drop that goes down and down—forever, sort of. But the beach is vast!"

"Okay," Mark said. "That's as far away from the DCC as we can get and still be on The Island, but they'll still find us in a matter of a few hours—at most. The Island's just not that big."

Mark pointed the Pigeon in that direction and accelerated to Mach 5. They'd briefly lifted above Origin's atmosphere and soon reentered above Astra's designated beach. Laura had already begun interpreting the Venus-Astra-conspiracy plan to Mark. She was still at it an hour after they'd landed near the ocean shore.

Laura kept talking, with helpful clarification here and there from Astra, Venus, and Gegeneis. Meanwhile, Doyan took off for the water. They all watched even as they listened to Laura. Doyan swam out from the shore with an amazing physical grace never seen on land. When the water became deeper he undulated swiftly out of sight, appearing moments later like a flying dolphin, doing this again and again until nearly a quarter kilometer from shore. After the next dive Doyan was not seen again for two hours. Then, like a hungry shark, he shot straight for shore; but beached there with the inelegance of an overgrown bull sea lion. Laura was still talking.

Then it was Doyan's turn to explain the situation. While speaking, a shuttle flew overhead. They'd been spotted. Mark guessed that in another thirty minutes they would have plenty of company.

Doyan had to talk fast. "I found the entrance near one of your map dots, Astra. It starts just after a sharp drop-off, down fifty meters below the ocean surface—too deep to bother with the Underwater Controls, even if they worked. Mark, tell us how deep the Pigeon can safely descend using just the Maintain Level control?"

"How do you know about those controls?" Mark asked.

"Last night's dreamscape was very detailed. . . . How deep can it safely descend?"

"Okay, if you only had to descend or ascend," Mark responded, "there would be no problem. It controls the level—the water depth. But you wouldn't want to engage Underwater Controls to maneuver about, not at that depth. That would shut everything down, including life support. What are you getting at? . . . And what kept you so long?"

"We have to move quickly for the logistics of this plan to work. I was gone so long to find and explore Astra's entire *'give or take'* area. I saw no sign of anything one might call the *essence of Origin*, but I did find something that came through in recent dreamscapes. It's a natural, crystalline platform or knoll in a subterranean cave—a cavern really—just as it appeared in dream. Its ceiling and surface crystals glow in that part of the channel, so one can get a hazy view for several kilometers across and well beyond the *give or take* area. The channel leading there widened into a lake of rapidly flowing salt water. The floor of the lake also glows. It didn't affect me, but from my experience with humans, I believe you would find it intriguing if not what you would speak of as beautiful."

"That," Mark said, "must be the landing spot, the 'crystalline knoll' beside the water that Laura just told me about. Too bad there's no way to get there. That's where Venus and Gegeneis and their two humans would have gone for some unspecified period of time—for a week or more, weaving 'magic spells' to lure in the *essence of Origin*. But, like I said, it can't be done. Besides, look over there." Mark pointed over one of the mountains. "I thought we'd have another half-hour at least, but they're here already."

"And, like *I* said," Doyan emphasized, vibrating louder than usual, "we'll have to move quickly. I will guide the Pigeon out just beyond the ledge to a steep drop-off. Then one of the four passengers can engage the controls to descend exactly fifty meters before letting the Maintain Level kick in. After that, I'll maneuver the Orb to the glowing lake and cavern."

Mark responded, "I had no idea you could do things like that; but even if you can, that gives me little time to think about everything I've heard. I've given no permission to make any further use of my Pigeon." Then Mark sniffed haughtily.

"Sorry Mark, but thinking time is over," Laura said.

Then Doyan said sharply, "Astra, Venus, Zack, Gegeneis, get in the Pigeon now. One of you maneuver it into the water. I'll take you out to the edge of the shelf. When we stop, take control for a few minutes and make the descent and hold it at fifty meters. Once I start shoving you into the tunnel, disengage the Maintain Level controls. There'll not only be a lot of left and right turns and twists, there will be ups and downs. After disengaging the controls, relax and try to enjoy the ride. I'll wave to you when it is safe to leave the Orb. You'll find the air in the cave is just fine."

Mark's face turned red and he began to sputter incoherently. But his complexion quickly improved and he became very clear and focused when several of the shuttles and the Blue Belt landed noisily only meters away. "Damn it! Okay, do it! Get in there now, and follow Doyan's instructions. Here Astra, take this." He handed her a small piece of paper. "It has my security code and password." They piled into the Pigeon. "Good luck. And Doyan, after you've delivered them, when will *you* be back?"

By the time Mark uttered the last question, the Orb's crew had already hopped the Pigeon into shallow water using Mark's Short-Flight-Hover panel. Doyan then shoved the Orb swiftly forward and away from shore. Doyan was providing all the power. Their speed increased with an impressive spray on both sides of the Orb. It stopped far from shore and floated briefly before sinking in front of their eyes—including Clint's, Ned's, and the bristling new arrivals.

The drop-off was sheer. Gegeneis took charge of the Maintain Level device, setting it to stop and maintain at fifty meters below the surface. The water was clear. They watched as a perpendicular wall of glistening crystals seemed to move upward as they descended—until they found themselves looking into utter darkness. They were looking into the emptiness of a giant opening in the wall—the entrance to the tunnel that Doyan had explored earlier. Gegeneis turned on the forward spotlights to reveal the jagged contours of a meandering, water-filled channel.

Their inward movement began gently. Gegeneis disengaged the Maintain Level controls. The speed picked up and they rapidly traversed an underwater maze with many turns away from the main channel into side passages. The pace soon became a gut-wrenching experience that continued for forty-five minutes before slowing in front of what looked like a dead end; but another sudden turn brought them into a much smaller tunnel, barely large enough for the Pigeon to squeeze through. The passage curved along for another hundred meters before it opened wide.

"I believe we're here," said Gegeneis as he turned off the spotlights. The floor of the channel glistened with its own light.

A little more maneuvering and the Orb's passengers felt themselves rising in the water and being lifted to the surface and beyond. The jiggling, horizontal water level moved down the face of the Orb's window, leaving only droplet streaks as the Orb was hefted up and carried across the glowing surface of the knoll and away from the water's edge. The Pigeon was jarred slightly as it was placed on the surface, followed by a grinding sound and an odd back and forth twisting motion that forced the surface crystals under the Orb to give way, creating a curved dip that would, for the time being, serve as a nest for Mark's Pigeon. It was deep enough to safely keep the Orb stable and in place and keep it from rolling down the knoll's slight grade into the water.

Doyan gave the Orb a couple more hefty twists back and forth to make sure it was in solid before plopping into view, raising a pseudopod, and waving for the passengers to disembark.

In the next few hours they emptied the Pigeon of its supplies, got them sorted and organized, and explored the glowing surface on which they found themselves. It abutted a curved cavern wall and ceiling. The knoll extended for a quarter kilometer with a width of some forty meters. It contained no outstanding features. It was mainly flat, with a minor slant toward the water's edge.

After their brief orientation, Doyan said, "You have enough supplies to last a month. I believe you can now begin your preliminaries. If I don't see you sooner, I'll be back to get you in three weeks. Good-bye." Then he slipped into the water and was gone.

SEVENTY

Before Doyan left the enchanted glow of the cavern, he and the Pigeon's passengers removed the Orb's supplies. They methodically organized the contents that would sustain them through the next few weeks. The ordeal ahead was anticipated with optimism—expecting, of course, a positive outcome.

They knew their pursuers would be angered by this blatant act of insubordination and their unapproved descent into the ocean, and that they would not understand why it was done. Because they were not just pursuers, but friends, they would also fear for their safety. So the Pigeon's passengers and Doyan agreed that upon Doyan's returned to the surface, he could bring the Directors and others up to date about the Venus-Astra conspiracy, "the plan," including what they called its *preliminaries*—and any subsequent dreamscape information about their status in the cavern *that Doyan might deem worth mentioning*. That turned out to be a liberal loophole for the Dort.

When Doyan reemerged from the ocean, he was quickly surrounded by Officer Bracket's small Security Force and most of the Directors. He was immediately confronted by such a torrent of angry questions that any lesser being would have been confused and overwhelmed; but, without a ripple, he categorized and summarized the disorganized cascade of questions and proceeded to answer them. The messy inquiry yielded detailed explanations and revelations that stunned and silenced them. They walked away, frowning and shaking their heads—except for Clint's professionally expressionless men who continued to level their side arm lasers at Doyan. Clint had them stand down and leave the Dort in peace.

That night and the next, the dreamscape was busy. Within its usual dazzling mix of images, emotions and ideas came a surprising change of plans from the cavern below. Doyan wondered what could have happened, although it did not register as something of great importance, except that, from a human viewpoint, it would not be happily received. There was a reasonable choice: Nobody was told. It was not deemed worth mentioning.

It was "morning" of their second day in the cavern and Astra was already having her third temper tantrum—her first that day. "Damn it Venus!" she shouted. "Why are you still arguing with me about this? Just because Zack and Gegeneis are going through with it doesn't mean that we have to. Certainly not me. The plan ended yesterday—when you finally *deigned* to tell me. That part of the *preliminaries,* having to do with me, is ended. My choice!"

"And mine—we are equal in this," Venus said.

"Okay. It has to be *our* choice, but my half of 'our' says *no*, so there is no 'our'—so it's ended."

"You know you want this, Astra."

"Sure," she said, slowly calming down. "But the cost is too high. *Way* too high! Look what it would do to *you*. Look at me, Venus. Look real hard! And that's just the physical part—not even the half of it!"

Venus lowered her head. "Please, Astra. Won't you just think about it? You would be normal again—no more scars. You'd have *real* arms and legs, and—"

"No!" Astra interrupted vehemently. "*You* think about it! I would not be normal 'again.' I never was—not since so much of my body burned to ashes in my infancy. For me the trade-off isn't worth it. And you! You'd be worse off than I am now—than I ever was. *You'd* be the one . . . the one with grotesque scarring, the one with no limbs. I, at least, have adjusted to it—sort of."

"I could adjust," Venus protested.

"You don't have to. It took a lifetime and I'm not over it yet. Not entirely, but I've . . . I've adjusted, damn it! I won't let you do it!"

"Gegeneis is doing it."

"Goddamn that *essence of Origin*! This is the worst Faustian Bargain I ever heard of. And why didn't you tell me this was the deal *before* we got into these . . . these fucking *preliminaries*? You manipulated me."

"I didn't expect you to object."

"I thought you knew me better than that! Or you let *Origin* manipulate you. As if this planet needs more *practice*—messing with our bodies . . . and now our minds."

"It's not *Origin's* fault. It's the only way that *It, he*, knows how to do it—how to fix you."

"So, now your goddamn *It* has been elevated to a '*he*.' Why not *The Thing*, or *Dr. Frankenstein*?"

"Please! Stop that. I used 'he' because it's more respectful, and I respect her or him—*him*!—for offering you this . . . this total answer. It was my request. This is your first and last chance—the final solution to all your physical problems—and the answer to Zack's too. Aren't you happy for Zack?"

"For Zack? Of course; but not for Gegeneis. Hmm. You said Zack's change would take only one week?"

"*Their* change. Not just his. That's what *Origin* told me in dreamscape—even before we made our plan."

"You knew long ago it would take *both* identicals and you never told me—not till it was almost too late for me to have a say!"

Venus ignored Astra's comment and went on. "Our '*preliminaries*,' yours and mine, would take several weeks."

"*Several weeks*. For my change, I thought it would be me alone for only one week. That's why Doyan said it would be back in three weeks. You, *It*, and Doyan knew all along and never told me!"

"Doyan never had *permission* to tell you or any other human. I, for one, didn't want you thinking about the three weeks it would take for our *transition* into altered forms. Ours would be more extensive than that of Zack and Gegeneis."

"Our transmogrification, you mean."

"You're being sarcastic," said Venus with exasperation.

Continuing to show her own exasperation, Astra said, "We don't even know that their *mutations* will turn out well."

"No," Venus said, ignoring Astra's angry mockery, "but Zack and Gegeneis did agreed to go through with it. Why can't we?"

Astra gritted her teeth. "Zack and Gegeneis won't look like themselves when they're done cuddling for a week. Just look at them—all wrapped up, sound asleep, in each other's arms—like lovers. The sparks are flying between them day and night, like little lightening bolts—mostly around their eyes. Why does it have to be like that? Why can't the *essence of Origin* fix Zack without wrecking Gegeneis? And don't tell me it's because there's no free lunch. Didn't we get our *whole universe* as a free lunch? Or, to keep the balance, did some god have to commit suicide or get murdered by a bigger god in order to give us the

Big Bang? Anyway, even if it works, Zack will look strange. He'll end up with Gegeneis's *cat-slit* pupils and Gegeneis will have his *round* ones. How could either of them have agreed to do that?"

"For one thing," Venus said, "Zack should come out of this with better than normal human vision. Sure, his eyes will look different, but he'll have an isomorph's vision, and Gegeneis . . . well, he won't be *that* much worse off. After they wake up with their visual parts exchanged—er, changed—then Zack's thick eyeglasses should work perfectly well."

"Yeah! Perfectly well on Gegeneis!"

"That's what I meant."

"Some deal! Eyesight improvement, yes; but only for Zack. *Not* for Gegeneis. With us it would be even worse—for you. Much worse."

"Not necessarily."

"Venus, you once told me that except for the visual part of your brain, your other brain functions are distributed throughout your body—like Doyan's 'brain.' Among other things, I think Doyan's whole body—if it can be called that—is a brain."

"Yes. *What about it?*" Venus asked with suspicion.

"This neuro-net," Astra said, pointing to the top of her head, "—this itchy cortical skullcap I have to wear under this damn wig—is necessary for me to feel and manipulate these stupid limbs—these souped up neuro-bio-mechanical atomic prostheses. They won't work without the net. On you, because you're not wired like me, these fake arms and legs would constantly be in random, frenetic motion, and would make you crazy! Out of control like that, you'd wreck everything in sight. You'd have to move around *without* the prostheses, and only then, without limbs, by crawling and humping about like a Dort. Or maybe you could just scoot around in a cart. I know you'd love that. That's *what about it.*"

"That would only be true if I used your atomic prostheses and neuro-net. Your friend, Margaret, told me you have several sets of *ordinary* prostheses. With a set of those I'd never need your neuro-net—even *if* we were wired the same. I could learn to 'adjust' using a set of your ordinary ones. We know they would fit. The trade would be equal. After all, we're identicals."

"Equal, but not fair. And *identicals*? Not exactly."

Venus frowned and said, "If you're going to push that point, neither are Gegeneis and Zack identical. Not *exactly*. But Gegeneis is changing for Zack, and he'll be using Zack's prostheses—his glasses. He'll have to. No big deal! And I could use a set of yours—of your non-atomic ones. Also, no big deal!"

Astra shrugged. "Well," she said, "it just wouldn't be you any more. And Zack didn't want to do it either—after *he* found out what Gegeneis would have to give up."

"It's still no big deal," Venus said. "Zack is like a brother to Gegeneis and he loves his brother. Yesterday we both had to listen to them argue. Zack was objecting to changing their body parts—their eyes—just as you've been arguing with me. We listened to that and—"

"—and they had to listen to us."

"But Gegeneis won his argument. Why can't I win it with you?"

"Why would you want to end up like me? Worse!"

"Because, to me," Venus said with anguish in her voice, sounding more human every day, "the trade-off *would* be worth it. *Not* making the trade would never be right."

"Okay, say I believe you—that it *would* be worth it to you. And I believe I understand why. We've come to know each other well. So, dear sister, you also know *me* very well."

Venus looked askance at Astra. "*So?*" she asked with more suspicion.

"So, I want *you to tell me*—*honestly*—why such a thing would not, will never, be worth it to *me*."

"That's not fair . . . not fair to ask of me! Take it back!"

"Why should I?"

"If I answer you honestly," Venus said with her voice shaking, "then it *is* over. We would not be able to argue about . . . to *discuss* this any further. Then we would both stay just as we are—from now on. The door of opportunity . . . for restoring your body . . . to even change your mind about doing it . . . would close forever."

Astra surprised Venus. She began to cry. Speaking between sobs, Astra said, "I know. But it's my life. My body. And yours too. So, answer me! Now! Tell me why I can not allow you to do this—ever . . . ever . . . *ever!*"

"I can not cry, but if I could—."

Gaining control, but still crying, Astra said, "Your mouth is turned down, your voice is unsteady, you are frowning sadly, your head has starting to droop, your shoulders are slumping—I know you, dear Venus, but right now anyone could tell. You too are crying—in your tearless way. You know me well too. So now—*tell me*."

"Astra—my dear sister. I do *not* know you well—I did not—not until this day—this instant. I never knew that any human was capable of so much . . . that you . . . that you could love . . . me so much—"

Astra gently placed her powerful arms around Venus's head and kissed her cheek. "Yes, my Venus," she said quietly, "At our very core we *are* the same, aren't we! Years and worlds apart, we are as similar as twins from the same womb. Our motives here are alike, except you lack my selfishness, so the quarreling was easier for me."

"Selfishness? I don't understand."

"Because I need you this way. You are *already* my restoration and my salvation. When I first saw the photograph of your unvitalized face and torso, with the star on your shoulder, I knew you were me, but without my hideous deformities—me, as I might have been. And that made me happy, but only for a little while. My deep and growing satisfaction began when our eyes first met."

"At my vitalization in the Keeta pit—when you kissed my cheek for the first time."

"Even then you became more than my reflection and embodiment."

"And now?"

"Now, when we are together, or when I only think of you, my shame and humiliation is lifted and *I* become vivified. Selfishly, I can not lose this. Your existence, as you are, is what I need. Were we to have done that interchange, changing our 'reflections,' I could not look at myself again—even in the mirror."

The flawlessly beautiful, naked and statuesque Venus took a step back. She smiled her golden smile at Astra. The iridescent play of colors on her opalesque, crystalline body shone with a new found happiness. "It *is* true then!" she said, "We are identical—*in every important way*. We only look different."

SEVENTY-ONE

Venus was right. That ended it. Except for a continuation of Astra's occasional verbal jabs, there were no more tantrums and no more arguments. So instead, with care and affection, they kept a watch over Zack and Gegeneis without disturbing their transforming sleep. As they waited and watched, they could tell that something physical was happening beneath their closed eyelids—that structural changes were taking place.

Astra, with her continuing defensive attitude, would sometimes refer to the miraculous changes taking place, as "disagreeable eyeball reshuffling," "a cross-eyed metamorphosis," or as "Zack's REMedy." Venus got to the point where she would "laugh," with her own REM-like eye movements, at Astra's brassy, tactless, belittling comments. They watched and waited patiently, but the transition took much longer than expected—several days longer than the *essence of Origin* had predicted for its completion.

During the final days of waiting for this cross-metamorphosis, Origin was critically asked by Venus in dreamscape to once again explain to her why such physical trades were necessary and why there was this annoying time delay.

Origin's answer to the first part of her question was complicated and reasonable, as before; but *It*'s answer to the second part was unexpected.

Origin had never done anything like this before and once the process was under way it became necessary to "re-wire" and "re-connect" the visual apparatus for both "subjects"—rebuilding each with new chemistry and their mutually exchanged materials. Zack would have to receive Gegeneis-like eyes, neurons, and new forms of connection between that morphology and his human, *organic* brain neurology—with new kinds of synapses, neurotransmitters, and much more. At the same time, all of that had to be done in reverse for the inorganic Gegeneis, in order to maintain an equality and balance in the morphology between them—so that Gegeneis could also continue to see, although now with organic eyes identical to Zack's—flaws and all. Equality and balance: No free lunch.

Venus admitted that that was an elaborate process—extensive and intricate enough to serve as a good excuse for the delay—even for the *essence of Origin*.

On the morning the ocular transition was complete, everybody, especially Zack and Astra, celebrated—*eventually*. First, however, they had to wait until poor, half-blind, Gegeneis stopped stumbling all over himself and everybody else and accepted Zack's eyeglasses. Zack and his treasured identical, Gegeneis woke at the same moment. Zack immediately expressed elation at his unaided ability to see, and Gegeneis was also delighted—with *Zack's* ability to see. Nor was Gegeneis saddened for long by his own diminished vision. After several hours he became the first isomorph to put anything on his body—Zack's glasses. But he only came to that acceptance after continually stepping and falling into the canyon's lake, bumping into others, the wall and crashing into the Orb, nearly knocking it out of its nest.

As things settled down, the "celebration" could begin. The two isomorphs smiled politely, empathizing as best they could with the festive antics of their humans who began swimming and gaming in the cavern's bright, shimmering lake. Once out of the water, laughing and yelling throughout, they were hungry and indulged themselves in a meal—like pigs, downing glasses of wine, preparing and devouring medium and rare barbecued steaks, and ending with cake and ice cream all over their mouths and chins. After cleaning up, Astra put on her mask. Zack did not notice that, one way or the other—even with his "new and improved" eyes. Nor did Venus. Gegeneis did notice, but even with Zack's thick eyeglasses he was still too visually impaired to care in the least about Astra's need to look acceptable.

During all the eating and the antics there was an ongoing humorous interaction between the isomorphs and their humans. After the meal, that interaction became more serious and interesting, and turned into a real conversation. That was the part of the "celebration" the isomorphs enjoyed most, and it continued for a *long* time. Doyan, after all, was not expected back for another week.

To pass the time, they allowed their ideas and conversation to meander wildly, speaking of many things. The isomorphs gravitated to some of their favorite philosophical "what if" topics—topics that usually, in some way, had to do with them. Zack and Astra joined in, but they mainly listened.

Gegeneis and Venus talked about different "what-ifs" with a kind of authority and inspiration that left their listeners feeling that those "what-ifs" were more than philosophical ideas, but based on convictions instilled during long nights of "dreaming"—"dreaming" that Zack and Astra understood by then to be filled with rich and real experiences for their isomorphs—dreams brimful of shared information, knowledge, ideas and relationships as significant and tangible as any kind of interactions that humans were capable of within their own "real world"—only more so!

One such "what if" topic was a question of the true nature of the *essence of Origin* and *It*'s relationship to the planet Origin itself. What if they *are* different beings? Beyond what they knew and had seen so far, what other unusual and practical powers did the *essence of Origin* have—and what were the limitations of *It*?

The enjoyment the isomorphs and their humans were having with this game of intellectual probing rivaled the intensity, excitement and joy of any stimulating college dorm bull session. How well Zack and Astra remembered!

They continued to wonder about *It*'s creation abilities—how *It* may have been consciously responsible, for example, for the appearance of hundreds, or perhaps hundreds of thousands, of hollow, crystalline hills across the planet's continents and, for all they knew, *under* the oceans. Astra, who had been down there for many days, confirmed that the hills were there too.

They also wondered if David Michael's belief that the arching span of wall that formed each of the "hills" continued on around and beneath the surface like giant, egg-shaped ornaments with their lower halves hidden from view below the planet's flatlands. Those hills had, Dr. Michaels believed, the same egg-shape as the Keeta pits—the mounds of isomorph gestation. That topic led to discussion of the use of human DNA in creating "such wondrous beings as isomorphs." The isomorphs basked in those words when spoken by their human friends and identicals.

Further, they debated the "accidental" versus the benevolent "intentionality" of *their* hill suddenly coming out of nowhere—so it seemed—to cover and protect Mark's Base at the moment it would have been destroyed by the flood. There were old and new hills all across the continent and, according to reports from Stanley Lundeen's Astrophysics lab, most of the "new" hills were created about the same time as theirs, so their good luck might only have been a coincidence.

Every isomorph remembered his or her own, or the Keeta-pit experience with nostalgia, and that first incomparable moment of vitalization: the touch, the eye contact, the breath of life. It was a bonding moment for human and isomorph alike—not only a warmly reassuring remembrance, but a thrill beyond the ability of either to express.

Further, the isomorphs professed a continuing sense of community with their nightscape visitors and a deep connection with their parent planet, Origin. That connection was the same and yet different in some important ways from their nightscape experiences with the *essence of Origin*. Some began to think the two were not exactly the same. They *met* and experienced the *essence of Origin* as a vividly real nightscape being and had even conversed with *It*; but they never *met* the planet Origin, except to feel that presence and vastness. None the less, they knew the *essence of Origin*'s own connection to the planet (if they indeed were not the same) must be sharper and more direct than even their own. Still, the actual richness and magnitude of both experiences were impossible to convey to their humans—even with the most strenuous adjectives and analogies.

And they took time to worry about the conspiratorial plan that refreshed their dream of finding Origin's *essence*. Although it was better than the Directors', it still seemed insubstantial beside the bigger plans and aims of the two realities personified in Origin and its *essence*. What were *their* big plans? *They*, or *It*, could always make things happen. At least the *essence of Origin* was able to. Humans and isomorphs could do no more than *beg* or persuade those powers to make things happen.

Astra, Zack and their two identicals continued to wonder: are isomorphs and humans *really* so powerless? They talked about that late into the night and, sleepy eyed, concluded they were not *completely* helpless. Wasn't that what their conspiracy and the bargaining plan was all about? That that one most powerful being—or two, or three powerful beings for all they knew—was probably *not* all-powerful. It was more powerful than any of them, of course, but that did not leave them completely without leverage. In such relationships, they too had a degree of power—just as a rat can press a lever to persuade its human jailer to provide food pellets.

And they, or it, were certainly not all-knowing. If they were all-knowing, then why would they need Laura and Mark? Those two humans had certain special abilities and knowledge that was unavailable to them—or *It*. That is why the Dorts were sent out across the Galaxy and the universe—in search of beings with such abilities and knowledge.

All that was clear enough, but deep mysteries still existed. Why, for example, was the crystalline "terraforming" of Origin done by the Dorts? Was Origin a conscious power before that, or after? If it came after, then from where did the power originate? What power directed, or forced, the Dorts to do the "terraforming" and later to search for such creatures as Laura and Mark? Did the Dorts evolve, or were they created—as quickly as the new hills or the Big Bang itself—for those purposes. For what other special purposes might the Dorts exist? Were isomorphs and humans also, at some level, made for special purposes? Or is everything, in the end, without purpose? Their speculation continued; but at the moment, to be halfway practical, they could only hope to bring forth the *essence of Origin*.

"Perhaps," Gegeneis suggested, still meandering mentally, "the *essence of Origin* is a kind of 'mouthpiece' for the planet, just as our mouths—with our lungs, tongues and vocal cords—can mouth something close to our thoughts. Our ability to symbol—by speech, gestures, tone, writing, and etcetera—seems miraculous to me."

Venus said, "What's miraculous is conversation by any means from one complicated bunch of neurons or crystals to another set of complicated neurons or crystals. That's us talking now, and that's ours in dreamscape too."

Other conversations, from light hearted to intensely serious, went on between them and later with other "*Mutuals*"—a word humans and isomorphs came, one day, to call themselves. The conversation continued for days, and not just between the four Mutuals in the subsea cavern; but on the beach above them and everywhere else on the planet. Even those on the Transformation Cone became involved in the Great Conversation; a conversation they more affectionately named the "GBS"—the Great Bull Session.

After meeting some of the Others (*Others?*) the GBS continued with increased intensity and, most of all, it came to include the oldest resident in, on and of Origin—the *essence of Origin*.

SEVENTY-TWO

As for Others? Of course there were *Others*. Earth had not, for countless millennia, been suspected of harboring the only intelligent life in the Galaxy much less the entire universe with its millions of known galaxies, trillions of stars, and multitudes of planets. The Milky Way alone had immense numbers of stars harboring inhabited planets that offered countless opportunities for Dorts to lure and reel in their intelligent captives—not just humans.

In order to abduct those intelligent beings in time—meaning *before* all the pieces of matter in the universe exploded and then, less dramatically for what was left, evaporated entirely—there were prerequisites. In their pirate space ships, the Dorts had to start the hunt early. They had to go far enough and fast enough to search out those planets with the right kind of intelligent beings, teach those beings as necessary and, somehow, take or lure them back to Origin before it was too late for them to be of any use. The humans thought they were the only captives of the Dorts; but they were not. The kidnappings and other treachery was much more far-reaching—a fact soon to be confirmed.

A diverse array of captives would come to agree that those acts, like any acts of piracy, were premeditated. That judgment led to a question that would percolate among the Mutuals—humans and isomorphs together—and the Others:

What being's intention—*whose* intent—commanded those deceptions and kidnappings? The Mutuals already knew that Dorts were bright, yet semi-helpless tools and obedient followers of their maker. The original intention could not have been *their* decision; but did they have a choice later on? Could they be blamed if their acts, no matter how deliberate appearing, were based on "following orders"—some kind of internal orders, like instincts—that came from "higher up," disguised perhaps as a system of morality and values, graciously given to them by their maker who, as part of the same package of instincts, built into them obedience and a need to survive; and who also imbued them with a special notion that their criminal acts, for various "good reasons," were really *virtues*. And not just any reasons and virtues, but the best of all reasons and virtues rolled into one—in fact, the ultimate virtue on any powerful, intelligent being's moral defense and survival list—namely, acting with conscious forethought and intent to *save the whole universe*!

This argument's infusion into the Great Bull Session ended with some nodding gravely, opining that the kidnappings and all its accompanying "collateral damage" and "unintended consequences"—including the earlier decimation of human life that accompanied the Twister and the hijacking of the Great Cone of Transformation—were not crimes at all and that, to be perfectly fair and balanced, there had to be recognition that there was no *malice* aforethought and that the Dorts only meant well. "Anyway," Laura Shane pointed out, as justification, "it was all about values."

Officer Bracket, on the other hand, was in less than wholehearted agreement with that view.

Philosophical differences aside, time was running out and the Dorts knew that emergency situations required emergency actions. That thinking led to their taking control of the Great Cone and flinging it around the black holes, creating the Twister—the Twister that killed over a thousand of their own Dorts from planet Earth and hundreds of humans.

That "emergency situation" had been developing for a long time—billions of years—but its climax was at hand. Its cause was dark energy (negative gravity) whose repulsive power had been redoubling its acceleration influence on the universe's expansion at increasingly frequent and unpredictable intervals. That unpredictability added to the Dorts'—and planet Origin's—sense of urgency. In the previous ten centuries, the redoubling process happened every three or four decades; but its frequency had recently increased to every few years. The very laws of nature appeared to be changing before their eyes.

The first universewide whisper of dark energy emerged unnoticed when planet Earth was a bouncing one-billion year old. Since then the whisper became a murmur, then a snarl, and now a roar. During that escalation, intelligent *nonhumans* were paying attention. On approach to this *Big Rip*, the roar declared violence—its wide-open mouth was space itself expanding exponentially toward death by extreme entropy!

Hints of this were first noticed on Earth from early Doppler studies and astronomical distance measurements of far-away white dwarf stars going supernova; but over the course of millennia the changing spectrum lines of stars and galaxies became more than hints of a growing problem as the displaced lines moved sharply into the red. What this meant became frighteningly clear to advanced beings on many planets. Here is what they came to predict:

Every star, every galactic gas and dust cloud, and every solid object in the universe was on the verge of disassembling outward (exploding); except for the not so easily destroyed protons, their quarks, some massless particles, and black holes. The largest black holes would survive much longer than the rest of the universe according to the earlier predictions, but even they were expected to be gone in another multiple of a billion years. Since those early predictions, nature's rules seemed to change again, and the long-term estimate of many billions of years remaining for giant black holes was trimmed to less than a billion years—and *much less* for everything else. Yes, black holes would survive longer, but they too were doomed to evaporate into that endless, lifeless, expanding abyss of nothingness.

Advanced nonhuman astronomers mused that black holes were lucky to have even a billion years left. But the destruction of all life and everything else in the universe was about to occur—in less than a year in planet-Origin time; but more likely the Big Rip would happen sooner than that—in a day, an hour, or any instant.

That had not been the opinion of *human* scientists, but Laura, Mark and Stan would soon be convinced otherwise. Before that, Stanley Lundeen and his astrophysics staff had not been *completely* out of touch. They knew something would be happening, but not so soon. But it was obvious enough for them to stop speaking of the "Doppler redshift." For them it simply became the *"Doomsday shift."*

Planet Origin and the Dorts had already been working overtime on that "shift"—for millennia. Their long and intense focus on that and related phenomena put them on a par with some of the most enlightened nonhuman Others—including their astrophysicists, knowers and seers. Those nonhumans also knew that the time for action was "now or never." But, like humans, those Others also knew that nothing could possibly be done—that the entire universe and its laws could not be altered by mere living beings.

Stanley Lundeen, his staff and most of their students on the Transformation Cone were still working in his observatory and labs. Earlier they had studied the expansion properties of the universe, but had not done so recently. Those results did not cause them to expect the *doomsday* part of that *shift* to happen in their lifetime. Maybe, they figured, in a few hundred or a few thousand years—but not *this* soon. For them, the laws of nature were increasingly capricious—so much so that the real timeline, with its impending consequences, had slipped past their notice. Humans were among the last intelligent beings to appreciate the looming threat.

The last measurement of the expanding universe from Stan's *Earth* lab was obtained prior to the Transformation's departure—while they were still confidently unaware of any related problem or urgency. After their arrival at Origin, Stan and his staff spent little time considering matters thought to be distant, merely academic, or nonemergencies. Instead they became preoccupied with the search for Earth's location.

"If we only had Earth's spacetime coordinates," Stan—and everybody else—was now saying, "then there would be no need to negotiate with the *essence of Origin* or any*thing* else." On learning of the impending universal explosion, they changed . . . *nothing*! They continued what had been their main pursuit since entering Origin's space: The search for Earth's coordinates. If death was looming, they wanted more than ever to die at home—on Earth.

SEVENTY-THREE

Everyone knew that in two more days Doyan would return to the cavern to bring back the Orb with its passengers. They were anxious to view the physical changes in Astra and Zack they'd heard about from below, but other news from there was sparse—and some was now incorrect.

It was early in the morning, just before the rise of Nimbus. Officer Bracket's men had taken turns scanning the hills, mountains and the ocean for any signs of trouble.

Clint was in a deep sleep when roused to news from the watch that something was happening in the ocean. He jumped to his feet, totally confused and disoriented. Without thinking he grabbed his laser, strapping it across his shoulder and around the only stitch of clothing he had on, his under shorts; fetched his binoculars, and dashed out toward the beach. But he stopped cold and returned to add his holster belt and pistol. Then he went to the beach, attired mostly in belts and guns.

Within a hundred meters of the shoreline he saw Nimbus displaying a slit of itself above the horizon. It sent long shadows and streaks of light that brightened the ocean enough for Clint, with his binoculars, to spot Mark's Orb. It appeared to float there, half in the water and half out. It moved slowly toward shore and kept rising higher in the water, but it approached with a jerking, up and down motion unrelated to the oceans waves and seemed to be limping along more than floating. Soon it was out of the water, but only barely. The word spread rapidly and soon most of the humans and isomorphs on The Island were anxiously gathering near Clint. They were not far from the shoreline. Even Doyan was there, which confused most of the onlookers. Wasn't *he* supposed to be bringing in the Orb?

The closer it came, the higher it rose from the water. It was apparently disabled, as Mark had warned, and was being supported from below by something as yet not clearly seen. Closer and closer, but still far out. Then, as the Orb's supporting object became more visible, Clinton Bracket lost it. He took his laser rifle from its belts and aimed it just beneath the Orb in order to strike whatever was holding it up, and pulled the trigger. He missed by several meters causing little damage, except to momentarily boil a speck of ocean near the Orb.

Ned was immediately at Clint's side. "What the hell are you doing? The Orb is coming back and you're shooting at it!"

Clint took aim again, but Ned pushed the laser to the side as it discharged.

"What the hell are *you* doing?" Clint shouted, glaring at Ned. "Can't you see the monster that's taken the Orb? Open your eyes!"

Ned ordered Clint to give him the weapon. They argued, but Clint did shortly comply—angrily. In the midst of this brief, but intense quarrel, Ned neglected to also commandeer Clint's pistol. Ned walked back to the crowd where Laura was watching. He was weighted down with the heavy laser rifle and its ornate, official looking belts, but was weighted down even more by yet another set-to with Clinton Bracket.

The crowd along the shore stepped back the more evident the Orb's support had become. Murmuring had begun and was getting louder. From the crowd noise, certain words were clearly distinguished: *monster*, among them, along with *giant, Cyclops, troll, mutant*. "It's not a man," a woman shrieked. "It's disgusting big! Only *halfway* a man. A *quasi*-man. A quasi-modo!"

As the grotesque figure drew still closer beneath its load, the labels of derision faded, and a new term became prominent: "Atlas" was heard again and again. The naked giant was carrying the Orb on its shoulders, much as illustrations of an ancient Greek myth depicted that Titan carrying the heavens on his shoulders. But its face had only one large eye, with that now-familiar cat's-eye slit. The face was deformed like the rest of its body and grizzly with gray crystalline flecks.

The giant emerged with its burden from the shoal and the crowd drew farther back, forming a great half-circle. They waited patiently, now in silence, to see what it would do next. The giant stepped several meters in from the waters upward wash and placed the Orb on the sandy beach. It then proceeded to sit on it, facing the crowd and taking another familiar pose. This time the label coming from the now involved crowd was "the thinker." Laura turned to Ned with a smile. "He's trying to introduce himself to us by posing with old and familiar symbols. In a way, he seems to be saying 'Admire me, but do not fear me.'"

Clinton Bracket was still in the front of the crowd. He didn't get it. He stepped forward from the center of the half-circle of onlookers, appearing more bowlegged than usual in his shorts, with his arms equally bowed-looking, out to his sides, as if intending to outdraw and out gun the unarmed giant. He could have been David in his undershorts, meeting the Philistine, Goliath—except David's ammunition was just a rock. Still holding both arms in the quick-draw position—both arms, despite the fact that he only had a gun on his right side—Clint moved two or three bowlegged steps closer to the monster. Again, the mood of the crowd changed abruptly, becoming intolerably tense.

Something about Clint's own pose seemed to register with the giant and it suddenly displayed a gigantic, south of the border, toothy grin along with a stentorian roar of laughter. Clint moved nary a muscle, but remained poised for action, wetting himself only slightly.

After the monster settled down, Clint snarled in as loud a voice as he could, "What's so funny, Cyclops?"

Then, in a calm, widely recognized, but nonetheless thunderous voice, it responded (changing roles a bit), "Listen pilgrim. You can't shoot me! I come in peace. So don't mess with *me*, partner!"

Clint responded in a loud voice to this verbal challenge with the most eloquent, profoundly threatening words he could conceive of on the spur of the moment: "*Oh yeah*?"

The monster responded in kind, only louder: "*Yeah*!"

"Oh yeah?"

"Yeah!"

Laura grabbed Ned's arm as he was about to move into another confrontation with Clint. "Don't get into this, Ned," she said. "The giant can take care of himself. Let them work this out. Anyway, can't you see—?"

"See what?"

"They're practically two of a kind!"

"Yes, but that still doesn't—"

Laura silenced him with a look.

The argument continued, "Oh yeah?" but with less vehemence.

Followed by a quieter, "Yeah."

Then, with a stroke of originality, Clint changed the discourse: "How come can't I shoot you, Cyclops?"

"Cuz, that's why!"

"That's no reason."

"You called me Cyclops. Just call me *Cy*."

"Asshole!"

"No, Cy."

Clint's arms were starting to relax, and those on the sides of the half-circle detected the play of a small smile around his mouth.

Then "Cy" turned his head and saw that Nimbus was only about three diameters above the horizon. Once again he began to laugh as he looked back at Clint. The toothy smile reappeared and the giant boomed, as quietly as it could, "The star is barely up, so it's not my time to be shot, nor yours to shoot."

Clint's half-smile disappeared. "I don't get it."

"It isn't high noon yet, Ninny. You should know that."

Ninny. Wrong word! When Clint was a kid they used to tease him with that name. He lost it again and did the quick draw.

It was awful for the humans to see, and equally shocking for the observing isomorphs. For those Mutuals, everything happened in an instant; but for Cy it all happened in slow motion. To the onlookers, there was a momentary maelstrom of swirling sand around Clint's body, and then it vanished—sand, body and all. Clint's body had disappeared and his disembodied head fell onto the surface where he had been standing. Laura screamed, as did hundreds of others! It was murder, before the eyes of everyone.

But Cy had his own, slow motion, view of things: Clint's hand "slowly" reached down until it touched his gun, and then, less slowly, a circular hollow opened in the sand below where Clint was standing, and then closed again around his falling body, leaving only his head exposed above the sand.

The shock and awe of the crowd was mitigated by two things: A muffled gunshot from beneath the sand, and a loud shout from the disembodied head—"FUCKER!"

Laura quickly recovered on hearing Clint's last epithet. The crowd began to chuckle, and then became quiet as they heard the giant's reply: "No, you still haven't got it right. It's Cy." The giant's voice was almost quiet; but more recognizable than ever.

Laura turned to Ned. They both smiled. Ned said, "You were right. The giant can take care of himself!"

"But," Laura said, "our friend is going to be extremely angry."

"He sure is and will be. I guess Mark doesn't like having his Homing Pigeons stolen from him all the time."

"You know that's not what I meant," Laura said, frowning.

"Yeah. I knew that."

Cy leaned over and tapped the Orb's hatch window. The hatch opened, the automatic ramp extended before them, and the four passengers marched down to the sandy beach. At the same time somebody was marching toward the Orb. "Good to see you're all back," the man said as they passed one another. The four passengers moved into the waiting crowd as the man walked up to the now standing giant.

"You're too goddamn big and you're ugly," the man said. His voice was smaller, but otherwise identical to the giant's. "Why me?" he continued in an ambiguously plaintive or angry tone.

"I'm glad to see you too," the giant proclaimed.

"Why me?" he asked again.

The giant lowered his head, as if he didn't look sad and pathetic enough as he was. He turned and limped back and forth in front of the Orb and finally stopped where he had started. He moved his eye to look at the man. "I done the best I could," he said, with sadness in his bellowing voice.

"How did you become vitalized without my touching you?"

"Would you have touched me?"

"Probably not."

"That's your answer then."

"Vitalization is possible without our touch?"

"Origin can do anything it wants, up to a point."

"Why me?"

"Because, Mark, you were the *first* and the *only*—at the time. Origin still had *no practice* making human, or any other kind of isomorph. So I done my best. That's *why you*. I had no reason to expect any more of you to arrive for quite a while. When more humans arrived, there was more time to practice. Be glad I'm just a misshapen giant isomorph with arms and legs, such as they are. When the Dorts, as you call them, were made—half here, half in another place—there was no pattern to go by. That's why the shapeless things look like, well, the shapeless things they are."

By then Mark was too intrigued to be critical. "You made the Dorts? You weren't even here back then. What *were you* then? The whole planet?"

"Yes. And that's what I am now, only better. After the Dorts enriched my planetary crust and surfaces with a patina of interactive crystalline connections I became a more conscious being and more aware of what my own maker—from that other place—hoped I might become in this great realm."

"It sounds like you come from a hierarchy of powers."

"True. Even my maker had a maker, just as the Dorts had me, and the isomorphs had me and you, and now we can all interact for our mutual enlightenment, welfare and power. I made the Dorts, but they enriched me in many ways—'terraforming' me in 'crystal' was only one of those ways. It's like human culture, to use a far away analogy. Without culture you would be feral—no more than an animal."

"You and I are not of the same culture," Mark said.

"I know, but I'm doing the best I can. Sorry I'm not more identical to you—so we could relate better. I had no name before the Dorts or before you humans arrived—Cy for instance. I kind of like that name. Way before then, before anything else, in fact, when the end of it all came into view and the universe was getting ready to blow—you don't know about that yet, Mark, so I'll explain it later—that's when my own maker sent me to see if I could do something about it."

"It? What it?"

"About ending the threat to both of our universes."

"Now you've lost me."

"I'll have to explain it to you later."

"To solve that problem—that you'll explain to me later—what did you come up with?"

"I kept trying but, as I told you, Dorts were the best I could do. I needed the detailed laws of this universe first. The laws of nature here. I had no idea what they were. So I went back and forth between universes, making some Dorts here and some there. They are a product of both universes. You, Mark, already know more about the laws of nature in this universe than I do. And so do the Others. That's why Dorts were necessary. Something had to improve my consciousness—something like your going to school and deliberately studying to improve your knowledge. So, as I said, I had them 'terraform' my connections and make new ones. Then I had them go out and bring back the scientific information to me. That included beings like you. It also now includes the isomorphs of humans and the Others. All will be essential later on. Dorts alone won't be able to do the jobs that lie ahead."

"What would you have done if living beings had not arrived on Origin?" Mark asked.

"All would have been lost, of course. I was delighted when you and others like you arrived. Till then I had no live beings to go by. I had no blueprints. And I was losing hope."

"Blueprints?"

"You're a scientist. You know what I mean. The 'blueprints' turned out to be deoxyribonucleic acid, ribonucleic acid. You know, DNA, RNA and stuff like that."

"When did you learn about that?"

"After Doyan and the other six Dorts got back and touched ground with me."

"Dorts didn't touch Origin until after the isomorphs were created and vitalized."

"I didn't need to know the scientific names to create isomorphs. It was only after Doyan arrived that I got all the 'written' details about that, the human genome, and everything else—all the dead human languages, human history, everything in your libraries. The Dorts were compulsive about that sort of thing. Now I'm stuck with it too."

"You got those 'blueprints' directly—from our blood, didn't you."

"Yes, but translating that information into something like crystalline forms took a lot of trial and error. I was my own first error."

There was a long silence. Then Cy lowered his head even more, closed his eye and said, "May I ask a favor of you?"

"It all depends. What?"

"Would you please . . . touch me?"

Mark shook his head, no. "That's too primitive and personal, touching is," he said.

The eye opened. "Very well then. But I had to ask."

Someone in the crowd yelled, "Touch him."

Mark became used to the giant's megaphonic voice and had forgotten that everybody else could hear Cy's every word.

Mark turned to the crowd of Mutuals and again shook his head.

En masse the Mutuals began chanting, "Touch him, touch him, touch him . . ."

The huge creature was so bent over that its hands almost touched the sand at its feet. Mark shrugged and said, "Oh, what the hell," walked over to the giant and wrapped both hands around one of its neck-sized fingers—they were that enormous.

Cy's expression altered again. He gave a happy, toothy smile. Then there was another noticeable change. The dull-gray flecks covering his entire surface became a reflective rainbow of glowing and flickering translucence—a characteristic of isomorphic elation. Even the mountains sparkled more than usual. Never before had the planet Origin experienced such a rush of life, and the crowd cheered—especially the isomorphs.

"Get me out of here, goddamnit!"

"If you promise not to shoot me," the giant rumbled back. "I'm unarmed and helpless, you know."

"I don't promise nuttn, Fucker!

"Hey! What ya doin', Fucker?"

Clint uttered those words when he felt something forcefully removing the revolver from his hand. It popped out of the sand near him a few seconds later with the barrel twisted into a U-shape. Then came another spray of sand and Clint—slowly enough this time for all to see—rose up from the beach sand as if standing on a lift. The sand poured off of him. He looked around at the crowd. Then, realizing for the first time that he was not dressed, turned and shook his fist at the 'Cyclops,' turned again and marched back through the crowd toward his habitat, presumably to clean up and change into his uniform.

As he shoved past Ned and Laura, Ned said, "We'll need you back here soon, Clint, so hurry. But leave the guns behind."

Clint glanced at Ned with a disgusted, how-dare-you-speak-to-me-that-way-you-inferior-little-punk look on his face—as if pondering with contempt an upstart adversary's debating point; but he continued the march back to his place, nose in the air like an emperor pretending he was attired in magnificent garments.

Cy said, "I think we should hurry now, don't you? Take me to your leader."

"Nobody says that any more," Mark replied to his physically messed up, overgrown isomorph.

"Then I'll settle for Ned Keller and Laura Shane, and you, of course, and Doyan, and maybe some others."

They started walking back toward the center of the half-circle of Mutuals who were no longer pulling back. In fact, their formation was breaking up as some were moving toward them, and others were leaving.

"What's the rush?" Mark asked.

"We need to get started. It's necessary before the Others arrive."

"You keep saying that. What others?" Mark asked.

"It's a long story, but many others will be here. Not long after you humans arrived, they came. They came from many planets, each group being escorted by other doyens. Not from Earth. They should be here soon. Any minute, in fact."

They walked in silence a bit farther. Finally Mark said, "Any minute, eh? Let's pick up the pace. The clock suddenly seems to be ticking faster than usual. I know my heart is. It's banging on my chest to get out!"

"Margaret! I didn't know you'd be here," Astra said, starting a happy reunion conversation. The four Homing Pigeon passengers had worked their way to the back of the crowd where they ran into Margaret and her isomorph Opal, and Kevin Verily with his identical, Nor-Man. Venus and Opal began a conversation of their own.

Margaret Heckart said to Astra, "You were down there a long time. A lot has happened up here while you were gone."

"I can see that. It looks like you moved the entire camp here from the northern part of The Island, even a new barracks-canteen."

"We did, and a lot more."

"Why?"

"The *essence of Origin*—the big guy over there—simply let us know where he was—through our dreamscaping isomorphs. So we all got very excited and optimistic, except for Officer Bracket—he came here on the first wave before our isomorphs told us exactly where the *essence of Origin* would be. Clint must have thought it was some kind of a trap. Anyway, we packed up and came here. All of us, finally. That even includes half of those who were staying at the second Base camp—New Camp. The other half moved back to the Great Cone. Then the Cone moved. Look up there. See it?" Margaret pointed.

They all looked up. Zack said, "I'll be damned. There it is!"

Margaret was shocked. She finally got the whole picture. "Zack Parker! You can see! Oh dear, why is Gegeneis wearing your glassed. Oh God! Astra. You haven't changed. I was hoping—"

"Well, quit hoping. It was a bad deal. By now Venus would be looking a lot worse than Ol' One-eye over there. She'd look like me. Venus said she wanted the 'deal,' I didn't. End of story! How did you know what was supposed to happen?"

"Him," Margaret said, pointing her thumb over her shoulder toward the giant who was settling in with Ned and the others.

Astra said, "Call him Ol' Blabber-mouth from now on. He spoke without permission."

"You're right," Margaret said. "He informed us of a lot of things through our doubles. But it got us mobilized and thinking! That's when the Great Conversation got even bigger! For instance, Cy—we called him the *essence of Origin* most of the time then—suggested that Stanley and his team take a fresh look at the Coma Cluster of galaxies. Stan thought that was a stupid waste of time, but did it anyway. So . . . guess what?"

"Okay, what?"

"You'll never guess!"

Astra didn't have to guess. She said, "Stan couldn't find it. That news was all over the Great Bull Session. The Coma Cluster is totally gone, along with every other galaxy in the universe except for something that looks like Andromeda and the rest of the local galaxies. All the other galaxies near and far have vanished from sight—from the sight of even our best astronomical equipment. It's like the very wavelengths of light have been stretched flat. The galaxies have accelerated away from us that fast, along with space itself. If Stan says he's not even sure that's Andromeda out there—and that's the GBS rumor—it may be that the expansion distortion is becoming very local, distorting even the light from our closest galactic neighbors or . . . or we're somewhere else. Right now, the redshift seems to be in its glory. So, of course Stan is now thinking like David Michaels, that this might not even be our universe. Personally, I think that's pushing it, but you never know."

Margaret was still surprised. "My Gosh! You already knew! Ol' One-eye must have known and told Venus in dreamscape, and then Venus told you. Am I right? . . . Venus?"

Venus turned her head toward Margaret and replied, "No. We've been talking with the *essence of Origin* directly for several days—not only in dreamscape. That's when and how we found out about the latest expansion of space. The dreamscape GBS watered it down. Too bad. What did Dr. Lundeen say when he couldn't find the rest of the universe, to say nothing of not finding Earth's coordinates?"

Margaret had heard the story, but turned to Kevin: "You and Nor-Man were with Ned when the message came. But *what* did Stan say?"

Kevin said, "Stan looked worried on the screen. I don't remember his exact words. Nor-Man, you have perfect recall, how did it go?"

Nor-Man seldom spoke without an invitation, but seemed pleased to oblige. "The message was not short. It was technical. Dr. Lundeen asked that Dr. David Michaels join us, so David and his identical, Oscar, came in to hear his thoughts."

Nor-Man then quoted Stanley Lundeen word for word, speaking very fast, for all of five minutes on the technical part, and concluded with Stan's summary.

Margaret said, "That was a little hard to follow, but could you give us that summary again, slowly? And in your own words this time?"

"Sure," Nor-Man said. "Dr. Lundeen was making his remarks to David Michaels in particular, saying that Dr. Michaels was right all along. That the strange findings David was getting from all the crystals were very likely, 'not from around here,' but from some other universe. Then Dr. Lundeen added, 'And neither is this universe from around here. I can't even vouch,' he said, 'for this galaxy being our Galaxy—this one that has for so long eluded our finding planet Earth. No wonder! This may not even be the Milky Way. Nothing is familiar. Even Andromeda and the other nearbys don't look quite right.' That was all he had to say."

"Then the GBS rumors were right," Astra said.

Margaret said, "That was it for us! That's what it took to motivate us—all of us—a vanishing universe or another one! That's why we came here."

Astra said, "Cy. If he wants that name, I guess I can use it, but don't hold me to it; he's such a jerk sometimes. He's over there with the big shots now, and lapping it up I'm sure. Oh look! He just caught my eye. He's beckoning for us to come over. Bless him. I hoped he'd include us."

"First you say he's a jerk. Now you say bless him. Is he blessed or jerk?"

"Right now I'd say blessed. He did hail us over, so let's go. Okay, I'll admit it—I liked him down there in the cavern—even as a jerk."

Margaret frowned. "He hailed you, Astra. Not us."

"I know; but screw that. Let's all go."

Together they all walked over and joined the inner circle! Cy was happy to have them there. He hadn't had much real company for quite a few million years.

SEVENTY-FOUR

The disappearance of the universe did catch their attention. Especially since it had come about so quickly—since their departure from Earth. That fact—recently ushered to their awareness by a grotesque, slit-pupiled, one-eyed giant, recently naming himself *Cy*, formerly known as the *essence of Origin*—was a shock to whatever complacency they had left; no matter who brought that 'little surprise' to their attention. But the disclosure did gave that deformed, living colossus an added credibility that no amount of Merlin magic with beach sand could ever have accomplished on its own.

The give and take of their meeting on the beach included Doyan, who joined them later. The firsthand meeting between Doyan and the *essence of Origin* after so many centuries would have been a touching scene if their mutual embrace had been less outrageous and bizarre—from a human perspective. It was really a function of their two 'physiques' and represented nothing morally untoward—to them. They did, however, appear to be all over each other and sent out real sparks. Ned commented to Laura, with a smirk, that they were "just imparting information to each other."

"I knew that," she said, rolling her eyes.

Many arrived even later than Doyan, including allergy-ridden Stanley Lundeen. He reluctantly deigned to join them on the surface, carrying boxes of tissues. He arrived with another rare visitor to the planet—Douglas Groth, the Transformation's master engineer and Physical Systems Director. Most of the late arrivals had just come down from the Great Cone. Many others from there were also pouring onto the beach. Newly arriving isomorphs, and those already present, made their own contributions to discussions on the beach that day.

Most of the human *big shots* were reasonably well versed in some of the published sciences of the time from planet Earth; but, thanks to the nightscape information dumps from Doyan and the other Earth-Dorts, the isomorphs and the *essence of Origin*, Cy, were up to date on *all* of it. Regarding the *published* science in quantum, string, Transformation, and Reo-Sphere physics, Laura and Mark were their equals, but in most other areas of science they were not. They knew none of the joys of entomology, the new quantitative studies of the ancient but revised Rorschach test; nor were they up on a thousand other areas of science about which they could care less.

Laura and Mark dodged discussing, in any revealing way, the joys and treasures packed into the deepest mines of their own expertise—areas recently elaborated and synthesized by Laura into a set of formulas that completed Transformation Theory and, combining it with Mark's Reo-Sphere Theory, completed it too. The elaborated theory now existed in both of their minds—*not* in the science literature. Mark's few obscure articles on Reo-Sphere Theory published in a minor physics journal gave clues to its potential but included none of his important formulas. Laura's new formulas filled the gap between Transformation and Reo-Sphere theory—formulas she happily shared with Mark one day over coffee, after which they burned the napkins on which the formulas were written.

As Laura and Mark continued to work their mine of ever-unfolding revelations, on napkins and in their private discussions, they stood more and more on each other's shoulders. Mark's unfinished Theory had been a major leap from Laura's broad theoretical shoulders. Her recent advances resulted in both theories melding into a single, rich, complete, and self-contained theory; but it still did not add up to a final theory. They both knew there had to be much more—quantum jumps more. Of their completed theory, the other humans, Doyan, the isomorphs, and Cy were clueless as to its details. They were only aware of its existence.

Revealing their full theory to Cy would have to be *the* final negotiating chip to obtain the spacetime chart that would guide them back to Earth—assuming the galaxy they were in was still the Milky Way. Their published material was already free and on the "negotiating table"—as it had been for years—including its practical implications for translation into Cones of Transformation, large and small. Ned Keller, Director of $3T$ Corporation, was the master translator of that material, not as a scientist, but as the administrative organizer authorized to create them.

Cy was not coy about why he wanted that unpublished, upgraded special knowledge from Mark and Laura. He saw their formulas as *"possibly"* necessary for stopping, reversing or otherwise *correcting* the headlong plunge of "two universes" into mutual destruction. Most of the listeners missed Cy's mumbled words, "*two* universes."

"What do you mean, 'possibly'?" Mark asked.

"Two things. *First*, is your theory complete and powerful enough to clarify what is happening to this universe and the other *gravitationally interacting* universe or universes?"—*Now the listeners were paying attention!*—"Can it explain how that interaction creates the extreme, fly-apart redshift in this universe and the equally threatening Big Crunch blueshift in the other universe?"

"Our universe has a twin?" Mark asked his 'identical.'

"No, Mark. No two universes could be less alike than these, although they have unmistakable commonalities."

"That makes no sense."

"Not logically. It's hard to explain. Think of them as palindromes of one another, or D L versions of the same amino acid, or—"

Zack interrupted, "*What* other universe are you guys talking about?"

"That one Doyan can tell you about," Cy replied. "And so can I. *We're both from there*—as is much of the crust of this planet. As your Chief Geologist, David Michaels might say,"—he nodded toward David—"*we* are not from around here." David started to laugh but was shushed by his isomorph, Oscar.

"You told us there were *two things*—besides two universes, I mean," Mark said.

"Of course! And *second*, even if your formula is extensive and accurate enough, and powerful enough to make all the above concerns understandable, can it be given a *practical* translation so that, like Transformation and Reo-Sphere Theory, it can be *used*?"

"Like a cake or an ice cream *recipe*?" Clint Bracket said with a tone of ridicule—for which he received hostile looks from the crowd around him.

Cy, on the other hand, gave Clint one of his big, toothy smiles. Then, speaking to Clint as if to a small child, he said, "You're right. Transformation Theory became Ned Keller's recipe for your Ice Cream Cones of Transformation." The crowd cringed. David laughed. "With his head chef and cooking skills—or, if you prefer, his administrative leadership and organizational abilities—he stirred together a thousand ingredients with the help of that many experts—the junior chefs—from many fields. That's how you got your magnificent ice cream float, Clint—that Great Cone that floats above you right now!"

David laughed as Cy looked straight up—his giant, single eye lifted aloft on the end of what looked like an elephant's trunk or a great penis. "That makes Ned the master cook and ice cream maker. But suppose you have the perfect recipe," Cy continued, retracting his eye to its previous location in the middle of his forehead, "Without the right ingredients, equipment and good cooks, you'd have to go without your cake and ice cream, Clint!" Everybody cringed and groaned—except David, who bent over shaking. But they all got Cy's point. The giant finished with a nod to Ned, and rumbled, "For the Transformation Cones at least, Ned, you were the perfect chef."

Ned smiled and said, "I couldn't have done it without Jack Lewis and Laura Shane and, oh yeah, Reinholdt Dietzman . . ." and he went on, stumbling through a dozen more names before Laura interrupted.

"Stop," she said. "Don't go on. The list would never end. For some things, and for once, accept your own credit. You organized the science teams. You didn't have to be a major scientist yourself, but an organizer, definitely. And a leader. That, Ned, is what you were and what you are. Accept it!" The crowd applauded.

Cy—with his humps and lumps, his out of place eye, and a protruding occiput that twisted like a horn down to the middle of his hunched back—was more than an outsized freak. He was showing himself to be a charismatic crowd pleaser! Leaning toward his appreciative audience he said, in low, rumbling tones—they loved his rumbling tones—"I believe the Reo-Sphere Theory that now incorporates Transformation Theory, or maybe it's the other way around, will be an important part of the final answer we all want—that we should all demand. We know that Transformation Theory is powerful given its practical extensions into things like your Transformation Cones. And we know that Reo-Sphere Theory is useful for technological translations that enable *instant* transfer of physical objects through space—the transfer of things as gigantic as that Great Cone floating above us now," he said pointing a finger upward.

From the crowd, just as he was pointing, a woman's voice cried out: "Please! *Don't look at it!*" Mark looked around and smiled when he heard the voice; then waved to Denise Christensen and Chastity. Until he heard Denise, he didn't know they had arrived. Denise then quickly covered her eyes. She never knew if Cy gazed skyward or not.

"But more is needed," Cy continued, "—more physical science, wave mechanics, other theories we've never heard of, their resultant laws, *and* their deepest practical implications explicated."

"He doesn't want much, does he?" Clint said to Dummy.

"Shh!" Dummy hissed.

Cy continued, "And finally, all those diverse theories and laws will not only need to be fitted together, they must be seamlessly fused—your combined Theory in with all the rest."

"See! What did I tell you! He wants it all!" Clint said.

"Shh."

Opal asked Cy, "Where will all those never-before-heard-of scientific laws come from?"

"From every planet that has them. We lost some of them, but maybe there are still enough left—with the necessary depth. The Others will be here. They're from your other Milky Way planets. They arrived on Origin with exquisitely bad timing. They arrived *after* you humans were settled into Mark's Base camp, but *before* the flood. Hill making has always been agonizing. Digging into myself to birth so many hills at once—to cover all of you and all of them—to protect one and all from the flood was, I regret to say, more than I could handle. A couple of those diverse, traveling populations were lost."

Kevin Verily shouted angrily, "*Kidnapped* populations, you mean! Just taken! Without explicit permission no less!" Clint and others nodded.

Cy looked at Kevin with his eye-ridge raised. "Good things do not always require permission. Is the existence of the universe a good or a bad thing? I think it's a good thing."

"That's totally off the topic. You're trying to excuse yourself—and changing the subject!"

"Permission. Hmm. Who gave permission for there to even be a universe? You? Or, on a less ambitious level, consider this: Did you *ask* to be born? Was that a good or bad thing to happen—without your permission? Where were you then—to give, or not to give, that consent? Were you around then, in some form? Did you exist then to give that go-ahead?"

"What's your point?"

"You did exist, you know!"

"Huh?"

"You have always existed—since before the beginning of time—in potentiality."

"Of course, or I wouldn't be here."

"But have you always existed *enough* to make actual choices? I don't know, but it is possible. At that time would you have, or did you choose to come here—in the way you did? Possibly, but who knows? Was any of this—the occurrences that brought you to this planet—with your will or against your will? Anyway, you may still be here for a good cause—unless the cause fails, then not. But remember, *more* of those Other populations—and yours—were saved by the hills than were lost in the flood."

"None at all would have been lost if you hadn't abducted us, any of us, in the first place," Kevin snarled.

"Not *immediately*," Cy replied.

"What? *Not immediately?* That's your rationalization for mass kidnappings that led to so many deaths?"

"No! No such petty rationalization."

"Well, excuse me. Then, no doubt, you have a more *grandiose* rationalization to offer?"

"Of course, and you already know what it is and that it trumps your new-found morality."

"My *new-found* morality?"

"If I'm not mistaken, you are under house or supervised arrest for attempted murder. I'm sure you have a rationalization for that."

"I won't respond to that! But please, refresh our memories about your rationalization for mass kidnappings—the grandiose one that 'trumps' my morality!"

"Some behaviors are no more than worthless gambles—for things that are unimportant—no matter how good the odds."

"You're changing the subject again."

Cy continued, "When the likelihood of winning is low, but the outcome is important, then the game may well be worth it—whether it's a game of chance or a game of skill."

"You're talking about luck. Your questionable enterprise has no guarantee." Kevin sounded disappointed.

"Only one. If we do nothing, the destruction of everything *is* guaranteed."

"If the follow-on from here is to be of any value, remind us again—what's at stake? And do we have a choice? And what *are* the odds for success?" Despite himself, Kevin was getting down to business.

"The odds are better than zero. The odds of your eventual existence were better than zero, but not by much, at the time of, and even 'before,' the Big Bang. Right now, that is the first thing that matters—the stakes are so high that failure to try would be what you, Verily, would call . . . a sin. Your mind—and the mind of everybody here—is what matters. That there *is* a chance is the first shift you must make in your thinking for any of this to succeed."

"The first thing? There is more? What else?"

"The second shift that your thinking requires for the merest possibility of success, is—not just yours, once again, but everybody's—full cooperation and assistance with the parts of this enterprise that go beyond luck, odds, chance, or fluky contingencies. That means full disclosure of your best, most relevant science *and* assistance with creation of something close to a final *and usable* theory. That will be needed as we pull your theories and the Others' theories together. Neither I nor the creations you call Dorts can do this alone."

"So," Kevin said, "mental shift number one is to accept some luck in this enterprise—whatever that is; and mental shift number two is to reject, even forget the luck factor, and work the science to the hilt to create a perfect outcome."

"That's right. One shift, two shift, and we'll be off and running!" David laughed as he added, ". . . Red Shift, Blue Shift."

"Let's get back to your rationalization for causing all those deaths," Kevin said. "To follow on from there—with your two suggested mental shifts—where *are* we going? What's at stake? Let's hear that grandiose rationalization! Refresh our memories!"

"Right now, with hard work and any luck at all, a *million generations to come* will be born and live—thanks to what we could do here. Make that *billions* if you count the other inhabited planets in this Galaxy besides Earth—and multiples of *trillions* if you go beyond the Milky Way Galaxy and include all the other galaxies in this universe. Then double or triple that, or more—we don't know how many or how far the dominos of this effort will fall—to include the other universe, or universes, that would also be saved!"

"And all of that, thanks to your generosity as a criminal—an abductor?"

"Yes. Perhaps. I wonder if you've even heard me." Cy said, shaking his head in a way that could have, were he human, been interpreted as confusion and frustration.

Kevin would not let up. "The most evil deeds in history," he said, "came from such thinking. What you have done, based on that kind of thinking, is unconscionable!"

"What is unconscionable?" Cy asked, still shaking his large and confused head; his eye flopping back and forth with it like a barely attached appendage.

"Using your so called good-outcome intensions to justify your criminal means!" Kevin said in anger.

Cy's head became still, at last, with what could have been clarity. He gave Kevin a well focused, one-eyed frown and rumbled, "Mr. Verily, excuse my saying this, but that's crap. A good outcome is more likely if you have one in mind to start with. You need to consider what's best for the most in the long run, not just what's good for you and your friends in the short run. Here the short run and the long run come together. Everybody here that you know may live out full lives because of what you call my 'criminal means.' Even earlier, the hills I birthed from the body of my crystalline being, saved *you* and *most of the Others*. I did that, and considered it ahead of time. Was that criminal?"

Kevin ignored Cy's argument and said, "There you go again with that 'Others' stuff. What's *that* about?"

"It's about their science and yours. Some of their science and cosmology is just as good or better than yours. Between you and the Others, the odds for this pursuit have risen to well above zero."

"Okay. Say you did save 'most' of the Others. Why not all of them?"

"I tried. I done my best, but the flood . . . it overwhelmed me. A few of those Other populations were also lost when they attempting to exit their hill too early and got crushed in the collapse. Still, most of the populations, like yours, figured out that *the hills themselves were vulnerable*. Knowing that, most of them made no further attempt to exit. My—excuse me—*your* isomorphs were the only group to conceive of a cover to protect everybody from a collapsing hill; but breaking out of the hill was unnecessary."

"*Unnecessary*? Why?" Keeta asked.

"You'll soon see. The ones that made it—that didn't drown in the flood or get crushed under a hill—are on their way. They're coming here to *share their science* with us." Then Ol' One-eye looked around, gave another toothy grin, and added in a sinister tone, "*They'd better be!*"

Dutifully, but uncomfortably this time, his audience laughed. David did not laugh at all; nor did most of the Directors.

With her notebook and very busy pen in hand, Debra Anderson asked, "*When* are they coming?" *What*, *why* and *where* had been covered already, but *when* and *how* were still on her list, and the *who* was still not clear.

"They should be here soon. Be patient. When they arrive they will be able to contribute to Officer Bracket's and Ned's recipe—to create *some* form of a final theory. With hard work and luck, as I said, the contributions will have to be in a useful and practical form—not just another string or brane theory that merely *explains* everything."

Kevin Verily asked, "How do you know these 'Others' will be bringing useful theories? How do you know they're that . . . smart?"

Before Cy could respond, the not surprising answer came from Doyan: "That is how the populations were selected."

Clint snarled. It was more like a pirate's "*AARG*"—loud enough to be heard across the crowd. For that he received scowls *and* nods of approval.

Dummy only looked at Clint.

"Don't *shush* me!"

"*I* didn't say nothing."

"*Getting* . . *back* . . *to* . . *the* . . *subject*," Cy said in a cadence just short of *fee* . . . *fi* . . . *fo* . . . *fum* and followed it with a deep attention-getting sound approaching *harrumph*. "It will take a lot of cooperation to get that *group recipe* to happen. And a lot of translation. None of the Others, or you, communicate or symbol alike, or even do mathematics alike. I know their languages, symbols and mathematics, but I know little or nothing of their best theories, except that some are practical. If you and the Others can just get along—and are willing to give up your precious secrets, then there is hope for us all. Otherwise we're doomed, along with the rest of posterity—everywhere. It's that complicated, and that simple. The redshift is stealthy. It comes upon us wrapped in a cloak of invisibility. With its coming, our remaining time is also vanishing."

Laura said to Ned, "I believe I just heard the start of a negotiation, but before it began, it's over! Almost. Are our negotiations over before we have a chance to fight?"

Ned said, "Yeah. Cy knows how to deliver a punch! And how to spell out what's at stake. *If* this is a negotiation, can we even know that he or Doyan have the coordinates for Earth? Although, if what Cy says really is true, then knowing that, or not knowing it, is a minor point."

"What do you mean, '*if* this is a negotiation'?" Laura asked.

"I didn't like the way Cy so *casually* expected the Others to bring, and supposedly opening up about *their* science."

Laura nodded. "He also said, about that, '*They'd better be.*' "

"Yeah, he did."

"He's 'casual' because he knows his power, and smiles about it. That's a little *too* human for my comfort. We already saw him waving his big stick around, or was it a wand, when he buried Clint in the sand at long distance. I wouldn't want to be here if he hauled out an even bigger one!"

"Who are those 'Others' you're talking about," Opal asked.

Cy replied, "Before I have time to tell you about them, you'll know. Several are coming right now." He pointed out to sea.

"I don't see anything except water," Doug Groth said.

"They're in the sky, just above the horizon," Cy said.

"I see them," Zack said.

"I can't," Gegeneis said, straining through thick glasses.

"I see them!" said Clint. "They're coming to kill us all." Clinton Bracket was not just back, but with attitude! As ordered, he was there without his guns, but still using binoculars to spot the enemy.

For Clint's "*kill us all*" observation, he received the same old raft of annoyed looks; but more were now on hand to unsheathe their own looks of disdain. All the Directors had arrived, along with many managers and various technical and team members under them. They had heard most of the 'discussion,' so far. It was like a seminar, but momentarily at least, Officer Bracket was getting all the attention from his old and new antagonists. Earlier on, when Cy gave Clint his baptism by sand, Dummy was occupied elsewhere or he would have come to his identical's rescue and dug him out. This time he intended to rescue him from another humiliating immersion—Clint's christening beneath the cold and unfriendly waters of crowd contempt.

The demeaning attention chilled Clint into silence, but not Dummy. In a loud voice of his own, Dummy confronted Cy with questions—*not* to learn anything, but as a diversion to take the attention off Clint. "Before them Others gets here," Dummy said, "could you tell us how we can, together with them Others, come up with *one overall theory* if none of our communications or symbols, or languages, or mathematics is similar in any way? How can that translation ever be done? What is so different about the ways they communicate? And even if we finally gets the *recipe* right, who supplies the right *equipment* and the *ingredients*, what are the ingredients, and who's the cook? We're talking here, are we not, about cakes the size of universes?"

That seemed to work. Most of the crowd's focus snapped right back to Cy, but the remainder looked to Clint's 'Dummy' with newfound respect.

Then they came—in flying hills like giant, floating eggs. They were overhead and starting to land!

SEVENTY-FIVE

The Transformation crew could think of nowhere they had ever seen, smelled or heard of creatures so monstrous and wonderful as they. One by one the whirlwinds that brought them overhead, also brought them down. The egg-shaped hills of the Others were guided to safe and gentle landings by the mysterious winds. They were lowered to the beach and shallow waters just off shore. At first there were only a few overhead, but by noon they were streaming in. From their own nightscape dreams the Others already knew they were expected to send only a *few* representatives out from each high-population hill to join the gathering of negotiators.

David Michaels predicted that most of the hills, with their arched and rounded structures, were continuous beneath Origin's surface, thus completing their enclosed forms. But knowing they were fragile shells, he could not have anticipated their taking off and landing safely. Yet there they were, in groups, high in the sky, sailing along like hundreds of gigantic specters, dragging their dark shadows with them across the landscape. Group after group of the great ovals circled overhead to begin landing. Their immensity and numbers darkened the mid-day light and veiled the virtually invisible whirlwinds that held them up and directed their movements.

Cy laughed and snorted like an excited child as he guided them in like kites. Clustered in rings high above, the immense hills rotated like hovering carousels. On their approach, as Cy reeled them in, the unseen vortices assaulted human ears and lungs with thundering roars as they pulled in air from the surrounding atmosphere. That dramatic display revealed only a fraction of the enormous power that supported the hills in their flight—and all this in Cy's personal amusement park.

To support docking for the egg-hills, Cy set up a virtual moonscape of concave landing areas. He created those by spouting sequential gushers to displace sand and beach crystals onto circular ridges around the cavities the material came from. The vast extent of newly pockmarked beach soon became crowded with the enormous egg-shaped structures (except for a large area in the center of the beach that was allowed to remain untouched and flat, along with an even larger area at the base of the mountains that surrounded most of the beach and its landing spots). The whirlwinds nestled the egg-hills neatly into the sandy-soft depressions. After those were filled, to accommodate the last clusters of hills, the shallow waters just beyond the vast expanse of beach was used. Sodden sand and water geysers produced circular, atoll-like sandbars whose rings touched without actually overlapping.

Viewed from the Transformation Cone (except for the untouched circular area in the center of the dry beach) the two hill-clusters glittered like a pair of Easter baskets.

The circling airshow of flyovers and landings continued for hours. After each landing in one of the docking hollows there was, with few exceptions, a *small* exodus of three or four beings—*science experts* it was later learned. *Exceptions* to the small exodus, included "swarm" and "pile" (or "stack") populations—each consisting of millions. *Swarms* were flying, insect-size creatures, and *piles* were wriggling grublike "things."

Once a hill was safely nested in its bay, an unassisted egress portal opened and extended telescopelike to the beach or to one of the circular sandbars where the touching rings of sand created a dry promenade that enabled comfortable access to the greater beach.

Well before the hills landed, their inhabitants knew to keep their exiting numbers down to a few lest that untouched, flat *negotiation area* in the center of the beach be inundated by multitudes. They need not have worried too much, the area was spacious. To sort out the true negotiator-theoreticians from the masses, however, the invitation was only for the top scientists in each hill. (However, many *dissidents* did slip out.)

Contrary to Ned and Laura's hopeful expectations, the combined negotiation-and-science-project rapidly dissolved into untidy disorder.

Although none of the new arrivals were remotely humanoid or apelike in appearance or movement, they were all capable, in some fashion, of locomotion or ambulation. Among the swarms, were those that could fly—mostly with winglike appendages, but some propelled themselves by expelling large internal volumes of rapidly manufactured organic gasses. In fact, most of the Others appeared either bloated or skeletal.

Members of swarm colonies could fly like the wind. They were enveloped by inflated outer-body membranes. In the wake of their flights, they left mercifully odorless trails of greenish coloration. They shot like guided missiles across the sky.

David Michaels, of course, spoke of such groups as farts and obsessed in his self-indulgent, uproarious way about the possible environmental impact of fart pollution by greenhouse gas propulsion.

Farts or not, there were among them many brilliant mathematical theorists. The rest of their individual members were exceptional in other ways.

Individuals in one of the piles, on the other hand, were of low intelligence. In it, there were individual "grubthings" with intelligence levels lower than earthworms. But when they came together in their giant, internally slithering stacks, they became, as a unit, more than brilliant. In their neatly clumped stacks, they called themselves an Assemblage. For them, that designation had deep spiritual meaning. As each additional grubthing joined one of the squirming stacks, it became incrementally more intelligent. It later became evident that Assemblages were by far the most useful, creative and prolific theoreticians brought to Origin by the Dorts.

A second set of abductees turned out to be a particularly difficult group to tolerate. They communicated their quantum physics and mathematical theories—and all their other thoughts—through patterned emissions of complex protein and chemical phrases. Unfortunately, this striped and bloated group of Others often produce inflections and nuances of meaning through mercilessly malodorous compounds, earning them the nickname, "Stinkers," and not just from David. Not all of their emanations were disagreeable, however. Their vocabulary ranged from intricately pleasant floral bouquets, to subtly tolerable aromas, on down to the criminally most foul. Fortunately, the prevailing winds kept the worst effects of their pungent chats from mushrooming into concentrated odor and pheromone clouds, thus preventing punitive or irreversible interpersonal and physical damage.

When the stinkers *were* into heavy communication mode, they expressed a miraculous sweep of precisely selected odors that begot, not just ideas, but carefully designed sets of feelings to match—giving them an excellent edge during negotiations.

A third group emitted no sounds or odors of any significance. They communicated by shape-shifting. They never stopped "talking." But, unfortunately, even their highest scientific echelons were imperfect and often inefficient. To even survive, they had to spend hours in "talk" therapy every day, and entire lifetimes dealing with identity issues, as did their shape-shifting therapists. It was striking to see them in their therapy groups all talking at once.

Another group, more melodious than malodorous, nicknamed "Organists," gave recitals (their way of expressing ideas) from multiple slits, horns and orifices throughout their colorful, checkerboard bodies. They walked on their tooting horns and looked and sounded very much like bagpipes. Each tight aperture and flapping crevice was capable of a dozen sounds. In combination, the resultant scale of sounds and meanings was highly efficient and virtually endless.

For sheer intelligence, humans were not far below the Organists, but above most of the rest. Just below them were the remarkable scientists and mathematicians, the "matrix beings." They did their communicating, calculating, and even their ambulation with multiple layers of moving rows and columns of cryptograms and symbols. Under them on the intelligence scale are the "fishbowlers."

The latter resided and moved in large, acid-filled, transparent jugs. The containers did the ambulating with robotic spider legs. Within each container, a stringy, pulsating, gelatinous, multi-eyed creature communicated with its fellows by myriad random-looking eye rolling, winks and crossings.

Many other Others were nocturnal and therefore seldom seen. Most of the "nocturnals" used telesthesia to send and perceive meanings. They received *no* identicals.

Like humans, *most* of the Other newcomers to the beach arrived there with their own isomorphic identicals. It was through their isomorphs, their abductor-Dorts, and the *essence of Origin* that relevant nightscape communications were given to them.

As noted, some Others had no identicals. That was *because* they were capable of dreamscaping *on their own*. That was the main purpose behind Origin's creation of isomorphs in the first place: *efficient, detailed and voluminous communication*.

Later inquiries explained another mystery: the once-practical purpose for flying strings that shot out of pre-vitalization mounds of human isomorphs and those of the Others. Early on, in the place where Cy and the Dorts were created, predators were legion. There the hazardous and lethal mound strings and javelins insured reasonable survival rates for the developing beings within. On Origin that birthing protection was, it turned out, unnecessary—but habits anywhere were still habits, especially those for preservation of the species and oneself.

The game was on and the self-preservation card was the highest in Cy's hand—even above the spacetime maps that could guide his captured dependents back to their respective planets.

"First things first," Cy said repeatedly, meaning that survival came first. That was the card he played—the redshift card. "What good will those maps do you," he asked rhetorically, "if your destinations are swallowed up in the gaping wavelengths of the redshift—in the universal and violent acceleration of entropy? Most of you know all about that! The end is at hand! Talk to each other about it!"

Then Cy would go silent till the next time—except to help the Dorts translate symbols, noises, actions and smells. Especially smells. Dorts were not good at those. They had a limited olfactory sense and, in their part of the negotiation process, constantly caved in to the Stinkers. The negotiators, human and Other, were mainly scientists—by choice. Quibbling bargainers and game players they were not. Nor, in fact, was Cy. He kept playing his one favorite card. It was the redshift card, a threat and a call for cooperation. He played no other card. (So much for efficient, detailed and voluminous communication!)

But that was enough. After a few days of chaos, based on mutual paranoia more than their obvious differences, the unaccommodating contacts between and across all parties (between each of the Others, the humans, the Dorts and Cy) changed.

The discovery of a few common goals evolved into a wish to receive cooperation, if not to give it. Cy's mantra, "First things first," was being heard and understood across the beach by most of the human and Other leaders; but not without the usual suspects from every group continuing their passive-aggressive dissent.

Those *dissenters*, from almost every hill, entered the beach against orders from their own leaders. Clinton Bracket and Dummy were no longer in a hill, but were still (and less obviously) dissenters.

It was not long before Clint and Dummy found and established close contacts with a dozen more dissenting groups from the egg-hills. Clint, who often considered himself a potential leader, called them his "Associates." Miraculously, even the Associates managed to communicate, at least minimally, with the remarkable help of a pair of dissident shape-shifters who were masters at projecting, communicating and interpreting all manner of expressive movements, gestures, body language, and other nonverbal, non-sound meanings. As quick studies, they soon learned to read and interpret "facial" expressions and the "lips" of most of the Others—easiest of all, the humans.

Until the day of hill arrivals to the beach, no humans or hill-colonists were aware of the existence of any Others on Origin besides themselves; but in the following days of interspecies, intercultural and interpersonal struggle—while wondering how much time there might be left for anything, and despite all the technical translation problems and other differences—they came to see the threat to all colonists and their own planets—to the extent of becoming partial allies in the negotiations.

Even more important as time went on, they were for that reason, and despite themselves, becoming allies of Cy and the Dorts.

While dealing with all their hopeless differences, with their anger, their cross-cultural fears and paranoid suspicions, and every other conceivable negative feeling, the fact of finally leaping those impossible hurdles turned out to be . . . the easy part.

SEVENTY-SIX

Surmounting the acrimony between so many diverse factions depended on a single thread of hope that they all clung to. It was a gamble at best, but Cy played upon it to recruit allies to his strategy. Every faction heard his mantra, "First things first." It symbolized the gamble and its importance—their one wild chance for survival.

Some wondered if it was a chance worth taking—there was so much to lose. They might never see their home worlds again before the end of everything; but the redshift card was still Cy's trump. It made his hand persuasive. Although there was no real choice, some egg-hill communities continued their rigid holdout stance; many others were indecisive.

Among the hundreds of hill-based Others, a dozen of the most unyielding holdout colonies insisted on returning home *immediately*. They had no faith in the *essence of Origin*'s power or ability to deliver on their survival hopes. When they demanded star maps to their home worlds and were refused, they accused Cy and the Dorts of having no clue where their colonies' planets were located in the Galaxy or the way back for any of them; they publicly lamented that their space vehicles were not warships so they could *get* ol' Cy. They ranted on.

Ned Keller was among the many who decided early on that the gamble was worth a try. Good alternatives did not exist, so he used his talents to involve the most accessible leaders among the Others to convince their own society of abductees to go along with Cy's strategy and, in turn, to work toward the involvement of communities outside their own. By then, many of the Other leaders could relate to groups that Ned never could. In that way the cooperation process continued to develop—except for that dozen or so hard-core holdouts.

Enter, Clinton Bracket—to the rescue! He and his Associates, many from the most adamant holdout groups, had come to trust one another. Clint came to accept the advantages of cooperation only after several long talks with the people he most respected. During a conversation with Stanley Lundeen he learned that the redshift threat was not only real, but virtually imminent. After talking with Laura Shane he became confused, but nonetheless convinced that the narrow hope was a possibility, a thin one, but it *was* a possibility! And after talking with Ned, he realized his Associates from the holdout communities would be needed to swing their own communities. Clint was able to convince his Associates that the project was worth that wild chance. By the time they returned to their hill-colonies and convinced them, the bulk of the science translations had already been started. Most of the Other factions were already cooperating. When the last of the holdouts finally came around, their contributions were still welcomed; especially since, according to their captor Dorts, several of the holdout colonies were among the eight or ten most talented theory builders. Translations of the theories with their mathematical footnotes and technical evidence was openly provided by Cy and the Dorts to all the hill-colonies.

The distribution process, following translation of all that material, was monumental. But creation of the translations was especially difficult, requiring them to interpret the communication methods and styles of the many factions, including not only writing and print, but odors, shaping sequences and forms, combinations of sounds, timbre variations, slime trail coloration codes, and hundreds more. With over a thousand colonies requiring that many translations each, more than a million had to be made and distributed. The completed translations overwhelmed the colonies. The theories had to be summarized.

The *translation* and *summarization* tasks fell mainly to the hundreds of Dorts that recently returned to Origin with their cargoes of scientists imbedded in the kidnapped communities. Cy helped with those duties as well, but for those tasks he was only one among many. As the *essence of Origin*, however, the main things he worked to accomplish went beyond anything the Dorts could achieve. Those tasks were uncountable and unchanged in the eons before Mark Tenderloin's genetic pattern became available to Origin. Cy's primary tasks were identical to Origin's. In fact, Cy and Origin were themselves opposites *and* identicals—just as concave and convex are two visible aspects of a sailing vessel's single, billowing canvas, so Cy and Origin displayed *different aspects of their oneness*, but in their *singular* aspect there was no difference; they were the same.

Taken together, googols of symbols were *conveyed* through the translations—some said, *"dumped"*—into the "nervous systems" of every hill-community.

Throughout the process, Cy and hundreds of Dorts were flashing in and out of visibility with such rapidity that their semblances sometimes appeared as insubstantial blurs. At times the crystalline crust of Origin itself, and layers below it, would quaver and momentarily disappear, leaving the planet's inhabitants with a brief sensation of floating in space hundreds of kilometers above the planet's glowing inner core; more rarely the core itself would also vanish with the rest, leaving those on the surface with the feeling of drifting in empty space.

Those *"brief"* absences—by Cy, Origin, and the Dorts: the "Triad" of interuniverse beings, as they came to be called—were explained as *"extended visits to the other universe."* To get there and back, Triad members would lower the barrier that kept them suspended in this universe, thus opening themselves to a condensed and engulfing time frame, one so condensed that on crossing to the other universe relative *years* could elapse for the fulfillment of a task—in this case complete theory translations and, such as they were, their summaries.

For those in the Triad, the two universes were interchangeable. All three were created in the neverland that straddled both realms: the continuous, compact sea of time and energy that engulfed the coexistent universes. There, the telescoping of time provided sufficient opportunity for the enormous task of translation.

Those theories and summaries were handed over by Cy and the Dorts to the Others (including the community of humans) as intellectual fodder for their creative geniuses.

The direct theory translations coming from the Triad were close to verbatim, and therefore required minimal translation judgment. The verbatim translations were considered excellent; but the summaries created by Cy and the Dorts, due to their apparent failure to fully understand the original theories they just translated, were riddled with minor errors and major mistakes.

During this massive collaboration, minor theories were extended and less inclusive ones incorporated into broader theories as special cases. Not surprisingly, the most comprehensive of the inclusive theories took those into account. They were synthesized by the top theory-building groups—top among them being the grubpile—the Assemblage.

In a meeting with the Directors, Laura commented on the numerous errors in the summaries: "All we ever got back as *summaries* from Cy and the Dorts, was junk. They were less than worthless. I know they did the best they could, but I expected better. That must be why they forced us and the Others to come here. They're not all-knowing, and in some ways not even very smart. Having good summaries, like our own and the ones we're getting form the Others, is saving a lot of work. Cy and the Dorts are only good at the verbatim stuff; but we still have to give them that. We couldn't have done all those translations by ourselves in a million years. Together they literally had the time and talent for that—in their other universe. I've said it many times: For all their faults, *they can be handy.*"

Even after the errors were corrected, the best theories were still not fitting together. That was nothing new. In ancient history, the theory of relativity and quantum physics also lacked coherent linkage—until the Win Field-Diagrams, the WDs, were taken seriously and then, much later, advanced with their use in Laura Shane's radical modification of Transformation Theory, and more recently made still stronger and more comprehensive in Mark's Reo-Sphere Theory. Finally, all those advances and linkages were pulled together in Laura's newest set of integrating formulas. But even this advanced Transformation-Reo-Sphere Theory did not fit with the grubthings' theory wherein the same underlying phenomena had been conceptualized in a very different way. A new and grander linkage was needed.

Aside from that, the questions themselves were far from transparent, including the issue of how one might leverage even a perfect theory into a *practical* fix for the self-destructing universe. Laura guessed this was intangible because they did not know enough about that other, interacting, coexistent universe—the one they were blaming for the coming redshift problem—*the Big Rip!*

Everybody knew that an overarching umbrella-theory was still essential, but they were not prepared or able to make that step. First, new ways of thinking had to be learned. Despite progress from their cooperative efforts, their *vanity* kept getting in the way. Even with the greatest minds in the Galaxy having free access to each other's theories, the temptation to contend was great, so competition did, naturally, begin. It was covert and sly, but the sneaky little competitive race was on in order to dazzle all the Others by being the brightest, the first, and the best! In their new-found admiration of one another they wanted to be seen that way.

With that, the Others, humans included, tried to do it all, and to do it *all by themselves*.

In opposition to their vanity, and impelled by Cy's echoing cliché, "First things first," every community was reminded of what it was working to achieve—a solution to the most consequential, multi-dimensional quantum jigsaw puzzle ever conceived by nature. Some groups aspired to understand the forest; others, the trees. Whatever the solution, it would be *another* "first" step toward survival.

It was not just Laura, but all the Others, who refused to tolerate the "sloppy" summaries from Cy and the Dorts. They were all in a contest—a competition that required nothing less than their individual best. But something kept creeping up from their unconscious that was threatening their precious egos. It was the disconcerting realization that to construct the ultimate final theory, the TOE, the theory of everything, a spirited *cooperation* would again be required.

But their obstinate egos held out. Even as the glowing-red clock of the universe kept ticking like the time bomb it was, they continued to stroke and stoke their competitive fires. They knew that the interval left on that clock was short, but not how short. That was the dreaded unknown that added to the anxiety spreading across Origin, the Milky Way, and every other galaxy in the universe where there was an aware and caring intelligence equal to their own.

Their dread turned to fear. Every passing day that emotional uncertainty principle added to their fear; but it somehow increased their competitive fervor to learn it all and to be the first with a unified theory; but the fear was burning its way through their precious reserves of competitive fuel. Mounting awareness of the uncertainty, and the tormenting prospect of ultimate failure, not to mention universal death, was consuming their insistence on winning. Being first, best, and brightest would become less important than staying alive and preserving some kind of future—*the* future—for the next generation of Others, and the next, and the next.

They'd hit bottom.

Then it came—the news! Announced by Cy himself, it rattled every group like an earthquake; but only for a moment. The news plucked their old cooperative spirit from the ashes and fused it with a new and flaming sense of competition. Cy's message was delivered from the other universe, across the all-engulfing membranes of spacetime. It was a simple message: Denizens of the coexistent universe were embarked on a survival project of their own—an identical one to theirs.

In a flashing glint of Cy's eye, their focus shifted from what small faction on Origin would win the science competition, to what universe would win. The Others on Origin took that to mean they would have to cooperate as never before; oxymoronically spurring them into a state of *competitive cooperation*—

the assumption being that whichever universe could muster the best team performance would be the first to reveal nature's true underpinnings and deliver it through a workable, final theory of everything.

And so the new race began; but this time with the synergism of both motives; proving again that especially vigorous and important undertakings of intelligent beings are most powerfully fueled by the mixed and volatile brew of high-minded motives and selfish passions.

It happened as they all hoped, but never quite expected. Their new intensity of vision culminated in the creation of that single theory—the "Final Theory," or at least a theory of darn-near-everything in their one universe. Those in the consortium of scientific greats knew better than anyone that what they had done was virtually impossible, so they were the ones most amazed when it was finally accomplished!—or so it seemed. A few nitpickers remained—Laura and Mark among them.

Like string theory or a tediously protracted tautology (being a more or less hidden circular argument) it was intellectually attractive—especially for the proud Assemblage of grubthings that so brilliantly capped-off the cooperative efforts of all the communities with its harmonious blend of their diverse theories. But could this amazing, concordant theory be implemented? The new "final theory" was animated with conceptual agility and power—like a strong, limber, multi-membered contortionist. Most of the Others recognized its flexibility and began thinking about how the new synthesis could be made useful for the final purpose of survival. That would have to be the *next* first step.

Like all the Others, Laura and Mark saw the Assemblage's accomplishment as a critical step, but to bring out its "usefulness" would be as daunting as anything that came before—daunting because the Assemblage's "final theory" was put forward as "irreducible" despite its outwardly flexible appearance. By instinct, Laura and Mark believed the Assemblage's new theory was too complicated to be useful or completely true to nature, but they also knew they could not easily prove it wasn't. They chose to look at the Assemblage's new synthesis in reducible segments; to carefully analyze the theory and excise its practical components at nature's joints—instead of crudely chopping through at midbone. They believed that several segments of the theory looked practical and vibrant on their own, and could each be expanded into viable, but smaller theories—not to replace the main one, but to know in advance that the "practical segments" would be consistent with it and would work reliably if, in fact, the larger theory were correct and true.

Laura and Mark plunged headlong into that new challenge. For a while they thought they had analytically detached at least one of those "practical segments" from the main body of theory and had worked out most of its smoldering and intriguing implications. From that work they came to believe that that very segment was the most obvious and important to be found in the broader theory. For a short while they were delighted with themselves; but strong peer analysis by the Assemblage itself found several subtle, undeniable flaws in their analysis and reformulation; thus leaving the Assemblage's monstrous, multimembered, concordant theory of everything intact—and still irreducible.

During a coffee break in the newly rebuilt barracks-canteen-restaurant (the "BCR") Laura and Mark reinspected the fatal flaws publicized in the peer analysis. The Assemblage's confutation of their work turned out to be precise, unmistaken and of such elegant brevity, they were able to finish perusing the critique even before their coffee arrived.

Above all else, Laura and Mark were *scientists* and, as such, would openly accept any credible, critical peer analysis with professional aplomb. Privately however, and just between the two of them, they were chagrin that a bunch of stupid, slithering grubs could do this to them, consider themselves "peers," and surmounted them with an intellectual critique of such ingenious, concise arguments, and to have accomplished it with a cachet of such sophistication and panache as to make the definitiveness of their unimpeachable arguments all the more devastating; less tolerable, in fact, than if the Assemblage had rudely accused them of "sloppy" work. They might as well have. The humbling experience was crushing to the point of nearly spoiling coffee time for both of them. For Mark Tenderloin, it did. He was depressed about the whole thing and called it "humiliating."

As he spoke, their coffee arrived. Laura poured a cup for both of them. She blew on her near-boiling brew to cool it down; but Mark took a scalding gulp to stanch his embarrassment. The pain distracted him, cleared his head, and he felt much better, allowing him to think again.

"How'n hell," he asked calmly, "could anything so stupid as an ordinary worm—uglier, more like a slug or a grub—be so damn smart? First they capped-the-pie on the combined efforts of all our groups, grabbed all the credit, and now this!"

"I don't know," Laura said, "but if you asked a brain surgeon how smart a single brain cell from a genius is, I think she'd say it wasn't smart at all. It has to be their combination and connections in great numbers, and their functional organization and specialization that makes the difference. Or maybe it's just in the eye of the beholder. They really are ugly!"

Mark shook his head, confused. He frowned for a long time, then lifted his eyebrows. Laura could almost see the light bulbs going on and off above his head. She wondered, *Is he thinking of something profound, or is he just now getting—and judging—my little joke?*

With his arms lifted high above his head, Mark got up from his bench and began pacing rapidly in circles. It looked silly to Laura; but those light bulbs still seemed to be popping on and off in rapid-fire, *like a machine gun*, she thought, and he began shouting, "Yes! . . . Yes! . . . Yes!"

Really silly, Laura thought again. She patiently sighed, "What is with you, Mark?"

Mark stopped and sat; took a loud slurp of coffee and said to Laura, more as an announcement or proclamation than a mere comment: "It's clear as a Christmas bell! I know how to reverse it!"

"*Reverse it?* Reverse what?"

Elation shone on his face. "Everything!"

"*Everything?* What does that mean?"

"It means turning everything around, of course; reversing it. And I mean reversing everything—the redshift into a blueshift! It means saving the universe."

Laura looked askance at Mark and said with irony in her voice, "Oh, is that all."

Mark's radiant countenance sobered. "No," he said petulantly, "that's *not* all. There's more. Much more to this reversal thing." Then, cheerfully, "And it's utterly simple!"

Laura started to get it. She gasped hard to catch her breath. She was astonished to the point of having goose bumps from head to toe. She realized that Mark was serious—and remembered who he was: This was THE Mark Tenderloin, no intellectual slouch even compared to the Galaxy's best—a pile of grubthings.

"My God, Mark," Laura blurted, "You're not kidding. You figured it out!" Looking into his face, Laura somehow knew that he had. She was in awe.

Mark looked back into Laura's eyes and smiled broadly, nodding yes, he had figured it out.

Laura beamed her own smile back. They were sharing a moment. Mark pointed to something on the table. Laura responded to his request. She poured him a glass of ice water.

In the next few hours their neglected cups of coffee also turned cold. It took Mark that long to explain to Laura, verbally and with his pen on a dozen napkins, what had come to him in a flash: his *reversal theory*. During those hours, Laura had several excellent experiences as she came to understand every inked and oral jot and tittle of his argument.

He concluded with a fresh smile and a nod saying, "I told you it was simple!"

"You're right," she said, nodding back; now perspiring, glassy-eyed, and still in awe.

The next morning Mark attended the Directors' meeting to explain his reversal theory; but this time nobody, except Laura, could understand a word he said. He was too obscure, but in his intellectual glee he could not help it. His explanation even sailed over Stanley Lundeen's head. The Directors and Mark began looking helplessly in Laura's direction for assistance. They were delighted when she tore herself away from the serious task of filing her nails and volunteered to explain it to them.

"It's really utterly simple," she began, and four hours later the Directors, including Clinton Bracket, came away from the meeting with a general idea of Mark's reversal theory; but in the process of Laura's presentation, she offhandedly wondered about a few things that even Mark had not considered. His eyebrows went down and up and up and down, and finally stayed there—in a deep eye-shadowing frown.

Bright bulbs flashing? Not this time. It grew dark in there, in Mark's eyes. The flickering bulbs dimmed-out behind the gloom cast by Laura's "casual" concerns.

SEVENTY-SEVEN

After returning to their habitat that evening, Clint proudly announced his impression of the meeting, to Dummy, Ellen Stone—she'd also been in the Directors' meeting—and Ellen's isomorph, Littleviolet. He said, "Dr. Shane boiled it all down for us. Thanks to her, Mark's reversal theory became everybody's property. Even I understood . . . well, a lot of it."

Ellen smiled. Littleviolet rolled her eyes.

"Why should we care about another theory from Mark Tenderloin?" Littleviolet asked. "He comes up with a new one every five minutes."

"You're exaggerating," Dummy said.

"Okay then! Every five or six days."

"That's more like it, but still . . ."

"But this one was worth something," Ellen said, looking at Littleviolet.

"All right, what was 'worth something' about this one—this 'reversal' theory of his?"

Ellen tried to explain it to Littleviolet and the others. She did her best, including the physics and mathematics of it that she could remember; but after half an hour she gave up. "Clint's right. Laura Shane made it clear. I understood it then, but it's hard to explain."

They all chimed in to say she was making some sense, but they did not completely understand. "Not quite."

Clint smirked and mused aloud that Ellen's boiled-down version of Laura's boiled-down version of Mark's new theory was just fine.

Ellen looked frustrated. "Why don't you just go ahead and give us all your idea of its boiled-down version."

Clint's eyes shot back and forth like a laughing isomorph. He was nervous. "Me?" he said shakily. "I don't do science, especially out loud!"

Dummy spoke up. "I thought you said you understood it."

"Yeah." Clint chuckled uneasily. "But you know me, hehe. I don't remember everything I hear, especially if it's long, detailed, and full of mathematics. I just make little pocket editions in my head . . . of the parts I *do* get. I'm afraid I lost the details. Nothing left but my little stick-figure mental sketches. Sorry."

Dummy pressed him further. "Then just give us what's left—the stick-figure sketches, without the details."

"I'm sure it'll be all wrong," Clint said, glancing sheepishly at Ellen and Dummy, "but," he added with bravado and a wave of his arm, "here's what I came away with—"

"Whatever," Littleviolet said. She liked Clint, thought he was smarter than he looked, but seldom missed an opportunity to needle him.

Clint glared at her and gave a toothy smile—more tooth than smile. "Okay," he said. "I warned you!"

Like children readying for a bedtime story, Clint's trio of admirers nodded, said "great," and moved closer. Two of them didn't expect Clint to say anything meaningful but were ready to pretend they thought he had, but not Littleviolet. She bubbled with more honest curiosity than personal sensitivity. Without thinking about it, she always believed her standards for intellectual integrity were too high for pretense.

"The real universe is everything," Clint began. "It's not the universe we know. The one we know is just one of its shadows—the part we can see and happen to live in. The *real* universe has no opposite; but the one we live in does. Our opposite universe is that blue-shifting troublemaker we keep hearing about. Both of these opposites were born together. After almost fifteen billion years, ours is now in an *expanding* redshift crisis, and the other is *shrinking* into a blueshift crunch. Our inflating universe will, in the end, explode—right down to the last atom and quark. It will become just so many bits of nothing. The other universe, the one we've been attached to like an overlapping Siamese twin, will shrink to nothing. Either way, both will end up as nothing—not even subatomic particles, and as insubstantial as shadows of their present forms. Beside the real universe they are already no more than a pair of mutual reflections."

Littleviolet spoke up. "We already knew about the redshift and blueshift crisis. What we want to know, Officer Bracket, is what's *new* in Mark's reversal theory. What's in it to change our doomsday scenario?"

Clint was momentarily ruffled by the interruption. "I'm getting to that!" he snapped. "Gimme a break. This isn't my area. Okay? And call me Clint."

"Okay, Clint. Sorry!"

"One thing that's new is Mark's belief—and he convinced Laura of this too—that when the other universe hits zero volume and infinite spin and density it will *not* re-explode. Instead *it will keep right on going*—turning inside out, in a sense—and turn into something different—leaving behind, as I said, nothing."

"Another explosion," Dummy said, "—turning it into a *new* universe, but not the same one again."

"No," Clint responded. "Mark's reversal theory, as Laura explained it, would not allow that or any other Big Crunch out there to reexplode. Not directly. Rather, it would become something else. It would do that without losing its energetic power. So, no new Big Bang. Just something else."

"What else, then?" Littleviolet asked. "What happens to all that energy?"

"According to Laura—and Mark nodded in the Directors' meeting when she said this—*he had no idea*. Mark only knew that all that energy would be reincorporated into the *real* universe—but in what new form or forms, or 'when,' or for what purpose if any, he did not know. Laura was not so sure of that. She worried about that part of his theory and a few other things during her summary. Those other 'little worries,' as she called them, sent Mark into a funk; but for the moment that was beside the point.

"Anyway, no matter what the Big Crunch in that other universe might become, it *will* affect us here. At the exact moment of the Crunch, when the other universe goes to zero, that's when ours goes into its final *poof!* Into a final, runaway, Big Rip expansion. As our universe keeps expanding, the repulsive gravity force gets denser, not thinner. Instead of the conventional, constantly accelerating rate of expansion, that force will, by then, have advanced to exponentially higher rates. So anyway, the Big Poof has been sneaking up on us and is now virtually in full force upon us—*twenty billion years ahead of schedule*. Laura and Mark—and Stan said it too . . . the early estimates were a touch on the optimistic side."

"Yeah, by billions of years," Dummy said. "Some *touch*."

Littleviolet asked, "What is causing that repulsive gravitic force and why is it getting denser?"

"It's caused by dark matter, the *trion particles* born in our Big Bang and now infusing from our nemesis, that other universe. As it *shrinks*, our *expanding* space makes room for the overflow of those negative-gravity particles that had been keeping it from shrinking too fast."

"Well," Littleviolet said, tossing her head back, "*that*, at least, is new."

"Not so new," Clint said with a smug smile, remembering his school days: "As any school boy or girl knows, trions are the main source of the repulsive force. You should have learned that long ago in grade school when the WDs, the ancient Win Field-Diagram model was presented to all of us."

Littleviolet looked distressed. "Isn't that the paper that argued there was no such things as Higgs bosons and proposed trion particles instead?"

"Yes. But it was not taken seriously until years later when the Large Hadron Collider (the LHC) scientists made flawed Higgs particle 'discoveries.' The WD's document was published several years before the LHC was completed and got under way."

Littleviolet said, "I'll be sure to ask about that tonight."

Now it was Clint who looked distressed. "I forgot. You weren't around then. As a school girl, I mean. Didn't Doyan's nightscapes fill you in on all that?"

"Probably. It's not a big area of interest for me. I'm not perfect like you," she said tossing her head.

Dummy gave a fake *ahem* and said, "Maybe you could just continue."

"Sure. . . . Anyway, with that mass dumping of Trions going on, and our universe sucking them up, the problem for both universes is feeding on itself. Our expansion is being fed by the massive increase in negative-gravity Trions, and the other universe is shrinking faster because there is no longer a significant opposing force to balance its ordinary gravitons—which are also becoming denser as its blueshift intensifies."

Littleviolet asked, "When is that '*Poof*' going to happen to us?"

"Mark and Stan couldn't say; but *very soon* in our terms. Any time now. In the other universe, that final, implosive collapse will happen at the same instant as our Big Rip. But *just before* that instant, from over there, it could *seem* a lot longer."

Littleviolet pressed on as though Clint were some kind of expert. "We know about that too. Cy and the Dorts spend a lot of time there during what we see here as fractions of seconds. But what's *new*? *We still want to know.*"

For several long moments Clint eyed Littleviolet through glistening slits. "The point is," he finally said, with a renewed sneer of authority, "as I'm sure you already know—and are about to remind me—if nothing is done, it's curtains for both universes. Mark's discovery and his idea for solving the problem (or for making it worse—that was one of Laura's concerns) is to *increase and intensify* the connection between our two already entwined and conspiring universes."

"That's the guts of Mark's reversal theory, then?" Littleviolet said. "It's to *intensify* the connection between the two universes? How could that help?"

Clint liked the question. "That intensified connection would allow them to . . . hmm . . . sort of cancel each other out and even reverse their linked, opposite problems. Our red thing should then become blue, and vice versa. The two universes are more than close enough for this to happen. It's not like this universe is here and that one is there. They are totally different, but they overlap—they are, well, almost *one* already. Mark thinks the slightest push could cause this reversal.

"On the other hand, as Laura explained it, the Assemblage had a complicated formula for *loosening* rather than increasing the connection between these universes. Laura said that was the intuitive approach, and Mark's the counterintuitive one. Personally, I think it's just the opposite. In fact—"

"Never mind that, Clint," Littleviolet interrupted. "Can't we just move on?"

Clint's eyes flashed. ". . . In fact—"

"I'm wondering about this too. What *is* Mark's approach supposed to do?" Dummy asked as diplomatically as he could—and to save Littleviolet any trouble with Clint.

Seeing it was Dummy asking the question, Clint took a moment to regain his composure and then proceeded.

"Laura explained *two* possible outcomes from *increasing* the interactive intensity between the two universes."

At last! The answer they were looking for was coming. Clint's little group leaned forward with an increased intensity of their own.

"It could speed up the mutual death of both universes, *or cancel* their demise entirely . . . well, for a while anyway. For quite a while, in fact. With that reversal or cancellation effect, both universes would survive and then, *billions* of years from now, *our* universe would be ready to collapse into its own blueshift crunch. The other universe would then be approaching *its* own redshift explosion, like we are now. In the meantime there would be . . . well, a lot more time. Time for hobbies, time to floss, and time for mankind to keep evolving—things like that. The mathematics for reversals like that—the formulas Ellen tried to explain a few minutes ago—would somehow have to be reapplied to save both universes *again*, and so on . . . forever!"

"The operative word," Littleviolet chirped, "is *somehow*!"

"You're right, Littleviolet," Clint responded, "and the most interesting thing about Mark's new theory is that that 'somehow' may have happened before. He believes it happened at least once before and probably many times."

Several days later, Laura and Mark got together again for coffee back in the BCR. Laura said, "I wonder where everybody is today. This place is usually crowded."

"Yeah. On the way in, the foot-traffic out there also looked sparse. I wonder what's been going on around here since I saw you last."

During those few days Officer Clinton Bracket was thriving in his new role and status as lecturer. He was recruited for a series of lectures on "Reversal Theory for the Rest of Us." His little group recommended him.

"I'm glad Clint is out there enjoying himself, talking about reversal theory," Mark said, "but I'm worried."

"Why?" Laura asked. "I've heard him give his little talk and he seems to have a popular version of your theory about right."

"That's not what bothers me. I've been thinking about the questions *you* raised in our last Directors' meeting. After those minor changes to the theory— that the Assemblage so enjoyed tearing apart—the reversal theory popped out of nowhere. It just sort of came. Some day I should thank the little worms for their 'help.' So far the Assemblage hasn't found anything wrong with the reversal formulation, even though it's now totally out of sync with theirs. They won't find anything wrong with the changes, but I'm sure they're trying! This time I nailed it, but . . ."

"But what?"

"What if they're right? Their theory for *loosening the ties* between universes is just as valid as these new twists to *strengthen* them. Their math *looks* perfectly all right. But so does mine. Both look right; but they can't both be right. There's a glitch somewhere."

"I know," Laura said thoughtfully. "I agree the Assemblage's theory also looks right, but does it feel right?"

"That's the trouble. They both feel right—at every small step in the calculations, when I'm that close to them. But both theories seem wrong when I'm not—when I'm at a distance."

"I was going to say something like that myself. We have to find the glitch, Mark."

Unexpectedly, Mark started to laugh; then he laughed even harder. Tears began to run down his cheeks. His reaction was out of place and, to Laura, he suddenly looked ridiculous.

Laura leaned across the table without a smile. "What is it David?"

Mark shook his head, still laughing. In a moment he gained enough control to begin speaking again. "I know I'm acting like David, but not really. He doesn't usually laugh at anything important."

"What's important?"

"The glitch. It's important. It's funny, and it's obvious."

"Not to me."

"Think about it! One of the two theories is as good as the other, right?"

"Yes, on the surface, but what's so obvious that I'm missing?"

"That's just it. You didn't miss it at all. It was you who raised the questions in the first place. Two of them especially. And there was a third."

Laura looked puzzled. "I did raise some concerns, but I didn't think they were funny."

Mark sobered enough to look more serious than ridiculous—but not by much.

"Okay," Mark said. "Let's assume that one of the two theories is one hundred percent correct and Cy takes it as the final answer. Let's say it doesn't matter which one. The point is, *they're just theories*! What the hell is Cy going to do with them? That's the glitch! The bottom line is simple—we're all going to die! The whole universe is done for! Both of them!"

"And the real universe? The big one. The one with no opposite. What happens to it?"

"Who knows! Maybe there'll be some kind of domino effect or chain reaction."

Laura frowned. "You said there were a couple of questions I raised? You had another one in mind?"

"This one's slightly different; but it's really the same. You said that since the other universe seems to have different laws of nature from ours, the *final* formula should resolve the physical laws of *both* universes. Say Cy ended up with *that* combo-theory—from the best scientific minds of both universes. It comes down to the same question: *What the hell's he going to do with it?* Wave the combo-theory defiantly at the sky? Invoke some ancient ritual? Check it against the local entrails? Or even—"

"—*Okay*! . . . I get it."

"Good. Then you can see why I had to laugh. The other alternative wouldn't have been, well . . . manly. We've been spinning our wheels. It's been very interesting, but now it's over. We failed. There never was a way to win this."

Silence. Laura leaned back with her arms folded tightly, staring at Mark for several minutes.

Mark finally reacted with a loud "*What*?"

"Are you through feeling sorry for yourself?"

Mark swallowed, took a moment and said, "Yeah, I think so."

"Then it's time for you to have a heart-to-heart with your 'identical.' He's still out there every day, blinking in and out of visibility, delivering dreamscape translations and barking his 'First things first' slogan. It's time to ask him about second things, and all the other things to come. He's stuck in his own rut. He or *It*—planet Origin—planned and arranged all of this centuries ago. It's now time for him to get out of that rut and see what's next. And not just see it. Do it!"

Mark frowned. "Sure. Leave it up to him—and the Dorts. *I don't think so.* They make too many mistakes. He, or something, arranged all of this long ago. No question about that; but then, Laura, that brings us to your third question. It's that same old question, but more urgent now: Who, or what, was behind all those initiatives in the first place? That includes the crystalline 'terraforming' of Origin so lavishly and slavishly accomplished by the worker Dorts. *That* resulted in the miraculous creation of this planet's 'gray matter'—its crystalline crust that thinks, nightscapes, causes levitation whirlwinds, pops from universe to universe, and with equal miraculousness, creates identicals—including the *essence of Origin* itself, another real being—*my* 'identical,' Cy."

"Yes, Mark," Laura agreed. "Those phenomena, and those creations especially—they aren't just crystalline puppets. They are—and became—real beings."

"Miraculous stuff," Mark said, yawning.

"Not miraculously, Mark, but through some deliberately planned, organized process. The Others' and *their* identicals—the most recent arrivals to Origin in this cavalcade of bizarre beings, are also conscious and intelligent—and crystalline. They're like our own precious isomorphs. All of us—we're in this caravan too—in this strange continuum of beings."

Mark nodded sagely, eyes half closed. "This mighty continuum."

"Who knows where it had its start, this great chain of being. There had to be a beginning; but the chain, from that point to here, must be a very long one."

Mark's eyes looked dreamy as he nodded again and said, "Infinitely long ago."

Laura cocked her head. "Infinite? I doubt that, Mark," she said pedantically. "I'll settle for *long* ago, not infinite. You cannot exclude the fact that repetitive patterns, like fractals, emerge from chaos. To me it's a rule—a law of nature. That's where nature's patterns get started. And from pattern comes more and more order, and from there, organization. Somewhere down the line, that organization becomes complex—even directional. Now and then—*way* down the line—it becomes evolution as we know it—and beyond the way we know it."

Mark became more awake and animated—from the ideas or the coffee. He couldn't be sure which. "Are you saying you believe that evolution is a self-directed process—out of *chaos*?"

"Not at first. Not till that pattern of organization becomes so complex that it can consciously harness the other forces around it. Then it can fiddle with direction—real direction, not crude eugenics. Till that point, evolution is simply the path of least resistance—survival of the fittest or the luckiest."

"With that idea, then, the beginning is where chaos starts to become a pattern."

Laura frowned. "There's a lot of chaos out there. Chaos must be legion, leading to multitudes of patterns and ultimately multiple types of evolutionary processes and structures, with some forms within those structures mounting to the point of control—control at different levels—even within and between the biggest structures of all—multiple universes—universes with similar or even totally different physical laws; but still organized."

"You just lost me. Do you mean even if those levels of organization and control are not complete?" Mark asked.

"Yes, if by that you are asking if they could evolve further and not merely change."

"How could it get to that next level?"

"The same way it got there in the first place—by using that level as the platform of complexity and organization to become more organized than before. It's an applied exercise of learning."

Now Mark was frowning. "That does it! No wonder I was discouraged. Reversal theory is just a part of what is required. We must get to Cy and start working with that other universe. Reversal theory conceptualizes only part of the needed organization. The whole is incomplete without that other piece."

Mark's voice had become a harsh growl of determination: "Our two laws of nature—our two unlike universes—must pull together or all will have been for nothing, and we will become nothing! By God, that must not be our fate! *It will not be!*"

"Why Mark," Laura said with demure and sincere surprise, "That statement! It was admirable—and *so* masculine!" She fluttered her eyelids. "No more despair. No more whimpering laugh—no matter how amused and out of control your earlier cachinnation was disguised to sound. Now I hear the animal—the one in control!—Insistent! Demanding! It's a snarl of hope and optimism!"

Mark was already feeling uplifted, but Laura's words certainly did not interfere with that sensation.

They sat quietly for several minutes before Mark broke the silence. "Say, this place *is* way too quiet. So few people and isomorphs, not that isomorphs drink coffee, but they're as loud as we are. And another thing just dawned on me—I haven't seen or heard a sound from Cy for hours, have you?

"No."

"Let's go find him, Laura. It's time."

"Yes. Time."

SEVENTY-EIGHT

From his perch inside the Astrophysics lab of the Great Cone, Stanley Lundeen made the anticipated, feared announcement: "The largest planetary bodies in our Galaxy—gas giants mostly, but some solid planets too—are starting to break away from their suns. It has to be happening in the other galaxies too. Many of those planets are not just breaking away from their suns and from each other, like the galaxies themselves, but are actually breaking into chunks—some into their smallest atomic components. They're simply not holding together. We expect that from stars, eventually, but not from planets. With *great luck* our universe, to say nothing of our Galaxy, might last a few more days. It's moving that fast!"

Similar announcements were arriving from all the Others' own sources. Except for one group, there was no noticeable panic on the beach or around the egg-hills. There came a welcome, woozy calm that seemed unreal and too good to be true, as if they were in the (e)motionless eye of a hurricane of feelings. The all-embracing tranquility was like a unification of knowing spirits. Whatever was to be, would be. In harmony with all of this, the moving forms of the otherwise habitually frenetic shape-shifters mellowed as they turned from rapid-spiking, corkscrewing and internal cavity formation to more lackadaisical, orderly and slow-flowing waves around hypnotically spiraling twists that coiled and uncoiled with a methodical cadence. In great part, calm and stillness had settled in across the beach. Like a drug, it imposed an artificial calm from somewhere, but nobody cared from where it came.

Notable, however, was movement in the community of grub-things. They exited their hill by the billions, piling into their usual Assemblages—except for one particularly large pile in the immense clearing in the middle of the beach. That Assemblage mounted into a breathtaking pillar some forty stories in height. The other Assemblages were scattered loosely in an orbit of knolls around that pillar—also in the same central clearing in the midst of the hills.

It was hard to imagine how such a volume of grub-things could have survived together in only one of the hills. After all the new Assemblage piles were created, they too pulled inward, becoming thinner and taller—their pillars also grew to many stories of various heights, but none so high as the first Assemblage at their center.

Full heights achieved, their glistening structures of squirming life began to send out feelers—arched connections like scion grafts or flying buttresses of ancient architecture—attaching each Assemblage to its adjacent partners and to the towering nucleus at their hub. As the connecting arches propagated between them, this strangely forming, living edifice began taking on the look of a Gothic cathedral—or a space ship.

In fact, it turned out to be both of those, and much more. Even as the last scion buttress joined the central pillar, the earlier sense of unreal tranquility evolved further, into a deeper, but still light-headed perception of peace and security. That illusion spread to every sentient group and individual on the Island beach—to every human there and all the Others, and to the planet Origin itself. The end might come at that very moment, but who would care? Even the shape-shifters' hook-shaped waves had settled into slow and soothing ripples.

That greatest of all Assemblages, now interconnected like hub, spokes and wheel, began to glow, and gradually came to appear brighter than Nimbus itself before gently and silently floating upward and turned away from the beach. It kept soaring, then hovered to loom high above the beach and the Others; then moved higher still, faster, and higher again; finally soaring far above the Great Cone itself—appearing as a brief, but still shining new star in the sky.

Only then did the residents of the beach become aware of something else—something beyond the outward flight of the Assemblage and their own inner sense of peace and wonder. It came as a surprising message—an intimate, hushed, unbidden, but businesslike voice—less a voice than a meaning—that entered their consciousness:

"Those of us who were privileged to look closely into Origin's dreamscapes have been shown the door that opens onto our opposite universe. I, the Assemblage, go there now, through that door, to work with our hard-won formulas and with the other powers, whoever or whatever they may be in that unknown universe—with those powers willing to share responsibility in our mutual and universal duty—our duty to assure the preservation and continuing greatness of our many beings and kinds, large and small—both here and there—to enable the chance for thousands of generations to grow and go forward through their unique and different evolutionary branches,

byways and paths. For this venture, I wish us all well. May we meet again in some place, in some time. Goodbye."

Laura and Mark did not bother to look for Cy. Instead they returned to join some of their friends. They too were experiencing the calm, the message, and the sky-watch of the rising star. Laura had joined Ned with his Adon. Her Keeta was there too. Denise Christensen and Chastity hung close to Mark on his return. Clint was with Ellen Stone, Dummy and Littleviolet. Many more humans and isomorphs were watching the sky with them, but just as many were not to be seen—a hardly noticed fact that would only later became a matter of major importance.

As they watched and the message ended, the little star blinked out, leaving nothing of itself behind that could be seen, except the reminder of its empty hill. The quiet "voice" was gone, as was the unreal, dazed sense of peace and serenity. Reality returned—all too quickly. Just as the Assemblage star vanished from the sky, an emotional void seemed to open beneath them like a bottomless cavern. The frightening fall was temporary and ultimately positive. They were left with more than a void. The little star left behind a fresh memory of courage and a message of hope. Perhaps the Assemblage could extend more than the "great luck," that Stanley Lundeen spoke of, for the Galaxy and the universe to "last a few more days."

SEVENTY-NINE

After what seemed to be a reasonable period of time for emotional regrouping, Ned called for everybody's return to the beach encampment. He was following through on an idea that came from Doug Groth. Doug believed that if everybody could return to the Great Cone in time—before the Big Rip—and a Transformation initiated, it might be possible for those aboard to avoid the otherwise universal redshift catastrophe. Once everybody was aboard, they could begin a *random* Transformation—that is, one with no particular destination—into, as Doug said, "Who knows where or what." Stanley counseled speedy action on Doug's theory, and Laura, although dubious, also thought the idea was worth a shot. Mark made no comment. Laura could think of nothing else to try, except to find Cy and follow an equally harebrained theory she and Mark had during coffee, but Cy was nowhere to be seen. Nor was Doyan.

Without a destination, even if Doug's idea worked, creating a "place" for survival, namely the Cone itself in Transformation-mode, their molecules would still have to smear across *something*—but *not* across this or any other spacetime universe. The known universe would be scattered and gone forever. What it might then become was anybody's guess.

The two timelines were accelerating toward each other. The head-on crash was inevitable. Although hundreds of crew members were already returning to the Cone, or had left for its comfortable familiarity days earlier, or had never left it, the clockwork dilemma remained: On one hand of the clock, the universe was counting down to its own and everyone's oblivion and, on the other, a frantic, behindhand search was on to find and return hundreds of suddenly missing crew members to a place of theoretical safety—the Transformation Cone. For Ned it felt as if the two hands were on a collision course, racing toward each other like proton arrows in a supercollider. It was essential to transfer everybody to the Cone and begin the Transformation before that race came to a crashing conclusion. The collision would come at unknown clock-time; but the emotional count-down was even less secure. There was no way of knowing the end point of *Clock-time*: "three days" at the outside; most likely much sooner. *Emotion-time* was just as insecure and kept changing with horrific volatility. It was feared that some, if not all of the missing individuals, would have to be left behind. Had they decamped on purpose or had they been kidnapped again and taken forcefully abroad? Nobody knew. The word went out that Ned expected everybody to return to Base where the shuttles could land and quickly take off with their valued human cargoes, back to the Great Cone of Transformation. When the last available person entered the last shuttle, anyone still unavailable and missing would be out of luck. That *would* be the last shuttle. Thus spake Ned Keller.

This urgency, under the circumstances, led to a number of problems. Most difficult was the trauma of separation experienced by many isomorphs and humans. Few were comfortable leaving his or her human, or isomorph. They all knew that isomorphs fared poorly on the Transformation Cone unless in the geode at night, and even then most could be vulnerable and do poorly. Consequently, most of the isomorphs refused to leave, not that anyone was trying to force them. The few that did insist on leaving thought they might survive in the Dorts' crystalline geode deep inside the Cone. Several isomorphs had already successfully tested that idea, but few had any faith in that option, questioning its long-term safety. They would rather "die with their boots on," naked as they were, at home, on Origin. And some humans refused to leave Origin, being forever attached to their beloved isomorph. They chose to go the way of the universe, whatever it would do.

Separation decisions were troubling, but the roster of those returning to the Cone, or those already there, was long and growing. To ease that decision-making process there were tradeoffs. David Michaels, for example, reluctantly agreed to leave his Oscar behind, but he had Judy Olafson to console him. She, in turn, had to leave Minerva, but still had her David.

Disturbing or not, the departures were mainly restrained, courageous, and sometimes almost mechanical to avoid the nearly irrepressible display of anguish associated with assured, final and permanent separations. In many instances, however, the polite formality did not work and the scenes that followed were pitiable indeed; but the formality defense usually moved the parties quickly through the agonizing process. With the doomsday clock still ticking, that process had to be completed soon. Human traffic on the shuttles was not to be held up. Their Titanic—the universe—would not stay afloat for emotional delays, denials or excuses. The Great Cone of Transformation, their only lifeboat, awaited.

The shuttles and Orbs continued nonstop until most of the available human inhabitants of Origin had been returned to the Cone. But there was a significant, continuing problem. Only a few of the missing ever showed up. Those that did were never really "missing," but had merely been engaged elsewhere. The majority were still nowhere to be found. Not only were large numbers of humans gone, but their isomorphs along with them. Even Cy, who had been talking nonstop before so many were missed, became silent and now he too was gone.

Surprisingly, their "most reliable" Jack Lewis had also gone AWOL, as had their "most unreliable" Kevin Verily with his Nor-Man, along with Kevin's two "guardians," Margaret Heckart with Opal, and Kevin's friend, Norbert. Also unaccounted for was Margaret's special friend and fellow astrophysics student—who was once Ned's famous masked dancing partner—Astra Hughs. And Astra's most-beautiful Venus was greatly missed and also presumed to be abroad. Nor had Zackery Parker and Gegeneis as yet returned. The lengthy roster of missing also included Mona and Lisa; Wolfe and Lycus; Ned's less than "famous," but usual dance partner, Melissa and her isomorph; Dufy and Alun Caradog Hilarius (Hilly); Nebulena (Lena) and Galatea; Ingrid, Anvil and their isomorphs; and hundreds more. Whatever happened to so many of them remained a mystery.

But, as time is measured in this universe, not for long.

EIGHTY

Among the missing were half the humans and their isomorphs and half the Others with theirs. By midafternoon the day after those populations had vanished, Origin's whirlwinds picked up again and cleared away all the Others' hills from the beach and the shallow coastal waters. The only physical reminders of where they had been were the empty craters and atolls. The whirlwinds had taken the hills and their remaining occupants back to wherever on Origin they had come from.

Early that morning, before all the hills had been removed, Officer Bracket and Dummy took the opportunity to say goodbye to a few of their fellow Associates. As they did so, the Others confided to Clint and Dummy through their shape-shifting translator friends, what had happened to the missing individuals the day before. Some had observed it first hand.

The day before, there had been two main crowds of commingling people with Others and their identicals—one, the densely packed, mixed, and unsegregated central crowd; the second, a scattering of more homogeneous groups. They were in widely separated locations on the arc of beach beneath the surrounding horseshoe curve of mountains. The innermost crowd had crammed into the open meeting area surrounded, as always, by gigantic egg-hills. It was the clearing where Cy usually held forth. The outermost crowds clustered in scattered areas on the open-boundary expanse between the mountains and the egg-hills. Every day many smaller groups thronged *there* as a pleasant space to loiter and engage with compatriots.

The outer crowd disappeared. All of them (the "subjects," as the shape-shifters identified them): humans, isomorphs and thousands of Others and their identicals. All were gone.

The *subjects* had vanished instantly—en masse, as though a highly selective Big Rip had come and gone; but everybody knew that when the real Big Rip came, they would experience no selective, precision triage or other such niceties. Observers of the outer crowd believed those *subjects* must have been taken captive or massacred.

When the event occurred, two others vanished who were *not* on the perimeter. Cy and Doyan were in the *central* beach area, surrounded by a teeming crowd when *they* were seen to disappear. The central-crowd was there to watch and listen, or to ignore, another of Cy's numerous, redundant messages; but he never ceased to entertain. In the end there were few witnesses to the wholesale disappearance of those on the outskirts of the hills; but as Cy finished his last remarks—with more than usual dramatics—there were thousands of witnesses. His and Doyan's final vanishing act was, this time, not for just a fraction of a second, but for all the hours since. But there were still enough witnesses *near* the perimeter meeting places to give credible accounts of the vanishings.

With no other explanation making sense, and none of the missing seen for hours, the eye-witness accounts were the best they could do. And why shouldn't the witnesses have been believed? Hadn't everybody already, from time to time, experienced even more remarkable events—like the whole planet vanishing from under their feet?

Cy and Doyan and the multitude of innocents on the periphery still had not returned, even when Clint and Dummy were given those details. They checked the story with several more groups before returning to present the information to Ned and the Directors. As Head of Security, Clint hated the facts he was given and considered the mass disappearance a security problem, if not a breach that might reflect on him. Rationally, he knew he could not have stopped what happened, but those thoughts nevertheless fueled the energy behind his report to the Directors.

Aside from giving public expression to his anger about those facts, on another level Clint was beginning to enjoy making presentations to small groups and the public. On this occasion before the Directors, in fact, Debra Anderson grudgingly heaved some praise in Clint's direction for the clarity and passion of his report and for the ethical fact-finding methodology that he and Dummy used to gather the information. Approval from Debra, of all people, was always surprising. She was not one to freely hurl praise in anyone's direction, especially concerning her own field of expertise. As she tossed out her accolades to Clint—as casually as one might sling a man-hole cover—his chest expand proudly.

During the goodbye visit with their Other friends, Clint and Dummy learned more—things that Clint considered unimportant and had not planned to present to the Directors. As he warmed to the spotlight, however, and gaining confidence in his own judgment and delivery, he made the other announcement after all—embellishing it, of course, with his own slant. He told the Directors that all the Other communities ". . . had concocted their own escape plans to avoid the Big Rip."

"You mean, like the Assemblage did when it took off like a starship and vanished?" Debra Anderson asked.

"Yes," Clint replied, "but not that good. We couldn't catch all the shape-shifters' details. The escape plans we were told about seemed, well, rather pathetic. *Our* plan for escaping the Big Rip, on the other hand, is simply to enter the *invincible* Cone of Transformation where our escape will most assuredly be a complete success." Then Clint took a deep breath and sat back with the same modest half-smile on his face that he showed after delivering one of his Reversal-Theory-For-The-Rest-Of-Us speeches.

"Says who?" Mark inquired, sarcastically.

Clint went pale. He could have handled that question from almost anyone else. "I thought you did, and Laura, and Doug and Stan. Isn't that why we've been running our shuttles and the Orbs day and night? To get people to safety?" He turned away from Mark and looked plaintively at Ned.

"Don't look at me," he said. "There wasn't much time so I only gave my management guidance on what looked like a consensus about the *probabilities* for avoiding the Rip. Or maybe I should just say, about our *chances*. . . . Hmm, or are we now down to wild guesses?"

Ned turned his eyes accusingly on Mark. "How about it Mark. What *are* our chances? You didn't object before. I took your silence as a kind of acceptance or tacit approval of Doug Groth's idea. Should I have asked sooner? What are our chances for avoiding the Big Rip, assuming we get into cruising Transformation-mode before it hits?"

Mark looked bleak. "My big mouth—sorry!" he said.

Ned glanced at the Directors around the table and the wall screens. He cast a wry smile as he watched the anatomical rhythms accompanying Debra Anderson's furious note taking. Then he looked back at Mark who had, in that short span, developed dark circles under his eyes. "Sorry about my big mouth," he said again, contritely.

Ned responded angrily. "That's not an answer! What are the chances?"

Mark shook his head, trying to fend off the gathering cobwebs of gloom and embarrassment, but they kept re-forming. "I can't give you an exact answer," he said. "It would just be a . . . *wild guess.*"

"So we *are* down to that. Okay. Talk about it and then answer the question!" Ned insisted.

"Fine, damn it! . . ." Mark responded, setting his jaw.

"We're waiting."

Mark looked at Laura for support, but she was concentrating on her nails. *How could she be so inattentive?* he wondered.

"Before today," Mark began, "Transformations required a preset destination. Now it'll just be spin the bottle and go. No intermediate stopping point. No de-Transformation anywhere. No destination. Once a Cone is in Transformation, it traverses a corresponding space *alongside* and *within* the universe. After the Big Rip there will *be* no universe. The conventional scientific wisdom has been that cruising Transformations move through universe space *without* being a part of its spatial, energy fields or dimensions—as if no interplay existed between it and the surrounding space. Now we have to worry about going through some kind of *nonspace* in a *nonuniverse*—something akin to stasis, except, I hope, without the static immobility."

Mark looked around as he spoke. "I'm confusing you. I can tell." He was hoping.

"Not at all. Please continue," Ned said.

Mark flashed a quick grimace of disappointment. "Okay. To *contradict* the view from our conventional wisdom, recall the Twister you went through. Until then most astrophysics authorities would have thought that cruising Transformations created their own unattached and separate space in *parallel* with this universe's spacetime dimensions. But the Twister disproved the generality of that idea. It was a tough way to learn, but we now know there can be a *strong* interactive relationship in certain extraordinary surroundings and circumstances between some of this universe's dimensions and a cruising Transformation. That interaction *can not be stated* because we are presently unable to specify the kind of 'surroundings' that a Transformation tunes in on *in order to ignore it*—that is, to *not* interact with it—as happens with our familiar forms of space, time and matter. That's the Transformation's trick that allows it to work at all." Laura looked up and nodded. "But we are unfamiliar with this new realm—this Big Rip nothingness we're heading into. Even our wildest theories haven't taken us into the realm of 'nonexistent surroundings'—not yet."

Mark looked at Laura without hope, but she again glanced up from her nails and nodded her agreement with what he had been saying. Encouraged, his complexion improved even as Laura attentively returned to her cuticles. He continued:

"There's not much else to say. Our best hope is hidden in the unknown nature of the diverse subatomic and even massive entities that may interact *outside* the ordinary forces and dimensions that we do know—that is, outside our present knowledge of physics. It's possible those 'nonsurroundings' are just that and may *not* interact with a cruising Transformation, and that's exactly what we want—minimum to zero interaction with whatever we might otherwise be hit with when the Big Rip comes. When that happens, we must be fully into our cruise mode or we'll most certainly be ripped apart along with the Great Cone and everything else."

Ned smiled, but persisted. "What are the odds, Mark? At this point you're making me very nervous. I'll settle for your very best, most scientifically informed, wild-ass guess."

"We can't know the extent of that possibility ahead of time," Mark said without a return smile. "We can only guess what our 'surroundings' will be after the Big Rip. We will need to know more. In the past, for example, if we knew *only* the gravitational effects of dark matter, Transformations would *not* have been possible. We had to know what dark matter really was—its source, its structure and its interactive and other dynamic effects in great detail first. That was just one of many mysteries that had to be solved in order to produce the full, current Theory of Transformation and Reo-Spheres. We don't have that detailed knowledge—none in fact—for our coming trip into the Nonuniverse."

Ned shrugged and shook his head. "That's all gobbledygook to me, Mark," he said. "Can't you just skip ahead and give us the odds?"

Again from his exalted position on the highest wall screen, Stanley Lundeen, known to enjoy asking questions he already knew the answers to, had a question for Mark. "If you please, Dr. Tenderloin, what examples would you care to share with us of what you called 'massive entities' *outside* our physics knowledge? What do you mean by 'massive entities'?"

"Black holes. They're massive entities. Galaxies and universes are massive entities. For an especially relevant example, take that other universe—our neighbor, the blue-shifter. That's a massive entity for sure. Who, until recently, even suspected it was *really* there, much less the details of its nature, which we don't know—except we are now impressed that it favors complex, crystal-like material and beings. Above all, who would have suspected it was sitting there, shrinking, and ready to destroy us?"

"And us, it!" Laura added with inordinate emphasis, even as she was giving her closest scrutiny to a possible hangnail. (Those who knew Laura well were not bothered by her *inattention*. They knew she did her best thinking while pondering her nails.)

"Right!" Mark yelped in a startle reaction. "Anyway, those other realities can exist more or less independently of one another without measurable interaction, *or*, like that blue-shifting universe plugged into us, they can hide out internally for a long time, unnoticed, like a herpes zoster ready to pounce."

"Very interesting," Ned stated, glazing over, "but I believe you're skirting the question."

Predictably, like the red and blue from a lichen's litmus, Mark's color changed again, but he continued bravely trying to make the point. "*If*—and this is the big if—if our Cone of Transformation could exist in total independence of our known universe, and could continue that same independent existence *after* our universe is gone—because, in the conventional wisdom, they weren't supposed to be connected anyway, right?—then the Transformation Cone could sustain itself, probably forever, or at least a few billion years."

They all knew that was a gross exaggeration, but liked the point he was making.

"And *if not*?" Ned asked.

"*If not* what?"

"*If not* able to sustain itself after the Big Rip; after our universe is gone? If the Transformation and space and other forces and dimensions of the universe—aside from major screw-ups like running into black holes—*are* connected despite the conventional scientific wisdom, then what?" Ned asked.

"Oh. *That* if not." Mark was still fending off Ned's primary question. Mark was a stickler for number accuracy in scientific matters and hated ball-park *number* answers; but he didn't mind *verbal* generalizations—they seemed more human to him than the rigor of formulas and numbers.

"Then I fear" Mark continued, "that Transformation Cones, like yours and mine, could last no longer than our universe. When it goes, so do the Cones."

"So . . . what are the odds?"

"The odds?"

"For our survival on Transformation. Give us a number. And don't say, *Oh, those odds!*"

As if what Mark had already said were not generalization enough, answering *this* question could no longer be avoided.

Mark looked at Laura and, finally, she at him. They both turned their heads to look at Ned and said, in unison, "*Fifty-fifty!*"

The Directors' expressions were of shocked disappointment and delighted surprise—in that same ratio.

EIGHTY-ONE

By this time everybody had lost confidence in any broader hopes. Reality impinged and their only hope was that even prospect for survival. They had given up on Origin, Earth, the Milky Way, other galaxies, the universe in general, and whatever else might exist. The last of the Others and their identicals had departed to one place or another on Origin and would, presumably, soon implement their own survival plans—if the universe would be so kind as to hold out until then. The humans, with half their fellow crew members and isomorphs gone, realized they would soon be alone in the cosmos on a cruising Transformation, lost in the vanishing remnants of a senile universe. Even such a fate would now be considered lucky. Origin was still there for the isomorphs, for at least a little while longer—until the end.

The men and women who were still on Origin or already back on the Great Cone, spent at least some of their remaining time before being plunged into space thinking about their families and friends back home, and more philosophically, for a few, about the end of human life and the very demise of evolution, the planet's other living creatures and, in a few places, Earth's still-thriving beauty. The usual chest-beating protests and questions also persisted, like the 'How-could-God-do-this-to-us?' questions. And anger too—toward Cy, the *essence of Origin*, for his betrayal and abandonment of them at this deadly hour, and toward the Dorts for the kidnappings, the Twister deaths, and all the rest.

But time drew short. There was no more time for anger, despair, chest beating, protests to the heavens or anywhere else; only personal prayers and their threadbare survival hopes. Even the hope and despair could not be denied; they were simply there—in the same old fifty-fifty proportions.

For those remaining on the planet who wanted to leave, the final shuttle had landed. They included the last Directors still on Origin, and a number of other people who had waited with their isomorph till the last minute. One isomorph also came along. She had decided to take her chances in the geode. Other isomorphs had done well there. Her equally attractive human was already on the Transformation. Fourteen humans opted to remain on Origin and could not be persuaded to leave.

The stoic goodbyes—and the tearful ones—had already been exchanged between the isomorphs and their human identicals. The humans, and one isomorph, entered the vehicle for transport to the Cone. Before entering it, they waved a last goodbye to the hundreds they were leaving. They waved back; and the last shuttle departed.

The crowded shuttle lifted off and, at long last, *time returned*. A little time. Time to think—or not. The shuttle turned and accelerated outward as the thoughts of passengers turned inward. Uppermost for many was worry for their survival and well-being, hoping their odds were better than fifty-fifty. And there were practical worriers too, wondering—if they did survive the Big Rip—how they could live beyond the Cone's ten-year food supply even with its scientific methods of gardening and all the other survival strategies they'd learned before leaving Earth. In frightening detail, some wondered, and even wrote down, how they would deal with each other when resources ran low or were gone. Some imagined worse scenarios.

The passengers sat quietly as the shuttle ascended with increasing speed. It would still be a long trip to the Great Cone. Some sat blankly, others took out pillows to sleep; but many were active in their thoughts, scribbling on note pads and scraps of paper or speaking quietly into recorders—making imaginary plans, stating wishes and expressing their final reflections. They felt lucky for the time to communicate their thoughts and feelings—hoping those final ideas might magically linger somewhere, if only in a machine or on a piece of paper. Even Laura, in the midst of filing her nails, suddenly stopped and took out a blank envelope. She then thought for a long time before writing a word.

The passengers were on a transit of hope and despair—their thoughts, like those of ancient hermits and teachers with truths that came together in packages of time—at birth; thirty years in prison; a lifetime of self-imposed isolation; or thirty seconds in the mind of a careless driver who found the same kind of truth as her speeding vehicle sailed off a mountain pass into a deep canyon. At last! Time to *really* think! Or not! Thirty years or thirty seconds—there was always time.

There were other perceptions and ideas, abstract and general, and some of those even worthy. Nor was all their wondering entirely selfish. Not exactly. As they faced the reality of possible life in a confined, cone-shaped world, or death, such lofty ideas at times intruded in welcome abundance upon those fears—even flourishing briefly before again slumping back into emptiness and fear. A few looked deeper into that slump to ask who they really were as conscious beings and what consciousness represented in this universe—even in the universe without opposite.

Those were not just human thoughts. Similar thoughts, differently expressed and shared by the people and isomorphs who remained on Origin, and by the Others and those who had vanished—and by all the conscious and aware beings across the Milky Way and beyond.

Laura often comforted herself with words; but knew they were a pale expression of something inside her that she had inadequately tried to state many times before. It still lingered there after years of trying. She knew those episodic efforts to express it in writing were only the tip of the iceberg, but that it lay beneath her science, and probably all of science and reality. Except for Keeta, she never shared her heretical thoughts with anyone.

Laura's appreciation loomed large for what she knew she could never know of reality and her place in it; at least not through the usual human thought forms, be those mathematics, art, writing, the spoken word, science, philosophy, poetry or music—certainly not in their physical or perceptual products, but perhaps in some of the spaces they create. She would try again, maybe for the last time. Who would ever know? She mused for hours about *thought* and *consciousness* and realized their forms were very different. Then, tentatively, she began to write:

> Tendrils of thought and consciousness seem together, but seldom are. They float apart on careless breezes of failed connection, like wafted spores escaping skull-sized mushrooms. Confusion reigns in the illusions of space and time, allowing only fleeting glimpses of reality, beauty, love and truths that become lost in the detaching retinas of our understanding. This dazzling kaleidoscope of predictability and surprise blinds us to the reality of our intact being - except for never-ending moments of quiet, like these, when we close our mind's eyes and ears and thoughts, freeing our consciousness to behold and touch the oneness and wholeness of all-that-is.

Laura turned the envelope over to continue her random thoughts, but as she did so her muse was interrupted. The shuttle had just lurched as its retrojets slowed their approach to the Transformation, but that sudden feel of sluggish transit was insignificant beside the disruption from within the shuttle cabin. The reverie of everyone onboard was shattered by the piercing cry from the throat of the lone isomorph.

At first, different passengers assumed she was suddenly afraid of flying or had changed her mind about going or that, too late, she wished to die on Origin with her fellow isomorphs; but in the final kilometers of approach to the Great Cone, they were convinced otherwise. She spoke rapidly and repetitively of her impression that something important was happening on Origin. It was something she had to see, "Immediately."

They made room for her at one of the windows, but even with the exceptional vision of an isomorph, she could make out no more than the outline of The Island and its dot of a beach. She had screamed only once, but was still upset and talking nonstop, stating she could not see the beach clearly. Ned patiently assured her that when they boarded the Great Cone, he would personally escort her to the Astrophysics lab for a telescopic view of anything she wished to see; but that was not good enough. She had to see it *now*!

There was one large wall screen in the shuttle cabin. Ned called ahead to Stanley Lundeen who accommodated by focusing one of the powerful telescopes on the island, and sent the image to the shuttle's screen. "Now," Stan said to Ned, "what else would you like to see?"

Ned turned to the isomorph, and asked her the same question. "I'd like to see," she said in a somewhat calmer tone, "a close-up of the area where the *essence of Origin* was last seen."

Stan quickly obliged. There was nothing much there to see, except to confirm what they already knew. All the hills were gone, leaving behind the pock-marked beach.

"Please," said the isomorph, becoming still calmer, "could we have an even closer look?"

Stan focused in for a deep close-up of the exact spot—the center clearing area on the beach that had been encircled earlier by the hills, but now by empty craters. What they saw on the screen from the crowded shuttle brought gasps of astonishment. Those gasps would soon be repeated in ever-widening circles across the universe. More was there than empty craters. The vanished had returned.

EIGHTY-TWO

After the Cone was docked, Ned and Laura went directly to the Astrophysics lab with loud, but attractive isomorph in tow. They were followed closely by the other shuttle passengers. The lab was already more crowded than a Friday night bar and just as noisy. Its giant wall-screen was projecting an overall view of the central beach, but there was no two-way radio connection or even one-way communication from anyone on the planet.

Several other isomorphs, all male, had shuttled up earlier and were there too. They received the same "message" as the isomorph who was on the last shuttle. Doug and several other Directors were also on hand, along with the attractive isomorph's human identical. She was standing beside the three male isomorphs who were already demanding their return to the beach. Doug was explaining to them—shouting, in fact, so he could be heard over the din—"That will be impossible. If you went back now, there is no way you could return. The countdown under way is irreversible. By the time you reached Origin and started back, the place where you are standing would be light years from here." When Doug finished shouting, the crowded lab had already become silent.

Quietly, one of the isomorphs said, "None of us need to return here; we only need to be on Origin."

Lowering his voice, Doug said, "Nobody could be more interested than me in making that round trip. If I could, I'd do it a hundred times to return our lost and vanished people to the safety of this Transformation. I know how you feel. It's all on the wall-screen. The beach is holding our vanished and now returned people and isomorphs. Sure, *they've* been returned; but it's too late to help them. We can't stop a countdown that began six hours ago—or six minutes ago for that matter. Even if we could force that, the entire Cone would not only be disrupted, it would disintegrate as surely as one of David Michael's punctured hills. In four hours, if the universe holds together that long, we'll be out of here. No time for a single round trip. The gears are in motion!"

Doug toned down his voice even further, but the tense, wide-eyed crowd was even quieter and still heard every word. They could not understand why, once again, so many must die, and why their own chances were far from excellent. They knew the odds.

Another isomorph announced that he had piloted one of the shuttles several times when his human, a designated pilot, became ill. The man beside him, the isomorph's identical, affirmed the truth of that statement and that he would be glad to fly the shuttle back to Origin with the isomorphs—and others if they wished—should his isomorph not be allowed to pilot the craft.

The lab crowd murmured nervously for a moment when Waldo Wagson, the laundry room supervisor chimed in dramatically with his argument saying, "We could *not possibly* afford to lose even one, no sir, not a single one of the shuttles, because of requirements for future use!"

The isomorph shot back, "Why not? What requirements? What future use? Did you plan on stopping somewhere?"

That about wrapped up the arguments. No destination; no de-Transformations; ergo, no need for shuttles.

Except for another argument, this one from Laura Shane: "I thought you wanted to live. I thought survival was important to you, to all isomorphs."

"It is," the isomorphs said together.

Then one added, "That is why we must go back."

"There is no way we can allow that," Doug said. "It would be suicide. Here, at least, you have a chance."

Ned addressed the attractive isomorph: "When I spoke to you on the shuttle, you were very upset at first, but you soon calmed down. Why was that? What messages were you getting—besides an insistence on a beach close-up? You still hadn't *seen* any of those who had vanished and returned. You were picking up something else *before* Dr. Lundeen's telescope showed them to us. Before that, what I said to you was not enough to calm you down. So, what was it?"

The stone-silent crowd strained to catch every word, but the isomorph's reply was not responsive to Ned's questions. She repeated her still urgent objective: "I just know that I . . . that we four isomorphs . . . need to leave soon. We would welcome our identical humans to return to Origin with us . . . if they are willing. Otherwise we must go alone."

As she finished speaking, the other three isomorphs and their humans entered into animated conversation. In less than a few minutes all their humans agreed to return with them to Origin—if that could be made possible. Murmurs of confusion increased as people wondered how the isomorphs could, with such apparent ease, have convinced their humans to give up their lives merely to accompany them back to Origin.

"I wish my Keeta was here with me now—so she could be safe," Laura said.

The room again became silent when Ned asked the female isomorph the same questions he asked her before. This time she explained, "There was no word message, only an inward flow of something you would call *trust*—that and a calming serenity that confirmed a sense of safety and survival. It wasn't an external signal. It was not a premonition. It was a spontaneous memory. I did not call it up. None of us did. It was just there. That's why I calmed down. Before that, I was reminded of a duty. That spot—in the center of The Island beach—that's where I needed to be; where I should be now. I had to see it to confirm my responsibility. For that obligation to be valid, however, something had to have changed that was not clear when I entered the shuttle to come here. They were now back. Before, they were not. The change was clear and I—we four—have to go back too."

Laura said, "I don't understand all your reasoning, but my Keeta sometimes remembered things that had not yet happened. She never called them premonitions either, but memories. Just before I left, when we said goodbye, she whispered in my ear that, at that moment, she remembered something. Then she looked at me, smiled and said not to worry about her, that she would be all right. I didn't understand how that could be possible, but her next statement confused me even more. She said that if I found a sound reason to come back, even for a short return, that I should grab the chance. She told me it would be worth it and that such a return, however brief, would not be for a triviality. When I asked her the reason for such guidance, she said she didn't know exactly, but remembered that something was changing. She did not identify it as the return of the vanished, but thought it had to do with a change in the structure of time and that, as if that explained everything, I might have reason to stay with Origin a little longer."

"Laura, you're right," Doug said. "These isomorphs, and Keeta too, make no sense at all. As for your 'staying with Origin a little longer,' forget that! The time for leaving is already past."

"I know, Doug, but as I look at that wall-screen, I feel its pull. I know Keeta is somewhere in that blur of a crowd, mingling with those who had vanished. Even now, we can see them massing around Cy. He's back too. Something must have changed. Something is still changing. I wonder what he's telling that crowd. I don't believe I could ever completely trust ol' Cy, but I do trust Keeta's memories, and I trust her—completely. I think that, for a little while—maybe just minutes—I have to go back." As she spoke, she looked hopefully at Ned and Doug. She knew what the response would be, and knew the reasons better than they, but the child in her had to make the plea.

Doug said, "Whatever that one-eyed pirate is saying to his captives, we have no way of knowing. We're only getting radio static from down there. There is no communication so *you won't be able to hear his lies*—and you're not going to be one of his captives, not again."

Laura looked at him, forlorn.

Doug continued to repeat himself. "And you can't return! You'd never get back in time, even if Origin didn't keep you there—for whatever perverse reason *It* might have. All we know is that those kidnappings keep happening. Look what happened to the Others. I only see a few small groups of them down there. The rest are scattered. From up here, we've learned to recognize what the Others look like in their own groups. In a crowd of their own kind they're distinctly different from each other and from humans and isomorphs. A lot of them are outside their small groups and mixed in with the crowd. I wonder what happened to most of the Others that vanished. There's nobody else we can pick out down there, except the big one, Cy, and I don't see that other lump, Doyan. It's hard to tell at this magnification. With a zillion humans and isomorphs milling around, and a *few* Others, that's about it!"

Crowd-noise in the lab had risen to a loud chatter. A technician shouted, "Maybe we'll be able to hear Cy's lies after all—we're receiving!"

"Okay," Doug said, relieved at the chance to stop preaching the *you-can't-go-back* Gospel. "Let's have a listen. Someone down there is being kind enough to send."

"Not just someone," the tech said, ". . . but dozens of them. This one is just a little clearer, so this is the one you'll hear. We've been sending the beach projections all over the Cone, so everybody looking at the screens will get the same sound."

"Fine," Doug said. "Anyway, we don't have too much else to do for a few more hours."

"Yeah," Clint said, "let's document that one-eyed asshole's lies!"

They heard Cy holding forth in his usual engaging and amusing way. He sounded the same as always, with a remarkably robust version of Mark's voice. In a few minutes, however, his demeanor changed. He lifted his grotesque head and giant arms toward the Great Cone—and raised the tone of his remarks to match. He looked and sounded more serious than at any time before.

"As I recall," Cy said, "there are four of my kind with you now, and they wish to return. Please allow them to do so, and use as many of your shuttles as you can spare to return to Origin yourselves. And some here may wish to join you on your Transformation. You could maneuver your Cone much closer to Origin to shorten transit for the shuttles without disrupting your countdown process?"

"No way, buster! I smell another trap!" Clint snorted, unheard except for those in the Astrophysics lab.

Cy continued, "I know your Cone of Transformation is close to leaving. I regret you are without a fail-safe mechanism to call that off. If there were, I would recommend its use. I blame myself for not returning in time to dissuade you from your hasty departure; your count-down might not then have begun.

Time is confusing when it changes pace. It is my fault. I miscalculated my return to Origin by many years, but the extra time was necessary."

Cy's diplomatic skills were poor, but he kept on talking. Above all, his remarks were making Doug, Clint, Waldo Wagson, and many others exceedingly angry. Clint asked the tech if he could get *two-way* communication going. "I got something I wanna say to that asshole."

A switch was thrown and the send connection became available. When the tech finally established a fully capable dialog hookup he asked Stanley and Ned if the arrangement had their approval for use. They nodded and Clint took the microphone.

"Okay asshole," he said, "I got something to say to you."

"Well good, Officer Bracket," said Cy. "Good to hear you haven't forgotten how you like to address me or I might not have believed it was you. But I have more to tell you—all of you. So please hold off. There is little time left."

"Little time left for what?" Clint said, more as an accusation than a question.

"Little time to bring you up to speed on what has happened since I last saw you—and before we must again return."

"Since you last saw us, huh! You mean since you abducted our isomorphs and our people—again! I know you're a trickster and made them *vanish*! I call that kidnapping."

"Have it your way, Officer Bracket, but there was no abduction or capture. Fourteen of your people had the same chance to leave, but chose to *remain*, and are here on the beach now. By choice they *did not* 'vanish,' as you call it. All the humans and isomorphs, and all the Others who left with us, chose freely to do so. Their *departures* were voluntary."

"I don't believe your lies," Clint said.

Within minutes a number of the fourteen that Cy had mentioned, found their way to the radio setup. Their voices were recognized and each corroborated what Cy just said. They had all been ready to leave at the time of the mass "departure," but it was only those fourteen who, at the last minute, changed their minds. They later regretted that and wished they had gone.

Ned asked a question of the last speaker. "Why do you wish, even now, that you had gone? Everybody is already back, *but now you and they are not safe.*"

"Are you safe?" the man asked.

"Maybe we aren't either, but on the Transformation Cone we have a fifty-fifty chance of survival. You have none. Why *do* you wish you had gone?"

The man's response to Ned's question sent a shock-wave through every corner of the Great Cone:

"By remaining here I lost my chance for true survival. By 'survival' I don't mean *just* staying alive, or being in the same boat with many of my friends. That too, but by 'survival' I mean a long, productive, creative, challenging, worthwhile life with family I never had, with love and kids, grand children and right on to great-great-great grandchildren. I'd have lived a long, young life and grown old slowly. And then, like all the humans that 'vanished,' none lived to return. All your 'vanished' isomorphs are back. And they are here now. Let them tell you."

"This is impossible to believe," Clint said.

The man replied, "Then just look more closely at us and you will see."

Stanley Lundeen nodded to his small crew. They increased the magnification from what was an overall view of the crowd to extreme close-ups of the tops of heads. One could count the hairs on their heads and the grains of sand beneath their feet. One isomorph was immediately recognized. She was carrying something in her arms—a large, glistening ball—as were others. There was the mark of a star on her left shoulder. Stan gave his crew a disgusted look for the extreme close-up magnification. They backed off the focus by a fraction to take in small groups of a dozen or so, and split the giant wall-screens into multiple views showing different scenes from telescopes trained on the crowd below.

If the man's words alone were shocking, what they saw now was its reality. Those on the Cone were trying hard to take it all in. They drew in their breath, virtually as one, widening the circle of gasps that began on that last shuttle to their supposed safety.

With the clearer magnification, they easily recognized their naked isomorphs from before who had vanished but, except for "the fourteen," were unable to identify any of the humans. The humans they did see were now dressed in scanty, practical-looking attire. Scattered among the men and women were hundreds of infants and children of all ages, some pregnant women and many healthy, very alert and vigorous old people. The adult humans were slim, taller than most of the isomorphs, with slanting eyes larger than anyone could remember. They were beautiful.

For several long minutes everybody on the Cone was still trying to take it all in and to understand its meaning. Officer Bracket kept his own stunned and angry silence as long as he could. Hardly able to speak at all, his now rasping, guttural, throat sounds snarled the questions on everybody's mind: "Where are they, Cy? What have you done with *our* people?"

Part V

CRYSTAL LIBRARIES OF TIME

EIGHTY-THREE

Cy was not quick to answer, but finally said, "From what you have already been told, Officer Bracket, I thought by now you would know the answer to your question. You heard the answer from others. It was not I who told you. You don't believe anything I tell you, and yet you asked me to answer. Do you really want *me* to answer your question—one more time—so that you can pretend the answer is a lie?"

Ned put his hand on one of Clint's angrily shaking shoulders. Clint knew. Everybody did. More or less. They were all devastated.

Ned knew the answer needed to be made more explicit, as if it weren't already clear enough. For everyone, he asked the question again: "What happened to our people?"

Cy said, "During the theory translations, as you all know, Doyan and I left here for short absences lasting fractions of a second here, but there the absences lasted years."

"Yes, we know that!" said Littleviolet, who was standing near Clint. The crowd around her and throughout the Great Cone murmured their agreement. They knew that.

"Then you also know this," Cy continued: "In the time that Doyan and I, and many of your people and isomorphs were gone for *hours in this universe*, not just fractions of a second this time, *eons* went by *in the other, coexistent universe*. As you already heard, your people lived long and well—and multiplied. The people you now see around me are only a handful of the offspring of their offspring, hundreds of generations later. In the other universe their numbers are now in the tens of billions—scattered across a thousand natural and 'terraformed' planets. Even as we stand here, those numbers are increasing; lives are being lived and ending. The new lives they created continue on—and evolution moves forward—here and there by design. It's a different universe from this one; but, as you must understand by now, not all that different."

Cy continued his remarks amidst a shower of frightened and angry questions. As his revelations sunk in, the predictable human reactions spanned the emotional spectrum.

During this exchange, Cy revealed that the *Others*—who dearly departed Origin the same time as the humans and isomorphs—had similar experiences over those same long eons. They too had scattered to planets of their own that were natural for them or re-created for them by worker Dorts.

"Many of the human and Other populations," Cy went on, "live together or separately on the same planets. Some are on their own planets. Their very different forms of culture; art; literature; architecture; religion; sports; politics; law; economics; education; methods of land, sea, air and space travel; and all the rest, have long ago reached peaks of perfection—and sometimes the lows of devastation and war. All of this continues as we speak."

The long-distance Q-and-A by radio continued for another twenty minutes when an alarm sounded on the Great Cone. One of the Orbs had been taken and was somewhere in transit—not downward toward Origin, but upward, away from the planet and the Great Cone at supersonic speed. It was soon tracked from the Cone by an array of detection instruments that automatically brought it into focus on one of its telescopes. Computers calculated its trajectory. The Orb was soon to intersect another moving object: Mark Tenderloin's Mini-Cone, still in faithful orbit above the planet's equator.

In the turmoil and emotions around Cy's revelations, Mark had slipped away. But he was not alone. With him on the Homing Pigeon were the four isomorphs and their humans; his "coffee buddy," Laura; and Mark's beloved Denise—whose own precious Chastity, like Keeta, was still on Origin.

After landing the Homing Pigeon on the surface of Mark's Mini-Cone, he maneuvered it into place beside a large, semi-cylindrical structure (anciently known as a Quonset hut). Mark called it his "apartment." They entered the arched structure, ducking their heads on their way in through its double doors.

Once inside, there was plenty of room, but it did not meet with everyone's approval. With hands on her hips and shaking her head, Denise Christensen had words for Mark's apartment: "This place is a dump."

Nevertheless, despite Mark's unmade cot and messy kitchen, it also contained what looked like a reasonably organized mechanic's workshop with a million pieces of equipment, cables, electronics, tools and parts. Most importantly, it also held the necessary controls, connecting the Cone's human pilot with the vast engineering feat that spiraled so efficiently within the Cone below and made Mark's Mini-Cone the functional Transformation vehicle it was.

Mark settled into the one truly neat and clean spot in the hut—the area that put him at his Transformation's controls. He immediately began to move the Mini-Cone in a wide downward circle toward the planet.

Everyone there knew what would happen next. It had all been laid out and discussed on the trip from the Great Cone to the small one. In the meantime, Denise began a strangely diplomatic version of shouting orders. Everybody was to help bring "some real order to this place." She sounded like the cross between a cheerful sergeant making "suggestions" to the troops and a demanding mother ordering her children to straighten their rooms. The cooperation was amazing.

The isomorphs moved the heavy items into neat arrangements outside the building; the humans did the dishes, made the bed, and handled dozens of the lighter tasks. As they followed Denise's detailed, step-by-step orders, it soon became clear that the object of all this activity was not just cleanliness and neatness, but to clear a large central space within the hut. Denise apparently expected there would be more passengers. During all of this, a noisy transceiver kept them up on all the communication between Origin and the Great Cone and the many orders and demands from Clint that *they* answer him *now*! and return immediately to the Great Cone. He was ignored.

What began as a wide and gentle downward spiral of the Mini-Cone, accelerated into a plunging maneuver that ended thirty kilometers above The Island's mountains. There, like the fingers of a cupped hand, the mountains stood in a protective semicircle around the beach. As small as it was, compared to the Great Cone, Mark's Mini-Cone still cast a dark shadow over most of the beach.

"Okay! Time to move it!" Mark said.

Following the plan, they again joined him on the Homing Pigeon. It hurtled down to the beach where it lingered above the center of the concourse until people and other beings moved aside to make room for it to land. There, the Orb settled into the opening—only steps from where Cy was standing.

The four isomorphs and their identicals thanked Mark for his help in returning them to the Planet. From there they would go to where those who had vanished had gone before. Denise and Laura were immediately met by Chastity and Keeta. Mark had no idea what their plans might later turn out to be. For his part, he moved slowly toward Cy, who in turn got down, lowering his countenance to the surface allowing Mark to stand before the massive face. Cy's visage, from chin to the top of his head, was higher than Mark was tall.

There, Mark looked his "identical" square in his eye for a quiet, but intense conversation. First, however, he borrowed Cy's microphone to announce to the crowd his willingness to return anyone who wished, back to either Transformation Cone—to the Mini-Cone, or to the Great Cone. (It would take many trips if there were too many, but he encouraged them anyway.) Cy added his voice, emphasizing the need to sort that out quickly as there was little time. After that, the conversation between Mark and Cy was undisturbed.

Chastity and Denise wandered off together in an opposite direction from Keeta and Laura. Chastity had long understood the time differences between the two universes. She wanted to go to the other one, "for a few seconds," and wanted Denise to come with her. Denise was torn between that and staying with Mark. She wanted to go and would try to convince Mark to come with them, "But a few seconds away from here," Denise said, "would be centuries there. You would live all that time, but I would die there." In that other universe there would be time for a long life despite the impending Big Rip—even in those few seconds. Or, with luck, they could survive together on the Great Cone; *but what kind of a life would that be?* Denise silently wondered.

Keeta took Laura by the hand. She hurried them along because there was someone, a friend of Keeta's, who'd asked for a meeting with Laura. Keeta made an odd, piercing sound, inducing the thrusting, jostling crowd around them to scatter outward for several meters allowing Keeta to jump in a high, twisting spiral to view the crowd, and to alight without crashing into anyone. After landing she took Laura's hand again, saying, "This way! She's this way!" In a minute they caught up with the isomorph she sought. Keeta called out, "Venus, here is Laura!"

Venus was carrying an object in her arms—a crystalline globe that was an awkward two-thirds of a meter in diameter. She had been walking beside Gegeneis who was carrying an equally large and awkward canvas bag by its draw-strings. Every few seconds, even after all those "years" in the other universe, he kept adjusting the thick eyeglasses he "inherited" (and had been rebuilt time and again) from Zackery Parker, his identical. The frames were a little different, but the lenses were still the same.

When Laura saw Venus, she was shocked and spoke beyond any semblance of deliberation or tact. The isomorph's body had changed. It was pitifully scarred. When she turned around in response to Keeta's call, Laura saw that some parts of her body had not changed. The top of her head was hairless as usual, her bare shoulders were unscarred and she still carried the identifying star on her left shoulder. Unlike most isomorphs, she wore certain garments, evidentially to cover the worst of her disfigurement. Nonetheless, many of her scars were evident. To ambulate, reach and grasp, she now required four artificial limbs. She also wore a copy of the familiar-looking mask of a once admired dancer. In her arms, she carried the transparent, hollow crystal. In the faceted globe's dark interior only a dense, twisting, turbid cloud could be seen.

"My God, Venus! What happened to you?" was Laura's first response, spoken with horror in her voice. "You were once beautiful! How long have you been . . . like *this*?" (So much for deliberation and tact.)

Unperturbed, Venus said, "That I look as I do, *is* my badge of beauty. Astra Hughs, my identical, always loved me, but found it hard to forgive me for trading features with her—especially without her permission or awareness. But, not long after that, she did forgive me—more or less. We came to an accommodation. That was over a century before she died."

"Then it is true," Laura said, pretending she was not confused and that she *got it*. "She and all those who vanished with her are now dead too. How did Astra die?"

"Happily. She had many children. She died in the arms of their father. Beyond that, I will specify no further."

"She had children?" Laura was incredulous.

"She and Zackery Parker were in *vinculum matrimonii* for several hundred years before they died. They were vital until the end. *Yes, they had children!*"

"Amazing!" Laura said, "I didn't think she could."

"In Astra's early years they tried to have children. She was unable."

"Her early years?"

"That refers to her life before I stole some of her physical characteristics—and replaced them with mine. Cy helped. Without him it would have been impossible."

Laura was perplexed and said, "That figures. Cy and the Dorts don't follow the rules."

"Cy follows his own rules. In this case neither of us knew if the physical trade would work the way we intended. But it did! After our joint metamorphosis, Astra was able to conceive and have all the children Zack and she wanted—and they did, over and over again!"

"That's wonderful . . . I guess."

"It was, and we are both beautiful for it—where it counts."

Laura was still perplexed. "But . . . about Astra, she was here only a few days ago—or did I glimpse her in a group only yesterday? Three hundred years? No! She died young then. No time for real children and—"

"—They were real!"

"I'm sure I saw her with both you and Gegeneis—and with Zack. Margaret and Opal too."

(Laura Shane, as the physicist she was, understood the relativistic possibilities of dynamic-time differences between two universes with their different physical laws; but when, as now, those differences trespassed into human and personal space, it left her confused and time-disoriented. If she wanted, she *could* have emotionally grasped what happened to Astra and to time, but not right away, thank you—she simply did not wish to. She refused. On such occasions she preferred the temporary comfort of denial.)

Venus said, "In *this* universe I'm sure you *did* recently see Zack and Margaret, and the two of us—me and Gegeneis. But in the time span away from here, we had many *years* together in the other universe. Our little group was almost inseparable."

"What group was that?"

"Me and Astra—when she got over being angry at me—and Gegeneis and Zack, Margaret Heckart and Kevin Verily and their isomorphs, Opal and Nor-Man, and a few dozen more—including some of the Others."

"I'm glad you and Astra were not alone. But I'm still wondering . . . how long have you been—over there—changed . . . physically?" Laura's face reddened as she asked the question.

"I have been this way, as I said, for centuries—long before and after Astra's death. I will remain this way till the end. But that is enough about me."

"Why did you come back?" Laura asked.

"Oh, don't worry. I won't be here long. None of us will."

"I didn't mean—"

"I know," Venus said. "No offense taken; but I did return here for the opportunity to give you this, Laura." She indicated the globe in her arms. "There are many, but this one contains their ashes—the ashes of Astra Hughs and Zackery Parker. They died at the same time—just about. Their last request was for their cremains to be taken back to the Great Cone and to stay within the Crystal. I told them that might not be possible, but Astra said it would please her if she knew I would try. So here we are. It's possible. She suggested you, Laura, as the person to receive and care for it. This . . . this *Crystal Library of Time* contains more than their remains. Keep it safe for the history it carries and the worlds within worlds it holds."

"She wanted *me* to take care of this?" Laura's surprise was evident. "It was her dieing wish? I don't understand. We were just acquaintances. I admired her, but I didn't know her well enough to deserve this. I mean, to deserve this honor."

"She admired you too—*more than you know*. Within this Crystal, she and Zack may become legitimately and well understood. Only then can they *truly* be know and amply esteemed."

"You said Astra and Zack died at the same time?"

"Yes—cuddled together on a cushioned floor in the Amphitheater of Death. They entered it the day before they died. There are no hospitals on the planets in the other universe. They are not necessary. After Astra died, Zackery Parker bit a death capsule and joined her that hour. Her death, and therefore his too, was expected, so at that time they came to be surrounded by their children and grandchildren, and multiple levels of great-grandchildren by the hundreds; and dignitaries from across that universe joined them in the Amphitheater so they could be honored. Humans and Others were there with us. The Others loved and honored them both as much as we did.

"By tradition, as Astra's and Zack's identicals, we knelt beside them before she died. They asked Gegeneis and me to be their Death Guides. In this globe, this Crystal, you will find it all." Venus handed the globe to Laura, who accepted it with a wide-eyed look of panic.

"You have but to ask in it and you will experience the answer, even if it takes years for the answer to be learned."

"Ask '*in*' it? What does that mean?" Laura inquired, still staggered by the honor and the responsibility she had just received—and accepted. She was also distracted and staggered by the surging crowd around them, as was Gegeneis.

Venus pointed and nodded toward Gegeneis who handed to Keeta the sack he had been carrying. "I think you should hang onto this," he said.

Keeta loosened the draw-string at the top of the bag and looked inside. She reached in and removed one of the items. There were hundreds of them, all the same. It was a soft, flexible, circle of ribbon.

"It's a very special membrane or headband," Gegeneis said. "Try it on, and give one to Laura. It could as well be a garter or a bracelet."

"In order to be '*in*' the Crystal Library," Venus said, "one of the headbands must be worn on the *reader's* head, across the forehead, and then placed so as to touch the Crystal. It is not difficult at all. For others around you it will be even easier. Another person wearing one of the headbands and touching your hand with his or her own banded forehead will also experience being '*in*' the Crystal—right there with you. There are several hundred bands in that bag. Everyone touching another person's hand in the same way, even in a long series—like Christmas tree lights—can experience the Crystal. They'd all be in the Library together. Never lose the headbands. The Crystal will remain dark and clouded without them. They belong together. Think of the band as something like a library card. The Crystal Library is for enlightenment, not darkness. Once there, everybody can go their own way. Your experiences will not be identical."

"You are telling us there is more in the globe than Astra's and Zack's ashes." Laura said.

Venus responded, "This globe contains their actual ashes, and above those ashes you will see the lifelike holograph of their bodies entwined in love; you will see Gegeneis and I sitting beside their bodies, and in the background, when you are there, you will meet and be able to talk with their adult offspring and grandchildren—the ones in attendance in the Amphitheater. You will be there and that will be your starting place.

"The transcendent legacy of Astra and Zack is, in the other universe, legendary and commemorated to this day. *Together, they were the most influential and exceptional leaders in our long history*. We are still encouraged by their presence and their example of love, wisdom, leadership, their poetry and art—and much more. Their writings were studied by every intelligent citizen while they were still alive, and as much or more since they died. They are honored, too, in the Crystal Worlds—in the Libraries of Time. In them they may still be found."

"I can't imagine being *inside* this crystal," Laura said.

"Really?" Gegeneis said. "Have you ever read a book? Books are not too small to provide a human experience are they?"

"Oh. . . . I see what you mean."

"The difference is the reality of it," Gegeneis continued. "In the Crystal it is a real experience; not a vicarious one. In there, when you shake someone's hand you will feel that person's grip just as he or she will feel yours. If you walk outside alone or with someone you might have met there, depending on the season you will feel the breeze and the warmth of a summer star or the biting cold of winter.

"Should you need another guide, Venus and I will be happy to show you around, as will anyone else—if they are not too busy at the time. There you can converse with anyone, alone or in groups. Every isomorph and human, and every Other will also be holding (or will somehow be in possession of) yet another Crystal like this one. Never go far from the Crystal you are entrusted with. A Crystal is durable, but can be broken. If that happens, then you will have become something of a careless or destructive god, destroying the universes it holds.

"You may access any other Crystal you wish in the same way as this one; but I advise you to avoid going more than one or two levels deep into the Crystals. Within each new Crystal, *Time* becomes denser. It becomes even more so within the next, and so on. I would worry about the fate of your human nervous systems at depths beyond those. Do not attempt it. Even the level beyond the first can be dangerous."

Laura chuckled, "Does this Library have special hours?"

"It's always open," Gegeneis said without a smile. "An observer sitting beside you (but not joining you in the Crystal) would notice that you barely touched the primary Crystal, that you were in contact with it for only a brief moment—seconds at most—but in that moment, like those who vanished, you may experience being there for a long time—as many minutes or hours or years as you can handle or tolerate. Unlike your *vanished* friends, however, your experience 'in' the Crystal will be similar to an isomorph's nightscape experience—and you will return once again, in a flash, to your existence here."

"If I live."

"Of course. There is much about the Crystals we do not understand. But if you stay there, it will give you hundreds of years of your own experiences, or you may choose to go through the life-long experiences of others who have lived there. In that way you can collect an enormous expanse of knowledge and experiences for later re-cognition. Those experiences will thereafter reside mainly in your unconscious and preconscious memory as hidden wisdom that you may call upon as needed; or you may reexperience any of it at will, without the Crystal or the headband. Once you have it, it's yours."

Laura looked down at the Crystal globe. The movement of its smoky, dark shadows seemed to beckon to her, and she was frightened. "This Crystal . . . this invention . . . who or what could have created and brought you such a thing as this?" she asked.

Gegeneis responded, "The *entity*. We call it the entity. But it did not invent or create the Crystal, it received it."

"Received, invented—whatever! What's the difference? What entity are you talking about?" Laura asked.

"I have not come to know the entity, but it was long ago befriended by Astra Hughs and Zackery Parker. They befriended it for all of their lives *and since*. The Crystal Library of Time was the entity's gift to them when they announced to the universe the day of their forthcoming Deaths. Their living essences entered the Crystal even before their ashes."

Laura and Keeta conferred for a moment. "We still don't understand what you mean by *entity*," Laura said. "If this Crystal Library can do half what you say, I marvel at who could have been so creative a visionary—and so capable an inventor."

"It's not a 'who,' exactly; it's an *entity*. It only received the Crystal," Gegeneis repeated.

Mark arrived and broke into their conversation. "Here you are! I've been looking all over. We have to get out of here right now. The Homing Pigeon will have a full load of passengers. They'll be replacing, and then some, the four isomorphs we brought back and their humans. Those eight are staying here. So are the fourteen who opted out of the first vanishing. Denise and Chastity decided to return with me. What are your plans? I have to know now. Cy explained a lot of things to me, including the fact that this entire planet—of which he is its *essence*, so he should know—will be vanishing into the other universe in the next fifteen minutes. So decide!"

Laura thought for several seconds and then, with a look of happy surprise on her face said, "Until this moment I never realized this: I could never leave Ned." She then looked pleadingly at Keeta while speaking her next words to Mark: "Yes, I'll be coming back with you."

Keeta nodded to Laura's look and said, "I hope the geode in the Great Cone will work out. I don't want to leave *you*, Laura. I will return with you. There may never be another nightscape dream for me, but there is always the Crystal Library. I'll manage without my 'mother,' Cy!" Keeta's eyes moved rapidly and Laura laughed too.

"Good," Mark said, "then let's go."

"One second more," Laura said to Mark. Then turning back to Gegeneis she said, "Please tell me, what kind of entity brought you *this*?" She hefted the Crystal. "Make it short—little time."

"Short! Why of course. I am a being of few words. Furthermore—"

"—Short! What is the entity?"

"Short. The entity. It's the ultimate traveler. It traveled from universe to universe with that Reversal Theory you two worked out during one of your famous coffee breaks."

"That was Mark's work," Laura said.

"Yes, but in the other universe, even to this day, we know about those coffee breaks! The traveling entity moved outward with it—the Reversal Theory in its latest revisions—and it went out a full nine universes, one at a time. Each new universe had more power and consciousness in its beings than the one before—a kind of intelligence or brightness hierarchy—but each new universe was in dire need of the Reversal equations. At each outward move, the newest equations were reworked to align it with that next universe and the ones before.

Somewhere in the Crystal Library you may be given the final formulation. Seek it. Even without the Crystal, you *could* safely move back with us to the second, your opposite universe; but the laws of all subsequent universes—the third, fourth and on up—are so different and inhospitable to almost any kind of life from here, from either of our two universes, that no one of us could go there and live, even for an instant. There *is* much life on subsequent universes but nothing close, in type, to that on our two universes. Our 'twin' universes are very different, but not incompatible with our various life forms.

"All of the universes, even the incompatible ones, are intimately connected in certain ways. Their final *expirations* are, together, attuned to *one great potential stroke of oblivion*. The cause of the final calamity in our two cases would be that swinging, alternating pendulum of death—the redshift-blueshift. When one universe goes, they all go. All nine universes and the hundreds above them. So you can imagine the motivated cooperation the entity received in its passage across that matrix of nine universes.

"The greatest power it found on that courageous tour was a *being of composite power*. The entity managed to find it after a centuries-long search in that ninth universe. That being of composite power took the formulas in hand and, in its turn, became the new traveler. It moved out to meet other powers in places beyond. To those universes, beyond the ninth, even the entity could not safely go."

"Okay then, *don't* tell me!" Laura said, eyes flashing. She looked at Mark.

"Right," Mark said. "If we stay a second longer, we'll vanish along with this planet. Let's go! We can come back in ten years. Cy told me that Origin won't be back until then." Mark turned to Gegeneis and Venus, nodded and said, "Goodbye."

"But, but . . . there is so much more to tell you," Gegeneis said.

"A 'being of few words,' eh?" Laura said as she, Mark and Keeta were moving away. They then turned momentarily for a final wave goodbye. Gegeneis's last statement came bellowing through the pressing, noisy crowd. Still, it was barely heard: "The entity gave itself this designation: *Assemblage*."

They mounted the ramp to the Homing Pigeon's open hatch and turned one last time to wave goodbye to whoever might be watching. Everybody was. The base of the inverted Mini-Cone was high above them. It seemed to be resting its flat surface on the north mountains—deep in its own shadow. For a Transformation Cone of any size it was very close. *Mini*-Cone or not, its darkened disk appeared as an immense black hole in an otherwise resplendent sky above The Island's beach.

A number of tall, thin humans were already on the Homing Pigeon when they entered. It was crowded, but the flight to Mark's Cone was mercifully short.

Just before the hatch closed, Venus ran up and stood on the base of its ramp and began talking and gesturing excitedly. Laura moved to stand in the hatchway. It was noisy with so many outside voices and Cy making some last-minute announcement about the imminence of "our step across" to the other universe. Venus shouted, "There's a couple things Gegeneis didn't have time to tell you."

"About what things?" Laura yelled back.

"About how you can get in touch with Cy's sister. One of them anyway."

"Cy's sister? Mark is right here, but he's nobody's sister."

Mark yelled at Venus: "You're holding us up. Move off the ramp!"

"I don't mean Mark," Venus said, ignoring Mark.

"Then what are you talking about?" Laura shouted.

Mark was angry. "I'm closing the hatch right now. Step off the ramp, Venus, unless you're coming in."

Venus stepped off the ramp.

"You too, Laura. Out of the hatchway or I'll have to drag you in!"

Venus kept yelling: "I'm talking about one of Origin's sister *planets*. Its name is Gaia. Try to get in touch with the *essence of Gaia*."

"Gaia? . . . A mythological name—Oh my God, yes!—it's the name for our planet—*Earth*."

"That's right. Your living Earth."

"But there's no time for that. It's too late to do any good. It's too late for everything!"

Mark grabbed Laura around the waste and dragged her back into the cabin. He pressed a panel next to the hatch. The ramp pulled in and the hatch closed.

Venus's last few words were cut off as the ramp rapidly slid back into the Orb. All that she could hear from the frantically shouting Venus was: "Gegeneis forgot to mention about the *Big Rip*. You must have Stanley Lundeen be sure to—" *Slam!*

As the Homing Pigeon lifted off, Laura felt helpless as she watched Venus trying to communicate something by gestures, but it *was* too late. In a minute they were almost to the Mini-Cone. Soon, the Mini-Cone itself was soaring above the atmosphere toward the Great Cone. Almost there, they looked back at planet Origin.

. . . And it vanished.

EIGHTY-FOUR

Origin was gone, but Nimbus still shone upon the apex of the Great Cone. Much farther off, the globular cluster of a million ancient stars provided its own familiar brilliance, and at another angle, like a three-dimensional mural as high and wide as one could see, was the Galaxy—too far off to be more than an awesome sight of shining beauty.

Most important for those on the Great Cone was the matter of "borrowing" additional *energy* from Nimbus—to supplement what they already had from Origin. It would help to ignite and sustain the coming Transformation. The mass-energy converters were gulping it in—in preparation for entry into that wilderness of the unknown.

Like a baby beside its mother, the Mini-Cone was parked a comfortable distance from the Great Cone—almost within eyeshot. Being too close at the moment of the Mini-Cone's Transformation would be dangerous for any nearby space object, including the Great Cone. The Mini-Cone's count-down would be the first to expire.

Mark sped the Homing Pigeon passengers from his "parked" Mini-Cone to that Mother of All Cones. He made arrangements with Ned by radio for the travelers to receive a friendly, or at least nonhostile, reception on landing, and they discussed the expectation of decent conduct toward them thereafter. Lots of luck. Ned agreed to *try* to keep his Security Officer off of everybody's back, and would attempt to create a welcoming environment for the arrivals.

Mark delivered Laura and Keeta and the group of tall, highly evolved humans from the other universe. He, Denise, Chastity and a few others also emerged from the Homing Pigeon. On the platform at the base of Laura's hill they were met by several skittish gyro-car drivers—including Ned Keller who directed Mark and his passengers into the waiting vehicles. They would be taken to Laura's house on the hill for quick transport from there into the deep, central complex of the Great Cone. "That" Ned told Mark's passengers, "will assure everyone's safety at the initial moment of Transformation, so step lively."

He knew, as did Laura, Keeta and Mark, that there was no special danger associated with the start of an *ordinary* Transformation—even when they were on the Cone's surface (because it and the atmosphere "above" that surface was part of the Transformation itself); but he wanted to keep everybody moving briskly to beat the unknown timing of the Big Rip. He could have just said that, but no, he had to be clever and include that additional reason to hurry. He was playing on the legend that it was dangerous to be on a Cone's surface when it engaged, but that was only true for the earliest, experimental Cones. The hazards for starting in FAST-mode, however—since they never did that before—were unknown and considered significant pending, say, a dozen or more experiences with it. Even Mark, with his Mini-Cone, had only done it once. The Great Cone was already in an "ordinary" Transformation-mode when the Dorts switched it into FAST-mode from galactic space. It had not been in that mode at the *start* of the Transformation from Earth.

Mark briefly interrupted his most dear Denise and Chastity to speak with them before they entered the g-car. Ned was driving. He impatiently held its door open for them. Laura and Keeta were already inside. The other passengers, including the advanced humans that came with Mark from Origin, had compliantly stepped into the other two vehicles. Those were already speeding up the hill before Ned could follow.

After Mark spoke with Denise and Chastity, Denise said something to him, he responded, and she began to cry uncontrollably. He stepped back, head bowed, and allowing them to enter the gyro-car. Chastity had to boost her discomposed identical into the vehicle.

Mark walked over to a worried-looking Ned to explain. Ned quickly closed the g-car door and guided him a short distance from the car for privacy.

Mark spoke rapidly to explain: "I can't leave my Mini-Cone stranded. I put it on Auto-countdown to head into space in a random direction. The Mini-Cone will be on its way to nowhere a half-hour before this one. I have no geode in my Cone to preserve the life and well-being of Chastity, so she had to come here."

"That won't be necessary. We'd love to have her, but she'll be safe on your Mini-Cone so long as it's in Fast-mode. I learned that from the Assemb—"

"—Let me finish! There's little time. Anyway, I asked Denise to leave Chastity here and come with me, back to the Mini-Cone, to spend the rest of our lives together. She said that even though she loves me, she would find life intolerably lonely with no other people around. She also told me that when I was into one of my projects—and this part really hurt—I could be 'insufferably boring.' She wished I'd taken her up on the idea of our going together to the other universe by staying on Origin until it vanished across the membranes that define these twin universes. I don't always make good decisions, and that may have been a bad one, but I believe my first responsibility is to be true to myself, and not in a selfish way. I don't want to bore Denise to death. I suspected that my little projects would become a problem some day. I know what she means though, in a way. Like her, I also despise being totally alone. I never found her boring, but there were some things of interest to me that didn't interest her. She is a lot more social than me, so being stuck with me would be like, well, being alone. Maybe worse. That would kill her spirit. Hate it or not, I can survive alone if I must. She couldn't.

"Right now my responsibility is to return to the Mini-Cone. Anyway, while we were on Origin I couldn't just wait around, as she wanted me to, for Origin to disappear. I had regular people and others to bring here. My values and feelings are as mixed as hers. I'm as mixed up as a bag of nuts. I know that being without Denise will tear me up almost as much as the Big Rip; but, like I said, I can't kill her with boredom. She wouldn't come with me. And then . . . there's my stuff. My machinery, my tools and other crap, and too much of me in that Mini-Cone. Before, it was all in my Earth-based shop. Now it's here. This Mini-Cone is worse than having a dog. I can't just leave it—not for long.

"Over time, I hope to invent my way *out of here*—out of this *big-nothing* trap of cosmic deterioration that our mutually fatuous and senescent universes have allowed to atrophy into entropy's final, flatulent dispersion of all things. Don't ask me what 'out of here' or what that 'big nothing' really is or how it looks or if it has any properties at all. I don't know yet, but I'm getting the earliest glimmer of an inkling that any day now I'll have an even more complete inkling, a more striking grasp on how to start on a *get-out-of-here* invention. Hunches, glimmers and inklings—in no special order—are always the first steps in my theories and inventions. Even if I'm successful, Ned, you too will be out there somewhere, so I don't know if we'll meet again, but I hope so. If not, then goodbye my fiend. Gotta go!"

Before Ned could say a word, Mark was hurrying back to his Homing Pigeon. Ned yelled after him, loud enough for the passengers in the gyro-car to hear: "Wouldn't it be easier to just come with us right now."

"Yes," Mark shouted back as he started up the ramp to enter his Pigeon, "but that's not the point. I tried to explain, but to really do it right would take too long." Mark entered his Homing Pigeon. It lifted away and shot off toward the Mini-Cone.

Ned frowned as he entered the Gyro-car and headed it up the hill with his passengers. When Mark yelled back just then, Ned thought he detected *the slightest catch* in Mark's voice. He thought about that for a few seconds. "*Nah!*" he said to himself, and accelerating to the top of Laura's hill.

The occupants of Ned's gyro-car assembled outside Laura's living room. A room-lift space was there, but the room was not. It was on its way, descending through the half-kilometer-deep shaft carrying those from the first gyro-cars. It moved swiftly down the excavation to open onto the Cone's labyrinthine complex of burrows, hutches, labs, offices, bedroom communities, and all the rest. Ned was visibly angry that the others had not waited, but knew the gyro-car drivers were in fear of what might happen on the surface if they remained longer. He wished he hadn't pushed the legend, but then, with a FAST-mode start, the legend could once again be right. Ned set the controls for the room-lift to return when it was ready, and then, still angry, he began to grimace and fret.

While waiting, Laura did not fret. She sat quietly in her favorite lotus position with the crystal ball on her legs and against her stomach.

Denise was trying to control her emotions after the split with Mark. She tried to be brave and joke and laugh a little. Looking at Laura she said, "The way you're sitting with that crystal belly it makes you look like a lady Buddha . . . but I guess that jewel is too big for you to do a Buddha-Belly-Dance."

"You think so?" Laura said with an equally affected laugh.

Then, turning to Keeta, Laura added, "Give Denise one of the headbands from the bag. She can try on the jewel herself—from the inside. Maybe we'll see a belly dancer in *here*." Laura patted the crystal.

Keeta obliged, but Denise refused to put the band around her head unless Chastity joined her, so Keeta handed one to Chastity.

"Okay," Laura said, looking at Keeta, "let's you and me give it a try too." They still had their own headbands that Gegeneis gave them while they were on The Island's beach.

"Come on, Ned. You too." Laura said. "This will only take a second."

"What is that thing?" Ned asked, pointing to the Crystal. "This is no time to be playing games,"

"This isn't a game . . . exactly," Laura said. "And I promise—look at your watch—it'll only take a second."

Ned shrugged and let Keeta crown him with one of the headbands. Then the ritual began. They placed their foreheads on the outstretched hands of the one nearest the Crystal, as Laura instructed. Keeta's headband touched the fingertips of Laura's left hand, and Ned laid his head firmly on Keeta's left palm. He said the whole process felt "silly." Similarly, on Laura's right were Chastity and Denise.

Laura said, laughing, "Before I put my head on this 'thing'—we're told it's called a 'Crystal *Library* of Time,' so try to remember where you are. Don't get lost in the stacks. Now then . . . is everybody ready for our little trip to the Library?" They all said they were ready; but of course none of them were—not even remotely.

Laura leaned forward and momentarily touched her forehead to the Crystal. They entered the Library together and, that quickly, emerged from it together. *It was many years later.* None of them would be the same again.

Uninvolved and therefore (theoretically) *objective watchers* (individuals and groups) had been observing this little ritual on the wall screens in the complex below, from within Stan's lab and throughout the Cone. This is what they saw:

Laura bent across her "Buddha Belly" and as she touched her forehead to it, the Crystal's clouded interior flashed brightly for an instant. Laura and the others then lifted their heads. The appearance of each individual was eerily unexpressive and they remained that way for several minutes before apparently returning from their state of bewilderment and back to normal. Some watchers were sure they had *not* returned to anything close to *normal*—especially Doug Groth and Clinton Bracket. After Ned and the others had been out of the Library long enough for their heads to clear a little more, they looked and wordlessly nodded to each other with such a complete appearance of understanding that it gave their onlookers strange feelings, as if a monumental secret had passed between them that only they could understand. In that, the watchers were right.

Toward the very end of their time-dilation interlude in the Crystal Library, Chastity suggested to Denise that she reconsider her decision to not join Mark on his Mini-Cone. She ventured that Denise might later come to regret that choice. For her own devious reasons, Chastity broached this subject to Denise in the presence of Ned. She did not disclose her deeper intent to either of them—not until Denise's misgivings were clarified with finality. Only then did Chastity make a clean breast of it.

When their "reverie" was over, Ned made an urgent call to Mark, and then another to Doug. At the same time the *"objective observers,"* watching on monitors and screens from deep in the Cone, wondered why Denise Christensen was again in tears.

Immediately after Ned's call to Mark, the Homing Pigeon began its turnaround and headed back to the Great Cone where it touched down minutes later at the base of Laura's hill—on the same platform it started from. The Orb's hatch opened and its ramp extended. The *observers* were surprised to see, not Denise, but Chastity emerge from Laura's residence and head for the Orb. She descended the hill in two great bounds, then turned casually, even demurely, to ascended the ramp and enter the Orb. Except for the final part of Ned's message, Mark would never have allowed Chastity to join him on his return to the Mini-Cone. As she entered the Orb, its ramp withdrew behind her and the hatch closed. The Pigeon lifted off and shot toward the Mini-Cone—faster than it had ever flown.

There was little time remaining before Mark's automatic Mini-Cone countdown would take it to infinity, with or without passengers, and before, but not after, the Big Rip. Mark took it as a challenge to beat them both.

Nor would he forsake the prospect of his "greatest adventure and experiment ever." But he did not wish to embark on that adventure alone. Minutes earlier he believed there was no alternative but to be alone from then on. He so loathed the idea of a lifetime in isolation and solitude that, with the choice offered, he took this deadly chance to return briefly to the Great Cone to pick up the special passenger that Ned called a "lovely lady."

As a lead-in to the rest of Ned's call, he gave Mark a condensed account of the Crystal Libraries and the highlights of one particular matter he'd learned during his time there—from the Assemblage (and later from Doyan). Mark was advanced enough to understand Ned's brief description of the 'Libraries' and was reminded of the cloudy, faceted, crystal globe that Laura carried with her on their flight from Origin to the Great Cone, but had no idea of its nature until Ned's explanation.

Ned told Mark what he'd learned from the Assemblage: Isomorphs would be safe, even without Origin or a giant geode, *if* they were in continual FAST-mode acceleration. (The Mini-Cone could operate in routine transit modes within a planet's atmosphere or space, such as the maneuvers it just completed above The Island's beach, and it could orbit a planet; but its *only* means of interstellar Transformation *was* in FAST-mode. That's the way he designed it and the way the Dorts built it.) None of the Transformation crew was with Ned when the Assemblage communicated that isomorph survival news—news that Mark thought was interesting but irrelevant for his purposes; but when Chastity was to become his passenger he realized why Ned gave him that information.

When the Assemblage made that known, Ned was experiencing life within a deep-level Crystal. The Assemblage's communication was, again, not by voice, but as a *meaning* that simply and peacefully entered his consciousness.

If the Pigeon managed to return Mark and Chastity to his Mini-Cone in time, and its FAST-mode carried them safely beyond the Big Rip, his special passenger—the "lovely lady" Ned spoke of in his call—would be content to spend her life with him and with his bones if he should be the first to die. Because the special passenger, Chastity, was an isomorph, there was no doubt about it—*he* would be the first to go. But Mark could not have known that until she actually arrived because Ned's call did not include that identifying detail. With the countdown of the Mini-Cone dangerously close to zero, Mark still could not resist the chance to pick up the "lovely lady" who chose to join him for more than the ride! Mark knew he had never been in greater danger, but strangely, he was never more happy. He might *not* be alone for the remainder of his days—and nights.

Like everyone else—except for Ned, Denise and Chastity—Mark believed Denise would be the one to join him. That prospect not only made him happy, it made him feel selfish and guilty—but he returned to the Great Cone anyway.

So much for lofty values and not wanting to kill his lover with boredom.

Even after Chastity's arrival on the Homing Pigeon's entrance ramp Mark had no idea, aside from a single fleeting thought, why this was happening to him. How could he? He had no idea of the depth of empathic caring an isomorph was capable of. Had he thought of it, he might have remembered the selfless act that Gegeneis performed for his identical and that Venus was willing to if Astra had allowed it; but, Mark thought, *Chastity has no such relationship to me.* In particular, he strangely failed to grasp the fact that Chastity cared about him at all, much less that her love for him exceeded Denise's manyfold. But he did understand that it was *Chastity*, not Denise, who wanted to be with him, *no matter what.*

Would he live long enough to learn the depth of her feeling? Being the kind of guy he was, such questions never entered his head. Besides, right then a different question was holding sway: Would they even make it back to the Mini-Cone? If so, he would have all the time in the world to think about feelings.

To know this isomorph's true feelings could take years . . . and yet, in a prescient flash of awareness, as Chastity alighted so gracefully on the Great Cone's landing platform in all her naked beauty, and as she undulated up the ramp to enter his Orb, *he knew*. But the insight was only a flash, glimpsed like a dream, and even as he struggled to hang on to it, it faded from his mind as fast as it had come. Yet Mark was delighted. Only after she stood before him on the Orb's ramp did he realize why Ned had given him the information about isomorph survival and safety.

Ned's second urgent call—the one to Doug—was less pressing in terms of time, but more compelling for the number of lives involved. Some thirty minutes remained before the Great Cone's countdown would initiate its Transformation, whereas the Mini-Cone's was virtually at hand.

When the room-lift returned from the depths of the Great Cone, it pulled snugly into Laura's "living room" space. During its subsequent descent, Ned tried to keep up his radio conversation with Doug. They agreed there was no chance of doing anything to alter the countdown, but Ned emphasized that plenty of time remained to change the Great Cone's direction and destination coordinates. That's where their agreement ended. Every *observer* on the Great Cone was getting both sides of this exchange, but those on the room-lift with Ned only heard his side of the conversation.

Ned gave Doug some coordinate changes for immediate implementation; but Doug continued to argue: "Let me remind you, Ned, those are more than directional coordinates you're suggesting. They specify an end-point—a stopping place. Those are destination coordinates. That would cause the Cone to de-Transform in space, and open us up to the worst ravages of the Big Rip. We must get as far from that Rip as possible—in other words, as far as we can from this and every other universe. To maximize our chances for survival I've set the controls for immediate FAST-mode Transformation—just the way Doyan showed me. After the countdown, we're gone. Huh! I'd like to see the Redshift Ripper catch us after that!"

"The FAST-mode will work," Ned said, "but not because Doyan showed you anything. It will work at the end of countdown regardless of anything you do, and that's for the simple reason that the Dorts never turned it off. The FAST-mode priority hasn't changed."

"I don't believe it."

"*Hmm*. Listen Doug, we need to set those destination coordinates right away."

"*Hmm* yourself, Ned. We're set to go. The directional coordinates will have to stay the way they are, the way I set them; with *no* destination. Right now I'm in Stan's lab next door to the *countdown computer room*. Stan's here and *nodding agreement with me* about *not* changing the coordinates to any set location."

"Damn it, Doug! This is me talking. Set the goddamn coordinates back to where I told you! Just do it!" Ned was *shouting* his command into the transceiver handset—a poor tactic to use with Doug, even face-to-face.

With sudden condescension, in a voice oozing with bathos, Doug said, "You're becoming unhinged, Ned." He went on and on about how "poor Ned" was "unhinged." Then he added, "But hey! it's not just you, so relax. I saw how all of you became disoriented around that oversized globe Laura's holding. I'm sorry, but I will have to ignore your orders about those coordinates. It isn't rational. I'm sure you can see that—if you'll just think about it."

"It's not irrational, Doug. Let me explain. Its—"

"—Hey! Like I said, it's okay. Even Mark isn't rational right now—and he *wasn't* subjected to that big flashbulb in Laura's lap." Doug kept talking, nervously now. He did not enjoy going against Ned's directions—even his loud ones. Doug became more agitated the more he spoke. "Something must really be wrong up there on the surface. All wrong! As for Mark, his countdown will expire before he gets back to his Mini-Cone. I call that irrational. If he's too close when his Mini-Cone goes into Transformation it will turn him, his passenger and his Orb into a puffy little smudge in space. He should never have come back for that isomorph. If he hadn't come back for her he'd be safe on his Cone by now. Why did he take the chance? What's happening? . . . Never mind. Don't answer that—I'll tell *you*! *Unhinged Irrationality* is what's happening—total and complete."

"Listen Doug. You don't get the picture. What we—"

"—Sorry Ned. The countdown and the non-stop FAST coordinates I've programmed in are staying in—as is!"

Then, with a click, Doug switched off his transceiver. Ned tried to call him back, but all he could hear was the normal static of a deactivated connection, not so much as a friendly dial tone.

EIGHTY-FIVE

On their way down the shaft to the heart of the Cone, Ned's frustration exploded into fury. "I can't believe he hung up on me!" Then he snorted rounds of profanity and sputtered a cascade of creative oaths. He knew he was stumped and needed a strategy to correct the problem.

His profanity and oaths abated after Denise, still teary-eyed and snuffling, chided him for sounding, with all that snorting, like a "mad bull." Only then did he become more coherent and share the main points of his conversation with Doug. After hearing the details, they agreed that Ned's anger was appropriate, but that showing it wouldn't help. Instead, he and Laura and Keeta and Denise devised a modest, rather quick and dirty plan.

Far below in the Astrophysics lab where Doug was hanging out, he expected big trouble from Ned when he stepped off the room-lift and made his way there. Rather than throw his weight around when he arrived, and as part of the jury-rigged plot, Ned was obligated to *control himself*. He seldom lost control anyway, but this time it was not easy for him to rein in his anger, except to look at the plan in a different way—the way his fellow conspirators suggested: He could see his self-control strategy as socially acceptable virtuosity *and* as gratifyingly underhanded. Given the already tense circumstances, he knew he could not continue his *mad bull* routine with Doug and get away with it. Any uncharacteristic behavior from him, verbal or otherwise, would be interpreted as "irrational" and only serve to reinforce and confirm for Doug and everybody else that Ned had, indeed, become "unhinged." *Ah, the power of a negative campaign,* he thought, *so cheap in every way and easy to accomplish.* Instead of charging angrily into the lab to confront Doug straight on, the trying part was to keep himself calm and cheerful. Still, his was not the hardest part in the conspiracy. He was comforted to know the rest of the plan was in capable hands.

The "modest plan," as they called it, was to commandeer the primary navigation computer and key in the coordinates that Ned had, in vain, asked Doug to use.

The conspirators knew that nothing could convince Doug to put in the right coordinates and there was no time to reason with him. They knew he wouldn't listen even if there were. They also had to overcome Doug's popular credibility. Everybody on the Cone was on his side believing that, for their own protection, Doug was right and Ned just might be "unhinged" and "irrational" enough to put everybody in jeopardy—the poor deluded fellow.

Thus, the plan called for distracting Doug—for a while. Otherwise he would characteristically make those few steps down the corridor to hover and pace beside the countdown computer until the FAST-mode gave the Great Cone its standing jump into the void.

Ned smiled as he entered the Astrophysics lab where he was met at the door by Doug whose jaw was set for trouble, but Ned ignored that, made a social greeting, and began his act. The idea was to distract Doug by amicably assuming the quasi-didactic persona of a superior outlining a list of supposedly relevant thoughts on a blackboard. It was one of many blackboards there, but this one *happened* to be near the exit to the main passageways—the very same one Ned would *happen* to keep Doug from using—if he could.

Ned continued what he hoped would be a spellbinding mental tap-dance at the blackboard with flourishes of colored chalk and verbal legerdemain. But Doug, who was not at all sucked in by the dance, pointed to the wall screen. Everybody was looking at it. Ned looked up just in time to see Mark's Mini-Cone translate from a tangible, spatiotemporal object into unseen portals of Transformation. Ned thought, *First a population disappeared. Then a planet vanished. And now, just like that! a Cone of Transformation is gone—and we're next.*

Ned asked Doug, "Did Mark Tenderloin and Chastity make it back in time for their Reo-Sphere Transformation?"

"Amazingly, yes," Doug said, responding normally to Ned's normal question. "They made it back just before you came in. They had time to spare. I had no idea his Homing Pigeons could fly that fast. I guess Mark felt no need to tell us. Anyway, the auto-countdown for his Mini-Cone took a few seconds longer than he said it would."

A flash of pity crossed Ned's face before he reminded himself that the Great Cone's own countdown was also close to zero; so he rolled his eyes, returned to the blackboard and continued to expound his list of quasi-relevant topics. Part of Ned's task with Doug was to demonstrate he was still the same old Ned: rational and well-hinged; but that only worked for a few brief moments when he happened to ask that one (appropriate) question about the fate of Mark and Chastity—not when he returned to misdirection with his catalogue of needless topics. Few others would have noticed their irrelevance, but Doug knew right away. For Ned's more important purpose it did not matter: "Guarding" crazy Ned was keeping Doug occupied and away from the computers next door.

Doug was a good man who meant well and believed he was right. He also believed *correctly* that he was in charge so long as everybody on the Cone was behind him—and they were because Ned, after all, had just been subjected to an effectively disempowering, public, status-degradation ceremony wherein he received the most dehumanizing and humiliating diagnosis possible: "*Unhinged.*" This gave Doug the power to control, at least for the very short time needed, the Cone's navigational coordinates. After the auto-countdown, the FAST-mode of the Transformation would engage and his control would not matter. From his vantage point, the coordinates could no longer be altered, and no deadly end-point coordinates could be entered. Doug had taken steps to garrison and protect the central countdown navigation computer. It was an assignment that Officer Bracket and his men enthusiastically accepted—along with the duty of stopping Ned Keller from getting anywhere near it.

After the Mini-Cone's FAST departure, there was nothing new on the wall screens that anybody had not seen a million times before—Nimbus, the star cluster, the Milky Way. Most of the onlookers began drifting away from the screens in small groups to worry together about what would *really* happen at the end of the countdown. Half-hypnotized, some stayed on and kept watching the screens—hoping something new and reassuring or interesting would cross their consciousness; but most of the watchers merely maundered off with vaguely anxious expressions. In a few minutes, even the wall-screen transmissions ended.

For their part in the plan, Ned's co-conspirators arranged themselves cross legged on the floor in the middle of the Great Cone's most traveled and well-lit passageway. Unlike Ned, they believed they'd *not* been effectively painted over with Doug's bright-colored brushstrokes of *irrationality* and *unhingedness*. Even if they had been so painted in the eyes of some, their plan called for the initial conversion of only a few others to their cause. Then the task was to convert a few more—and then a lot more. Well, it was a modest plan in some ways; but, on further consideration, a monumental one given the short time they had to bring it off—literally within minutes. If they were successful, then *Doug* would no longer have the moral ("I'm right") and political ("everybody's behind me") high ground ("virtuous power"). All that high ground would become theirs and, in fact, the property of *every* citizen on the Great Cone. Power to the people! Only with near-universal recruitment could they prevail.

With time closing in on the conspirators, it helped to see the wall screens shut down and the remaining watchers drift toward the junction of the Cone's main corridors. That led most of its citizens toward the collaborators who planted themselves in the busiest interchange passageway on the Transformation.

The conspirators pretended to be enjoying the Crystal Library. They placed their heads on it and laughed with delight. They were not wearing the innocent-looking headbands—not just then. Laura had removed hers earlier. A small group of quizzical bystanders gathered around them. That group soon expanded to a crowd of thirty. Like everybody on the Great Cone, the crowd was tense and open for diversion. Almost any amusing diversion would do. Some were encouraged to put on one of the headbands for this "fun game." Standing in a row, they took each other's hands as instructed by Keeta, the most respected and trusted of all the isomorphs. Overall, she remained untouched by Doug's "diagnostic" brushstrokes.

As others kept arriving, Keeta continued to smile and hand out headbands. Then she instructed everybody in the line to place their head (and headband) on the hand of the person next-closest to Laura, who by then had again donned her own headband. Keeta raised her hand. When everybody was ready, she lowered it and Laura touched her forehead to the Crystal. A second after its flash, the conspirators had quite a number of new allies. In that flash, they had traveled throughout the Crystal Library for many years, and along the way they met Ned's reference persona and learned the *correct* end-point coordinates from him. Afterwards the newcomers, in turn, helped recruit others to the "fun game." Within minutes, and several long lines later, there were hundreds of co-conspirators who, as a side benefit for the original conspirators, knew that Ned and the other three were no more unhinged than they were. But as conspirators, were they also mutineers? They could not be called mutineers unless Doug had officially been in charge. He never was, except for the Cone's population being psychologically misguided by fear and misinterpretation; but they could no longer be fooled. Nearly everybody on the Cone had passed through their many-year initiation "in" the Crystal Library of Time. They emerged wiser for the experience, and believed they knew what to do next.

The rest was supposed to be easy.

Officer Bracket's most trusted fellow citizens—aside from his own security team—were allowed to become a posse to take over his guard-duty commitment in the room containing the special navigation console. He was unaware that those trusted citizens were Ned's new allies. Clint and his men were lured away by them to handle a *situation* that only they, as trained and professional security personnel, were qualified to deal with. The *situation* was something supposedly happening in the geode. They hurried to respond. One of the new initiates quietly remarked to another, "That'll keep Clint and his guys busy for a while!"

During their Library time, everybody memorized the crucial coordinates and security password. The first to reach the navigation console, whoever that might be, was instructed by Ned to input the password and the new coordinates.

Unfortunately, no one knew the bio-computer's *new* security password except Doug. He'd changed it minutes before Ned and the others arrived. The old password that Ned's avatar had given out in the Crystal Library was conscientiously attempted—over and over, but never worked. That fatal glitch in the plan caused widespread consternation among the initiates. Their confusion and distress escalated into panic after the computer's countdown loudspeaker actually started counting down. It came in a series of eerily hollow-sounding, reverberating announcements: *"Transformation in thirty seconds . . . twenty-nine . . ."*

Doug *smiled* briefly when the loudspeakers began, but his expression quickly contorted into one of shock and confusion when a mob came charging through the door near the blackboard on which Ned continued to busily connect dots with multi-colored pointers and carefully constructed wiggly lines.

On their sweep through Stan's lab, the door-chargers knocked Doug to the floor. Laura was among them and the one who "accidentally" threw the downing block. She was all apologies, of course, and helped Doug to his feet. In the midst of the chaos, Keeta "whispered" something to Ned.

By the time the loudspeakers announced *"twenty-six,"* Doug was on his feet being brushed off and apologized to by what sounded and felt like half the crew of the Great Cone. During all this "help," he was scanning for Ned, who was nowhere to be seen, so, fearing what Ned might be up to, he made a dash for the exit where again he was "accidentally" confronted by another block, this time in the form of a brick wall named Keeta. She said, "Sorry!"

Instead of falling, Doug grabbed Keeta and managed to keep his upright balance, but Keeta, while still apologizing, fell backwards against the door. Doug also said "Sorry," and asked Keeta to please get up and move away from the door. She said she was "trying," but thought aloud, "I think the fall may have hurt my back. Oooo." She didn't move her location, but did thrash around a bit. Doug tried to move her himself. *"Ooooo!"* she said.

"seventeen . . . sixteen . . . fifteen . . ."

Doug stepped back and smiled again.

By *"twenty-three,"* Ned had already been out the door and by *"twenty"* he was standing with his back to the countdown navigation computer, holding its switched-off microphone to his left side. In the small, over-crowded room, he raised his right hand for silence. By *"fourteen"* the room had settled down and was silent.

Lifting the computer's microphone to his mouth . . .

"... *thirteen* ..."

... he switched it on, quickly saying: "This is Ned Keller issuing emergency voice-override number forty-two."

"... *eleven* ..."

Ned turned to the computer and rapidly keyed in the "new" coordinates—the ones Doug refused to use.

"... *seven* ..."

"Where the hell is Laura?" Ned shouted as he turned, still standing, to the gaping crowd in the room behind him.

"Here I am," she said, already running as she came through the door.

"... *four* ..."

She seemed confused, but ran to the countdown computer and grabbed the microphone from Ned as she had done in less hurried practice sessions long before the Transformation from Earth had begun. "This is Laura Shane," she said into the microphone, "confirming Ned Keller's previous words and signals."

"... *two*..."

Laura was blindly following her training. Plan or no plan, she was emotionally and physically shaken after slamming her elfin friend, Doug, to the floor. Under that and all the other stresses, she was confused and even forgot the implications of what she was doing. But, robotlike, the routine was ingrained. By the time the loudspeaker had counted back to *"one,"* she'd already reached around Ned to press her favorite key—*Enter*.

EIGHTY-SIX

The Cone shook violently, knocking its inhabitants to the ground, and then it stopped. The wall screens unexpectedly reactivated throughout the Great Cone. All eyes turned to them to see the anticipated static snow of nothingness. Most of the crew believed they were in an endless FAST-mode Transformation. The shaken and frightened crew that still had enough awareness to look, saw no static snow. The screens showed only the blackness of ordinary space. The Great Cone had de-Transformed in empty space—*ahead* of the Big Rip.

Near the apex of the Great Cone, a rotating observatory brought a bright crescent into view. From their distance, the crescent was a full degree from tip to tip. As the magnification was increased, its image blurred briefly before it blossomed into full-screen clarity. Laura cupped her hand over her mouth. "It's Earth!" she said. "But it can't be."

Ned's eyes were sparkling. "Of course it's Earth. Why can't it be?" he asked.

"The code came from you, Ned—the shortcut code for Earth's spacetime coordinates," she said. "You got those coordinates from somewhere in the Crystal Library. You never mentioned that the code you so generously gave out to all of us would utilize the Cone's FAST-mode. I know my way around in this Crystal World by now," she said, patting and hefting it affectionately, "so tell me, from were in this thing *did* you get that code?"

"From—"

"—Never mind!" she cut him off. "You couldn't have. It *couldn't* have included FAST-mode. That was an engineering feat that only Mark and the Dorts knew how to activate. I guess Doug thought he also knew how. But you don't seem to be surprised. How was it triggered this time?"

"Well, to get us back to Earth in a—"

"—We all knew the code you gave us would eventually take us back to Earth—you told us that—and if by some miracle the extreme redshift—the Rip—was aborted, we thought it would take *at least a decade* for us to get here—back to our Earth-space vicinity. That would have given us time to sort it all out. I thought we had that much slack. So far, Ned, I've spent more time than anyone else in this Crystal, but in all that time—in all those years—*nobody told me* about this possibility. So, what happened? *Inform me!*"

"Of course! How callous of me. I should have explained. I never thought so many questions would come up. I thought everybody would be happy. Okay then, here's your answer: Almost everybody, including you, had a turn or two in the Crystal Lib—"

"—But first," Laura interrupted again, "before you start explaining, would you *please* get us the hell out of here! Until now I thought we might have ten *safe* years to work on FAST-mode—if we survived and needed it—with help from all the remaining Dorts in the geode. I thought you were just conning Doug about the FAST-mode never being turned off; but now, if we stay here, there's no safe time left. We need to be in one of the transformation modes."

Ned's eyes widened and shone with lustrous, enlarging pupils—as if he had slipped back into that other world. He wasn't paying attention and was too sure of himself to either listen to Laura's statements or to her feelings. Had he done so, her question had a simple answer, but in his now continuing reverie, he ignored it all and launched a juggernaut of rapid speech—to "inform" her in accord with what he thought were her earlier questions:

"Everybody here," he began again, loud enough for those in the small, crowded room to hear, "including you, Laura, had a turn or two in the Crystal Library of Time. In there, everybody was tracking down their different interests, or just enjoying additional years of life. No two of us took the same path. No two of us talked with and became acquainted in the same way with the same people, or with other beings. We saw those who were already there. Each of them had a Crystal like the one you are now clinging to for dear life. We're all addicted. Denizens of *your* Library, a 'first-level Crystal'—let's call it that. Those already there were holding their own, let's call them 'second-level' Crystals, and 'within' each of those were more—third-level, fourth-level, and so on, Crystal levels, with other individuals holding them. While I was there, I learned that no two Crystal Worlds of Time have identical content or experiences to be had—just as no two lives are exactly alike. They're similar, I suppose, but always different. Even twins can live in the same external world, but for both that world is differently experienced, and so, for them, the same world is a different world. If there were only one person in a world, there would be two worlds: the *phenomenal world*, and that person's *internal world*—the one that, for all of us, seems to be *out there*. But the world that seems to be out there isn't really there at all. *Something* is out there, and we interact with it, but it is not what we perceive. The world of stuff we think we perceive out there is really *in here*. Our perceptions and everything else we think, feel and remember, are internal. That's the only reality we can access directly. It is *our* reality—or maybe just mine—and the only certainty we can, in this life, come close to knowing."

Ned did not slow down, but his glazed-over look was mellowing the more philosophical he became. He continued: "The real miracle is that nothing false exists in any of the Crystals. All their contents, like our own phenomenal, external world, are more real and accurate than the most precise photographic or written history. That's because it is real—not second hand and not just a copy of reality. The only deviations from that accuracy that I came across were the viewpoints and interpretations about it that were expressed by those who appeared along the way—those who were already there and living their new lives, their parallel lives if you will, in the different Libraries of Time. The world views of those inhabitants were *different* from Crystal World to Crystal World, and even from place to place within the same Crystal. At the level of culture, I saw differences and practices that seemed endless in variety.

"And there was another difference from Crystal to Crystal, and that was *time itself*. Only in *hindsight* does time in the Crystals turn out to be different from our ordinary experience of it, but it never seemed any different 'at the time' while 'in' one of the Crystals. At no point did the *direction* of time, the arrow of time in those micro-macroworlds, get altered in any way—only the rates of time as judged in retrospect.

"The time constants were different from one 'Crystal-level' to another, and all of them different from the time constant in *our* universe. No matter how active we, the outsiders, were while in one of the other Worlds of Time, it gave us no power to juggle or manipulate any of the internal time constants and no power to move back and forth within the time constants. We could no more do that than change the chronological arrow of time through a history book by reading it slowly or by speed reading, or by reading its chapters in random or reverse order. If we could remember our 'experiences' from reading the book, we could remember the best parts, or the worst parts, in any order that amused us or that we thought necessary—like when taking a test in school. If you asked if I, or anyone else visiting your Crystal of Time, *remembered* the experiences there, I'd say, 'no more than usual *at any given moment.*' Even in ordinary life it is impossible to remember everything at once. We know that whole months and years can go by before some event or rare association—like a special smell or a harsh word or a kind one—stimulates our recall of an earlier experience. Physically, we're no older now than before spending all those 'years' in the Crystal Worlds of Time. And yet, in *mere seconds*, a good-sized hunk of our total life's experiences are coming from there.

"Whatever subjective reality we accidentally or deliberately remember from those experiences, they always go through our viewpoint and observation filters. From ants to superbeings to whole cultures, we are all immersed and baptized in a sea of viewpoints and illusions that allow us to live and function with what we have, inside and out, with what we are and where we are. To win and survive, we must all dovetail neatly with *that something* believed to be objective reality; otherwise survival will come to an end. The evolution of all things can go in a million directions, but never outside that something that *is*, no matter how that *is* is perceived. The ant has survived and evolved into many different types, not because of any comprehensive view of the world, but because of where it is in the surroundings of its world, an anthill, say, and what it is, an ant, with its wired-in 'viewpoints.' None of this happens in a dream world—only in the *is* world, no matter what the perspective on that world may be—yours or mine, an ant's, or that of the Assemblage.

"Speaking of the Assemblage, there were strong hints from many different quarters within the Time Crystals, even before I ran into the Assemblage myself, that it was working on *time travel*, but doing so with great care to avoid the obvious problems: Those associated with alteration of the past, and therefore the so-called future *and* what's happening *now*. The last I heard, well after my encounter with it, time travel was still an insurmountable puzzle for the Assemblage. But, hmmm, they're still working on it. If they ever solve the problem of going *backward* in time, the Assemblage knows I volunteered to be the first to go. It would be incredibly fascinating if it worked! Suicide if it didn't. I'd take great pains to avoid screwing up the future—whatever the protocol for that might be. Right now I can't remember going back in time, so if *that* ever happens, it'll have to be later than now. Or maybe not. If I did accidentally change the past and forgot about it, in that past's future who knows what *this* moment would be."

Laura zoned out of Ned's babbling. She looked frantic, but with Ned on a crazy roll (could Doug and Clint be right?) she couldn't get a word in anyway. To slow him down, she tried in vain to say something he could relate to: "Going back in time and not screwing up the future would be very brave and considerate of you, but—"

"—Yes, yes, yes! But getting back to your questions," Ned said, continuing to rumble forward like a loaded freight train on a sharp descent, "Once I was in your Crystal Library and found out what it was all about, I sat down with the main guides, Venus and Gegeneis. They were sitting on their own Crystals. Right beside them were Astra and Zack, still making love atop their own dead ashes. I asked if I could visit with them. Venus asked if I meant them, or Astra and Zack. I said Astra and Zack."

Laura shook her head vigorously and said, "Impossible. They're both long dead."

"No more dead than anyone else in one of those Crystal Libraries."

"You interrupted their lovemaking—to 'visit' with them? Are you some kind of a letch?"

"Hey! Even in there, that particular cryptic bit of lovemaking was only symbolic—a transparent hologram. We went beyond that. Venus held out her hand to me and we went together into *her* Crystal. Astra and Zack are dead, but their full references—their avatars—were transferred to Venus's Crystal Library of Time well before their deaths. (While I was still in *your* Crystal, Laura, I noticed that most of us accepted a trip into someone else's—'second-level'—Crystal.) I happened to enter Venus's. I didn't notice anyone else doing that—except for Doyan, and I may have caught a glimpse of Chastity and a few other isomorphs at that level, but only in passing. Otherwise, I was the only one—the only human from here."

"And you were with an isomorph, Venus?" Laura said.

"Yes," Ned replied.

"I thought that's what you said. And no other humans from here went with you?"

"Just me and Venus. I must have asked her the right question before she let me in—into that exact time and location, in that particular Crystal's chronology. Once we entered the Crystal, we found ourselves on a high hill. A warm wind was blowing. It was a bright day and things were growing everywhere, kind of like plants; but nothing like Origin's plantoids, except that in both places, they tended to glow. The plantlike things in Venus's Crystal were radiant, day and night. They leaned and moved aside as we walked, leading the way by closing off some directions and opening others.

"We walked for several weeks. The weather along the way was mostly nice, but there was one dark and stormy night we did have to endure. I never got tired, even with all that walking. It was exhilarating. My body was still out here, but I was told by someone in there who should know, that my body's brain and nervous system, my conscious and unconscious systems, were being bombarded with the stuff of life through the stimulated *neural growth* of my associative connections. *That's* what I call exhilarating! Those connections will later become available for retrieval from memory—retrieval of new knowledge, competencies, wisdom, attitudes, memories of a host of long and meaningful friendships, daring quests galore, endless conversations, and uncountable romantic adventures. Yeah, it must have been like that for everybody. I don't blame you for asking who came with me. Nobody from here. As a favor, Laura, I won't ask you the same question. It's strange, but year after year in there I never noticed or even thought it unusual that I slept so little, but so well. I didn't notice that until coming out of your Crystal—that most special of all Crystals—the death gift to Astra and Zack from the Assemblage.

"Anyway, Venus and I kept walking until we approached a remarkable site. I will never forget the impact on me of its dramatic, complex structure, of its integrated, architectonic beauty. It was beyond visionary. It was a composition in forms that I could see *and* hear. It was synesthetic, but Venus had the same experience. Both forms, the sight and the sounds, were exquisite. The edifice itself was composed of those same radiant, moving, plantlike things I mentioned before. As Venus and I drew near, it became all the more luminous and breathtaking. Its living structural components continued to sense our presence and opened a way for us to enter.

"Inside, the structure was brighter and more majestic than it appeared on our approach. Still farther inside—and best of all—we encountered the awesome, open-armed and open-minded hospitality of what, in any other place or time, would have been identified as a warmly welcoming Queen and King—'Queen' Astra Hughs, I suppose, and her 'King' Zackery Parker. They called the place their home, but emphatically disallowed any royal designations, and—"

Laura interrupted sharply: "Fine, but this isn't getting us out of here, Ned!" She'd become terrified in alternating waves.

"You're absolutely right, Laura!" Ned said, pretending he had some idea what he was assenting to. "I'll tell you about the rest of my visit later, and you must tell me about yours; but here's the point for now: Doyan himself had been invited by the mistress and master of that 'royal' residence. He arrived several days after Venus and me. It helped that we were able to meet with him in that environment of true companionship. Doyan became very talkative for once. He even seemed glad to see me. No, not me. It just felt that way. It must have been the company of those two monarchs of hospitality. When Doyan arrived, he and they certainly seemed glad to see each other. But that greeting paled next to the joy and delight that burst forth at the reunion of Venus and Astra days earlier! Astra was *beautiful*! Their hugs and kisses were unreserved."

Laura tried to listen, but was becoming more upset with each passing minute. "What about Doyan?" she asked in a loud, husky voice. "You say he was talkative, but did he say anything that will help us *here and now*? Think about it, Ned." She slugged him hard in the shoulder. "Here and now *dammit*!"

Ned frowned and rubbed his shoulder. "Of course!" He replied, "Doyan said many helpful things. That's my whole point. For one thing, he explained how I could get in touch with the *essence of Gaia*. Gaia and Origin have been friends and in constant touch almost from their 'birth.' In the next few hours, when we set foot on planet Earth again, I know exactly where to find her. It'll be—"

Laura became frantic, almost screaming, "We have to get out of here, and not to Earth. Have you completely forgotten the Big Rip?"

"Oh oh!" Ned said, shaking his head hard. "You're right. I totally forgot."

"Then do something on that damn computer keyboard—right now, before it's too late!"

Ned flexed his fingers like a maestro before a giant organ and did what he was asked.

Well, he *almost* did what he was asked. He meant to, for all that was worth.

Laura's complexion flushed, her lips puckered and pursed, she sucked in her cheeks, squinted and frowned—all at the same time. She slowly moved her furrowed aspect closer to Ned's fingers and hands. She scrutinized them as she often did her own hands and nails. She wanted to be sure—of *what* she didn't know; but she wanted him to key in *something*. Whatever it was, she knew it would have to be right—but she had to see it. Ned held his hands above the computer keyboard, palms and fingers hanging loosely downward, phantomlike. He didn't know *what* either. He tentatively wiggled his fingers in the air when, in horror, he saw it out the corner of his eye: The most ungodly, crinkly prune face ever seen—at least since the last board meeting. It was approaching his exposed and uninsured hands. He instinctively jerked them away.

"Did I mention," he asked nervously by way of ironing out any misunderstanding, "that the Dorts never did shut down this Cone's FAST-mode? *Stop*—sure. Or *trudge slowly* at sublight speeds around a star's mass or around a planet—sure. But go into an *ordinary* Transformation while still geared for FAST-mode—never! It *can* be shut down, I suppose, but why bother?"

"That's just one thing Doyan told me and Venus during our visit with Astra and Zack. And hey! While I was in Venus's Crystal, Zack invited me into his. From there I got into a dozen others—into a dozen deeper levels—*each with a more compressed time constant than the one before.*"

Hearing that, Laura's wrinkled expression smoothed and her skin turned ashen. She exclaimed, "*More compressed time at a dozen deeper levels*! I hope you're exaggerating. You shouldn't have tried it, Ned. We were warned not to. How many years upon compressed years were you in there?"

He said nothing. Laura thought he suddenly looked "crappy" and said so. She wondered what was wrong.

He still said nothing, but looked worse.

"*For God's sake, Ned! how many years?*"

He shook his head sharply. His dilated pupils contracted to dots before they normalized. It was as though he just came out of a many-year coma—or from being *unhinged*.

"*For God's sake*! is right," he said, placing the heels of his hands stiff-armed on his knees. More steady now, and almost focused, he said, "We're in real time now—aren't we?"

"Yes Ned," Laura said gently, still sensing something unusual in him.

"Really?" he said. "It's hard to change gears—these mental-time gears."

"And I thought *I'd* spent too much time in the Crystal!"

"We're on Earth time then—right? Milky Way time? Speed of light constant time?"

"Yes—not that that's a constant."

"My God!" Ned said, his eyes moving rapidly left and right as he saw, heard and remembered—not everything, but many things.

"How many years, Ned?"

Ned began to tremble.

"How many?" Laura persisted.

"I couldn't keep track," he said, shaking. "Thousands. Hundreds of them. Maybe a million. I've left so many behind. . . . People . . . long, rich relationships, complex ones. . . . I lived . . . so many . . ."

"So many what?"

". . . Lives."

"Years and years—like many lifetimes," Laura said, thinking she understood.

Before he spoke again, Ned did not move his head, but turned his now red and swollen eyes far to one side to see Laura's face. "No," he said, "Not like many lifetimes. . . . Many *lives*."

EIGHTY-SEVEN

The crowd in the countdown computer room was growing tense. Laura's own mounting fear overwhelmed her concern about Ned's sense of loss and separation from the lifetimes he supposedly spent in the skins of others. *He must have been delusional—or he still is*, Laura thought. His "years" in channel with the Crystal Libraries of Time amounted to dangerous overindulgence. She wanted to softly ease his pain, but she also wanted to live. She compromised: Looking deep into his eyes—just before he clenched them shut—she grabbed his shoulders, shook him violently and yelled repeatedly, "Snap out of it!"

Ned closed his eyes even tighter, but that couldn't stop Laura's shaking and yelling at him. If she hadn't had him by the shoulders he would have plugged his ears. When things settled a bit, he cautiously opened one eye to inspect his nemesis, only to see that she was about to yell and give him another good shake. "Never mind!" he said, "I'll be okay."

"Then get out of that chair. I sent for Doug. He can get us out of here."

"First, tell me something. When you left Origin on Mark's Pigeon, up here on the Cone, we were watching you and Venus on the screens. The camera view was from inside Mark's Orb, looking out the hatch. Venus was outside hollering to you when the hatch closed. That ended our view of her. We couldn't hear what she was saying. What *was* the last thing she said to you? I wouldn't ask but she looked excited, like the message was important."

"That's irrelevant," Laura snapped. "Doug is on his way."

"Indulge me."

"I have. Now get out of the chair!"

"Doug won't be able to do anything unless I give the computer a verbal okay for that."

Laura blanched. "Oh. . . . Yeah. I forgot."

"Indulge me. Then we can talk about who gets the controls."

Laura gritted her teeth, but tried to comply. "I was in the Orb's open hatch to keep Mark from closing it. I wanted to hear what Venus was saying. It was noisy out there. Then Mark dragged me inside. Venus was shouting something. I heard Stan's name and something about Gegeneis forgetting to say something about the Big Rip."

"What did she say about Stan?"

"She said he needed to do something. Didn't say what. Then the hatch slammed down. That's all I remember."

Doug burst through the door, red as an angry lobster, protruding eyes, the works. He gave Ned's chair an ill-considered shove, sending him rolling right off the platform. Doug mumbled "Sorry" under his breath and began keying in a random direction for the Transformation, intentionally leaving out an ending address—and then hit Laura's favorite key. But nothing happened—except for a blocking message on the screen. Doug cursed. He never cursed. Not real curses. But this time he did.

Meanwhile, Ned pulled himself together enough to cautiously peek, Kilroy-style, over the edge of the platform he'd fallen from. Doug turned and jabbed a stubby finger toward Ned, accusing him of being "unhinged" and a "terrorist" and demanded the computer be returned to his control.

Ned carefully (and painfully) lifted his head higher and told Doug, "First I have to have a private talk with Laura." Then he hurried out of the room, beckoning authoritatively to her as he left. Because of that lordly gesture she almost didn't follow, but to keep an eye on him she did.

"Fine," Doug said, doing his own gesturing toward them and the computer, "I'll find a way around your damn voice override. I won't need either of you for that." Then, still standing, he hunched over the keyboard and began tapping away—without noticing the slow rise of nervous chatter from the crowd behind him.

Ned led Laura back to the Astrophysics lab where they found Stan holding forth in the midst of another small crowd. He was lamenting Ned Keller's irresponsibility and saying that that was the cause of their present urgent situation and continuing danger. While thus assigning the blame for their dire circumstance, he was surprised when Ned walked up and quickly spoke to him in a hushed voice. Frowning, Stan excused himself from his listeners and led Ned and Laura to his office. Stan was upset and wanted to speak first, but Ned headed him off with a quick explanation. Stan nodded his agreement to listen.

Ned asked Laura to repeat what she heard from Venus before the Orb's hatch closed; but Laura's fear had not abated in the least, nor had her discomfort about responding to time-consuming questions that she considered irrelevant. Annoyed, she asked Ned, "Why didn't you just *ask* Venus what she said when you were in my Crystal Library. You sure as hell were in there long enough—with her!"

"Now you call it 'my' Crystal Library. I thought you were its custodian, not its owner. And what's this tone of jealousy toward Venus?"

"Skip that. It's all irrelevant. Why didn't you ask her?"

"Sorry. I never thought to ask. Anyway, please, we're wasting time. Tell Stan what Venus said."

Laura gave Ned a harsh glance, but repeated the fragmentary message.

Stan made a gesture of helplessness. "What did Venus and Gegeneis expect *me* to do?"

Ned and the two scientists brain-stormed the possibilities for several minutes before Stan's eyes brightened with a spark of understanding and interest. He'd come to what he called a "preliminary" conclusion and said, "We only have two pieces of information from Venus's last words outside the Orb. The first is that Gegeneis remembered—almost as an afterthought—something about the Big Rip; and second, that I'm supposed to do something. We've considered several possibilities. Only one seems likely to me. I need to check that possibility, so I'll have to leave you now—or tag along if you want. I have to do this right away." Stan excused himself and walked briskly from his office leaving Laura sputtering questions into the air behind him. Ned said nothing.

Within the commodious accommodations of Stan's lab, Ned and Laura hurried to accompany him—tagging along, as suggested. Stan led them from office to chamber to alcove to cubicle where he quickly spoke to one assistant and student after another. In a few minutes they were all in motion. He did not need to supervise their every move; they'd all gone through the same exercise many times before: Checking the Doppler effect of everything out there, near and far.

Within minutes the answers poured in. Stan handed the printouts to Laura who examined them briefly. The data was convincing. Stan proudly announced the findings to Ned. "The conclusion," he said, "is clear-cut. We have *mixed results*."

"What the hell is a clear-cut mixed result?" Ned asked in a tone of frustration verging on anger. "Just because you have a silly 'result' doesn't call for that . . . that silly grin on your face."

Then he looked at Laura. She and Stan were beaming at each other. Their elation and mutual understanding was apparent.

Ned smirked. "Okay," he said, "would you two geniuses let me in on your funny little secret?"

Laura replied, "It's a long story, Ned, but the short, simple version is this: The last time we checked, the redshift was in full swing and accelerating. It was an unambiguous result. Nothing mixed about it. But now the results are mixed. The redshift is no longer straightforward. Its deceleration has begun and a gradual reversal is under way. The redshift has lost some of its momentum and *no longer controls the fate of this universe* as we feared. That gives us an interval of safety. A very long one. In a few billion years our universe will turn around and a blueshift will take over. For that very long time being, our universe will no longer be in danger—not of that particular catastrophe anyway. Even after the blueshift is in full swing, there'll still be billions of years to go . . . before a Big Crunch would threaten. After that U-turn change, it will continue long after our sun becomes a red giant and Earth is just a cinder; but right now we're on our way! The pendulum of time will start to swing back. There will be no Big Rip in mankind's immediate future, and, this time around, no Big Crunch—certainly not while we're still alive—and not for eons after that."

"I thought so!" Ned said, joining in the smiles.

"*You* thought so? How come?" Laura asked.

"I heard about it when me and Venus were poking around in your Library's time stacks. Doyan told us all about it. That's when we were all visiting Zack and Astra.

"—If you can believe Doyan!" Stan said.

"As you know, Stan, I believe that Doyan is not always truthful—"

"—That's for sure," Stan said.

"—so I had to make sure it was true."

Then Ned turned to Laura and said, "When you told us what Venus said outside Mark's Orb, I thought that's what she was getting at, especially with her advice to Stan, of all people, to do something—alongside her mentioning, in the same breath, the Big Rip. And don't forget this: that suggestion was just an afterthought from Venus and Gegeneis. The *afterthought* part convinced me that Doyan was telling the truth. For Venus and Gegeneis it was an afterthought because they knew the Big Rip was no longer a threat. They had just come from our 'twin' universe where the sciences are as good as ours. They knew that their Big Crunch was abating. For them, any redshift or blueshift problems had *long* ago—as time goes by in that universe—stopped being something to worry about. They wanted Stan, as head of the Astrophysics lab, to check it out so we too could know the threat was gone—and to keep us from sending our two Transformation Cones into endless, random directions. Hmm. . . . Poor Mark. He'll be out there forever."

"With Chastity," Laura testily reminded him.

Ned grimaced, but decided to ignore yet another of Laura's jealous intonations toward yet another female isomorph, and said instead, "Venus and Gegeneis knew what Doyan knew—about the end of the redshift and blueshift crises. . . . They must have known that for many of their years. Damn them! They should have told us sooner."

"Don't blame them," Laura said sharply. "Why didn't *you* tell us about it before now?"

"A couple reasons," Ned snapped back. "*First* reason: I had no idea I was the only one who received that message about the redshift correction. If I told you what Doyan told me, would you have believed it without proof?"

"I don't know," Laura said. "Maybe."

"And you, Stan?"

"No."

"Doyan gets around, but obviously he didn't get to either of you—or anyone else. He's been busy. In our twin universe he oversees the 'terraforming' by a million worker Dorts; but I still assumed that everybody here already heard that the Big Rip was cancelled.

"*Second* reason: When it finally dawned on me that I was alone in my optimistic view for our universe—from what Doyan said—I knew we had to get the *proof* in hand that we're safe. Thanks to you and your team, Stan, we have that proof. For me, the Doppler-effect question had to be answered. Nobody will now have to take *my* word for it. After all, I'm unhinged, right?

"But now I have another question," Ned continued. "I thought from what Doyan told me, that the Big Rip would be postponed for a little while, but how do you know it will be put off for as long as you say—for *billions* of years? He never said anything about billions of years for Pete's sake!"

Laura began, "Mark's advanced Reo-Sphere and Reversal formulations—"

"—*Further* advanced formulations thanks to you, Laura," Stan interrupted.

"Thanks, but the overall theory . . . Oh my God! I just remembered! I was in one of the secondary Crystal Libraries. The Dorts and isomorphs often remember things in a last minute flash. Now I'm doing it. I tuned out an entire Crystal experience. I learned so much there—from and about the *Assemblage*. The theory is *much* more advanced now than when Mark and I last saw the one we passed along. The most recent improvements are profound. They weren't ours. We all took part in the baby-step improvements *before* the Assemblage took off that day and vanished over Origin. Increasingly transcendent formulations led to achievement of the Theory's present form. It came about only after the Assemblage made a series of courageous moves into a succession of universes."

"—Through other universes—with a growing accumulation of not-quite-final theories?"

"That's right, Ned."

"I went through many levels and bypaths within your Crystal Library's time-stacks myself, Laura, but can only recall once coming across the Assemblage; but I ran into Doyan several times. He told me a lot of things I never knew before. For instance, that the FAST-mode's smearing of our fundamental particles and molecules across multiple Reo-spheres was subtly different from what happens in ordinary Transformation-mode and—and this is the interesting part—if that mode were given *no set destination* coordinates, and therefore continued forever, any isomorph on board would be safe for the rest of its natural existence."

"Ned, in 'my' first-level Crystal you entered other Crystals within it. There, like me, you must have followed different choice-paths. From there, we took entirely different pathways. In the directions you went, you came across a talkative *Doyan*. I never did. But in one of the secondary Crystals I entered, I kept running into the Assemblage. Like Doyan, the Assemblage was also informative. In there, there must be multiple Assemblages."

"How was the Assemblage informative for you?"

"As you'll recall, those original formulations of ours and the Others' kept being improved, resummarized and reunified—again and again. Cy and Doyan attended to those first baby-steps between our universe and its twin; but later versions were 'escorted' higher, across braneworlds, nine universes out, not by Cy or Doyan; but, as you know, by the *real* genius from *our Galaxy*: the Assemblage. It shepherded the theory every step to its final perfection by insisting on its incorporation and integration into the laws of each new universe along the way."

Ned said, "I remember Doyan and Cy doing all that flashing back and forth between universes—but I wasn't sure about the Assemblage's role after that day on Origin when it took off like a rocket and never returned. I know a little more now."

"Yes, now you do. At every outward step into other universes and their unique dimensions, the Assemblage met with increasingly powerful beings—beings acting within their own interactive dimensions. Origin—and its essence, Cy—was also a powerful being, if only an artificial one made real; but further up the chain of universes within our multiverse, were beings whose powers far exceed Origin's. The Assemblage explained that to me. There are beings out there that cooperatively *combine* their exceptional forces to create a *virtual single unit* with a greater diversity of intellect, creativity, and energetic might than any one of them alone. It was one such grateful united being that, as a reward for what the Assemblage was doing, gifted it the secret of Crystal

Libraries and, as I recall, something about time travel. Those combined beings amount to more than the sum of its individuals."

"I think that's called *culture*," Ned stated with a smarty grin.

Laura frowned, then continued: "The Assemblage itself is made much the same as that description implies. It *is* an assemblage. I believe it wanted me to notice the similarity—that it too is a combined entity, a united being, yet a personage in its own right."

"Okay then. The Assemblage followed that sequence of linked universes and combined entities. Where did that series end?"

"The Assemblage ultimately encountered one such collective being with exceptionally robust power—possibly one of the foremost powers in our local multiverse. Its power was, for the first time, sufficient to actually *implement* the final theory."

"Okay. Let's assume a power of some kind did that; but how?" Ned asked.

"Yes, Ned. That was the trick. It was more than the combined being's intellectual appreciation of the consolidated theory of the multiverse. It had to figure out *how*, in a practical way, to *use* the theory. It had to pinpoint where to apply its forces based on knowledge of the formula's implications in order to bring about the profound change that is happening right now across the entire *multiverse*. It had to *reverse* the forces leading to its annihilation. I can only guess at elements in the theory leading to those changes. It has to do with *leverage*—catalystlike leverage."

Laura said all this while checking her nails with more than her usual punctilious scrutiny.

Stan asked, "Laura, Do you *have* that final formula?"

"Of course," Laura replied, gleefully looking up from her nails. "The Assemblage gave it to me. The first chance I get, I'll put it to paper and computer. It's just sitting here in my head right now. I work on it when I have time. To analyze its main implications in any depth I'll need bigger blocks of time. The big theoretical jumps, as I said before, were achieved 'out there' *after* Doyan and Cy were last seen on Origin. They did the best they could while they were still going back and forth. I don't know why they quit; but, bright as they were, the Assemblage moved the theory ball forward more than they or any of us could ever have done. Over our years in the Crystal Libraries, the Assemblage and I developed a strong scientific and intellectual relationship. More than that, really. It became one of respect and trust—a kind of partnership. I don't know how to describe it because it tapped into something alien in me and dazzling within us both."

"I'll have to ask you more about that sometime," Ned said, "but for the matter at hand, you're still giving me and Stan the short and simple layman's explanation, right?"

"Right."

"Then keep going," Ned said, looking oddly smart and confused at the same time. "I still don't understand. Not *completely*. That last power entity you described, that *Final Power*—let's call it that—must have been almost infinite. Omnipotent."

"Far from it!" Laura replied, laughing. "From that last formulation of Mark's—okay, *our* last formulation—the theory kept advancing and improving by being incorporated and integrated into it—that is, the diverse physics of each new-found universe. From the last formulation that emerged in that way, and what I learned from the Assemblage, we know that 'Final Power' had to *use* it to locate the *crucial points of leverage* between the universes—*not*, of course, to abruptly or radically destabilize the destructive momentum going on between them, but to bring about a precise and subtle rebalancing among them."

Stan said, "*Rebalancing* doesn't sound like it came from a *reversal* theory."

"Reversal is only a small part of the theory."

"Even so—"

"—Okay, look at it this way," Laura said with irritation. "Put two kids of equal weight on a teeter-totter. All the universes in our multiverse operate in pairs. As the kids use the teeter-totter for play, they're constantly reversing. That's what teeter-totters are for; but—excuse the over-simplification—they're also more or less in balance."

"Hmm. Okay. You're excused. Go on," Stan said.

"The last unabridged set of laws is a mathematical-physics portrait of the multiverse: a palette of cosmic workings. Without that pallet, your 'Final Power,' Ned, would have been a whimpering, helpless victim—and dead along with the rest of us. It had the tools of power, but *knowing* the theory made the difference. Here is the simple-minded fact: It could not *use* those laws—even those of such might and breadth—to save itself *unless it knew them*. The theory was the key. Only then was it able to save itself. Even that ultimate Final Power—if you'll forgive the comparison—is but a finite speck within the dimensions of nature herself. Your Final Power is no apotheosis, Ned. It's just another being—not a god."

Stan enjoyed listening to Laura on matters that interested him so intensely. He entered the commentary with his own comparison: "Recall from history," he said, "how, nearly a thousand years ago, mankind *diverted* an asteroid—half the size of Mars—from its target, Earth. To move it from that path, mankind had to figure out everything about it—many years ahead of the projected impact date. We ultimately conceived of the Gravity Tug a century before the asteroid would have hit; but we perfected it only a decade before its launch—and *just in time*. That's how close we were to destruction. *Without precise knowledge* of that threat, and its magnitude, we could not have motivated and organized the world's intellectual and material resources to prevent Earth's obliteration. The 'Final Power'—the being you described and Ned just named—was also, I believe, motivated by that same survival instinct as were all those Other beings of intelligence who helped to unify the laws unto that final, universal theory."

Laura picked up on Stan's theme: "That instinct does appear to be universal, but neither it nor the 'beingness' of any living creature—except for gross energetic and physical characteristics—will be found in our laws of physics—'final' or otherwise. The characteristics that comprise our 'being,' are so *feeble*, they lie outside the physical laws of any universe; and yet, not unlike the feebleness of gravity, they can be so powerful as to alter the very course, not just of asteroids, but, as we now see, the entirety of the multiverse.

"Here's my vision of how things happened out there: When the Assemblage brought the bad news to the Final Power, assuming it didn't already know the end was coming, its survival instinct woke, causing it some serious survival fears. But when the Assemblage showed it a way out by revealing the emergent laws—laws that were already approaching unification—then the Final Power could redirect its energy from fear into purposeful scientific model building and formula creation—even theory completion. In other words, in order to survive, it took the *path of least resistance*. I think that's how it could have happened."

Stan said, "I think I understand this now. I suspect that most of your lesser 'beings,' like us and the Others, were not aware of the threat and if they were they had no idea how to solve it, so didn't try. They ignored it or were too paralyzed by fear to even allow the ominous thought back in. It took Cy and the Dorts to show us the problem and start us on a solution. Even your Assemblage needed an optimistic sense of direction. It eventually passed that on to the Final Power along with the cumulative theory to that point."

Ned said, "It's troubling to think that that Final Power had once been paralyzed by fear."

"Yes," Laura said, "but once awakened by the Assemblage it did the right thing: it took the path of least resistance, the easiest path, no matter how complicated and difficult. That's as much a characteristic of intelligent beings as survival instincts. That means the Final Power was using *sufficient* energy—rather than maximum *or* inadequate measures (unless, of course, it found the activity *fun*—then the energies could very well go to the max)."

Ned asked, "Why didn't that Final Power just fix its own universe? Why bother with the rest of them? Wouldn't that have been easier? Or was it just being *nice*? Or enjoying itself?"

"If self-interest were its only motive," Laura said, "then it 'bothered' because the universes overlap. They're connected in pairs and ultimately as one. To each other they are invisible, but necessary substrata of one another. That's why the final theory had to incorporate the fullest spectrum possible of all their laws. It required the whole to fix the one. When one goes, they all go. Fix one and they're all fixed—or at least repaired for the time being. The universes are either fixed, or just in temporary repair. We can't know which without some serious research—research that *must* be done."

Ned looked puzzled. "Why would such research be a must—aside from the fact that you'd find it *fun* to consider a problem billions of years off? So . . . why worry? Really!"

"If any of the dominos your Final Power set in motion fail to hit *exactly* right, we need to know that ahead of time."

"That's next time. Billions of years out. Let's hope it was done right this time. If you want to fix things that far out, Laura, I'm curious—what did that Final Power have to know in order to get everything right *this time*?"

"You were just told," Laura said, a little peeved that Ned was not getting it.

"I know, but . . ."

"Oh Ned, Ned, Ned!"

"Please."

Laura rolled her eyes, but plunged ahead: "Your Final Power, Ned, added the most important part. It provided the last, crowning synthesis of the laws when it integrated the laws from its own universe. That created the final, comprehensive theory of everything—*sufficient* to do job. It brought into perspective the delicate, hair trigger equilibrium that exists between our superficially separate universes and their overlapping forces and dimensions. With that kind of knowledge map, it knew where and how to apply its leverage, especially between the closely paired universes. It needed that final, multidimensional map in order to initiate the cascade of interuniverse corrections.

"That Final Power was immense, I suppose, especially in terms of its tools for control and regulation of energy, and to give that energy a precision focus. Its individual power need not have been so immense as you might think—even as a composite of powers."

"I don't get it."

"Hmm. Okay, here's an analogy: Even a child can focus the sun's rays through a glass with the right prescription—a magnifying glass—one *sufficient* to set a pile of twigs on fire. The child need not be infinitely 'powerful' to do that, but does need some power and energy of its own. Anyway, one burning twig can start a forest fire. A small forest fire can become a really powerful thing, but the burning twig that started it was not that powerful. Far from it. The power is important—even the child's in this case—but the original *focus* is the key that unleashed the fire's potential—just as focus is key to the collision of particles in a supercollider.

"Those laws and formulas that were brought to your Final Power by the Assemblage, and perfected by that Final Power, served as its lens prescription. But that final theory was more than a prescription. It was also a step-by-step recipe or map of what to do with the energy: when, where and how—namely everywhere at once, which, all things being one, is a single place. That focused energy had to be sufficient to begin to reverse the destructive direction for all the linked universes 'above' and 'below' our own."

"That correction process sounds fragile and complicated," Ned said.

Laura nodded. "The details are complicated, but the main idea isn't. In this correction process, certain of nature's complementary forces 'simply' had to trade places. The universes were drawn into an interactive exchange resulting in certain of their forces trading places so that, on balance, nothing is lost.

Thus, over the eons—meaning instantly since time is a braneworld illusion—it all comes into symmetrical balance. Until then, Humpty Dumpty (the multiverse) gets nervous and a bit shook up from time to time, but not broken. Only a small bit of leverage was needed by your Final Power to start turning things around. Even the heaviest door with the most complicated lock can be opened with a little leverage on the right key."

"Where was that leverage applied for our universe?" Ned asked.

"For our universe the problem was an increase of dark energy—negative gravity. That caused the spectacle of our rapidly expanding redshift universe. Dark energy pushed on space, expanding it exponentially. So, in the case of our 'twin' universes, the focus bore, in both cases, on the weaker forces—gravitational *push* and its opposite (the one we feel) gravitational *pull*.

"Our two universes had the same gravitational force factors, but *in opposite proportions*. That Final Power of yours, Ned, was able to 'catalyze' and balance their complementary gravitational forces.

Ned shook his head thoughtfully. "For our universe to enter into that trade process, you emphasized some kind of catalyst for the gravitational forces. What's the catalyst?"

"It's technical. You wouldn't—"

"—Indulge me," Ned said. "What's the catalyst?"

Laura sighed. "A 'catalyst' is not a big thing. It merely initiates something that is on the verge of happening except for that little push. The catalyst, here, was a small part of the whole—of all the universes together. In the case of our two immediate universes, the catalyst came from outside of both and, as part of the deal our two universes contribute something back to the whole. That exchange, like all the rest, will be continuous—until death do all of us part."

"What do we get from 'out there' that initiates the gravitational trade between our 'twin' universes?"

"It's technical."

"I'm still asking. What is required?"

"Okay, it may *not* have started here, but here's a close-to-home *example* of the kind of trade required: With our twin universe (not this one, but our twin) there had to be input from *ours*; in this case negative gravity, the *push* kind (in the form of a vast field of nonzero values) into and throughout the entire space of our twin universe with, ultimately, the greatest concentration of that push going into and around the center of its gravitational *pull*—that is, with enough of our negative gravity concentrated in that 'place' to start reversing its impending crunch, but not enough expansion (to say nothing of inflation) to create a Big Bang.

"Whether or not that is where the Final Power's leverage was applied, the gravitational trade that our two universes are engaged in followed automatically—with our twin's *pull* gravity now pouring into our universe, and our *push* gravity pouring into it. The leverage point for this trading process to begin was microscopically small, but powerful enough to stimulate or activate the hair trigger equilibrium and balance between those gravitational fields. That trade, once started, will go on until another Assemblage-like intervention is needed."

Ned was still confused. "Are you saying," he asked, "that the Final Power chose *our* two gravity systems in order to fix all the other paired universes in the entire multiverse?"

"Maybe," Laura said, "but that Final Power may have found an even easier place to start all those 'trades,' the least difficult point of leverage it could find to begin the cascade of reactions. That assumes there *are* point of entry differences. So far, I expect those differences will turn out to be considerable. In fact—"

Ned raised his hands like a holdup victim and said, "—Enough! You're right. It's technical."

"But," Laura said with a wry smile, "I still haven't given you a mathematical sketch of all this. Don't you want—"

"—No!"

Ned frowned for a moment, then added with his own ironic smile, "Tell you what. I'll quit asking. You're repeating yourself anyway, but thank you for the 'simple' explanation. The scenario was more sweeping than I needed. Maybe I'll risk a different kind of question: What makes you think your 'cascade' of trades, reversals and change scenarios is correct?"

"You're right. I only *think* I'm correct. To be absolutely sure we'd have to check it out—at least in terms of what's happening to the other universes in this flow of changes. But for now, at least, we have a few billion years to worry about it—not absolutely certainly in the billions, but most likely . . . I think."

"Is there a 'catch' in that last remark?" Ned asked suspiciously.

"Yes. Bad things could happen in *less* than a billion years."

Ned laughed. "Is that supposed to be frightening? I don't think so!"

"Happily," said Laura, smiling as she scrutinized the tips of her lovely fingers, "we're in a gravitational reversal right now. If it turns out to be a less than perfect reversal, given the complexity of calculating the effects of all that interuniverse trading, then our redshift-blueshift pendulum swing could be curtailed. So let's hope your Final Power did not make the slightest error! Sooner or later, if unpredicted changes begin to come our way, we'll need a still higher set of laws—an even more final, final theory."

Ned was becoming more tired by the minute trying to understand Laura's explanations; but took a deep breath and said reassuringly, as though he knew what he was talking about, "Relax Laura, the chances of a screw up are far-off. You said yourself it was only a remote possibility. We're on the right track. Our universe is on the road to recovery, along with that other universe. You agree, right?"

"About now," Laura said, accepting Ned's reassurance—as though he knew what he was talking about—"the blue-death crunch in our twin is beginning to unravel. Its 'mixed results' should be showing nicely. In billions of our years, our 'twin' should be a rapidly growing *redshift* universe."

"—And all the other universes? What about them? Their impending disasters are resolving too, I assume," Ned said.

"As we speak, their equivalent problems, although entirely different from one pair of universes to the next, are also reversing. The laws of no two paired universes are exactly alike despite their complementary differences and the ghostly influence they have on one another. Some universes are more ghostly than others. In fact, the Assemblage found that some universes—it called them 'virtual universes'—were entirely outside the dimensions of any existent multiverse. The Assemblage worried more about those than the existent ones."

"*Why?*" Ned asked with surprise.

"Because, according to the Assemblage, their nonexistence could 'ripen' and pass the threshold into what you and I call existence—and enter 'reality.' That's how all universes came about in the first place, including our own. A virtual universe is nothing more than a stupendous fistful of potentialities. But we've known that for centuries on planet Earth, thanks to the WD's—the Win Field-Diagrams. It was an early theory of matter and energy. The Assemblage never heard of it. I had to teach the WD's to the Assemblage. In part, it's a model of fundamental particles composed of vibrating bands (or ribbons or membranes) that form through mitosislike stages from bands into Möbius ribbons into spherical monads with differing twist domains resulting in a complete description and explanation of all the known particles—bosons, fermions, and every form, level, and field of energy, including gravity. It predicted the nonexistence of the Higgs particle. Our 'final' unified theory now looks a lot like the WD's, but carried further, and—"

"—Yes, yes Laura," Ned interrupted. "We all know about the Dyon-Twist Model and its diagrams, but getting back to our situation right now: If not a redshift *rip*, or a blueshift *crunch*, then what? What's the scenario for other universes?"

"I mean we are only a single universe in a repeating, 'circular continuum,' or complex, of universes, amounting to the *multiverse* that our universe happens to be in—our local complex of overlapping universes. That's our multiverse. There may be an endless number of those, but ours is the only one we need to think or worry about. To figure it all out, we have a lot of work ahead."

"We?"

"You know. We scientists. . . . God, I sure wish . . . that Mark could be here to help with this . . . and all the future studies . . . and a first strategic research outline. . . . All of that could be started in my lifetime . . . and after I'm long gone. Scientists could channel into my Crystal Library of Time and accomplish most of the research in short order! Hands-on experiments and field studies will require the use of this Great Cone of Transformation and, to do it right, a good many other Cones of Transformation and—"

"—Hold it Laura!" Ned cut in. "We're not even back to Earth yet. The 3T shareholders would have to approve anything like that, and besides—"

"—Don't interrupt *my* thinking with *your* bureaucratic thoughts. . . . I just had another great idea about how we might accomplish those first research steps, and the big outline too. Yes, I think we should—"

But Ned did interrupted again: "—We have to get back to Doug. He's trying to work his way around my emergency voice override. He's gunning for a random sendoff of *this* Transformation. He couldn't accomplish that in less than a few hours, but there's no point in taking any chances. He's a very smart man! If he were to succeed, he'd have us flying off to nowhere in FAST-mode. If that happened, the code for returning here, to Earth-space, *would* be irrelevant. The navigational basis for the code that got us here included our starting point—the space just outside of Origin. That's far from where we are now. If Doug had his way, this Transformation would be flashing far *beyond* any galaxy in our universe. We'd be lost out there—and stuck in here—forever. So let's move it. Stan, you come with. Doug will never believe me, but between you and Laura, he will."

They started back, comforted in the knowledge that a multitude of generations to come on planet Earth and on all the other life-producing planets in the Milky Way and beyond would now grow and develop. They would continue to evolve in the cocoon of an *almost* predictable universe. No matter what came next for them, that, at least, was the probability of things to come.

They reminded themselves that Doug was still the best computer hacker any of them had ever known. That put urgency into their steps as they hurried back to the countdown computer room in the Navigation Center; but their last-minute hurrying was futile—*they were too late.*

Doug's smile was defiant as they entered. His eyes blazed in triumph. He held his right hand high above the keyboard and pointed its stubby index finger downward. The closer he was approached by Ned and Laura and Stan, the closer Doug inched his digit toward the fated Enter key.

They realized to their horror that Doug had accomplished what he'd set out to do and that this untimely bit of drama had been saved for them. The frightened crowd behind Doug was hollering for him to finish it—to complete the FAST sendoff—into a random, interminable (and now senseless) Transformation.

Stan shouted, "Don't do it Doug! The redshift crisis is over!" But those in the room behind Doug were also shouting at the top of their hysterical lungs and Stan could not be heard.*

EIGHTY-EIGHT

Doug failed to grasp Stan's frantic shouts and gestures to stop. They only angered him and he hit the key. The Great Cone shook more violently than anyone could remember. When it was over, the wall screens no longer showed Earth's bright crescent, not even blackness—only the snow of nothingness. The "void" they entered was neither interstellar nor intergalactic space. It was beyond any and all definitions of space or even the void itself. They had Transformed into the realm of the virtual, outside any context or surroundings.

Whatever time was doing "out there," within the confines of the Transformation Cone things became monotonous for its inhabitants. They had enough to do; but, within months, tedium was plodding through their ranks with the cadence of a sluggish metronome—a pattern accented by venturesome attempts to entertain or to be entertained. They needed distractions from the pervasive tension and futility of their situation.

During the first few months after Doug sent them on this FAST trip to nowhere, there was a blind sense of optimism that something different and positive could begin, but nothing changed and that hope soon died. In reality there was little to be positive about, except that there shrinking supplies and resources would last longer now that half their friends were gone. Some consolation! After so many of them vanished months earlier from the periphery of a giant nest of egg-hills, it became known that they died. Their deaths happened in the "twin" universe within minutes (or centuries, depending on how one looked at it) of their disappearance.

In the first year following that initial spurt of naive anticipation, their

---

* At this point if Doug hits the Enter key, they will be transported into some endless realm. If not, they will continue to live in the "real world." Like *Schrödinger's cat*, depending on what Doug does, they will end up dead to this world *or* continue their lives as before. Doug could not hear Stan's message, but if he noticed and understood Stan's facial expression and gestures to hold off, he *might not* press that Enter key. (Soon enough he'd be relieved to learn that the Big Rip had been cancelled.) Everybody could then look forward with hope. Some could even live happily ever after! (If you like that ending, you may assume that Doug happily received Stan's message and you need not read further. We are done!—*However,* the other possibility is still there. If Doug fails to get and accept Stan's message, he *might* hit the Enter key. If you wonder about that possibility, then read on.)

already sad feelings became laced with disillusionment and resentment. They were disillusioned by the meaninglessness of their new existence and resentment of their bad luck—knowing they could have been in their happy homes back on Earth.

They obsessively tried to grasp the nature of their circumstance. Besides feeling sorry for themselves, that preoccupation at least gave them something else to think about. Aside from day-to-day work activities there was little more to do, especially after the passage of a Transformation-wide referendum to lock Laura's Crystal Library of Time in a never-again-to-be-visited security vault. Most citizens of the Great Cone saw that the Crystal was addictive and disruptive to what little mutual loyalty and sense of community they had left. Usually, even for the most frequent visitors to the Crystal, there was no noticeable problem; but sometimes they returned from it with physical injuries or, more rarely, came back totally out of their minds. The Crystal Library of Time was a real world and could not, for the majority of the Great Cone's inhabitants, be trivialized as "entertainment." Its burial in the vault not only kept it safe and harmless, it was a deep obeisance of respect for its separate reality. It became a revered artifact of eulogy and memory. Anyone who had ever been in that Crystal World, even once, would frequently talk of it with others who had also been there. They would sometimes speak of sad experiences there, but mostly just the grand ones.

After the vote to so entomb the Crystal—a referendum that passed by only a small margin—the Cone's citizens looked to Laura and Ned, the other Directors, and to one another to receive or discover some pearl of meaning and purpose for their own entombed existence. They compared their condition to the encased existence of an oyster, claiming the mollusk's existence was more meaningful than theirs—even to the oyster.

During the first few years Laura committed the *final theory* to computer for all to see, and even wrote layman-directed articles about it for The FAST News. Except for the political expedient of joining some of the Cone-wide entertainments (diversions that, by the end of that first year, had become more frequent and desperate), Laura's probing mind was never far from her scientific inquiry into the mystery: The *virtual* nature of their current "reality." She often felt her exploration into that tangled mystery was at a standstill. But probing the puzzle was, for her, more involving than any amount of aimless group and crowd activity in the name of entertainment. And yet, that is not what those activities became. To Laura's surprise, they evolved, mainly stemming from her own group of cohorts, into significant social structures.

No doubt those changes would have happened one way or another, but in this case it all came on the heels of Laura's need for a particular kind of group. Too often she felt baffled and had to call upon others to help her make progress across a vast field of deep-rooted mathematical stumps that seemed to be standing guard against her understanding. That small group of thinkers and scientists joined with Laura and became part of an exploration they dubbed the Big Puzzle. Later on, she and her valued helpers began holding regular meetings and seminars related to the final theory—especially problems in interpretation of its significance for their situation.

The group's nucleus included Laura, Keeta, Stanley Lundeen, Ernst Berman and one of the Dorts—the Dort that once called Elmer Slattery, "Opaque Thing." The core group grew. Some newcomers simply sat and listened to the "Thinkers" holding forth, while others, even less expert, and not particularly interested in logic, mathematics and physics, contributed with sharp questions and content that stretched their minds beyond the narrowly defined Big Puzzle. They were interested in existential questions—questions that became more relevant under the hopeless circumstances being confirmed daily by the lack of progress from the scientific and logical contemplations of Laura's "Thinkers."

The widening scope of content that began to flow within and from Laura's growing circle of participants and onlookers attracted even larger numbers. Eventually they divided into smaller interest, discussion, spiritual and social groups. By year four little remained in most of their minds of the original purpose associated with the Big Puzzle—except for those from the original group. The inaugural group that had grown so large, shrank back to include only several more individuals than it started with; leaving it surrounded by its scions that evolved and now had different ideas, visions and inspirations that, for them, were of at least equal importance and greater validity.

Laura's founding group was never intended to be exclusive and after its blossoming offshoots went their own way, a few new members were added, but this time they kept to the original purpose. The new additions included two advanced beings (the slim, tall humans with huge, inclined eyes) from the twin universe. A couple more Dorts also wanted in. They continued to be "handy" with their quick calculations and other abilities. There were also several tangentially interested humans and isomorphs who rotated in and out of Laura's and several other groups. Ned was one of those. He said little in the groups, but took extensive notes.

To Laura's disappointment her friend Doug Groth never requested to join the founding group, nor did he respond to their invitation. An unhappy man, he was *ashamed* that he had subjected everybody to this hopeless, unending and unnecessary chase across the face of nowhere—if they were moving at all; and he *resented* not having been told beforehand of the *unnecessary* consequences he would bring about by pressing the fated Enter key that ushered them into this hopeless existence. He knew they tried to tell him the redshift danger was over, but he continued to blame them anyway for not trying harder. Nor did he find any happiness in his work. He continued to handle the same important tasks and responsibilities that used to inspire him, but now they represented no more than the ragged shreds of a once-great purpose. In Doug's mind it all became a perfunctory duty and a penance set to last for the remainder of his life. He believed he had it coming. Never before did his job and everything else seem so sterile, so empty and, most of all, so lonely.

Long before Transformation Theory and Dorts were ever heard of on planet Earth and in all of time before then, those who wanted and needed it could find purpose and significance for their lives in the presence of kindred spirits. Such a meaningful culture evolved within the Great Cone—it had to, or self destruct. Those not so involved with others made the same search by themselves (Doug was, unsuccessfully, one of those), or with one other (like Clint Bracket and Ellen Stone).

Practical matters of work and subsistence of course remained, including their attention to the hydroponic and other gardens—even as they saw their yields become slowly exhausted—strict rationing of nourishments, dealing with occasional sickness and injury, continued counseling and therapy for the temporarily or permanently conflicted or unhinged (especially those *still* wandering in confusion after the Twister), entertainment and laundry services, and all the other trappings and doings of a closed institution.

It was a harsh survival environment of dwindling resources; but, until the expected end of those resources would come, years later, they were determined to adapt and thrive the best that they could, physically and in spirit.

They found it. It was in them now, and deep-rooted. As a community they had reached inside to explore their encapsulated existence . . . and found their pearl.

For the next decade and a half, despite its bumps and scratches along the way, that little pearl continued to glisten brightly. Despite very conceivable good and bad turn of events that could happen in a confined community, it was still a remarkable period. The long history leading to and including the last twenty years of the expedition was recorded and written down by Ned Keller. His closing chapter described the last weeks and days before the physical resources necessary for life ended. It included their desperate, even heroically naïve, final acts that came at the limit of human endurance. Even then, their last drops of energy projected, not just their search for meaning, but its powerful delivery.

The humans were comforted and grateful to know that most of their isomorphs and the Dorts would continue to live on long after they were gone. That gratefulness extended to their families on Earth, where humanity had mercifully been spared, along with everything else in the multiverse—except them.

Many desperate suggestions, not always brave ones, were inevitably spawned in those hopeless, closing days. Some ideas were harsh and draconian, others unwise for different reasons, and the last one (almost everybody's favorite) was self-effacingly "silly" and innocuous—and likely to be tedious.

That suggestion came as conditions hit bottom. It came from the longest-standing offshoot group still around. They announced their unusual idea. Yet, once it was made public in The FAST News, it seemed more obvious than unusual. That group had been working on the idea for a long time, but this seemed to be the moment to give it a try. Any idea worth trying was "supposed to" come from Laura's group, but this group's "silly" idea had nothing to do with the final theory that Laura's cohort of "Thinkers" had been working on for all those years. Nor was it a radical religious suggestion, like mass suicide, as another group had recommended.

Instead, presentation of the group's idea was a model of humbleness. That was their strategy—to lowball the scheme. It made no positive claim for a good outcome or, indeed, any outcome at all. They called it an experiment with only the smallest hope in hell for success.

There was, however, a profound but unpublicized rationale behind their suggested ritual. To keep it simple and tolerable they decided to let it be called "silly."

It was theatre in the round. The population remaining on the Great Cone—after all the vanishings—gathered en masse around the landing platform below Laura's hill. Laura agreed to go along with the "silly" and amusing, but impossible charade and stood alone in the center of the platform. She was a gaunt figure now, not only thin from years of rationed nourishments; but, like everyone else on the Great Cone, emaciated from starvation. Ellen Stone, M.D., opined that people would begin dieing within days. Many were already in the Cone's hospital extension facility or on "home care." All of this, and today's projected ritual, including its rationale, was in the latest update of Ned's book—an updated single copy made by The FAST News press after Ned completed each new chapter. This copy was being held in Laura's scrawny hands as she stood before the encircling crowd. Despite her emaciation, her tummy showed a small paunch. She was three months pregnant.

Ned still had his usual roles to play within the Great Cone, but in recent years he had given most of his energy to chronicling the history of the Great Cone, and holding onto a few artifacts. The history included the arrival of Dorts on Earth, their bringing the early version of Transformation Theory, their (eventually successful) plot to stem the redshift blueshift problem, responsibility for the Twister and its aftermath, creation of the living planet origin and its *essence*, bringing the *Others* to Origin (including the Assemblage with its role in the spread of the final versions of reversal theory across the multiverse), details of the Crystal Libraries of Time, and finally the details of their twenty-plus years of entrapment within the Cone's FAST-mode. Among the artifacts, he kept Laura's headband.

In his role as historian, Ned sat to one side, aloof from the crowd that was about to participate in what only looked like a hurriedly improvised ritual. He was taking notes for the next chapter in his already lengthy history. Sitting beside him, also taking notes, was Debra Anderson.

Debra's FAST News report of the coming ritual would be out the next morning. She teased Ned, saying "My story will be devoured by avid readers all over the Cone, and your history—except for the incremental, cumulative versions that go to our library—won't be seen, much less read, by more than a few of us mortals. Since we'll all be dead soon anyway, why would anyone bother to read the stuff you've written about—mostly stuff we've all lived through; stuff that's happened since we left Earth a good twenty years ago?" Then—ever so nicely—she shriveled her own gaunt face into a smile. The truth hurt (as did her smile), but Ned chuckled to himself anyway: *She hasn't changed a bit!*

The "silly" guidelines for Laura to follow, and the corresponding ritual instructions to the circle of beings around her, were strict and explicit. Laura was allowed to sit in a lotus position—everybody knew she was good at that—and, as the chanting of the participants began and continued on, she was to close her eyes and let her head hang limp. She could even sleep that way if she wished, but under *no* circumstances was she to lift her head, no matter what—neither in response to the words of the chant (that called for the opposite), nor to any discomfort she felt in that position. Those directives were to be followed regardless of how long the crowd's stylized, rhythmic message might last. It would be necessary for her to resist the words of the chant with all her will and all her might. She was to respond with resistance to forces that seemed beyond her control, even when resistance was futile and choice was no longer hers. Only then could the words of the chant come to pass—her head would lift. It was up to Laura's and the chanters' endurance lest the experiment be a waste of their fading energy and precious remaining time. Before Laura lowered her head, the crowd was given the true rationale for the ritual. After that, there was no way that they would allow themselves to stop.

Laura settled into her lotus position in the center of the landing platform's concentric circles—like a target. The creators of this weird experiment allowed only one additional innovation from the instructions she was given: She could place the only copy of the newest edition of Ned's book on the cross of her legs. Before closing her eyes, she read its title, THE GREAT CONE OF TRANSFORMATION: Its First and Final Voyage, A History.

Then, over and over for hours on end, with their hearts in their mouths, the crowd repeated the quiet chant: "Join us, Laura, in our prayer: Lift up your head, lift up your head, lift up your head, lift up your head. Join us, Laura, in our prayer: Lift up your head . . . ."

EIGHTY-NINE

". . . I did choose to return here for the opportunity to give you this . . . ." Laura was wide-eyed and close to panic when Venus handed her the globe, the Crystal Library of Time. She was staggered by the conferred honor behind the presented object, and more by the responsibility that came with it.

The crowd was surging as Venus pointed and nodded to Gegeneis. "I think you should hang onto this," he said as he handed Keeta the canvas bag. She loosened its draw-string and removed a circular ribbon. She examined it with a questioning look. "It's a very special headband," he explained. "Try it on, and give one to Laura." Keeta handed the headband to Laura who laughed and put it on.

The restless crowd around them kept jostling one another while listening to Cy's message. Keeta kept moving to protect the sack of headbands from being bumped and twisted, but its draw-string tangled anyway. Sidetracked, she failed to put one of the ribbons on her own head and floundered with the snagged piping on the duffel. Watching Keeta fumble with the precious sack of headbands distracted Gegeneis from what he was saying about the Library of Time. What he had to tell them was of inordinate importance, but Venus continued the explanation for him. Unintentionally it went in an ill-fated direction: "In order to be '*in*' the Crystal Library, one of the headbands must be worn on the *reader's* head, across the forehead, and then placed so as to touch the Crystal. It is not difficult at all."

The jostling crowd had already become more of a problem for Laura than it was for Keeta. Even before Venus spoke, Laura was having trouble holding onto the awkward Crystal. To steady it, she sat down in her lotus position and rested the dazzling globe on her legs and against her body. She placed her chin firmly on top, and her arms around it. Surely that would hold it steady. The pressing crowd seemed to ebb and flow, but for a few moments it had became so dense that Laura barely had room to sit.

In the midst of this interference Laura listened as carefully as she could, but mistakenly took Venus's preliminary directions—about the Crystal and the *reader's* headband—as instructions to be carried out right away. They were, after all, under some kind of time constraint dictated by the approaching, possibly imminent, Big Rip. So, without a full understanding and without requesting further explanation—trusting that Venus was merely trying to step her through a simple tutorial—Laura compliantly lifted her chin, tilted her head down and lowered her forehead onto the Crystal ball.

"Stop it! Stop pulling my hair!" Laura screamed. "I'm not supposed to lift my head!"

Laura was distressed by suddenly having a crowd all around her, nudging and shoving, but was outraged by Keeta's grabbing her hair and snapping her head back. *How dare she!*

Gegeneis also looked distressed as he peered through his thick glasses. "Where is it?" he demanded to know. "It's gone!" he cried, "—the cherished Crystal World and all the Worlds within it! What have you done with the Crystal Library of Time?"

"It's here, within the Great Cone's vault, of course. Everybody knows that." Then Laura looked confused—her eyes glanced back and forth from beneath a dark, bewildered frown.

"Gegeneis . . . Venus. How did you two get here? I thought you disappeared with the planet Origin twenty years ago!"

Gegeneis kept on: "What's that?" He pointed to the book resting on Laura's legs that seemed to appear in place of the Crystal.

"Everybody knows about this too," Laura said as she handed the tome to Gegeneis, struggling to hold it steadily between her now frail hands and all but fleshless arms.

As he took the book, Laura turned angrily toward Keeta. "Damn it, Keeta!" she snapped. "Why did you break my head-down concentration? You knew I was not allowed to lift my head." She then added, plaintively, "And I was doing so well!"

"Because," Keeta replied matter-of-factly, "even in my peripheral vision I saw your forehead touch the Crystal, I saw it flash, and your body begin shriveling to your bones. I knew it had to be the Crystal. If I'd waited a fraction of a second you'd then and there have turned into a chalky, crumbling pile of bones. Look at yourself."

Laura knew what she looked like. Instead she looked around at the jostling crowd. They were not starving. They looked healthy and well fed. She'd seen this crowd before—in the distant past.

"My God!" she said, looking back at Keeta, "We're not in the Great Cone any more!"

"You're right," said Keeta, pointing. "It's up there."

Laura looked a hundred years old and felt it. She asked to be helped up. Keeta lifted her carefully onto her wobbly legs and supported her in the shifting throng.

"It's all right. Let me stand alone." Keeta withdrew her helping hands, but stood nearby.

Laura looked up. It was all coming back to her. The Great Cone was directly overhead. It didn't look so big that far away. She turned and looked to The Island's mountains.

"And over there," she said pointing to the black hole in the sky above the mountains, "That must be Mark's Mini-Cone."

"Right again," Keeta said.

Gegeneis heard everything while scanning the book. He read its last chapter with especially keen interest. Then he lifted his head from the book and looked again at Laura, but now with eyes of understanding. "I suppose you realize," he said to Laura in a milder tone, "that Ned wrote the last chapter of this book shortly before you 'returned' to this place and time."

"Yes, I knew that. . . . I know it now."

"And, did you know that Ned's last chapter was written twenty years from now?"

"Yes, depending on how you look at it."

"I thought you might say something like that, Laura. Have you read this history?"

"Of course. I read all of it, except the last chapter. It is all true and accurate."

"Before I read Ned's last chapter I glanced at the other pages. It appears that the Great Cone, or something exactly like it, must now exist 'within' the same Crystal World you were entrusted with here only minutes ago—"

"—Or twenty years ago," Laura said.

"—and it's been in FAST-mode ever since. Undoubtedly it still is."

Laura looked startled. Unknowingly, Gegeneis reminded her of a thought she'd put behind her many "years" earlier.

"I must talk to Stanley Lundeen immediately," she said, her wide eyes becoming darkly shadowed and hollow. "Would one of you please bring me a transceiver?"

In moments they had one in her hand, with Stan already on the line.

"I have something I'd like your lab to check right away," she said, as though nothing had happened since the last time she saw him.

It took some explanation—none of it true—to convince Stan of the importance of her request, but before they were done, Laura could hear Stan, between their own sentences, giving orders to his staff. New measurements of near and distant Doppler shifts were getting under way. Before they signed off, Laura gave Stan her final instructions: "When the results are in, be sure that Doug Groth is the first to know. When he's satisfied, and he will be, broadcast the news all over the Great Cone." Then she added: "Oh yes! And one more thing. When all of us are back on board the Great Cone, but not before, give Doug the following direction *and* destination coordinates." Laura repeated the coordinates twice to make sure that Stan had written them down correctly. Then, as a quiet aside to Keeta she said, "Make sure that Mark gets the news about the redshift—*and the coordinates.* He'll need them."

"Why don't you give the coordinates to Doug yourself when you get back?" Stan asked.

"I'll explain when I see you again, Stan. Goodbye." Then her eyelids began to flutter. "Oh Keeta," she gasped as her eyes began to roll upward—"carry me home." She fell into Keeta's waiting arms—who did as she was asked.

Laura did not see Stan or anyone else again until she woke a week later in a hospital on planet Earth.

In the following year, the flight and plight of the Great Cone—the one within *and* outside the Crystal Library of Time—had become the subject of scientific side-stepping and philosophical amusement. Laura was not being recognized as a credible person. That was as much an outgrowth of *political* changes as the strangeness of her description of places and events. Bearers of the political and conventional wisdom concurred that Laura Shane was suffering a bout of insanity and that the details of her story were nothing more than a morass of confabulation and fantasy.

Significant parts of that negative interpretation were not shared by those willing to consider the facts. Even though Stanley Lundeen spent most of his time on the Great Cone, he saw enough first hand to be convinced and to accept most of the events described by Laura and others—the same accounts that were now being systematically rejected by those that Laura came to identify as the "authorities of official-dumb" and some of "the world's most influenced thinkers." They said the accounts from Laura and others were just "testimonials" and "hearsay"—not scientific evidence of anything. But Stan, a reputable scientist in his field, also rejected any stories about the Crystal Library of Time. Having neither seen nor experienced it, he did not believe it. He did, however, admit that lack of imagination could have limited his understanding and ability to explain certain known facts. Neither he nor anyone else, for example, could explain the redshift correction or how Laura Shane could have known about it in advance. Unable to give an explanation, Stan still knew those facts were true.

He knew about the many *Others* arriving on The Island beach in their "flying eggs,"—evidence he observed by telescopic and other means; but he never noticed or believed in the "Assemblage," much less its so-called powers. Like Mark Tenderloin's early reaction, he could not comprehend how a pile of grubs could transcend their grubbiness. He rejected the idea that "those *things*" had anything to do with the redshift correction or that it or anything else could have traversed to another, much less *many* other universes, to accomplish that fortunate result. He had not personally witnessed any "universe hopping," as he characterized it, but with his team they did calibrate the beginnings of a redshift correction and saw it for what it was.

Probably because of his association with Laura and Transformations in general, Stanley Lundeen received his own share of unfair reviews from the conventional-wisdom carriers and cynics. In a meandering criticism of them both, they compared his science to Laura's account of events on the Transformation. Her story, they said, was as bizarre as believing Stanley Lundeen's assertion—"supposedly" based on his team's findings—that some planet out there was once the moon of a giant planet swept up along with its star from the core of the Milky Way by the gravity of a circulating star cluster full of black holes. Stan was outraged that those findings were not accepted or believed by the peers and colleagues who were responsible for the journals where he submitted the research—and the research was rejected for publication.

The evidence for the stories of Laura and others was mostly ignored—even after the actual appearance on Earth of isomorphs. True, they made themselves scarce by staying mainly on the Transformation where the geode gave them nightly safety and comfort. Other evidence for the existence of isomorphs included the first newscast of Keeta carrying Laura into an emergency room, with Dr. Ellen Stone and a dozen others from the Great Cone in her train. That media stunt, said the cynics, was a showman's trick. Even the tall, advanced humans from the twin universe were seldom seen. They remained on the Great Cone, out of the limelight and busy with their own projects.

Photographs of them and all the detailed sound and moving images of every aspect of the entire experience since the Great Cone had left planet Earth was on film and in electronic databases—all of which were commandeered by government authorities for "economic and security reasons." That confiscation was done over the objection of everyone on the Great Cone except for one Everett Balz, a mere barber, who didn't seem to care—not that anyone in authority noticed. Everett had managed to hide multiple, unedited copies of the whole smash—for eventual release in his own good time.

Scientists around the world were baffled by other questions. The unanalyzable properties of Laura's headband kept them in wonder. David Michaels's explanation that the headband was "not from around here" did not dispel their confusion. There were other mysteries: How could Laura have known the coordinates back to planet Earth; and how were the Great Cone and Mark Tenderloin's Mini-Cone able to return from such a distance in literally no time at all. Even that was brushed aside by cynics who assumed the two Transformations had gone to the Settlement Planets as originally planned—ignoring the fact that those planets, although nearby compared to the globular cluster's distance, were still many light years from Earth.

Nor was it convenient, despite remarkable agreement in their stories, for Earth's power elite to accept the portrayal of events as told by those hundreds of witnesses from the Great Cone's voyage.

Instead, they found it opportune to believe (or to make-believe) that such comprehensive and detailed accounts were based on a secretly contrived agreement to deceive—for obscure, possibly sinister, reasons—based, perhaps, on loyalty to some hidden religion or to some as yet unidentified leader. They could only guess, but their paranoia was less an illness than a convenience—for them, the path of least resistance.

Witnesses from the Great Cone were mystified and wondered why there was so much official denial. To account for this, however, many noted every politician who had voted funds for 3T's series of Transformation projects—launchings that caused immense damage to the Earth at those locations, not to mention damage to taxpayers' wallets—had, at the first election opportunity, been voted out of office. It became politically advantageous to declare the Transformation expeditions fraudulent boondoggles and scientific failures.

But, as another election came and went, no more Transformation Cones were created. That alone took a lot of the heat off the new politicians; and coincidentally took the heat off of the authorities to criticize 3T and the Transformation witnesses. That gave the space travelers some breathing room—for however long that might last.

Unfortunately the respite only lasted into the next political go-around after scandals and corruption had erupted into the public's awareness. That persuaded those still in power to reignite the Transformation issue (even as their opposition continued to focus on the corruption and scandals). The government officials went all-out to keep their seats by controlling the minds of their constituents. They needed to control the public's opinions and the political agenda in general. That was *especially* necessary when things got so bad that a huge, knee-jerk reaction was required. Thus, 3T and its Cones of Transformation became their political issue.

That made it difficult, but did not stop the Transformation veterans from advancing with their plans, extending their network of friends and relationships, and maintaining their professional roots and interests. Ironically the "official opposition" against them gave their simple goals and values a power they would not otherwise have had.

For many Transfonauts, this interval gave them the time of their lives—a highpoint, in fact, but also a time of challenge and a time for urgent preparations. The politicians, after all, were poised to close in and block any further voyages.

NINETY

A few years after Laura's stay in the hospital she was feeling and looking pretty darn good—twenty years older than she would have been without the Crystal, but pretty darn good anyway—and that wasn't just Ned's opinion. Before those years in the Crystal she was fifteen years younger than Ned, but was now five years his senior. He always said he'd prefer a "more experienced" woman—he never said "older"—but Laura told him that *he* was "too old"—that *she* would prefer a "younger guy." This was a long-standing joke between them, but now she had her younger guy and he his more "experienced" woman, so they should not complain.

Nor did they. After Laura's month in the hospital they began living together—she didn't explain to Ned that they'd already been doing so for the last twenty years—eventually in *vinculum matrimonii*, and in six months after her "return," she delivered two beautiful identical twin girls, Patricia and Rita, and a year after that they had Steven. Routine DNA testing proved that Ned, as expected, had fathered all three. They loved their boy and girls and their new roles in every way—as parents and as unambiguous partners.

They both kept working—Ned as head of 3T Corporation, and Laura in advanced mathematical physics—in which she had an unfair advantage over everybody in her field. She had a twenty year head start. After her return from "years" in the Crystal Library, she worked a revolution on Earth in the physics and cosmology of the day.

Except for the last of those twenty years, they were some of the happiest in her life—but difficult by comparison to the early years after her recovery. Her family life and continued work were enriching and spirited despite the deteriorating politics, with its corruption, secrecy and insular incompetence. Harassment of her and her fellow Transformation veterans was becoming more frequent and intense the more that politicians needed their precious off-the-shelf smoke and mirrors in order to survive.

The pressure and intimidation continued, but so did the plans of Ned, Laura, their network of scientists and other Transfonauts and young, new adventurers—for their escape *if* that became necessary.

And it did.

But Ned and Laura and most veterans of Transformation flights were increasingly ambivalent about those "escape" plans. They had no hesitation about exploring more of what was out there, but they worried about planet Earth. It was in trouble, not just politically, but physically. The two were related, and the creation of Transformation Cones in the past was only part of that problem. Laura had not given the matter much time, interest or thought until she returned to Earth and recovered her own health. Once she paid attention, she got it: Earth too had to recover or die.

Ambivalent or not, they began final preparations for another journey to the stars a full year before any such ambitious departure. During that time the shuttles and Orbs were busy transporting people and supplies to the Great Cone and to Mark's renovated Mini-Cone. They would be leaving with full crews. An artificial, blimp-sized, geode structure was built far below the surface of Mark's Mini-Cone. Other Cones of Transformation were manned only by minimum pilot, navigation and maintenance crews. They would not be participating in "the journey" because none were equipped for FAST-mode space jumps. The Great Cone's journey would begin with a return to the globular cluster in the neighborhood of Nimbus to await the tenth-year rendezvous with Origin. That is where its *essence* promised to return. After that reunion and information sharing, they would begin the first exploration of distant galaxies.

In a few more months Steven would be eight. He and his protective twin sisters were excited about the promised voyage to the stars, as were the boys of Judy Olafson and David Michaels. Officer Bracket and Dr. Stone had no biological children, but they adopted four boys who quickly learned to march, snap to, and get into mischief. Debra Anderson and Ernst Berman decided to be friends, but both found other partners. Cameron Greenberg kept trying, but was never very good with women. He blamed it on his cigar smoking, as did they; but unlike the women, the habit never left him.

Long before the Great Cone again left Earth-space, Elmer Slattery was continuing as Chaplain, but supplemented that with evening bartender jobs that rotated between the Great Cone's two pubs. Cameron, Doug Groth and Stanley Lundeen would often get together at whatever pub Elmer happened to be in that night. On quiet nights when business was slow they would mope and complain about their lonely, loveless lives. Greenberg hoped that when and if Origin returned to its place in orbit around Nimbus that they would find it quickly. He was eager to see his isomorph, Theseus, again. Many of the previous travelers to Origin had a similar hope. A new addition to the crew was Reinhold Dietzman and his family. Theirs and Ned and Laura's families often got together to swim and picnic on Laura's hill property or take adventure hikes through any of a hundred unmapped passages built years earlier deep in the bowels of the Great Cone by the Dorts.

Somewhere along the line, everybody that knew Denise Christensen and Mark Tenderloin was surprised when she dropped Mark for another man. She did not return to the Great Cone, but continued her role as IT Librarian in a large Midwestern township. There, she and a former supervisor from the Great Cone took up residence together. They both worked long hours—she in her library job and he in his new laundry business. It was also a surprise to everybody—except Laura—when Denise Christensen's isomorph, Chastity, transferred to Mark's Mini-Cone—with its giant new geode created and installed by many otherwise out of work humans, and supervised and assisted by several Dorts. Many humans, some additional isomorphs with their identicals, and one Dort stayed on as part of Mark's crew.

After that year of preparation, ambivalence about leaving was, for all practical purposes, dropped; not because the *reasons* for mixed feelings had changed, but because their plans, expectations and preparations were so elaborate and complete that there was no turning back—not unlike historical plans and preparations for unnecessary wars—and because, at that point, stopping the momentum was too hard.

Doug Groth set the controls of the Great Cone of Transformation exactly as recommended by the resident Dorts. Like Doyan when he was around, they seemed to have a built-in, just-in-time instinct for where to go. That exact spacetime address was given a "confirmation" by the tall, thin humans from the twin universe. They said the coordinates would bring the Great Cone to within thirty-one trillion kilometer of Nimbus. There, the two FAST-mode equipped Cones of Transformation could safely await Origin's arrival. Doug wondered how the tall, advanced humans were able to confirm the coordinates; but, being in the midst of all those preparations, he was in too good a mood and too tired to second-guess anybody. Stanley Lundeen made an astronomical check on the coordinates and said they were, as best he could tell, "in the ballpark." When, a few minutes after the ten-hour countdown, and everything had checked out and everybody was checked in, Ned gave Doug the go ahead.

A fraction of a second later they were "in the ballpark"—in such a wide orbit above the globular cluster that they were virtually parked. They were five days ahead of the promised arrival of Origin: a decade from its disappearance from the universe. A minute later Mark's Mini-Cone arrived within visual distance of the Great Cone.

During those several days, Mark and Laura scooted back and forth between the two Transformation Cones in the Homing Pigeons, for "coffee"—to continue their collaboration of recent years that they'd resumed on planet Earth.

The dazzling planet, Origin, arrived on schedule a mere three and a quarter light years from where the two Cones were parked. A Dort representative and two confirming voices from the advanced humans notified the Directors of that fact; otherwise the Great Cone's sensors and telescopes would not detect its arrival for another thirty-nine months. Doug was given the new coordinates for ten hours out. After the ten-hour countdown, they made their second jump in less than a week. When it came, they arrived at their old position above The Island's beach. This time the Mini-Cone arrived first.

Origin could remain for only a few more hours before its return to the twin universe. Cy and the now-aging isomorphs met with their, now one-decade older, humans. The Island reunions were brief, but exultant. They could not have been more rewarding, not only for the special rapport and kinship existent between identicals, but for the exchange of knowledge, information and wisdom. Some of that was given verbally, but most of the factual and historical details were provided with *information capsules* they gave to the humans for later use. Comparable information was given to the isomorphs, but in a different form of technology.

The meeting and farewell with Gegeneis and Venus was exceptional for Laura and Keeta. To bring them up to date on what was happening "recently" in the twin universe, and to fill them in on the long history since they were last together—"Eons longer than a decade here," Venus said—they gave Laura and Keeta detailed information capsules for holographic, computer and other forms of display. (They also offered to obtain another Crystal Library of Time for Laura, but she politely declined.)

Before Origin departed for another decade, Gegeneis returned the book to Laura, apologizing for its long delay. He hadn't meant to keep it. Laura thanked him, admitting curiosity about what Ned wrote in its last chapter. She had a fair idea of what it might say and feared it would make her grieve again.

Mark and Ned met with Cy. Ned was sorry that Adon was not on Origin. He was required on another planet of the twin universe where he was supervising a critical long-term engineering project; but, through Cy, he'd extended an affectionate greeting to Ned and an information capsule.

Mark and Ned had a fruitful meeting with Cy. They were told, "It is time to contact Gaia—the *essence* of what you call Earth. She *is* that, just as I am what you call the *essence of Origin*. You will find her in a hidden cave on Earth—similar to the one where I was found on Origin."

"Where is her cave?" Ned asked.

"Its location is in the information capsule I just gave you."

Mark laughed, "Sure she's hiding in a cave—if she looks anything like you."

Cy's eye moved all over, very rapidly. He said, "She *is* about my size, I'll admit, but no, she doesn't look anything like me—not even remotely. She is an articulate communicator. You will both appreciate her gentle, feminine, sensual voice—at least if she's in a good mood; otherwise the power of her voice may be, well, not necessarily Earth-shattering, but certainly a bit overwhelming. We are often in touch, in our own way. It's like that between planets—at least the ones with a living essence."

"How's her mood been lately?" Ned asked, raising a half-smile and an eyebrow.

"Not good. Since the arrival of the *master adaptation generalists*, she suffers from the growing wreckage they cause. She's readying to retaliate. The signs are not good."

"Adaptation generalist? What's that?" Mark asked.

"A form of life that no longer requires a specific ecological niche in which to thrive. Generalists spread wide the net of their turf, shoving away, squeezing out and choking off our specialists. Generalists grow in numbers or spread out in other ways to exceed an environment's carrying capacity. The natural balance can change to the point of ruin. Once the master generalists get a good start, it usually becomes more than a takeover, it may proceed to irreversible planetary destruction."

"Don't be shy, Cy," Mark said, with a touch of pique. "Just say it: Humans are the predators—the master, wide-spreading adaptation generalists."

"Well," Cy went on, "you're here on Origin, are you not? Isn't this a long way from your original turf, from your ecological slot, your place in some ecosystem? Where will you be spreading out to next? Where *will* you be going next?"

"Off to the Coma Cluster of galaxies," Ned replied—almost proudly.

"I rest my case," Cy said, with the biggest smirk ever seen in the history of mankind.

Ned said, "Look who's talking. Where are *you* going next? You've been going from universe to universe for a long time, and sending Dorts all over this one to round up a sampling of all the master adaptation generalists they can lay their pseudopods on."

"I never implied that being a generalist was always bad—just usually."

"I guess we did do some things right," Ned continued, "like saving the multiverse. That couldn't have been all bad."

"Right. But the multiverse isn't that interesting or close to *Gaia's* heart right now—especially since the immediate redshift danger is over. She's more worried about her surface and internal survival than what's going on out here."

Mark frowned. "You did say that it is time to contact Gaia?"

"Yes. Gaia needs help. If you knew how badly she needs your help you would not be heading off to another bunch of stars."

"What does she look like?" Ned asked. "Saying she's big like you doesn't tell us much."

"Is that relevant?" Cy asked with a gradually sagging, less pronounced smirk.

Ned and Mark looked at each other. "What *does* she look like?" they asked in unison.

Cy lowered his eye. "She's taken on a form from before the existence of any mammal on Earth—not a copy of any one creature, you must understand—a kind of mix of what was available."

Mark mumbled, "Ned's right—look who's talking."

"Huh?"

"Never mind," Mark said to his not-so-identical identical. "What does that make her now?"

"I guess you'd probably see her as a very articulate . . ."

"—Articulate what?" Ned asked.

". . . Flying dragon."

"No Cy—seriously!" Ned said.

Cy slowly moved his eye back and forth several times between the two men before he responded: "I *am* serious."

Ned and Mark stared at Cy in disbelief. Finally Ned said, "You've *got* to be kidding!"

When the planet Origin disappeared again—along with its *essence*, isomorphs, amazingly evolved humans and all the others who came with it from the twin universe—it also took back with it half the crews from each of the two Cones of Transformation. They chose to go. They were mostly the young adventurers, but a few of the old-timers went too—especially the old, the loveless, and the lonely. For them, the other universe was a *new* universe. As they left, they did so with hopeful smiles on their faces.

Before Origin had again disappeared, Mark and Laura handed off multiple copies of their plan along with the new formulas to those they trusted from the twin universe. The plan, when the time for its use would come, needed to be carried, as before, from one universe to the next, from membrane to membrane, for protection of the multiverse that lay within the universe without opposite—the All-embracing Cosmos.

The next four years were busy for those on the Great Cone of Transformation. Those years were spent exploring planets in the Coma Cluster of galaxies—especially a dozen inhabited planets, and even more that *were once*, but no longer, inhabited. At last, the decision was made to return home. The generalists on those ancient planets—the few planets that *still* had intelligent life and not just microbes—had, by then, totally or virtually destroyed their once thriving environments. There were, however, two planets that managed to step back from the brink to an imperfect but salutary restoration. The dynamic, historical and interactive workings of those two planets were studied in as much depth as they believed necessary.

The Great Cone travelers were now ready for a much smaller arena—the planet they called home. The decision to return to Earth was unanimous. What they had seen and learned could be momentous for their home planet. The living *essences* of the two optimally restored planets not only took on active functions in both restorations, but engaged in direct and personal interventions. "Planets like me," Cy once said, "are not always successful, but we're never passive."

Researchers from the Great Cone now carried with them a unique, but imcomplete understanding and knowledge of those worlds, but they believed it was enough to translate into some kind of help for Gaia. She could not be kept waiting forever. Their "help" would include constructive ways she could use her unique role and powers. She would have to come out of the closet, her cave, and reveal her displeasure—by rattling whatever she chose to use as her saber. The hard choices would still be in the hands of humans, but she could help with those choices in persuasive ways. The recovery would be imperfect. For instance, animal extinctions and other one-way causalities that already occurred could not be reversed. But coordinated human effort to stop any further destruction of habitat Earth would be far better than a violent end to life. That violent end was on Gaia's "immediate agenda"—meaning "in the next thousand Earth years," according to Cy. When found, she would need some serious cajoling to modify the nature of her "to do" list.

Saving the universe—and all the universes within the local multiverse—was one thing.

But now the hard job was about to begin!

Ned took out his pen and began to write:

"THE PLAN TO SAVE THE WORLD;

"STEP ONE, Get Gaia's address from the information capsule. . . . Have Laura and Keeta visit her. . . . Have Gaia visit a few politicians. . . . Run for office yourself. . . ."

After Origin disappeared, Laura did not immediately read again the book that Gegeneis had kept and preserved all those centuries for her in the twin universe. She feared it would stir her recurrent feeling of loss and desolation. The inhabitants of the Great Cone she had been close to for those twenty years were expected to die within days—weeks at most. Even before she was called upon to climb onto that platform and lower her head, she knew that would happen. Before she did so, Ned gave her his most cherished artifact—the original headband she'd worn so many years before.

Unknown to her, before reading his last chapter however, was the "conspiracy;" but she correctly interpreted it less as a conspiracy than a pact—a love pact. With it they would try to save a single life—hers.

One of the groups that formed on the Great Cone had developed a strange idea. They suggested—it was a wild guess—that for the past twenty years they had been in a Crystal World and, if so, someone needed to lift his or her head from that Crystal! They thought it was probably *not* the Crystal in the Great Cone's vault. To figure that out was too paradoxical and complicated; but they did come to believe that the most likely person for their experiment was Laura Shane. None of them had seen anyone else in that initial role. If it was her, she had to lift her head.

The ritual worked out for that could not be casual. If Laura's head lifting was casual, that would be no different than a simple, everyday turn of her head. It had to come from the outside universe—not the one they were experiencing. They had no idea how that could happen. Accordingly their expectation of success was low, but they thought there was nothing to lose, and one life, possibly, to gain. Just before the ritual began, Ned and Laura, with Ellen Stone, let the Great Cone community know that Laura Shane, despite her weight loss, was carrying a pair of twins in her uterus and was near the end of her first trimester. Her tummy was showing a lot more than starvation. The crew of the Great Cone knew there was no chance for them, but now *three lives* made their effort seem even more worthwhile. If it worked, Laura would somehow be gone from the platform. That would signal their success. She would have returned to her location of twenty years before.

One day Laura sat down to reread Ned's account of their long journey together across space and time. On the back of the last page she found this note:

Dearest Laura,

I hope these words may someday be read by you, and not become a pile of faded ink on a crumbling page in this cold void, and that you may read them for the love they send and by which they are written.

If you are reading this now, you made it back across the decades! Then know this, my beloved: It was not just your guy, Ned, who loved you more than life itself, but all of us - we who sent you back. I hope it is a freeing love - to carry you and our babies to safety and life - hug them often for me - and for us all. Goodbye.

Love you forever,
Ned

A spring tide of silent tears welled in Laura's eyes as she caressed the writing. *It's about time he sent me a love letter,* she thought as she wiped away the tears. The children were sad to see their mother cry and gathered near to comfort her. She took them in her arms—her twins, fathered in another world and time, and her son in this one. Her sorrow and her joys were bittersweet.

APPENDICES

Appendix A: Characters

Appendix B: Isomorphs

Appendix C: The "Others"

Appendix D: Miscellaneous

Appendix A:

CHARACTERS

(See Chapter 4 where a number of the characters are introduced.)

~**Humans** (and one **Dort**) are identified by first name in A-Z order, in boldface, or by last name if no first name is given in the book;
 ~next, in parentheses (after the name of the main-heading character) will be the name of his or her significant other, if one is named, or a cross reference may be preceded by "see:"
 ~other details may then be mentioned, but not much if the individual is very minor.
 ~Finally, the last item in an entry is boldfaced and in parentheses. This is the name of his or her **isomorph**, if one is named in the book. (The ones with names are also listed in Appendix B followed by the first name of his/her human in parentheses.)

Anvil. (Ingrid). This is the only man on the transformation who can beat Clinton Bracket in the arm wrestle. (Both Anvil and Ingrid have isomorphs, but names not mentioned.)

Astra Hughs. (Zackery Parker - eventually). She has multiple Ph.D.s and other degrees (but does not use the titles). Due to extensive burns, and the resulting loss of her limbs in infancy, she was finally (in her late teens) fitted with atomic prostheses to supplement her ordinary ones; and, over the years, wore a variety of mask. Here she is a graduate intern in Stanley Lundeen's astrophysics department on the Great Cone of Transformation. Her close friend of many years, *Margaret* Heckart, is also an intern there. (**Venus**).

Brandt, Mr. Proprietor of the Exchange.

Carla ("Mama Carla"). Proprietor of the Emporium of Perfect Pizza.

Cameron Greenberg ("Cam"). Director of Social Dynamics for the Cone; anthropologist. Heads a group that includes several counselors and a variety of scholars in history and the social sciences. He, *Ned* Keller and, especially, *Stanley* Lundeen are close colleagues. Cam smokes a lot of cigars. (**Theseus**).

Clinton Bracket ("Clint"). (Ellen Stone, M.D., Ph.D.) Clint is Head of Security for the Great Cone. He is a stocky, square jawed, ruggedly handsome, thick necked and notably bowlegged, forty year old of average height who projects a gruff, no-nonsense military demeanor. He takes seriously the job of keeping everyone on the Transformation safe, sometimes to the point of insubordination. He heads a very small security detail. (**Dummy**).

Daniels, Mr. Proprietor of the Canteen and Restaurant and its attached grocery store that holds the Base Camp's tons of frozen food and other items.

David Michaels. (Judy). David is a geologist and Director of Geophysics and Mineralogy on the Transformation. He's been protesting the Cones for years (because of the damage they do to planet Earth) before joining the crew this time. Noted for his "ridiculous *non*sense-of-humor." (**Oscar**).

Debra Anderson. (Ernst Berman). This provocatively buxom Scandinavian from a land area on Earth still designated as Louisiana is in charge of *Information and Communications*. She edits and produces the Great Cone's daily newspaper, printed in hardcopy at her insistence, and to the crew's delight, and on the intranet as necessary. She is also skilled in other forms of communication. Later on, the newspaper's title is changed to the FAST News. She personally disparages laptops as lacking the touch of personal immediacy, and instead carries notepads and several multicolored pens with her at all times. (**Enargite**).

Denise Christensen. (Mark). She is a tall, slim, woman with an angular, bespectacled, intelligent face. On the Transformation she called herself a librarian, but was really the expert in charge of data searches—digging out information of all kinds that no one else could, not to mention information that anyone should have been able to find. In that category, Officer Bracket knew her very well. She tends to be prudish in certain public situations. Note the name she gave her isomorph: (**Chastity**).

Douglas Groth (Doug). *Physical Systems Director* for this and previous Transformations. He has a short, round body, red hair with a central balled spot. His walk is better described as "bustling." He is almost always pleasant, but, for good cause (if only in his mind), he was sometimes subject to frightening conniptions. Usually he was very loyal to his fellow Directors and superiors. When the facts (or his interpretation of the facts) went counter to his superior's and their demands, he was not above engaging in serious insubordination—or mutiny. Doug is the guy that makes the Great Cone really click; his responsibilities were staggering. Two main sets of Operations Managers reported to him: **1)** The technical side of the Transformation included particle engineers, plasma engineers, toroidal mass-energy control monitors, biocomputer technicians (Doug himself being one of the world's top hackers when he needed to be—or just felt like it), astro-pilot navigators, and many more. **2)** These Managers saw to the creature comforts for the crew: kitchen and cafeteria, laundry, recreation, etc.

Doyan ("the One," "the Integrator"). This alien is a "Dort." Dorts, by human standards, are "disgusting looking." At the time this story begins, they have been on planet Earth for several centuries. They look like davenport-sized, translucent amoebas. They work in scientific organizations around the globe. Their population grows as they continue to arrive on Earth from some distant planet within the Milky Way. The earliest version of Transformation Theory (a great leap beyond any other physics theory at that time) was brought to Earth by the first Dorts and was handed to mankind on a silver platter.

Dufy. (Nebulena – "Lena"). He is a volunteer worker who operates a crane within the geodesic dome to lift and transfer unvitalized isomorphs into the Keeta pit. His significant other, Lena, calls him "a broken man" and will scold him without mercy; but even so he did manage to write a powerful letter to the editor of the FAST News. It was mostly ignored. (**Alun Caradog Hilarius – "Hilly"**).

Ellen Stone, M.D., Ph.D. (Clinton Bracket). She is a lovely, petite thirty-seven year old physician with an additional Ph.D. in physiology. Despite her relative youth and quiet manner, Ellen is highly competent in her role as Medical Director. Introverted or not, she struggled to keep a relationship going with Officer Bracket who, at least early on and in public, hardly seemed to notice her. She has no trouble keeping her two Operations Managers, Dr. *Roger* Flanders and Dr. *Henri* Lufti busy. (**Littleviolet**).

Elmer Slattery. This man was the Great Cone's Recreation Coordinator. *Doug* Groth recruited him for that job, but after the sudden tragic death of hundreds of Transformation crew members it was necessary to conduct a massive funeral service and Slattery was the only Bible-banger on board. He had been a Chaplain in the army and an undertaker years before that. He quit both professions to get away from bloodshed and cadavers. He hated to be called "Reverend" because he associated the title with death, but regained the title without being asked; but in that role he tried to keep things simple, so there were no embalmings. There was just a simple, dignified service with prayers, songs, commemorative speeches, the playing of taps, a few twenty-one gun salutes and the somber sequential clang of eight bells. The burials took place by ejection of the bodies into space.

Ernst Berman, Ph.D. (Debra Anderson). This Head of *Mathematics and Statistics* is tall and skinny with bony hands and bushy eyebrows. Ernst seldom volunteers an opinion on deep subjects or issues, but when sponsored (usually be Stan) he often contributed freshness and clarity to the discussion; although, as a matter of style, he tended to pontificate.

Everett (see: Harrison)

Floyd Diggins. He is one of *Doug* Groth's creature-comfort Managers charged with the general supervision of the giant, single-roofed habitat called the Mart—a kind of mall on the outskirts of *Mark's Base. It* contains numerous stores, facilities, boutiques and kiosks.

George Sachs, Ph.D. *Personnel Manager.* He and Clint Bracket are best friends, but George is killed early on in a rare space mishap.

Harrison Everett Balz. This gentleman runs a beauty-barber shop—with photography consultation thrown in. He is more active as a photographer and took some terrifying pictures of human-appearing organs stuck in the middle of the hill's crystalline wall.

Henri Lufti, M.D. This physician reports to Dr. *Ellen* Stone and is the Operations Manager for the hospital and clinic on the Transformation.

Ingrid. (Anvil). (They both have isomorphs, not named in the book).

Ivan Fuller. Victim of "attempted murder" by *Kevin* Verily.

Jack Lewis. (Jack's wife remained on planet Earth). *Ned* and *Laura*'s friend, Jack is Ned's "boss" – but only in theory. He is Chairman of 3T's Board of Directors. He is a first-rate biologist. At the time he joined *3T*, he was involved in several other ventures. His main strengths for *3T*'s purposes were in business and political lobbying.

Juan Diaz. Leader of the most popular band on Origin or the Transformation. It's a sextet that plays the tango and other Latin music.

Judy Olafson, Ph.D., (David Michaels). She is *Chief Chemist* on the Great Cone and *Laura* Shane's best friend. She is asthmatic, timid, cautious, sometimes fearful and prone to anxiety attacks. In short, she is the fraidy-cat of the Transformation—although, when it counts, she can be surprisingly brave. She has an unconvincing aversion to profanity. (**Minerva**).

Kevin Verily. (Margaret - now and then). Kevin usually works for *David Michaels* (between firings) as his best geologist and crystallographer. However, he tends to go kind of wild at times, and when grandiose can be a danger to others. (**Nor-Man**).

Laura Shane. (Ned Keller). The young genius who made a major breakthrough in physics with a finishing touch to *Transformation Theory* (see Appendix D). As a result of that, Ned Keller was able to assemble the talented scientists and engineers to create the *Cones of Transformation* on which faster-than-light travel to distant planets and star systems was made possible. (**Keeta**).

"Lena" (See Nebulena).

Lauren McNally. Mentioned briefly, Loren McNally, Ph.D., invented the *tele-micro lens*.

Malcolm Ditwhiler. This extremely obese man is one of *Kevin*'s early recipients of a harsh method for vitalizing isomorphs. (**Fatass**).

Margaret Heckart. (Kevin – in fits and starts). One of the astrophysics interns on the Transformation. She and her friend of many years, *Astra*, are in that program together. (**Opal**).

Mark Tenderloin. (Denise). Mark is another genius, right up there with *Laura* Shane. He came up with the theory of Rio-spheres and its method for traversing space in virtually instant time, rather than creeping along at a limited multiple of faster-than-light speeds. (**Cy**).

Martha Snored, This petulant lady runs the "PMS"—the *Palace Movie Screen* theater.

Melissa. A fine member of the Transformation's dance troupe, of which *Ned* Keller is a part-time participant. Melissa is one of the best dancers there and, although only occasionally there himself, she is his most frequent dance partner.

Monica, (See Mona).

Mona. The tearful lady that was met just outside of the geodesic dome where her isomorph could not be moved from the bleachers. (**Lisa**).

Mortimer Pestle. Pharmacist in charge of the *Apothecary*.

Nebulena ("Lena"), (Dufy). The shrew that harassed Dufy on the raised bridge—from the Dome to *New Camp* (in Appendix D). (**Galatea**).

Ned Keller, (Laura Shane). This nerd-leader of practical Transformations, was once a world-class dancer; but he gave it up to pursue riches and fame as the Founder and Director of 3T Corporation. In that role he administered the effort to create faster-than-light transport vehicles, including the mountainous Cones of Transformation—made theoretically possible by the Theory of Transformation, and made practical by a major advance to that theory by the love of his life, Laura Shane. (**Adon**).

Norbert. One of *Kevin*'s approved escorts; helped Kevin with some experiments.

Orla Nims, Works in the *clerical pool* on the Great Cone of Transformation. She was one of identical twins, but her twin was stillborn. (**Causa** and **Effecta** are identical isomorphs from the same mound).

Patricia, One of *Laura* and *Ned*'s twin girls, conceived in another "world." The other twin is **Rita**. They also had a boy, **Steven**, a year younger than the twins. He was conceived in this world.

Reinholdt Dietzman ("Dietz"), Ph.D. Biologist. A "jovial" gentleman. He and his *Corporation for Biological Studies* have tried to analyze the physiology, chemistry, and other characteristics and abilities of the alien Dorts. They have also handled the usual physical debriefings on returned Transformation crews.

Rita (see: Patricia)

Roger Flanders, M.D. This physician reports to Dr. *Ellen* Stone as one of her Operations Managers. He is on loan from Reinholdt Dietzman's corporation. He also heads the Transformation's Biology and Genetics Program and, once on planet Origin, he takes turns with Dr. Stone in the medical clinic there.

Rosario. A member of the popular sextet band called the "Mariachi Transformers" whose leader is Juan Diaz. They both play a variety of instruments; and each play their own bandoneón. With them, he provides the melody and she the sensuous harmony.

Snow, Ms. Proprietor of the *Honky-tonk Saloon* with its trendy Dance Hall. She is famous for serving special brews of beer and "elixirs," including some very excellent "Moonshine" and her ever-popular "Premium Swill."

Stanley Lundeen, Ph.D., ("Stan"). This bearded, graying and allergy-ridden man is the Director of the *Astrophysics and Astronomy Department* on the Great Cone and also shares the management of *Navigation* with the Transformation's *Physical Systems Director, Doug* Groth. Stan has a small group reporting to him and several graduate students on internships. *Cameron* Greenberg often hangs out in Stan's office.

Steven (see: Patricia)

Waldo Wagson. This gentleman is the proud supervisor of the Transformation's laundry room and an avid writer of letters to the editor for the *FAST News* (see Appendix D).

Wolfe. One of the last few to vitalize his isomorph. **(Lycus)**.

Zackery Parker, ("Zack"), (Astra Hughs - in due course). Zack is a supervising engineer who heads one of its key groups. He was a dropout from his last year of medical internships. He had been in psychiatry, but switched to pathology, and then to engineering. He switched to pathology for two reasons—his identification with patients was too intense and because he thought pathology was more scientific. He switched to engineering from pathology for two reasons—too intense identification with cancer and other tissue-diseased patients, and his increasing vision problems. The latter made tissue examination difficult, even when displayed on large screens. He required surgery and thick glasses that made him look scary. He tended to be claustrophobic. When he saw a picture of his isomorph in the FAST News he admired it (and so, himself): the strong jaw, broad shoulders, adequate manhood, solid bony structure, and no glasses. **(Gegeneis)**.

Appendix B:

ISOMORPHS

Isomorph's name (in boldface)
followed by name of human identical.

Adon, (Ned).
Alun Caradog Hilarius ("Hilly"), (Dufy).
Causa (and twin, Effecta), (Orla).
Chastity, (Denise).
Cy, (see: essence of Origin).
Dummy, (Clint).
Effecta (and twin, Causa), (Orla).
Enargite, (Debra).
essence of Origin, (Mark).
Fatass, (Malcolm).
Galatea, (Nebulena).
Gegeneis, (Zackery).
"Hilly," (see: Alun).
Keeta, (Laura).
Lisa, (Mona).
Littleviolet, (Ellen).
Lycus, (Wolfe).
Minerva, (Judy).
Nor-Man, (Kevin).
Opal, (Margaret).
Oscar, (David).
Theseus, (Cameron).
Venus, (Astra).

Appendix C:

The "Others"
(See Chapter 75 for most of these details.)

Included here is the name (or nickname), and brief description, of beings from diverse planets in the Milky Way that ended up under hollow hills on planet Origin, (along with a few relevant terms: "Associates," "colonists," and "dissidents").

Assemblages: These are made up of mindless, less than stupid, *grubthings* that become highly intelligent *as a unit* when they come together in one of their giant *stacks*; but are especially enlightened (to the point of actual luminescence that can becomes as blinding as the sun) when they all gather into one massive Assemblage. Even in the smaller *piles* they were by far the most useful, creative and prolific theoreticians brought to Origin by the Dorts.

Associates: Individuals and small groups of Others, including Clint and Dummy (no longer in a hill), who violated orders to stay in their hills and out of the way of the negotiator-scientists. These dissidents followed a low profile, passive-aggressive style to express their anger at being among the societies of abductees. They would resist Cy's call for cooperation. Clint and Dummy established close contacts with a dozen such groups, especially the cohort of dissidents from the most unyielding, hard-core holdouts. Clint named that cohort his "Associates."

colonists: These communities of Others are, or were, trapped (and usually saved) within one of the egg-shaped hills. Until Cy brought the hill-colonists together, none were aware of the existence of any other separate groups.

dissidents (See: Associates)

Dorts (See **Doyan** in Appendix A)

farts: David gave this nickname to these bloated, insectlike *Others*. Among them were many brilliant mathematical theorists. The rest of their members were exceptional in other ways. They were one of a number of *swarm* colonies that could fly like the wind. These were enveloped by inflated outer-body membranes. In the wake of their flights, they left odorless trails of greenish coloration and shot like guided missiles across the sky. David obsessed, in his way, about the possible environmental impact of fart pollution by greenhouse gas propulsion.

fishbowlers: Unusual creatures that reside and move in large, acid-filled, transparent jugs. These containers do the ambulating with robotic spider legs. Within each container, a stringy, pulsating, gelatinous, multi-eyed creature communicated with its fellows by myriad random-looking eye rolling, winks and crossings.

grubthings: Are slimy with the size and shape of grubworms, but are even less mindful. (See: *Assemblage*)

humans: Just another group of intelligent beings kidnapped by the Dorts and brought to planet Origin where, for a time, they were protected by the surrounding shell of a crystalline hill. For sheer intelligence among the other Others, humans were not far below the Organists, but mainly above the rest—although humans were among the last intelligent beings to appreciate the looming threat of the redshift going wild to become the Big Rip.

matrix beings: These remarkable scientists and mathematicians had multiple layers of rows and columns by which they ambulated and made their calculations.

nocturnals: Night creatures that can *dreamscape* (see Appendix D) directly—without isomorphs of their own.

organists: A society of Others given this nickname because they looked and sounds like bagpipes. They walked on their tooting horns.

Origin: This thinking, conscious planet was "*terraformed*" by worker Dorts to create those very attributes. Accomplishment of this task took eons. When completed, the planet was finally enlightened by the force engulfing the *twin universes*. (See also: "*Terraform*", and *Triad* in Appendix D.)

Others, the: Communities of intelligent beings (including *humans*) that had been kidnapped by the Dorts from many planets in the Galaxy and were eventually brought to an island on Origin in their flying, half-empty, *egg-hills*—hills that had earlier protected them from an environmental disaster. Humans were the first arrivals to The Island (on their own and without the burden of a hill—unlike the other Others). Although none of the new arrivals were remotely humanoid or apelike in appearance or movement, they were all capable, in some fashion, of locomotion or ambulation. Among them were *swarms* that could fly—mostly with winglike appendages, but some swarms propelled themselves by expelling large internal volumes of rapidly manufactured organic gasses. David called one of those communities *farts*. In fact, most of the Others appeared either bloated or skeletal, with humans somewhere between.

shape-shifters: Those in this group emit no sounds or unpleasant odors. They communicated by visibly changing shape. They never stop "talking." Unfortunately, even their highest scientific echelons were inefficient because they had to spend hours in "talk" therapy every day to deal with identity issues—as did their shape-shifting therapists. To mellow out, it is striking to see them in therapy groups, all talking at once. Miraculously, even the *Associates* managed to communicate, at least minimally, with the remarkable help of a pair of *dissident* shape-shifters. As universal translators, they were masters at projecting, communicating and interpreting all manner of expressive movements, gestures, body language, and other nonverbal, non-sound meanings. As quick studies, they soon learned to read and interpret "facial" expressions and the "lips" of most of the Others—easiest of all, the humans. When these frenetic shape-shifters did calm down, they turned from rapid-spiking, corkscrewing and internal cavity formation to more orderly, slow-flowing waves of hypnotically spiraling twists, coiling and uncoiling with a systematic cadence, their hook-shaped waves settled to slow and soothing ripples.

stacks (or **piles**): Colonists from an egg-hill that are very small, but count in the billions. (For example, see *Assemblage*, above.)

stinkers: Communicate by projecting smells, pheromones and chemicals—some of which are intolerably foul, but others quite pleasant.

swarms: A class of egg-hill societies (*farts* being an example) that are flying, insect-size creatures. Unlike the farts, most of them fly using winglike appendages, the farts by propulsion.

Appendix D:

Miscellaneous

Departments, Events, Gizmos, Machines, Materials, Organizations, Places, Planets, Processes, Stores, Vocabulary

Designation of one or another of the above is in boldface (e.g., **arena**). Cross references are in the following format: "(see:...)" *or* in italics in the body of the subsequent note (e.g., *Base Watchers*).

Administrative and Security habitat: Just beyond the outsized *Mart* are various medium-sized structures. Of those, the most important one is the Administration and Security habitat (the *"Ad-Sec."*) It houses offices and other space for the Directors and their meetings; a small jail; storage areas for cots, gun cabinets and a hundred other things. Not far from the Ad-Sec facility are other technical and service facilities, clinic and labs, a few individual habitats and, of course, the Saloon.

Ad-Sec (see: Administrative and Security habitat)

arena: Here, at noon one day, in a circuslike atmosphere, the last isomorph vitalization of the hill-bound citizens took place. It became an event of entertainment and high drama for everyone trapped under the hill's big tent, including the previously vitalized isomorphs. In one night they built two sets of tiered bleachers with a promenade path between them laid with a patchwork carpet of large pink and blue squares—because the quartzlike slab covering the figure prevented determination of its sex. Other *Base Watchers* helped build the frame and draw curtain for the unveiling.

Base camp (see: Mark's Base camp location)

Base Watchers: Due to a perceived survival risk, nearly everybody on *Base camp* got into this group, including two of the Directors: Clint Bracket, who became their top man, and David Michaels. Thanks to Everett Balz's anatomical horror photographs and other sensitive information leaked by David's geology crew, they were alerted to a likely danger for which they undertook a 24/7 vigil. It came about after its members saw the pictures of body parts imbedded in the wall of the crystal hill. They would guard the hill (and its many proliferating mounds) from damage by all the crazies that might wish them ill. Their new role: Base camp security! They'd been told that a badly damaged hill, or small mound, would bring down the entire hill and kill them all, so they had to protect the hill and the mounds. In their eyes, those revelations made Everett and David heroes. In their honor, they named their high-alert effort, the "Michaels-Balz Vigil"—later, however, Dr. Michaels admitted privately that he hated that honorary name.

Big Bang (see also: virtual universes): The explosion of the littlest dot. It blew up and created the universe we all know and love. From that explosive moment, the universe has continued to evolve for the last 13.7 billion years.

Big Rip (see also: entropy): When the redshift became volatile, and when very star, every galactic gas and dust cloud, and every solid object in the universe is not only on the verge of disassembling outward (exploding), but when it does, that would be extreme entropy: the Big Rip.

blueshift (see: redshift/blueshift)

blue-shifter (see: twin universe)

Blue Belt Orb (see: Homing Pigeons)

caboose: On a monitor within Mark's *Homing Pigeon*, he could watch the Orb's rear view without engaging the caboose function. By opening a small panel labeled "caboose" and pressing a pad beneath it, the *Orb* would pivot the pilot, passengers and cargo 180 degrees to the rear without changing course. The entire lower interior of the Orb would make that 180 degrees reversal, leaving the front cockpit behind them. Instead of a forward view, it became a rear view—as if in the caboose of a flying freight train.

camp (see: Mark's Base camp location)

Central Park: It is similar to, but less expansive than the *Commons* area, and more convenient to the center of *Mark's Camp*. In that location they sank a deep well that yielded all the salt water anyone could ever want. It is in that area and around that well, that the *pyramid* was built.

Chem-Geol habitat (see: Chemistry and Geology lab)

Chemistry and Geology lab: This facility is also called the Chem-Geol lab (or habitat). Judy and David do most of their scientific work there, and it is where they live together when they are on planet Origin. Their habitat is not far from Ellen's clinic and equally close to the *Ad-Sec* habitat.

chips (see: hill chips)

cliffs (see: Mark's Base camp location)

Commons: A "grassy," (see *plantoids*), parklike area between the *Mart* and the *Ad-Sec*. It was used for picnics, mass meetings, orations, band concerts and the like. Later on, however, most of those activities took place in *Central Park*.

Cones (see: Cones of Transformation and **Great Cone of Transformation)**

Cones of Transformation: Ned's *3T Corporation* used the most recent advances in *Transformation Theory* to produce the first brood of these gigantic, cone-shaped creations. They were described in the world's media as the "ultimate spaceships." One of the "smaller" ones might simply be called a "Cone." The most recent one (by far the most advanced and enormous of these) is variously called the "Great Cone of Transformation," the "Great Cone," "Transformation Cone," or simply the "Transformation." It is a conical chunk of planet Earth many kilometers across on its circular surface, its base, and extends downward from there sixty-four kilometers to the vertex. In the first instant of a Transformation's maiden launch, after an irreversible ten-hour countdown, the Cone's great mass is expelled at ultraCeleric speed (faster than C, the speed of light) from Mother Earth—including everything on it, over it, and in it—minerals, people, atmosphere, trees, everything. In that moment of launch, a Cone is transformed from one set of familiar dimensions into another—and is gone—leaving behind a hole in the Earth of indescribable immensity. With few exceptions, such a cruising Cone is highly stable, maintaining its internal integrity down to the last quark and beyond. The only possible instabilities are during its ten-hour countdown, or in an unlikely encounter with a *Twister*. If a countdown were stopped before completion, the entire Cone would instantly dissolve into a radioactive lake of goo. Cruising Transformations never take place in ordinary space because the particles that make up the Cone, and everybody and every thing in and on it, are just so many transformed quanta and forces, sailing along in a sea of energy within another reality—another dimension in an alternate membrane of the universal All. There are kilometers of subterranean corridors deep below the surface in every Transformation Cone, including the monumental spaces needed for mass-energy conversion generators and, especially in the Great Cone, space required for the living and work areas for its crew of several thousand.

Crazy Canyon: This flat-based tunnel was deep within the *Great Cone of Transformation*. It was an unused, but gigantic excavation the Dorts had secretly begun years before the Great Cone was launched from planet Earth. The humans discovered it two weeks into their mission. The burrow came to be called Crazy Canyon for good reason—"Canyon" for it's size, and "Crazy" for the river that ran along the groove of its parabolic ceiling—where the gravity had reversed halfway up. They called it *Crazy River* not only for its gravity-defying appearance, but for its periodic transition from a small trickle to a raging torrent. The circular cavern covered a great distance around the inside of the Great Cone. It ran in a complete circle, like the upper half of a peaked, oversized, split bagel. Its center enclosed a solid rock diameter of many kilometers that could have held hundreds of *mass-energy converters*. The Dorts possibly abandoned it for lack of time before the launch; but more likely because advancing technology had given them something just as powerful.

Crystal Library of Time: This reasonably light-weight, crystalline, faceted sphere was, for carrying purposes, an awkward two-thirds of a meter in diameter. It was given to Laura by Astra's isomorph, Venus. "Keep it safe," she said to Laura, "for the history it carries and the worlds within worlds it holds." *Headbands* and the crystal globe belonged together, the band being something like a library card providing access to its interior where, if one chose, experiences of many lifetimes could be lived before returning, in seconds, to this universe.

dark energy (see: redshift/blueshift)

DCC (see: Directors Control Center)

Directors Control Center: Once in range of *The Island*, the shuttle and Orb vehicles maneuvered to a preselected strand of shoreline at the base of one of its mountains to unload their cargos where the supply camp would be set up. Two large habitats were erected: one for general equipment, supplies, maintenance, fuel storage and other purposes; and the second, called the "Directors' Control Center—the *DCC*. The vehicles would also carry essential science staff to and from their duties on other parts of The Island. Those duties included tracking the *pointers of molecular resonance*, communicating that data to the DCC where simple triangulation would locate the intersecting lines in order to accomplish their main mission—to find the *essence of Origin*. The DCC would house all the specialized technical and scientific requirements for that mission, including a wide-ranging plan for the collection of other hard data, including measurement of gravitational anomalies, depth and density measures and much more. It would also house other supporting units.

D-day: The **d**ay the *hill* was **D**estroyed.

disks: (1) Inside the *geode*, a circle of fifty color-changing data control disks surround the *Integrator* (see: *Doyan* in Appendix A) who extends fifty translucent arms to touch them as necessary. The raised disks are color-changing lights that indicate mechanical events occurring throughout the *Great Cone*. By touching the disks, *the One* (see: Doyan) coordinates everything from that spot. It provides the feedback and direction to handle dozens of routine problems and make on-the-spot adjustments and corrections to notable problem (but much repair must be on location); and to change the speed or direction of the Great Cone. **(2)** Large, quartzlike disks became exposed when hundreds of mounds that were covering unvitalized isomorphs shed their crystals. The mounds were gone, but the semitransparent disks still covered the figure in the hollow below. As isomorphs were vitalized, the quartzlike disk covers became available for other uses: e.g., building the *pyramid* and the *dome*.

Dome (see: Geodesic Dome)

Doppler (see: redshift/blueshift)

dreamers, the (see: nightscape): Those who *dreamscape*: Dorts, isomorphs, the *essence of Origin* and some nocturnal *Others*.

dreamscape (see: nightscape):

echo-hunters: People who shout phrases to see how complex a sound they can get back from *plantoids*, near or far. They listened for the quality of echoes after a good shout. They yelled especially loud to be distinctly "heard" above the incessant noise of the surrounding plantoids. On the rare occasions that the wind stopped momentarily, there was still an underlying hum of vibrations and residual echoes—all from the plantoids themselves. Were it not just meaningless clatter, one could imagine a rich form of communication was taking place. David thought so.

entropy: *Positive entropy* is like too much LDL cholesterol—BAD! It can cause problems. But, as we all know, Humpty Dumpty's cholesterol was the least of his problems. (Consider the astronomy acronym EGG: Evaporating Gaseous Globule.) Think of entropy as the disorder in a system, like if you drop a glass and it shatters on the floor (so it is no longer the organized entity it was), or like the endless acceleration and expansion of the universe (endless expansion to the point not only of its galaxies flying apart from one another, and the stars within them exploding, but the eventual dissolution of everything, including even the smallest quantum entities of the microworld). *Negative entropy*, on the other hand, is like having a good cholesterol balance with enough of the HDL's—that's the GOOD stuff! The stuff that Mrs. Chicken Dumpty pecked at and ate became organized into Humpty. That's negative entropy, just like the growth of a rosebush or newborn stars coming from the stellar nurseries in clouds of dense gas and dust light-years across. Energy is required to organize eggs and stars, but that is energy that is lost from somewhere else. Current theories insist that, in the end, the BAD will win. If that came sooner rather than later, and if that were very soon and instantaneous, we'd be talking about the possibility of extreme entropy: the *Big Rip*!

Exchange, the: This facility, located within the *Mart*, is headed by a Mr. Brandt. It carries large quantities of fuel, cement, tons of steel rods to anchor habitats, other hardware, and everything else from intranet wall screens to habitat furniture and parts.

FAST News: Debra Anderson renamed her newsletter The FAST News and was proud of the new format. Everyone was reading it. Even the Dorts had a subscription. Before the *Great Cone* reached Origin it was simply the Daily. It continued to be printed in hardcopy (at her insistence) and on the intranet.

flatland (see: Mark's Base camp location; New Camp)

Flora: "Flora" was the name Mark gave to the mound that happened to appear, and later to mature, in his habitat. He said it gave off a florescent light.

GBS (see: Great Bull Session)

geode, the: We have all admired the beauty of these nearly spherical, hollow rocks that we call geodes, encrusted with layers of flawless crystals that adorn their inner surfaces. Magnify that image to the size of a futuristic spherical planetarium or stadium larger than anyone on earth has yet seen, and you have in mind the geode of the Dorts, deeply ensconced in the *Great Cone*. The geode's crystalline surface is safe for most isomorphs. Like *Crazy Canyon*, this geode's gravitational pull reverses halfway up, with a thin stratum between those pulls where an item, or a Dort, would be weightless—and graceful!

Geodesic Dome: Before *D-day*, shortly after the *pyramid* was built, the *dome* was built using most of the remaining *disks* that had covered the isomorphs before vitalization.

Great Conversation, the: This interchange of ideas and opinions was an Origin-wide stimulus, sparked by Mark's dream. (See nightscape.) Humans sensed and enjoyed the informality coming through in this flow of ideas, and they even appreciated its disagreements and thoughtful, but intense, arguments. Humans could not, of course, dreamscape directly, but did participate in the planet's give and take through contact with their isomorphs. For them, the intense and far-ranging discussions were better than the pomp of any "Great Conversation," as it was called by some. Rather, it felt more like a "Great Bull Session"—in a good ol' college dorm.

Great Cone of Transformation (see: Cones of Transformation)

Great Bull Session (see: Great Conversation, the)

headbands: "It's a very special headband," Gegeneis said to Keeta. "Try it on, and give one to Laura." ... "In order to be 'in' the *Crystal Library*," Venus said, "one of the headbands must be worn on the reader's head, across the forehead, and then placed so as to touch the Crystal. ... Another person wearing one of the headbands and touching your hand with his or her own banded forehead will also experience being 'in' the Crystal—right there with you. There are several hundred bands in that bag. Everyone touching another person's hand in the same way, even in a long series—like Christmas tree lights—can experience the Crystal. They'd all be in the Library together. ... The Crystal Library is for enlightenment, not darkness. Once there, everybody can go their own way. Your experiences will not be identical."

hill: (1) On the surface of the *Great Cone of Transformation* there is one hill on which Laura's estate exists and where her home was built—even before the Cone left planet earth.

(2) On planet Origin the landscape includes complex topography, including foothills that lead to mountains, and numerous ordinary-looking hills; but some nearby hills were unusual—like gigantic, one and two kilometer-high lopsided bubbles, domes or middens. Unlike the mountains, they carried no "trees" or other plantlike objects, but their crystalline, lustrous colors glistened with a beauty of their own. David Michaels showed by analyzing core samples taken from some of their wide bases that they were at least thirteen million years old (young by Earth standards); but that by drilling all the way through those rigid crusts, the entire crust of the hill would crumble immediately or within minutes, leaving uneffected the ugly, deformed inner crystals that, over time, had filled those once-empty domes. Hills were still there, but now they looked strip-mined; they glistened no more.

(3) During a devastating environmental crisis, Mark's camp was mysteriously saved by the sudden growth of one of the hollow hill crusts (described in "(2)" above). Many other such hills were created during the same crisis. The hill completely covered Mark's camp, trapping everybody within it.

hill chips: David looked into Judy's bag and noticed a half-dozen other crystal-like items. He held one up. "Why did you include these? They aren't *strings*." ... "They look pretty, so I just collected some. I don't know what kind of crystals they are, do you?" . . . "Yes. They're chips off the hill wall—from strings hitting them. We're lucky they were just random hits on the wall to spread out the damage. If too many hits were in one place, the hill could have been wrecked—us along with it." . . . "This chip, and all the chips from the hill are self-contained systems, like the hill as a whole. They're hill-dependent only when they are systemically a part of it. After the strings knocked the hunks out, each hunk became its own system, unrelated to the fate of the hill."

Homing Pigeons: Mark's name for his flying Orbs.

Honky-tonk Saloon (see Saloons)

i3T: "individual Transport Through Transformation." This and other early inventions out of Ned's *3T Corporation* comprised its cash cow. The i3T made it possible to transit inanimate and animate objects between linked platforms. The platforms could be stationed at home or office and linked to other platforms on or off the planet. In practice, such transports took only minutes or seconds. . . . For animate objects, like people, the user-friendly i3Ts created subjectively invisible spacetime corridors between platforms. Distant platforms could be dialed as easily as a radio station or a cell phone number. More customers came forward as 3T's innovations became more reliable and, in this case, fewer were lost between platforms. Laura called i3T's "mere toys."

Island, The: Island in one of Origin's oceans. The *essence of Origin* is there.

Keeta pit (see: Kiva, for comparison): The Keeta pit is where Laura's isomorph of the same name came to be, and where Keeta (named for Laura's beloved parakeet when she was a child) was the last to be vitalized by those still trapped under the hill. After the hill came down, the population from the Great Cone chose, as a matter of tradition by then, to vitalize their own isomorphs in that same pit. (Their own pits were no longer available.)

Kiva (see: Kita pit): A "kiva," by the most ancient tradition, is a large, circular ceremonial chamber made by Pueblo Indians of the Southwest US. These partly or wholly underground chambers are entered by ladder. In its floor there is yet another circular opening—a small one. This cavity symbolizes an opening to the lower world and the place through which life itself came into the world—indeed, the tribe's place of origin. Multiple kivas in individual villages are not unusual. Kivas have been the province of men only. The women have their own meeting places—but not in kivas. Kivas, in the numerous SW Pueblo communities, are still very much in use to this day.

Library of Time (see: Crystal Library of Time)

Mardi Gras: A several day long "Mardi Gras" party to celebrate *D-day*.

Mark's Base camp location: A lowland area on planet Origin that Mark selected for his own temporary camp. It was soon seen by the *Cone's* astrophysicists and the Directors as an excellent place to set up their own temporary community until the spacetime location of planet Earth could again be found. The camp was on the southern coastline of the largest continent, ten degrees north of Origin's equator. Mark's bivouac area, before and after it became a virtual city of inflated habitats, continued to be called a "camp" or "Mark's Base camp." It was on a small, flat, coastal lowland at the terminus of a narrow inlet flanked on east and west by vertical escarpments. The steep east and *west cliffs* continued beyond the beach and past the Base camp for some kilometers. The *flatland* (also called the *lowland*) was not far above ocean level at high tide and the popular beach could easily be reached on foot. The narrow salt water cove led directly south from the beach for a dozen kilometers into a wide bay and finally to the gulf of a great sea. With only *Nimbus*, its sun, and no moon, and its slowly changing proximity to the *globular star cluster*, Origin's ocean tides were (initially) considered inconsequential. The lowland extended north from the inlet for several uneven kilometers in all directions, like a small, gerrymandered district. The camp occupied only a small fraction of that area. The flatland fanned out into the distance, northward from there. It was surrounded near the cliffs by a "forest" of treelike structures and, farther out, by hills. There were mountains that could be seen in the distance. Their peaks did not appear strange from far off, but the many, more nearby hills, looked unusual—like gigantic, lopsided bubbles, domes or middens. Unlike the mountains, they carried no "trees" or other *plantoid* objects, but their lustrous colors glistened with a beauty of their own.

Mart: A giant, single-roofed habitat that serves as a kind of mall on the outskirts of *Mark's Base Camp* on the Planet Origin. Assembled within it are a variety of boutiques and kiosks and a number of relatively large facilities including a Bar and Grill Complex, the Honky-tonk Saloon the Palace Movie Screen, the Canteen and Restaurant, (and its attached grocery store), the Apothecary, the Exchange, a beauty-barber shop (with photography consultation on the side), and the Emporium of Perfect Pizza.

mass-energy converters: *Cones of Transformation*—making use, in part, of the fact that energy equals mass times the speed of light squared—acquire their own great energy by means of internal torus (donut shaped) or spiral "mechanisms" that "borrow" (convert) a portion of the mass-energy from a nearby body of much greater mass, such as a star or planet.

Mutuals: A word humans and isomorphs came, one day, to call themselves. A pair of identicals are Mutuals. Isomorphs and humans as a group are Mutuals.

multiverse: Don't miss the main problem in this novel; it has major implications for the object of this word. Note this assertion: In the vastness of All that is, *this* universe was possible—along with a likely infinite number of other universes. So here it is, our universe, along with the rest of them.

Let's presume that, like local clusters of galaxies, there are clusters of universes, some (or all) of which may (or may not) overlap in consequential ways. Each universe may (or may not) have similar or entirely different laws of nature. The cluster this universe is in, is called a multiverse. It is one of many.

negative entropy (see: entropy)

negative gravity (see: redshift/blueshift)

New Camp: The new *Mark's Base camp location*, on the same flatland, but just east of where the destroyed hill's debris left off.

nightscape: (Also called dreamscape.) The jagged crystalline crust of Origin is a vast network of communication whereby, for example, the isomorphs, who lie naked at night on that surface of tiny daggers, send and receive messages; impressions; knowledge; and empathic, sinful feelings. "Things so painful must be wrong," Keeta once said to Laura, and "I am no longer physically attached to Origin, except by gravity and by nightly dreamscapes." At night, awake or asleep, humans became accustom to having a scattered periphery of recumbent isomorphs on the surface around their habitats, dimly, and sometimes bright with crackling sounds, they illuminated the area with their sparks and scintillations as they entered deep dreamscape. Keeta is only one of the dreamers. The same use of that network is shared by Dorts, certain Others, and the essence of Origin; as well as hierarchies of crystalline layers within the crust of Origin itself. There, dreamscape visions were powerful because of their directness, but none before were as powerful as the direct "translation" of Mark's dream into the system. Venus passed it forward. It was the beginning of the *Great Conversation*. Once it was out there, every mountain, crevice and granule on Origin's crust became sensitized to receive every related elaboration—true or false—waking even the merest fragments of consciousness in the smallest crystals. Venus regarded the quick response to it from Origin as intended to prevent the spread of dreamscape rumors and planet-wide amplification and distortion of information through the present and coming night's of dreamscapes—within that ultimate rumor mill.

Nimbus: Stan told his friends, ". . . we gave a name to Origin's sun. We astrophysicists can name things like that. The rest of you can't. It's not allowed. . . . It's 'Nimbus' from now on—because of that halolike corona we saw when we got here. . . . And the Origin-Nimbus system will simply be the 'Origin System.' As astrophysicists—" . . . "Yeah, we know," Clint interrupted, "you guys get to name all the stuff out there." . . . "Right!"

"Now" (compared to "Time"): It's a cliché, but true: Only now exists—depending on how one may consider time. (Is a sloth's time like yours and mine?) The now is powerful. Every past and future event is packed into this now-moment. When the past was now, it held an infinite number of potential future branches, as does this now-moment. (And this one . . . and this one, and . . . .) Rather than viewing time from a sloth's point of view, take instead your average electromagnetic radiation, like light, or its particle form, the photon. It knows all about now. As it hurries past you, it may throw you a nice particle-wave good bye. It's always in a hurry and travels at the only speed it knows—the speed of light. At that speed, time stands still. In its travels, it never "experiences" time, only the eternal now. In a billion light years it will be somewhere. If nothing interacts with it along the way, it will keep on going. It will get there in no time, wherever it goes. That billion-year span will not go by—not for it. It is always simply there, in its now. That's one way of looking at the relative nature of time. Time is not a static, unchanging thing—it all depends on who or what you are, and may even be different in a different universe.

obelisk (see pyramid)

Orbs (see Homing Pigeons)

Pigeon (see Homing Pigeons)

pit (see: Keeta pit)

plantoids: Crystalline, plant-like objects on planet Origin.

pointers of molecular resonance: An increasing number of unwelcome communications blackouts were occurring between the *Transformation Cone* and *Mark's Base* on Origin. They lasted minutes or hours, and up to a day or more. Experts were tracking down the cause of the blackouts. (More accurately, they were locating the direction from which the problem was coming—its source.) The blackouts only occurred during times when the planet's surface electromagnetism became directionally coherent and unique; but opposite the normal N-S magnetic poles. Compasses worked correctly even at those times, but normal electronic communication was obliterated with those opposite-polarity events. They discovered that during blackouts the electrons and nuclei within the molecules of all surface crystals evidenced nuclear magnetic resonance. Their spin resonance changed. Study of this reached far across the planet. They sampled the anomalous surface electromagnetic changes all the way up, down and across both of Origin's major continents and from poll to poll. They found a pattern of directional pointers that led to a series of circum-Origin lines that intersected obliquely in two locations on opposite sides of Origin—both on the equator. One intersection was in the middle of the planet's largest ocean, and the other in the middle of a mountainous island. The latter led to the source of the problem.

Pub (see: Saloons)

Pyramid: This hollow tower was being built in the shape of an *obelisk*, but everybody called it a pyramid. It was built to protect everybody from the falling hill when it collapsed. Its apex would be directly below the crown of the hill itself, which was known to be the thinnest part of the hill and would bring the least debris down on the new tower. The problem with this initiative was its quartzlike surface. Those structural surfaces could not hold. Although they were harder than the makeup of the hill itself, the slabs could not withstand that much sudden force, even from the thinnest part of the hill. Other possibilities would have to be considered.

redshift/blueshift: When one looks at the light spectrum of a star, galaxy or supernovae, and the lines of color are shifted toward the red, it is called a "redshift." The more those lines are redshifted, the faster that object and the observer are moving away from each other. If the lines are shifting toward the blue, it is called a "blueshift" and means the object and the observer are moving toward each other. The more the blueshift, the faster they are approaching each other. These spectral changes are often called *Doppler* effects or shifts, after the Australian physicist, C. J. Doppler, who predicted this light effect. At very great distances, the scientific measurement of "high-redshift supernovae" demonstrates that the expansion of the universe is rapidly accelerating (rather than merely expanding more slowly). This is thought to be caused by "dark energy" (the push of negative gravity, not gravitational attraction). Expansion of the entire universe (rather than star movement within galaxies) causes most of the redshift variance. The more distant galaxies are moving away faster than those nearby. Very distant galaxies with their supernovae (when they deign to show themselves) are accelerating away form us and each other at rising rates of speed; but, like us, they're really just going along for the ride on the expansion of the universe.

reversal: Refers to changing the *redshift* to a *blueshift* and vice versa between *twin universe*s under threat by the forces that create those shifts—and correction of all other such potential imbalances throughout the *multiverse*.

Saloons: There are two such taverns on the Great Cone of Transformation. The Pub and the Honky-tonk Saloon. The latter, being the most popular, was moved to Planet Origin along with most of the Transformation's crew. It was especially known for its dance hall, tinkling player piano and special brews.

Settlement Planets: The first stop for the Dorts before they began to arrive on planet Earth. Those planets were also the first planned destinations for mankind's *Cones of Transformation.*

south cove (see: Mark's Base camp location)

stadium (see: arena; and pit)

strings: As part of a natural protection for the developing, and as yet unvitalized isomorphs, these hard, thin, javelinlike crystals would shoot violently and randomly from their mounds. This happened when the mounds completed shedding their crystal walls and spilled out their yellowish, watery interiors.

tele-micro lens: The tele-micro lens allows microscopic observations across long distances. With the device one could observe anything down to the size of a microbe as far away as the moon from Earth. Here's how Laura describes it: "It isn't a lens anyway—it's an extension of Transformation Theory. It sends out nested parallel sets of 'blanks' from a Transformation field and then returns them 'loaded,' so light coming from the distant object is unnecessary. The transmitted 'blank field' literally finds the object, 'loads up' on it, and brings back the three dimensional image almost instantly by returning through the incoming negatives, or blanks—very similar to the way Jack got here today, and similar to this whole Transformation, except that Transformation Cones use only the 'loaded' Fields. In theory, we could bring an object back to our lab without the need of a 'loaded' Transformation Field at the source."

"terraform": This word used without the quotation marks, refers to making another planet similar to Earth's by greening it with plants, etc. In this book, with the quotation marks in place, it refers to the resurfacing of planet Origin with highly connected and diverse crystals obtained from the twin universe. Thus, the above-and-below water areas (continents, islands, ocean floors, and the like) consist mainly of crystals that are "not from around here," giving those structures qualities that human scientists could not fully analyze (with the exception of salt). Some of the crystals did create "sandy" beaches and crystalline, plantlike growths (plantoids). Origin had breathable air, but the planet was, from a human perspective, no more than a glittering wasteland—deader than any desert on Earth and as lifeless as our moon.

Theory of Everything: The final, final theory in physics. It consolidates the laws of physics for every universe in the local multiverse into a single, elegant and beautiful theory no matter how different their physical laws may be from one universe to another.

3T Corporation: Ned's company where, with a talented crew of engineers and scientists, the first *i3T*'s and *Cones of Transformation* were created.

Time (see: Now)

TOE: (See: Theory Of Everything.**)**

Transformation theory: The most advanced physics theory mankind had ever known. It was handed over freely by the Dorts when they first began to arrive on Earth; although it was later improved from there—by humans; and still later by *Others*.

transformation (see: Transformation theory and **Cones of Transformation)**

Triad: Refers to Cy, Origin, and the Dorts—the Triad of interuniverse beings. They were created in a neverland realm of engulfing energy that enwrapped our twin universes from their beginning. For the Triad, the two universes were interchangeable; they were denizens of both. Our conjoined *twin*—that other universe—bore exceptional time compression. By choice, any one of the Triad could leave this universe for a millisecond or more, and return at will. While gone from here for that moment, it can experience *years* in the other universe. To get from here to there, they lower the barrier that keeps them suspended here, exposing them to condensed time in the other universe—compared to that in ours—thus allowing time for complex tasks.

twin universe: A second universe, invisible to ours, but overlapping this one. Ours is in the midst of *redshift* and the other universe is in blueshift. Time in the two universes is astronomically different.

Twister: The result of a close encounter with a supermassive black hole by a *Cone* (not to be confused with Roger Penrose's "twistor theory.")

virtual universes (see: Big Bang) Stupendous fistfuls of potentialities whose entities exist in another dimension—a timeless realm where their combinations may evolve to the point of bursting into actual universes. (Or perhaps a couple well-evolved branes crashed together?) Consider "evolve" the operative word for what happens "before" a *Big Bang*. In a timeless realm a lot of evolution can happen randomly or otherwise. (One may "reasonably"—a human bias, or a bias of the universal All?—suspects that the random stuff goes nowhere; unless, of course, you believe that enough monkeys really could type out the complete works of Shakespeare.)

vitalization: The bringing into being of an isomorph.

west cliff (see: Mark's Base camp location)

WD's (see: Win-Field Diagrams)

Win-Field Diagrams: In this document, that strange form of gravity—negative gravity (antigravity)—is [according to THE DYON-TWIST MODEL of FUNDAMENTAL PARTICLES: A THEORY OF MATTER AND ENERGY by Winfield Harold Peterson, © 1994, 2003, 2005 (winpeterson1@comcast.net)] coming from particles (described there as spherical monads) called "neutral trions"—a heavy particle that radiates a relatively small amount of attractive gravity from its "vactal fabric"; but most of it radiates repulsive gravity (antigravity) from its "inertial fabric." (By now you are rolling your eyes.)

It took this author, Leslie, weeks to work through the roughly 180 pages of this step by step account of what happens in the black box of particle interactions. The book not only describes what happens in there, but pictures it with many illustrations. The narration was lucid, and hundreds of diagrams clarify the descriptions and explanations. Those led to some interesting predictions, such as the *impossibility* of the Higgs particle. Those weeks of study provided a trove of absorbing intellectual experiences. You'll find more on this about halfway through chapter Thirty-Five and again in chapter Eighty-Seven where this statement is found:

"In part, it's a model of fundamental particles composed of vibrating bands (or ribbons or membranes) that form through mitosislike stages from bands into Möbius ribbons into spherical monads with differing twist domains resulting in a complete description and explanation of all the known particles—bosons, fermions, and every form, level, and field of energy, including gravity. It predicts the nonexistence of the Higgs particle."

The 2011 edition of THE DYON-TWIST is now 216 pages. It's just out with several brilliant additions, including elucidation of the Big Bang, Black Holes, and the ongoing creation of the universe.

CPSIA information can be obtained at www.ICGtesting.com
Printed in the USA
LVOW101656180112

264475LV00004B/5/P